Secret lives of the
men and women
THE OFFICER FACTORY

The General and his secretary— he slaved to produce Nazi soldiers . . . she begged to be treated as a woman

The Captain and his cadets—he admired their iron discipline . . . and loved their athletic young bodies

The wife and her warriors—her husband was only half a man . . . but she had her choice of a thousand others

The Lieutenant and his conscience—did he dare expose a murderer . . . knowing he was an important Nazi?

As the "thousand-year Reich" totters under the shock of war, these men and women live their lives, fight their private battles for sex and power in this magnificent new novel by the author of "The Revolt of Gunner Asch."

The
OFFICER
FACTORY

HANS HELLMUT KIRST

▲ PYRAMID BOOKS • NEW YORK

THE OFFICER FACTORY

A PYRAMID BOOK—published by arrangement with Doubleday & Company, Inc.

PRINTING HISTORY—Doubleday edition published January 1963
Second printing . . . . February 1963
Mid-Century Book Society selection, January 1963
Pyramid edition published . . January 1964

© 1960 by Verlag Kurt Desch Gmbh, Munchen-Wien-Basel

English version © 1962 by William Collins, Sons and Co., Ltd.

Library of Congress Catalog Card Number 62-7652   All Rights Reserved

Printed in the United States of America

Originally published in German under the title **Fabrik der Offiziere**
by Verlag Kurt Desch, Munich

PYRAMID BOOKS are published by Pyramid Publications, Inc.,
444 Madison Avenue, New York 22, New York, U.S.A.

CONTENTS

CONTENTS

CONTENTS

CONTENTS

IN MEMORY OF THE BETRAYED
GENERATION AND AS A WARNING
TO THE YOUTH OF TODAY.

THE
OFFICER
FACTORY

1 *A LIEUTENANT IS BURIED*

WITH GREATCOAT FLAPPING, Lieutenant Krafft hurried across the graveyard like a startled bird of ill omen. The mourners eyed him with interest, sensing the possibility of a diversion from the otherwise interminable boredom of the funeral ceremony.

"Let me through, please!" muttered Lieutenant Krafft discreetly. Skillfully he wormed his way between the group of officers and the open grave. "Let me through, please!"

Nods greeted Krafft's request, though no one made room for him, possibly in the hope that he would fall into the grave. That at least would have been a step in the right direction. For nothing, except perhaps an endless church parade, makes hardened soldiers more restless than a long funeral, and at least at a church parade it's possible to sit down with a roof over one's head.

"What's the hurry?" asked Captain Feders with interest. "Have we managed to produce another corpse?"

"Not yet," said Lieutenant Krafft, pushing past him. "As far as I know."

"At this rate," observed Captain Feders blandly to all within earshot, "we'll soon be able to pack up as a training school and set up as undertakers—a limited liability company, of course."

Although even here Captain Feders didn't seem to care what he said, he kept his voice low. For the general wasn't far off.

Major-General Modersohn stood at the head of the open grave, a tall, erect figure with clearly defined features. He stood there utterly motionless.

Modersohn was the sort of man who seemed not to notice

13

what was going on around him. He never even glanced at the hurrying figure of Lieutenant Krafft, and showed no reaction at all to Captain Feders' remarks. He stood there as though posing for a sculptor. Indeed all who knew him cherished the thought that they would some day see him as a statue.

Major-General Modersohn was always the center of any gathering he attended, and wherever he was, all color seemed drained from the surroundings and words rendered meaningless. Heaven and earth were reduced to the status of a back cloth. The coffin at his feet, poised on boards over the open grave, was now little more than a stage prop. The group of officers to his right, the bunch of cadets to his left, the aide-de-camp and the course commander two paces to his rear—all were reduced to more or less decorative marginal figures: a mere framework for a successful portrait of the general painted in cool, firm colors without a touch of garishness or ostentation. The general was the spirit of Prussia personified—or so at least a lot of people thought.

He was a past master in the art of commanding people's respect, appearing to be altogether above all ordinary human feeling. The weather, for instance, was a matter of supreme indifference to him, though his uniform was quite another matter. And even if the ice-cold wind which swept across the graveyard had started blowing solid blocks of ice, he would never have put up the collar of his greatcoat. As for putting his hands in his pockets, it was unthinkable.

He set a permanent example to his officers, who were left with no alternative but to follow it. They stood there now freezing miserably, for it was very cold and this ceremony seemed to be dragging itself out to an inordinate length.

Yet the more restlessly, the more hopefully the gathering eyed him, the more stiff and unapproachable did the general seem to become.

"Unless I'm very much mistaken," whispered Captain Feders to those beside him, "the old man's hatching up something really frightful. He's shut up like an oyster—the only question now is: who's going to force him open?"

As Lieutenant Krafft continued to make his way forward to the group in front, the officers' interest quickened visibly and they began to nudge each other surreptitiously. Their hope was that the lieutenant would eventually find himself confronting the general, with all the inevitable dramatic consequences that would entail.

But Lieutenant Krafft was wise enough to avoid offending a statue. He had found that it was almost always more prudent to stick to the regulation way of doing things, so he now turned to Captain Kater, in command of the head-quarters company, and said, "If you please, sir, the army chaplain is delayed—he's sprained his ankle. The medical officer is with him now."

This announcement upset Kater considerably. It seemed to him extremely painful that he should be forced to become the hearer of an unpleasant piece of news from his company officer in this way—before all the assembled officers too! For Kater knew his general. He knew that, probably without ever saying a word, he would give him a cold, penetrating look tantamount to a devastating reprimand. For a ceremony was in progress here, planned down to its minutest detail and brooking neither interruption nor delay. Lieutenant Krafft, or the stumbling chaplain, whichever way you liked to look at it, had landed Kater in an embarrassing situation. In an effort to gain time, he was foolish enough to ask, "How can the man have sprained his ankle?"

"Probably tight again!" said Captain Ratshelm, seething with righteous indignation.

The ADC cleared his throat warningly. And though Major-General Modersohn continued to stand there without batting an eyelid, the dashing Captain Ratshelm sensed that he'd been reprimanded. He had meant well enough, but had expressed himself incorrectly. After all, he was at an officers' training school. The welfare and instruction of future officers had been entrusted to him, and it was one of his duties to express even undeniable truths with immaculate care.

So with some courage and therefore slightly excessive volume, he declared, "When I said 'tight,' I should of course have said drunk."

"The chaplain can't even have been drunk," said Captain Feders, the tactics instructor, whose mind worked very fast although not always in the pleasantest way. "It only requires the most elementary logic to see that. He is in fact almost always drunk, and so far no harm has ever befallen him. He might say his guardian angel sees to that. If, as now appears, he has sprained his ankle, then it may be presumed that he is *not* tight, or if you prefer, drunk, and is therefore having to do without the assistance of his guardian angel—and his ankle has given under the strain."

General Modersohn now turned his head. The process was a slow, menacing one, like a gun barrel feeling its way towards its target. His eyes remained expressionless. The officers avoided his glance and stared with a show of solemnity at the grave. Only Feders looked inquiringly at his general, with a barely perceptible smile on his lips.

The ADC kept his eyes and mouth shut tight, feeling that a storm was about to break over his head. It would probably not amount to more than a word from the general, but it would be violent enough to sweep the graveyard clear. Astonishingly the word remained unspoken. And this stimulated the ADC to still further thought. Slowly he came to the conclusion that the chaplain's particular denomination must have something to do with it—presumably the major-general was of a different faith. That is, if he had one at all.

Suddenly with a slow circling motion the general raised his left arm and looked at his watch. Then he lowered his arm again.

And this relatively meager gesture conveyed a terrifying rebuke.

There was now no alternative for Captain Kater but to push his way forward to the general. He was followed by every pair of eyes in the place. Both the officers and cadets were counting themselves lucky they weren't in his shoes. For Kater was responsible for the smooth running of the ceremony—and the ceremony wasn't running smoothly at all, which in the general's eyes constituted a devastating reflection on his abilities.

Kater summoned up all his courage, praying that he would manage to pass on the message without his voice quavering or trembling or breaking unexpectedly into a falsetto. For he knew from experience that what mattered most was to deliver a message in clear, ringing tones and without a trace of hesitation. The rest then usually took care of itself.

Anyway Captain Kater, the officer commanding the headquarters company, was merely telling the general something he knew already, for after all he wasn't deaf. In fact his ears were reputed to have all the sensitivity of sound locators.

Major-General Modersohn took the message calmly enough, immobile as a lonely rock at the bottom of a valley. But then came the moment Kater had been dreading. The general pushed back the peak of his cap with a brusque gesture, and said briefly, "Take the necessary steps."

The officers grinned broadly. The cadets craned forward eagerly. But Captain Kater seemed to break out into a cold sweat. It was his job to see that the necessary steps were taken without delay, but what were they? He knew that there were at least half a dozen possible courses of action open to him, but at least five would prove to be the wrong ones—in the general's eyes at least, which was what counted.

Lieutenant Krafft couldn't help feeling a certain sympathy for Kater. This was because he still didn't know the captain well enough, since he had only arrived at the training school two weeks before. But Krafft was a shrewd fellow and was picking things up very quickly. The most important thing was to abide by regulations and carry out orders—it was the only way to show the requisite briskness and decision. Whether the regulations made sense or not, or whether there was any point in the orders, was of secondary importance.

It was in that spirit that Captain Kater now promptly issued an order. "Ten minutes break!" he roared.

This of course was a hair-raising piece of stupidity, a real Kater idea. The officers were barely able to conceal their delight, always glad to see others make a bad mistake because it bolstered their own self-confidence. Even the cadets shook their heads, while the valiant Captain Ratshelm simply muttered indignantly, "Idiot!"

The general, however, turned away and seemed to gaze with utter indifference at the sky. He didn't say a word. But he thus gave his sanction to Kater's order all the same. Why he did so was his own secret, though there were at least two possible explanations. The first was that the general didn't want to give Kater a dressing down in front of the cadets, who were his subordinates. The second was that the general respected the sanctity of the place in which they found themselves. The relevant army regulations were very specific about this.

The main thing was that orders were orders, and therefore in many people's eyes sacred.

At any rate, there it was: a break! A ten-minute break!

Major-General Modersohn turned away and walked a few paces in the direction of a small rise. His ADC and the two course commanders followed him very respectfully at a short distance. And since the general didn't speak, neither of them spoke either.

The general surveyed the horizon as if trying to devise a plan of battle. He knew every inch of the landscape here. The River Main wound between gentle hills covered with vineyards, and, down below, the town of Wildlingen looked as if it had been built out of a box of bricks. Towering above it all was Hill 201 with Number 5 Officers' Training School perched on the top. The cemetery lay rather to one side but was within easy reach, exactly fifteen minutes' march from the barracks, which was convenient for the return journey too.

"A nice bit of ground," said the general.

"Really very nice," Major Frey, commander of Number 2 Course, assured him hurriedly. "And an astonishing amount of room in it too, General. In this respect I don't think we need anticipate any difficulties, unless we're subjected to air raids. But even then we'll manage somehow."

The general had been referring to the landscape. The major had meant the cemetery. Now they both fell silent, to save any further misunderstandings.

The officers had acted on their own initiative and had broken ranks on a signal from Captain Feders. He left the ranks and withdrew to the rear—to stretch his legs, as he put it. He disappeared behind a yew hedge.

The officers began wandering about in groups. No one could take exception to that, for the only thing that mattered was to follow the general's example. If he stretched his legs, then they might too.

"Lieutenant Krafft," said Captain Kater resentfully, "how could you do such a thing to me?"

"What do you mean?" asked Krafft, quite unperturbed. "I didn't sprain my ankle, did I? I'm not responsible for this ceremony, am I?"

"In a certain sense yes," said Kater angrily. "For as an officer of the headquarters company you're my immediate subordinate, and any responsibility that I have you share with me."

"Certainly," said Krafft, "but there's a small point you've overlooked. I agree I'm responsible to you, but then you're responsible to the general. And rather you than me!"

"It's fantastic!" growled Captain Kater. "How could they ever have sent a man like you to an officers' training school!"

"Oh well!" said Krafft cheerfully. "You're here, after all!"

Captain Kater gulped. He only had to make a mistake and even junior officers started abusing him. But he'd show them. With a quick look at the general, he positioned himself by way of cover behind a tree, then pulled a flask out of his pocket, opened it, and took a drink to give himself courage. He didn't offer the flask to Krafft.

But just as he was putting it back into his pocket he suddenly found himself surrounded by a small group of officers headed by the inevitable Captain Feders. They, it seemed, were in need of warmth too.

"Now come on, Kater, try and show a little friendly spirit," said Feders, with a grin. "Hand that flask of yours around. It shouldn't really set you back much—with those vast supplies you've got."

"I would like to remind you that we're in a cemetery," replied Kater with dignity.

Feders said, "We can't help it if the general suddenly takes it into his head to hold a slap-up funeral just as if it were peacetime. After all, this is war. Heaven knows how many times I've eaten with the dead. So pass your flask over, you old hypocrite! You're responsible for this break, you might at least make it as pleasant as possible."

The forty cadets of H Section stayed where they were, unable as yet to avail themselves of the privileges of officers. It was not for them to take their cue from the general and wander about as they pleased. They needed a direct order to be able to do such a thing, and this of course was not forthcoming.

So they just went on standing there, at ease, three deep, rifles by their sides, steel helmets on their heads—forty incredibly young, smooth faces, some of them with the eyes of experienced old men and hardly a man among them more than twenty. These were the youngest of the whole course.

"Where the hell do the officers get the drink?" said Cadet Hochbauer to his neighbor. "There hasn't been an issue of schnapps for a week."

"Perhaps they're just very economical with it," suggested Cadet Mösler with a grin. "I'll tell you one thing, though. If I needed anything to make me want to become an officer, I'd find this flask a most convincing incentive."

"But it's downright dishonest," said Cadet Hochbauer severely. "It shouldn't be allowed. Something ought to be done about it."

"Why not just blow up the lot," suggested Cadet Rednitz. "Then there'd be a mass funeral, and at least that way we wouldn't have to keep running back and forth to the cemetery."

"Shut up," said Cadet Hochbauer roughly. "Keep your lousy remarks to yourself, or you'll have me to reckon with."

"Don't get excited," said Cadet Rednitz. "I sized you up long ago."

"Silence, please!" said Cadet Weber. "I'm in mourning here, and I'd like a little respect for the fact!"

Gradually the excitement among the cadets began to subside. They looked around cautiously; the general was a long way off, and the officers were still stamping their feet up and down to keep warm. Meanwhile Captain Kater's flask was empty. Captain Feders was still keeping the company entertained with witticisms. The presence of the coffin seemed quite forgotten.

But one of the officers was Captain Ratshelm, a valiant and tireless father to the cadets, and commander of Number 6 Company, of which H Section formed part. And Ratshelm, though standing on the other side of the grave, continued to cast frank and friendly glances in their direction.

Captain Ratshelm eyed his cadets with real fatherly affection. True, they had begun to raise their voices, but in that he chose to see a sign of their soldierly qualities. They had come here to accompany their section officer, Lieutenant Barkow, on his last journey, and he was delighted to note that they were not behaving like a lot of women, but almost like real soldiers for whom death was the most matter-of-fact thing in the world—an ever-present traveling companion, the truest of all comrades as it were. And though it wasn't quite fitting to laugh in his face, a certain composure in his presence was thoroughly desirable. Or so Ratshelm thought.

"At the front," said Cadet Weber, spitting vigorously, "we barely needed five minutes for a burial—apart from digging the grave, that is. But here, back home, you have to make a huge great box. I've nothing against it, mind you, except that if it's going to be done with all the trappings, then you might as well do the thing really properly and include an afternoon off, which is something I could use. I've got myself a nice little girl lined up down in the town—Annemarie's her name. I've told her I'll marry her when I'm a general." There were further signs of restlessness among the cadets at this. But most of them simply stood there half asleep, moving their frozen toes about energetically inside their boots. To stamp their feet for warmth would have been going too far, but there was nothing wrong with rubbing their hands together, and someone in the rear rank had even gone so far as to stick his deep into his greatcoat pockets.

Only the front rank, exposed as it was to the full glare of publicity, was unable to do anything but maintain the correct at-ease position. Some actually managed to give the impression that they were staring sorrowfully at the coffin. But in fact they were doing no more than note the details of its construction—the imitation oak (pine presumably), the shoddy metal fittings, the drab paint, and the crudely made feet. And for the umpteenth time they read the inscriptions on the wreath ribbons, most of which were red and bore a swastika. The inscriptions were printed in gilt or jet-black lettering:

To our beloved Comrade-at-arms Barkow—Rest in Peace—The Officers of Number 5 Officers' Training School.

An unforgettable instructor—with respect from his grateful pupils.

"God knows what sort of section officer we'll get now," said one of the cadets, gazing thoughtfully out across the confused landscape of crosses, headstones, mounds, and bushes which made up the cemetery.

"Ah, what the hell!" said another harshly. "We got rid of Lieutenant Barkow and we'll get rid of anyone else who comes along. The main thing is for us all to stick together—we can do what we like, then!"

"There's nothing I wouldn't put beyond these fellows," declared Captain Feders, the extremely knowledgeable and perceptive tactics instructor, to the world at large. "I wouldn't put it beyond them to blow their own section officer sky high. Lieutenant Barkow wasn't a fool, and he wasn't tired of life. What's more, he knew that equipment inside out. It was only his pupils he doesn't seem to have known, and perhaps that was where he made his mistake. I warned him several times. But there's no hope for that type of obstinate idealist—they understand nothing of life as it really is."

"He was a first-rate officer," protested Captain Ratshelm energetically.

"Exactly!" said Feders, kicking laconically at a stone. It rolled into the open grave.

Ratshelm was unfavorably impressed. "You don't seem to have much reverence," he said.

"I hate the vulgarity of this whole official-funeral business," said Feders. "And all this endless petty lying over the body of a dead man makes me sick. But at the same time I keep asking myself: what's in the general's mind? He's up to something or other, but what is it?"

"I'm no general," said Ratshelm.

"You'll soon be one, though," said Feders aggressively. "The rottener the times, the easier it is to get promoted. Just look at this bunch of officers—they do everything they're told. All with the fine precision of machines, whether in the mess, the classroom, or at the cemetery. Utterly reliable—that's the only thing to be said for them. You can rely on imbeciles, too, in a way."

"You've been drinking, Feders," said Captain Ratshelm.

"Yes I have, which is why I'm so mild and agreeable. Even the sight of Captain Kater engenders friendly feelings in me today."

Captain Kater was walking restlessly up and down among the tombstones like a cat on hot bricks. He was trying to think how he could get on top of the situation. He felt almost inclined to appeal to heaven, and indeed to that very department which concerned itself with the affairs of the padre's particular faith. But he soon abandoned all hope that the Lord Himself would set His servant's ankle to rights in time.

He kept gazing longingly at the entrance to the cemetery. Finally he asked Lieutenant Krafft, "Do you think there's any chance of the padre turning up in time?"

"Not much," said Krafft amiably.

"But what the hell are we doing here, then?" cried Kater in desperation.

"Well, my dear fellow," said Captain Feders, "you have, as always, a number of alternatives open to you! For example you can extend the break. Or you can postpone the funeral. Or you can find a substitute for the padre. Or you can tell the general that you have nothing to tell him. On the other hand, you can quite simply drop dead, and thus be rid of all your troubles."

Kater looked about him savagely like a wild boar at bay. The officers regarded him with considerable interest; after what had happened here at the cemetery, he no longer seemed such a formidable figure. Lieutenant Krafft, it seemed to them, had maneuvered Kater into a position from which he would find it difficult to emerge unscathed. Presumably Krafft was after his job. After all, this was the way things usually worked; one man profited from another's mistakes.

But an expectant hush suddenly settled over the mourners. For Major-General Modersohn had turned back toward the funeral party, letting his shark's eyes sweep over them until complete silence reigned. Then he stared straight at Captain Kater.

"Break over!" cried the latter immediately.

The general nodded almost imperceptibly. The officers fell in again and the cadets froze in their positions. Otherwise at first nothing else happened at all.

A silence which was not indeed without a certain solemnity now settled over the funeral party. Only Captain Kater could be heard, breathing heavily beside Lieutenant Krafft.

"For God's sake, then!" said the general.

Kater started with dismay. The ceremony was his responsibility, but he couldn't think what should be done with it. Feeling increasingly inclined to hand the solution of this problem over to Krafft, he turned on him a look at once peremptory and imploring. "Carry on then Krafft!" he whispered, and as if to give further emphasis to the order, for there could be no doubt that this was what it was, he pushed Krafft to the fore.

Once again Krafft almost stumbled into the open grave. But he pulled himself up just in time, and said to the cadets stationed beside the coffin, "Let him down!"

The cadets immediately obeyed. The coffin rattled down into the grave, and frozen earth fell on top of it, while those present followed this utterly unexpected turn of events with mixed feelings.

"We will now join in silent prayer," proposed Lieutenant Krafft. Fortunately this rather vague formula had the suggestion of an order about it. And the mourners seemed to adapt themselves to the proposal at once. They lowered their heads, stared at the ground, and tried to maintain suitably solemn expressions.

Hardly any of the officers thought for a moment about Lieutenant Barkow lying in the now almost invisible coffin, for few of them had ever seen much of him. Lieutenant Barkow, like many of the instructors, had only been at the school a few weeks. He had been an erect, rather aloof figure, with an expressionless youthful face, fishy eyes, and a mouth that was always tight shut. An officer of the sort you find in picture books; the faithful youth of Germany—resolute, prepared for anything. Even for this. What could be more logical?

One of the cadets muttered, "He asked for it anyway." From a distance, at any rate, it sounded almost like a prayer.

"Amen," said Lieutenant Krafft loudly.

"Dismiss!" said Major-General Modersohn.

This order of the general's caught everyone completely by surprise. It was like a pistol shot fired at point-blank range. The mourners looked up, some rather put-out, others genuinely disturbed. The order was not without its resemblance to an unexpected kick in the pants. Moreover it was issued to people who were ostensibly saying their prayers.

Only slowly did the utterly unheard of nature of the order begin to dawn on the more experienced members of the funeral party—it was an order directed against the ceremony itself. For the earth had not been thrown in, the wreaths had not been laid, and the volley had not been fired over the grave. The procedure which had been so carefully planned and rehearsed four times had been abruptly broken off at a single word.

A word, however, which there was no gainsaying.

"The officers are dismissed." As second-in-command, the officer in command of Number 1 Course gave the order without delay. It was a good chance to display initiative. It would not escape the general's attention, for initiative was something to which he attached particular importance. "Cadets will return to their billets. Further duty as per timetable."

The funeral party broke up almost at once. The officers moved off in ones and twos toward the entrance to the cemetery. Captain Ratshelm immediately took over command of his company.

Captain Kater stood there for a few seconds rooted to the spot. Then he moved off in the wake of Lieutenant Krafft, for whom he was planning a massive rebuke. For how was Kater to continue to exist in this training school if he couldn't find a scapegoat? He had never failed to find one before.

Major-General Modersohn alone remained behind.

The general took a few paces forward and stared into the grave. He saw the dark brown wooden planks onto which the earth had fallen. All around him lay dirty trampled snow. Somebody's heel had ground a scarlet wreath ribbon into the slush. It lay there encrusted with mud.

The hard, inscrutable face of the general gave nothing away. His lips were set in a thin, straight line. And his eyes were closed, or so it seemed. As if he wanted no one to see what he was thinking.

As the officers and cadets marched down into the valley toward their barracks they looked back from the great bend in the road and saw their commanding officer still standing in the cemetery in the distance—a clear, slim silhouette, menacing against the ice-cold, snow-blue sky, as if frozen in his unapproachability.

"There's going to be a damned cold wind blowing in the next few days," said Captain Feders. "Because I don't care what anyone says, there's something odd about this whole business. The general isn't the sort of man to mind about ordinary, everyday stupidity. If he shows he's angry, then it means that some really gigantic row is brewing. But what, exactly? Well, we'll be finding out all too soon."

2   *A MATTER OF RAPE*

"MY DEAR LIEUTENANT KRAFFT," said Captain Kater, who was making his way through the barracks with his company officer toward the headquarters building, "a training school is a highly complex organization. And compared with our general the sibyl herself was little more than a slick fortuneteller."

"That's why I can't understand how you of all people got here," said Lieutenant Krafft frankly.

"I didn't choose this post," said Captain Kater with a somewhat weary smile, "but since I'm here, this is where I intend to stay. Do you follow me? I wouldn't like you to build any false hopes in that respect. For that would make things too unpleasant for you and too exacting for me. If you're wise, then, you'll try to get along with me."

"What else can one do?" said Lieutenant Krafft cheerfully. "I'm neither clever nor hard-working. I have no ambitions and I'm all for a quiet life."

"A bit of a one for the girls, too, I dare say," the captain suggested with a wink. He mistrusted Krafft, as he mistrusted everybody on principle. People were always trying to get things out of him. The general wanted discipline and a knowledge of the regulations, the officers wanted bottles of schnapps and extra rations, and this fellow Krafft, it seemed, wanted his job. It was difficult to hold younger, inexperienced officers back when they saw a chance of treading on their superiors' heels. And the officers of the military training school were an elite who were not only burning to make a career for themselves but also had it in them to do so. However, there were always girls.

"We mustn't exaggerate," said Krafft. " 'Girls' is going too far. One's quite enough for me. Every now and then."

"You will find me quite human about that," the captain assured him. "And I always say: every man to his own tastes. But let's get one thing straight; I am in command of the headquarters company and you're allotted to me as company officer. We're clear about that, aren't we?"

Together they walked through the orderly room of the headquarters company with Captain Kater leading, as was only right and proper. The clerks, a corporal and two lance-corporals rose to their feet. The one member of the female staff, however, remained seated, and in a most provocative manner too. Kater pretended to take no notice of her.

Yet it did not escape him that this attractive girl—a certain Elfrida Rademacher—had eyes for no one but Lieutenant Krafft. She smiled at him with such direct intimacy that he and she might have been the only two people in the world. Kater looked away.

"A cup of coffee?" asked Elfrida. She said this in the direction of Captain Kater, but winked at the lieutenant as she did so. Krafft winked back. Slowly the icy cold of the cemetery began to thaw from his limbs.

"Yes, fine, make some coffee," said Kater generously. "Put some cognac in mine, please."

In this way Captain Kater demonstrated his individuality of taste. He never let slip an opportunity of reminding his associates of his individuality—at least as far as drinks were concerned.

"I'm badly in need of a cognac," he continued, collapsing noisily into the chair at his desk. He motioned Lieutenant Krafft to a chair beside him. "After that farce at the cemetery I need something to fortify me. Though I say so with the utmost respect, the general's becoming a bit of a nightmare. What is it he wants? If we were to make as much of a fuss as this over everyone who got killed we'd hardly be able to get on with the war. And without cognac, life would be utterly impossible."

"Yes," said Elfrida brightly, "the war gets harder and harder every day." She spread a cloth on top of the desk and brought in two cups of coffee. "The best thing will be if I just put the bottle of brandy down as it is."

"What do you mean by that, exactly?" asked Kater, suspicious as ever. The eagerness with which Elfrida made the suggestion led him to fear the worst. "Is something else wrong?"

"Trebly wrong, you might say," said Elfrida frankly, arranging the glasses and beaming across at the lieutenant.

The captain managed to overlook this. His seat creaked beneath him. The air reeked of cold cigarette smoke, and the foul smell of soap and water and rotten floor boards was all about him. Somewhat nervously he adjusted his stomach and folded his fat little fingers over it. Then for the first time he looked straight at Elfrida Rademacher, his excellent, multi-purpose secretary, with an expression of weary exasperation.

This girl Elfrida Rademacher was certainly not uninteresting to look at, though she was a little full in the figure and her dress bulged prominently in a number of places. She was a little like a horse, though perhaps with a rather cowlike temperament. In any case there was a full-blooded rustic quality about her, suggestive of haystacks and rustling woods —all things, admittedly, to which Captain Kater attached little importance, for he was a pretty cold fish. He was, alas, no longer in his first youth, though this sometimes lent him a spurious air of virtue.

"Out with it, then, Fräulein Rademacher," he said, lighting a cigar—a specially mild Havana. "You know I'm a very understanding sort of person."

"Well, you'll need to be, this time," Elfrida assured him, winking at Krafft again, and running her tongue quickly over her lips.

"Come on, Fräulein Rademacher," said Captain Kater impatiently, "fire away."

And quite casually, as if she were talking about the most natural thing in the world, she said, "Someone was raped last night."

Captain Kater winced. Even Lieutenant Krafft pricked up his ears, though he had long ago resolved never to be surprised by anything that this war for the glory of greater Germany might have in store for him.

"It's disgraceful!" cried Captain Kater. "Utterly disgraceful the way these cadets behave!"

"It wasn't one of the cadets," Elfrida Rademacher informed him amiably.

"Not someone from headquarters company, I hope?" asked the captain, even more perturbed. Rape committed by one of the cadets would have been just tolerable, inasmuch as these were not directly under his command. Presumably the girl would concern him, for all civilian employees were his responsibility.

But if the incident should turn out to involve a member of the headquarters company, it would be disastrous. In fact it might seal his fate altogether. Coming on top of the events at the cemetery it might even get him posted to the front.

Kater therefore glanced straight at Krafft, automatically preparing to implicate him in his troubles. The situation was grave indeed. First a man of God who sprained his ankle at the crucial moment; then a defender of the Fatherland who was foolish enough to be caught in the act of rape!

"What's the name of the fellow who's done this to me?" he demanded.

"Corporal Krottenkopf. He's the one who was raped," announced Elfrida Rademacher, smiling with genuine pleasure.

"I'm always hearing about this Corporal Krottenkopf!" cried Kater desperately. "But really it's absurd! It's just not possible."

"It's the truth," said Elfrida. She was obviously thoroughly enjoying herself. "The rape of Corporal Krottenkopf took place some time in the early hours of this morning between one and three A.M. In the basement of the headquarters building, too, in the communications center, by three of the signals girls on duty there."

"But it simply can't be true!" cried Captain Kater. "What do you think, Lieutenant Krafft?"

"I'm trying to envisage it from a practical point of view, sir," declared Krafft, shaking his large bucolic head in amazement. "But I'm afraid my imagination doesn't seem to run to it."

"Disgusting!" cried Kater, meaning not so much the incident itself as its possible consequences. "What was this Krottenkopf fellow doing at night in the communications center anyway, even though he is the signals corporal? And how is it that three of these women were all in the communications center at the same time? There are never more than two on duty at once at night. And why did they have to pick on Krottenkopf? Aren't there enough cadets in the barracks who would be only too glad to satisfy their demands? Quite apart from which, why did it have to happen in duty hours!"

Captain Kater refilled his glass to the brim, and his hands were trembling so much that the cognac spilled onto a document on his desk, forming a tiny aromatic lake there. But Kater couldn't have cared less about the document or the lake of cognac. All he could think of was this appalling affair of the rape and the complications it was likely to lead to. He tilted back his glass, but its contents might have been water. There was nothing he would have liked better than to get drunk on the spot. But he had to make a decision first, and it had to be the best possible one in the circumstances. In other words it must be a decision which would save him work and worry, and enable him to shift the responsibility from himself to someone else's shoulders.

"Krafft," he said, "I hand the investigation of this affair over to you. The whole thing seems to me utterly incredible, but we've got to try and get to the bottom of it. I hope you follow me. I simply cannot believe that anything like this could possibly take place in my headquarters company. Biologically speaking it's improbable enough, but militarily it's unthinkable. It must be a mistake."

Having said this, Kater prepared to leave, confident that officially he hadn't put a foot wrong so far. He had taken the requisite steps for an occasion of this sort, handing the matter onto someone else and seeing that it was properly investigated. If mistakes were made now, the responsibility would no longer be his. And if Krafft were by any chance to come a cropper in the process, so much the better.

Yet before Kater finally left he turned to Krafft and said; "There's one point you oughtn't to overlook, my dear fellow —and that's this: why does Krottenkopf wait until now, this afternoon, before reporting this filthy business? Regulations say he should have done so first thing this morning at the latest. What does the fellow think he's doing? Who does he think he's dealing with? See that he's severely reprimanded! A man who breaks regulations like this is always suspect."

Krafft felt a certain respect for Kater as he watched him go. He was certainly a cunning creature—though there was really nothing so surprising about this, for how otherwise would he have managed to hold his job at the training school?

Kater's suggestion that Corporal Krottenkopf, the plaintiff, had broken the regulations was as low as it was cunning, for it put Krottenkopf at a disadvantage from the start.

"I really feel like throwing the whole thing back in Kater's face!" said Lieutenant Krafft.

"Is that all you feel like doing?" said Elfrida, sidling up to him.

"Perhaps we ought to close the door!" suggested Lieutenant Krafft. He was standing very close to Elfrida.

"What's the use?" she said with a slight huskiness in her voice. "It hasn't a lock."

"How do you know?" he asked quickly. "Have you tried it before?"

She laughed softly and snuggled up close to him as if to stop him from asking any more questions.

He put his strong arms around her and her body yielded willingly. She closed her eyes and leaned back against the CO's desk, at the same time pushing the coffee cups to one side with an unfaltering hand to prevent them from falling to the floor.

"No one will come in without knocking," she said. "And Kater's in the officers' mess by now."

Lieutenant Krafft looked down past her to the desk, where there was a writing pad with a note scrawled on it: "Call RO 25/33." Presumably this meant: call Rotunda, the landlord of The Gay Dog, and get him to deliver twenty-five bottles of the '33 vintage. But Krafft closed his eyes as if to forget the letters and figures, as if to forget everything except the strength of the life within him.

They were soon panting desperately, while outside a group of cadets could be heard singing, "There is no finer country in the world." With its sturdy ground bass of tramping boots, this song made a good deal of noise, and this was helpful, for barrack walls, not being built for eternity, are usually pretty thin.

"I can't wait for tonight!" said Elfrida.

But all Karl Krafft could do was nod.

Corporal Krottenkopf, the alleged victim of the rape, was waiting for Lieutenant Krafft in the corridor. He gazed up at his superior officer with a tortured expression, and then, stooping slightly, bowed his head in shame.

Yet this Corporal Krottenkopf was no sensitive plant, no delicate youth, or mother's darling. He was a man with a protuberant nose, full fleshy lips, apelike hands, and the powerful hindquarters of a stag.

"They called me up in the middle of the night," he related mournfully and with a great show of indignation. "They called me up and told me that the external exchange was out of order. I told them they could go and get—well, you know. . . . They said, 'Well, not down the telephone.' That should have put me on my guard. But I was thinking solely of my duty, of the fact that the exchange was out of order, and of what the general might say if he wanted to telephone. It just didn't bear thinking of. It's the sort of thing that can get a man sent to the front. Well, anyway, along I went, for duty is duty, after all. No sooner had I reached the basement, though, than they set upon me. All three of them, like wild animals. They simply tore the clothes off me, boots and all. And that had them panting a bit, because my boots are damned tight—anyone who hasn't the knack has to pull like hell to get them off. But these women stopped at nothing!"

"All right, all right," said Krafft, who had no wish to go into any further details. "But why are you coming to me only now? It must have occurred to you first thing this morning that you'd been the victim of a brutal rape?"

"Yes, well," said Krottenkopf, grinning to show that he was speaking as man to man, "I'm not inhuman. I'm not a petty-minded sort of fellow, you know; never have been. I enjoy a visit to a decent brothel like the next man, and when these women set upon me like this I thought to myself: Now then you're not going to have any hard feelings about this. When someone's had more to drink than is good for them, it works on the brain and makes them randy as a rattlesnake. Right, then, I said to myself, forget all about it. It's a hard war, and casualties are inevitable in war. I'm a sensible sort of fellow, you see. The unpleasant part of the business only developed later. Now these beauties won't address me by anything but my Christian name: Waldemar they call me! And that's going too far. They've lost all sense of discipline. They spend their whole time giggling and making personal remarks and actually laughing at my orders. They call me darling! Would you believe it? They call me darling in front of the rank and file. And not just the three who were involved yesterday evening either, but the rest of them as well! The entire communications section! And as a corporal, even as a man, I'm not prepared to stand for that."

"Right," said Lieutenant Krafft. "I'll look into it, that is if you really insist on pressing the charge, Krottenkopf."

"I'm not insisting on anything," the corporal reassured him. "But what else am I to do? The whole barracks is laughing at me, and calling me Waldemar! . . . And my real name's Alfred! Please do something about it, Lieutenant."

"You don't think you might possibly have made a mistake?"

"You'd better ask the three harpies themselves about that. They know best, after all."

Captain Kater had retired to the officers' mess in search of strength and succor. The mess was his own undisputed territory; kitchen, cellar, and all the personnel here were his direct responsibility in his capacity as the officer commanding the headquarters company. Apart from him, the only other person who had the right to give orders here was the general —though there was little danger of his putting in an appearance during the afternoon.

"Well, now, gentlemen," said Captain Kater briskly, "what can I offer you? Don't be shy, just tell me what you'd like. A funeral like that takes it out of you—you need something to pull you around afterwards. Personally I'd suggest an armagnac, straight from the cask—twenty years at least in the wood."

The officers took his advice, for at least Kater knew something about drink, having spent a good deal of time in France.

Kater insisted on paying for the round. It didn't cost him much, for there weren't many officers in the mess at the time, only a handful of tactics instructors and a few company commanders. And, in addition to them, the training school's guest of the moment, a certain Wirrmann, judge-advocate by profession, temporarily seconded to the inspector of training schools and posted to Wildlingen-am-Main to investigate the death of Lieutenant Barkow.

This pillar of military justice was a spry little fellow who seemed more interested in the contents of the officers' mess cellar than anything else. Thus he and Kater got along famously, and Wirrmann found himself with a glass that was full to the brim.

"Well, gentlemen," said Kater joining the officers, "what a funeral this afternoon! I don't know who one would prefer to find oneself up before—one's Maker or the general."

"I must say you'd make a splendid corpse," said Captain Feders cheerfully. "No question of it—the funeral would make a most happy affair. One's only got to think of all those supplies of yours that would be automatically released."

"Captain Feders," said Kater icily, "I'm surprised to find you in the mess at this time of day. Besides, you're a married man and your wife may be waiting for you."

At this, Feders seemed on the point of losing self-control altogether. All trace of humor vanished from his face. The officers eyed him warily, for everyone knew his Achilles' heel though few would have risked wounding him there. Kater had acted carelessly, to say the least.

Feders began to laugh, but there was a raw, dangerous edge to the sound.

"Kater," he said, "if you're surprised to find me in the mess at this time of day, all I can say is that I'm even more surprised to find you here. Normally you should be in the pigsty of yours by now, trying to keep some sort of order there, to put it mildly. But presumably you've delegated the job to someone else—this fellow Krafft, I suppose. He's got a broad back certainly, so broad in fact, Kater, that he could quite easily carry you off altogether if he felt like it. This fellow Krafft's no fool and if I were in your shoes, Kater, I wouldn't be feeling too happy at the moment."

This remark went home all right, and the captain rose to his feet. "What an irrepressible fellow you are, Feders!" he said condescendingly in an attempt to laugh, but it didn't sound very convincing. Kater left, saying that he wanted to go and inspect some stores that were arriving.

No sooner had Captain Kater arrived in the officers' mess kitchen and taken a shot of something to boost his morale than Judge-Advocate Wirrmann appeared on the scene.

"Anything worrying you, my dear Kater?" he asked sympathetically.

"Nothing important," Kater assured him.

"Then," said Wirrmann, "you should find it all the easier to confide in someone who is well disposed toward you. You can rest assured, my dear fellow, that if it's justice you want you've come to the right address."

"Now, ladies," said Lieutenant Krafft, beginning his interrogation, "I'd like you to try and forget both that I'm a man and that I'm an officer."

"That won't be easy," said one of the three girls.

"Do your best, all the same," Krafft advised them. "Imagine I'm a sort of neuter, a personification of the law, if you like. You can talk to me freely, without any false modesty."

"We don't have such a thing anyway," said another of the girls.

Lieutenant Krafft now found himself at what might be called the scene of the crime, that's to say in the communications center in the basement of the HQ building. Chairs stood in front of a row of switchboards, above which were circuit diagrams with the inevitable poster: "Beware! The enemy is listening!" There was a table in one corner on which stood coffee cups, a jug, and an electric kettle. The latter was officially forbidden throughout the barracks, but since it was Captain Kater and not General Modersohn who was responsible for the ban, no one paid any attention to it.

In another corner stood a camp bed—the *corpus delicti*, so to speak—a shabby, battered, rusty iron bedstead, with a mattress and some blankets on it.

Krafft confronted the three girls behind the switchboards. Their figures were well developed and their faces pretty and innocent-looking. Their honest, friendly eyes regarded him with curiosity. Though the eldest of these girls was barely more than twenty, they were neither particularly embarrassed nor excited, seeming to have no sense of guilt at all.

"What can you have been thinking of, ladies?" asked Lieutenant Krafft warily.

"Absolutely nothing," said one of the girls, which sounded convincing enough.

"Right," said Krafft. "I admit the business demands no particularly strenuous intellectual effort, but some sort of thought process is unavoidable. For example: why exactly did you have to pick on Corporal Krottenkopf?"

"Oh, anyone would have done," said one of the girls, managing to smile at Krafft, "and this Krottenkopf just happened to be handy."

Lieutenant Krafft found he had to sit down. The whole affair seemed to him either fearfully complex or else amazingly simple, which sometimes amounted to the same thing.

"At any rate," said Krafft finally, "you did lay hands on him, didn't you?"

The girls looked at each other. They seemed to have come to a pretty careful agreement about what they were to say. Krafft couldn't really take objection to this. He had no particular wish to start a major judicial process. So he simply smiled at the astonishing girls encouragingly.

"It's true," said one of them, a pretty little thing, with a wide baby smile and frank honest eyes, and a sort of roguishness about her reminiscent of her grandmother's era in the First World War, "it's true we took his clothes off, but we then meant simply to throw him out as a sort of demonstration. The trouble was, he wouldn't budge."

"You mean," said Krafft in amazement, "this was simply a sort of demonstration!"

"Exactly!" said the unbelievably innocent-looking girl. "Because it's time something was done about the situation in these barracks. There are nearly a thousand cadets and fifty girls here, and no one's allowed to take any notice of us at all. Wherever you go there's supervision and closed doors and we're surrounded by sentries. All we're asking for is a certain amount of social life. We just don't want to vegetate! But human beings mean nothing to this general, he doesn't take the slightest notice of us. And all this had to be said! That was why we picked on Krottenkopf—not because we wanted to start anything with him but because we wanted to draw attention to the situation. Now do you understand?"

Lieutenant Krafft was beginning to see the funny side of all this, though he was determined to tread warily.

"Listen a moment," he said, "I want to tell you a story. When I was a boy and still lived in the country, some of our geese one day waddled across some relatively clean washing put out to dry by our neighbor, who immediately lodged a complaint. Now there were a number of possibilities. First, the geese themselves were wicked. Secondly, they had been deliberately driven over the washing. Or thirdly, they had simply strayed there. The last explanation was the simplest and the best and it wasn't difficult to make it sound plausible. After all, wicked geese or geese that had been maliciously inspired could lead to all sorts of trouble. Trouble of the sort that geese don't usually survive. Now is the moral clear? Or do I have to make myself still clearer?"

The girls eyed Krafft carefully, and then exchanged glances among themselves. Finally the innocent-looking one, who was probably the sharpest of the three, said, "You mean we should simply say it was some sort of mistake?"

"Well not a mistake exactly," advised Krafft, "but you might perhaps have been playing a trivial if daring practical joke, an innocent sort of tease to get your own back on your tyrant Krottenkopf. Only unfortunately the tease rather got out of hand in a way you couldn't have foreseen. In this way you shift the blame from yourselves without actually putting it onto anyone else. If it was a sort of joke, well, perhaps a few long faces will be pulled about it, but no one's going to lose his head. If, however, it were a serious matter, if there were any question of assault, or something as perverted as rape—then good night, sweet ladies! That could end in jail. Which in certain circumstances can be even more unpleasant than life in barracks."

"How nice you are," said one of the girls gratefully, while the others nodded vigorously. They realized at once that they were lucky to have been allowed to jump back from the fire into the frying pan. "One could really get along with someone like you."

"Maybe," said Lieutenant Krafft. "But don't get it into your heads to pursue the matter further next time you find yourselves bored with night duty and in search of a little diversion."

When Lieutenant Krafft got back to his desk in the headquarters company he found someone waiting for him. This was a slight little figure of a man with the quick agile movements of a squirrel, a pointed nose, and the darting eyes of some bird of prey.

"Allow me to introduce myself," the little man said. "My name's Wirrmann—judge-advocate. I am interested in the Krottenkopf case."

"Who told you about that?" asked Krafft cautiously.

"Your superior officer Captain Kater," explained the little man quietly but firmly. "Besides, it's all over the mess by now, and being discussed in a rather unsavory manner, which is hardly surprising. All the more reason for getting it dealt with and out of the way as quickly as possible. Your superior officer at any rate sought my advice and I was prepared to give him my fullest support. The case interests me, from both the legal and the human point of view. Perhaps you will let me know how your inquiries have been getting on."

Krafft had had just a little more human interest than he could take in such a short space of time, and now felt the urge to be human himself. Furthermore he found this man Wirrmann unsympathetic, and even though there was this squirrel-like quality about him, the man's sanctimonious courtroom voice jarred on his nerves. Krafft therefore turned on him roundly and said, "I don't regard you as having any authority to act in this case, Herr Judge-Advocate."

"My dear fellow," said the latter, and his eyes narrowed, "whether or not I have any authority to act in this case is hardly for you to determine. Apart from which I am acting with the consent of your superior officer."

"Captain Kater hasn't told me of this—either verbally or in writing. And until he does so I must act according to my own judgment. Which means that I'm working on this case alone until I receive further instructions—perhaps from Major-General Modersohn himself."

"Then you shall certainly have them, my dear fellow," replied Wirrmann promptly. And his voice now sounded like a rusty scythe being whisked experimentally through the air. "That is, if you insist."

Krafft looked at the wiry little man with a certain amount of apprehension. Not even the threat of Major-General Modersohn, the terror of Wildlingen, seemed to make much impression on him. These court-martial fellows were gluttons for punishment.

"Well what about it?" urged Wirrmann. "Are you going to let me in on your inquiries voluntarily, or do I have to bring the general into it?"

"Bring anyone you like into it!" said Krafft, losing his temper. "The commander-in-chief of the Wehrmacht, for all I care."

"Let's start with the general," said the judge-advocate quietly, whipping around suddenly like a weathercock in a powerful gust of wind, and vanishing from the scene.

"I suppose I can pack my bags now," said Lieutenant Krafft to Elfrida Rademacher. "My brief stay at the training school seems to be over."

"Did someone see us?" asked Elfrida anxiously.

"If that were all," said Lieutenant Krafft, "at least it would be something worth being thrown out for."

"In any case I could always say I tried to rape you. That seems the latest dodge."

"Too true," said Krafft. "A dodge, what's more, that's going to give the general a nasty shock."

"Nothing's capable of giving him a nasty shock," declared Elfrida emphatically. "He wouldn't turn a hair whatever happened. On one of his rounds recently he went into a room where a couple were making love. And what did he do? He walked straight through the room without batting an eyelid."

"He didn't say a word?"

"Not a word. It wasn't necessary. He recognized them both at a glance."

"And had them thrown out?"

"Made them get married."

"Even worse," said Krafft apprehensively.

"They're said to be very happy," said Elfrida, looking out of the window with a smile.

By this stage in his career, Lieutenant Krafft himself was incapable of being shaken. Yet his quarrel with the judge-advocate could have only one result if it went against him, namely expulsion in the direction of the eastern front, though just at the moment any direction would be a welcome relief from the circus he found himself in. The general could roar at him to his heart's content. The lieutenant had already been roared at quite a bit without suffering anything worse than a slight strain on the eardrums.

After just half an hour, most of which he spent smoking

in the lavatory, Krafft received the anticipated summons to the general. Surprisingly enough, Modersohn didn't insist on the lieutenant reporting to him in the usual way in full-dress uniform. The Major-General merely wished to speak to Krafft on the telephone, and it was to be a telephone conversation of bewildering brevity.

"I understand," said Modersohn without further ado, "that you have refused to allow Judge-Advocate Wirrmann to take part in an investigation you're engaged on."

"Yes, General."

"Why?"

"Because I didn't think the judge-advocate had the authority to act in this particular case, General."

"Good," said Modersohn. And that was all, for the present at least.

3   GAMES FOR H SECTION

THE YOUTHFUL VOICES of the cadets rang through the gymnasium, where a powerful smell of male sweat hung on the air. Captain Ratshelm, the officer commanding Number 6 Company, was personally supervising the three sections under his command, as he always did when they were down for sports or games. Dressed in shorts and a sleeveless shirt he cavorted happily about among his cadets, lending them encouragement and, in so far as he could, setting them an example. For he had a slight tendency to corpulence, and the rosy pinkness of his skin stood out in contrast to the brown sinewy torsos of the cadets.

H Section was the one he was particularly interested in. For it had been bereaved by the sudden death of Lieutenant Barkow and was thus temporarily without a section officer. Until the general appointed a successor to the dead man the company commander voluntarily took on the job himself.

Ratshelm was always happy when he could get into slightly closer contact with his young cadets, being particularly fond of a game of handball, in which he would hop around, grabbing the ball for himself and barging one of his young comrades out of the way in order to get a better shot at goal. With their damp glistening torsos rubbing against him and the sharp animal tang of their sweat in his nostrils, he felt his heart full of strength and joy and deep sense of comradeship. And this was particularly true whenever his eyes lit upon Cadet Hochbauer.

"A lovely pass!" he shouted across at him. "More like that one!"

"This fellow Hochbauer's in training all right," said Cadet Mösler knowingly. "For a creep up the CO's arse."

Cadet Mösler had a reputation as a wit. The advantage of this was that almost everything he said was taken as a joke, which saved him a good deal of trouble one way and another.

"Hochbauer'll have to look out, though," said his neighbor Cadet Rednitz thoughtfully. "There's plenty of competition."

"Yes, you have to make certain sacrifices to become an officer," declared Mösler, not forgetting to grin inanely.

They were standing rather out of the limelight, right at the back of the field. Mösler was a wiry little fellow with darting eyes which spent most of their time on the lookout for anything in skirts, while Rednitz was a medium-sized, slim figure who, however, moved like a bear and was almost always smiling about something, though hardly ever laughing. He had already learned not to do that.

"Scandalous we don't have women training to be officers," said Mösler. "I'd be only too willing to play games with them!"

"Bad enough with some of us carrying on like women," said Rednitz. "Or do you want to sleep your way into a commission?"

"It depends on who with," said Mösler, grinning. "I wouldn't mind a comely young major of thirty or so. It wouldn't be the worst sacrifice one could make for one's Fatherland."

"Half time!" cried Captain Ratshelm. "Change sides!"

The two teams changed sides, and Mösler and Rednitz promptly found their way to the rear again. They had no objection to leaving the main part of the field to the keener sportsmen.

Though Mösler and Rednitz were both only twenty-one, they had already acquired a certain amount of military experience, having developed a sixth sense which told them when their superior officer's eye was upon them. They instinctively positioned themselves where the danger of being spotted was slight. Captain Ratshelm was now out in front of them, pleasantly distracted from his supervisory duties by the game and his sporting companions, and Mösler and Rednitz found his back a comforting sight. Now and again they would make a perfunctory move in one direction or another, even occasionally actually pursuing the ball. But this was only because the cold January air left them little option. They had no wish to work up an unnecessary sweat, but they had no wish to freeze either.

"Hochbauer'll get his commission all right," said Mösler.

"Could become a general," agreed Rednitz, "if the war lasts long enough and he finds enough superior officers to fall for him."

"Coming over, sir!" cried Cadet Hochbauer in clear, ringing tones. "Into the center!"

"Right!" cried Captain Ratshelm. Skipping forward with what he imagined was remarkable elegance he caught the ball and sent it hurtling into his opponents' half of the field, where for some reason or other one of the cadets dodged aside and the ball went into goal.

Yet another point scored. The captain's team were well ahead, as was only to be expected. Once again Ratshelm felt that his own remarkable versatility had been overwhelmingly demonstrated.

"They can't beat us now!" cried Hochbauer happily.

"Our opponents are putting up a great fight, though! All honor to them!"

This man of honor, Captain Ratshelm, a professional soldier and an officer out of deep conviction, was utterly dedicated to the training company under his command. He had three sections under him all together, G, H, and I, each of which had on its strength forty cadets, one section officer, and one tactics instructor. It was Ratshelm's gift to be able to unite in his own person all those qualities required to produce the officers of the future. There was no field in which he was not an expert; he was planner, instructor, educator, all rolled into one, and above all a true comrade-in-arms. Although himself only a few years older than his cadets, he felt like a father to them, and the love which he so devotedly bore them was a father's too; or so at least he convinced himself.

"Well done, Hochbauer!" he cried, puffing slightly as he scored yet another goal. "A lovely pass!"

"You were beautifully placed again, sir!" replied Hochbauer, his eyes shining with admiration.

It would never have occurred to Captain Ratshelm to feel

flattered, it was enough for him that he was appreciated. True he had a fatherly love to bestow, but in return he looked for nothing but respect, and he never had the slightest fear that the depth of his affection might in any way constitute a threat to discipline.

Just then the ball hit him full on the side of the head. He swayed slightly, and for a moment it looked as if his legs were going to buckle under him. However, though his head was throbbing fiercely, he managed a sporting smile in the best officer tradition.

"Sorry, sir," called out Cadet Weber from the other side of the field. "I didn't mean it to be so hard."

"Foul!" cried Cadet Hochbauer, springing to the captain's defense at once.

Cadet Weber (Christian name: Egon) was a broad, burly fellow, as solid as an old-fashioned piece of furniture. Panting heavily he now pushed his way forward, laboring somewhat with a sense of insult, for he, too, had his ambitions as a sportsman.

"How would you know what was foul," he said to Hochbauer, "since you don't know what's fair?"

For a moment it seemed as if Hochbauer was going to spring at him. But then he looked across at the captain, who, though still nursing his head, was not prevented from doing what he conceived to be his duty as a sportsman.

"Weber," said Captain Ratshelm severely, "no arguing while the game's in progress. You're sent off!"

"Greetings, fellow sportsmen," said Cadet Weber, trotting over to Rednitz and Mösler. "Have you heard? I've been sent off. Not a bad trick for getting a spell of rest, eh? I'm going to patent it."

"I'm afraid," said Cadet Mösler, "that if your friend Hochbauer has to choose between you and the captain there's little doubt where his choice will lie."

"Who cares?" said Weber indulgently. "The main thing is I managed to give Ratshelm a crack on the head—all in the spirit of the game of course—and I've earned myself a breather as a result."

"All the same," Rednitz reminded him, "Hochbauer did say it was a foul."

"He's right, too," said Weber, quite unabashed. "I have no hesitation in playing foul in that sort of game, but I'm not going to admit it to those bastards."

This was typical of Cadet Weber (Christian name: Egon), whose imperturbability and disarming frankness allied to a bulldog-like temperament made him the least vulnerable of men. With such a remarkably thick skin he could count himself a useful soldier.

"What about a game with the medicine ball?" he suggested.

Mösler and Rednitz agreed—medicine ball was easily the best way of avoiding trouble; it kept one warm without requiring any effort, rather like the friendly sort of games that children play.

The three cadets retired from the game of handball altogether, without anyone noticing them. Ratshelm was still in the thick of things, playing with great abandon and setting an example which he felt sure everyone else would follow. He didn't exactly suffer from a sense of inferiority.

"Heard the latest?" Cadet Weber asked.

"What's that?" asked Rednitz with a smile. "Apart from the fact that your friend Hochbauer thinks you don't play fair."

"Oh hell," rejoined Weber good-naturedly, "I know you can't stand Hochbauer, but I can't think why!"

"You know quite well why," put in Rednitz.

"My dear fellow," said Weber calmly, "my sole purpose here is to survive the course, not to go around awarding people marks for character. As far as I'm concerned, anyone here can be as pure or sink as low as he likes—all I care about is becoming an officer. To hell with everything else!"

Rednitz smiled. He picked up a medicine ball and threw it to Mösler. Their evasive action was already under way.

"Well," asked Mösler, "what's new on the Rialto?"

"Something pretty big!" Weber assured him. Rednitz looked at him curiously, and he added, "Or so it seems to me. It looks as if the women have got out of hand!"

"That's nothing new," said Mösler speaking as an expert, "but which particular women do you mean?"

"The ones here in barracks!" said Weber. "It's said they're rushing about naked all over the place."

"Only in the showers, surely," said Rednitz. "Where else?"

"You may well ask!" said Weber. "In the basement of staff headquarters—in the communications center, I'm told. Rows of them. Three at least, if not five. No one's safe, they say. Further information later. Makes you think, though, doesn't it, fellows?"

"Man!" said Cadet Mösler with something like solemnity. "This seems to demand a maximum effort on our part. I suggest the formation of a raiding party for tonight!"

"Carry on without me, fellows!" Captain Ratshelm called out to his cadets.

"We'll manage," Cadet Hochbauer assured him. "Thanks to you, sir, we can't lose." And several of the cadets nodded enthusiastically.

Captain Ratshelm had scored enough points. His companions had the right to score, too, and he wasn't the man to spoil their fun. Besides, he was feeling rather tired. He was panting hard and had a slight stitch in his right side—life at the front, it seemed, had taken its toll of him. He withdrew to the rear—not far enough to disturb Cadets Mösler, Weber, and Rednitz, but far enough away to be able to watch Cadet Hochbauer.

In Ratshelm's eyes Cadet Hochbauer was the very model of what an officer should be. He already possessed an outstanding personality, and his mind was alert and precise. He had plenty of energy and endurance, and was both keen, resourceful, and respectful. In short, this fellow Hochbauer was endowed with all the qualities of a born leader of men. The inevitable callousness of youth would fine down in time, and his idealism, which was rather lacking in sophistication at the moment, would learn to make the unavoidable compromises.

Ratshelm paused to look across at the two other sections, G and I, where a familiar sight met his eyes. Lieutenant Webermann was circling his flock of cadets with the tireless energy of a sheepdog; Lieutenant Dietrich on the other hand had so positioned himself that he could take in all his cadets at a glance. They used different methods but achieved the same result, keeping their cadets on the move without setting any particular examples themselves. This was why they were wearing thick track suits, whereas Ratshelm, stripped for action, was a true sportsman and a fitting companion for the cadets.

Thinking along these lines, Captain Ratshelm suddenly noticed that it was extremely cold in the gym. He was even shivering himself, so he decided to order a run around the hall.

He beckoned the section senior over to him and said, "Kramer—in five minutes we'll bring the games to an end and finish with a general run."

"Hear that?" said Cadet Mösler to his friends Rednitz and

Weber. "They're off on the Idiot's Handicap in five minutes. They can leave us out, though, eh?"

This went without saying. A run around the hall wasn't for old soldiers like them. This wretchedly taxing marathon trot was part of the captain's basic routine, the principal item in his act, in fact. Captain Ratshelm stood in the center of the ring, while they all trotted around him for at least fifteen minutes.

To avoid this, Cadets Mösler, Weber, and Rednitz went up to Kramer, the cadet who at present held the post of section senior, and Mösler said, as if it were the most obvious thing in the world, "Kramer we'll see to the equipment—all right?"

"What, again?" demanded Kramer irritably. "All three of you? You three always want the cushy jobs! I won't stand for it indefinitely, you know; people will start asking questions."

"If that's all they start asking questions about," said Rednitz amiably, "you can count yourself lucky."

"Are you threatening me?" asked Kramer indignantly. He was head sergeant and wanted to be shown a certain amount of respect. If people only asked him for this sort of thing politely, he was almost certain to agree pleasantly enough. But the behavior of these three cadets was beginning to look very much like blackmail. "You look out!" he muttered. "These hints of yours will land you in trouble. You can't prove anything—Lieutenant Barkow died a completely natural death."

"It depends how you look at it," said Weber. "Death is always the most natural thing in the world, one way or another."

"We'll have a talk about it some time," announced Mösler with a grin. "Today we just want to spare you any unpleasantness—and we're the only people who can. For if we don't look after the sports equipment you can be sure you'll be short a medicine ball."

Kramer was quite smart enough to realize what was being hinted at here. The three of them had obviously managed to hide a medicine ball away in such a way that only they could find it again. If he wanted to save himself a lot of trouble and embarrassment he had no alternative but to give in to them. He muttered an obscenity under his breath before giving the order. "Mösler, Weber and Rednitz are to see to the equipment."

Which meant that for these three the games period had

ended before it had begun. It would have taken an inexperienced recruit less than ten minutes to collect and return the sports equipment, but since these were old soldiers, a good half-hour would be required. And by that time the circus performance would be over.

"Friends!" said Cadet Weber. "We must now discuss our plan of campaign—we've lots of time for it. I must say I can't get the idea of those women out of my head. I take it as a personal affront to my virility that these wretched little girls should be running around so pathetically dissatisfied."

"Let me have your attention a moment, fellows!" said Captain Ratshelm after looking at his watch. "We've just got time to sharpen up our wits a little, in accordance with the principle *mens sana in corpore sano,* you know. You all understand what that means?"

There was hardly anyone who didn't understand what that meant. It meant that before his last great closing number, before the last communal exertion of the day, Captain Ratshelm intended to indulge in a little theoretical work. Noncommissioned officers might be content to know *how* a thing was done, but officers needed to know *why* it was done. It was to this end therefore that Captain Ratshelm collected his cadets around him in a semicircle and asked searchingly, "Why actually do we play games?"

"I often ask myself that!" whispered a cadet at the back.

Captain Ratshelm ignored this, chiefly because it never occurred to him that anyone would have dared to whisper in his presence. He gazed straight into the keen, eager faces of the cadets. For one of the slogans of the training school, laid down by the course commanders, stated that there were no questions to which an officer did not have the answer.

Ratshelm looked at Hochbauer with a momentary tingle of pleasure at the cadet's fine, upstanding appearance. His fine blue eyes, betraying both confidence and humility, radiated his respect for his commanding officer. Siegfried must have had something of the same look when his glance rested on Kriemhilde. And Hochbauer thrust his powerful, manly chin slightly forward, a gesture equivalent to the raised hand of the eager schoolboy denoting that he was burning to be asked.

"Well, Hochbauer?" asked the captain. A shiver ran down the cadet's spine, as he sprang to attention in exemplary fashion, looked his superior officer straight in the eye, and spoke out, "Games steel the body, sir, but a healthy body contains a healthy mind as well. Games make one versatile, and versatility is one of the finest qualities in the German character."

It was as if the answer had been turned out by a machine —curt, crisp, and precise. In short, beyond reproach. Ratshelm was very pleased. He nodded and said, "Good, Hochbauer."

Hochbauer seemed to swell with pride and happiness, though his face remained admirably self-controlled. He stayed as rigid as ever, with the merest flicker of a smile playing about his lips. But his eyes radiated warmth. He bared his teeth slightly, almost imperceptibly. They too were splendid and he would have made an admirable toothpaste advertisement: Healthy teeth denote a healthy mind—Officers prefer Blendol.

But Ratshelm continued his theoretical instruction with the question, "Are games an officer's concern?"

"Only in so far as his subordinates have to play them," whispered the cadet at the back.

But a cadet in front gave the required answer. "An officer is concerned with everything that promotes military efficiency, instills discipline and maintains and indeed develops a high standard of general fitness. Games are an excellent way of improving military discipline. A good officer organizes games and takes part in them himself, he has to set an example in everything."

Ratshelm decided that that would do. The excellent answers were fully up to the standard of the earlier performance. He had every reason to be content with this section of his and could only hope and pray that the successor of the late Lieutenant Barkow would prove worthy of them. Such firstrate human material deserved the greatest possible care.

Captain Ratshelm now gave orders for the run around the gym to begin, planning that it should last about twenty minutes. To guarantee a good steady pace he put Hochbauer in front, and to prevent any weakening in the center, made Kramer, the section senior, bring up the rear. Off they trotted in this formation.

Letting his glance wander up from the cadets' legs to their faces, Ratshelm was surprised to find the correct expression of enthusiasm missing. In vain he searched for that fine eager glow of manly zest which should have distinguished the officers of the future, particularly those whose privilege it was to grow to their full stature under his tutelage.

But perhaps the sudden death of Lieutenant Barkow had depressed the cadets. It might have been, too, that the regrettably incomplete funeral ceremony of the early afternoon had made an unfavorable impression on them. Then there was the unpleasantness of the investigation being conducted by Judge-Advocate Wirrmann into the Barkow affair—an unavoidable procedure, perhaps, but one well calculated to bewilder them.

Thinking along these lines, Ratshelm found the situation deeply moving. Young men who had been selected to be officers, he told himself, needed to be shown the importance of *esprit de corps* in the circle to which they aspired. So, acting on a spontaneous impulse, he once again gathered H Section about him.

The cadets showed an extraordinary willingness to respond to their commanding officer's summons, which provided a welcome break in the exhausting marathon. Most of them were curious too; for they had soon discovered that Captain Ratshelm was utterly unpredictable. The man also had a way of talking as if reading out of some military textbook, which certainly had its funny side.

"Right. Now, just give me your attention, all of you," said Ratshelm impressively, the very picture of an officer determined to give his men a thorough grounding in their subject. "Today we've buried our section officer, Lieutenant Barkow. He was a good man. Now we all have to die in the end, and a good soldier must be prepared to do so at any moment—officer or not, of course. So far so good. But our soldiers don't only have to fight and die, we also have a paper war to fight. And this has its points, even though I won't discuss them in further detail just at the moment. Anyhow it's a necessary part of things that when a man dies there should sometimes be an investigation. But an investigation of this sort is a pure matter of form. Do you follow me? There's nothing more to it than that. Certain things just don't happen among officers. Understood? And just to make myself completely plain to the blockheads, Lieutenant Barkow died a natural death, a soldier's death, one might say. It was an accident, and that's all there is to it. Anyone who thinks otherwise hasn't yet understood the meaning of being an officer, and he'll find he has me to reckon with! About face! Double march!"

* * * *

Intermediate Report No. 1

The Curriculum Vitae of
Lieutenant Karl Krafft,
or The Problems of Respectability

My name is Karl Krafft. I was born on November 8, 1916, at Pöhlitz, in Stettin, Pomerania, son of a post-office inspector called Joseph Krafft and his wife, Margaret, whose maiden name was Panzer. I spent my childhood in the town of my birth.

The sky is dark, as it almost always is, and it rains a lot. I have gray eyes and the mirror I see them in has lost its sheen. The houses in the street are a muddy gray, the same color as my father's face. When I kiss my mother my hands wander across her forehead; and her hair is stiff and dry, gray as old silver, almost as gray as lead.

When it rains, dull gray, milky gray water runs through the streets. We run bare-foot and the water comes up to our ankles. Our hands scoop sand and earth from the garden and mud from the street and we knead it together and compress it into a doughlike mass, build dams with it. And the water rises, forms a pool, spreads and overflows the pavement, threatening to invade the cellars. People curse us, and we laugh; then we trample down the dams and run off until we can no longer see or hear the people cursing us.

Once again water is flowing. And this time it's the river at the edge of the town, called the Oder. The waters rush past sucking and churning up the earth and the sand, driving them before it, as we stare into the swirling current. We fold up huge banknotes on our knees. These banknotes have lots of noughts on them and we fold them into paper boats. They float and bob giddily about on top of the water, turn drunkenly around and around, bump into each other—but the important thing is, they float. This paper money makes wonderful boats.

"All the money's any use for is to wipe your arse on!" says a man, who's my uncle. "No," says my father, "that isn't true!" "Everything printed or written, all paper in short," says my uncle, "is only fit to wipe your arse on." "You shouldn't say that!" cries my father indignantly, "at least not in front of the children."

Father doesn't talk much. Mother hardly talks at all. It's always very quiet with us in the little house. Only when there's discussion of what my father calls "higher things" does he get at all excited—talk about the Fatherland for example, or the postal service. "When many men love and honor a thing," says my father, "then you can be certain that it's worthy of love and honor—you mark my words, my son." And then my father is suddenly standing at attention in the middle of our little garden, for the head of the post office, Herr Giebelmeier, is passing by. "Very fine, Krafft," Herr Giebelmeier shouts at my father. "Really very fine—your flowers are like so many soldiers standing there. They make a brave show. Carry on, Krafft!"

"We're going to paint this little house of ours," says my father after thinking for a long time. "We want to make a brave show of it!" And so my father buys whitewash and lime and two paint-brushes—the smaller one for me. And we begin painting it blue—bright blue, the color of the sky. And then once again the head of the post office, Herr Giebelmeier, comes past and says "What on earth are you doing there, Krafft? What's all this about?" "I'm smartening the place up a bit, sir," says my father, standing to attention. "But you can't do that," says Giebelmeier firmly, "that sort of thing's much too ostentatious, it's too garish, man. If only you'd chosen post-office yellow, I might have come around to it—but sky blue! It positively screams at you! Anyway, all I can say is, it's certainly not right for any official of mine."

"Very good, sir," says my father, and when Giebelmeier has gone my father says to me, "He was an officer of the reserve, you see." "I don't see," I say. "What's the connection between an officer of the reserve and house painting?" "Later," says my father, "you'll understand that too." And our house stayed gray.

In 1922 I began going to the primary school in my home town. My marks were always indifferent, but I steadily made my way up through the eight forms.

My books are tattered and well thumbed. They are covered in smudges because my hands are sweaty and not always clean. They're full of penciled scribbles: underlinings, marks, words written in, drawings, little men sometimes, and once even a woman, as I had seen her drawn on the lavatory wall in the railway station, with thighs apart and mountainous breasts. Every time I see this picture I feel ashamed because it's such a bad drawing.

One of our teachers called Grabowski catches sight of this

picture. We always call him "Stick" because he seems inseparable from the cane he carries. "Look at that—the little swine!" says Stick delightedly, waving his cane about in front of my face. "A dirty little swine, eh?" "I copied that," I tell him. "You can see it on the lavatory wall in the station." "Listen to him," says Stick. "So you've been looking at filthy drawings in the lavatory, eh?" "Well, yes," I say, "you can't really help it." "Now my lad," says Stick, "I'm going to show you what you can help and what you can't. Bend over. Bottom in the air. Trousers tight. Right." And then he beats me with the cane, until he's panting for breath. "Right," he says, "that'll teach you, you little stinker!" And I think to myself: Yes, that'll teach me—I'll never let him catch me with a drawing like that again.

"Always be obedient," says my father. "Obedient to the Almighty and to the authorities. Then you'll have a clear conscience and your future will be assured." But the new authorities deprive him of his living because he's been obedient to the old authorities.

"You must learn to love," says my mother. "To love nature and animals and men too. Then you'll always be happy and cheerful." But when my father falls on hard times she cries a lot. Her way of loving sometimes makes me sad. From then on she is never happy or cheerful again, even when my father is given the chance of obeying the new authorities—though this makes him very proud.

The faces of the teachers all seem the same to me because their mouths all go up and down in the same sort of way. The words all sound very smooth and polished and all get written down at one time or another. Their hands, too, all seem the same; their fingers are mostly curled around a piece of chalk, a fountain pen, a ruler, or a cane. Only one of them is different. His name is Schenkenfeind. He knows a lot of poetry by heart and I learn everything he recites. And some more besides. I don't find this particularly difficult and Schenkenfeind is liberal with his praise. I even learn a poem about the Battle of Leuthen which has fifty-two verses. And Schenkenfeind says, "A fine poem!" And I believe him because he seems so sure about it. He actually wrote the poem himself.

There's a schoolmistress called Scharf, who comes and sits beside me on the bench. She is soft and warm and her limbs seem made of rubber and I am overwhelmed by a desire to seize hold of these limbs to find out whether they're really of rubber or not. But I don't—because she's close to me and I can smell her. I move away from her, feeling sick. "It's stuffy in here," I say. "There's a nasty smell." She gets up abruptly and never looks at me again. This suits me fine because I don't like her at all.

Some days later I catch sight of her one evening in the park, while I'm trying to trap glowworms. But this woman Scharf is lying on a bench in the dark with the teacher called Schenkenfeind, the man who writes such vast long moving poems. But the things he's saying now sound very different. He is saying the sort of things that Meerkatz the man who drives the beer dray says to his mare. Anyway I no longer want to learn from him any more.

"Man must learn if he is to hold his place in life," says this fellow Schenkenfeind. "I don't want to learn," I tell him. "No," says the teacher, "you'd rather go sniffing around the place, creeping about the park and spying on the lovers there —I saw you! You have nasty dirty thoughts, but I'll soon drive them out of you. As a punishment you'll write out ten times the beautiful poem *On Eternal Constancy*. And what's more you'll go and apologize to your teacher Fräulein Scharf, at once." But I don't go and apologize.

When I left my primary school in 1930 I went first to a commercial school in Stettin. After that I worked in the estate office of the big Varsen estate at Pöhlitz, where I was mainly concerned with the payroll and the issuing of supplies.

The old woman who lives in one of the attics above us passes me on the stairs, goes on down, and then suddenly stops. She stops, and collapses as if her legs had snapped like matchsticks. She lies there without moving, like a bundle of rags. Slowly I go up to her, stand in front of her, bend over her, and kneel down and look at her. Her eyes are yellow and staring; her thin mouth, with its dry, cracked lips embedded in a web of wrinkles, is twisted open and a thread of saliva runs down onto the dirty floor. She is no longer breathing. I put my hand over her shriveled breast at the place where the heart should be, but it is no longer beating.

Giebelmeier, the head of the post office, gives father a dressing down in front of everyone in the middle of the post office, because of some express letter which hasn't arrived quickly enough. Quite by chance I happen to be standing there behind a pillar. And Giebelmeier roars and gesticulates and gets purple in the face. But father never says a word, he simply stands there, small, hunched, and trembling.

Rigidly at attention. He looks up rather shiftily at Giebel-meier, who stands stiffly and proudly in front of him, roaring his head off. And father remains silent, abject.

That evening Father sits there silent as ever, and asks for a beer, which he drinks in silence. He asks for another beer. And then another. "Karl," my father then says to me, "a real man must have pride, a sense of honor. Honor is the all-important thing. One must always defend one's honor." "Oh, yes," I say, "but sometimes one has to remain silent and accept abuse for the sake of a quiet life." "Never," says my father indignantly. "Never, do you hear? Take me, for example, my son. Today in the post office I had a row with the head, this fellow Giebelmeier. He started shouting at me! But he came out of it badly. I told him off. Gave him a regular trouncing!" "Well done, Father," I say, and leave the room, because I feel ashamed for him.

I hold my friend Heinz's hand, which is cold as ice. I raise his head and turn it around slightly and see the rent in the skull and the watery blood and brains running out, all yellow and gray. Gently, I lay my friend's head back again and my hands are sticky with blood. And then I look at the weapon on the ground, a .98 rifle. And the end of the bullet has been filed off. He hadn't wanted to live. What has to happen to make a man not want to live like that, I wonder. And I can't get rid of the thought.

The girl snuggles up to me; I feel her body through the cloth of my suit. All I can see is the gleam in her eyes, but I feel her breath on my face and the moistness of her lips, and my hands slide down her back, brushing the boards of the fence against which I'm pushing her. A wave of passion comes over me, and I no longer know what I am doing. Then I have a great feeling of exhaustion and hear a voice asking me, "What your name?"

"It was two hundred hundredweight of potatoes," I tell the accountant in the estate office. But he doesn't look at me and simply repeats, "It was one hundred hundredweight. Do you follow me?" "No I don't," I say. "We delivered two hundred hundredweight." "But only a hundred are being entered up," says the accountant. "And we enter up what I say. Is that clear? Perhaps you've heard something about the crisis in agriculture, Krafft? It may have occurred to you to wonder how we keep our heads above water? And here you are wanting to let the State—a State like this, I ask you!—wanting to let the State swallow up all our hard-earned cash! It's suicide. Put it down, then: one hundred hundredweight! Enter that up." "Enter it up yourself," I tell him, pushing the books toward him, "and kindly keep that crisis-in-agriculture stuff to yourself in future!" "Krafft," the accountant then says, "I'm afraid you're not really cut out for this profession. You can't take orders from people. You don't co-operate." "I'm not going to make any false entries," I say. "Look here," says the accountant, "are you trying to accuse me of fraud? Just look here, will you—what's written down here? What have I written? Two hundred! There you are, you see. I only wanted to test you. And of course I'm not going to stand for it if you're going to start suspecting me and accusing me of dishonesty. You're not a person one can work with. I'll have to draw my own conclusions!"

One evening my uncle says to my father, "Your son Karl doesn't seem to have understood the signs of the times. He goes to church too little and makes no preparations for a family. As a result he's beginning to get ideas into his head. He'd better be sent into the army. They'll soon knock some sense into him there."

I began my military service in 1937. When my two years were up I was made a corporal and released, only to be called up again shortly afterward in the summer of 1939. I was with the colors at the outbreak of war, promoted sergeant after the Polish campaign, and commissioned as a second lieutenant after the campaign in France. During the campaign in Russia I was given command of a company, was promoted lieutenant, and then at the beginning of January 1944 was posted to the officers' training school. I hold the following decorations: Iron Cross First Class, Iron Cross Second Class, the Close-Combat Clasp in silver, and the Wound Badge in black.

Corporal Reinshagen, who's in charge of my training as a recruit, has many fine qualities and is a born soldier. He's a fine upstanding fellow, full of drive and possessed of an iron will, but not exactly a pillar of the Church. Thus for example he knows all the relevant military regulations backward, but no others. However, I also take care to be well informed on various aspects of military regulations, particularly those sections dealing with the treatment of subordinates and their right to lodge complaints. Sometimes I quote these at him and he doesn't like it. One day I turn my knowledge to practical advantage, and hand him a comprehensive and carefully worded complaint. About himself! To be passed on to higher authority. At first he simply bellows at me. Then he grows noticeably milder, and even displays a certain friendliness. "You can't do this to me," he says disarmingly. "All you've got to do is to behave decently," I reply. And he promises that he will.

Girls in the few hours we're allowed off duty—mostly picked up in the bar called The Anglers' Rest: servant girls, shop girls, typists. A dance or two, a drink or two, a short walk to the nearby park, and then and there quick but basic satisfaction. Back again for another dance or two, the whole experience washed down with beer. And then back to barracks, until next Saturday evening.

Then Eva-Maria. An official's daughter. Picked her up in the movies—some film or other with a broad-shouldered woman with a lion's mane of hair and a deep male voice growling love songs. A diversion urgently required—fortunately Eva-Maria is sitting beside me. She takes me home—a clean, well-kept home, a decent place. Her parents are away. Wonderful carefree hours. A strangely intoxicating sense of happiness. And as I make my way back late, very late, to the barracks, I feel an overwhelming desire to sing at the top of my voice. I'm so happy! But the night has no sequel, not for me at any rate. "Don't let's get sentimental," she says. "But I love you!" I cry. And it's the first time in my life I've ever said such a thing. "That's what the others say, too," declares Eva-Maria. Then she goes off with one of the others.

I stand at night in the street of our little garrison town and listen into the darkness. And I raise my eyes to where a soft light shines behind a curtained window. When I close my eyes I see her before me, I see everything she does and everything that happens to her. I see her smile, radiant with happiness and pleasure and at the same time dread. I see her quivering mouth tortured with desire, see her breasts as she covers them with her hands, see the rounded curves of her body. And I close my eyes, and now it is myself who am with her in that one night I spent with her.

And I say to myself, "I'll never again tell a woman I love her. Never."

Then comes the war. A man ducks down in front of me behind the rim of a well, all cramped as if doubled up with pain. His hair sticks out from under his cap. He's frightened and his body and clothes are covered in filth. I get him in my sights at a range of about sixty yards and raise the barrel of my rifle toward his temples, where he has an unruly tuft of hair. Slowly I curl the forefinger of my right hand around the trigger, but I can't bring myself to shoot. I can't do it. The man behind the rim of the well shoots, though. And a fellow beside me shudders, stares for a second into nothingness, then spurts blood from between his eyes and collapses.

"Here's an extra loaf for you," Sergeant Taschenmacher tells me. "I don't want it," I answer. Sergeant Taschenmacher has pinched two dozen loaves from the ration truck for his own private consumption. "Come on," he says amiably, and he can be very amiable when he wants, "don't be a wet blanket, go ahead and pocket the loaf. It may come in handy. You can even get yourself a real virgin with it if you feel like it—I'll throw in a suitable address for nothing. You see how generous I am!" "Sorry," I say. Now he's much less amiable. "Look here," he says, "are you out of your mind? What is it you want? Two loaves? Well, all right then." "No," I say. "Well three loaves, then," he says angrily, "and that's my final offer." "I insist that the two dozen loaves go where they belong," I reply. "And that's *my* final offer. If they don't I'll report the matter." Cursing, Sergeant Taschenmacher loads the two dozen loaves up on to the truck again all by himself.

The child wants to come to me; it raises a hand and opens its little mouth. But the officer chases both mother and child away. Then he sets fire to the farm, theoretically to give a better field of fire. The smoke billows softly, nauseating, toward me, wreathing itself in foul, thick, yellow and green waves about my face. And I stand there motionless, trying not to breathe and listening to the choking sobs of the woman and the gasping of the child. But I neither move nor breathe. "You have to kill to prevent yourself being killed," says the officer. "That's the law of war, you can't get away from it."

"Please go and see my wife," one of my comrades asks me. "Take her this parcel, I've saved a few rations. Give her my love and tell her I think about her all the time." And then I find myself sitting beside this wife of his. I've got a lot to tell her and she's very happy as we sit there having a drink together. I make a move to go, but she won't let me. "It's so nice together here," she says. It's warm in the room and getting warmer all the time and she says, "Make yourself at home, it's so nice together here." Well, fine, so I take off my tunic. But why does she then have to take off her blouse and stockings? Ah well, it is warm, and it's very nice being together, as she says, and besides she has utter confidence in me. I like this and we have some more drinks. She comes closer and suddenly says, "Do you always take so long or have you just forgotten how to do it? Or is it that you just don't like me?" "That's it," I say, "I don't like you." And I hit her in her beautiful, stupid, wanton face.

"You're an officer now," says my CO, "and I hope you'll prove worthy of your commission, Second Lieutenant Krafft." "I'll try to, sir," I answer.

A hundred and twenty men are delivered into my hands, entrusted to my care. I march with them, sleep with them, and share my food with them. We also share our cigarettes, perform our natural functions together, and kill together, shoulder to shoulder, day and night, month after month. Some of them leave me to be replaced at once by others—quite a few die. Some die accidentally, others as a result of an order, others because they no longer want to live. Death is with us all the time. But it always passes me by. Am I being spared, and if so, for what?

"You're a lieutenant now, Krafft," says my commanding officer, "and I hope you'll prove worthy of your promotion." I hear him say this but I make no answer. What does it mean: to be "worthy"?

Home again, or rather what's called home, for the once-enchanting little town is now barely recognizable. A hydro-electric plant has sprung up apparently overnight, with huge pipes and boilers covering an area of several square kilometers, and there are lots of little houses for the engineers, wooden barracks for the workers and office employees, and houseboats on the Oder, old barges, floating barns for the slave laborers and others. From time to time some of these can be seen in the distance dangling from a gallows on deck—hanged for sabotage, espionage, or various other things. Police and security units are interspersed among them. Finally there are twelve antiaircraft batteries in the vicinity. But worst of all are the bombs. In exactly thirty-five minutes one night my little home town ceases to exist, and my parents are dead.

Looking back down the years there seems just an endless series of battles and corpses and copulation, murder and sex. In Poland, in a western suburb of Warsaw, a half-charred, stinking house, and in it a woman called Anja—two days. In France, in Paris, some hotel or other in Montmartre near which I found Raymonde—four nights in six weeks. Russia, Jasnaja Poljana near Tula, where Tolstoy lived; in the museum there, a girl whose name I never knew

—twenty minutes. And all for food, or for schnapps, or for passes of one sort or another. Almost always followed by remorse and disgust with oneself. Never once anything like real love, even when the girls were German, as for instance on some night train journey, or on a truck transporting members of the Women's Auxiliary Corps, or in an operating tent while the doctor slept off his drunkenness.

But then comes a girl who disturbs me profoundly, a girl whom it's a pleasure to be with and into whose eyes I can even look afterward. She has a wonderful, redeeming sort of laugh which banishes all remorse or disgust. I find myself emotionally involved, or at least become aware of a deep need in which lust is strangely unimportant. The whole thing is rather worrying, after all that's happened down the years, and the most frightening thing of all is that I sometimes feel tempted to say what I've determined never to say again: "I love you!" But I won't ever say it again, not even for her. This girl's name is Elfrida Rademacher.

4 AN EXERCISE POSTPONED

"GENTLEMEN," said Major Frey to the assembled officers, "I have to inform you that the general intends to work out a tactical exercise at the conclusion of dinner this evening."

"All alone?" asked Captain Feders immediately, with an amiable grin.

The major amended his statement with a certain sharpness.

"The general and the rest of the officers!"

Frey didn't like being interrupted by subordinates, particularly when they put him right. This fellow Captain Feders sometimes behaved as if he were the only person who knew anything about soldiering. Still, one had to show him a certain indulgence. In the first place Captain Feders was unquestionably the finest tactics instructor in the school, and secondly he had a very sharp tongue. Finally there was the extremely painful matter of his wife. All in all it was better to avoid a clash with him, for Feders was a dangerous man.

Or at least Feders had a dangerous way of putting apparently disarming questions. He always wanted to know everything, including whether the person he was asking really knew anything at all.

"Has the object of the exercise been announced yet, sir?"

"No," said the latter.

"Do we know how long it's likely to last?"

"No, we don't," said Major Frey rather crossly. With two completely innocent-sounding questions Feders had demonstrated to the rest of the officers that the major was little more than an office boy as far as General Modersohn was concerned.

"Right, then," said Feders. "Let's all go back to school again. One thing's certain at least: the chances of a good night's rest are just about nil. Once the general starts this exercise he won't stop until quite a number of heads have rolled. Well all I can say, gentlemen, is enjoy your dinner!"

The officers assembled in the mess anteroom looked thoroughly gloomy. There were more than forty of them in all, including the two course commanders, the company commanders, the tactics instructors, the section officers, and the administrative group of planners and organizers. The general's lightning decisions seemed to hang over them like menacing storm clouds.

Knight's Crosses were flashing all over the place. Not a chest in sight that didn't boast an Iron Cross at least. Close-combat clasps, anti-tank badges, campaign ribbons, war-service and long-service medals—such things were a matter of course. The German Cross in Gold was nothing out of the ordinary. And the faces above this brilliant splendor were mostly serious and grimly professional, marked by a certain uneasiness, sometimes even anxiety, about the eyes, though seldom indifference.

"Gentlemen," said Captain Feders, "I suggest we start. After all, the general always begins his meal punctually regardless of whether everyone's there or not."

"Not very funny, Captain Feders," said Major Frey, commanding officer of Number 2 Course, sternly. None of the other officers seemed to think it funny either. Even in the bright electric light their faces looked black.

The most silent group of all was that in the immediate vicinity of the dining-room door, where the victims of the evening's *placement* were standing. This *placement* was worked out in the most intricate detail before every meal by the ADC, in collaboration with a corporal who had been a schoolmaster in civilian life. The principle was that every officer should take his place at the commanding officer's table in strict rotation. It was an honor which no one was spared. Only occasionally did the general choose his own dining companions, and then always to the considerable disquiet of those concerned. This was exactly what had happened now.

Captain Kater felt a weakness at the knees and a queasiness in his stomach, for the place on the general's left had been reserved for him. One glance at the rest of the *placement* made the special significance of this clear. Judge-Advocate Wirrmann was seated on the general's right, while another place was reserved for Lieutenant Krafft immediately opposite.

"Well, gentlemen," said Captain Feders, going up to the victims with a show of interest, "what's it feel like to be on the menu this evening?"

"I'm pretty tough," said Lieutenant Krafft. "Quite a mouthful for anyone, I think."

Feders looked Captain Kater up and down with some hostility. "I must say if I were the general I'd prefer a nice streaky slice of wild boar myself."

"However, you're not the general," muttered Kater angrily. "You're simply a tactics instructor here, and a married man, what's more."

"But what's all the fuss about, gentlemen?" pleaded Judge-Advocate Wirrmann. "Anyone would think this *placement* was an affair of state."

"It's a rather a special situation here," said Feders. "You must know that one glance from our general may easily be the first step on the road to a state funeral. You're up against serious competition here, Wirrmann. You merely apply the law. The general makes it."

"Not for me, he doesn't," said Wirrmann, permitting himself a slightly condescending smile.

At a signal from the mess senior sergeant the orderlies appeared with the soup, and carried it past the officers into the dining room.

This was a sure sign that the various scouts posted along the route had spotted the general's approach. The few people who had managed to engage in conversation fell silent. The officers fell in, the junior ones automatically stepping to the rear while the more senior prepared to confront the general.

"Gentlemen, the general!" cried Major Frey. It was a superfluous announcement. The gentlemen were already standing rigidly to attention as if turned to concrete by their sense of discipline.

Major-General Modersohn approached with measured strides, accompanied by his ADC, to whom no one seemed to pay the slightest attention. The officers had eyes only for their general, who came to a halt exactly one pace inside the threshold and surveyed the assembled company. It was as if he were thinking of counting them and registering them individually. Only then did he bring his hand up to the peak of his cap and say, "Good evening, gentlemen."

"Good evening, sir!" the officers replied in chorus.

The general nodded, not so much acknowledging the greeting as ratifying it. For the voices had been nicely in harmony, and adequate in volume. "At ease, please," he said, and the officers complied immediately. Or at least they relaxed sufficiently to push the left foot slightly forward and to one side. But no one dared to speak.

Major-General Modersohn now took off his cap, and unbuttoned and removed his greatcoat, handing first one and then the other to an orderly standing stiffly at his side. The general utterly refused to allow himself to be helped in any mundane activity of this sort.

The officers followed their general's every movement with the keenest interest, and watched him take a sheet of paper from his cuff, unfold it, and read it. It seemed almost as if he were taking in one of those telegrams which start wars. Finally the general looked up and said, "The subject for tonight's tactical exercise will be a major outbreak of fire in the barracks."

And with that, consternation really set in. This was a subject full of all sorts of hidden surprises—the more experienced officers realized that at once. If it had been a question of organizing a raiding party, maneuvering companies into position, or if necessary even bringing up whole divisions, they could have managed it. But a major outbreak of fire in barracks had no place in the training curriculum at all, nor had they ever had the slightest practical experience in this field.

"Well, I hope you've all made your wills, gentlemen?" said Feders delightedly, under his breath. "Because I'm afraid this major outbreak of fire in the barracks is going to cook quite a number of people's geese for them."

The mess sergeant appeared, a sort of headwaiter with military training. Behind him two orderlies opened the swing doors leading into the dining room, whereupon the senior sergeant stepped up to the general much as if he were approaching royalty. He came to a halt, thrust out his chest, laid his fingers down the seams of his trousers, and said, "I beg to inform the general that the soup is on the table!"

Modersohn nodded briefly with that touch of affability he always reserved for his lower-ranking subordinates. The forty-six officers made way for him at once and he strode through them into the dining room. Those who had been commanded to sit at his table followed closely at his heels, while the others poured in behind them. And still no one dared to say a word.

This dining room was not without a certain Germanic splendor, having a slightly worn lime-green carpet, and walls paneled in an imitation oak veneer appropriately decorated with a pattern of oak leaves. In the middle of the room hung a sort of brass chandelier with ceramic candles, while around the walls were portraits of so-called war leaders and statesmen of recent German history—all in imposing proportions befitting the subjects. At the upper end of the room, at least three times the size, hung a portrait of the Führer in oils.

"As usual, gentlemen, quite informal," announced Major Frey quietly. For the general always left trivial matters of organization to his immediate subordinates.

The officers dispersed, informally as usual, to their various tables, with the company commanders and a sprinkling of tactics instructors positioned close to the general. After them came the section officers, followed by the rest: three accountants, or rather quartermasters, two doctors, an engineer officer from the transport section, and a civilian specially attached.

Major Frey said, "I beg to report to the general that the officers are all present for dinner."

Major-General Modersohn nodded almost imperceptibly and sat down. His forty-six officers did the same. The general grasped his spoon. The forty-six officers did likewise. The general drove his spoon into the soup. The rest of the company followed his example.

They ate in silence at first, a silence punctuated only by occasional sucking noises. For the general neither said a word himself nor gave anyone else permission to speak. Every now and again he would throw a searching glance at his officers, noting that none of them seemed particularly to relish their food—a fact which could not be attributed solely to the thin insipidness of the potato soup. The officers were desperately trying to prepare themselves for the tactical exercise to follow—the major outbreak of fire in barracks. And the effort rather took their appetites away.

Only when the second course, a dish of beef with *haricots verts,* arrived did the general turn to Judge-Advocate Wirrmann and, speaking with a slight drawl, say, "So you wish to undertake a second case in my command even before completing the first?"

Wirrmann felt relieved at thus being asked to speak at last. He perked up at once and said, "My investigations into the causes of Lieutenant Barkow's death remain of course my chief concern, General. As for this matter of rape——"

"This alleged matter of rape," Lieutenant Krafft corrected him, in discreet but unmistakable tones.

The general eyed the lieutenant shrewdly for a moment, before going on with his dinner. Clearly he wasn't going to allow anything to escape him.

The judge-advocate continued hurriedly. "All right then, this alleged rape. But as far as that's concerned, I have simply wished to make my expert knowledge available—an offer which Captain Kater seemed delighted to accept but which Lieutenant Krafft seems to view with disfavor."

"Not without reason either," said Lieutenant Krafft, quite unperturbed. "For the facts are still obscure, and nothing has yet been proved."

"Excuse me, please," put in Wirrmann. "Since you're not a lawyer, you're hardly in a position to judge that."

"Maybe," said Krafft stubbornly, "But I've been put in charge of this case, and I am therefore dealing with it as I think right."

"As you think fit," corrected the general, without looking up from his plate, and concentrating wholly, it seemed, on the potato before him.

This unexpected remark struck his table companions temporarily dumb. Captain Kater choked on a mouthful of beef. Wirrmann subjected the general's remark to the closest possible scrutiny, trying to decide what to make of it. Krafft was merely astonished at the sharpness of Modersohn's hearing—the general, it seemed, was alive to every nuance.

Finally Wirrmann said, "A case of this sort, General, requires expert opinion even more than the usual routine sort of affair. I therefore consider it my duty to lend Captain Kater my assistance. You see, it's quite different from some everyday offense such as refusing to obey an order, or theft from a comrade, or desertion—the most trivial details can be of decisive legal importance in a case of this kind. According to the relevant paragraph of the Military Code there are three fundamental requirements for rape: the complete act itself, the use of force, and the absence of consent. Take one point for example, the importance of which most laymen would overlook: the underclothes. The question here is, Who removed them? How much resistance was offered? Were there in fact any underclothes at all?—and if not, from what point in the proceedings?"

"Herr Wirrmann," said the general without raising his voice, but with extreme asperity, "we're eating our dinner."

The judge-advocate's mouth shut tight. His lips, which were thin enough in any case, now became no more than a slit in his face. He blushed to the roots, feeling like a schoolboy humiliated in front of the whole class, an experience which hadn't come his way since he'd been in the sixth grade. The other officers were discreetly enjoying the situation.

The general calmly went on with his dinner. Lieutenant Krafft put his knife and fork together, and for the first time examined Modersohn more closely. He saw a long, angular skull, as rough as a piece of pumice stone, though the features were clear and distinct. The few lines in his face ran very deep down from his nostrils past his mouth to his chin. His eyes were a steely gray, and he had a high forehead with close-cropped white hair. Krafft was tempted to think of some noble but unpredictable Prussian stallion.

"Gentlemen, we shall now retire," said the general, getting up from his seat.

"The tactical training exercise," announced the ADC fussily, "will take place in this room in fifteen minutes' time."

"Well, Judge-Advocate," asked Captain Feders amiably, "did you enjoy your dinner?"

"A little too strongly spiced for my taste," said Wirrmann, laughing as if he had a sense of humor. But his laugh sounded anything but genuine, for he was a man who took himself desperately seriously.

Most of the officers had withdrawn to the lobby to get out of the general's field of fire, and they now took advantage of the break to smoke a quick cigarette. At the same time they tried to ferret out information about the projected exercise, chiefly quizzing Captain Feders.

"Gentlemen," said Feders defensively, "I'm utterly in the dark about this myself. How should I know what's meant to happen if a major fire breaks out in the barracks? Until I've had further details of the scheme, I shan't be able to think of how to cope with it. I may be tactics instructor in a training school, but I'm not exactly a clairvoyant yet."

The officers' restlessness increased and they enveloped themselves in thicker and thicker clouds of smoke. Through the open doorway of the dining room they could see the orderlies transforming the place into a sort of classroom with a blackboard at the rear and two map stands beside it, and the general's tablet in front, like a headmaster's desk. The officers' tables and chairs were arranged like school benches.

"Well anyway," said Judge-Advocate Wirrmann, "I'm glad to be spared this."

"And I expect you'd be gladder still," said Feder, "if you had permission to put those three strapping girls under your microscope."

"Captain Feders," Wirrmann rebuked him, "as far as I'm concerned this is a purely professional matter and the fact that it happens to involve three females of doubtful repute is of complete indifference to me."

"I don't quite see how you can separate the one side of it from the other."

"I am a lawyer, Captain, after all!"

"Exactly!" said Feders gaily. "If you were a doctor, or a psychiatrist, or even a gynecologist, I'd say fine, this is his job, this is the sort of thing he's used to. But when a lawyer whose only experience so far is with old sweats comes along and starts peering under three young girls' skirts —then my dear sir, I can hardly help laughing up my sleeve."

"You're letting your imagination run away with you," replied Wirrmann. He would have liked to add that the general was too. But he held his tongue. He bore these insults with dignity, though he wasn't going to forget them. He knew this type of officer inside out. Consciously or unconsciously, a man like Modersohn encouraged all sorts of subversive ideas. On principle he, Wirrmann, had to regard such people with the utmost suspicion. "You lack confidence in the responsible machinery of the State," he said before he left.

As he watched him go Captain Feders said, "You have to hand it to him—he's no fool. And that could mean trouble."

"Officers are requested to take their places for the exercise," cried the ADC.

The officers didn't wait to be told a second time. They quickly stubbed out their cigarettes, brought their conversations to a close, and went into the dining room, which had been turned into a classroom for the officer elite. They took their places and eyed the general expectantly.

Major-General Modersohn sat at his table working like a headmaster at his desk, quite undisturbed by the entrance of the officers. He was looking through the documents which the ADC had collected for him, and there was a writing pad beside him on which he was making notes.

The ADC now made the further announcement that Major Frey, commanding officer of Number 2 Course, would be in charge of the exercise.

This marked down the first victim of the evening. Others would follow later. For a tactical exercise of this sort had a dual purpose: first, to work out in theory some situation that might arise in practice, but secondly to permit special tasks to be allotted to as many of those present as possible. Once this was done the business of fighting a major fire could be worked out step by step. Each participant had to describe both concisely and comprehensively exactly what he would do in the emergency, or alternatively cause to be done, if for instance he had charge of a party detailed to prevent the fire from spreading, or of one of the brigades themselves—or simply of a supply store. And thus it would go on throughout the entire night, if Modersohn felt like it.

Captain Feders, that experienced tactics instructor, found his companions waiting on his every word. "The man who'll really catch it is the one who has to play duty officer," he told them.

"Duty officer," read the ADC from the pad on which the General had been making his notes, "Lieutenant Krafft."

Krafft only just managed to suppress an oath. He was an old enough hand to realize that he'd got the most thankless task of the whole exercise. The general had obviously had his eye on him and the thought worried Krafft.

"May I have a copy of the guard regulations?" he asked.

The general nodded, and the ADC had the guard regulations handed to Lieutenant Krafft. The officers regarded with interest the man who seemed likely to be the scapegoat of the evening—though without sentimentality, for someone had to be the victim and this time it just happened to be this fellow Krafft. One could hardly hope to interrupt a general's dinnertime conversation and get away with it.

The ADC had now finished reading out the list of those participating in the exercise, and no one, it seemed, had been forgotten. Everyone had been allotted a role of one sort or another or at least the supervision of some role. The officers found themselves sweating with anxiety. The traps were set, but who, apart from Krafft, would fall into them?

The ADC announced the opening situation. "A major fire is presumed to have broken out in the region of Number Four Company. Origin unknown. Scale so far unknown. Day: Sunday. Time: zero one thirty-eight hours. The exercise begins."

Captain Feders grinned happily, for he had spotted the pitfalls at once. "Number Four Company," he whispered to his companions, "is almost bang in the middle of the barracks—what a marvelous chance for a fire to spread! What's more we're caught in the sacred silence of a Sunday morning with almost everyone still away on late pass. What possibilities! There'll be some smoke here all right, I can sniff it already."

"If you please, Major Frey," said the ADC at a glance from Major-General Modersohn, "the exercise has begun."

"Alarm!" cried Major Frey in slightly strained tones, and they were away. All Frey had to do now was to find someone to carry the game on. "Number Four Company area is on fire, then. What is Number Four Company going to do?"

"I pass on the alarm," said the officer in charge of the company. "I, in my turn, alarm the duty officer."

All eyes now turned toward Lieutenant Krafft, who leaned back in his chair. He was determined not to let himself be stampeded. He wasn't going to be the lamb led to the slaughter by sheer weight of numbers. "Are these guard regulations to be regarded as authoritative?" he asked.

"Of course," said Major Frey at once. "They're the official regulations."

"Does that mean that I have to obey these regulations?" continued Krafft subbornly.

"But of course, man!" cried Frey with some sharpness. He felt most indignant. "Regulations are there to be obeyed. Every order has the authority of law, and a written order is the law itself."

Krafft made it clear from his expression that he regarded

the Major's pronouncements as the last word in stupidity. The officers sensed a sensational development. With a mixture of hope and alarm they looked from Krafft to Major Frey and from the latter to Major-General Modersohn. The general observed placidly, "The guard regulations are to be regarded as authoritative, Lieutenant Krafft."

"Then, General, this exercise has no foundation in reality at all," said the lieutenant. To those present it seemed little short of an attempt at suicide. "Because these guard regulations just don't make sense." The heavy silence which now fell across the room seemed to be waiting for a flash of lightning to shatter it. Even the happy grin on Captain Feders' face partially froze. Then Captain Kater gave an indignant snort. The evening had reached another climax.

With a remarkable softness the general said, "Would you explain that a little further, please, Lieutenant Krafft?"

Krafft nodded rather wearily. He had shown the courage of a lion so far, but it now threatened to desert him as suddenly as it had come. He began to have a panicky feeling that he had gone too far.

"Well?" asked the general with devastating politeness. "I'm listening."

"General," said Lieutenant Krafft finally, "these guard regulations are not only imprecise in certain respects but on a number of vital points they actually contradict each other. For example the order in which the fire hydrants are to be used is given as numbers one, two, three and four, but this is senseless, considering the actual position of these hydrants. If the duty officer were to go by these regulations, he'd have to waste an enormous amount of valuable time rushing back and forth all over the place. Because there's only one possible sequence for the effective use of the fire hydrants, which is four, one three, two."

"Anything else, Lieutenant Krafft?" asked the general, still very softly.

Krafft brought forward four further points to demonstrate the defects of the guard regulations: inadequate alarm system, incorrect inventory of fire extinguishers, wrongly stored explosives, and a shortage of picks, spades, and axes in the guardroom equipment. "If the duty officer were in fact to go by these guard regulations the entire barracks would be burned down before there was a chance of getting a single hose into play."

"Let me see, please," said the general.

The guard regulations were handed to Modersohn, who turned over the pages and skimmed through the relevant sections. His face remained a mask, as imperturbable and detached as at dinner. All eyes were turned toward him and the general accepted this as if exposed simply to the rays of the sun.

Then he raised his head, looked at Krafft, and asked, "When did the defects in these guard regulations first strike you, Lieutenant Krafft?"

"Three days ago, sir," said Krafft. "When I was duty officer."

"In that case," said Major-General Modersohn, "I should have known about this at least two days ago. You neglected to put in the necessary report. You will report to me at ten o'clock tomorrow morning."

"Very good, General!"

"In point of fact," said the general, "these guard regulations are utter nonsense. It's impossible to work with them. A new edition will be ready in a few days, until which time the exercise is postponed. Good evening."

5 *THE NIGHT OF THE FUNERAL*

THE BARRACKS which housed the training school lay on a long ranging hill above the River Main, which the ordnance survey maps marked as Hill 201. To some people this point was the center of the world. Down below in the flat trough of a valley lay the little town of Wildlingen, which twisted away in an endless series of narrow little streets like intestines. Everything was bathed in pale blue moonlight. A blanket of snow lay on the ground. The night was gripped by a leaden sleep.

The war was a long way off, so far off that it had left Wildlingen-am-Main untouched. Yet hidden away here in this out-of-the-way place the future seeds of professional destruction were now being manufactured. For the time being, however, the vast machine of the training school had come to a standstill. Both the engineers and their tools were resting. For though the war itself knew no sleep, the warriors themselves could not do without it, and for more than a few this sleep was no more than a prelude to death itself.

But death on the whole kept away from training schools. Why should he bother to disturb a process which served him well enough in the end? Here he was sparing with his victims. He merely put in an appearance now and again in a purely routine sort of way as if to remind people that he was in fact everywhere. The ages of those who lay in the cemetery at Wildlingen-am-Main halfway between the town and the barracks were high for the most part, and a certain Lieutenant Barkow of twenty-two struck an almost jarring note, though even this error of taste was soon to be rectified.

In any case the moon was quite indifferent to where it shed its light. It looked down on all things equally as it had done since the beginning of time, on lovers and corpses, on the old town and the new factories of war. Human beings might write poetry to it, stare at it, or revile it as they pleased. It waxed and waned, disappeared and rose again. The sentry on guard at the barrack gates was no more than a speck of dust, the old town a writhing worm, the training school itself just a hollow nutshell.

But within the training school a thousand people were breathing away. A thousand people slept, a thousand digestions were at work, a thousand bloodstreams performed their sluggish tasks. Millions and millions of pores filtered the air like the cleansing units of so many gas masks.

No glimmer of light made its way through the blacked-out panes. Behind the closed windows the sickly smell of warm bodies mingled with the odor of blankets, mattresses, and floor boards, while this and the various other smells of the night merged into a heavy, suffocating atmosphere which slowly enveloped the sleepers in the small, overcrowded rooms.

Not everyone, however, was permitted sleep, or even sought it. For some it was forbidden.

The cadet on guard at the gate, for instance, felt cold and tired and bored, but beyond that felt nothing. "To hell with the whole rotten business!" he muttered to himself.

He didn't quite know what he meant by this. He only knew that he had to become an officer, though he had long ago ceased to bother about why.

He was getting through his course, in which sentry duty was laid down as part of the curriculum. And that was that.

"Aren't you tired?" Elfrida Rademacher asked the girl sitting on her bed. "When I was your age I'd have been asleep for hours by now."

"But you're only a few years older than me," said the girl. "And the later it is the more wide awake you seem to become."

Elfrida Rademacher looked into the mirror and slowly combed her hair, watching the girl behind her as she did so.

This girl had been in the barracks only a few days, a supplementary posting for number one kitchen, detailed for elementary duties during the hours of daylight only. For this girl, whose name was Irene Jablonski, was little more than sixteen years old and her age was of course taken into account.

"Are you going out now?" she asked.

"I still have something to do," said Elfrida, trying to sound noncommittal.

"I can imagine what that is," said the girl.

"You should try not to let your imagination run away with you," said Elfrida sharply. "Then you'll sleep better."

Irene Jablonski made a face and threw herself down on her bed. She felt grown-up now and wanted to be treated accordingly. Then she suddenly felt frightened again. It was true that she had been sleeping worse and worse lately.

Elfrida pretended not to notice the girl, who was one of the five with whom she shared this room. A pretty, slim, fragile little creature, with large eyes and a well-developed bosom which proclaimed her maturity though she still had the face of a child.

"Can't I come out with you in the evening sometimes?" the girl asked.

"No," said Elfrida firmly.

"If you won't take me with you I'll go out with the others."

She meant the other four girls they shared the room with, two of whom were employed on communications duties, one in the record office, and the other in the sick bay. They were all experienced, mature girls, carefree to the point of indifference, which was hardly surprising after two or three years in barracks. They were already asleep by now, though only two in their own beds.

"I can do anything you can," said Irene sulkily.

"No you can't, not for a long time," said Elfrida. "You're much too young."

She glanced around the room, which contained the usual sort of barrack-room furniture, though not of the lowest type. More NCOs' standard than other-ranks'. There were even bedside tables, which were normally the prerogative of officers. Yet everything was standardized, even though the pattern of uniformity was slightly modified by rugs, paper flowers, and ornaments, which gave the room an unmistakable atmosphere of femininity and showed that they hadn't yet given up altogether.

"Listen, now," said Elfrida to Irene Jablonski. "It might be a good thing if you forgot all about the thing that seems to be most on your mind. You're too young for it and too vulnerable. I was just like you once. And I did just all the things you long to do in your heart of hearts. Well, it wasn't worth it, see? It's pointless."

"But you go on doing it, don't you?"

"Yes," said Elfrida frankly. "Because I still hope that it may prove worth it in the end."

"But won't one always go on thinking that?"

Elfrida nodded. She turned away, and thought to herself, Without hope one's done for; where would one be without it? And softly she said to herself, "He's different from the others, I think."

Captain Ratshelm allowed himself no rest, and interpreted this as his sense of duty.

He had made all his preparations for the following day's work, had written a long letter to his mother, and had then sat listening thoughtfully to the final sounds of the day which invariably preceded the sounding of lock-up—the scampering of bare feet in the corridor, the water running in the washroom and the latrine, a brief exchange of conversation, a joke or two, the hearty laughter of young men, all followed by the footsteps of the duty officer passing through the billets, brisk footsteps marked by a faint clinking sound as an iron-studded heel struck a flagstone. A few sharp orders, and then a sort of forced and artificial stillness.

The rule was that any cadet who from then on (2200 hours) wanted to sleep was to be left undisturbed. Undisturbed, and this was an important qualification, by his companions. For of course visits from superior officers, practice alarms, or special searches might disturb him at any hour of the night. Anyone who wished to work, though, could do so up to 2400 hours, the one condition being that he wasn't to make a noise under any circumstances.

This was Ratshelm's great moment.

For the captain had established it for himself as a principle that the cadets should know just how solicitous he was for their welfare. He applied this principle by a carefully formulated plan known only to himself, which he put into action first thing in the morning immediately after reveille, when he supervised the morning wash and early games, and again now, late in the evening.

Ratshelm strode briskly from his room, down the corridor, and out through the main door of the building. He continued across the parade ground and the main thoroughfare of the camp, around an ammunition dump, and up to a set of wooden barracks, where H Section enjoyed temporary accommodation. The barracks were gradually becoming too small for their purpose, and additional huts had therefore had to be built to house the most junior of the officer cadets. Those in H Section were naturally the first to suffer, though in Ratshelm's eyes there was nothing wrong with throwing them all together like this. His one cause for regret was that they were some distance away, though this also meant that more checks were required.

Ratshelm entered the narrow corridor of the barrack block and looked eagerly about him. He was disappointed by what he saw or rather failed to see. The rooms were fitted with glass windows above the doors, but in none of these was there a light. It seemed that the cadets were already asleep. This indicated that none of them was making a point of working late, though such a thing was expressly permitted by the regulations. Ratshelm shone his flashlight along the numbers on the doors, until he came to number seven.

The four cadets who lived here were in fact asleep, or at least showed no signs of not being asleep. One was even snoring in his bunk, while the others lay there like logs, paralyzed with exhaustion, dead to the world. Anyhow, Ratshelm's expert glance noted at once that the room was nice and tidy, and his eyes shone with appreciation. He flashed his flashlight across the beds, and found himself looking into a pair of eyes that stared back at him wide awake and radiant.

"Aha, Hochbauer," said Ratshelm softly, going closer, "so you're not asleep yet?"

"I've only just stopped working, sir," replied Hochbauer equally softly.

The captain smiled to himself rather as an art expert smiles on finding himself before the most valuable picture in a gallery. He considered himself fortunate to be entrusted with such magnificent specimens of humanity.

"What have you been working at so late, Hochbauer?" he asked with interest, and his pleasant baritone voice was full of fatherly good will.

"I've been reading Clausewitz," said the cadet.

"Admirable stuff," commented Ratshelm with approval.

"I'm afraid, though, sir," said Hochbauer confidentially, "that there are one or two things I'm not quite clear about. It's not Clausewitz's fault, but there are just a few points I don't quite understand."

"Well, my dear Hochbauer, you can always come along and see me about them. Any time, after duty. Tomorrow evening would suit me. You know where I live. I'll be only too pleased to help you. That's what we're here for!"

"Thank you, sir," said the cadet happily, and throwing out his chest he braced himself in the bed as if coming to attention. His night-shirt opened across his chest revealing his identification discs and the glistening texture of his skin.

Ratshelm nodded and left, seeming suddenly to be in a great hurry. Probably his sense of duty called him.

Major-General Modersohn sat at his desk, with the harsh light of a lamp falling across his angular features. It was almost as if a wax figure were sitting there in his place. But the general was working on a file in front of him on the cover of which the words "KRAFFT, KARL, LIEUTENANT" were written in large capital letters.

Modersohn occupied two rooms in what was known as the guest house, adjoining the officers mess. He used one of these for work and the other for sleep, and in all the time he had been there had never once used either room for anything other than the purpose for which it was designed.

The general sat at his desk fully dressed. It was difficult to imagine him with his shirt open or his sleeves rolled up. Even his orderly seldom caught a glimpse of Modersohn in his suspenders or his socks. As far as the general was concerned, soldiers were either dressed or undressed; "improperly dressed" was a term that simply had no meaning for him. Thus for him it was the most natural thing in the world that he should be sitting alone in his room in the middle of the night as impeccable in appearance as if he were on parade or on a tour of inspection.

The general's tunic, which was made of worsted and was slightly worn at the elbows, even a little shiny in places, was nevertheless immaculately clean and buttoned right up to the neck. The golden oak leaves on both sides of the collar of his tunic seemed to glow magically in the light of the lamp. The German eagle on his left breast looked worn and faded. No decorations were visible, although Modersohn possessed almost every one there was. But the general preferred to make his authority felt by his personality, rather than by getting himself up like a Christmas tree.

Yet there was a subtle difference in the general's expression now, a bleak acknowledgment of the fact that he found himself completely alone. He seemed almost lost in thought as he gazed at the documents before him.

Carefully he read through each of the personal reports of which they consisted, before comparing them together. Then he came to the conclusion that a lot of bunglers had been at work here. For according to these reports, the man who was now Lieutenant Krafft had always been quite unexceptionable, a good soldier—almost one might say a fine one—always keen and reliable. But there must be something wrong with that.

The general read the reports through again, this time systematically searching for specially revealing turns of phrase and oblique marginal references, which in due course he found. Almost imperceptibly he smiled.

For example in the report on Krafft as a corporal he found the words:

. . . remarkable for his obstinacy—his feeling for discipline still leaves something to be desired—determination is his strong point . . .

And in the report on Krafft as a lieutenant were the words:

. . . good at solving problems on his own—very self-willed —plenty of energy but not always put to the best uses—a first-class leader of men with the ability to render really outstanding service under a superior officer who knows his job . . .

The last report written shortly before Krafft's transfer to the training school offered the following instructive comment:

. . . of a rather critical turn of mind—an extremely useful if not altogether comfortable subordinate with a strongly developed sense of justice . . .

Only a few words extracted from a superfluity of neutral meaningless formulas, cheap generalities, and empty clichés. But these few words made it clear that Krafft was something out of the ordinary. He had been posted suspiciously often, and yet almost always with words of commendation. It looked as if people had praised him highly in order to be rid of him the more easily. And now he had landed here at this training school—in the domain of Major-General Modersohn, popularly known as the iceberg or the last of the Prussians.

Modersohn closed Krafft's personal file. The notebook which lay near to hand remained empty. The general closed his eyes for a moment as if to rest them from the harsh light of the table lamp. His face still revealed nothing of what he was thinking. But the ghost of a smile remained.

Then Modersohn rose and went into his bedroom, where there was an army bed, a chair, a cupboard, and a washbasin—but that was all.

The general unbuttoned his tunic and pulled out a wallet, which he opened. He stared at a photograph, about postcard size, which was the portrait of a young man—an officer with an angular face and large, frank, inquisitive eyes. It was a solemn face, but one which at the same time evinced a quiet determination.

When the general looked at this picture something approaching warmth came into his eyes, and the severity of his expression was replaced by a look of distant sadness.

This was a picture of Lieutenant Barkow, who had been buried the day before.

Lieutenant Krafft was also unable to sleep that night. However, it wasn't his conscience that kept him awake, but Elfrida Rademacher.

"I hope no one saw you come," said Krafft rather nervously.

"What if they did?" replied Elfrida with apparent indifference, sitting down beside him on the bed. She thought she knew what men liked—cheerfulness, brightness, and above all no fuss and bother.

"What will the other girls you live with say?"

"Just what I say about them when they don't sleep in their own beds. Nothing at all."

Krafft listened to the night, but there seemed no risk of being disturbed except by Elfrida, who now began to take off her clothes.

Krafft found the moral atmosphere prevailing in these barracks really quite remarkable. The remarkable thing was that such an atmosphere should be possible in the domain of a man like General Modersohn.

"They haven't invented a cure for it yet," said Elfrida, pulling her petticoat up over her hips. She did this as if it were the most natural thing in the world, which, Krafft reasoned, seemed to show that she'd had a certain amount of practice.

He found it difficult to make this girl out. It was true that everything had been quite simple from the beginning, completely uncomplicated, delightfully straightforward. But Krafft could sense that she wasn't quite what she pretended to be. He was always catching himself thinking about her. Well now, he said to himself, it was possible that she wasn't so much seeking pleasure for herself as wanting to do him a favor. There was a suspicion of charity about the whole thing.

"Haven't you any misgivings?" asked Krafft.

"Why should I have?" she replied. "We like each other. That's quite enough."

"Quite enough for me certainly," said Krafft. "But what if Captain Kater finds out how you're spending your nights? After all, he's officially responsible for you and the other girls."

Elfrida began to laugh. It was a completely frank laugh and dangerously loud at that. "This fellow Kater is the last person who can afford to set himself up as a guardian of morality!"

"Have you had some sort of experience with him then?" asked Krafft, noting with astonishment that the idea made him slightly unhappy.

Elfrida paused for a moment. She straightened up slightly, before turning her dark eyes on him and saying, "I've been here for two years now, ever since this training school was started. I'm living here with more than forty other girls in a special separate corridor of the headquarters building— we even have our own entrance, in fact. All day we work in the stores and in the workshops. We are women civilian employees called up for military service. We come into contact with men day after day; there are a thousand of them all around us. So it's hardly surprising that from time to time we feel the need to spend our nights with them too."

"Well, all the same, I'm glad you selected me from the thousand or so others."

"I did so for a number of reasons," said Elfrida, taking off her stockings. "First because your billet and mine are in the same building, which makes matters a lot easier. Then because the two of us work in the same place, in the headquarters company, which makes it easier for us to arrange to spend our free time together. And then there's another reason, Karl, a by no means unimportant one—I like you. That doesn't necessarily mean I love you. I'm against big words like that, and anyway they've become very small in these times of ours. But I do like you very much, and that's the only reason I'm doing what I am doing. In any case Captain Kater has no place on my list—which isn't all that big—and he never will have."

Almost hurriedly, Elfrida stripped off her brassière. Krafft looked at her longingly, burning with desire and wanting to stretch out his hands and seize hold of her at once, but she pushed him away and looked at him almost sadly.

"I'm not exactly a model of virtue," she said, "I don't need to tell you that. But I don't want you to think that my being here and the ease with which everything has developed between us is all just a matter of course. There's more to it than that."

Her breath was coming in short gasps and he misinterpreted the sign. "Come on!" he said impatiently.

Elfrida shook her head.

"There's more to it than just that," she repeated with a slight huskiness in her voice. "I feel something almost like fear. I know it sounds silly to say that, but from the very first I had the feeling that we only had a short time together. Don't laugh at me, Karl. I know nothing can last for long in this war. Everything comes and goes, one loves and is unfaithful, wants to forget and is forgotten. All right, one has to accept that. But it isn't just that, not this time."

"Come on," he repeated, and put his arms around her.

And so he never heard her when she said, "I'm afraid for you."

"It just goes to show," said Captain Kater, thoughtfully. "One doesn't hesitate to do one's duty, yet how is one rewarded? With misunderstanding! One finds oneself in trouble! And all because a certain person likes to think of himself as the last of the Prussians and to attach more importance to military regulations than to ordinary human qualities."

Captain Kater was sitting in the far corner of one of the rooms at the back of the officers' mess, with the soft light from a standard lamp shining full on to his moonlike face. A well-rounded bottle of red wine stood before him, while opposite sat Wirrmann, the judge-advocate. Both looked worried, and stared morosely at the bottle of red wine, which deserved happier faces, being one of the noblest Pommards ever ripened in the sunshine of France. Kater still had a few more cases in the cellar, but he was tortured by the fear that he wouldn't have the chance to enjoy them.

For the general seemed unwilling to leave him in peace. In his own eyes, Kater was a goodhearted fellow and a successful organizer. But Modersohn seemed unable to appreciate that sort of quality. There probably wasn't another man like Modersohn in the entire Wehrmacht: and yet he of all people had to be the commanding officer of the training school at which Captain Kater had the headquarters company!

"The general seems a very self-willed man," said Wirrmann, using the formula with the utmost circumspection so that it seemed free of both provocation and reproach.

This was typical of Wirrmann's tactics. He was always very careful in his choice of words, nearly always sticking pretty close to protocol. But the underlying tone made it clear to Kater how Wirrmann was thinking.

Judge-Advocate Wirrmann, seconded to training-school inspection duty, an experienced lawyer and trustworthy servant of the Reich, a naked sword of justice with more than two dozen death sentences to his credit, he of all people had been humiliated by Modersohn as if he were no more than some incompetent petty official. And in front of all the other officers too! Kater could hardly help seeing in Wirrmann a potential ally.

"Between ourselves," said Kater, leaning forward confidentially, "the general isn't only self-willed—there's simply no telling what he'll do. Though I say so with respect, he seems utterly unappreciative of the joys of living. The finest wines, the best cigars, mean nothing to him, nor does he cheer up in the slightest at the sight of a pretty girl—"

"But you can't help noticing the interest he takes in certain young officers," interjected Wirrmann. And he smiled knowingly as he said this—a smile, as he thought, of extreme subtlety and of the greatest gentleness, as if he imagined himself to have lifted a sad corner of the truth.

Captain Kater choked, so that the wine spilled on his uniform, but he took no notice of it. He was thinking hard. The judge-advocate's comment had sounded harmless enough, but something about the way in which he obviously intended it to be taken put him on the alert.

Warily Kater asked: "You mean—?"

"I don't mean anything," said Wirrmann at once. "I wasn't even hinting at anything. I was merely turning over in my mind the thought that, with the exception of course of our Führer, no human being's decisions are impeccable, unless of course he should be fortunate to have the law to guide him. All I was really getting at was this: even generals cannot be devoid of certain human sympathies."

"And these have their dangers. Yes, you're right there." Kater nodded agreement. "Quite often to the disadvantage of decent, honorable men, sound reliable officers for example. In my own case there's the additional factor that this man Krafft is after my job as CO of the headquarters company. It's the only explanation of his behavior."

"Well, yes," said Wirrmann slowly. "The general isn't your friend exactly. And this Krafft seems a fairly cunning and ruthless fellow. He may even succeed in pushing you out—a key job like yours is well worth having. But if Krafft is in fact to be your successor, then it can only be with the general's approval—that is, it can only be something he himself wants to happen."

"Which isn't altogether out of the question," admitted Kater. "For what does the general know of my particular abilities? I do my duty at least as thoroughly as he. But he seems quite unable to appreciate the fact. The man has his limitations—of course I'm speaking quite confidentially between ourselves. All right—he knows a thing or two about strategy and tactics. But he hasn't grasped the simple truth, valid for thousands of years—for as long as soldiers have existed, in fact—that a soldier who is hungry and thirsty is only half a soldier."

The judge-advocate disapproved of the crude hints Kater was dropping of his carelessness and lack of restraint, but he didn't hesitate to exploit the situation.

As if savoring the heavy bouquet of the wine, he said, "Things would certainly be very different—and not for you alone—if this training school had a commanding officer with whom one could work more pleasantly."

Kater stared at the judge-advocate. Hurriedly he filled up his glass and drained it at a draught. His moon face shone with new hope. In his mind's eye he could see the crates of wine he had stocked up for the benefit of both his brother officers and of himself, and imagined himself enjoying the fruits of his industry and ability, undisturbed and free from care. And he asked, "You think that might be possible?"

"It depends," said the judge-advocate casually.

"On what?"

"Well," said Wirrmann carefully, "I'm assuming of course that you realize that the only thing I'm interested in is the pursuit of justice."

"Of course, that's taken for granted," agreed Kater readily.

"My dear Captain Kater," said Judge-Advocate Wirrmann, "what we need is something to go on. Just something to start with will do. The very possibility of an offense is sufficient grounds for opening a case, and once a case has been opened it usually means that the man is automatically relieved of his duties. There are two points in particular I have in mind. First: the person of whom we are speaking has never categorically indicated his enthusiasm for our political system and our Führer. This could prove of considerable significance. Secondly: the person in question shows a remarkable interest in everything connected with Lieutenant Barkow, that's to say personally connected with Lieutenant Barkow. Now why is that? What lies behind it. Have we something we can go on here? Give the matter your attention if you're seriously interested in remaining in charge of the headquarters company here!"

"Follow me, men!" whispered Cadet Weber. "No hanging back. A potential officer must be a match for every situation."

Cadets Mösler and Rednitz slunk across the camp with Cadet Egon Weber threading his way through the darkness about ten to fifteen yards ahead of them. All three were keeping in the shadow of the transport sheds, avoiding the main thoroughfare of the camp and the sentries' patrols, as they headed for the Kommandantur building.

They groped their way through the night, bent double. Their pockets bulged, for they were loaded down with bottles, and one of them cupped a burning cigarette in the hollow of his hand.

"Steady, man," said Cadet Rednitz, not bothering to lower his voice particularly. "We mustn't overdo it; let's have something to keep our strength up first."

"We've lost too much time already," objected Mösler. "We shouldn't have bothered about Hochbauer. Why did you have to go and tell him what we were doing! You know he's against this sort of thing."

"One needs to keep in with Hochbauer," said Weber approvingly. "He's bound to be our next section senior and he'll be twisting Captain Ratshelm around his little finger in no time."

"Man," said Mösler thoughtfully, "when that day comes we're for it."

"Hochbauer's all right," Egon Weber insisted.

"And you, Weber, are a damned fool" said Rednitz amiably. "As you'll find out for yourself one of these days. Want to bet?"

They paused when they reached the cookhouse. Standing in the shadow of a supply shed they looked across at the Kommandantur. The moon obligingly hid itself behind a bank of clouds.

Cadet Egon Weber uncorked a bottle and took a mighty swig. Then like a good comrade he passed the bottle on, while Rednitz kept a lookout for the enemy—a patrolling sentry or an officer.

"What are we going to do if we're caught?" asked Cadet Egon Weber.

"Look silly," said Rednitz.

"And what are we going to say?"

"Anything that comes into our heads—anything but the truth, that is." Rednitz liked to turn everything that happened into a joke. Mösler on the other hand was a person who spent his time systematically in pursuit of pleasure and wasn't particularly choosy where he found it. Cadet Weber simply did everything he was called upon to do from attending a church parade to visiting a brothel. All that was needed was to appeal to his sense of comradeship and his physical strength, and then there was nothing he wouldn't do. As a result he was remarkably popular with everyone and his commission was a virtual certainty.

"For instance what if we run into the duty officer?" asked Egon Weber.

"Then," said Rednitz reaching for the bottle, "the best man among us confronts him and sacrifices himself for the others. I imagine that will be, you, Weber, because I don't expect you'll want to let anyone else deprive you of the honor."

"All right," said Egon Weber, quite undismayed, "let's suppose that happens. Then the duty officer will want to know what I'm doing here."

"With a bottle?"

"You're sleepwalking of course, Egon!"

"But that's the whole point!" insisted Rednitz. "Without a bottle there wouldn't be anything odd about you."

"What's all the nattering about?" said Mösler impatiently. "Why are we hanging about like this? Let's get on to the girls."

"Steady now," warned Rednitz. "If we don't think things out carefully and watch what we're doing we'll be in trouble. I'll go ahead and see how the land lies."

"You just want the best girl for yourself," said Mösler suspiciously. "That's not playing fair."

"And anyone who doesn't play the game," said Egon Weber, Section H's champion wrestler and always spoiling for a fight, "will have me to reckon with."

Rednitz found himself powerless against such arguments. He had no alternative but to act in accordance with the principles taught him by Captain Feders: every operation once set in motion is to be carried through to the bitter end, provided no decisive alteration of strategic considerations demands a change of plan.

"Alteration of strategic considerations" hardly came into it, for there wasn't an officer in sight and the sentries were all dozing in their various corners. But down in the basement of the Kommandantur sat the poor little love-sick maidens of the communications center.

The events of the night before had been all around the barracks by the late afternoon. Cadet Weber had learned certain details from the man in charge of the sports equipment. This man had received his information from a corporal in the kitchen. He in turn was a close friend of the clerk in the orderly room, and the latter was himself a close friend of the raped corporal in person. In short, first-class addresses, relatively accessible. To the rescue then!

"Right, come on," said Cadet Rednitz, sounding the advance.

Mösler and Egon Weber followed him excitedly, holding their bottles by their necks and swinging them like hand grenades. They crouched low as they hopped across the concrete road of the barracks and disappeared into the Kommandantur, determined to take the communications center and the girls by storm.

When they got there, however, they found others there before them.

Captain Feders, Section H's tactics instructor, sat enveloped in thick clouds of cigarette smoke, thinking, writing, and smoking, in a state of complete exhaustion. He tried to concentrate on his class's subject for the following day: transport of an infantry battalion by rail. But utterly without success. And sleep wouldn't come to him.

The night seemed to be filled with a dull roaring, as if of distant aircraft, or trains running continuously on the other side of the hill. But he knew this was an illusion. The darkness all about him was empty save for the wreathing cigarette smoke, the bare walls of the room, and the floor boards, which let in the cold. No sound reached his ears— none of the sounds of life around him—the breathing of a thousand sleeping men, their groans and muffled heart beats under the bedclothes, the gurgling of water pipes, the scraping of the sentries' boots, the panting somewhere or other of a couple of lovers. He knew that all this was there, but heard none of it.

Captain Feders, the tactics instructor, was one of the cleverest men in the training school, the sort of man who could never help trying to tie people up in knots, and who was always being tempted into sarcasm, being a great scoffer and fond of debunking for its own sake. Whenever he sensed that he had any sort of audience he wore a permanent, cold, ironical smile on his face. But when he was alone, as now, he was a tired man with a haggard face, whose eyes showed him to be tortured and desperate.

He listened anxiously, wanting to hear something only in order to prove to himself that what his reason told him was there really existed. He drew at a cigarette—he heard that. He blew the smoke out of his mouth—he heard that too. His wife lay in the bedroom. She must have been tossing about restlessly, pushing the blankets away, breathing noisily —but however hard he listened he heard nothing.

"It's as if everything were dead," said Feders to himself. "Everything seems to be decaying."

Marion, his wife, had been called up for military service like all the other women in the barracks. The previous officer in command of the training school had arranged for her posting to Wildlingen-am-Main, simply as an act of generosity. He saw to it that the couple got a small apartment in the guest house, for Frau Marion Feders knew how to exercise her charm.

The present commanding officer, Major-General Modersohn, tacitly accepted the situation. It could hardly be supposed that he would allow it to continue indefinitely. For Modersohn didn't seem to recognize such a thing as private life, and certainly not at his training school. This suited Feders, particularly in the circumstances, though he hadn't the strength to tell his wife openly.

He forced himself to concentrate. He wanted to hear her, in order to realize again—over and over again—what a desperate senseless business it all was. But he heard nothing. He got up, went over to the door that led into the bedroom, opened it, and switched on the center light.

And there lay Marion, his wife, with her short, bright blond hair. The bedclothes had slipped from her strong, sunburned shoulders, and he noted the clean sweep of her hips and the magic of her skin glistening with the sweat of sleep.

"Are you coming to bed?" she asked, blinking, and rolling over onto her back.

"No," he said.

"Why don't you?" She was so sleepy that her lips hardly moved.

"I just wanted to get a book," said Feders, picking up a book that lay on the bedside table. Then he turned his head abruptly, put out the light, and left the room.

He returned to his desk and stood in front of it for a while. He put the book aside and stared at the harsh light, at the billowing clouds of smoke from a couple of dozen cigarettes, and beyond, into the darkness which seemed to lie in wait for him. And in that moment it finally became clear to him that life—his life at any rate—was rotten and useless. Hardly worth bothering to do away with.

The moon rose higher. The hard silhouette of the barracks melted in the pale frostiness of the night, until all outlines disappeared. Roofs seemed to become flatter; roads merged with patches of lawn into an indeterminate grayness, and it was as if the walls of the place simply sank into the earth. A flat uniformity seemed to absorb everything.

The thousand human beings there were now lost to the world. Hardly a man among them was not sunk deep in oblivion. Even the sentry dozed wearily. He had lost almost all sense of his surroundings by now. The utter emptiness all about him was like some infinite extension of his own state of mind. The most comfortable of all worlds to guard would have been one in which all life was extinct.

As the hours slipped by they stripped the sentry of all personality; of his vague emotions, his cautious appetites, his rare flickerings of purpose, and his overwhelming despondency. He merely patrolled his beat: a mechanical being with a brain that was already asleep.

The hills above Wildlingen-am-Main on which the barracks now stood had once been covered with vineyards, where, barely two centuries ago, a wine had been bottled under the lable "Wildlinger Galgenberg." A dry, fruity, full-bodied wine, so the connoisseurs said. But then times had changed for the worse, and people turned from wine to schnapps, which made them drunk more quickly.

Then, however, times had become great and heroic again, as the newspapers and radio stations never ceased to proclaim. The German people, it was said, had once again become conscious of their great and glorious traditions. And so, one fine morning in the year 1934 a truck drove up onto the hills. Army officers, engineers, and officials looked, nodded, and gave the word. Wildlingen was found worthy to become a garrison town, a decision which caused great joy to the citizens of Wildlingen, who liked to serve the nation, particularly when they were well paid for doing so.

Two years later the barracks were built, and soon afterward an infantry battalion moved in, and money started rolling into the pockets of the citizens of Wildlingen. Tears came into their eyes when they beheld their valiant soldiers. And the birth rate rose astonishingly.

When war came the infantry battalion was replaced by an infantry reserve battalion. Otherwise there was little change. The brave citizens no longer wept from emotion, but the birth rate continued to rise, for procreation and death proved themselves effective partners.

In the second year of the war the barracks above Wildlingen were transformed into Number 5 Officers' Training School, whose first commanding officer was Major-General Ritter von Trippler, later killed on the eastern front. The second commanding officer, Colonel Sänger, fell victim to a prosecution for a misappropriation of Wehrmacht property. The third commanding officer was Colonel Freiherr von Fritschler und Geierstein, who was relieved of his duties for demonstrable incompetence and given a post in the Balkans, where he was highly decorated. The fourth commanding officer was Major-General Modersohn.

Major-General Modersohn now lay quietly asleep in his bed, breathing regularly. It was almost as if he were ceremonially laid out in his coffin, for there was no situation in life in which Modersohn's attitude was not exemplary.

Wirrmann, the judge-advocate, was also asleep. He lay there breathing heavily, as if packed between documents and covered with the dust of many courts-martial. Kater, commander of the headquarters company, had fallen into a similar sort of heavy sleep. Three bottles of red wine kept all his worries at bay.

Elfrida Rademacher still lay beside Lieutenant Krafft. And their expressions made it clear that they hoped the night would never end.

Captain Ratshelm smiled in his sleep. He saw himself in his dream standing beside a pure, vigorous young wife in a meadow full of flowers, surrounded by a troop of adorable healthy children. And all of them, both spouse and progeny, were cadets—cadets of his training school, on his course, cadets of his company—his very own cadets!

But none of the cadets were dreaming about Captain Ratshelm, not even Hochbauer. He hardly ever dreamt. If he occasionally gave in to daydreams while awake, these were shot with reds and golds and browns, and they revolved around visions of titanic glory, of mighty achievement, and renown. Every imaginable sacrifice for the great goal! In times of desperation, his beloved Führer had wielded a housepainter's brush; he too was ready for a similar sacrifice, if there were no alternative.

Cadets Mösler, Rednitz, and Weber had gone to sleep in a great state of dissatisfaction. They had been deeply disappointed to find the terrain they coveted already occupied. But they hadn't given up hope. After all, the course had only just begun—a mere twenty-one days ago. Eight full weeks still lay ahead of them, and they were determined to make the best possible use of them.

Captain Feders still couldn't get to sleep. He stared at his watch; the hands crawled around with appalling slowness. He closed his eyes. And he felt how lust reached out with quivering tentacles into nothingness. And he saw only a hopeless void. All was dead. Life was a mere transition between death and death. All was rottenness.

The sentry on the gate yawned.

6 *A SECTION OFFICER REQUIRED*

"I was told to report to the general at ten," said Lieutenant Krafft to the girl who looked up to see what he wanted.

"Then I must ask you to wait until that time, Lieutenant."

Krafft looked pointedly at his watch. It was five minutes to ten. He drew attention to the fact and even tapped his wrist watch.

"Quite correct," said the girl with friendly aloofness. "You're five minutes early."

The name of the girl he was speaking to was Sybille Bachner. She worked in the general's anteroom under Bieringer, the ADC, who however wasn't there just then, being busy probably checking the bread ration for his commanding officer. Anyhow, Sybille Bachner seemed determined to apply the general's principles, and simply left Krafft standing there.

Krafft promptly sat down in the ADC's chair. He crossed his legs and eyed Sybille Bachner with interest.

After a while he said, "So you're the general's principal assistant, so to speak. You'll notice I choose my words with care."

"I'm employed here as secretary, Lieutenant, and that's the full extent of my duties or obligations. Anything else you'd like to know?"

There was a certain tolerance about Sybille Bachner's smile. She seemed quite used to being eyed like this and having to submit to questions.

"How long have you been in this outfit actually, Fräulein Bachner?" inquired Krafft.

"Longer than the general," said Sybille, giving him a cool, impersonal smile. "Isn't that what you want to know, Lieutenant? The general neither brought me with him nor applied for me to be posted here. He simply took me over."

"In every respect?"

"My duties weren't limited in any way."

Sybille Bachner said this quite ingenuously, straightening a stack of paper on the little typing table beside her as she did so. She seemed anxious to get on with her work, which

87

gave Krafft plenty of opportunity to observe her more closely.

This girl Sybille Bachner occupied a rather special position among the women in the barracks, for she worked in a proximity to the commanding officer that made discretion imperative. A room of her own was intended to help her preserve this quality. But unlike most of the other women's rooms this did not lie in a separate corridor of the headquarters building but in the so-called guest house. Not so far away from where the general himself lived.

This prompted a good deal of speculation. With anyone else the inference would have been obvious. But with Modersohn things were different. Few people found themselves able to imagine that a general like him could be beset by ordinary weaknesses, and those that did were influenced primarily by Sybille Bachner's looks, which seemed to make absolutely any sort of weakness understandable. For she was a dark, Latin type of beauty of about twenty-five, and her skin was soft and the color of apricots and her large eyes were black as night. Silky hair framed her face like a shawl, a face dominated by slightly prominent cheekbones and a soft, sensual mouth.

Krafft stopped eying the Bachner girl as soon as it became clear that she was interested only in work. Secretaries in important posts in anterooms were usually interested only in work, and he hadn't noticed a single gesture of hers, or heard one word, which suggested that she wished to be treated as someone who had the commanding officer's ear. She was neither ostentatiously formal nor absurdly refined. And in any case for him she represented simply a brief encounter soon to be forgotten, for he felt sure that before many minutes were up, his short stay at the training school would be over.

"It's ten o'clock, Lieutenant Krafft," said Sybille Bachner pleasantly. "Go in, please."

"Just like that?" asked Krafft in astonishment. For the Bachner girl had neither left the room nor made a telephone call. Neither had any little bell been rung, nor message been given her. She had simply looked at the clock.

"It's ten o'clock," said Sybille Bachner, and her smile broadened slightly. "The general thinks punctuality very important and keeps to his daily schedule exactly. Go in please, Lieutenant, don't bother to knock."

Sybille Bachner was left alone in the general's anteroom,

looking at the walls, which were hung with nothing but training schedules. Documents, files, regulations lay all over the place—on the ADC's table, on her own table, on shelves, on the window sills and even on the floor. She was literally surrounded by work. She pulled open one of the drawers. In it lay a mirror in which she looked at herself thoughtfully. She felt depressed by what she saw. She was gradually growing old, wasting her life here among papers and the rattle of typewriter keys, stuck in one of the culs-de-sac of the war.

She heard footsteps approaching and hurriedly closed her drawer again. The ADC came in. Her looking-glass face vanished and she shifted a bundle of papers in front of her.

"Well," asked Lieutenant Bieringer, the ADC, "is this fellow Krafft with the general?"

Sybille Bachner nodded. "He was only five minutes early," she said, "and didn't seem particularly overawed. On the contrary, he was even rather fresh."

This was really a compliment. Most people seemed to regard the anteroom as the antechamber to hell, and those who gathered here were either anxious and nervous, or else absurdly stiff. They usually arrived at least ten minutes early in order to make sure of being punctual. Krafft, then, at least was not one of this servile minority.

"Fresh, did you say, Fräulein Bachner? Do you like him?"

"I found the man extremely sure of himself."

"Not a bad start," said Bieringer.

"I wasn't thinking of starting anything," said Sybille Bachner abruptly.

"But why not?" suggested Bieringer. "You know what a high opinion I have of you, Fräulein Bachner, and my wife loves you like a sister. We're worried about you, though. You work too hard and are alone too much. Don't you think it might be good for you to allow yourself a little relaxation?"

Sybille Bachner looked the ADC straight in the eye. Bieringer's smooth, rather pale face wasn't much to write home about. He looked rather like someone who was hoping to be a teacher, and was certainly not what could be called a soldierly type. But he was a man with a sixth sense for everything that concerned the general, taking the place for him of a calculating machine and a whole bundle of notebooks and thus preserving him from a vast amount of unnecessary work.

"Herr Bieringer," said Sybille Bachner, "I'm completely satisfied with my job here. I find no need of any relaxation."

The ADC pretended to be very busy with a file of documents.

"Well," he said slowly and with a certain wariness, "that is only as it should be. After all, the general is wholly dedicated to his work too. And he has no need of any relaxation either."

"Kindly keep any unnecessary remarks of that sort to yourself, Herr Bieringer," said Sybille Bachner indignantly.

"By all means," said the ADC, "by all means, that is in so far as they are unnecessary. Believe me, my dear Fräulein Bachner, I've known the general a long time now; since long before you knew him. You can be quite sure of one thing: he neither has any private life nor ever will have any. And if you're clever you'll find yourself someone who will distract you in time from any false hopes you may be entertaining—someone like this fellow Lieutenant Krafft, for example. Always provided, of course, that this fellow Krafft stays with us. But that's for the general to decide."

"Lieutenant Krafft, sir, reporting as ordered."

Major-General Modersohn was sitting behind his desk, which was placed exactly opposite the door. The seven yards or so between him and the door was covered by a plain green hair-cord runner. In front of the desk stood a single hard chair.

The general was busy making extracts from a document and didn't seem to want to interrupt his work. He merely said, without looking up, "Come in, please, Lieutenant Krafft. Sit down."

Krafft obeyed. Modersohn seemed to be making quite a fuss of him. All he had expected was two or three annihilating sentences, a curt and brutal ejection in the unmistakable language of a pure-bred Prussian.

But the general seemed to be taking his time.

"Lieutenant Krafft," began Modersohn, looking straight at his visitor for the first time, quite impersonally yet with the intensive scrutiny of someone who is a complete master of his subject, "have you any idea why you were posted to this training school?"

"No, General," said the lieutenant truthfully enough.

"Do you think your ability had anything to do with it?"

"I don't suppose so, General."

"You don't suppose so?" drawled Modersohn. He never liked this expression. An officer didn't "suppose" anything —he "knew," he "assumed," he "held it as his opinion." "Well?"

"I assume, General, that my ability was not the decisive factor in my posting."

"What was, then?"

"An officer was due to be posted from my unit and the choice fell on me."

"There was no reason for this?"

"I don't know the reason, General."

Lieutenant Krafft didn't feel entirely at ease. He had come prepared for a severe dressing down from the general, not for an interrogation. So he tried to fall back on the traditional technique of the old soldier and acted dumb, answering everything as shortly as possible, and neglecting no chance of appearing to agree with his superior officer.

This was a technique which usually saved considerable time and trouble. Not with Modersohn, however.

The general pulled toward him a writing pad that lay on his desk. "Have you seen your personal file, Lieutenant?" he asked.

"No, General," said Krafft in some astonishment but also truthfully enough. Modersohn was slightly taken aback by this. (Not that anyone would have realized the fact. His hand, which was on the point of thrusting the writing pad away again, merely stopped for a second.) For the general knew the form. Personal files were theoretically "Secret," but there were always ways and means of getting a look at them if only one were determined and smart enough. And this fellow Krafft was smart, the general could see that. So there was only one conclusion to be drawn, namely that he had had no wish to take a look; his personal file was a matter of indifference to him. Presumably he knew from experience how haphazardly these accumulations of paper were compiled.

"Why do you think you were made an officer of the headquarters company in this training school and not an officer among the cadets?"

This was a question that Krafft had often asked himself. He had been posted here nominally to train cadets, but had immediately found himself stuck with Captain Kater and all the other canteen heroes. Why this should be so he had absolutely no idea.

"I assume that there was just one officer too many for the course, General, and that one had to be transferred to the headquarters company, that it was just a coincidence that it happened to be me."

"There are no coincidences of that sort in my command, Lieutenant Krafft."

Krafft should of course have known this. But since the general seemed to be asking for frank answers to his questions, the lieutenant didn't hesitate to give them to him after his fashion.

"Well, General," he said, "I assume that I'm regarded as an awkward sort of fellow, and there's even a certain amount of truth in that. Wherever I go, I find myself posted again almost at once. I'm gradually getting used to the fact."

The general was not impressed. "Lieutenant Krafft," he said, "I gather from your personal file that certain differences arose between you and your former regimental commander, Colonel Holzapfel. I wonder if you would be so good as to enlighten me further about this."

"General," Krafft replied almost lightheartedly, "I had occasion to lay certain information against Colonel Holzapfel regarding misappropriation of ration supplies. The colonel used to move about with his own baggage train, and not only thought it proper to withhold rations from the front-line troops but also deprived them of military vehicles in order to transport his spoils to the rear. The colonel was court-martialed, severely reprimanded, and posted elsewhere. It was his successor who transferred me to the training school."

"You had no misgivings, Lieutenant Krafft, about laying information against a superior officer?"

"No, General. For it was not a superior officer against whom I was laying information but a swindler."

The general did not indicate what he thought of this answer. Without further introduction he suddenly asked, "Have you concluded your investigations into this alleged rape of the day before yesterday?"

"Yes, General."

"With what results?"

"A summary of evidence on a charge of rape would not be justified by the facts. The three girls maintain, plausibly enough, that at first they merely intended to play a joke. They couldn't foresee that it would get out of hand. Moreover, three empty bottles were found in the scene of the alleged crime. Corporal Krottenkopf admits to having drunk one of these all by himself in the course of the proceedings. A detail which effectually rules out rape. The whole affair should be dealt with on a disciplinary level."

"All those involved in the incident will be posted within twenty-four hours," said the general, as if talking of the weather. "All in opposite directions—each at least two hundred miles away from the training school. Inform Captain Kater of this. I shall expect to hear that the order has been carried out tomorrow morning."

"Very good, General," the lieutenant gulped.

"Furthermore, Lieutenant Krafft, you will in the course of today relinquish your duties as officer of the headquarters company to Captain Kater, and take charge of Section H for Heinrich. I myself will announce your appointment as section officer at noon today. You will commence your new duties first thing tomorrow morning."

"Very good, Herr General," said the lieutenant, quite unable to hide his astonishment.

Major-General Modersohn had lowered his eyes, a fact which Krafft registered with relief. The general made a few notes on a pad and pushed it way to his right. Then he reached for a new pad and began to make notes on that too.

Krafft now began to feel himself wholly superfluous. After this scare he felt badly in need of a brandy. What's more, Captain Kater would be only too glad to stand him a whole bottle, for one consequence of the order the general had just issued was that the commander of the headquarters company seemed temporarily to have escaped his threatened posting.

But still Lieutenant Krafft did not receive his dismissal.

The general completed his notes, and looked at a file which had been lying in front of him the whole time. He opened it with a certain solemnity, and eyed Lieutenant Krafft keenly.

"Lieutenant Krafft," said the general, "you know that the last officer in charge of Section H for Heinrich was Lieutenant Barkow?"

"Yes, sir," said Krafft.

"And you know that Lieutenant Barkow met his death accidentally in the course of a training exercise?"

"Yes, sir."

"Do you also know how this accident occurred?"

"No, General."

Modersohn drew himself up and leaned back very stiffly in his chair. He placed his hands and his forearms flat on his desk and his finger tips touched the thin red file in front of him.

"What happend was this. At fourteen hundred hours on the twenty-sixth of January Lieutenant Barkow was scheduled for engineer work with Section H at the sound-locator post. A ten-pound charge was due to be exploded. Lieutenant Barkow was unable to reach cover before the charge was detonated. He was almost completely torn to shreds. What do you make of that, Lieutenant Krafft?"

"I hardly knew Lieutenant Barkow, General."

"I knew him better," said the general with a slight huskiness in his voice. "He was an excellent officer, dedicated to his work, and, in spite of his youth, an extremely sensible man. He was an expert on all types of equipment, and particularly on explosives. He had already carried out a number of complicated bridge demolitions on the eastern front."

"In that case, General, I don't understand how this accident could have happened."

"It wasn't an accident," said the general. "It was murder."

With a quiet gesture of finality the general had played his trump card.

"Murder, General?"

There seemed no place for such a word in the sober atmosphere of that room. It didn't go with the general's face. It simply didn't belong here.

"I wish it hadn't been necessary to use such a word," said the general. "You're the second person I've used it to. The only other person who knows what I think is Judge-Advocate Wirrmann. I had the inspector of training units second him here to carry out a full investigation."

"And does the judge-advocate agree with your theory, General? Does he think it's murder, too?"

"No," said the general. "But that doesn't alter the fact that it was. Cold-blooded murder. I know this indirectly from Lieutenant Barkow himself, because before his death he was dropping unmistakable hints which I dismissed at the time as utterly impossible. But all his conjectures have been borne out by the facts. Right, then, you will concern yourself with this affair, Lieutenant Krafft. I will put all the relevant documents at your disposal, and you will examine all the evidence. You will be able to discuss anything you like with me. And of course I don't need to emphasize that the whole matter is entirely confidential."

"Why are you telling me this, General?"

"So that you can search for and find the murderer," said Modersohn. "He can only be in Section H, that's to say in your own section, Lieutenant Krafft. And I shall expect you to complete your task successfully. You can count on my support. That is all for today."

* * * *

Intermediate Report No. 2

THE CURRICULUM VITAE OF
CAPTAIN ERIC FEDERS,
OR PATTERNS OF ACCIDENT

Born on July 17, 1915, in Aalen, Wurttemberg. My father was
Constantine Feders, a Protestant pastor. My mother was Eva-
Maria Feders and her maiden name was Knotek. I grew up
in Aalen.

The first thing I can remember clearly is a pair of folded
hands, and a voice that always seems to be intoning. The
words of this voice are full of beauty and meaning. This is
my father: dark clothing, snow-white linen, a solemn, dignified face. A strong smell of tobacco comes off him making me
feel slightly sick. But then on Sundays, the smell of sour
wine as well. A full, rich laugh when I am touched and
looked at.

Organ sounds all about me—triumphant, tempestuous,
rumbling ominously. A continuous assault on my eardrums.
Finally a muffled, high-pitched whistle, a stifling yell, a rasping rattle. Father holds me up against the air valves of the
organ. "Splendid!" he cries. "Isn't that splendid!" And I
cry, too, wildly, desperately, continuously. "A pity," says my
father with disappointment. "He isn't musical."

Mother is like a shadow, very soft, very quiet, very gentle,
even when she cries. But Mother cries only when she thinks
she is quite alone. And she is rarely alone, because I am
there most of the time, behind the curtains, in the corner by
the cupboard, under the sofa. And then I come out and ask,
"Why are you crying, Mother?" and she says, "But, my boy,
I'm not crying." Then I go to my father and ask, "Why is
Mother crying?" and my father says, "But my boy, Mother
isn't crying! Are you crying, Mother?" "Of course not," she
says. And I say, "Why do people tell lies here?" And then my
father beats me, because I have broken the Fourth Commandment. There isn't a commandment which says thou shalt not
lay hands on children.

The son of Hörnle the manufacturer is always wanting to
play with me because he's not allowed to play at home in the
factory. At Hörnle's place they roll and cut sheet metal, and
every now and again a finger and a hand get chopped off
as well. In church, of course, nothing like this can happen. Besides there's no one to keep an eye on us here ex-

cept when a service is in progress. But Hörnle is always wanting to climb up into places, preferably into the tower where the bells are and where he likes hanging out of the little belfry windows—first with one foot, then with both, and finally with his whole body. "You do the same," Hörnle says to me. "If you don't you're a coward!" "I don't know whether I'm a coward or not," I say. "I only know I'm not an idiot." And this is true. Because Hörnle loses his balance and breaks every bone in his body.

"How could such a thing happen?" cries my father. "Why didn't you watch out?" "Why should I watch out?" I ask. "I wasn't hanging out of the window myself." "My God!" says my father, "what sort of a son have I brought into the world?" And I ask myself the same question.

In 1921 I went to the primary school in Aalen and in 1925 to the secondary school, where I finally graduated in 1934, one year late. Apart from getting a year behind in this way there was nothing exceptional about my schooldays.

In the church jumping competition I manage eight feet six. This is in fact a local record, but then along comes a fellow from Göppingen who's staying here for the summer holidays and does a whole two inches higher—though only after a good deal of training. These church jumps are performed on the end of the bell ropes. You pull at the rope and let yourself swing up with it. The person who pulls hardest reaches the greatest height and incidentally produces the finest peal. Bets are laid, too, and my friends almost always win. "You little blasphemers!" my father shouts at us, when he discovers why his bells are always ringing so merrily.

Schnorr, an assistant master at the secondary school, is a frequent visitor to our house. "He's a highly educated man," my father tells me, "and you must show him respect. Besides, he's a friend of mine, and later when you go on to secondary school he'll be your teacher. So see you treat him with respect!" But I can't stand this man Schnorr. He keeps on asking me questions like how much does nineteen times eighteen make, or how do you spell engineer, and what was the date of the Battle of the Teutoburg Forest. And every time I see him he has more questions for me. I try to keep out of his way as soon as he shows up.

Almost worse than this fellow Schnorr is a girl of the neighborhood called Marion Michalski. This girl Marion pesters me wherever I go. She will never believe what I say about anything and even doubts my church jumping record. The worst part about it is that Marion is three years younger than me and is really just a little child. But she won't leave me alone. She has pigtails and a silly laugh and always thinks she knows better. But there are some things in her favor; she's the daughter of the burgomaster for instance and he can give orders to the police, which can be a great advantage.

When I go on to secondary school this man Schnorr is my teacher. Which is bad. For now I can no longer keep out of the way when he shows up, and he keeps on asking and asking questions. But soon I learn always to give him some sort of answer, even if, according to Schnorr, it isn't always the right one. "That son of yours isn't much of a scholar," Schnorr tells my father. This worries my father very much and he starts drinking heavily; and Schnorr is worried too and drinks even more heavily than my father. Then a glassy look comes into his eye, his speech thickens, he dribbles and slobbers and slips off his chair. "He's not feeling well," says my father heavily. "Take him home." And I take my sled because there's snow outside. We load Schnorr onto the sled and I drive off into the park, where I put him down beside the war memorial. In my view it's the business of the police to take him on from there.

From that day on Schnorr asks me many fewer questions than before. Sometimes he acts as if I weren't in his class at all. But he doesn't keep this up for long. I notice he pays more and more attention to my written work. Just before I'm due to be moved up to the next grade, he finds seven mistakes, underlines them in red, and writes at the end, "Poor." And this puts an end to my chance of a move. But I find some red ink and underline two more mistakes—where there aren't any of course—and then go up to Schnorr and say, "Excuse me, sir. There are nine mistakes marked here, but I've only made seven." Schnorr says, "Impossible," counts them up again, blushes almost as red as the ink, and then says, "You're quite right. It's wrong. I'm sorry." And then he crosses out the two extra mistakes. "Excuse me, sir," I continue. "I got 'poor' for nine mistakes then surely I must get a better mark now that I've only got seven, or isn't that right!" and of course I do get a better mark and I'm moved up after all.

The church becomes our stronghold. I've had extra keys made for every lock in it at the verger's expense. I caught him one day trying to pinch the Communion wine, since when I've been able to do what I like with him. And we squat there on the carpet talking of God and the world and of life, particularly the latter, and drinking a great deal. Until this bitch Marion Michalski comes and forces her company on us. What is it she wants anyway?

"This man Ley is a filthy pig," I say in front of the whole class. So Schnorr can't overlook the remark but has to go to the headmaster about it. The headmaster runs to the local education authority. A commission is set up to investigate the matter. But I say, "There's absolutely no doubt about it, this fellow Ley is a filthy pig." "Remember now, Feders, you're talking about one of the leaders of the Reich!" shouts the school inspector. "I'm talking about a filthy pig," I say. "Because this man Ley pissed out of a car as it was passing a whole group of Hitler Youth, who had to jump aside to avoid getting wet. I saw it with my own eyes!" "One doesn't say things like that," declared the inspector decisively. "No true German boy would believe such a thing!" This is the year in which I am not moved up, ostensibly because I'm weak in history.

The best thing about Schnorr is undoubtedly his wife. She always smiles when she sees me, and her smile grows warmer and warmer each year. When I'm in my last year, she's particularly friendly. "You've grown into a fine young man," she says when I bring the exercise books to the Schnorrs' apartment. "Let's see if you've any muscles?" "Quite a lot," I say. "All over." And she feels them for herself. She had plenty of time for this because Schnorr is teaching that afternoon. Her voice grows husky and her eyes grow large. She seems to lose her balance for a moment and I catch her and lay her on the couch. "Stay with me," she says. And I do because she shows me everything I want to see and teaches me a lot of things I know nothing about as yet. Then she says: "What are you thinking about?" "About the written work for the matriculation," I answered. "Can't you find out what the questions are going to be?" "I'd do anything for you," she says. And she does it.

"Shame on you!" says Marion Michalski indignantly. "How can you do such a thing! And with her of all people! Shame on you! I never want to see you again. Never!"

"You make me ashamed of you," said my father. "It can't go on like this. You need to have some order and discipline knocked into you. You must go into the army."

In 1935 I volunteered for the Wehrmacht, with the intention of becoming an officer. After the usual two years' basic training I graduated first from the Military Academy in Potsdam and in 1938 was promoted second lieutenant.

It's all quite simple; I have useful muscles, a strong heart, and my lungs would outdo a pair of bellows. I can run faster, jump further, march longer, than most men. Nothing tires me.

It's all quite easy, so long as one remembers one simple basic principle: stupidity is trumps, the stupid represent the norm. The most primitive oaf of a ranker has to be able to understand what's going on—everyone else has to adjust their point of view to him. Even in his sleep the soldier must be able to shoot effectively or do whatever else is demanded of him—then everything's fine. For a convoy always proceeds at the speed of its slowest vehicle. An army is as good as its most half-witted private. This has to be understood if life is to be tolerable. You have to appreciate this standard if you are to achieve a corresponding sense of superiority. Soldiering is based on the lowest common denominator—its highest peak is represented by a slick mediocrity.

Practically speaking, that is all you need to know. The soldiers among whom I find myself remind me of a patient herd of cattle—useful material for the slaughterhouse of war. The noncommissioned officers above me who bellow and nag, bluster and bully, are simply, either by inclination or instinct, the leaders of the herd. The officers I'll be mixing with, who spend their time organizing, planning, supervising—they're simply the designers, the engineers, the switch controllers for large concentrations of human machinery. Ah, my friends, a man who has grasped all this isn't going to be impressed by anything.

But it's only the Wehrmacht which functions along clear, simple, predictable lines like this, not life itself. That's a complicated business even if it doesn't always seem so. An example of its complexity is provided by Marion Michalski. She's there when I get home. She follows me around even if I don't want her to. She bothers me whenever she can. "What is it you want from me?" I ask her. "I want anything you want," says Marion. And she says this as we're walking through the park on the way to the movies. There's a full moon above us. I can see her face very clearly in all its details—her eyes, staring at me, her lips slightly parted, and the whole framed by her long loose hair which reaches below her shoulders. And then there's the smell of chestnuts in bloom, and, growing stronger and stronger, the scent of Marion's skin as she comes closer and sidles up to me. "I want anything you want," she repeats. And I say, "I want to make love to you, here, on the grass." "Then do," she says. "It's time you did!"

Everything would be easy, child's play, one could cope with everything with one hand tied behind one's back, if it weren't for this girl Marion. One's military duties—barely more than a primitive way of enjoying oneself. Preparing to become an officer—ridiculously easy, kindergarten stuff. The various exertions on the barrack square, on maneuvers, on the ranges—all child's play to Feders. Even as a corporal I know more than any lieutenant. And the girls of the garrison towns of Stuttgart, Tübingen, and Göppingen are nice and pretty and uncomplicated. It's positively touching the trouble they take. "Show me what you can do," I say. And they say, "What's the matter with you? Who are you trying to forget?" And I say, "I've already forgotten whoever I wanted to forget."

But it isn't true. I can't forget. However hard they try, no one comes up to Marion. With Marion everything's always so easy. Nothing is ever awkward or goes wrong. I come to her and there she is. I want to make love to her and she's ready for me.

Then I am promoted second lieutenant. When I come home Marion is waiting at the station. She comes up and stands in front of me and looks at me. "Marion," I say, "will you marry me?" "Yes, you idiot," she says, "I've always wanted to. Even as a child I wanted to."

I married Marion Michalski in the spring of 1939. At the beginning of the war I was given a company and after the campaign in France was promoted first lieutenant. After being wounded in January 1943 I was made a captain and was posted to No. 5 Officers' Training School. Decorations: Knight's Cross, etc.

Death appears on the scene, physical hardships increase, everything grows more and more unpleasant, but otherwise war brings little change. The methods remain the same. That's the mistake. Because no war follows the same pattern as the previous one. I get my company across the bridge over the Marne. I rally the remnants of two other companies whose officers have been killed. I secure the hill on the far side of the river. "Withdraw all forces immediately," radios the divisional commander. I radio back, "A withdrawal is tactically senseless and could only be carried out with heavy casualties." "I order you to withdraw your troops at once on pain of court-martial," radios the general. And I radio back, "Strong radio interference, staying put." The next day the divisional commander is in a towering rage. Every other word is "court-martial." The day after that I'm awarded the Knight's Cross. "You haven't deserved it!" says the general. "But I've got it all the same," I reply.

My leave with Marion, my wife, is one long ecstasy. We only have one room, and we hardly ever leave it. We lie in bed together far into the morning and get back again in the early afternoon. The fourteen days race by. "I'll always love you," I say. And Marion says, "I'll never forget what it's like to be with you—it's wonderful." "But when I'm gone, Marion?" "I'll never forget what it's like!"

The MO stands in front of my bed and asks, "Well, and how are we today, Captain?" "What's the matter with me?" I asked him. "Please tell me quite honestly—what is the matter with me?" "Well," says the MO, "at any rate you're lucky. You'll get over your wound, it could have been much worse." "Please don't keep anything from me, Doctor, I want to know the truth." "It's quite simple," says the other finally. "In a few weeks' time everything will be more or less normal for you—you'll be able to skip about like a two-year old, except for one small detail. But believe me, my dear fellow, it's a loss which becomes more and more tolerable with the years."

7 THE MAJOR'S WIFE IS INDIGNANT

"EVERYONE HERE toes the line sooner or later, Lieutenant Krafft," said Captain Feders. "Either from cowardice, discernment, or plain adaptability."

He and his newly appointed section officer were making their way together out of barracks and down the hill toward Wildlingen.

"I'm not much of a games player, I'm afraid, Captain. I've never been very good at toeing the line."

"But you'll learn," said Captain Feders with conviction.

Major Frey, the officer commanding Number 2 Course, had issued invitations to a "modest little dinner for a small circle of friends." Now it's true that his dinners were always modest, but the point here was the "small circle of friends."

For Frey had a wife, and she had ambitions as a hostess, though what exactly these were remained obscure.

"She must have read about an officer's social obligations in some novel or other," said Captain Feders. "But she must also have overlooked the fact that that particular piece of trash was written in the days of the Kaiser."

"I don't find anything very remarkable about that, Captain. The Kaiser's days are after all halfway to modern times. When I was at the front I had a regimental commander who behaved like Attila, King of the Huns."

This man Lieutenant Krafft began to interest Captain Feders. He seemed a decent, solid sort of fellow. But the question one couldn't help asking oneself at once was how long would he manage to survive at the training school? Feders felt sure that the first stick was about to be broken over Krafft's back this very evening. He knew the major's wife only too well.

"My dear Krafft," said Captain Feders with a certain amusement. "What is the heat of battle compared with the hatching of social intrigues at home? In battle a man's life is snuffed out like a candle, and that's that. But here one is roasted over a slow wood fire to a beautiful golden brown. With kind words considerately lavished on one into the bargain."

"And is everyone a potential victim for these primitive rites? Is no one safe?"

"Really, my dear Krafft," said Captain Feders flippantly, "you must try not to confuse your terms. There's nothing primitive about this, it's a question of tradition."

"Sometimes the same thing, isn't it, Captain?"

"Of course, my dear fellow, it can be. Tradition is, among other things, the finest excuse in the world for the lazy-minded, a blank check for those half-wits who conceal their own incompetence under the dead weight of all that's been handed down to them. But you shouldn't underestimate these people, above all in terms of numbers. Quite a lot of our educational methods date back to Frederick the Great. Clausewitz is regarded as a modern author and Schlieffen as a model of genius. And if the worst comes to the worst, even the experiences of the last war will come into their own—the war, that is, in which they say we weren't beaten, but which we indisputably lost. As for a great part of our accepted social conventions, they go back to the turn of the century!"

They kept in step as they walked along. The barracks lay behind them in the pale light of evening: a broad, bulky shadow dominating the horizon. The houses of the town looked tiny by contrast, like formations of coral that had attached themselves to a rock. The fact that the town had been there several centuries before the barracks was no longer evident. Mountains of cement had desecrated the landscape, and the modern concrete piles of a number of business houses and blocks of apartments were beginning to destroy the lovable old face of Wildlingen-am-Main.

"Tell me, my dear Krafft, you're quite a boy at the hand kiss, I expect?" said Captain Feders.

"Is this a military training school or a dancing academy?" asked Krafft.

"You *are* naïve, my dear fellow," said Feders with a smile. "You don't seem to realize why Major Frey, our officer commanding Number Two Course, has invited you."

"Well, not to give any pleasure to me, I'm sure of that. But perhaps he merely wanted to fulfill his social obligations."

"Hell!" said Feders. "The man just wants to put you through your paces, that's all."

"And for this purpose he introduces me to his wife?"

"Exactly. He wants, among other things, to test your manners as an officer. Because in the major's view it is only officers with impeccable manners who are fit to instruct officers of the future. But it's the major's wife who has the last word. Which is why, my dear fellow, a full-blown formal hand kiss will be not only an act of politeness but also a first convincing proof of your social capabilities."

"Quite funny that," said Lieutenant Krafft cautiously.

"You'll be finding plenty of other things to amuse you here before you're through, you can be sure of that. Officially the hand-kissing is quite optional, but in Major Frey's eyes it is a natural obligation. Particularly where the major's wife is concerned—she was a von Bendler-Trebitz, you know. Right, then—the charming lady will extend her tiny hand toward you. You grasp it, but without exercising undue pressure. Then you bend over it, Krafft. And for God's sake, and the major's, don't make the mistake of drawing this charming tiny hand toward you as if you owned it, this would be looked upon as little short of an attempt at rape. You bend over it then and keep yourself at a distance of at least three feet from the lady. You then click your heels and without pursing the lips or even wetting them, sketch out a hand kiss. Somewhere between a quarter and an eighth of an inch is regarded as the correct distance. Now have you got that my dear fellow? Try it out today. For sooner or later you'll have to teach it to your cadets in the etiquette class. It's all part of the curriculum, you know."

"I'm afraid you're right," said Lieutenant Krafft. "We'll be having a lot of fun together."

"I never cease to admire you, Felicitas," said Major Frey to his wife. "It's really fabulous the way you manage to arrange everything."

Frau Frey lowered her eyes modestly. "Oh, it's really nothing," she demurred.

This was true—it really wasn't very much. The table was laid, the wine stood ready, all just as usual, and, as usual, none of these preparations were the work of Frau Frey, but of her niece, as the major knew perfectly well.

This niece, a poor relation who looked like one and on whom Frau Frey had graciously taken pity, worked in the Frey household as a servant. She was a capable, willing, undemanding sort of girl, and although Frau Frey didn't actually pay her any wages she hoped to find a husband for her, an officer, in due course.

"What sort of man is this Lieutenant Krafft?" asked the major's wife.

Frey didn't quite know the answer to this, though this didn't prevent him from telling her. "Average," he said. "Possibly a little above the average. We'll manage to make something of him. Sooner or later everyone comes to heel."

"Married?"

"Not as far as I know."

"I'll take a closer look at him," said Frau Felicitas.

The major nodded meekly. He knew what that meant. She would take a closer look at this fellow Krafft to see if he would do for their niece, Barbara Bendler-Trebitz.

"Barbara!" cried Frau Felicitas peremptorily, and their niece appeared at once.

She had a round, friendly, innocent moon face with shy eyes. "Here I am," she said agreeably in a soft chirpy voice.

"For goodness' sake, take that apron off before the gentlemen arrive. You should take more trouble with your appearance, child. Wear a white apron. And try and move gracefully."

"Yes, of course," said Barbara, and disappeared.

The major watched her go with a sad shake of his head, which naturally wasn't intended as any reproach to his wife. This would have been unthinkable, for he had nothing but gratitude and respect for her. She came from a really high-class family and was the owner of a sizable property in Silesia, which was being run at the moment by an impoverished relative who was exempt from war service.

Frey had in fact a great deal to thank his wife for. For instance it was positively touching the way she helped him in his career. No commanding officer could have had a more devoted wife. And then again, there was the loving care with which she had furnished this house: Wildlingen-am-Main, Marktplatz 7. An old, elegant, romantic building in the Franconian style, solid and sound, and yet at the same time cozy and with a charm all its own, it might have been built specially for Felicitas Frey *née* Bendler-Trebitz.

"This girl Barbara," the major ventured to remark. "She's a nice girl, but remarkably uncommunicative, don't you find?"

"She'll make a good wife and mother."

"Oh yes, of course, of course," admitted the major. "But she ought to dress with a little more style. I mean her figure really isn't bad at all—quite the contrary, in fact."

"Archibald," said the major's wife, "you don't mean to say you've been eying the girl?"

"Not intentionally of course," the major reassured her. "But after all she is running around under my nose all day long. Besides, I'm thinking of her future, too, and if I'm to be quite frank, I think Captain Ratshelm would be preferable to Lieutenant Krafft."

"Don't you worry your head about that," said Felicitas Frey. "This is a woman's business. If Krafft turns out to be a man of the world with really decent manners, why shouldn't we bring him into our own little inner circle?"

"I'm afraid, though, that this fellow Krafft isn't really a man of particularly fine feeling. He's more Captain Feders' type."

"That wouldn't do," said the major's wife. "And if that's so, then obviously you can't have the two together in the same section, the one as tactics instructor and the other as section officer. Anyway Captain Feders hasn't got anything to give himself airs about with his wife leading that sort of life. It's disgraceful, really disgraceful. You can't have that sort of thing in an officer's training school. But we'll have to discuss that later. We mustn't try and take on too much at once. First of all I'll take a good look at this man Krafft."

"Welcome, welcome to my humble hearth!" cried Major Frey. "So glad you could come. Come in, gentlemen. Take your coats off. Make yourselves at home."

The major was wearing a simple field tunic, which both conveyed an impression of sterling worth and at the same time demonstrated the extent to which he felt at ease. His Knight's Cross with oak leaves flashed brilliantly even in the dim lighting of the hall, and his face was beaming with good will.

Feders and Krafft took off their things and Krafft was introduced to the major's niece. He shook a hot, damp hand and, smiling pleasantly, looked into a face paralyzed with embarrassment. Feders made a jovial remark or two and the girl ran off giggling.

"Captain Ratshelm was just ahead of you, gentlemen, so that now the party is complete. Do come in. My wife is most anxious to get to know you, my dear Krafft."

"The feeling is mutual," declared Feders, noticing with delight that at this the major looked slightly annoyed and Lieutenant Krafft extremely embarrassed. An amusing evening seemed ahead.

The major piloted the two gentlemen into the drawing room, where Captain Ratshelm stood gesticulating animatedly to the major's charming wife Felicitas Frey *née* Bendler-Trebitz.

"Right, in you go!" whispered Feders, pushing Krafft forward.

The major's wife smiled graciously at Lieutenant Krafft and immediately held out her hand expectantly, a stately, elegant figure, standing beneath some sort of ancestral portrait. She had a face like a sheep's and the bold curve of her fleshy nose was something which it was impossible to overlook. Her eyes gleamed with the weary majesty of some mountain eagle. Her skin was faded, but a lot of makeup had lent it a dull, silky gloss which gave the impression of extending over her entire body and certainly was in evidence on her hands, one of which, having been so briskly extended toward him, was now seized by Lieutenant Krafft. He gave it a relatively gentle squeeze and even shook it slightly. His bow seemed to him quite adequate. An icy glint came into her eagle eyes.

But Lieutenant Krafft merely said, "Good evening, Frau Frey."

"Splendid," said Feders with enthusiasm. "Quite the real thing!"

"Our friend, Lieutenant Krafft," said the major, trying to act the man of the world, "will have to find his feet here of course, but I don't think that'll be too difficult for him, with the spirit prevailing under my command. Aren't I right, my dear Ratshelm?"

"Yes indeed, Major," confirmed Ratshelm instantly as one might have expected. "We're very proud that we can teach the young cadets here a good deal more than the mere basic principles of their trade. We make it our endeavor to grasp and mold the entire personality. Krafft will soon get the hang of this."

"Anyhow," said the major with friendly condescension, "I want to welcome Lieutenant Krafft most sincerely to our ranks, as a fellow fighter for our great and good cause under what one might call our training school slogan: Officers First and Foremost!"

"What can I offer you, gentlemen?" asked the gracious lady of the house, who had turned slightly pale but had lost none of her air of majesty. "Would you care perhaps for a small glass of port?"

Captain Ratshelm thanked her humbly, signifying that this would be most acceptable. Captain Feders announced enthusiastically that the charming lady's offer was an extraordinarily happy idea. Krafft merely managed to nod.

And Major Frey remarked, "A true German mistrusts everything foreign, unless of course it's something to drink!"

Captain Ratshelm laughed heartily at his course commander's witticism.

The dinner was, as they had been told, a modest one. Lieutenant Krafft had the honor of sitting next to the lady of the house. That was not altogether a pleasure, though, for while the other guests were able to devote themselves to their platefuls of sausage and share such butter as was available among themselves, Lieutenant Krafft found himself subjected to a barrage of questions.

"Are you married, Lieutenant?"

"No, Frau Frey."

"I should say, from your age, you really should be by now. You must be almost thirty, aren't you? Here we always say that a family tie does an awful lot for a man's moral standing, and if it's up to an officer to set an example, how much more must this apply to those who train officers! Now tell me, are you engaged? Do you by any chance carry a picture of your fiancée on you? I always think that's such a nice thing to do. I'd love to see it, if you have one."

"I'm afraid I'll have to disappoint you there, Frau Frey," said Krafft evasively, not hesitating to shelter from all this curiosity behind what he regarded as a white lie. "I was indeed once as good as engaged, and the girl came from an excellent family. But the tie was brutally sundered by the war."

Captain Feders choked and spluttered and Captain Ratshelm regarded him with disapproval. But the major just went on eating. Since his wife was paying no attention to him he had no need to conform to her dietary regulations.

"The young lady died, then," declared the major's wife. It was obviously difficult for her to imagine anything but death sundering such a tie.

Lieutenant Krafft choked on his slice of bread, which under the penetrating glance of his hostess he had dared to spread with only the thinnest layer of butter. As he choked, his head went forward, and she accepted this as tacit confirmation of her assumption. He felt certain that she would express her sympathy for him. As indeed she did. But she went further than that, for after all she was more than just a woman, she was the wife of a senior officer, and known to the cadets as "the Commanderess." So to her conventional expression of sympathy Frau Frey added the following remark. "It must be very sad for you of course, but this mustn't make you despondent or prone to that numb state of helplessness which I believe is usual among vulgar people and ordinary rankers in their distress. However, so long as you remain one of my husband's officers and colleagues I shall of course take you under my wing."

"I'm most obliged to you, Frau Frey," said Lieutenant Krafft warily.

"Every week I hold a social gathering at which those officers who are still bachelors can meet the young unmarried ladies of good family of Wildlingen. You must come to them in the future, Lieutenant."

"Oh that's really too much, Frau Frey," said the lieutenant, overwhelmed. No woman had ever tried to assert such a vigorous and possessive hold over him before. This was more than mere friendly sympathy, it was social welfare positively being thrust down his throat. The lieutenant swallowed the so-called pudding which followed the "cold plate," a tart of some sort or other, and as he did so he looked irritatedly across at Captain Feders, who seemed to be thoroughly enjoying himself. Lieutenant Krafft leaned forward slightly, spreading his legs apart under the table rather like a Japanese wrestler searching for a hold. As he did so his right foot struck the table leg. That's to say Krafft thought it was the table leg. But shortly afterward he became aware of a certain warmth and then a yielding quality, whereupon he drew back sharply. It was not the table leg at all but the leg of the gracious lady herself with which he had come into contact.

Frau Felicitas never flinched. Her self-control was astonishing. She merely lifted her fine sheep's nose slightly, as if smelling a bad smell.

"So sorry, so sorry," said Krafft in embarrassment.

"I think," said Felicitas Frey loftily, "that it's now time for the gentlemen to have their smoke."

"A good soldier," the major assured everybody, "is never off duty. Which is why, gentlemen, you will hardly be surprised if I take this opportunity to talk a certain amount of shop."

"No indeed, that doesn't surprise us at all, Major," Feders assured him.

The gentlemen were sitting in the venerable, leather armchairs, which creaked painfully every time anyone moved. Beneath their feet was a carpet lavishly adorned with a pattern of roses. They were surrounded by plush and excessively heavy and ornately carved dark brown furniture—no mistaking this for anything but a smoking room.

As a pure matter of form the major held out to the officers an ornate silver-plated rosewood box well-stocked with cigars. Captain Ratshelm and Captain Feders, both of whom knew the form here, declined with thanks and asked permission to smoke their own cigarettes. Only Krafft grabbed mechanically at the box. To make matters worse, once there he seized on one of the major's showpiece cigars. The major managed to keep his hospitable smile intact. He merely frowned slightly at the same time. Yet as Krafft bit off the tip of the cigar with his teeth and spat it thoughtlessly out onto the carpet, the major shuddered. Not for the sake of the carpet, but because such a degree of contempt of good manners hurt his finer feelings.

"I'm so sorry," said Lieutenant Krafft, "but sometimes I find I completely forget the difference between a drawing room and a foxhole."

"When I was at the front," said Captain Ratshelm, "I had a CO who always used a snow-white napkin at meals even in the front line itself. Whatever happened he never ceased to be a man of culture."

"When he dies a hero's death he won't exactly smell of eau de cologne," said Feders.

"Gentlemen," said Major Frey, "I find that there are certain things which can't be joked about. In particular those things that are what one might call sacred to us." And he fingered his Knight's Cross with oak leaves as if to reassure himself (*a*) that it was still there, (*b*) that it was straight and clearly visible, and (*c*) that it could therefore be admired.

"Let us never forget, gentlemen, that the high moral purpose which is one of the fundamental tenets of soldiering should be with us at all times, for once a soldier always a soldier. And an officer of our stamp is the soldier *par excellence*. But to get down to business. On my course, my dear Krafft, there are three companies of three sections each, and each section has one tactics instructor and one section officer. And I may say that my officers are among the finest in the entire Wehrmacht. You are now about to take your place among them, since tomorrow morning you will be taking charge of Section H for Heinrich. And I venture to suggest that it is one of the finest sections of the whole company. Aren't I right, Captain Ratshelm? As company commander you must be in the best position to judge."

"Oh yes, that's so, Major. I'd even say it's the finest section we've had for a long time. There are a number of first-class men in it on whom I pin great hopes. As tactics instructor, wouldn't you agree with me, Feders?"

"Oh, completely," said the captain. "Section H for Heinrich consists of a lot of stupid, arrogant, underhand oafs. They're lazy, greedy, cheeky, stupid, mad for women and decorations. When I'm teaching them they can't tell the difference between a hand grenade and a field kitchen, a machine gun and a ration pack, orderlies and orders. They're interested primarily in food, and only secondarily in ammunition. And their faith in a certain former corporal seems more important to them than any proper appraisal of a given situation."

The major smiled. And Captain Ratshelm tried to do the same. Lieutenant Krafft was merely astonished. Captain Feders' utterly uninhibited statements bordered on high treason. Krafft sucked pleasurably at his cigar.

"Our beloved Captain Feders," said the major with a curt laugh, though his eyes were like pin points and his smile frozen as his voice grew sharper and sharper, "Our beloved Captain Feders is very fond of using bitter words and cutting expressions, and in fact has quite a reputation for them. But all of us who know him well realize how he means these things to be taken. He likes to pile on the irony, so to speak, rather as Blücher and Wrangel used to do. He has, however, sufficient tact to confine such remarks to a most intimate circle, which is really a sort of proof of his confidence in us. His prodigious capabilities as a tactics instructor help us to be indulgent toward him. If I've understood you correctly, Captain Feders, what you mean is this. The cadets of Section H, whose tactics instructor you are, are still deficient in a number of soldierly qualities and riddled with human weakness. They're badly in need of some first-class tactical training, which after all is the point of an officers' training school. Their faith in our Führer is gratifyingly pronounced—an indispensable prerequisite indeed for their careers as officers— yet this cannot be regarded as enough in itself. Isn't that so, Captain Feders—isn't that what you meant by your remarks?"

"Yes, Major, exactly," said Feders impassively.

The major smiled indulgently. He could hardly help admiring himself. He was more than just a soldier, he was a diplomat as well. He might well be on the threshold of a great career. His work at the training school would be an excellent first step toward it. "Well, my dear Krafft, how were you thinking of handling your cadets?"

"Strictly, but fairly," said Krafft, unable to think of any other platitude just at that moment.

"What methods of instruction were you thinking of employing?"

"Whatever methods are currently in use here and you consider correct, Major."

The major nodded. The last part of Krafft's answer was particularly gratifying. The fellow was adaptable or at least was prepared to be, which was always the essential prerequisite for good, fruitful co-operation. But what the major liked to think of as his restless spirit of inquiry wouldn't leave him alone. "Which method do you prefer, Krafft?" he asked. "Skillful persuasion, instruction by example, or drilling things into people by force?"

"Whichever seems suitable in any given instance, Major."

Again the major nodded. This time he wasn't exactly displeased by Krafft's answer, but he wasn't particularly happy about it either. The fellow was suspiciously evasive and simply wouldn't allow himself to be pinned down. The major would have to be careful. The existence of one Captain Feders among his officers was unsettling enough. Two such people in one and the same section spelt trouble.

However, the major was spared further speculation, because at that moment his wife, Frau Felicitas, poked her by no means insignificant sheep's nose into the room, smiled, and said quite brazenly, "What a pity you gentlemen have to leave so soon! But of course you have a heavy day tomorrow."

"Archibald," said the major's wife, "I don't like this man at all."

"I can't say I'm exactly enthusiastic about him either, Felicitas dear," agreed Frey with alacrity. "But unfortunately I can't always choose the people I work with. And the fellow has been positively forced on me."

The major suppressed a yawn and tried to look interested. He usually took notice of her advice, though it wasn't always possible for him to follow it. But one thing was clear; Felicitas was remarkably good at sizing up how useful and valuable a subordinate was going to be. The quality was inbred in her, so to speak, for several of her ancestors had been generals, important landowners, and ministers of state.

"The man has no manners, Archibald. He doesn't know how to kiss one's hand, and he has no conversation. He eats untidily, scatters ash all over the place, and never once addressed me as 'ma'am.' "

"Most regrettable," said the major.

"Not that I overestimate the value of social conventions, Archibald. But you know my view—people with properly trained minds have good manners as well. This man Krafft may well be very capable, but then so are a lot of artisans. A true officer needs to be more than just capable. In short, Archibald, I have considerable misgivings."

"So have I, Felicitas, my dear! But what am I to do?"

"You could talk to the general, it's still not too late. Tomorrow, though, when this man takes over the section, it could be too late."

The major lowered himself heavily into an armchair. The telephone stood just beside him. He had a problem to wrestle with now. He certainly wanted to protect himself from harm and also not to disappoint his wife. But it wasn't so easy to get the general to change his mind, for he always required absolutely conclusive arguments.

"Did you notice how he looked me up and down, Archibald?" the major's wife now asked with a shudder of indignation.

"He looked you up and down?"

"Almost as if I were one of those terrible women. I felt utterly ashamed. A positively animal look, Archibald. I regard him as quite shameless and utterly degenerate."

"But my dear Felicitas," said the major in some confusion,

"he probably only wanted to flirt with you a bit. You should laugh at that and take it as a compliment—an unfortunate compliment perhaps, but at least the right idea was there. He simply tried to make eyes at his commanding officer's wife, in order, in his rather clumsy way, to get you to like him."

The major took one look at his wife and felt sure that he was right. Her qualities were unmistakably more of a spiritual nature. But then he began to have slight doubts. Not everyone, he told himself, was made like himself, with his sense of duty, his moral irreproachability. He had known how to sublimate his instincts in action. But even among his own officers there might easily be people who were inclined to go astray. He had even read of a singular addiction in some young people for older women, and there was nothing he wouldn't put beyond Krafft.

"He looked at me as if he wanted to undress me!" insisted his wife with a great show of indignation.

The major shook his head sadly. "You must be mistaken, Felicitas," he went so far as to say.

"I don't make mistakes about that sort of thing," she insisted. "And if all that isn't enough for you, then I won't keep the rest from you: the man tried to molest me in an unbecoming manner under the table."

"Inconceivable!" said the major. "An unfortunate accident, perhaps."

"It can't all be accident!" cried Frau Felicitas bitterly. Then she walked over to the door, opened it, and called, "Barbara!"

Barbara, the girl who was both niece and maid, appeared at once. A shabby apron was tied round her, for her day's duties were by no means over. She blinked and looked past the major at Felicitas. She waited.

"Barbara," said Felicitas imperiously, "what was the matter when you were helping the officers into their overcoats just now? You let out a shriek and then giggled like an idiot. Why?"

"Oh, nothing, nothing at all," said Barbara, blushing.

"Aha!" cried Frau Felicitas. "Lieutenant Krafft was standing just beside you. Did this man pinch you by any chance? And if he did, where?"

"It was nothing," Barbara insisted. "Really nothing." She looked down.

"That'll do," said Felicitas Frey. "You can go back to your work now."

Barbara left with visible relief. The major watched her go,

thoughtfully. She did indeed have a remarkably fine figure. And Krafft had noticed the fact on the very first evening, the depraved fellow.

"Well?" asked Felicitas insistently. "Aren't you going to do anything about it? It may be too late by tomorrow."

Major Frey nodded gloomily. Then with an air of determination he picked up the telephone and had himself put through to the barracks. When after a slight delay the switchboard at the training school answered, he gave his name and rank. Then, clearing his throat, he asked to be put through to the general.

"Modersohn," said a clear, quiet voice almost at once.

"I'm terribly sorry to trouble you at such a late hour, General . . ."

"Don't waste time explaining," said the general. "Get to the point."

"General, on mature reflection I have decided to request you most earnestly to countermand your appointment of Lieutenant Krafft to be section officer of my Number Six Company."

"Request refused," said the general, and hung up.

"What always fascinates me," said Captain Ratshelm, "is the elegance and sophistication one finds in Major Frey's house."

"And what fascinates me," said Feders, "is the colossal narrow-mindedness that prevails there."

They were walking up the hill toward the barracks, a picture of harmony, it might have been thought. In the center walked Captain Ratshelm, to his right Captain Feders, to his left Lieutenant Krafft—men engaged in the training of officers, striding easily along, in amiable conversation.

It was a bright, clear night and the snow crunched beneath their feet. Everything around them seemed mildly enchanted—the sharp outlines of the trees, the houses like dolls' houses, a sky full of twinkling stars. A typical German winter's night, thought Ratshelm. Then he turned to Feders again and said cordially, "You've got it all wrong, Feders my dear fellow. Our major and his worthy wife are cherishing eternal values. They are upholding all those things that it is so essential to preserve—home, dignity, social intercourse."

"Nonsensical sham, nauseating twaddle, an eye on the main chance!" declared Feders. "These people are living in a mad world of their own, and of course they're not the only ones."

"Excuse me, Feders," said Captain Ratshelm indulgently but in a mild tone of rebuke, "you're talking about your own major, you know."

"I'm talking about a state of mind that I call narrow-mindedness," said Feders stubbornly. "It's a widespread defect, like short sight. No one with it sees further than his own limited horizon."

"My dear Feders," said Ratshelm, trying to calm him down, "we should strive to live our lives in a spirit of loyalty, humility, and unselfishness."

"Tripe!" cried Feders abruptly. "What we should do is keep our eyes and ears open and see this world as it really is, with all the muck that's in it, and all the blood. What matters is to be able to see beyond the horizon. Over there behind Hill Two Hundred and One lies Berlin, and a few thousand human beings die there almost every night, torn to shreds, suffocated, burning and bleeding to death. A few hundred miles further on is the eastern front. While we're busy kissing hands and grinning inanely, thousands of men are dying there, crushed by tanks and burned by flamethrowers—and here we are entertaining ourselves with polished social conventions."

"You're a bitter man, Captain Feders," said Ratshelm. "I can understand why."

"If you're going to harp on my marriage, then I'll really go to town on you."

"I shall take care not to do that, Feders," Ratshelm hastened to reassure him. "I merely wanted to try and explain my point of view. But sometimes, you know, you really are a difficult person to get along with."

"Only sometimes, unfortunately," said Feders. "Most of the time I am paralyzed by weakness, fatigue, and disgust. Above all I am quite unlike our friend Krafft here, who seems able to walk in his sleep. Or do you have a melancholy streak in you?"

"A streak of something or other," said the lieutenant, "but I'm afraid it doesn't run very deep. Do you remember that girl Barbara—how she laughed!"

"So she did!" said Feders, suddenly recovering his spirits. "I'd almost forgotten about it. The little thing squealed like some kitchen slut who's had her bottom pinched."

"I don't understand," said Ratshelm in bewilderment. "I imagine you two gentlemen are talking about Fräulein Barbara Bendler-Trebitz, Frau Frey's niece. She laughed, certainly, but what's so special about that?"

"The point is why she laughed," declared Feders. "She laughed because our friend Krafft did in fact pinch her bottom."

With a sense of outrage Ratshelm said, "How could you do such a thing, Lieutenant Krafft? I find that downright vulgar. And in that house, too!"

"Well," said Krafft, "maybe you do, but the little girl enjoyed it! In that house too. Quite instructive, really. Or don't you think so?"

" 'Request refused,' was all the general said. Nothing else."

Major Frey, man of the world and hero of many battles, sat there shattered. A curt rejection of this sort from the general could have quite unforeseeable consequences. The general had always been a difficult man to approach, yet he, Frey, had never before known him quite so hard and uncompromising.

"I'm afraid," muttered the major, "that I've just made a mistake that's going to be almost impossible to put right. And it's all the fault of this Lieutenant Krafft!"

"I had a feeling," said his wife, with undertones of triumph in her voice, "that this man's appearance was going to lead to little good."

"Maybe," said the major uneasily, racking his brains for some way out of the situation, "but at all events it would have been better if you hadn't interfered!"

"But you know my reasons for doing so," she said in astonishment. "And you've accepted them up to now."

"Perhaps I shouldn't have," said the major suddenly. Yet he quickly saw that it was pointless. He avoided his wife's eyes, for he felt that she had let him down badly.

His glance wandered restlessly over the rose-patterned carpet. He just hadn't been sufficiently on the alert. He should have taken her idiosyncrasies into account more. She was inordinately sensitive about certain things. She could talk for hours on end about illness, wounds, and death, but the simplest physical contact was sometimes enough to bring her to the verge of unreason.

There was a nobility about her, of course, an unmistakable nobility, the major was in no doubt of that. But on the delicate subject of sex, what she liked was tenderness, the shimmer of romance, chivalrous devotion, soft music, and the willing attendance of courtiers. She was deeply sensitive. And honorable, too, uncommonly honorable. But she was utterly lacking in all sense of reality. Damn it, officers weren't a bunch of minnesingers—certainly not this fellow Krafft who was responsible for the mess he was in now.

"Felicitas," said the major, "I think you shouldn't overdo your role as a paragon of virtue, not when grim realities are at stake. My God, do try and realize that a training school like this isn't a hothouse for sensitive plants!"

Felicitas looked at her husband as if he were some workman who had forced his way into her house. She raised her great sheep's nose majestically into the air and declared, "That is no way to speak to me, Archibald."

"Oh, really!" said the major, who still hadn't recovered from the shock of Modersohn's two words. "If you hadn't come out with these idiotic sexual complexes of yours, I would never have incurred the general's rebuke."

"I pity you," she said, "and find it lamentable that you should try to shift the blame for your own ineptness on to me." The sheep's nose rose still higher into the air, looked even more majestic, then described a hundred-and-eighty-degree turn and was borne out of the room, a convincing picture of indignant pride. A door slammed and the major was alone.

This Lieutenant Krafft, thought the major bitterly, is not only endangering my marriage but has brought the general down on top of me as well. To hell with this man Krafft!

8 *THE CADETS MAKE A MISTAKE*

"HAND GRENADES ready for the new man!" cried one of the cadets brightly. "Out with bayonets and pen nibs—it's a matter of life and death! Idiots and suicides to the fore!—soldiers take cover!" The speaker looked around for applause, but no one laughed. This was no time for trying to be funny. A new section officer marked a new chapter in training, perhaps even a new start altogether. And this was nothing to joke about.

The cadets of H Section were entering classroom thirteen in ones and twos. They took their places, unpacked their brief cases, and laid their notebooks out in front of them. All this was done surely and mechanically, as when a knob is turned in a factory, or a lever's position changed at the ring of a bell.

Up to this moment in the day everything had gone like clockwork—reveille, early games, washing, breakfast, cleaning out of rooms, marching to class. But now the complications set in. Unforeseen developments might lie ahead. No one could be sure of what would hapen. A wrong answer could result in a bad mark, every false move might prejudice one's chance of a commission.

"Listen here!" cried Cadet Kramer, the section senior. "This new man's name is Krafft, Lieutenant Krafft." He had learned the name from one of the course commander's clerks. "Anyone know him?"

No one knew him. The cadets had had their work cut out getting to know their former section officer, their tactics instructor, their course commander, and all the other people who had a say in whether or not they were to become officers. No other officers interested them.

"In one hour at the latest," said Cadet Hochbauer with an air of superiority, "we shall know exactly how to behave. Until then it's best to reserve judgment. And don't let anyone try and suck up to him too soon!"

This was to be taken as not just a hint but a warning. The cadets around Hochbauer nodded. What was more, there was some sense in the injunction, since it was never advisable to put too much faith in a superior officer whose business was to put them through their paces for several weeks on end.

On this particular morning, therefore, the cadets of H Section were unusually quiet. They slipped uneasily into their places and looked nervously across the bare room toward the instructor's desk and the blackboard.

At the middle desk in the front row sat Cadet Hochbauer, and beside him the section senior. The two conversed together under their breaths. Hochbauer gave Kramer advice, and Kramer nodded agreement. Cadets Rednitz and Mösler naturally sat right at the back of the room. Of all those present they were easily the calmest, for they had invested practically nothing in this course to date, either physically or spiritually, and as a result had nothing to lose.

"What are we getting so excited about, children?" asked Rednitz jovially. "It's quite possible that the new man will be completely accommodating. It's possible too that he'll have limitations, or be blessed with more than his share of stubbornness. In any case the man's an officer, so we must be prepared for anything."

"We're going to wait and see," said Cadet Hochbauer in a

tone of rebuke. "It would be a mistake to jump to conclusions, don't you think, Kramer?"

"A great mistake," said the section senior.

"But what if the new man's like Lieutenant Barkow?" inquired Mösler.

"Then," said Rednitz, "we'll again have to put our trust in God, our Cadet Hochbauer, and the effectiveness of a fast-burning fuse."

Hochbauer jumped to his feet and drew himself up to his full height. The cadets in the front row backed away and formed a ring of spectators. An uneasy silence settled over the room, broken only by the shuffling of feet.

Hochbauer walked down the center gangway to the back of the room, followed by Kramer, the section senior. Two other cadets, Amfortas and Andreas, joined the procession, though more to cover the rear than for any other purpose. The room was poorly heated, but the temperature seemed to have risen appreciably.

"Now what's all this melodrama so early in the morning!" cried Mösler, looking around for some way of escape.

Rednitz had also risen. He looked rather pale, but managed to convey a certain air of lightheartedness nevertheless. He waited until Hochbauer was standing in front of him and then made an effort to broaden his friendly smile. He wasn't afraid, being too well acquainted with the freakish twists of fate at the front to have any fear of this posturing youth. And although he was about the same age as Hochbauer, he felt himself almost an old man by contrast.

"Rednitz," said Hochbauer in an unmistakably menacing tone, "I don't like your nasty insinuations."

"You don't need to listen to them!"

"I regard my honor as at stake over this," said Hochbauer.

"If nothing else," said Rednitz.

Cadet Rednitz looked around at the flat, pallid faces of his companions, and found little support there. But he was grateful for Mösler's hand on his arm, and noticed that the bull-like Weber, Egon, was maneuvering into position, though less out of loyalty than at the prospect of a fight for its own sake. The net effect, however, was likely to be the same.

"You will apologize to Hochbauer," Kramer ordered Rednitz, and Amfortas and Andreas nodded energetically. "This has gone beyond a joke."

"I think we both agree on that," said Rednitz. "The problem is to convince Hochbauer."

The cadets watched the dispute with rising misgiving,

sensing unnecessary complications. Things were difficult enough as it was, on the course, without having dissensions in their own ranks, which were just a dangerous waste of time.

The majority of the cadets respected Kramer as their section senior. He had spent a good deal of time as a corporal and thus had the necessary experience for the job without being clever enough to rule by intrigue. He was in fact a relatively decent fellow, a real plodder, and they could hardly have found anyone better.

But the cadets also tolerated Hochbauer as deputy section senior, having quickly realized that he was one of the ambitious ones of this world. There was no way of stopping him or placating him except by letting him have his own way. That he also happened to be a powerful athlete and an expert in ideology were additional reasons for letting him have his head.

These, then, were the basic considerations in the minds of the cadets. The line of least resistance was their chief concern; and life simply had to be taken as it came. This was why the provocative attitude of Rednitz and Mösler seemed nothing short of irresponsible. The instinct for self-preservation alone demanded that such outsiders should receive no support.

"I'm waiting," said Hochbauer, looking at Rednitz as if he were some sort of louse.

"As far as I'm concerned," said Rednitz, "you can wait there till the cows come home."

"I'll give you five seconds," said Cadet Hochbauer. "After that my patience will be exhausted."

"Be reasonable, Rednitz!" implored Kramer. "After all we're all comrades here, all in the same boat. Apologize and it'll all be forgotten."

"Out of my way, Kramer!" cried Hochbauer firmly. "One has to talk plain German with people like this!"

Kramer still wanted to act the peacemaker, but Hochbauer pushed his way forward, followed by his bodyguards Amfortas and Andreas. Then everyone stopped where they were and listened.

"Look out! He's coming!" cried a hoarse, excited voice.

This was Cadet Böhmke, a poetically inclined individual who in consequence found himself allotted every sort of dreary special duty. This time he had been posted as lookout.

"Look out!" he repeated.

"Attention!" cried Kramer with relief. "To your places, men!"

Captain Ratshelm walked into the classroom followed by Lieutenant Krafft. Cadet Kramer reported, "Section H for Heinrich—forty men all present and correct, sir."

"Thank you," said Ratshelm. "At ease, please!"

"Stand at ease!" cried Kramer.

The cadets pushed their left feet forward and sideways and waited. Each knew perfectly well that the order Captain Ratshelm had just issued was an imperfect one. But he could afford to do that sort of thing; he wasn't on the course.

He corrected himself. "You may sit down."

"Be seated!" cried Kramer.

The cadets sat down very correctly, with their hands on the desk in front of them in the prescribed manner for the presence of officers. They now began to cast a wary eye on Lieutenant Krafft, without, however, for one moment forgetting to give the impression that their whole attention was riveted on Captain Ratshelm, the senior officer present.

Captain Ratshelm now addressed them with gusto. "Gentlemen, I have the honor to introduce to you your new section officer, Lieutenant Krafft. I know you'll give him your full respect and confidence."

Ratshelm looked about him with a challenging air of optimism, concluding with the words, "Lieutenant Krafft, I hereby hand over to you your section and wish you every success."

The cadets watched the ceremony with mixed feelings, noting the exchange of handshakes between the two officers, the radiant look on Ratshelm's face, and the tough smile on Krafft's. Then Ratshelm strutted from the room, leaving H Section alone with its new section officer.

The cadets couldn't make much of him at first. Outwardly he bore a certain resemblance to a bull. His face wore a serious expression, and his glance seemed to sweep over them indifferently. He seemed to have no particular quality that one could pick on, which rather increased their uneasiness. They had no idea yet who it was they had to deal with. And yet everything seemed possible, including of course the worst.

Lieutenant Krafft saw forty faces staring up at him, forty vague, colorless, identical faces in which he found it quite impossible to make out the details. Somewhere in the back row he thought he discovered a pair of friendly eyes for a moment, but couldn't find them again when he looked for them. Instead he saw passive indifference, watchful reserve, and cautious mistrust.

"Right, gentlemen," said the lieutenant. "We must get to know each other. I am your new section officer, Lieutenant Krafft, born in 1916 at Stettin, to be precise, where my father was an official of the post office. I worked on a large agricultural estate as farm foreman and as accountant in the estate office, and was then called up in the Wehrmacht. And that's about all. Now it's your turn. Let's begin with the section senior."

This increased the cadets' misgivings considerably. They began to feel they were being victimized, for they had expected their section officer to start straight in on the lesson, in which case the lieutenant would have had to hold the floor and they would have been able to take their time sizing him up. Instead of which, here was this Lieutenant Krafft demanding from them solo performances which could only have one object, namely to bring each one of them in turn under scrutiny. And what, after that, would they know of their new section officer? Nothing. That he wouldn't have gathered anything very much about them either didn't seem to occur to them.

Meanwhile the section senior had risen to his feet and in his hoarse, slightly rasping voice, obviously accustomed to giving orders, announced curtly, "Kramer, Otto, cadet. Born 1920 in Nuremberg. Father, fitter in a photographic works. Regular enlistment. Corporal."

"Any further interests, Kramer? Particular aptitudes? Hobbies?"

"None," declared Kramer honestly, and sat down, feeling rather pleased with himself. He was a simple soldier and nothing more, and it seemed to him important to have made that clear. He was sure he'd made a good job of things. He always was, until someone of higher rank pointed out the contrary. But this happened rarely enough.

Krafft's glance switched from the boorish face of Cadet Kramer to that of the man beside him. He saw a youth whose clear-cut, winning features had a certain nobility about them, and he said encouragingly, "Right, then, next please."

Cadet Hochbauer rose to his full imposing height and said, "Cadet Hochbauer, Lieutenant. Christian name: Heinz. Born 1923 in Rosenheim. My father is in charge of the political training school at Pronthausen, holder of the Pour le Mérite. After matriculating I volunteered for the front. Special interests: history and philosophy."

Hochbauer said this all very much as a matter of course, without attaching any particular importance to it—almost in a offhand way, in fact. But he watched Lieutenant Krafft carefully to see if his words had made any impression, and seemed to detect that they had. The lieutenant's eyes rested thoughtfully for a while on Cadet Hochbauer.

"Next please," said Krafft.

"Cadet Weber, Egon, born in 1922. My father was a master baker in Werdau which is where I was born, but my father is no longer alive, he had a heart attack at work in 1933 just after being nominated master tradesman of the district— he'd been a Party member from 1927 or '26. I learned baking too—we've got a number of different branches—and my hobby is motor racing."

Figures, names, dates, particulars of places and professions, clues, explanations, statements of fact—all these political, human, military details formed a confused buzzing sound in the room, which seemed completely to bemuse Krafft. By the sixth place name he had already forgotten the first. By the ninth surname he could no longer remember the third or fourth. He stared at the desert of faces in front of him—bony, flat, round, long, and podgy. He listened to one voice after another—honest, rough, sharp, gentle, rasping voices—and they all merged into this one indeterminate buzz.

Krafft noted the amount of wood there was in the room, taking in the paneled wall, the beams of the ceiling, and the floor boards—wood everywhere, worn, scratched, battered, from yellowish brown to brownish black. The smell of pine-wood, turpentine, and dirty water was all about him.

Krafft realized that this method of his was neither bringing him any closer to his section nor enabling him to gain any particularly penetrating insight into them. The hour crawled by with lamentable results. He looked at his wrist watch and longed for the time to be up.

The lieutenant's increasing sense of misgiving automatically transmitted itself to his section. The cadets too longed for the end of this hour that had brought them so much boredom and confusion. Disgruntled looks came over their faces as they began to shift restlessly about in their seats. Some, who had already said their piece, relapsed into sullen brooding. One even yawned—a long-drawn-out yawn that was distinctly audible. But the new section officer seemed not to notice this, which the cadets took as another bad sign.

Only two more of them, thought Lieutenant Krafft, and then it'll be over. And automatically he said, "Right, next please."

Cadet Rednitz now rose to his feet, smiled pleasantly, and

declared, "I must get the lieutenant to excuse me, but I'm afraid I'm not in a position to give him the extensive information he requires."

Krafft gazed at Rednitz with some interest. The cadets stopped wriggling about in their seats and also turned and looked at Rednitz, thereby turning their backs on their section officer—an unusual sign of disrespect, which the lieutenant appeared not to notice. This made Kramer, the section senior, particularly indignant. He began to fear for the preservation of discipline. Discipline was his responsibilty, and provided he had the support of his superior officer it was perfectly possible to maintain it in the requisite manner. But if this Krafft was going to let the cadets turn their backs on him, it would only be a matter of time before they were talking in the ranks or sleeping in class. Lieutenant Krafft on the other hand regarded Cadet Rednitz's behavior as a welcome diversion. His spirits recovered slightly, and he asked in some amusement, "Perhaps, Cadet, you would be so good as to explain just why you can't give me this information?"

"It's like this," said Rednitz pleasantly. "Unlike my fellow cadets here I'm afraid I can't produce an official father, and so I can't say what his profession was."

"Presumably what you mean, Rednitz, is that you are illegitimate?"

"Yes, Lieutenant—exactly."

"Well," said Krafft cheerfully, "such things happen from time to time. And it doesn't seem altogether a bad thing—especially when one realizes that official fathers are by no means always the best. I hope, though, that this minor deficiency won't prevent you from giving me at least a few other particulars."

Rednitz beamed. He liked the lieutenant. But there was another reason for his undisguised pleasure. He could see Hochbauer's angry face glowering at him, and this alone made it worth the little extra trouble.

"I was born in 1922," declared Rednitz, "in Dortmund. My mother was a housemaid to the director of a big firm, though it would be unwise to draw any particular conclusions from that. I went to the primary school, spent a year at technical school, and another year at higher technical school. In 1940 I was called up into the Wehrmacht. Special interests: philosophy and history."

Lieutenant Krafft smiled. Hochbauer looked black. He regarded Rednitz's statement that his special interests were also history and philosophy as a personal insult. Some of the cadets grinned, but only because their section officer had smiled, thus giving them something to go on.

But Cadet Kramer got to his feet and in his capacity as section senior said, "May I draw the lieutenant's attention to the fact that time is up now?"

Krafft nodded, trying to conceal his relief. He did up his belt, put on his cap, and made for the exit.

"Attention!" roared Kramer.

The cadets jumped to their feet rather less briskly than at the beginning of the period, and came to attention with a certain sluggishness. The lieutenant saluted the room briefly and went out.

"Impossible," muttered Cadet Kramer. "If he goes on like this the whole section will go to pieces."

The cadets looked at each other for a moment, and then burst out laughing with relief. The prevailing mood was excellent, and more than a few of them now found themselves facing the remainder of the course with a certain equanimity.

"Well, Mösler," asked his friend Rednitz, "what do you make of him?"

"Yes," said Mösler thoughtfully, "what do I make of him? He's not unsympathetic—but that's not much to go on. My grandmother's quite sympathetic too."

"Fellow sportsmen," said Cadet Weber, Egon, pushing his way closer. "This much is certain—he seems an energetic sort of type, and yet acts like a sheep. Now, what is one to make of that?"

Böhmke, poet and thinker, merely shook his head a number of times. All in all he would have found it difficult to give any very clear opinion of Krafft, and indeed no one asked him for one.

Kramer, the section senior, made an entry in the class log, sensing complications ahead. This fellow Krafft hadn't even signed the book confirming the subject and duration of the class. Kramer saw that they were in for a period of disorganization and indiscipline.

But in the group around Hochbauer joy reigned supreme. Amfortas and Andreas even went so far as to convey utter contempt when the new section officer's name came up. "A complete nonentity, eh, Hochbauer?"

The latter nodded vigorously. "We'll soon have him where we want him. He'll either be eating out of our hands within a week or be fit for nothing but a pension."

9 A JUDGE-ADVOCATE SPEAKS OUT AGAINST HIS WILL

"FRAULEIN BACHNER," said Lieutenant Bieringer, the general's ADC, "we've known each other quite a time now, I think?"

Sybille Bachner looked up from her work. Bieringer pretended to be preoccupied with the notes he was putting in order. "Is something wrong?" she asked.

"What could be wrong here?" cried the ADC, with an expansive gesture. "But I'm worried about your private life again."

"I haven't any. You know that!"

"Exactly!" said the ADC. "No one can live by work alone."

"Except the general."

"Fräulein Bachner," said Lieutenant Bieringer, "the general is married to the army. He's not a normal man at all—he's a soldier. And you're a woman, not just a secretary."

Sybille Bachner smiled, but there was a serious look in her eyes. She sat up straight and pushed her chair back. Then she asked outright, "What are you getting at this time?"

"Well," said Bieringer rather hastily, "I was wondering what you might be doing this evening, for instance."

"Are you offering to take me out?"

"You know I'm a married man," said the ADC.

It seemed to Bieringer only right to point this out occasionally. For though he and his wife lived together in barracks, in the guest house, few people knew her. She was expecting a child, and never appeared at an official function. She hadn't once been into the staff headquarters building where her husband worked, and had never once telephoned him during working hours. She simply might not have existed. And it was not least on account of this very strict reserve that Bieringer loved her dearly, though only after working hours, of course.

"All right then," said Sybille pleasantly, "I'm doing nothing this evening, but why do you want to know?"

"You could go to the movies," said Bieringer. "There's a comedy of some sort on there, people even say it's quite funny. Or perhaps you could go for a walk. I know at least forty officers who'd be delighted to escort you."

"What's all this in aid of?" said Sybille resentfully. "I just haven't arranged anything. Anyway the general may need me—he's got a whole pile of work to do."

"The general only needs you if you're not otherwise engaged. I'm to make that explicitly clear to you."

"Good," said Sybille Bachner, "you've made that clear. Now what?"

Bieringer shook his head, and his gesture could have been interpreted in a number of different ways. He cleaned his spectacles carefully, looking at Sybille as he did so with his gentle watery eyes, and said finally, "So you're prepared to work overtime again?"

"Of course, Lieutenant," said Sybille briskly.

Bieringer felt a certain misgiving about this keenness of hers. For Sybille Bachner was said to have had something of a past. Between her and the previous commanding officer there had been something more than a mere working relationship.

But then Major-General Modersohn had been made commanding officer of Number 5 Officers' Training School, and Bieringer had confidently assumed that Bachner's days in staff headquarters were numbered. But it wasn't long before an unexpected development took place; Sybille Bachner proved herself a first-class worker. And she didn't seem to make the slightest effort to extend her influence beyond the general's anteroom. The general therefore tolerated her and said nothing, though the ADC remained on the alert.

"The general would like a talk with Judge-Advocate Wirrmann at nineteen hundred hours. Also with Lieutenant Krafft. Also at nineteen hundred hours."

"Both together?" asked Sybille in astonishment.

Lieutenant Bieringer took care not to look at her, for he could not have helped conveying a certain reproach. His order had been clear enough. Any expression of private opinion was unnecessary. He was the best possible ADC the general could have had.

Sybille Bachner dropped her eyes. Her long, silky hair hung down each side of her face like a curtain. She reminded Bieringer of some tender portrait by Renoir in which the streaming tresses caught by the rays of the sun told of a voluptuous indolence. Bieringer found this combination of thoughts rather unsettling. For he was on duty, after all, and a happily married man and expectant father into the bargain.

"I rather think, Fräulein Bachner," he said cautiously,

"that you should try and get yourself a slightly more severe hair style."

"Has the general been complaining about my hair?" she asked with a flicker of hope.

Bieringer looked at her reproachfully, pityingly. "Fräulein Bachner," he said, "you're not a soldier—why should the general show any interest in your hair?"

"Order and cleanliness," declared Captain Kater, "are what I set store by. And in that I'm second to none."

Captain Kater was inspecting number one kitchen in his capacity as commander of the headquarters company. All kitchens in the barracks area came under his jurisdiction.

Parschulske, the kitchen corporal, accompanied him on his round, respectful and attentive. His conscience was never wholly clear, and his fingers were in almost every pie. Astonishingly enough he was as thin as a rake.

"I've taken the liberty of laying the table as usual, sir, so that you can check the rations and sample the quality of the food."

Kater nodded. He went into the storeroom, prodded one or two sacks, and satisfied himself as to the contents. Then he pulled open a drawer or two—and suddenly stopped dead in his tracks, for he had caught a glimpse of something pink hidden in the semolina.

Captain Kater pushed his hand deep into the semolina and felt about in it. And there he found three lengths of sausage. Three large, fat, juicy lengths of sausage, each weighing about six pounds.

Kater said nothing for the time being. He removed his hand, let his eyes sweep over Parschulske, the kitchen corporal, who was standing stiffly to attention, by his side, and moved on into the kitchen, where the table was already laid.

Here he sat down and examined the food in front of him —cold roast beef, fat sausages, creamy portions of cheese. All this was there to be sampled for quality, taste, freshness, general condition, and whatever else served as an excuse. Kater cut himself a slice or two here and there. It was his principle never to act precipitately. There were always considerable advantages in keeping people guessing, and he was, he thought, a master of such tactics. He had left the kitchen corporal completely in the dark as to whether or not the pilfered sausages had been spotted—as to whether or not they would have to be accounted for.

For the time being, the wretched Parschulske didn't know

where he stood, and felt distinctly uncomfortable. He therefore abused the cook for stealing the rations.

But the cook wasn't going to take that; he immediately laid the blame on the various kitchen assistants. "What if a few sausages have been stolen?" -he said. "It could have been anybody, or is there a label on them saying who took them?"

"But in the last resort," said the kitchen corporal, "it's my responsibility!"

"Don't worry, Captain Kater will allow an extra helping or two to confuse his memory."

But Captain Kater just thoughtfully ate on. He was still trying to decide what he ought to do about the sausages. A short note to the general, perhaps. In this way he would be able to demonstrate both correctness of approach and a certain skill in detection. But there were also advantages in putting the kitchen corporal under an obligation to him.

And while Captain Kater thus turned over various possibilities in his mind he let his glance sweep across the kitchen —over kettles and coppers and tables to the female kitchen personnel. Strapping, buxom girls, most of them. They might have been specially fattened for the job. Not his type. One of them caught his attention, though, a new girl who looked at him with large inquiring eyes. Presumably, thought Kater, it's a surprise for her to find her superior officer here.

Affably he beckoned her over, still holding his knife in his right hand. The girl hurried across at once. Obviously there was nothing she had wanted more than to be noticed. This delighted Kater.

"Name?" asked the captain affecting a sympathetic, paternal expression.

"Irene," she said. "Irene Jablonski."

"Stationed here in barracks?" asked Kater, observing with increasing interest the splendid curve of her bosom. This feature was all the more remarkable, since in every other way her fiigure could be described as neat.

"Yes, sir, in barracks," said Irene looking at him hopefully. "I'm in a room with a number of other girls, but none of them works in the kitchen."

"How's your stenography?" asked Kater. "Can you type? Know shorthand?"

"I can learn anything," Irene assured him, beaming at him as if he had been her rescuer. "I learn very quickly—really. I can be taught anything. But anything."

"Well," said Kater, "we'll see."

Lieutenant Bieringer, the ADC, hung up and stared thoughtfully in front of him for a few seconds. Then he said, "The general wants you, Fräulein Bachner."

"I'll go right in," said Sybille.

Bieringer did not look up at her. There really was something suspiciously keen about her. She was a good worker and he didn't want to lose her, but he would most certainly lose her if she were to try and break through the barrier of reserve with which the general surrounded himself. He adjusted his spectacles, picked up a bundle of papers and left the room. The ADC was on his way to the routine weekly conference with the course commanders, at which the training plans for the following week were settled.

Sybille Bachner, however, went into the general's room without knocking, in the usual way. She saw Modersohn sitting at his desk exactly as she had seen him sitting there every day of the week for the last six months—in the identical position and the identical uniform, practically motionless.

"Fräulein Bachner," said the general, "I'd like you to take a shorthand note of my conversation with Judge-Advocate Wirrmann and Lieutenant Krafft, and to type it out immediately afterward. No carbon—no one else to see it."

"Very good, General," said Sybille. She stood there waiting, a picture of devotion.

"That is all, Fräulein Bachner," said the general, bending over his desk again.

Sybille's eyes shone darkly. She turned to leave, but hesitated for a moment at the door, then stopped and said, "General, I don't expect you'll have time for dinner this evening, shall I get something for you?"

Slowly the general raised his head, with a cool lack of surprise. He stared at Sybille as if seeing her now for the first time. And with a flicker of a smile he said, "No, thank you."

"Not even a cup of coffee, General?"

"Thank you, no," said Modersohn. And the flicker of a smile quite suddenly disappeared. "If I need anything like that, Fräulein Bachner, I will inform you at the time."

And with that, this semiprivate conversation—the first for six months—was quite clearly at an end. The general was already at work again, once again surrounded by that wall of reserve, like a wall of bulletproof glass, which so unnerved his colleagues.

Sybille withdrew, neither perplexed nor surprised. She had

grown used to Modersohn's idiosyncrasies over the course of time.

There had been much she had had to get used to. The general's predecessor here had been a jovial, condescending sort of man of the world who knew what he wanted and got it—a boisterous, benevolent despot, an uninhibited, demanding character with whom she had finally been on intimate terms.

With the advent of Modersohn everything had changed overnight. The officers of his entourage froze in the icy atmosphere with which he surrounded himself, and either kept out of his way or crawled around him like eager watchdogs.

In this way Sybille Bachner got to know each of them pretty well, and saw all her illusions scattered like balloons in a storm.

"May I break in on this idyll?" asked a remarkably friendly voice from the door.

It was Captain Kater. He smiled through the half-open doorway—warily, benevolently, confidently. For Sybille Bachner was alone in the room, a fortunate coincidence which enabled him to demonstrate what a jovial, goodhearted fellow he was.

"It always gives me pleasure to see you," he declared, extending a hand toward her. This, too, was something he did only when no one else was present.

"What can I do for you?" asked Sybille Bachner with some reserve.

"Your very existence makes all other needs superfluous," Kater assured her exuberantly. He had worked out this phrase some time before. This Bachner girl was important, she had to be flattered.

"Is there any information I can give you, Captain? I'm afraid Lieutenant Bieringer isn't here at the moment. But if you have a message for him, I can take it for you."

"I have a problem, my dear Fräulein Bachner, which may in the end prove somewhat complicated—I wouldn't like to say yet."

"You wish to speak to the general, Captain? I don't think that's possible just now."

"I'm sorry about that," said Captain Kater with visible relief.

This was probably the best solution, for the time being. It saved him from having to make a decision. It was in fact a development on which he'd been reckoning.

"If it's something particularly urgent . . ."

"No, no, not at all!" the captain hastened to reassure her. "I really can't say that. It will be enough, my dear Fräulein Bachner, if you could simply confirm if necessary that I have been here."

Sybille Bachner saw at once what was up; the captain wished to cover himself. A familiar situation. Types like Kater were always wanting to cover themselves—by little memos, by pushing responsibility onto others, or by pretending that they had made every effort to deal with some matter, though alas in vain.

"I have an uncommonly high regard for you," Kater assured her, winking confidentially. "It's a real pleasure to work with you. And I'm certain the general knows how to appreciate you."

This was a clumsy piece of insinuation. For what Kater meant was that after all the general was a man too. But Captain Kater—so his wink conveyed—was a gentleman and knew how to keep his mouth shut so long as it seemed politic or profitable to do so.

"Captain," said Sybille Bachner coolly, "I shouldn't like to think I've given you occasion for the slightest misunderstanding."

"But of course not!" cried Kater with an expansive gesture. "Quite the contrary! There's no question of any misunderstanding."

"May I once again assure you," said Sybille Bachner, "that I am not in a position either to take any decision or to influence one. My job here is simply that of secretary."

"You're made of sterling stuff!" cried Kater with enthusiasm. "You must stay like that. Don't you think we ought to be friends? And if there's any little wish you should have, no matter how private—come to me." And in the next breath he added, "What did you say the general was doing?"

"He's expecting Herr Wirrmann and Herr Krafft," explained Sybille, caught off her guard. The next moment she was appalled by what she had revealed.

Delighted with his cunning, Kater said quickly, "Well, if you should want someone you can really trust—don't hesitate to come to me. You can rely on Kater, you know."

"You're keeping me from my work, Captain," she said coldly.

Kater didn't take offense. He drew a little closer and smiled at her. "I knew a girl once," he said, "a fine girl she was, all you could ask for. And she had an affair with a lieutenant-colonel—a really spendid fellow, one must concede that. The two of them got married later. They had no alternative. There had been too many witnesses, you see. There's not much one can do about that."

"How awful!" said Sybille Bachner indignantly.

"You can't really go wrong if you're clever about it. I know a thing or two. And if you should need any advice, my dear young lady, you always know where to find me."

"Herr Judge-Advocate Wirrmann," said Major-General Modersohn, "I should like a report please on the progress of your investigation into the death of Lieutenant Barkow."

The general stood with Judge-Advocate Wirrmann and Lieutenant Krafft before him. At the back of the room at a little table of her own sat Sybille Bachner with a shorthand notebook in front of her.

Wirrmann began evasively. "Might I be allowed," he said, "to draw the general's attention to the fact that I consider it inadvisable just now to make such a report in the presence of a third party?"

"I note your point," said the general. "Would you kindly begin your report?"

Sybille Bachner took down every word in shorthand, including all the various flowery turns of phrase. As far as possible she kept her eyes on the three men before her as she worked—the upright figure of the general, the court-martial expert, wily and tense, and Krafft, relaxed almost to the point of slovenliness. For Krafft imagined himself unobserved, and felt superfluous here, though he was wrong on both counts. Sybille Bachner saw that the general was noting every one of the lieutenant's reactions carefully.

"As far as any investigations into the matter are concerned, General," Wirrmann began, choosing his words carefully, "I'm inclined to think they can be regarded as closed. Apart from the preliminary summary of evidence against person or persons unknown, drawn up by yourself, General, I had the following relevant material at my disposal: a sketch map and three photographs; a stores inventory; the doctor's post-mortem; three affidavits from experts, including those of two officers who had concluded their engineering training and had had practical experience of explosives at the front. In addition, nine personal statements, two of which came from the officers on the teaching staff of the training school, the remaining seven from cadets who can be regarded as eye-witnesses."

"I'm familiar with the documents in the case," said the general. "What interests me is the result of your investigations, Judge-Advocate."

Wirrmann nodded. It was plain from his expression that he felt offended. Once again the general had obviously intended to humiliate him.

"Well, General," he said, "after an exhaustive study of all the available documents, and after a thorough examination of all doubtful and debatable points, or points that were from my point of view obscure, I have come to the following conclusions. Lieutenant Barkow died a violent death. It was caused by the selection of a fuse for the charge which was not only a fast-burning one but of insufficient length. The only real point to be decided was how this fast-burning fuse, of insufficient length, in fact came to be employed. Now here a number of alternatives present themselves. First, a fuse of insufficient length was selected through inadequate expert knowledge. This alternative is excluded because Lieutenant Barkow was an officer of considerable experience in this field. Secondly, the correct and properly selected length of fuse was replaced by another which detonated the charge prematurely. In this case the only possibility is that one of the cadets was responsible. By the very nature of things, however, this, too, it seems, can be excluded or at least regarded as extremely improbable. For the cadets' statements, all tally. Moreover there seems no indication of what must always be the decisive factors in such cases—motive and opportunity. For which, thirdly, the final and only logical conclusion that presents itself is that it was an error, a mistake, an accident, which caused Lieutenant Barkow's death. *Ergo,* his death was accidental."

"If you really believe that," said the general sharply, "you're incompetent. But if you only pretend to believe that, then I must regard you as a liar."

Sybille Bachner looked up from her note-taking in amazement. Never before had she heard Major-General Modersohn use such strong words, so deliberately designed to cause pain. Even his most extreme and devastating disapproval had always been expressed with relative restraint. Sybille Bachner took a deep breath. Her hand trembled slightly—but she went on writing, as she had been told to.

Lieutenant Krafft, however, sat up with a start, and began to listen intently. He looked from Modersohn to Wirrmann with secret delight. And gradually it began to dawn on him that what he was watching was an extraordinarily thrilling and potentially dangerous drama. It was as if he were honored with a special seat in a box.

The judge-advocate blushed as red as a beet. His composure was astonishing. An expression of deep distress appeared on his face, to be replaced by one of bitter reproach. What he seemed to want to convey was that he had been lamentably misunderstood. More than that, he felt as if he had been treated as a mere insignificant subordinate.

"General," said Wirrmann in a choked voice, "may I be allowed once again to draw your attention to the fact that I consider it hazardous to make this report in the presence of a third party. Particularly with respect to the points which it now seems cannot avoid being discussed."

"I repeat: I take note of your suggestion, but I do not accept it. Kindly come to the point."

"The general really doesn't wish to rest satisfied with my conclusion? Even when I assure him that it represents the best and indeed the only acceptable solution in the cirumstances?"

"Even then not."

The judge-advocate mopped his brow with a large red-and white-striped handkerchief. The general stood there immobile as ever. Krafft now leaned forward slightly, and Sybille Bachner hastily grabbed another pencil—her first one had broken.

"Naturally," said Wirrmann ponderously, "it is possible to draw other conclusions from the documents before us than those which have led me to the final assessment of my investigation. In fact, as the general may have presumed or indeed known, there is a motive of a sort, which could exclude the possibility of an accident or at least render it doubtful. Yet I dare not examine this motive, General—or rather it would involve more than mere daring to do so, it would be a fatal mistake!"

"And why, Judge-Advocate?"

"General, I'm not quite clear what was the exact nature of your relationship with the deceased Lieutenant Barkow . . ."

"I was his commanding officer—that suffices."

"Very good, General—whether that suffices or not is of course not for me to decide. But if the general should compel me to look for a possible motive, then this might be found in the abundant and indisputable proof that Lieutenant Barkow repeatedly made subversive remarks about the war effort, and that he used expressions hostile to the Führer and Supreme Commander of the Wehrmacht which could be categorized as high treason. These, General, are crimes which inevitably incur the death penalty. It could be said that this violent death of his saved him from one more shameful."

"So that's it," said the general almost inaudibly.

Then Major-General Modersohn slowly turned around, went over to the window, parted the blackout curtains, and flung the windows wide. It was a clear blue ice-cold night outside—moonless and starless. The darkness glowed strangely. It was almost as if this little square of artificial light were the only window giving onto the whole world—a world which froze in icy rejection of all things human. The people in the room shuddered at the cold draft of air.

After a while the general swung around and faced his visitors. His complexion seemed to have turned a shade paler. But this could have been explained by the eerie lights reflected from the snow which poured in through the wide-open windows.

"Thank you for your remarks, Judge-Advocate," said the general. "I note the fact that you regard your investigations as closed. Your duty in my command is thereby concluded. You will report back to the headquarters of the inspector of training first thing tomorrow morning. I hope you have a pleasant journey, Judge-Advocate."

Wirrmann stood up. He saluted and left the room. Both pride and satisfaction were evident in his gait. He felt confident now that victory was his. Casualties had been heavy, but victory was his! And he felt sure that next time he would not only beat this dangerous opponent but destroy him altogether.

"Fräulein Bachner," said the general after Wirrmann had gone, "please hand me your shorthand note."

Sybille Bachner went and put her shorthand pad down on the desk in front of him—it wasn't customary to hand anything directly to the general. And standing just in front of Modersohn, Sybille thought she saw an expression in his eyes that she had never seen there before—an expression of sorrow. As she realized what it was, a wave of feminine sympathy overwhelmed her, threatening to sweep away all her precariously maintained reserve. "General," she said in embarrassment, "if there's anything I can do . . ."

"Thank you. That will be all for today, Fräulein Bachner," said the general, in a tone which brought her back to earth again immediately.

Sybille Bachner then also hurried from the room. It was as if she were trying to escape from herself. She shut the door clumsily behind her.

"Lieutenant Krafft," said the general, looking pointedly at his section officer. "That's it, then. Your task is clear."

The general seized the pad on which the shorthand note of the conversation had been taken. He tore up the pages with brisk gestures—once, twice, thrice. Then he let the scraps of paper slip from his hands to the floor.

"Lieutenant Krafft, you will now act as if I were in your place."

* * * *

Intermediate Report No. 3

THE CURRICULUM VITAE OF
CAPTAIN JOHANNES RATSHELM,
OR FAITH AND SALVATION

I, Johannes Matthias Ottokar Ratshelm, was born on November 9, 1914, the son of a druggist, Johannes Ratshelm, and his wife, Matilda (maiden name Nickel), in Eberswalde in the province of Brandenburg. A year later my mother died and I spent my childhood and youth in the house where my father had his drugstore.

I am sitting on a carpet—a large, thick, square carpet. This carpet is red, the same color as the ball which lies on it. My doll is there too—it no longer has any clothes on but still has some hair left. Her name is Johanna, which is what my father called her. And at the edge of the carpet lies Johann, a big shaggy, white and yellow dog, who is there to watch me. Every time I try to leave the carpet he comes up and pushes me back with his muzzle. He also does this when the ball rolls away or when I try and creep away myself because I've wet my pants. Johann watches all the time. He's quite kind, though, very gentle and quiet. But I'm afraid of him—afraid he'll bite me. He doesn't bite me though. He simply stands there all the time in front of my bed so that when I wake up, there he is looking at me, and I think to myself, he's going to bite me! And I wish he would bite me, so that I could die or he would go away. But he doesn't bite.

My father is quite big and dark and very, very handsome.

He has an apparatus of some sort and I'm always having to stand or sit or lie down in front of it. This apparatus has an eye and is called a "camera," and it's the reason why I'm always having to change my clothes, even to wear girl's clothes of silk and velvet, and transparent things too. "He's sweet," they say when they see me. "He's as pretty as the Blue Boy," says my father. "He's like a painting come to life." And the "camera" stares at me with its one eye and clicks and stands there, sometimes giving off a flash with a nasty smell that makes me cough.

There are a lot of women in our house, though none of them is my mother, and none stay there very long. They come and go all the time and I never get used to any of them. I call each of them "aunt," as my father tells me to. They're all over the place—in the kitchen, the drugstore, the sitting room, and also in the bed where my father sleeps. They're fat and thin, blond and brunette, good and bad, noisy and quiet, and they wear white blouses and aprons, and dresses and shirts, and sometimes nothing at all. Sometimes they moan like wild things, and when I tell my father this he hits me. "You're having wicked thoughts," says my father. "You're spying on me all the time. Why do you do that? Do you enjoy it?" "No," I say, "I don't enjoy it—it's disgusting." "You're having wicked thoughts," says my father, "very wicked thoughts. Do you realize that?" I do. "You ought to be ashamed of yourself!" And I am.

I attended the primary school in my home town from 1920 to 1924. Then I went to secondary school hoping to graduate, which I succeeded in doing in 1933. I lost my father in an accident in 1925, and from then on was brought up by my father's sister, Frau Constance Ratshelm, the widow of a doctor.

The primary school teacher called Gabler is a great beater; and those he doesn't beat, he fondles. But he often beats my friend Klaus and then fondles him afterward. He seizes him by the hair as he sits on the bench in front of him until Klaus cries out with pain. Then he laughs, hurriedly, unnaturally, and pulls Klaus's head toward him, half closing his eyes, and at the same time opening his mouth slightly as my friend's head touches his thigh. And these violent swinging gestures—this pushing and pulling, pulling and pushing—drive me mad. The blood rushes into my cheeks, and I clench my fists. And I jump up as if something inside me were forcing me to my feet, urging me forward, toward the exit, out into the open. But then I sit down again, clenching my teeth.

I hear cries in the night. I jump out of bed and run in the direction of the cries into my father's bedroom, where I see him lying all doubled up across the bed. The bed is white, but his body is gray, and in between on a level with his head, there's something bright red and sticky. The woman in the room is screaming like mad. Slowly I begin to understand what it is she's saying. "It's not my fault," she yells. "He's ill! It happened quite suddenly!" There is blood on her nightdress. "Get a doctor!" she screams. I get a doctor, who says, "Too late," adding, "Hemorrhage—bound to come sooner or later."

My Aunt Constance never lived in our house. She only came there once, to get me when Father died. "Don't ask questions," she says. "You wouldn't understand the answers I'd have to give you. We'll sell the drugstore. The proceeds will pay for your education, and it'll be a good education. Because that's what you need, and it may not yet be too late. In any case you can count yourself lucky that things have turned out like this, because you'll now be living a normal healthy life for the first time. I'll see to that."

"Show me your hands," says Aunt Constance. And I show her my hands. She wants to see my teeth and my ears and my neck too. Every Saturday I have to have a bath. And my aunt stands there watching while I soap myself and rinse the soap off. "If your body's not clean," she says, "you can't have clean thoughts either."

Her name is Erna. She lies on the sofa next to my chair. I watch her hand slip from my knee and reach up to the light switch, and although it's dark I see her lying quite clearly before me. I see her brown face, consisting only of a mouth and eyes, of huge, dark, rather slanting eyes that are always moist, of a mouth which I now feel on mine, a warm, wet, sucking mouth exploring mine. And her hands are everywhere, stroking me, tearing at me, clawing into me. I shut my eyes and let myself fall, and I fall into an endless abyss, only to be pulled up abruptly and violently; a harsh light is shining down on me. And I see her hand on the light switch, see her beneath me, look into those huge, wide staring eyes that are now like a wild animal's, out for blood. And I'm seized with shame and fear and misery and wrench myself free. I plunge out into the night with her laughter ringing in my ears.

"All women are tarts," says my uncle, the sea captain, who pays us a visit during one of his shore leaves. "Never forget that and you'll go far, or at least further than most of the others. Because in the true heart of life, my boy, there's no place for women, they just stand around smelling bad. Believe me, they're useless for the really important things in life. They can't rule a country, steer a ship, or above all wage a war. Only in bed do they sometimes have their point. Which reminds me there's something I want to discuss with the maid. Send her up to me, will you?"

After graduating in 1933, I thought at first of falling in with my aunt's wish and taking up medicine. But eventually it is my own wish to become an officer that prevails. In 1934 I volunteered for the army. In 1938 I had the honor of being promoted lieutenant.

In the old days and in the Middle Ages, experiments could be carried out only on animals—mainly dogs and monkeys. This was due to the reactionary attitude of the Church authorities. But today we dissect human corpses, because anatomy is the science of the structure of the living body and its components. There is what is called general anatomy and so-called topographical anatomy, and this last leads on to applied anatomy. All this is very complicated, very difficult, and very laborious, apart from which there's usually a terrible stink all the time as well. I am all for cleanliness, for life itself, for beauty, for everything that's elevating. But I find none of this in anatomy.

"The living body," Simone tells me, "is much more interesting and instructive than any dead one, don't you think?" I agree. Simone, like me, is doing her first term of medicine, and her father is a famous surgeon in Paris. "Would you take to pursue your studies on the living body?" she asks. "Yes," I say, "that would be very interesting." "Then let's undress," says Simone. And we do so. After a time Simone says, "But what are you doing? Are you a man —or what?" So I start behaving like a proper medical man. After all, that's what she suggested. But suddenly she doesn't seem to like it. Which just goes to show how inconsistent and unpredictable women are—French women in particular.

For the first time I no longer live alone in a room—seven

other men share my life with me. We get up at the same time, wash together, run down the corridors together and across the barrack square and over the countryside. We wait and march, freeze and sweat, shoulder to shoulder, thigh to thigh. We curse, sing, laugh, and talk—eight bodies reacting as one from the moment of waking to the moment of sleeping. It's splendid how well we understand each other, how well we work together, how closely we belong to each other. Even if everyone doesn't realize this, even if it isn't always absolutely clear, nevertheless it's the truth. An experience of something one can call only community of spirit.

Lieutenant Waldersee is my great hero. A man like a tall fir tree, slim and slender and evergreen in outlook, full of warmth and friendship, a true comrade-in-arms who nevertheless always commands respect as an officer. He can perform a circle on the high bar in full uniform and make a sixteen-foot long jump in his boots. His hobby is racing cars, and he knows almost all the military regulations by heart. One couldn't think of a better friend.

Her name is Erica, and she is charming and good and beautiful. Besides, she's of good family—her father's a major, though on the retired list. He has an automobile agency, but a first-class one, Mercedes in fact, with a large number of army contracts, and our Führer himself likes to travel in this type of car. This is a great honor. "Erica," I say, "the most beautiful thing in the world is a home, a wife, and a splendid number of children. An exemplary family life, you know—strict, decent upbringing and a permanent atmosphere of trust and harmony. A truly "German" atmosphere in fact, in the best and fullest sense of the word. What do you say to it?" "When?" asks Erica. "As soon as I get my commission!" I say.

Then I'm a second lieutenant. And I rush to Erica and say, "I've got my commission now!" Erica says, "That's fine. You've got your commission and I'm pregnant." "But that can't be so," I say. "Why can't it?" asks Erica. "I'm not pregnant by you of course. There are others, and they don't wait until they get their commissions."

In 1939 we were forced into war. I was immediately given an infantry company, though I didn't have the luck to contact the enemy at first either in Poland or France. In 1940 I was promoted first lieutenant and in 1941 I was made Regimental ADC. During the advance into Russia I was

*temporarily given command of an infantry battalion, and
with this in December 1941 I frustrated enemy attempts to
break through south of Tula. For this I was honored with
the German Cross in gold. Shortly afterward I was promoted
captain and posted to No. 5 Officers' Training School.*

And there they sit, the prisoners of war—thousands of
them, broken and disheveled, guarded by me and my men—
quaking symbols of defeat, the end of a senseless, criminal
piece of provocation, the refuse of fallen pride. They are no
longer soldiers, just miserable wretches. Can they ever have
been soldiers, though? No! No soldier could sink as low as
this. Their eyes shift greedily, their hands grasp trembling at
food and cigarettes, and they stink to high heaven in their
rags. What an astonishing contrast with my own men, who
guard them—clean, high-spirited, clothed in decent uniforms.
Correct in their behavior too. None of the prisoners are
maltreated—and if they are, then it is no more than a spontaneous reaction to animal provocation. "Men," I say whenever an incident occurs, "don't let these scum provoke you.
Never forget that you're Germans and that this implies certain
obligations. So don't shoot the first time, men, or give them
the bayonet. A blow with a rifle butt sometimes works
wonders. Be humane, even though many of them don't de-
serve it."

My regimental commander, Colonel Pfotenhammer, is a
hell of a fellow. Tremendous sense of humor wherever he
is. Never happier than when in the front line. "B-r-r-rm!" he
says, whenever a shell bursts. Sometimes he complements
this word with a brief sound of another sort which always
gives rise to a great deal of merriment. He should have had
the Knight's Cross long before—the divisional commander
got his during the campaign in France. But even over such
a thing as this, Colonel Pfotenhammer retains his wonderful
sense of humor. He's the born front-line soldier, to be
found wherever the fighting is thickest. He makes tremendous
demands of all his officers, noncommissioned officers, and
men, and can't stand the sight of lowly servants. An unforgettable New Year's Eve in 1914, a huge fireworks
display put on by Colonel Pfotenhammer; mortars first, followed by tracer from machine guns with flares over the lot.
But the enemy doesn't play the game—he shoots back with
multiple rocket guns. The colonel is right up in the front
line as always and has a magnum of champagne with him,

plus real champagne glasses. *"Prosit,* comrades!" he cries to us. *"Prosit,* Colonel!" we chorus back, standing there like trees in the storm of steel. And Captain Kwadlitz, a fine fellow and a great joker, full of champagne and the spirit of New Year's Eve, jumps up out of a foxhole and lets down his trousers. "A New Year's greeting for you over there!" he cries. Well—a bit vulgar perhaps, but a wonderful gesture of contempt. Good God, what fellows we were!

"We've got our backs to the wall now!" says Colonel Pfotenhammer. "Now, my dear Ratshelm, show the sort of stuff you're made of." The colonel finds Major Wagner at the Pelikowka crossroads. "Coward!" he yells at him. "I'll have you court-martialed, Wagner!" The major wants to take his battalion back, to retreat in fact. "You take this lot over!" the colonel says to me. So I take command of the battalion and barricade the crossroads. Not another bastard *can* come through! So they have to fight—under my command. And I'm right up in front with my men all the time— hand grenades in my belt, automatic pistol slung around my chest. In the end the men fight like lions. The casualties are terrific—on both sides, of course. But the crossing is held all night. Then the tremendous pride when the colonel gets the Knight's Cross. "I've largely you to thank for this, my dear Ratshelm," says the colonel with true chivalry. "And when the time comes I won't forget it." He was a man of his word. Because later I get the German Cross in gold pinned to my breast for the incident.

Victory celebrations at regimental staff HQ, behind the lines, some days later. Crates of bottles. Stirring words. The spirit of comradeship flourishes. In the early hours of the morning Colonel Pfotenhammer, my beloved CO, embraces me and kisses me calmly on both cheeks. His speech is thick. "You're destined for great things, Ratshelm, my fine fellow. You will be sending us out officers we can rely on. I know of no one better than yourself for the job, Captain Ratshelm. In the fight for decency, honor and discipline, then, the training school calls!"

10 *UNORTHODOX METHODS*

THE TIMETABLE laid down two hours of drill. The three sections of Number 6 Company—G, H, and I—stood on the barrack square while Captain Ratshelm, the commanding officer, circled around them like an efficient sheepdog.

Lieutenant Krafft's section senior reported in the regulation manner. As Krafft had anticipated, Cadet Kramer proved to have plenty of authority. His voice easily filled the barrack square and echoed back from the walls of the various buildings. He wasn't, of course, the only one with this degree of volume at his command. The entire barrack square now rang with noise.

Krafft took inspiration from the din which now came at him from all sides to pose a fundamental question. "How essential is it to have a clear, carrying word of command?" he asked.

"Very essential, Lieutenant," cried the cadets, after overcoming their initial surprise. The question seemed to them not only superfluous but downright idiotic, though of course they kept their opinion to themselves. However, there was a certain degree of levity discernible in their reply.

"Why?" asked Krafft.

They were stumped by this. Well, why indeed was a clear, carrying word of command essential? Ridiculous question! This was something that was just self-evident and required no further explanation. The man wanted an explanation, though. All right, then he should have one—but what?

They racked their brains for a while, thrashing out the matter, and finally coming to the conclusion that it was just customary practice. The majority seemed inclined to accept this rather vague formula. A considerable discussion was soon in progress, threatening to develop into a full-blown argument. The section senior, Kramer, felt indignant. Even Captain Ratshelm, at the other end of the barrack square, noticed the hullabaloo going on in H Section and rather uneasily stalked closer.

"Gentlemen, please!" called out Lieutenant Krafft, realizing that he'd have to put a stop to this. He saw that if this section of his was not to get the better of him from the

144

word go, he would have to insist on discipline. "We will agree on the following method. I ask a question, you answer it. But you only answer when you're asked a question direct. Is that understood?"

"Yes, Lieutenant," muttered the cadets, docilely enough, though they were in fact delighted. Their section officer seemed to be turning out to be none too bright.

The cadets had never known such an innocuous drill period before. Not even under Captain Ratshelm, who had his human side after all, and certainly not under Lieutenant Barkow, who had been very strict with them. This Lieutenant Krafft, however, seemed more interested in theory, and a little discussion group. Well, this suited them all right.

"Cadet Hochbauer," said Krafft. For he noticed that this Hochbauer was the only one who had not so far taken any part in the general discussion.

"Yes, sir?" Hochbauer looked at Krafft inquiringly, pretending he didn't know what his section officer wanted of him, and affecting equal politeness and curiosity. He despised the lieutenant, and not simply because he himself was rather taller than Krafft. Yet he did so only with a certain circumspection, for carelessness was not one of Hochbauer's faults.

"I'd like you to answer my question, Hochbauer."

"Well," said the cadet, with a condescending air, "an officer must be able to give orders which are clear, brief, and to the point. Some of these orders are given in the form of a word of command, and not only on the barracks square and in open country but in confined spaces as well. These commands must be able to make themselves heard above other commands being given in the vicinity, above other sounds such as that of motor engines, and of course also above all the inevitable sounds of the battlefield. For this reason it goes without saying that an officer needs to have a clear, far-reaching word of command."

"Very good Hochbauer!" cried Captain Ratshelm, who had come up in the meantime. And the company commander immediately turned to Lieutenant Krafft and said, though somewhat discreetly, "Please, my dear fellow, do get on with the practical work. The other sections have already been at it for some time, and we haven't got all day, you know."

"Very good, sir," said Lieutenant Krafft rather sloppily.

"I don't want to interfere with you in any way, Krafft; I shall be off at once. You must feel yourself completely free. Please don't regard my suggestion as a rebuke—rather just as the advice of an old hand."

"Yes, sir," said Krafft, making no attempt to conceal his astonishment when Ratshelm, who said that he didn't want to interfere, nevertheless continued to stand there.

"You should play yourself in gently here, Krafft. Don't try and overdo things, nothing flamboyant—just the good old orthodox methods."

"The good old orthodox methods—right, sir."

"But you seem to have made a good start, apart from all this chatter. You've obviously summed things up here pretty well, by getting on with the excellent Hochbauer so quickly."

After this broad hint Ratshelm did in fact take himself off. Meanwhile Lieutenant Krafft had finally grasped the real nature of his job here, which was simply to act as supervisor. He had no need to give any orders himself, simply to superintend the orders given by his cadets. His job was to let others do the work. The first thing, then, was to nominate a cadet to take over the section, and his choice fell upon Weber, Egon, a man who could undoubtedly be trusted to deal with the primitive business of drill in a relatively uncomplicated fashion.

Weber, Egon, had the elementary corporal's technique at his finger tips. He planted himself in front of the cadets and shouted, "Section H for Heinrich will take its word of command from me."

Weber then split the section into four squads and nominated four squad leaders. These in turn nominated four deputy squad leaders. Weber shouted, "Drill by individual squads! Basic movements and wheeling! March off! Drilling commence!"

And a fairly tolerable sort of barrack-square routine was immediately set in motion.

Krafft looked across the bare, bleak parade ground to the barrack buildings. With their rows of narrow, lusterless windows they seemed to be staring with tired resignation into space. It was a clear, frosty February day though the sky was overcast. Only on untrodden patches of grass was there still a little dirty snow.

Lieutenant Krafft looked across to the two other sections, trying to see what method their officers were using. And he was astonished at what he saw.

Lieutenant Webermann, a small, wiry officer with the

husky but penetrating bark of a terrier, kept his own G Section permanently on the move. They were at the double more often than not, and only very rarely came to a halt.

Lieutenant Dietrich, on the other hand, a large, broad-shouldered man who moved slowly, kept his section—I Section—quite simply at a standstill. They just stood there, properly dressed and with the correct number of paces between ranks, writing in their notebooks.

But what on earth has that lot got to write about, Krafft asked himself. And why are the others running around like a pack of hounds? And an uncomfortable feeling began to steal over him that here indeed he was no more than a beginner.

Captain Ratshelm had disappeared from view. He was standing in the latrine which served the parade ground, though even this did not prevent him from keeping an eye on his flock, for there was a slit at eye level through which he was able to squint out into the open.

Meanwhile Lieutenant Krafft's section had begun to practice saluting. In his capacity as section leader, Egon Weber wandered proudly around from squad to squad without ever actually intervening. The feeling that he could intervene if he wanted to was quite sufficient for him.

The cadets themselves got on with their work in peace without overexerting themselves. The individual squad leaders gave commands and shouted continual reprimands at the tops of their voices, as had been the custom from time immemorial, but hardly anyone paid any attention to them. The cadets were taking things easy. Besides, they were subject to a certain amount of distracton, as Krafft quickly recognized.

This distraction was understandable enough, for a horde of females were disporting themselves on the field beside the parade ground. These were the women and girl civilian employees housed in barracks who were being organized by an experienced member of the German Girls' League, employed at the training school as assistant to the medical officer. There, then, was all this womanhood hopping and dancing and leaping about, with breasts bobbing all over the place, and the cadets found it difficult to ignore the fact.

"This view interferes with my marching," said Cadet Mösler. "How can one possibly drill properly in a situation like this?"

"Control yourself," said Cadet Egon Weber. "I'm in command of this section. You can't just boycott me and stare across at the women all the time."

"Come on now," said Mösler. "See if you can't get us close in there. Let's try and exchange a few telephone numbers."

"Mösler," said Weber, very much in his capacity as section leader, "I see that you urgently need to be excused. All right, off you go—but don't stay longer than five minutes."

Mösler made off without first reporting to his section officer, who had his hands full anyway, trying to decide how best to get the work to proceed.

Webermann and Dietrich, the two other section officers, had also noted the danger. Which meant that they had promptly dealt with it. About turn—it was as simple as that. Their cadets now stood with their backs to all this female distraction.

Krafft reacted in a similar manner. He summoned the scattered reconnaissance groups back with a blast on his whistle, and the cadets gathered about him.

Behind them—and thus directly in Krafft's own line of vision—the women continued to leap about the field. They were playing handball now, and among the players Krafft recognized Elfrida Rademacher, who was easy enough to distinguish from the rest and seemed well aware of the fact. Even from a distance she struck one as being uncommonly well proportioned.

Krafft found it difficult to prevent his own attention from being distracted. He tried to concentrate on his cadets.

"Any questions about saluting?"

They looked at their lieutenant with misgiving. They weren't used to asking questions themselves; especially not on the parade ground. They were used to being asked questions, or given orders, or sworn at, or occasionally even being praised—but in the asking of questions they had had no practice at all. They looked around to see if there might not be at least someone among them who was keen to respond. Krafft waited patiently.

Cadet Rednitz raised a hand. As always, he was in the rear rank. "Is the word salute to be understood in the sense of a salutation, Lieutenant?" he inquired.

"The sense in which it is to be understood is laid down in regulations, Rednitz," declared Krafft, trying to look as unconcerned as possible. "Next question, please." Now it was Cadet Mösler's turn. The slightly odd answer given by the section officer had made him curious, and he wanted to find out if this were just a shot in the dark or whether there was some method in his madness.

"Lieutenant—what about the following case; as a cadet, I'm going along the street when I meet a ranker in the company of a woman married to a major. Should I salute first—salute the major's wife that is—or should I wait until the ranker salutes me?"

"That depends," declared the lieutenant agreeable. "If she is a major in her own right, then of course you salute first—since you find yourself confronted by a superior officer. If, however, she is merely married to a major, then you have no obligation to salute her, unless of course you happen to know the major's wife personally. In which case politeness bids you salute her. And just one other thing, Mösler; to an officer—and you will be an officer one day—a major's wife is not a woman but a lady."

The section grinned broadly, and this grin covered a certain amount of genuine astonishment. It was the first time they had ever heard words used quite like this, at the training school at least. When Captain Ratshelm laid down the law it was simply a parade of military virtues. Lieutenant Barkow used merely to quote regulations, all of which he knew by heart. Captain Feders, on the other hand, their tactics instructor, used words like a sledge hammer. But this fellow Lieutenant Krafft didn't seem to fit into any of the familiar patterns. The man even turned out to be quite witty, though he certainly didn't look as if he was. But this of course could mean complications.

Krafft glanced hurriedly over the heads of the cadets to where the women were still disporting themselves. His eyes were searching for Elfrida and eventually found her on the edge of the sports field with a medicine ball under her left arm. She too seemed to have been on the lookout for him. She raised her right hand and waved. This was a touching display of intimacy and affection, but hardly the thing for a parade ground.

Nevertheless the sight gave the lieutenant pleasure. "We'll have a short break now," he said.

The cadets looked at him in bewilderment. Their section officer's moves seemed so unpredictable that it was damned difficult to tell what he was up to. Kramer, the section senior, made his way forward anxiously to where Krafft was standing, and said respectfully, "I beg your pardon, sir, but it's for the company commander to decide on breaks during drill."

"Right, then," said Krafft. "We'll practice deep breathing. Carry on, please!"

"Come, come," said Elfrida Rademacher to the little girl called Irene Jablonski. "Don't let your eyes pop out of your head. You're much too small for that."

"My brothers are all soldiers," said Irene dreamily.

"Of course it's very nice that you should love your brothers," said Elfrida. "But that doesn't mean that you have to fall in love at once with everyone else who wears the same uniform."

"You're quite right," said Irene.

There was something deeply sad about the way she said this.

"It's not all as simple as you think," said Elfrida, looking across to the parade ground and trying to identify Karl Krafft. She hadn't spoken to him since he had been made section officer, three days before. For not only had his spare time been considerably reduced, but what was worse, his quarters were no longer in the headquarters building. His new room was in the barrack block with his cadets, because a section officer, being part of his section, had to be in a position to supervise them day and night.

"I do envy you," said Irene Jablonski. "You've really got everything I wish for. But I don't begrudge it you."

Elfrida Rademacher swung her medicine ball gently to and fro, smiling as she did so, for her eyes were following Lieutenant Krafft as he walked up and down in the distance, smoking a cigarette. It seemed as if he, too, was looking across, but it was difficult to tell from his face under the brim of his cap.

Their relationship like everything else here was now subject to barracks regulations. He couldn't go to her room— there were five other girls who slept there, among them the romantic little Irene Jablonski. And she couldn't go to his room, where forty cadets could hear them. They thus seemed condemned to park benches, large trees, doorways, or the back of the war memorial. But perhaps they might also succeed in finding some shed or empty classroom or even a hotel room. After all, it was the beginning of February, and the cold was a poor match-maker.

"Keep lively, girls, keep lively!" cried the instructor. But hardly a girl listened to her.

"Elfrida," said Irene confidentially, "I'd love to be like you one day."

"You certainly look stupid enough to be," said Elfrida.

"You know," said Irene, "officers are so different."

"You're quite right," said Elfrida. "Their uniforms and their boots are made of better quality than those of the NCOs and men."

"And a man like Captain Kater, for instance," went on Irene. "You could really trust someone like him, couldn't you?"

"What makes you think that?" asked Elfrida very suspiciously.

"He had a conversation with me recently in the kitchen when he was carrying out an inspection there. He asked if I could type. And I told him I could easily learn to. I learn terribly easily, I told him."

"So it seems," said Elfrida dryly.

"Right, gentlemen," said Lieutenant Krafft when the break was over. "Let's get on with it. Our subject is still saluting."

"Excuse me, sir," one of the cadets standing beside Hochbauer asked immediately. "Why is it that in the Wehrmacht we salute by raising the hand to the cap?"

"Well, because it's the usual practice," said Krafft, on the alert at once. The question gave him evident satisfaction. The break had paid off. The conversation that had been taking place in the meantime had put the cadets just where he wanted them—right into his lap.

All unwittingly the section had once again started up its idle chatter. Like a lot of washerwomen, thought Kramer. This fellow Krafft had hardly been in office forty-eight hours and the section had turned into a rabble. In two days, discipline had gone to hell, and it would need more than a few witty remarks to put it right. To make matters worse, the clique around Hochbauer was now busy undermining the last vestiges of the lieutenant's authority.

"Excuse me, sir," asked another cadet, from roughly the same quarter, "wouldn't it really be more sensible if the same type of salute were valid for the whole of Germany?"

"Certainly," the lieutenant agreed at once. "The various Party organizations have but to adopt our style of salute."

Hochbauer himself now intervened in this game of question and answer, asking cunningly, "Doesn't the lieutenant think the style of salute used by our Führer should be compulsory for all Germans?"

"But my dear Hochbauer," said Lieutenant Krafft, still amiably enough, though in a tone of gentle rebuke, "surely you don't want to cast doubts on the greatness of our beloved Führer?"

Cadet Hochbauer was taken aback. He had the painful sensation of having had the wind knocked out of him—all in good fun, of course, but with deadly accuracy. That this should happen to him of all people, who glowed with veneration and admiration for the Führer, was quite unbelievable! Or had he misheard? Had his words been misunderstood? Or had he perhaps not expressed himself clearly? Hochbauer simply didn't know what to make of it and looked about him in utter amazement. Then he croaked, "How do you mean, exactly, sir?"

Krafft gave his cadets plenty of time to enjoy the situation, in so far, that is, as they were able to. For not everyone appreciated the cut and thrust involved. Krafft had been provoked and had sprung to arms after his own fashion. He had even wished to be provoked. What he hadn't quite expected was that it would be done in quite such a clumsy way.

This fellow Hochbauer and his friends were still children, really, with all the stupid courage and idiotic arguments of blind adherents to a cause. They needed gradually to be made to understand that it was a mistake to try and take advantage of such an old hand as himself.

So, like some indulgent schoolmaster, Krafft said, "Well, Hochbauer, you know of course that our beloved Führer is not only the leader of the Party and all its various organizations, but also Reich Chancellor and commander-in-chief of the Wehrmacht as well. You know that, don't you, Hochbauer?"

"Yes, sir," gulped Hochbauer. He still couldn't quite understand what was going on here, though one thing was certain— he had been humiliated—he, the cadet who had hitherto been acknowledged as the man who best understood and most admired his Führer in the whole section. It was exactly as if a boy in the sixth grade had been asked whether one and one make two and which letter of the alphabet followed it.

"Well, now," said Krafft, "if you know that, my dear Hochbauer, then it'll occur to you that our Führer could, if he wanted, without further ado, order his own type of salute to be introduced into the Wehrmacht. If, however, he has not done that, then it's presumably because he doesn't want to. Or do you think, Hochbauer, that the Führer might not be in a position to give such an order? Do you think perhaps, that he might meet with resistance in the Wehrmacht and find soldiers who might refuse further allegiance to him? Do you really think that? Are you trying to tell me that the Führer has enemies in his own ranks, against whom he needs to be on his guard—whom he even fears? Is that what you're trying to tell us?"

"No, sir!"

"Well, there you are, Hochbauer! All is clear, then. A little more confidence in our Führer would do you no harm."

And with that the lieutenant handed the section over to the cadet whom he had designated as leader. All he did was to order them now to practice rifle drill in close order. Facing the last of the classroom blocks, what's more, which meant with their backs to the sports field.

Weber bellowed out his orders at the top of his voice, thus industriously collecting good marks for his final rating. Hochbauer now treated his rifle to a series of resounding slaps. Mösler and Rednitz grinned thoughtfully to themselves. As far as the drill itself was concerned nothing went right, and Kramer, the section senior, was in despair again.

"This fellow Lieutenant Krafft seems something of a wag," said Mösler, grinning happily. "I think we may be going to have quite a bit of fun with him."

"Who knows," said Rednitz thoughtfully. "I've got the feeling we may be going to catch it from him." They allowed themselves a short break and listened to Egon Weber's orders without responding to them.

"It's great that he should have picked on Hochbauer like that! Side-splitting, eh, Rednitz?"

"Not at all," said Rednitz looking very thoughtful. "I've been making a careful study of this Lieutenant Krafft. He's not at all what he makes himself out to be."

Lieutenant Krafft stood slightly to one side, having pulled out his notebook and started writing in it, all of which looked very impressive from a distance. But Krafft's mind wasn't on his notebook at all. He was well able to rely on his memory, and his notes were merely an excuse. He was in fact glancing over them in the direction of the sports field toward the girls.

"Not a very pleasant sight," said Captain Ratshelm, who had stalked up close behind Krafft to keep an eye on him. "No grace, no spring—the flesh all fat and flabby. Don't you agree? And what's more, distracting us from our drill. While we're on the subject, by the way—the subject of drill I mean—how are you getting on with your section? Broken the ice with them yet? Beginning to get the hang of them?"

"I really feel I'm little more than an observer at the moment, sir."

"You must enter into the spirit of things with them, my dear fellow. I'm talking to you as someone with experience of training cadets. You must set an example to the men, one they'll feel inspired to follow. A shining example—it's the most important factor in the formation of a soldier's personality. The lads must feel that they want to become a Blücher or a Clausewitz, whichever suits their disposition— or even a Krafft or a Ratshelm, for that matter. So shine away, my dear fellow! And don't bother yourself with discussion and theory; wars aren't waged by philosophers, you know, but by men of action. Get me, Krafft?"

"Completely, sir."

Captain Ratshelm nodded, convinced that he had expressed himself very effectively. Yet something was still wrong. His face wore an anxious expression, for he failed to detect in Krafft the grateful and spontaneous response he would have liked. And Ratshelm let his glance wander over toward H Section, over all that splendid manly material. A glint came into his eye as it rested on Hochbauer. His sense of duty, however, forced him to extend his inspection to the rear rank as well. And what he saw there upset him considerably. The cadets were drilling without any punch, without zest, without interest, even. Where was the wonderful fire which he himself had lit in them? Some of them were even openly conversing together.

"Some of your men," said Ratshelm, reproachfully, "seem to choose to mistake drill for an opportunity for a cozy chat. Don't you notice that?"

"Yes," said Krafft pleasantly. "So I see."

"And aren't you going to do anything about it?"

"But why should I?" asked Krafft, almost flippantly.

Captain Ratshelm frowned. His voice sounded incredulous. "What did you say?"

"I said why should I interfere? I merely note the fact."

"And what about discipline, Lieutenant Krafft?"

"Discipline can hardly be part of the curriculum in an officers' training school. I mean it isn't something you can teach."

"But it's something you can insist on!"

"When necessary, yes—but hardly permanently. The soldier too often finds himself unobserved for that to be possible, and then he'll always do what he wants to, what he feels like doing, what he can get away with. And I like to watch him doing this as much as I can. Don't you find one can deduce a great deal from such observations?"

"I find your views very peculiar," said Ratshelm stiffly. "Very peculiar indeed."

Captain Ratshelm drew himself up and looked significantly into the distance. A difficult resolution was forming in his mind. There seemed nothing for it but to burden his course commander, Major Frey, with his doubts. His sense of duty demanded it.

In short, this Lieutenant Krafft didn't seem to him to be the right sort of person to turn men into officers.

11 AN UNHAPPY MAN

CAPTAIN FEDERS looked at Lieutenant Krafft with some misgiving.

"You claim to be a man of sensibility, I believe. All right, you suggest a game of chess, but why? Do you want to avoid my eye?"

"I want a game of chess with you, Captain, if you feel like one."

"And what else? No ulterior motives? Not just being inquisitive? Has someone put you up to something? And if so, who?"

"Really, Captain," explained Krafft calmly, "I don't know what you're getting at. I come here into the reading room quite by chance, see you sitting in front of a chessboard, and wonder if you'd like a game. But I don't want to force myself on you."

"Sit down," said Captain Feders. "Let me take a good look at you. Who knows how much longer I may have the chance of admiring the heroic soul beneath your cowlike countenance! If you carry on like this you'll be out of here on your ear within the week. There are some people who are already preparing your departure for you, you know."

Lieutenant Krafft sat down without further ado. He enjoyed talking to Captain Feders, whatever the circumstances. After all, the two of them were working together in the same section, and were thus paired off, so to speak.

"I'm only an average player," declared Krafft. "You'll have to make allowances for me."

"I'll do nothing of the sort," said Feders. "You suggested the game, and we'll get on with it without any quarter asked or given."

They were sitting in a corner of the so-called reading room in the mess, in the light of a standard lamp with a faded salmon-pink silk shade. A crude set of chessmen stood arrayed on the wide expanse of board.

They were not alone in the large, long room, which was rather like a veranda in a country hotel, with the tables arranged one after another along the window. Two of the other tables were occupied. At one of these a group of young section officers were playing a card game. At another, Captain Ratshelm sat with two brother officers of equal rank to whom he was holding forth in a manner which appeared to give them food for thought.

"Do you see those fellows over there?" Feders inquired.

"Who do you mean?"

"The gentlemen at the corner table on the left apparently engaged in conversation."

"Yes, I think so. Captain Ratshelm keeps looking this way."

"Of course," said Feders. "What else do you expect him to do!"

"I suppose," said Lieutenant Krafft, calmly arranging his men on the board, "that Captain Ratshelm thinks he ought to keep an eye on me for purely service reasons. He doesn't seem too satisfied with my work as section officer."

"You really are a supreme ass, my dear Krafft," declared Feders, opening the game. "You're going around everywhere with your head in the clouds whether it's in the mess, on the barrack square, or in the classrooms. What do you think you're doing?"

"It's quite simple," said Krafft patiently. "I'm looking after these officer cadets in my own way."

"My dear Krafft," said Feders, clearly irritated by what seemed to him to be mere clumsy ignorance. "Where on earth have you been these last few years while the war's been on? You seem to have been somewhere on the other side of the moon. Or have you been able to fight the war your own way too? Have you been able to have your own way about anything these last few years? Of course not!"

Lieutenant Krafft looked carefully across at the other tables, but for the moment no one seemed to be listening. Presumably everyone had heard this sort of monologue from

Feders before, or they simply ignored it. In cases like this, decent officers behaved exactly like society ladies when a risqué joke is being told; they acted as if they simply hadn't heard, and in this way saved themselves the need to feel indignant.

"Your way of doing things, Krafft," said Feders, "is by no means the training school's way. Here you've got to adjust yourself to the fact that others call the tune—your company commander, your course commander, the commander of the training school itself, the inspector of training schools, the commander-in-chief of the army, the supreme commander-in-chief of the Wehrmacht—all composers of some authority, I would point out. Believe in the Reich, the German people, and the Führer; be ready to starve for them, to take upon yourself every hardship, and to die. Those are the only words to the tune, and the only instrument that's really required is a drum."

Captain Kater appeared, wearing his broad, expansive officers'-mess grin. Anyone who had no business to be in the mess at that hour of the day was now at his mercy, though he was always prepared to show mercy provided one showed him due respect in return.

Kater made for the table where Ratshelm and his companions were sitting. He had a sure eye for the senior officer in his mess at any given time. But he stopped short when he saw Captain Feders and Lieutenant Krafft together.

Kater took up his stance in front of them and said, "Well now!"

"Kindly spare us your intellectual observations," said Feders, making a bold move with one of his chessmen.

"You in the mess, Captain Feders, at this time of day. When you have a home and family, as it were."

"Clear off," said Feders roughly, "you're bothering us."

But Kater thought he had reason to feel on top just then. The gentlemen at the other tables were following his performance with some interest and the proper amount of respect. Kater positively basked in limelight such as this.

"Ah yes," he went on, "I'd quite forgotten. Today's Friday."

Captain Feders withdrew the hand he had stretched out toward one of his men, and Krafft saw that it was very slightly trembling. The muscles stood out on Feders' jaw, showing that his teeth were clenched.

Krafft simply didn't understand any of this. Why was Feders getting so excited? Why had he been so very nervous right from the start? What was wrong with what Kater had said?

"Kater," said Captain Feders with menacing softness, "if you don't clear off at once I'll tell a story about a certain officer who forcibly undressed one of his subordinates, a female subordinate, which of course makes the matter understandable but doesn't excuse it. You can be sent to the guardhouse for that, you know. Which is where I'll have you sent to allow me to get on with my game of chess, if you don't look out."

Captain Kater cleared off at top speed, muttering a few words which nobody caught but which sounded like some sort of attempt to save his face.

"What did you say he'd done?" asked Krafft in alarm.

"I don't know!" said Feders, carefully advancing his knight and thus endangering Krafft's queen.

"But you accused him of something quite categorically."

"Probably quite accurately too," said Feders calmly. "But what do I care? He annoyed me and I wanted him out of the way. So I thought up something or other, and since one can be sure that Kater has anything but a clear conscience, almost any accusation strikes home—that's what you call tactics, my dear fellow. But watch your game. You'll be mate in three moves if you don't look out."

Krafft tried to concentrate on the game of chess, but without success. Then Feders went into action again.

"Orderly!" he shouted across the mess. "Bring me a bottle of brandy and put it down to Captain Kater."

Krafft again succeeded in saving his queen, though Feders was after it with his bishop at once. Then he grabbed the bottle of brandy and half filled two tumblers. Krafft hurriedly withdrew his queen to the back of the board.

"All the same," said the lieutenant cautiously, resuming their former conversation, "officers are after all human beings, too, individually with the most diverse points of view, talents, and characteristics."

"And how!" cried Feders. "You could say the same of dustmen and road sweepers, for that matter. You'll find them all there as well—drunks, god-fearing bullies, well-meaning friends of humanity, faithful Nazis, followers of the Kaiser, socialists—some of them even all these things at once. They put the emphasis wherever it suits them at the time."

Krafft grinned. "You'd put an officer on a par with a road sweeper, Captain?"

"Well, yes, though I may be doing the road sweepers an

injustice. But they have their orders too. Sweep the streets! Fortunately for them that's fairly simple. Officers' orders on the other hand are to wage war. And that's a little more complicated. You can't do that with a simple word of command; you need mountains of rules, regulations, and instructions, simply to make it all as foolproof as possible against personal feelings of any kind or second thoughts. The machine has to function smoothly, the conveyer belt has to be kept running. And where the factory regulations seem inadequate or beyond comprehension, the word of command is all-powerful—the word of command which must be obeyed without question."

At this point Captain Feders resolutely sacrificed a castle. He wanted to get up close to the opposing king. Regardless of losses he broke through Lieutenant Krafft's defense with complete success. But it didn't seem to give him much satisfaction. His nervousness, his almost frenzied tension showed no signs of abating. Over and over again he looked at his wrist watch, apparently reluctant to trust the sluggish movement of the hands.

He called one of the mess orderlies over again. "I want to know the exact time."

"It'll be seven o'clock in a few minutes, sir," said the soldier on duty there as a waiter.

"Listen man," said Feders angrily, "I didn't ask you for a prophecy, I wanted to know the exact time to the minute."

The orderly disappeared, and was back again almost immediately. Hurriedly he said, "Six fifty-six precisely, sir— I got it from the radio."

"Can one trust the radio?" asked Feders.

"The time signals at least, sir."

Feders laughed out loud. He liked the answer, the man might have been one of his own pupils. But instead he spent his time carrying bottles of schnapps and plates of food about the place. Well, perhaps that was better than bothering oneself with a lot of officers. Smarter, perhaps, too. Pleasanter at least.

"Don't, however, misunderstand me, my dear Krafft," said the captain significantly, draining his glass. "I am neither rebel nor reformer; I am merely trying to define the limits within which it's possible to operate. You've obviously got a lot of woolly ideas about how to train people, Krafft, and of course that's all nonsense. An officers' course of this sort lasts eleven weeks; the war allows us no more time. What do you hope to achieve in these wretched weeks, Krafft? Do you hope to change people, to mold individuals, build personalities? That's all a lot of crap! Even if at least eighty per cent of the cadets prove miserable failures, at least eighty per cent will become officers. The quota has to be met. Or do you imagine that we here at the training school would let ourselves be reprimanded for incompetence? Of course not! So we keep the conveyer belt running. And all we can do in the short time available is to stuff the cadets' heads with the simplest basic principles. And the most important thing is that we get into their heads for good and all the fact that orders are orders."

Feders looked at his watch again, and then bent almost hurriedly over the chessboard. He moved right into the cone of light cast by the lamp. It cast harsh shadows on his clever, puckered face, carving in it deep ravines, which made it almost grotesquely unrecognizable.

"Right," he said, "take that queen of yours out of the way. It's time we finished the game."

"You're thinking of something else," said the man, sitting up slightly.

"No, I'm not," said Marion Feders. "But I'm uncomfortable. Your arm's in my way."

"It's been behind your neck all the time," said the man, "but you've only just noticed it."

"I'm just beginning to wake up," said Marion Feders. "You know I'm always a bit on edge when I wake up."

They were lying in the little apartment in the guest house, which belonged to Captain Feders. Marion Feders stared at the ceiling. The man beside her stretched comfortably. His hair was still elegantly waved, but there was a dreamy look in his eye and his well-shaped lips were parted sensuously. His name was Seuter, a lieutenant and section officer in Number 1 Company, nicknamed the Minnesinger. His Christian name was Alfred. Women and his friends called him Freddie.

"Do you find me very disappointing, Alfred?" asked Marion Feders.

"No, of course not," he reassured her.

"I sometimes think I'm so appallingly ungrateful."

"Don't worry, my dear," he said lazily. He took this last remark of Marion's to apply to himself. "Don't worry, everyone has their off days."

He sat up a little further and began to look at her. She lay on her back blinking up at him. The shaded light from the bedside lamp gave her body a pinkish tinge.

"I know my hips aren't good," she said. "They're too fat."

He let his hand glide expertly over them. "I don't find that," he said. "They're feminine. A real man likes that."

"Please, you're hurting me."

"You're so tense sometimes. Sometimes I have the feeling that you're fighting against yourself."

"Please stop. Take your hand away."

"That's what I like," he whispered into her ear. "You always resist at first. But then you suddenly change and become wild and abandoned. That's what I like about you."

"No," she said, "please, it's too late already, Alfred. I'm sure it's too late. Look at the clock please."

"Afterward."

She sat up suddenly. For a second he took the movement for some sort of passionate gesture. Then she slipped to one side, grabbed the bedside lamp, and tore away the dark red cloth that hung over it, casting a harsh light onto herself and the clock on the table.

"It *is* too late!" she cried in agitation. "What did I tell you? It's already after seven."

"Oh hell," he said impatiently, trying to draw her toward him. "Five minutes one way or the other won't make any difference now!"

"Do you see what I mean now, Krafft?" asked Captain Feders.

He had won the game of chess without difficulty.

"Is it slowly beginning to dawn on you, Krafft, how idiotically you're behaving here? You converse freely with the cadets, address them intelligently, try to instill into them individual qualities, as if you were some sort of stock breeder —and what on earth's the point of it all? Stuff the oafs with rules and regulations until their eyes start out of their stupid heads. Get them so that they'll obey you automatically. That's the only way to get anywhere."

"Thanks for the tip, Captain," said Krafft. This Feders was the most headstrong officer he'd ever met, with the exception of Major-General Modersohn. "You've given me something to think about."

"My dear Krafft," said the captain, draining his glass with a self-deprecating gesture, "I won't say I have a soft spot for you, but I'm sorry for you. You're a man who still retains a certain amount of faith in himself. But you'll only be able to keep it, here, if you take care to hide it—otherwise it'll be knocked out of you right away. And that would rather spoil any fun we might have together."

"I certainly shouldn't like to miss that, Captain."

"Good. Let's hope we'll be having some. But it'll hardly have escaped your notice that you're not particularly popular either with Captain Ratshelm or with Major Frey. In itself that's a point in your favor. Practically speaking, though, it's proof that you're lacking in adaptability. And here that means a posting to the front at the very least. Besides, Krafft, I'm primarily concerned with the bunch of cadets whose section officer you are and whose tactics instructor I happen to be. I don't want to have to deal with a horde of pampered, enlightened youths. I want material I can work on. Anything else is a waste of time."

With this, Captain Feders got to his feet, put the cork on the bottle of brandy, which was still half full, and jammed it under his left arm. Krafft stood up too. "A stimulating evening," he said.

"We mustn't let it be over yet," said Feders after a short pause. "Come along with me, if you feel like it. I want to show you where and how I live, and I'd like to introduce you to my wife."

"Thanks very much," said Krafft, "but I won't disturb you."

Feders looked him straight in the eyes with a rather sad expression. "You don't want to—a pity. But I can understand it. And of course I don't want to force you."

"I'd love to come," said Krafft honestly. "You must believe me. But I have an appointment."

"A girl?"

"Yes," said Krafft.

"And you couldn't postpone this appointment? Just for an hour? I'd really be delighted if you'd come. What about it?"

"All right," said Krafft, "I'll come."

"You won't regret it," said Feders, who seemed very pleased. But quite suddenly he turned serious, and added gravely, "One way or another, you won't regret it."

The corridor of the so-called guest house was long and narrow, a dreary place with a brown runner of coconut matting on the floor and dull gray-green paint on the walls. There were doors at regular intervals. The whole atmosphere was like that of some provincial hotel thrown open for the season.

"I live right down at the end on the right," said Feders, pointing in that direction. The door he had pointed to opened.

An officer stepped out into the corridor and closed the door carefully behind him. Then he looked up and saw Feders and Krafft standing in the corridor, and started. He drew himself up to his full height, narrowed his eyes slightly, and started walking toward them.

Feders had turned pale. He took Krafft by the arm, but more as a gesture of friendliness than as if he wanted to stop. The captain needed only a short second in which to regain control of himself. And quite inconsequentially, but in an almost genial tone, he said, "There are actually some faces which the good God seems to have produced on the conveyer belt, at least I can't tell them apart. In point of fact I'm capable of distinguishing even one hedgehog from another—which the hare in the race in the fairy story couldn't do; but these standard uniformed faces have me floored."

In the meantime the officer had come nearer. It was, as Krafft recognized, Lieutenant Seuter of Number 1 Company, known as the Minnesinger. Krafft didn't find him particularly sympathetic, and Feders seemed not to want to take any notice of him at all.

The Minnesinger somewhat surprisingly brought his hand up correctly to the peak of his cap. Feders stared at the wall with apparent indifference. Krafft returned the salute rather absent-mindedly, but definitely enough.

After Seuter had walked stiffly away, Feders asked brusquely, "In the picture?"

"I don't know all the officers in the training school yet," said Krafft, hedging. "I've got my work cut out trying to get to know our cadets."

"Don't pretend you don't know what goes on, Krafft," said Feders tensely. "Everyone here in the training school knows about it, it's common knowledge. I can tell from the way my so-called brother officers look at me. I hear them sniggering behind my back. Even a sod like Kater has the nerve to make cracks about it, and sometimes I even have the feeling that the general himself regards me with pity."

"I don't know what you're talking about," said Krafft adding, "and I don't want to either."

Captain Feders thrust his chin forward as if scenting the air. His eyes had a cold, distrustful look. He stopped where he was, as if reluctant to enter his own home.

"All right," he said finally. "It may be that you really don't know what I'm talking about. But you'll find out sooner or later. You'll have every detail whispered to you, until you blush either with embarrassment or with malicious delight."

"I've got very bad hearing when it suits me," said Krafft. "And besides, I find it rather cold here in the corridor. So what shall we do? Go into your apartment or go back to the mess? After all, you've got to let me have my revenge for that game of chess I lost. Besides, the brandy bottle isn't empty yet. We could throw dice for the contents."

"Spare yourself these dodges, Krafft, and give me the chance at last to show you the skeleton in my cupboard. Much better that I should enlighten you than that others should."

"Captain," said Krafft, "I think it's easy to overestimate what others know or think they know about us. Apart from which, I do my best to respect other people's private lives, largely because I want them to do the same for me."

"I'm quite sure you do," said Feders with forced jocularity. "But what about your sense of duty as a soldier! And the interests of the greater German people! So in with you, then, brother officer and fellow German."

Feders flung open the door of his apartment. His wife appeared and started to run toward him, but stopped when she caught sight of a strange officer behind him. She stared at both of them, and as she did so pulled her dressing gown together across her bosom.

"Don't worry," shouted Feders, and pointing at Krafft he added, "these aren't reinforcements—just my latest subject for experiment—Lieutenant Krafft, about whom I've already given you such a bad report."

The slightly tense expression on Marion Feders' face relaxed and she tried to smile. She came up to Krafft and held out her hand. Her eyes scrutinized him closely. "I'm delighted to meet you at last," she said.

"Right, then!" cried Feders, pushing them both into the living room. "And Krafft will be delighted to have something to drink. All we need are glasses to begin with, because we've brought a bottle with us. There's a second bottle in the bathroom, in the medicine cupboard, if I'm not mistaken. Or have you in the meantime put it to better use?"

"I'll get it at once, and the glasses," said Marion obligingly, and hurried out. Feders watched her go.

"Well," asked the captain, watching him keenly, "do you like the look of my wife?"

"She's your wife," said Krafft cautiously. "What I think of her is quite irrelevant."

Feders laughed and uncorked the bottle. "You needn't be afraid, Krafft. But all right—we'll formulate this question slightly differently. What do you think of my wife?"

Krafft saw that he could no longer evade the question. Feders was determined to get an answer, so why shouldn't he give him one? "Well," said Krafft candidly, "your wife is what's called attractive. She seems very good-natured and at the same time rather unhappy. That's about all I can say at the moment."

"Right, then," said Feders grimly. "I'll fill in the picture for you slightly. My wife is very tough, because in spite of the cold she runs around without many clothes on. Besides, her watch seems wrong. Or else she hasn't had time to look at her watch!"

"I'm sorry," said Marion Feders from the door.

She was carrying a tray with two glasses and a bottle on it, and cast an imploring glance at her husband. Feders, however, avoided it. "I'm sorry," she repeated.

"There's nothing to be sorry for," said Feders fiercely. "Certainly don't feel sorry for me. Everything's quite in order—not the best order, perhaps, but in order nevertheless. I'm even deeply grateful for the existence of this bottle."

She didn't seem hurt. "You won't need me any more this evening, then," she said.

"No," said Feders. "You can go and get some rest." He added softly, "You must be in need of some."

"You're a born father-confessor, Krafft," said Captain Feders, draining his eighth glass. "You draw confessions out of people like a magnet. And one has the feeling one can trust you. Which should worry you."

"My skin is thicker than an elephant's," said Krafft. "And if I so wish, my memory can be as short as a fly's."

"That won't help you," said Feders. "Nothing will help you in the long run. For one day even you, Krafft, will recognize the senselessness of the life we lead, and then it'll drive you mad too. I'd very much like to witness this remarkable sight."

They were alone, after spending almost an hour talking together evasively. But there was already a strong bond of sympathy between them.

"We ought to talk more quietly," said Krafft. "We'll disturb your wife. She must be asleep in the next room by now."

"She's my wife. And so nothing disturbs her any more."

Feders let his shoulders droop, and stared absent-mindedly

at the light. His mouth hung open slightly and a little saliva trickled from the corners. His hands shook slightly, as he reached out for his newly filled glass. He poured the alcohol violently down his throat and choked. Brandy trickled over his chin onto his Knight's Cross.

"You should have seen me a year ago, Krafft—a picture of Mars himself! And I say that not to flatter myself, but in order to explain things to you. I knew I'd become a general or a corpse one day. I would have preferred the former, but the latter held no terrors for me. And in Marion I had found the perfect wife for such a career, not least because she could always make me intoxicatingly happy. And so, besotted with happiness, I plunged headlong into this career and felt I was doing triumphantly well. Then one day a shell splinter caught me in the groin and unmanned me altogether."

Krafft, who had been about to pick up his glass, froze with his hand halfway to it. He stared at Captain Feders in amazement, at the sweeping dome of his forehead, now glistening with sweat, behind which waited a calculating brain capable of reacting with the speed of lightning. A brain capable of deadly thoughts, capable of working everything out with infallible mathematical precision.

Feders always made a point of trying to see every possible consequence of a course of action. With him, nothing was ever unpremeditated, as Krafft now recognized with some sense of shock. Before him sat a man in danger of bleeding to death from wounds self-inflicted by the razor-sharp machinations of his own brain.

"Is this occasional, enchanted, messy quarter of an hour really so important?" asked Krafft eventually.

"It makes all the difference," said Feders. "A man can lose an arm or a leg, a lung, or even part of his brain in so far as he has one, but if he loses his sex, he ceases to be a man."

"Perhaps he only ceases to be a bull, a stallion, a cock, and is thus freed from a good deal of unpleasantness. His life becomes simpler, less complicated, calmer. Isn't nature said to provide its own compensations? If a man loses his sight, his hearing becomes sharper, his sense of taste develops, his imagination increases."

"All lies!" said Feders morosely. "All pious, impertinent, idiotic lies! Morphia for the soul, soothing massage for the mind! At the best, well-meaning words of comfort—and of course that's something—but mostly, in war at any rate, that sort of talk has another motive behind it. This is really just the age-old method by which cunning statesmen get things their own way. Filth and misery are pleasantly cloaked by decorative words like Fate, the Will of God, Honor, Providence, Sacrifice, etcetera. All these phrases are indispensable for those who lead a nation astray or wish to do so. Sacrifice! They talk of sacrifice all the time—for the Fatherland, for freedom, for peace, for whatever happens to suit their purpose. They peddle cheap sympathy and pay their bills with other people's honor. It's an expedient and highly successful method, tested and proved over thousands of years. I know that death and mutilation belong to war and soldiering, as a fish to water, and the man who puts on a uniform, though he can hope for a Knight's Cross, ought also to be prepared for a different sort of cross or even to have his testicles shot off. I was always quite clear about that, in theory. But just start lying there and staring at the ceiling, knowing that you are helpless, powerless, wholly unmanned, and things look very different."

Krafft didn't know what to say at first. Automatically he seized the brandy bottle, poured himself a full glass, and drank it to the dregs. The brandy tasted like water.

"Don't try and belittle sex, Krafft," said Feders. "Never belittle it. The urge is one of the principle factors in our existence, one of the really decisive elements—perhaps the final secret of creation."

"The thirsty man always dreams of water, the hungry man of food, the lonely man of a woman or a friend. What's missing always seems the thing that's most desirable. Yet anyone who thinks at all knows there's no such thing as complete fulfillment. The satisfaction of the senses can never be more than a brief moment of transition."

"Don't try and put that crap over on me, Krafft. You know quite well what it is that keeps us soldiers going. Among soldiers there's nothing that comes up more blatantly or persistently than sex. They're at the mercy of a compulsion. It's the only real topic of conversation, and they talk about it all the time because they're under pressure from death. The fear of death is one pole of their existence, sexual desire the other. *Love and War* was the name of the magazine that turned the troops of the First World War weak at the knees. The urge for recognition and the sexual urge, the ecstasy of power and the ecstasy of sex, death, and procreation—these are the forces that everyone carries within him, my dear Krafft." The expression in Captain Feders' eyes slowly turned into a glassy stare. He gazed ahead motionless for a few seconds. Then he drank another glass of brandy, rose heavily to his feet, and dragged himself off, swaying slightly, to the door that led into the bedroom.

Feders opened the door with a certain amount of caution, stopping in the doorway, leaning forward, and looking in silently for several seconds. Then, in an exhausted voice, tortured and yet tender, he said, "She's asleep."

Krafft had got to his feet. He didn't know what to do. He felt a need to go up to Feders and put his arm around him.

But Feders so far hadn't made the slightest gesture of intimacy. He had merely made a number of provocative explanatory statements.

The captain turned around, and looked at the lieutenant through half-closed eyes. He pulled the door to behind him almost roughly, and said, "Why don't you sit down, Krafft."

Krafft sat down.

"Are you trying to spy on me or something?"

Krafft shook his head helplessly.

"Because I'd advise you not to," said Feders.

A considerable period of time elapsed. A heavy silence lay over the room. In the distance a radio was blaring out the Love Song Waltz of Johann Strauss—it was being played by a brass band and sounded vulgar and obtrusive.

Eventually, leaning his back against the bedroom door, Captain Feders said gravely, "Well, now you know it all, Krafft. This is the rule of life. But of course this rule, too, has its exceptions and I'm one of them, having drawn my own deductions from such an appalling situation. I have indeed lost what are called my manly powers, but I've compensated for them by my will and reason. Are you with me so far, Krafft?"

"Why are you trying to explain to me something I don't want to have explained at all?"

"No excuses, Krafft, you just listen. I'm giving you priceless material for a conversation in the mess. You see, it's like this: if you lose a limb there are artificial limbs, and similarly if you lose your manhood there are also substitutes. The Minnesinger performs this function for me. I chose him and persuaded my wife to accept him. He is simply a body, nothing else. My wife and I are wholly agreed about that. He's an instrument, a substitute organ, an emergency solution. A stupid, vain, polished ape, with wonderful muscles and the brain of a fly. His existence is a safeguard against humiliating tortures. Is that clear to you, Krafft?"

"No," said the latter. He felt tired and sad. "Nothing is clear to me."

"Then why do you drag all this out of me, Krafft?" asked the captain, swaying nearer. His eyes wandered from Krafft to the brandy bottle and back again. "Why do you force your way into my confidence and lead me up the garden path like this? Why do you sneak around me like this with your malice and hypocrisy? Are you trying to make a fool of me, Krafft?"

"I honestly want to try and understand you," said Krafft, staring into a face distorted with drunkenness and pain. "But I'm afraid my understanding works rather differently from yours."

"You're trying to make a fool of me!" roared Captain Feders. "Get out of my sight and don't let me ever see you in here again! I've had enough of people like you! Sods and swine! That's all this filthy world consists of. Go on, get out!"

"Good night, Captain," said Krafft. He felt desperately miserable.

12 *A LESSON IN ETIQUETTE*

"FRIENDS" said Lieutenant Krafft, addressing his cadets, "as you are aware, one doesn't necessarily need to know all about a subject; the important thing is to be able to talk about it. And so we come to our theme for today: etiquette."

The class proceeded orthodoxly enough at first. The section officer posed the right idiotic questions. The cadets gave him the right idiotic answers. Morale generally was good. For the theme was in no way a tricky one, and in a way even had its entertaining aspects.

For example: who introduces whom to whom first? The gentleman is always introduced to the lady first, of course. But what about differences of rank and seniority between the gentlemen? Here alone the variations were almost inexhaustible. For a cadet could meet a captain who was going out with a corporal's wife. (Only in theory of course, as Krafft didn't neglect to add.) Then a lieutenant found himself face to face with a general who in turn found himself with the lieutenant's sister—a little closer to reality this; at least it was just the sort of problem one concerned oneself with in respectable officers' circles.

"Are good manners just a question of chance?" asked Krafft, looking over to Hochbauer.

"Not for an officer, Lieutenant," declared Hochbauer promptly.

"Doesn't it seem a bit absurd," Krafft then asked warily, "in the middle of a war seriously to bother oneself with forms of address, hand kissing, and all that sort of thing?"

"It can't be absurd," said Amfortas, one of Hochbauer's satellites, "because after all, this theme is laid down as part of the curriculum."

This was an argument which was always effective; even Krafft didn't dare to ridicule it. He grinned.

As usual, the cadets took constant notes. Only Mösler stared absent-mindedly into space; he was busy cleaning his fingernails under the table—in his view, a practical contribution to the theme under discussion.

Next to Mösler on the rear bench sat Cadet Rednitz, whose notes ran as follows: Age more important than youth—females always before males, except on stairs—officer's wife worth more than a corporal's wife—seniority decisive, rank equally decisive—a true gentleman not only takes his pleasure and keeps quiet about it, but also lets others take their pleasure and keeps quiet about it, in so far of course as no infringement of service regulations is involved.

"Is there in fact a prescribed manner in which officers should sit in latrines?" asked Cadet Mösler in the innocent tone of someone anxious to learn, interrupting the cleaning of his fingernails.

Lieutenant Krafft quite unconcernedly asked his cadets to give their opinion on this. "Well, Hochbauer?" he asked.

Hochbauer rose to his feet. He was intelligent enough not only to see that Mösler's question was in itself a direct provocation, but also that it was no accident that Krafft had chosen him to answer it. It was up to him therefore to dominate the situation and not look ridiculous.

So he answered seriously enough, "The officer is distinguished from the rank and file not only by special qualities such as character and intelligence, but also by certain external characteristics. For example: his uniform, his badges of rank, his equipment—and so on, down to his underclothing. The officer eats in his own mess too. He also makes use of special latrines, which have their own locks on them. Even in the field there are special messing facilities for officers, and similarly portable field latrines, or at least special separate compartments in the general latrines, or if not that, then regulation times for officers' use. The officer has certain privileges, which may be regarded as a modest compensation for the greater duties he has to undertake."

"May I just enter a modest objection," said Cadet Mösler. "Cadet Hochbauer's remarks seem to me to be purely theoretical. I would say that there are some situations in which it is quite impossible to make distinctions of rank. Thus, if one may take the example before us, an officer stinks the place out neither more nor less than a simple soldier."

Once again a violent dispute arose, threatening to split H Section into two camps. If the fronts weren't altogether clearly defined, this was because no one had yet been able to establish exactly what the section officer's own opinion was, and this made it difficult for most of them to take up an uncompromising position. Krafft merely smiled, with something like an air of patience. He let his cadets have a completely free hand, at the same time keeping them under close scrutiny.

Slowly the dispute simmered down, with the usual comforting conclusions: . . . something to be said on both sides . . . in certain circumstances . . . it all depends. Thus they all ended just as clever or as stupid as they'd begun, and everyone was happy. The lieutenant, however, having gone this far, determined that with so much absurdity already in evidence there should be no half measures.

His cadets listened carefully as he said, "Let's take the following case, now. You have accepted an invitation from your commanding officer—something which naturally goes without saying, unless you happen to be lying on your deathbed at the time. There is dancing. You ask the wife of your commanding officer to dance, something else which naturally also goes without saying. Good manners demand it. Your offer is accepted, and you whirl her away. While you are dancing your monocle slips from your eye and, obeying the law of gravity, and accelerated by the energy of your steps, falls straight down your commanding officer's wife's magnificent and ample décolletage. What do you do?"

The cadets listened attentively. It was up to them to work out the solution to this problem, and they had no choice but to take it seriously.

Serious reflection about this sort of nonsense, as Krafft well knew, was a special hobbyhorse of Major Frey's. The affair of the monocle and the bosom had been one of the problems which baffled officers' messes at the turn of the century, but its great advantage was that it offered an un-usually wide range of alternative solutions—three at least—and was thus, to Major Frey's way of thinking, a useful sharpener of the wits. Krafft smiled. "Well, Amfortas?" he said.

Amfortas was sitting next to Andreas. As Krafft had discovered, this pair were the closest allies of the Greco-Germanic Hochbauer. They even had certain external character-istics in common, though they seemed somewhat thinner, paler, and smaller. In fact they were just different enough to make them seem like plaster casts of the original.

"I'm listening, Amfortas! Don't leave us awaiting the lightning flash of your intelligence too long. Well, what would you do?"

"I'd say excuse me," said Amfortas, helplessly.

"And then?" asked the lieutenant softly.

"I'd say excuse me," maintained Amfortas in slight con-fusion. "There's nothing more I could do."

"And your monocle?" asked Krafft, noting with pleasure that a certain spirit of amusement was spreading among the cadets. "What about your monocle? Is it to stay where it is? Are you going to ask for it back? Do you anticipate that it will be returned to you? Or what?"

The situation was too much for Cadet Amfortas. Discom-fort gave way to anxiety. His answer had been unsatisfactory, which was bad enough in itself. But now he couldn't think of any answer at all, and that was far worse. For in this way he was contravening one of the most important basic maxims, which laid down that there was no situation in which an officer found himself at a loss. Amfortas felt sure he was bound to collect a lot of bad marks here.

"And you, Andreas, what would you do?" asked Krafft.

"I'd ignore the matter entirely, sir," said Andreas with grim determination. "I'd act as if nothing had happened at all."

"What's that?" asked Krafft in apparent amazement. "You'd ignore the matter? You'd let your monocle fall down some-one's bosom and then try and carry on as if nothing had happened?"

With that Andreas was destroyed on the ground, so to speak. The section started to show signs of restlessnes. They were afraid they might have been a little premature with their outburt of hilarity. The problem under discussion seemed to contain all sorts of hidden traps.

"Right, then," said Krafft. "Let us pull the whole thing together a bit. There are a number of alternatives. First of all, one excuses oneself. Secondly, one ignores the whole matter. Thirdly, one tries to regain the monocle. But how? Does one make a grab for it? Does one ask the commanding officer's wife to do so for one? Does one wait until the monocle reappears of its own free will? And then again, if one does excuse oneself—what form of excuse does one use? If one ignores the whole matter, how in fact does one do so? If one starts searching for the monocle, how exactly? Well, Hochbauer, what would you do in this case?"

"I feel sure, sir," declared the latter, "that with me such a thing would never happen. I would have maintained a respectful distance."

"But it had happened, Hochbauer! Or have you perhaps failed to notice that the problem I've set you is both clearly formulated and precise?"

Hochbauer, too, had fallen into an elementary trap and didn't know what to answer. What's more, he felt certain that whatever he said the lieutenant would have no difficulty in finding a counterargument and this realization made him very bitter. He fell silent, trying to maintain his silence with dignity. But he thought he sensed a gradual loss of influence and authority among his fellow cadets. And he decided that something would have to be done about it.

Krafft felt satisfied. Once again he had got through a class relatively pleasantly. He said, "Between now and tomorrow morning I'd like each one of you to work out a short appreciation of the problem before us. That will be all for today. The period's over."

The cadets left the classroom in small groups and formed up into a squad on the path outside. Even though the distance to the barracks was only a few hundred yards, these had to be traveled in proper formation.

Kramer, the section senior, did his best to get his men to fall in correctly. But this was no easy task, for the cadets were now thoroughly absorbed in this question of the bosom and the monocle.

"What is one to say?" muttered Amfortas to his friend and comrade Andreas. Both looked toward Hochbauer.

"It's really quite simple," said Hochbauer seriously. "Whenever I find myself confronted by a problem I ask myself, What would my Führer say to this!—and everything is then quite easy."

"And what do you think your Führer would say to this?"

"Can't you guess?"

"No," declared the two of them truthfully.

"Well try and think about it a bit!"

The section moved off toward the barracks in which they were quartered. Kramer felt compelled to call for silence several times, but he did so in vain.

Some felt that this additional work was unnecessary. Others felt certain there was a catch in it somewhere. Others maintained that they saw in this a subtle attempt on Krafft's part to check up on their whole pattern of thought and action.

"But it's always like that," said one of them gloomily. "The officers just want to make trouble for us; it's all they care about. There's only one thing for it—to co-operate at all times. And if someone wants an essay from me on how to put lavatory paper to the best advantage, he shall have it!"

The cadets let their imaginations run riot. A décolleté bosom was after all rather out of the ordinary as a classroom topic.

Cadet Weber, Egon, the strong man of the section, declared, "I would simply hold the commanding officer's wife up by the legs until the monocle fell out and then say 'I'm deeply obliged to you, ma'am'!"

"Too formal!" maintained Mösler. "All you say is 'With your permission, ma'am'—and quite simply make a grab down her bosom. Very discreetly, of course."

"And if it's some old harridan?" one of them asked anxiously.

"Just the same!" declared Mösler. "On humanitarian grounds! And if it also happens to be the commanding officer's wife it might even lead to promotion."

"Or a posting to the front," said Rednitz.

"None of you have any sense of poetry in you," said Böhmke, the dreamer. "You're all so obvious. But here in fact is a wonderful opportunity for adventure, not unworthy of Boccaccio. In order to regain possession of the monocle so charmingly concealed somewhere on this lady's person, there's only one thing for it—to make a conquest of her. And I don't mean just seize hold of her crudely as you usually do, but pay court to the lady, flatter her, confess your tender passion to her, and when she finally undresses . . ."

The cadets roared with laughter. Kramer looked about him, but fortunately there wasn't an officer in sight so he didn't need to intervene.

"Dismiss!" he cried with relief when they reached the barracks.

The cadets pushed their way into the corridor. The day's work was over. Their conversation at once took on a coarser note altogether. Mösler was already wondering what would happen if the monocle were found in the commanding officer's wife's panties.

Hochbauer received these remarks with increasing displeasure. "Really insufferable!" he cried with contempt.

"Exactly what I feel about you!" returned Mösler.

Again the cadets roared with laughter, and Hochbauer said to his friends, "They'll laugh at any rotten thing now. But they'll see sense in the end." Hochbauer was extremely dissatisfied with his fellow cadets. All in all it hadn't been a particularly good day.

"I think," he said to his friends, "something will have to be done about this. Common decency demands it."

"May I have permission to speak, Captain?" said Cadet Hochbauer, both smartly and humbly at the same time.

Captain Ratshelm sat beneath a standard lamp in an armchair in his room, which was extremely stuffy from the central heating. He had taken off his tunic, and his shirt was partly unbuttoned over his chest. The red of his suspenders shone vividly. His socks were a grayish white. He radiated a relaxed, manly geniality.

The cadet said politely, "I hope I'm not disturbing you, sir?"

Captain Ratshelm sketched a generous gesture of welcome. He closed the book he had been dipping into between naps, a work of military history about the battles of Frederick the Great.

"You're always welcome here, Cadet Hochbauer, as indeed are all the others, too, for that matter. That's what I'm here for. Take a seat, sit down beside me. Would you like a cigarette? No? Quite right! Smoking is a sign of nerves. I only smoke very occasionally myself, and then only when in company. But what's troubling you, my dear fellow? What's on your mind?"

Hochbauer sat down in a chair beside the captain, looked at Ratshelm's pink, sweaty chest and interpreted it as a sign of confidence, if not indeed intimacy.

"As you well know, sir," he said confidentially, "I devote myself in my spare time to certain private studies which to some extent might also be said to be in the line of duty."

"Yes, I know that very well and welcome the fact, Hochbauer. What's on your mind?"

"Prince Eugen, sir, was a Frenchman in the service of Austria. Graf von Moltke was a Dane who won victories for Prussia. Might one perhaps, ought one perhaps, to maintain that these two war leaders were to some extent forerunners of the Greater German idea of a united Europe?"

"A most excellent thought!" agreed Captain Ratshelm. "And one that has already occurred to me. These ideas of yours are first-rate, Cadet Hochbauer. After all, it's not just Germany and the countries associated with her whose future is at stake today, but something far larger than that."

Hochbauer smiled gratefully. For some time they chatted together pleasantly on this almost inexhaustible topic. Carried away by it all, the captain laid a hand on the cadet's knee, a clear sign of the enthusiasm he felt for the subject.

Then, however, Hochbauer confessed slightly shamefacedly that there was another problem on his mind which he couldn't quite straighten out. "I don't really know whether I ought to burden you with it, sir, or not."

"Come along, no false modesty, my dear boy," said Ratshelm encouragingly.

Hochbauer told him of the commanding officer's wife in the décolleté dress and the monocle which dropped from the eye of the waltzing cadet. Hurriedly he added, "Naturally I don't expect you to solve the problem for me, sir. But I must confess that the incident in question struck me as very remarkable."

"Hm," said Captain Ratshelm, thoughtfully looking down at his socks.

"If I may say so I find the whole thing distasteful," said Hochbauer. "For me the very thought of such an incident has something almost nauseating about it."

Ratshelm nodded, trying to visualize the situation. A bared bosom—soft, white, swelling flesh . . . and the captain too found it almost nauseating. Thoroughly revolting, in fact.

"I'm with you there, Cadet Hochbauer. A strong sense of shame is always a sign of high morals, I find."

It was a pleasure to both to find themselves in such complete agreement. Yet the captain never for a moment forgot his sense of duty. Here in the presence of a subordinate he was not going to blame the section officer or even criticize him. Such a thing would have been utterly irresponsible.

"I am grateful to you for being so understanding, sir!"

"My dear Cadet Hochbauer," said Ratshelm, "I know how

to value the confidence my subordinates put in me. And I can only hope that they will always continue to do so. For there's an old, well-tried saying which runs, trust for trust—or alternatively, loyalty for loyalty! Do you follow me?"

Cadet Hochbauer nodded. He felt that anything he could say would be superfluous. He even acted as if, from emotion, words failed him.

Ratshelm buttoned up his shirt, and pulled on his tunic and his boots. Strictly in a spirit of hearty comradeship he clapped Hochbauer on the back—a little low down the back, to be sure, but his hand only rested there for a moment.

"I'm not a man to make big promises," he said. "But something will be done, you can rest assured."

"Can I speak to you for a moment, Captain Feders?"

"No," said Feders. "I'm not available—at any rate, not just to anyone."

Captain Ratshelm, in his capacity as the responsible officer in command of the company, always make a point of sticking closely to the correct procedure. He never went over anyone's head, unless there were special grounds for doing so. And for this reason he had first sought out Captain Feders, who as tactics instructor had an equal responsibility in this matter.

But Feders wanted to be left alone. He was playing billiards by himself. This way he could win every game.

"It'll only take a few minutes," said Ratshelm, "and it's about something I must beg you to keep quiet about."

"All right, Ratshelm, I'm keeping quiet."

"But that's not what I meant, Feders," said the company commander with some irritation. "I meant that what we discuss must remain between ourselves, an official secret, so to speak. I'm worried about Lieutenant Krafft. In fact I have considerable misgivings about him. I don't like his methods. He seems to be lacking in the necessary seriousness of purpose. I even get the painful impression that he makes fun of things that ought to be sacred to him, or which at least he ought to regard as a matter of duty. Quite frankly, Feders, what do you make of Krafft?"

"Don't bother me. The man's a beginner, Ratshelm," said the tactics instructor crossly. "I see red whenever I think of him. And at the moment I'd like to be able to see fairly clearly—I happen to be playing billiards."

"That's a thoroughly negative attitude, if I may say so."

"Ratshelm, you're a most perceptive fellow. It should therefore be clear to you by now that you're in my way here."

"What a clown you are, Feders!"

"Maybe, but unfortunately I never yet succeeded in getting anyone to die of laughing."

"May I ask how you are?" enquired Ratshelm courteously.

"Very well, thank you," said the major's niece. "And you?"

"Thank you, I'm very well too!"

This conversation, conducted with the utmost gravity—and indeed why not?—took place in the hall of Major Frey's house at number 7 Marktplatz, Wildlingen-am-Main. Barbara Bendler-Trebitz, lady's companion, niece, and maid of all work, was welcoming the unexpected guest.

For the major had first to remove his slippers and put on proper shoes, while the lady of the house was busy arranging her hair in a series of elegant buns before a genuine Venetian looking glass. So in the meantime Barbara, the housemaid-niece, had to do the honors.

She was clearly a very willing sort of girl. She helped Ratshelm off with his greatcoat. She even brushed his uniform here and there to remove the odd speck of dust or thread or fluff. Ratshelm thought this was going rather far, but found it touchingly feminine. Meanwhile Barbara was brushing his back with long low-reaching strokes of the brush.

"Thank you very much," said Ratshelm, rather embarrassed.

"It's a pleasure!"

The appearance of the major saved Ratshelm from having to reply. His Knight's Cross shone brilliantly and there was a cordial ring in his voice. "You know," he insisted, "you're always a welcome guest in my house."

A moment later Frau Felicitas Frey assured Ratshelm of the same thing. "Would you care for a glass of Madeira?" she asked.

The major recognized this offer as a sure sign of approval. For some inexplicable reason Felicitas regarded Maderia as the acme of drinks, and it was offered only to specially selected guests and to himself. But the major didn't begrudge the captain his Madeira. For he knew that he could quite safely entrust to Ratshelm not only a company of cadets, but his wife as well. With him at least there was absolutely no danger that he would overstep the limits of decorum.

"You're a man of principle, Ratshelm," the major assured him. "I set a lot of store by that."

"Oh, really," said the captain with self-deprecating modesty, "one does one's duty as best one can."

"It's a pity you're not married, my dear Herr Ratshelm," said the major's wife thoughtfully. "Really a great pity. You're a born family man—devoted, dignified, firm of purpose."

"Well," said the major, trying to put a stop to this, "Ratshelm has his hands full with his cadets at the moment, and with some of his officers too. Aren't I right?"

"As always!" Ratshelm assured him appreciatively. "You have an uncanny knack of spotting trouble in time, sir, a real eye for that sort of thing."

The major smiled, flattered, at the same time raising his hands in a self-deprecating gesture. Frau Felicitas, however, threw her husband a glance which was anything but admiring. She felt ruffled, for he had interrupted her train of thought.

"Fire away, then," cried the major encouragingly. "Trust me. Let the cat out of the bag."

"It's rather a delicate matter," said Ratshelm. "And not really for a lady's ears."

"I am a commanding officer's wife," said Felicitas firmly. "And as such I participate in everything which concerns my husband's position."

"Thank you, dear," said the major.

"So you can talk quite openly, my dear Herr Ratshelm." Felicitas smiled in anticipation. "After all, we're people with experience of life, aren't we?"

Captain Ratshelm nodded, and began to tell his story, though he made no attempt to conceal his revulsion as he did so. The example which Lieutenant Krafft had chosen for his lesson in etiquette was, he made clear, both painful and repellent to hm.

The major smiled at first. "Come, come," he said jovially. "A rather broad joke certainly, but not really anything out of the ordinary. In my days as a cadet—and I graduated first!—we laughed ourselves silly over exactly the same ludicrous situation. Ha, ha, ha, ha, ha!"

But as he caught sight of the stiff indignant face of his wife, his laughter died away. With her unerring feminine instinct she had seized at once on the really shameless aspect of this affair. "How could you laugh at such a thing, Archibald? Don't you realize what this man Krafft is up to? He's trying to make me ridiculous and to undermine your authority!"

"But how do you make that out?" asked the major in bewilderment.

"How do I make that out?" she cried with furious scorn. "This man is talking about the wife of his commanding officer —about me, that is! In front of forty cadets he maintains that I wear shamelessly décolleté dresses. He uses the word bosom quite openly—with reference to me! Into these young, unsullied minds he plants the idea of making immoral approaches to a lady. And you, Archibald, you find it something to laugh at!"

"The man doesn't seem to me fit to be a section officer," declared Ratshelm with honest regret. "And it's not only this story that tells against him—about which, incidentally, he is getting the cadets to write an essay—but in my capacity as company commander I've a number of other complaints to make. Captain Feders, our tactics instructor, entertains a similarly unfavorable opinion of him."

"Feders can't exactly be regarded as a paragon of virtue and morality," said Frau Frey. "But if even he takes exception to this person then it's really time something was done."

The major nodded. "Really regrettable," he said. "Really most regrettable."

"It's a disgrace!" said Frau Felicitas. She seemed most upset. "Such people might perhaps just do for the training of raw recruits, but that the fate of valuable young human beings like these cadets should be entrusted into their hands seems deplorable!"

"They are indeed the most magnificent material, ma'am," Ratshelm assured her. "You really ought to see these young people—one's heart goes out to them."

"All right, Ratshelm," said the major. "You've convinced me. But will the two of us be able to convince the general?"

They conferred half the night. Carefully they drew up their program point by point. By the end they had convinced themselves that their arguments were unanswerable.

"What'll prove decisive," said Ratshelm, "is that the general can't tolerate any sort of slovenliness under his command."

"Of course, of course," said the major, rather more doubtfully. "But we're taking a risk. We can never be sure in advance what the general's going to do."

"This time he can't fail to be convinced by your arguments," said Felicitas.

The next morning Major Frey and Captain Ratshelm asked to see Major-General Modersohn. The general received them immediately. "Come to the point at once, please," he said.

The two officers laid all their complaints against Krafft before the general, choosing their words carefully. Finally they gave him a detailed description of the example Krafft had chosen for his essay subject. They felt sure the general would find this highly objectionable.

When they had finished they looked at Major-General Modersohn expectantly. The latter, however, stared through them unmoved, as if they were made of plate glass. It seemed to them they could hear the snow falling outside as if it were rain.

Finally the general said slowly, "The solution to the problem posed by Lieutenant Krafft is a simple one. A cadet doesn't wear a monocle. If he does he's a fop. But if he's a fop then he can't become an officer—at least not under my command. I thank you, gentlemen."

And that was all.

* * * *

Intermediate Report No. 4

THE CURRICULUM VITAE OF
MAJOR ARCHIBALD FREY,
OR FREEDOM THROUGH RESOLUTION

My name is Auguste Wilhelm Archibald Frey. My father was Auguste Ernst Frey, a respected grocer in Werdau, Saxony. My mother was Maria Magdalena Frey, born Ziergiebel of a land-owning family of some importance. I was born on May 1, 1904, in Werdau, where I spent my childhood and went to school.

A small, slight shadow of a woman—this is my mother. An equally small but much broader shadow always behind her —this is my father. Mother has the face of a shrew, and Father looks more like a hamster just before hibernation. Mother is always quiet and prays a lot. Father almost always makes a lot of noise. His shop is small and dark, but stuffed to the rafters with goods. There are even crates in the kitchen, and packets of washing powder are piled high in the lavatory. But the cartons of candy and the till itself are kept under the bed where my father sleeps. And when he is asleep one of his hands is almost always hanging down protectively over where the money lies. Besides, my father is a very light sleeper, as has been proved.

The pastor is a mighty man in my mother's eyes. My mother would do anything for the pastor, my father thinks. To my father the pastor is just another customer, who sometimes buys wax candles and, at Christmas, all sorts of food to distribute as gifts. Father sells everything it's possible to sell, and not only groceries. I'm allowed to sing in the church choir after the pastor has ordered oil for the lamps from us. This according to Father, brings him in about seven marks. But my mother gives ten marks to the church, so the pastor has a net profit of three marks—as my father doesn't stop saying for weeks. "Perhaps I'll let you go into the Church," says my father to me. "It seems to be a paying business."

"There are two bells in the shop, one on the door and the other on the till. The one on the door rings loud and shrill, the one on the till with a soft silvery tinkle. Both can be heard quite clearly in Father's office, which is also part of his bedroom. And when the till rings he's always there at once. But when both bells ring together, the one on the door is much louder and if one also clears one's throat at the same time, the bell on the door is the only one that can be heard. This has been proved too. But there's never much cash in the till, and when Father notices that anything is missing he becomes firmly convinced that he is financing almost the entire Church on his own, which of course is a considerable exaggeration. Mother in fact has a great deal of Christian patience, as well she needs to have.

The little girl's name is Moldner, her Christian name Margarete, and she is the darling of the whole town. When the pastor sees Margarete, he always smiles so that you can see all his teeth. These are in a very bad condition, due perhaps to the fact that the dentist is of another faith. Even the teacher sometimes calls Margarete "our little darling." The district judge has stroked her and called her "curly-head"; and the barber on the corner grins when he sees her and pipes up, "Well now, Fräulein, what can I do for you?" This Margarete is just about the same age as I am, and squints and has fat legs. And she hasn't any curls at all, though she certainly has plenty of hair, in the same way as horses have manes. But her father owns the cotton factory which mass-produces socks and underclothes, and her father's brother owns the big hotel in the market square with the café and the restaurant. So Margarete has always got a piece of tart, or some chocolate, or a piece of bread and sausage, or lemonade, or even money. I am glad to protect her and stop others taking things from her. And she is very very grateful to me for that.

Little Margarete Moldner's father's brother, the hotelkeeper, is a nice man, and is my godfather as well. He comes on the scene just as I am beating up a particularly cheeky boy two years younger than me who has insulted Margarete by saying she wets her pants, which is a lie—we know, because we've checked up. Anyway, I'm beating him up and the hotelkeeper says, "You're a good lad!" And I say, "I won't let Margarete be insulted!" "You're a fine fellow," he says. "A real little cavalier. And besides, aren't you the son of Frey the grocer?" I confirm the fact that Frey, the grocer, is my father, and he says, "Perhaps I could do some business with your father from time to time. Ask him his price for a sack of sugar, will you?" And Father is beside himself with joy. "A special price," he says, "thirty-four marks a sack." "A special price," I tell the hotelkeeper, "thirty-six marks a sack." "Fine," says the hotelkeeper, "I'll have three sacks."

Margarete is a little beast. Somehow she discovers that I've earned first six marks and then another eight. Now she wants to tattle—only she can't decide who to tattle to, her uncle or my father. But Alphonse, a friend of mine, gives me a good piece of advice. He tells me to do what he did with his brother's wife. And this doesn't seem a bad idea. So I say to Margarete, "Don't do that. I only earned the money in order to buy you a present." "Really?" she asks. "Word of honor," I say, and spit three times. "What are you going to give me?" she asks. "Something particularly beautiful," I say, "such as only fine ladies have. But there's something I'll have to see first." And we go into the wood behind the brick factory and there I make her show me all sorts of things. She even thinks this funny. So that's what it's like! I think it funny, too, only I don't say so. Though after all she is a little beast and wanted to get me into trouble. So I say to her, "If you ever start getting cheeky again, I'll tell everyone what you do with the fellows in the wood. And then you'll see what happens."

"Idiot!" says my father to me when he hears about it. "Ill-favored son, miserable child! How could you do such a thing! Are you out of your mind? Have you forgotten everything I've ever taught you? Do you want to ruin me? The little girl is a manufacturer's daughter, and her uncle owns the hotel. You don't irritate people like that, you stay friends with them at all costs!"

I ended my primary schooling in 1918, after playing my own modest but active part in the war for the Fatherland. Then I

*went on to secondary school, and left it for purely economic
reasons in 1923 with a middle level certificate. After a number of hard years in which I was forced to take up a responsible post in heavy industry, I decided to become a soldier.
In 1925 I entered what was then the Reichswehr, determined to take up an officer's career if possible.*

"The Fatherland needs guns," says the teacher, "so you
must collect metal." Which is what we do. I am in charge of
my class's collection campaign, which proves a success.
Finally I take charge of the whole school's campaign. Cop-
per and lead are the most important metals. Sometimes we're
given gold as well. The giving isn't always entirely voluntary,
unfortunately. But in the interests of patriotism we help to
improve our citizens' attitude of mind. We've still got a
considerable store of metal when the war comes to an end,
though now it's a question of concealing such valuable material from the various Allied snooping commissions. Father
lends us a good deal of help, though not always entirely
unselfishly, which leads to violent differences of opinion between us. "In this way I'm financing your secondary education," says Father. "Which is in Germany's interests, too,
in the long run." And I let him convince me. Our beloved
Fatherland is suddenly crawling overnight with speculators,
black marketeers, and war profiteers. True values have to be
maintained at all costs.

Dark, troublesome times! The Fatherland, they say, is
down, but not shattered or destroyed, only disarmed. Red
flags spring up everywhere; there's a rotten spirit abroad.
The mob runs through the streets; a boilerman from Moldner's cotton factory becomes burgomaster, and in Berlin
there's some master saddler or other who calls himself President of the Reich. All officials cringe and crawl. All cringers
and crawlers change their coats. The Reds grab all the best
jobs. Mother is labeled clerical, and Father is proclaimed a
dirty capitalist, though he's making hardly any profit at all.
But in the end he is accused of bartering sacks of sugar with
the brother of Moldner the manufacturer, that's to say the
hotelkeeper, one of the Kaiser's men. In short, things begin to
go badly. There's hardly any demand even for precious metals, and anyway stocks are diminishing rapidly. "Poor Germany!" is all one can say, and, even as a schoolboy, do
one's duty.

As consolation there are German women. Edeltraut for
example. Edeltraut Degenhart, the widow of an officer. Her

husband had been a cavalry lieutenant, in command of a supply unit at the end, specially engaged in the transport of metals. It was said that he had refused to allow mutineers to rip the insignia from his shoulders, and had preferred death instead. So he died. Defending his honor, said his widow. Of alcoholic poisoning, some subversive wretches said, in their usual undermining sort of way. In any case, even if there was some truth in what they said, inasmuch as Lieutenant Degenhart had preferred to drink the bottles of schnapps entrusted to him rather than let them fall into the filthy hands of the enemies of the Fatherland, he had done his duty to the last. His youthful widow, however, lives on in our house, mourning nobly, and urgently in need of consolation. Fortunately I have time at my disposal—school is over, and a suitable profession has not yet been found for me.

"This Frau Degenhart interests me," says this fellow Korngiebler. I maintain an attitude of reserve. I've noticed him following Frau Degenhart around, and his intentions have been unmistakable from the first. "This Frau Degenhart is a lady," I tell him. "So much the better," says Korngiebler. "I'd very much like to get to know her." "And what exactly do you mean by that?" I ask. It's true I'm only twenty and he's at least twenty years older, but of course I know something of the world. I've been around with a manufacturer's daughter, I've done business with a much respected hotel-keeper, I've taken a prominent part in large-scale collecting campaigns, all in spite of my care, so I'm perfectly entitled to ask, Who is this fellow Korngiebler and what does he want? "I represent a well-known firm with an exclusive business," he says. "Supersil, the washing powder for every housewife— we can't get rid of it fast enough. So you won't lose by this. Can you arrange an introduction to the lady for me?" "If, as I believe, the matter is of some importance to you and your intentions are honorable, there's no reason why I shouldn't."

They marry—the officer's widow, Edeltraut Degenhart, and Korngiebler, the commercial representative. I am a witness at the ceremony. Extraordinarily impressive the whole thing. Though not exactly a church ceremony, there's a piano and a violin playing Tannhäuser, and a champagne breakfast. Korngiebler is overcome with emotion. Confesses to me, after a night of carousal, "I didn't want to at first. At first I merely wanted . . . well, you know. However—

and when it was all over, with all that it entails . . . and even if it's only a girl, I shan't mind. It won't make any difference to me—you can't go wrong with Supersil. Feel really proud. Got you to thank for it, Archie. She's a woman who'll be a credit to me. Increase the turnover. Not really necessary, but it can't do any harm. You must come into the business. No, none of that—we could use you. Isn't that so, Schatzi? Schatzi nods, you see."

So I begin organizing—one wagonload after the other, truck after truck. Right-hand man of Supersil's chief representative in the Chemnitz area. There's nothing particularly difficult about the work, and it doesn't take up too much time, at least not for someone who's a born organizer. So I have plenty of opportunity to study, particularly to study life. Moreover I prove myself worthy of this fellow Korngiebler's confidence and friendship by devoting myself most attentively to his wife. This leads to misunderstanding, though. "Archibald," this fellow Korngiebler says to me, "you've been in my wife's bedroom!" "Certainly," I say. "I wanted to speak to her." "But I wasn't in the house and you were there for hours." "Perfectly true," I say in all honesty. "I was simply waiting for you." This is the absolute truth, but he doesn't believe me.

My friend Alphonse's comment on this case is, "You're too honorable; it's a disadvantage sometimes. You shouldn't have told this fellow Korngiebler the truth. Those sort of people can't take it. They want to be lied to. What you should have said was, Your wife has now got to the state where she seduces everyone in sight. And what would have been the result? He would have turned her out of the house, but you would have remained his right-hand man."

Still, one can only be oneself. Honor and truth are more important to me than anything. No word of protest, of indignation, or contempt falls from my lips as his mercenary soul reveals itself in all its nakedness. He repudiates our friendship. More than that; he kicks me out of the business. And still not content, he concocts every sort of malice about me in his lust for revenge. He even maintains that I—I of all people!—have been embezzling funds, or at least lining my own pocket. It's an example of how blind and repulsive the greed for profit can make such people.

But this ends my career as a salesman. Time has meanwhile made considerable inroads on my father's modest fortune. I feel nauseated by these rats who swarm everywhere, endeavoring, without any sense of shame, to enrich themselves in this hour of Germany's need. My whole being craves fresh air. So I enroll in the Reichswehr. My dear friend Alphonse is already there.

In 1925 I was privileged to be accepted into the Reichswehr in spite of my age; a number of influential people sponsored me. I followed the normal career of a professional soldier, being promoted in the regular way on all but one occasion. With the arrival of the new era there began a systematic expansion of the Reichswehr, which eventually became the Wehrmacht. In 1931 I was elected to serve the Fatherland as an officer.

What a splendidly characteristic picture, this photo of 1925 with me and my comrades in our plain gray uniforms. There is the outer courtyard of the castle at Dresden, its principal turret in the background. And in the foreground: ourselves—Number 6 Section—gathered around our corporal, whose name—how could one ever forget it?—was Schweinitzer. And here is the special thing about the picture: one can see a smile on Schweinitzer's face, something one never normally saw on the barrack square. And he, as you will notice if you look closely, is smiling at me. Yes, at me. And though I won't say I was a magnificent soldier, yet I wasn't a bad one either.

I was made room senior while still a recruit. By my second year I was the best rifleman of all the rankers in my entire company. In the same year I was made an assistant instructor. Only a year later I became section leader and led the company choir, though I had no particular gift for music. In short I was what you might call a first-class all-rounder. Best handling of a rifle at rifle drill, greatest powers of endurance on route marches, highest scores in rifle competitions. On top of that, a good swimmer, a good runner, a good cyclist. And I was several times commended for my excellent knowledge of military regulations. But despite all this I always remained close to my fellow soldiers.

Happy hours of good fellowship in the inn known as The Kaiser's Rest. So called because the owner's name was Kaiser and he let rooms. The chief attraction was the dance every Saturday, where we NCOs would have our regular table to ourselves. In fact it would be a stag party until just before midnight—just us men, drinking beer, making speeches, eying the girls. Good, solid talk, toasts—mainly from me, all in keeping with the unwritten law of our table, which ran, Free time is time for fun, and the spirit of good fellowship shall reign at least until midnight, when the girls come up for discussion. What fun we had! And the great gamble was always who would have which girl after midnight. Rank counted for nothing once the dancing started. What was particularly remarkable was that, whether corporal, sergeant, sergeant-major, no one tried to pull his rank on evenings such as this. The same close bond of comradeship embraced us all.

Lieutenant Pökelmann sends for me, a magnificent officer, a fine man to have over one, and very popular. There's nothing peculiar about him sending for me because he's the officer in charge of recruits, and I, as sergeant and section leader, am his right-hand man. But it's late—almost two o'clock in the morning. I report to him in his flat on the second floor of company headquarters—entrance on the landing. Pökelmann gives me a broad grin. He is in bed with a girl—there are clothes and a few bottles in front of the bed. "My dear Frey," says Lieutenant Pökelmann, "you're somebody one can trust, aren't you?" I assure him I am. First we have a drink. The good Pökelmann can hardly take any more, but the girl, a lively little thing who works as an assistant in a record shop—His Master's Voice—still has plenty of life left in her. "Frey," Pökelmann says, "escort the little lady out of barracks, will you, but in such a way that nobody sees you." And then he turns over and goes to sleep. But I carry out his wish, and one hour later escort the girl out of the barracks, unobserved. For it so happens that my friend Alphonse is on guard that night.

"My dear Frey," Lieutenant Pökelmann says to me a few days later, "you're not only reliable but you have a sense of chivalry and tact. The little girl was full of your praises, and it seems you're discretion itself. I've had my eye on you for some time, my dear Frey. You make a fine soldier and you seem to be an equally fine human being. In addition to all this you seem to be a thoroughly sociable sort of fellow. In short, it is my view that you're cut out to be an officer. We'll see what can be done about it."

Already by 1935 I had been promoted second lieutenant, after a number of courses through which I passed with flying colors. By 1938 I'd been promoted first lieutenant, partly as a result of my work as adjutant to a training battalion in Leipzig. At the beginning of the war I had the good fortune to take part in the campaign in Poland with

command of a company, and there I won the Iron Cross
First and Second Class. My engagement to Frau Felicitas
Bendler-Trebitz took place at Christmas in the same year.
After the campaign in France, in which I was awarded
the Knight's Cross, I married the lady in question, and then,
after service on the home front, was posted in 1943 to No. 5
Officers' Training School as course commander.

A fine atmosphere in the mess. The commanding officer
was an officer of the good old school, a bachelor, too, who
combined a subtle appreciation of pretty women with a
really sophisticated social sense. An unforgettable first summer party in the mess, extending over the terrace and the
garden. Bright moonlight, balmy night air, the enchanting
sounds of a select military band playing Mozart, Lehar,
Herms, Niel, behind yew hedges. Smart mess uniforms, fash-
ionable evening dresses, bubbling champagne, a splashing
fountain, and there beside it Herr Bendler-Trebitz, landowner
and lord of the manor of Gross- und Klein-Marching, lieutenant of the reserve, in service with our regiment. A nice
man certainly, but nothing compared with his wife, whose
Christian name was Felicitas, and who managed to combine
astonishing charm with nobility and dignity. And the commanding officer, though a confirmed bachelor, cries out
in enthusiasm, "What a woman!"

Hard, unremitting duty of every sort, which nevertheless
proves one long uninterrupted joy. Building for the future
with all its problems—hard weeks, but among them great
moments of relaxation too. And all the time this magic sensation of organizing, of being passionately involved, this
delight in detail. A far cry now from the mercenary spirit
that had once ruled one's life, gone forever the turbulent
youthful phase of storm and stress, almost forgotten now the
minor mistakes and peccadilloes which had been an inevitable part of the sick atmosphere of a republic condemned to
death from the start. All was now crystal clear: self-
improving drill, far-sighted study, a wide-ranging awareness
of responsibility—in short, full consciousness of what it
meant to be a German. And in the rare moments of leisure an
ever-recurring and unforgettable picture—Felicitas!

Friendship with Bendler-Trebitz the next time the reserve
took part in maneuvers. Not a great man, but a good one.
Not exactly what you'd call a full-blooded soldier, but a
really nice fellow. My first invitation to the estates of Gross-
und Klein-Marching. A magnificent property. The impres-

sion previously made on me by Frau Felicitas is reinforced. Seconds in which no word passes but in which looks say everything. No avowal of love, not even a hint of it—simply a demonstration of straightforward, seemly, and respectful friendship. Then the unforgettable May 27, 1939, the conclusion of three days' spring maneuvers. A tremendously good officers' party which lasts right through the night. And as soon as dawn breaks, horse racing. All the sporting instincts of the younger officers are unleashed. Lieutenant-of-the-Reserve Bendler-Trebitz is among them. Zero five forty-eight hours; somebody falls. Laughter at first. Then silence. The fall is fatal. Our friend Bendler-Trebitz is no more. The commanding officer turns to me. "See that his widow is informed."

Then, shortly afterward, almost like a stroke of luck, comes the war, enabling one to get over the tragedy and forget. Continuous fighting all the time—nothing but fighting. For the Führer, the German people, and the German Reich. And for Felicitas, I have to admit in my heart of hearts.

Still, only a few curt postcards from the field as we go from victory to victory . . . the first man to win the Iron Cross Second Class . . . continually advancing . . . again the first to win the Iron Cross First Class . . . no one can dispute our victory . . . permit me . . . respectful greetings.

The first Christmas of the war—in 1939, spent on Frau Bendler-Trebitz's estate. Uncommonly festive, a service in the village church, distribution of presents to the servants, Christmas dinner among a small select circle, with turkey and burgundy. And afterward champagne—just for the two of us. Rustling silk, a crackling hearth. The light of the flames falls on my decorations, and on Felicitas' pure, flushed countenance. Our hands join, quite tenderly and yet with a powerful underlying urgency. And outside in the Silesian winter's night they're singing carols. In the morning we look upon ourselves as engaged.

Brilliant campaign in France! I earn a special reputation for building bridgeheads. Wherever my men and I gain a foothold, there we stay and can't be shifted—not even when savage colonial troops are hurled against us. Glorious fighting spirit. We mow down the tanks in front of us. Slight unpleasantness caused by a painful dispute with an antitank unit which claimed to have destroyed some of the tanks in our bag. Only minor casualties, hardly worth mentioning.

Then the Knight's Cross! Much rejoicing, though some

are envious. We press on regardless, until France lies at our feet. Utterly hopeless soldiers—except for those units confronting me. Then weeks of one long victory celebration. Paris! But I control myself, participate only modestly and in a spirit of curiosity.

For I have but one goal in mind—Felicitas! Felicitas Bendler-Trebitz of Gross- und Klein-Marching, a thousand acres in all with some of the most magnificent breeding stock in Germany. I take her by the hand, and she is mine.

13 *CERTAIN DEMANDS ARE MADE*

"I'D LIKE TO SEE Lieutenant Krafft, please," said the general to Sybille Bachner. Official duty was over for the day, and the headquarters building was beginning to empty.

Sybille Bachner got on to Number 6 Company orderly room and said to the clerk on duty there, "Lieutenant Krafft is requested to report to the general."

The clerk told the orderly corporal and the orderly corporal told the duty cadet. The general's request had meanwhile transformed itself into an order. It now ran, "Lieutenant Krafft is to report to the general."

The duty cadet went in search of Lieutenant Krafft, and announced, "The lieutenant is to go to the general. Immediately!"

This didn't sound particularly encouraging. But encouraging sounds weren't really what one expected from the direction of the general. Krafft nodded as if it were the most natural thing in the world for him to be summoned to commanding officers at all hours of the day.

"Did you say immediately?" he asked.

"Yes," said the duty cadet. "Immediately! It's of the utmost urgency—that's what the orderly corporal said."

"But presumably it will be all right if I just put on my trousers first?"

Krafft was determined not to let himself be surprised by anything, not to let anyone upset his equilibrium. It seemed to him that he had nothing to lose—or rather, so far as he could see at the moment, nothing to gain.

"Right," said the lieutenant, "I'm coming immediately. That's to say in about a quarter of an hour."

The cadet took this simply as a slip of the tongue. He knew that no one kept the general waiting a second longer than was absolutely necessary. But the affair no longer concerned him; he had fulfilled his errand.

Lieutenant Krafft took his time about dressing—ordinary service uniform. Then he rang up Elfrida Rademacher and said, "I expect I'll be a bit late."

"Anything special, Karl?"

"The usual, I expect. Either a severe reprimand or I'll be chucked out. I've got to go and see the general."

"Has Kater had anything to do with this?"

"I hardly think so," said Krafft cheerfully. "This looks less like a backstage intrigue than a straightforward piece of disciplinary action. But the important thing is that you should wait for me."

"With the greatest impatience," she assured him.

"I've been told to report to the general, Fräulein Bachner."

Sybille looked up amiably at Lieutenant Krafft. This was some progress anyway, though still a long way, presumably, from the intimacy of a smile.

Krafft stood by the door waiting. Sybille Bachner gave him a searching look, and then said, "I don't think it was a question of reporting, Lieutenant. The general merely expressed a wish to see you. So you can leave your belt, gloves, and cap here with me in the anteroom."

"You're sure you're not making a mistake, Fräulein Bachner?" he asked.

Sybille Bachner gave a friendly shake of her head and looked at her watch. "Patience for another three minutes, please. The general is just finishing a document."

"And how will you know when he's ready?"

"The general always allots a specific period of time for everything he does, and informs me or the ADC accordingly. Only when we need to know, of course."

Krafft discarded his superfluous gear, and as he did so asked, "Do you have fun in your job here?"

Sybille looked at him in astonishment. "Fun?" she exclaimed in bewilderment. "What do you mean by that?"

"Nothing," Krafft reassured her hurriedly. "It was an unnecessary question."

"I quite agree," said Sybille, looking at him with some misgiving. Then she asked, "Do you know why you're here, actually?"

"Not exactly," said the lieutenant. "But it'll be something stupid I've done—I provide a wide range of choice."

"So do the others," said Sybille. "Only they don't always realize it."

"They're lucky," remarked Krafft.

"Herr Frey and Herr Ratshelm came to see the general this morning," said Sybille Bachner.

"Thanks for the tip," said Krafft. "What can I do for you in return?"

"That's quite simple—forget what I've just told you."

"Already forgotten, Fräulein Bachner. And is there nothing else I can do for you?"

"No," she said.

Her days succeeded each other with deadly monotony. The same thing on each of them: getting up at 0630 hours, 0730 hours breakfast. Work from 0800 hours to 1800 hours. 1830 supper. And after that the inevitable overtime or what went by the name of free time; i.e. mending underclothes, washing stockings, occasionally writing a letter to her parents, now and again a book or a radio concert, from time to time a visit to the movies in the little town below— mostly alone, but sometimes with the ADC's wife.

"You can count on me if you ever need me," said Lieutenant Krafft.

"Thank you," she said. "But I don't need anyone."

"Oh, come on—you're only human."

"Please, Lieutenant Krafft, the general is waiting."

"And what conclusions have you come to, Lieutenant Krafft," asked the general, "after studying the documents in the case of Lieutenant Barkow?"

The lieutenant started. He hadn't been prepared for this. He took three seconds to adapt himself to so surprising a question. Hurriedly he suppressed the arguments he had prepared for the anticipated discussion of his class on etiquette with particular reference to the problem of the bosom and the monocle.

But it didn't escape him that the general's next move was something almost unheard-of: he abandoned his usually stiff, erect attitude, turned his chair around slightly, and crossed his legs.

"At the critical moment," reported the lieutenant, "Section H for Heinrich was divided into two groups. By far the largest group, thirty-two men in all, was already under cover. The remaining eight men helped Lieutenant Barkow with the final preparations for the explosions. In the preliminary preparations—packing the explosives, measuring the length of fuse, introducing the detonator—the whole section had taken part. In the final preparations—laying the charge, connecting the detonator to the fuse, opening up the point at which the fuse was to be lit—only a small group was employed for safety reasons."

"Everything is quite straightforward so far."

"So far, yes, sir. But then, with all preparations concluded, this was what happened. One of the cadets in the group that was by far the larger of the two sprained his ankle. Lieutenant Barkow went over at once and established that the accident in fact was no more serious than that. He then returned to the site of the explosion. As usual, he placed the end of the fuse against the head of a match, and ripped the two together across the face of a matchbox. The eight men ran for cover. Lieutenant Barkow, trusting to the time which it had been calculated it would take the fuse to burn, rose slowly to his feet and equally slowly began to walk away. But then suddenly the explosion occurred."

The general leaned back. He seemed to have closed his eyes. And Krafft too seemed to see what the general saw: eight cadets scurrying for cover against a pale blue sky, greatcoats flapping, arms swinging, feet pounding, and faces stiff and gray in the pale light. A lieutenant standing upright, a thin, sharp silhouette, then walking with remarkably controlled, measured strides and a wry smile on his face at the haste of the men scuttling for cover. And then an ear-splitting explosion, a sudden bright jet of flame, and the lieutenant is hurled into the air with devastating force, his shattered body dashed face-downward to the ground. Everything is wrapped in a cloud of dust and smoke. Then silence.

"Who were these eight?" asked the general quietly.

"Cadets Kramer, Weber, Andreas, Böhmke, Berger, Hochbauer, Mösler, and Rednitz, sir."

"And the man who sprained his ankle?"

"Cadet Amfortas, sir. The sprained ankle turned out later to be only bruised."

"Is there medical evidence?"

"No, sir. Cadet Amfortas didn't report sick. The bruising, though alleged to have been painful, was only temporary. Cadet Amfortas says that he didn't really think it necessary to go to the doctor. Now of course it's too late to get an expert opinion on the matter. There are, it's true, witnesses who maintain they saw the discoloration of the skin."

"Is that all you've found out, Lieutenant Krafft?"

"That's all so far, sir. At any rate that's the only material that's of any use in the entire forty-page document."

"And what other steps have you taken?"

"None, sir, or rather no definite ones."

An icy gray gleam came into the general's eye. "And how were you thinking of proceeding, Lieutenant Krafft?"

"I am trying to get to know the cadets in my section, which seems to me the best basis for further investigation. It'll take time, of course. . . ."

"And time is just what you haven't got."

Lieutenant Krafft said nothing. The general began to resume his usual position. He put both feet on the floor and sat up very straight.

"You haven't got much time, Lieutenant Krafft—especially if you proceed at your present pace. Your company commander and the officer in charge of Number Two Course are neither of them enthusiastic about your performance to date."

Lieutenant Krafft still preferred to remain silent. He was tempted to answer that his superiors' lack of enthusiasm for him was reciprocated, but there would have been little point in this.

The general said, "Within the next few days, possibly even tomorrow, I'm expecting a guest whom I'm going to give you to look after, Lieutenant. This will be Frau Barkow, the mother of the dead lieutenant. I've entrusted this task to you for two reasons. First, you're Lieutenant Barkow's successor—you'll be in the best position to explain to his mother how her son lived here and what he did. Secondly, you have in my opinion special personal qualifications for the job."

"What can I tell Frau Barkow, sir?"

"The official version."

Krafft thereupon felt himself to be dismissed. He rose to his feet, and the general nodded to him confirming the impression. The lieutenant went over to the door preparatory to springing to attention in the approved style. But the general raised a hand.

"Krafft," said the general, and this almost intimate form of address didn't seem to come easily to him, "I hope I can rely on you. But that doesn't mean to say I'm always prepared to shield you in whatever extravagant follies you commit. Only on one specific point—and you know the one I mean—can you count on my unequivocal support. I wish to see the murder of Lieutenant Barkow avenged. For that I need you. And I therefore expect you not to take any unwise risks. Don't let me down, Krafft!"

The lieutenant sprang to attention without replying.

"Lieutenant Krafft," said the general finally, "please don't forget this; your task is clear and your time is short, and you no longer have any way of avoiding it."

"Do you happen to have a brandy within reach, Fräulein Bachner?" asked Lieutenant Krafft.

Sybille Bachner looked at him closely.

"Or anything else one can drink? Methylated spirits would do!"

He felt sure of getting a firm refusal. Instead, she said, "If there's nothing else for it then I can help you. I think in the circumstances I can take the responsibility." And without more ado she fetched a bottle and a glass out of the ADC's desk.

"Tell me, excellent one," asked Krafft, leaning against a filing cabinet slightly exhausted. "How does the general react when someone fails to respect his wishes or instructions?"

"I really don't know, Lieutenant," said Sybille Bachner. "Such a thing has never happened so far."

She held a well-filled glass out toward Krafft and looked at him in a friendly, inquiring sort of way. The lieutenant drank the glass down at a gulp. Comforting warmth trickled though his veins. Yet he felt no real relief.

"What sort of role am I meant to play?" asked Krafft angrily. "Am I some sort of blindfolded padre armed with an automatic pistol? Or a Santa Claus who hangs hand grenades on the Christmas tree? What do you take me for, Fräulein Bachner?"

"For a man who's clever enough to see that the general never makes unjustified demands."

Sybille Bachner now smiled slightly. She's as sparing as the general with her expressions of feeling, thought Krafft—it seems to be a quality that rubs off. But at any rate she smiled. Certainly in this room she had experienced every imaginable reaction from officers who had just been flattened by the general—the proud, the stupid, the faithful, the cringers, the stuck-up, the fools, the unconcerned, the intriguers—and all said, "Very good, sir." And Sybille smiled.

"Perhaps you ought to devote rather more of your time to your general, Fräulein Bachner—in a human way, I mean." Krafft intended no harm. He felt provoked, and wanted someone on whom he could unload part of his resentment. "You ought to try cheering him up, he seems badly in need of it."

"That's a mean thing to say," said Sybille Bachner.

"Oh, really," said Krafft losing patience. "I've already told you once you shouldn't try and play the icy virgin around here. After all you're not made of typewriter keys. You're a woman! Why don't you behave like one? It would be a blessing for all of us—for the general too."

"Perhaps you'll take the opportunity of telling this to the general himself next time you see him!" said Sybille Bachner with great control. She seemed to have turned rather pale, and her little fists were tightly clenched.

Although Krafft sensed that he had once again made himself an enemy, her remark sobered him and restored his sense of proportion.

"You're quite right, Fräulein Bachner," he said. "And I'm a cowardly swine. I shoot my mouth off here all right, but I should really be doing it on the other side of that door."

"You're improving," said Sybille Bachner.

"People expect too much of me," said Krafft. "I'm a wretched sort of ass, really. And what's worse I know it! You don't realize how I envy those others who sleep with a clear conscience, confident that the eye of the good God—or even the general—rests on them with satisfaction. But in times like these you need the simplicity of a child if you're not to find the prevailing state of affairs utterly nauseating."

"I'll gladly give you another brandy," said Sybille Bachner, and she smiled again, though this time her smile was free of mockery and even revealed a certain affection.

"You're not so bad," said Krafft. "But perhaps you don't realize it."

"Well, I do now," she said lightheartedly.

"Good, well don't forget it again."

"Look in here from time to time to make sure I don't."

The ground floor corridor in the staff headquarters building lay still and deserted, like the interior of some factory at night. A blue-painted bulb burned dimly, its light only just managing to reach as far as the bare walls and dark doorways.

The administrative offices, which were situated in this corridor, were empty of human beings. Only through the keyhole of the library came the gleam of an almost imperceptible ray of light. Elfrida Rademacher was waiting there for Karl Krafft.

"I'm sorry," he said, "I simply couldn't get here any earlier."

"You're here now anyway," she said, "and that's all that matters."

Elfrida Rademacher didn't complain. She never asked questions. She wasn't the sort of girl who went in for moods or hysterical scenes or fits of gloom. In fact Krafft realized that he was a lucky man.

"It's got very late," he said, looking around the library with an experienced eye. He checked the blackout curtains, locked the door, and hung his cap over the keyhole. Then he took off his tunic and draped it around the table lamp. Finally he collected all the cushions he could lay his hands on, together with some mats and typewriter pads, and arranged them into a bed. Elfrida handed him the blanket she had brought and he spread it out.

"Watching you, one might almost think you did this sort of thing every day of the week," she said.

"Well, dismiss such thoughts," he muttered. "Help me spread this blanket out."

She knelt beside him. "Do we have to whisper?" she asked.

"You can shout if you like," he said. "That is if you feel like having spectators."

Elfrida realized that in the circumstances secrecy was indispensable. She sighed. "Now at least I see some of the point of marriage," she said.

Krafft didn't altogether like the sound of this remark. Talk of marriage always made him feel uncomfortable. So he changed the subject and said, "A clever idea of yours, getting hold of the library like this."

"Oh, plenty of others have had the idea before me," she said. "The corporal in charge tactfully rents the place out in return for cigarettes."

"Quiet," he said suddenly, seizing her by the arm.

They listened. Nothing stirred in the silence of the night. They could hear nothing but the sound of their own breathing.

"You're particularly cautious today, Karl," said Elfrida.

"I wouldn't like to lose you, Elfrida, that's why."

"You'll never lose me if you don't want to. And this library isn't the only place where we can meet, after all. A friend of mine who works in the tailor's shop is married and has a little room down in the town, with her husband of course. But he works on the railway and so is away a lot. And this friend of mine likes to go to the movies. So if we pay for her ticket and give her something to smoke or drink as well, she'd let us have the room for an hour or so every now and again."

"Not a bad idea," agreed Krafft. "I find it too uncomfortable here in barracks, and it's too risky too. My position's precarious enough as it is. If I get caught in a compromising situation like this I'm done for."

"Come on," said Elfrida with a smile. "Don't let's wait till they catch us."

She lay back and pulled him toward her. Krafft breathed in the scent of her body and slipped his hands expertly over it. He knew it well, though somehow it always seemed new to him.

At that moment there came a knock on the door.

The lovers started up in terror. It took them a second or two to force themselves back to reality. Krafft signed to Elfrida to stay still. He himself rose cautiously to his feet and called out, "Who's there? I don't want to be disturbed. I've got work to do."

"Come off it," cried a jovial, rather ponderous voice. "Is that what you call work?"

There seemed to Krafft to be something familiar about this voice. He looked across at Elfrida, who nodded to him and began to smile as if relieved. She got up and stood there nonchalantly, still half undressed. Finally, hardly troubling to lower her voice, she said, "Captain Kater—who else?"

"Come on, open up, Krafft," blustered Kater quite genially from the door. "I only want a few words with you."

"I'm sorry, Captain," said Lieutenant Krafft through the locked door. "I must ask you to respect the fact that I'm not alone."

"But I know that, my dear boy! I even know the lady's name. My regards to Fräulein Rademacher; she needn't feel embarrased for my sake."

"One moment, please," said Lieutenant Krafft, helping Elfrida on with her dress, and looking around for his boots.

Elfrida didn't seem a bit embarrassed. She seemed almost to be enjoying the situation. And as she folded up the blanket she said gaily, "What's he got on us?"

"I really didn't want to disturb you," Captain Kater reassured them.

Some sort of order had by now been restored to the room. Kater entered jauntily, wearing his most accommodating smile and carrying a square-shaped bottle of what was presumably Cointreau under his arm. He looked up at each of them, at Elfrida in an intimate paternal way, at Krafft knowingly, understandingly, as man to man.

"I'm really terribly sorry if I'm too early," exclaimed Kater with a wink. "But I wanted to be quite sure not to be too late."

"How did you know we were here?"

"But really, my dear fellow, one isn't as stupid as all that; one has one's sources. Why don't we sit down?"

The captain moved fussily about, switching on the center light, drawing three chairs around a desk, and placing the bottle of Cointreau on top of it. He motioned them toward it.

Elfrida sat down. Krafft found that the bottle, which was almost full, made the captain's presence somewhat more endurable, and so sat down too.

"I'm really your friend, you know," Kater assured him, fishing three schnapps glasses out of his trouser pocket. "I have nothing but your best interests at heart."

"Then you shouldn't have disturbed us."

Kater let out a bleat to show that he had seen the joke and liked it. He filled the glasses to the brim and pushed one over toward each of them.

"You mustn't think," Kater assured them, "that I would ever turn a situation of this sort to my own advantage unless formally compelled to do so. In general, I'm what you might call a gentleman of the old school. I know when to keep my mouth shut. And I wish you every conceivable joy from the bottom of my heart."

"On what terms, Captain?"

Kater didn't reply at once, he found himself distracted for the moment. He couldn't keep his eyes off Elfrida, who was quite unconcernedly straightening her stockings. She'd had to put them on again in too much of a hurry and they had slipped sideways. She stretched out her legs, first the right and then the left, lifting them slightly so that the tops of her thighs became visible. Her hands slid playfully, almost tenderly, along them. And while thus engaged she looked up into Kater's face. He grabbed hurriedly for his glass.

"Here's to us!" he cried, drinking, and choking as he did so.

Krafft smiled at Elfrida and drank too. He had seen at once what Elfrida was up to; it was her way of getting her own back for the interruption. Finally with a sudden gesture she pulled her skirt over her knee and reached for her glass.

After they had drunk, Captain Kater cleared his throat

and said, "Why should I want to make terms? Nothing could be further from my mind. It's true I've caught you both *in flagrante delicto*, but why should I exploit that fact, so long as we remain good friends? Of course I could make things difficult for you, my dear Krafft, one way and another; there are a number of people who are not exactly well disposed toward you. They'd be only too delighted to pick on this little incident, for which there are other witnesses besides myself—the corporal in charge of these rooms, for instance, whom you bribed with cigarettes. But don't let's talk about that!"

"All right, come on," said Krafft grimly, for he realized he had fallen into a trap. "What is it you want from me?"

"Nothing, my dear fellow, really nothing. Not for the moment, anyway. But I'll let you know in plenty of time when there's any little thing you can do for me. And you, too, of course, most excellent Fräulein Rademacher. Yes, and what I also wanted to know, my good fellow, was this. I understand you're to look after Frau Barkow when she arrives tomorrow?"

"I understand so, Captain."

"This interests me—me and a number of my close friends. For purely legal reasons, so to speak, and reasons of national interest, though of course that won't mean much to you. What's certain so far, anyway, is that the general has got his staff to reserve a room for Frau Barkow—the best room in the best hotel. What's this lady coming here for, actually?"

"To visit her son's grave and to see how he lived here, and where he worked—what else, do you suppose?"

"But rather a lot of attention for the next of kin of one dead soldier, don't you think? Where would we be if every funeral were immediately followed by a visit to the training school with a special officer's escort and dinner with the commanding officer? It must mean that there's some quite special, quite private, relationship here."

"What makes you think that?"

"Do you think I haven't noticed that the general has developed an unusual interest in the case of Lieutenant Barkow? Why is he doing that? Just because he's the commanding officer here? Or because Lieutenant Barkow stood particularly close to him? I mean in a human way. Intimate, one might say. Get me?"

"You believe him capable of that?"

"I believe anyone capable of anything," said Kater, refilling his glass. "Look here, my dear Krafft, the general always lived like a monk. He's supposed to have never so much as laid a finger on the pretty Sybille Bachner. But when this Lieutenant Barkow turned up here he saw him several times. More than that, he even received him in his private rooms, which no one else ever visits. And quite candidly, and wholly between ourselves, my dear fellow, I'll tell you something else. The general requested Lieutenant Barkow for his training school in the first place. What do you say now?"

"That I couldn't care less about the whole affair! That's all I have to say, Captain."

"As far as I'm concerned, my dear fellow, you can say and think what you like and do whatever you want. Alone or with Fräulein Rademacher. But if you succeed in discovering the exact nature of the relationship between the general and Lieutenant Barkow, I shall be blind and deaf so far as this evening's concerned. Do I make myself clear?"

"Crystal clear. Beyond any possibility of misunderstanding."

"Then we're agreed. Let's drink to our future cooperation! But now I won't disturb you any longer—you'll certainly want to be left alone for a while. Quite undisturbed this time too. I guarantee you that. You can keep the bottle. So—sleep well, my dears!"

14 THE PRICE OF IT ALL

"You just lie there," said Marion Feders to her husband. "I'll do everything."

"I can't sleep anyhow," said Captain Feders.

"Just lie there all the same. Look at the ceiling and try and doze."

"That's no good," said Feders. "I start thinking when I do that."

"Then think of something pleasant."

"I can't," he said. "There isn't anything pleasant."

The first faint light of the new day came through the window into the little apartment. Feders blinked and turned over. But now it wasn't the light that worried him, but his wife standing by the washbasin.

Feders rolled over onto his back. It was a dull, leaden-gray morning. The heaviness of the night still hung about the room. He closed his eyes.

The morning sounds immediately seemed to grow louder —water being splashed onto a human body and dripping down it while busy hands rubbed the skin, soap being picked up and put down, the padding of naked feet. And these feet—Feders heard them clearly—crossed the wet floor, walked over a carpet, slid into slippers, and could be heard again on the stone floor.

"Wrap your dressing gown well around you," he said. "Put a towel around your neck and another around your head."

"I'm not cold, Eric."

"Do it all the same," he said. Feders hadn't looked at her. He always knew what she was doing and what she wasn't doing. He could keep his eyes shut and see her clearly in front of him. All that was necessary was that she should be somewhere close.

"I'm sorry," she said, looking at him full of remorse.

"You've nothing to be sorry for," said Feders. He continued to look at the ceiling, seeming to see Marion's face there. "You haven't the slightest reason to apologize for anything, as far as I'm concerned."

"Good," she said, and went into the next room. "I'll put a towel around me."

With tired, mechanical gestures she prepared the coffee. Her face was gray and flaccid.

Then through the open doorway she saw that Feders had got up. He went over to the washbasin and stripped to the waist. And she looked at his heavy but well-proportioned shoulders, his powerful chest, his sure, sinewy hands. She went over to the door.

"You're beautiful," she said.

"You look after the coffee," he replied without looking up.

"I love you!"

"I know, in the same way as one loves a picture or a piece of music." He spoke with bitter mockery.

"You want people to hurt you."

"A wounded man has to bear pain. You can't get away from that. Besides, the water for the coffee is boiling, and that's the most important thing at the moment. I have to get to work."

"What is it you want from me?" she asked uneasily.

"Nothing but breakfast at the moment."

"I have only to see you," cried Captain Feders to Lieutenant Krafft, "to be reminded that this world is by no means the tragic place it generally seems to be. How do you intend to entertain me today?"

"There's something special I want to ask of you, Captain."

"A bad start!" said Feders. "I'm no Santa Claus."

Captain Feders was standing by the window in the corridor of the classroom block smoking a cigarette, for he had just announced the usual break between two tactics classes. The cadets stood about in groups at a respectful distance, puzzling over a so-called "brain teaser" their tactics instructor had set them in case they found the break "too boring."

"May I attend your next class, Captain?"

Feders looked amused. "You don't mean to say you wish to check up on my methods and capabilities!"

"No, I think I know enough about them," said the lieutenant. "I merely intend to take a closer look at some of our cadets, if you'll let me."

"But you see this flock of sheep day in and day out, from first thing in the morning till last thing at night. Don't you have enough of them?"

"When I'm with the cadets, Captain, I'm busy either supervising them or teaching them. I've gradually discovered how they react to me and my way of doing things. Now I'd very much like to know how they behave with other officers."

"And so you come to me of all people, Krafft? Even though you know I'm not in favor of the individual approach. With me everyone reacts exactly as I want him to, and not as he wants. But if you really want to see this, then, by all means."

"I'm much obliged to you," said Krafft. And he said it almost respectfully and with a certain diffidence. "All I want is just to be able to sit in a corner."

Captain Feders gave the lieutenant a searching look, and a deep furrow appeared across his brow. "It is of course ludicrous for me to suppose that you might be wanting to spy on me," he said. "In your situation that would be absurd. Besides, I don't think you're capable of it. Stupidity yes, but meanness, no. Even though you've managed to discover a good deal about me one way and another."

"If you wish to talk about that, Captain . . ."

"I don't, Lieutenant. But I'm not avoiding the subject either."

"I've been thinking over all you said to me the other night.

And I believe that in your position I would think and act in much the same way as you."

The furrow on Feders' brow grew deeper, and he clenched his teeth, but a new light came into his eye. He said nothing, presumably because at that moment some of the cadets walked past. Then he looked out at the weak February sunshine creeping slowly across the dirty snow. Finally he turned to Krafft and asked:

"Do you know the Villa Rosenhügel?"

"No, Captain."

"I'll show it to you, Krafft, and then you'll know more about me. It'll be anything but a treat for you, but you'll find it instructive. I can guarantee you that."

"I'm always ready to learn."

"So I see. It seems to me you've grasped even the really important point of learning from other people's stupidity and meannesses. But let's get on with the class now. Got any special requests? I mean do you want me to lead out any particular cadets for you? Don't stand on ceremony. Just give me any names you want."

Lieutenant Krafft hesitated for only a moment before pulling a slip of paper out of his sleeve and writing eight names on it, and then at the last moment a ninth. He handed this slip of paper to the captain.

Feders cast a quick glance at the list and broke into a smile. He looked at Krafft in astonishment, as if he were some fabulous animal.

"Just like you, Krafft! Exactly as I thought—you're tilting at windmills."

"I think it would be truer to say I'm on a rat hunt."

"You're a Don Quixote," said Feders stubbornly. "But I've always had a weakness for him. Come on, then, I'll put a little wind into the sails of your windmill for you."

"Class, attention!" cried the section senior.

Captain Feders entered the classroom like some sort of commander-in-chief and waved the section senior aside before he could make his report. The cadets slumped into their places.

Feders offered Lieutenant Krafft his chair, but the sorely tried cadets had no time to puzzle over the presence of their section officer. Captain Feders provided an immediate diversion with his opening questions.

"Kramer, what's our subject for today?"

The latter jumped up as if stung by a wasp and cried, "A company is moving into new quarters. Fighting on home territory, or on maneuvers. What sort of billet does the officer reserve for himself?"

"Rubbish," said Feders crisply. "Kindly listen more carefully in the future. We're not on a hotel-management course here. We don't reserve rooms, we requisition them, allot them, appropriate them."

Thus at one stroke the section senior, the experienced corporal of many years' service, was laid low. Yet no one seemed particularly affected, Krafft saw this clearly. Each cadet was busy with his own thoughts. All sat there ready to leap to their feet; and their faces showed that for almost all of them it would be a leap in the dark.

In an astonishingly short space of time Krafft learned how right they were to be so hopelessly resigned to their fate.

"Right then, Amfortas—what sort of billet do you appropriate as an officer? Always assuming that you do ever succeed in becoming an officer. Speak up, man. What sort of billet?"

"The one I'm allotted."

"Utter drivel, Amfortas!" said Feders with biting sarcasm but without raising his voice for an instant. "In general the job of requisitioning billets is carried out by a corporal. No officer allows himself to be "allotted" a room by a subordinate. He selects one for himself. But what sort does he select for himself, Böhmke?"

"The officer always takes over the worst billet, sir," cried the cadet resolutely, "because he has to set an example."

"But not an example in stupidity, man! You're at an officers' training school here, not a camp for aspiring martyrs."

Captain Feders laid about him with devastating accuracy— quick, cool, and precise. Krafft realized at once that there was no one in the section who was a match for their tactics instructor, or if there was he was taking pains to conceal the fact. Feders not only made it crystal clear to his men that an officer was always right, but also showed them how he must set about convincing his subordinates of the fact.

The cadets stared at the captain like rabbits at a snake. Of course certain nuances also made themselves felt. Some cadets, like Amfortas, Andreas, and Berger, simply demonstrated their blind subservience. Others, like Kramer, Weber, and Böhmke, subordinated themselves to authority unconditionally, or at least without putting up any sort of fight. Still others, like Mösler and Rednitz, searched for loopholes, but even they didn't have much hope. And one or two others, like Hochbauer, seemed to want only to be put to the test, without any allowance being made for them.

The captain's next victim was Cadet Berger, who like all the others shot up in his place like a jack-in-the-box. He had pale blond hair and was tremendously keen. He assumed a rather unnatural attitude and took a deep breath as if about to burst. "I should take over a billet of medium standard," he said. "In order to underline the sense of community, of comradeship with my men."

"You're not called upon to underline anything, idiot. You're not an accountant. The only true sense of community is to be found in a common grave, and you don't demonstrate the spirit of comradeship by your choice of beds. Next. You, Rednitz."

"I would take over the best billet, of course," said the latter unhesitatingly.

"Why, Rednitz?" pursued the captain immediately. "Anything to do with the fact that it's about the only choice now left to you?"

"Because only the best is good enough for an officer, Captain."

"Very convenient for you, I'm sure. I suppose you'd like to fight your war from the officers' mess? Never take the field without a portable phonograph, a crate of wine, a liberal supply of eau de cologne, and an officers' brothel, eh? Nothing but the best for you, I suppose. If that's the reason you want to become officers, gentlemen, your prospects aren't very bright."

Captain Feders played this devastating game for a full quarter of an hour. In this astonishingly short space of time he had made mincemeat of all nine cadets on Krafft's list. All the other cadets were by now thoroughly intimidated. Only now did Feders allow them to voice one or two suggestions to which he was prepared to give partial approval.

And the final answer went something like this: The officer takes over the best billet because he has the most to do and therefore has to make do with relatively short periods of rest—in other words just because he *is* an officer and not an NCO or a ranker.

The cadets scribbled furiously away with their pencils. It was as if they wanted to get this sort of information down once and for all, so that they could then safely take it to war with them.

When this matter had been dealt with the captain gave

the order, "Maps out! Message pads ready! We're using number six seven four."

If possible, the cadets now looked even more worried than before. However, they tried to convey the right impression of cheerfulness and keenness. Any outward signs of depression lost them marks at once. Major Frey had made this unmistakably clear to them at the beginning of the course, with one of his celebrated "maxims for all occasions."

Captain Feders would never have used such words. He couldn't care less what his cadets thought of him. The only thing that mattered to him was that he should have them under his thumb. Whereas hitherto he had merely initiated a number of local individual actions, he was now moving over to an attack on a broad front, with the assistance of map number 674.

This belonged to the series commonly known as the "Dunces." For they had been prepared as elementary teaching media. They did not show any of the usual features and were divided up into special numbered "zones" in which certain areas were enclosed by red and blue circles and squares. These could at will be designated by the teacher either as zones that had been cordoned off, or as assembly zones, operational zones, etc.

Captain Feders said, "Movement of a company from assembly zone A into action against zone F. I want you to give the necessary company orders, please. You have fifteen minutes, starting from now."

The captain placed his watch down on the desk and appeared to devote himself to the study of some manual in front of him, but instead of reading he was really keeping a close eye on the cadets.

Lieutenant Krafft was doing the same thing. He turned from one to the other. Mösler and Rednitz were copying from each other quite shamelessly; Böhmke stared in a helpless trance into space; Weber was sweating blood trying to think what to say; Andreas and Amfortas wore expressions of extreme determination, though it wasn't at all clear what they were determined about; Hochbauer seemed to be one of the few working away with real concentration, presumably because he knew exactly what he was about.

When thirteen minutes had gone by the captain said, "Time's up, Kramer, collect the work please, but not Mösler's or Rednitz's, which'll be worthless—they've been copying from each other. In my classes everyone produces his own muck, and I'd like you all to take note of the fact!"

And while the section senior was busy grabbing the answers from those cadets who were still trying to make last-minute corrections, the captain began dictating, "Tomorrow's task: In the newly occupied position at zone F seven, Number Two Section is eliminated. Provide the necessary replacements from combat, ration, and baggage supply lines; formulate the relevant company orders. Right, that's all. Off with you. I don't want to see a man in the place in two minutes' time."

In two minutes' time the classroom was clear of everyone but Feders and Krafft. The captain said, "You can take a look through this muck of theirs if you like. Take it to your room with you."

"You'll be wanting it back at once, of course, Captain?"

"Hell, no!" said Feders, packing up his things. "Though I might possibly use it as fuel for the stove, I suppose."

"But don't you tell them what's wrong with their work next day?" asked Krafft in slight astonishment.

"I tell them how it should have been done, which is quite enough. These fellows' efforts are all hopeless—if they're not utterly wrong they're incomplete or imprecise in some way. And they know this perfectly well, which is why they're shitting in their pants with fright. Which, in turn, is exactly the effect I wish to produce. And why? To give them a foretaste of the hell which awaits them as officers. I want to make them realize the full depths of misery they're in for. They and all of us. Come with me to the Villa Rosenhügel and I'll show you what I mean. I've ordered a car, it'll only take us half an hour."

The car which Feders had ordered was a small Mercedes convertible, and half an hour later it drove out of the barracks. A heavily muffled lance-corporal was at the wheel, wearing a fur cap with the ear flaps down and ear muffs underneath. Feders and Krafft sat behind wrapped in their greatcoats. It was icily cold and their breath froze on the air.

Skirting Wildlingen-am-Main, they headed for the main road to Würzburg. Low, gentle hills were all about them, and snowdrifts created a melancholy effect.

"Damn cold," said Feders. "I must get the cadets to understand what it's like when the ground is frozen as hard as this. Blast effect is increased terrifically and the digging of graves made much more difficult."

They soon left the highway again, for a delightful little side road leading toward Ipfhofen. A magnificent wine was grown hereabouts, but the hills were bare and bleak now, and the posts between the vines, in their rigid regularity, were like the endless rows of crosses in a military cemetery.

"What do you think of Hochbauer, Captain?" asked Krafft cautiously.

"Far and away the best man in the section," said Feders unhesitatingly. "He's got a real gift for tactics. Thinks clearly, knows what he wants, plenty of determination. And however much you may dislike him, Krafft, he's a born officer."

"What do you make of his character?"

"I don't care a damn about that, Krafft. What's the point of bothering about character when the only thing that matters is ability, energy, and powers of endurance. The most important thing for an officer is to be able to give orders quickly, clearly, sensibly, and of course correctly. Character alone will help you neither to hold a position nor to take one."

"But surely there are certain qualities . . ."

"Which are of absolutely secondary importance, from my point of view as tactics instructor. What is it you want of an officer, Krafft? Goodness, understanding, love of his fellow men, decency? Loyalty? Devotion? Come off it. That's not the way to start wars, and certainly not the way to win them. Qualities of character indeed! Try looking for such qualities among your superior officers, you fantasist. Best of all start right at the top with your supreme commander-in-chief. I beg your pardon, Krafft?"

"Never mind," said the latter.

"I agree with you," declared Feders. "Let's stick to our cadets, then. Believe me, Krafft, if there's one quality an officer has to have it's toughness. It's your only chance in war. War is merciless, cruel, nauseating, and in it one either dies or one survives; though that isn't quite the whole story, Krafft, for there are some who survive even when they're done for, as you'll be seeing for yourself in the next half hour or so."

They drove on in silence through tiny little winegrowing towns which still breathed the air of the Middle Ages—forgotten corners of a land heading fast for destruction, pastoral idylls in a world strewn with corpses and now invaded by this field-gray convertible, a wholly foreign object, like some beetle crawling across a nursery floor.

They followed a turning off the road, until they came to a villa which stood on a hill in front of them. A place of retreat, it seemed, steeped in romantic charm, looking in the distance as if it were tied up in the silvery gray ribbon of a bend in the River Main.

Feders spoke acidly. "Don't you feel there's something missing? The sound of harp strings or the merry ring of sleigh bells perhaps, for it's winter, after all."

At the first sight of this delightful villa Krafft felt prepared for anything. A discreet officer's brothel perhaps, or a concealed supply dump, or even a secret experimental station. The place seemed deserted.

"This villa," said Captain Feders looking toward it, "is like a sort of church for me. Last night you saw me at the end of my tether, a babbling, whimpering, helpless wreck of a human being. But I don't often get these depressions, and when they do threaten to attack me I fly here. The man in charge of this place is the only friend I have in the world."

The closer they got to the Villa Rosenhügel, the clearer it became that it was situated in a zone of complete isolation. There was a barrier across the road, beside which was a notice saying "No entry," and a little further on here was a high, single-strand barbed-wire fence.

The car came to a halt. Feders jumped out and went up to the gate, where there was a speaking tube. He pressed the buzzer.

"Name please," grated a harsh voice from a loudspeaker.

"Captain Feders and two companions."

"Pass, please," said the voice after a pause.

Feders jumped into the car again. There was a whirring sound and the gate opened automatically. Slowly—speed limit ten miles an hour—the car moved up to the villa. Feders and Krafft climbed out. The driver of the car stayed where he was. Despite the cold he seemed to have no wish to accompany the two officers, possibly having been forbidden to do so when he came here before. He stamped his feet and lit a cigarette, putting the burnt-out match back into his pocket.

"This is our destination, then," said Captain Feders. "Or perhaps really I should say here we are, at the end of the road."

The hall, which was painted off-white, was empty. Its stone floor was partly covered with sacking mats. There was that pungent, stifling smell in the air which immediately revealed the building's identity; it was a hospital. A military hospital. But one dominated by a heavy silence.

Then, hurrying toward them out of the shadows, there appeared a large, lean man in officer's uniform. He was wearing a white coat opened down the front, which flapped about him. There was a curious rocking quality about this person's movements, though they were quite unrhythmical. His head seemed to hang from his shoulders at an unnatural angle.

And as this man came closer, Krafft saw that he had no face. Above his shoulders hung a pale pink, swollen lump of flesh, in which one eye gleamed disproportionately large —a bright blue eye that was at the same time both shrewd and benevolent.

"May I introduce my friend Dr. Krüger," said Feders formally. "Lieutenant Krafft, one of my brother officers."

The doctor put out a hand to greet Krafft. It was a sensitive, very finely jointed hand, with elegant fingers full of tenderness and strength, the hand of a violinist or a surgeon.

A slit opened in the swollen lump of flesh which had once been a face. (And what sort of face must it once have been, if the beauty of the hands was anything to go by?) The doctor said, "It would be presumptuous to welcome you to this place, Herr Krafft. But what I usually say to the very few visitors who come here is, try not to despair, all the same."

The lieutenant looked around uncertainly at Captain Feders, and the doctor, catching the look, asked, "Haven't you given our guest any idea of what to expect here, Eric?"

"Of course not," said Feders. "He's got to learn to see the world as it is, however painful the experience. What you'd call shock therapy, I think, Heinz."

Doctor Krüger nodded thoughtfully. Then he looked at Lieutenant Krafft as if about to give him a medical examination. His eye flashed crystal clear. Again the swollen slit that had once been a mouth opened.

"My friend Eric Feders and I have known each other since our schooldays. We were always inseparable. We had the best school reports, did best at games, were the most popular dancers, married the most beautiful women—and were both mutilated by the war at almost the same time. Ever since then we've tried to discover a new and different life together; but still can't get away from the old one. Every now and again Feders feels the understandable need to try and find someone who can understand us, and brings him here."

"No lectures please, Heinz," said Captain Feders. "All I've discovered about this fellow Krafft is that he's got a reasonably useful brain which I don't want to see atrophy.

But it's full of rather woolly ideals, and the only way to remove them is by a brutally ruthless piece of surgery."

The doctor's single eye now seemed to be smiling at the lieutenant. And in his subdued voice, which was entirely without intonation of any sort, he said, "If, Herr Krafft, you've never seen what I am about to show you or perhaps don't even know of its existence, then you will be appalled. No other reaction is really possible. And perhaps it's as well for you to know that you can see but can't be seen. You're separated from what you see by a sheet of glass which from the other side appears to be a dark wall. The voices you hear come from loudspeakers which we've installed for our own purpose. If you hear no voices, it means these loudspeakers are switched off. Come along, then, my friend."

The doctor led the way, followed by Krafft, with Feders bringing up the rear. They walked through the off-white hall into a narrow corridor, the walls of which were smooth and cold and dazzlingly bright. Suddenly they came out into a sort of shed, where the doctor opened an iron door and motioned Krafft inside.

The lieutenant entered a narrow room in which a man in a white apron was sitting. His spine was twisted at an awkward angle and he was hunched forward almost motionless. His head seemed to be sunk deep into the shoulders as if he had no neck. The man, who was terribly deformed, had a job here as a hospital orderly.

In front of him stood an apparatus consisting of switches, a clock, an amplifier, and a microphone. The hospital orderly turned his body in a series of twitches and looked up at the newcomers. Then as if wishing to attract the lieutenant's attention, he twitched around again and looked across at the long wall. Krafft followed his gaze and saw a wall entirely made of glass, which was rather like a shop window. Behind it was a room with greenish walls and beds in it—simple narrow beds with tall sides like children's cots. All of them were freshly made and empty.

Krafft looked and saw a number of bundles hanging from the ceiling; clumsy, angular, box-shaped bundles dangling there helplessly in space. They were wrapped in a striped pale material—material rather like pajamas, and were enclosed in harnesses made of webbing or leather, like wide-meshed nets holding a ball.

These bundles, as Lieutenant Krafft now saw, moved to and fro—not all of them, but some, slowly turning from one side to the other as they swung through the air. And these bundles had heads. Human heads. These were human beings hanging there.

"My patients," said the doctor softly just behind Krafft.

These were bodies with heads but without limbs, wrapped in pajamas, trussed up in harnesses, and suspended from hooks like meat at the butcher's.

"I have two more wards like this," said the doctor.

These human beings seemed to be talking to each other. They opened their lips—one to the breadth of a mere slot, another quite wide. A third mouth seemed to gape open as if laughing. Or was it a yawn? Or a scream? It was impossible to tell, for all this took place in a sinister, breathtaking silence. The hospital orderly had switched off the loudspeakers.

"They are creatures like all other human beings," said the doctor. "Only they can neither walk nor take hold of things. They are deprived of the power of movement and are therefore helpless as children, though with the minds, the feelings and the needs of twenty- and thirty-year-old men."

The lieutenant felt as if all strength were being drained from his body. His limbs seemed to turn to water, there was a great emptiness in his brain that made him reel. He felt a hand grasp him and steady him.

"Basketmen," said Captain Feders. "The final fiendish cruelty devised by war. Many of these people lack not only arms and legs, but lungs, throats, stomachs, aural passages, and sexual organs."

"Stop!" said Krafft in an agonized voice. "Stop. It's enough!"

"These men," said Captain Feders, "are counted as dead, or missing, fallen for the Fatherland. But they're alive, all right —that is, if one can call this life. And if by any chance they should not one day be translated for medical reasons or on grounds of comfort to what must undoubtedly be a better life in the hereafter—how are they to complete this so-called life of theirs on earth? In their baskets? Helpless as infants? Hopeless, no longer even capable of committing suicide. With neither woman, nor friend, nor family, to look after them, no one but soldiers, the archaccomplices of war, themselves deformed, disfigured, and mutilated."

Krafft turned away. His face was ashen gray.

"And now, Krafft," said Captain Feders with passionate intensity, "see if you can be completely lighthearted for a

single second ever in your life again. If you can, then—"
He fell silent.

"Come on," said the doctor, gently leading Krafft out.
"Don't say anything. Just think about it. Then perhaps I'll
see you here again one day, and will bid you welcome."

15 *A LADY SHOULDN'T FORGET HERSELF*

"Archibald!" cried the major's wife.

Her husband didn't answer. He was never there when she
needed him, as she had been noticing more and more often
recently. The guest list for her party lay before her, and it
presented her with a special problem.

"Archibald!" she called out again.

With a certain relief she heard a door shut. Footsteps could
be heard shuffling down the corridor. The major came into
the bedroom.

Frau Felicitas was at him at once. "Archibald," she said,
"I have an urgent matter to discuss with you."

The major sat down on his bed to change his socks. Hearing himself addressed in this rather peremptory tone he
looked up resentfully. Since getting to know Modersohn, he
had wished that, as with the general, people could only speak
to him when he had given them express permission to do so.
But after all he wasn't a general, and what's more he was
married.

"Yes, what can I do for you, my dear Felicitas?" he asked
co-operatively.

"Can't we leave this Lieutenant Krafft out?" she suggested.

"I'm afraid not," said the major with some regret.

"He'll upset my little party altogether," pleaded the major's
wife.

Her evening parties took place every other Friday. These
occasions had been entirely her own idea. The major had
merely had to agree to them, and had been willing enough to
do so, for in this way the wife of the commanding officer of
Number 2 Course proved not only that she was the first
lady of the training school but also that she knew how to
wield a corresponding influence.

"I wish I could spare you this fellow Krafft," the major
assured her, "but there's a question of principle here, my

dear Felicitas. So far, in a most wonderful way, you've never made any exception of anyone, and in spite of considerable difficulties you've always managed to make your parties a success."

Frau Frey nodded thoughtfully.

"You must know, Archibald, that I've invited only seven young ladies so far." In her view this was the most the society of Wildlingen had to offer. "But if this Krafft person comes there'll be eight unmarried officers all together, which is one too many."

"Aha," said the major with some interest.

"Of course," said Frau Felicitas, "every officer must escort his own lady, or there'll be a serious danger of flirtations getting out of hand."

"Well, what about your niece, Barbara?"

"Out of the question!" she said. "Barbara will be badly needed in the kitchen. I couldn't possibly do without her. Besides, you'll simply have to get an orderly from the mess as well, or we won't be able to manage. Can you do that, by the way? Or doesn't your influence extend that far?"

"Of course I can," said the major promptly. To doubt his influence was tantamount to an insult, as Felicitas knew perfectly well. It was in fact the surest way of getting anything she wanted from him.

"To come back to this fellow Krafft, Archibald—couldn't duty prevent him from coming?"

"It will indeed, my dear Felicitas, if the evening train from Würzburg doesn't arrive on time. Krafft has been detailed, by no less a person than the general, to go and meet a certain Frau Barkow at the station and accompany her to her hotel."

"By the general himself?" asked the major's wife, raising her voice slightly.

"You mustn't think that this influences me in any way, Felicitas. Quite the contrary, I may say. Considerable differences have arisen between the general and me, these last few days. We no longer altogether see eye to eye on a whole number of matters, and this would conceivably have far-reaching consequences. Moreover, Lieutenant Krafft is a real thorn in my flesh. If I had my own way, I wouldn't even pass the time of day with him, especially since he spent nearly the whole of this afternoon gadding about the countryside without so much as a by-your-leave, with Captain Feders of all people."

Frau Frey looked at her husband, who stood before her in his stockinged feet simulating a friendly interest in her problems. She knew him well; too well, she sometimes thought. Of course, he cared about the general, whatever he might say. And this fellow Krafft did seem to enjoy Modersohn's protection. The major considered it advisable to respect the fact, however reluctantly. The passiveness of her husband's attitude disappointed her. She was afraid it was becoming more and more pronounced these days.

"You ought to put on your slippers, Archibald," she said. "It's not good either for you or your socks to run around like that."

"I was going to have a bath anyway," said the major, excusing himself. He hurried from the room, and Frau Frey watched him go anxiously.

There was a knock at the door. Barbara came in and said, "There's a cadet outside who's come from Captain Ratshelm."

"The excellent Ratshelm," said the major's wife, pleasantly touched. "So chivalrous. A real man."

"I don't see it," said Barbara.

"Perhaps you and I mean something rather different by the term," said Felicitas.

"Perhaps," admitted Barbara. "I don't in fact happen to find Captain Ratshelm particularly manly."

"Barbara!" cried the major's wife indignantly. "How can you say such a thing? Captain Ratshelm is a first-class officer."

"That may well be," said Barbara calmly.

Felicitas Frey regarded her niece with evident disapproval. What sort of girl was she? She had absolutely no poise! But she was useful in the kitchen, which was something.

"We'll talk about this some other time, Barbara," she said snubbingly.

"By all means," said Barbara. "Shall I show the cadet in now?"

"Not into the bedroom! The sitting room, of course. Yes, show him in."

The cadet was extremely handsome, as the major's wife noted at once. The very picture of German manhood, and with impeccable manners too.

"Excuse me, ma'am," said her visitor with pleasant formality. "My name is Hochbauer. Cadet Hochbauer, Number Six Company, Section H for Heinrich. I've brought a few books from Captain Ratshelm."

Frau Frey smiled with delight and gave the cadet her

hand. He stepped boldly forward, bowed slightly, and gave it a gentle pressure.

Felicitas Frey noticed that his glossy hair was carefully combed and parted on the left. His high forehead clearly indicated a purposeful thinker. And the straight honest eyes below it, the slim nose and well-shaped mouth might, she fancied, have been those of some royal page.

"The excellent Ratshelm!" said Frau Frey. It was all she could think of to say. "Please sit down, Herr Hochbauer. What lovely things have you brought me?"

"The very flower of German literature," said the cadet sitting down politely in front of her. He opened the brief case which lay on his knee. "An anthology of our spiritual heritage, ma'am—Johst, Jelusich, and Blunck."

"How lovely," said Frau Frey, taking the books from his hands. And as she did so she thought, they're not a man's hands yet, they're much more the tender, sensitive hands of some noble boy. "Do you read much yourself?"

"From time to time," said the cadet cautiously. "Whenever duty permits. And duty naturally takes precedence over everything else. Though it mustn't of course prevent one from participating in the intellectual life of the nation."

"How true!" agreed Felicitas Frey, and hearing her husband letting out the bath water she added in some confusion, "Perhaps we can talk about all this rather more fully some other time."

"It would be an honor for me, ma'am!" Hochbauer assured her gratefully.

He stood up and once more bowed over her outstretched hand, clasping it gently. Striking tenderness, noted Felicitas. The gesture gave her great pleasure. She felt honored, and the feeling did her a world of good.

"Have you had someone in to see you?" asked the major, entering in his bath wrap.

"You shouldn't run about the house with so little on, Archibald," she said almost solicitously, for she was in tender mood. "You must remember that Barbara could come in at any minute. I wouldn't like her to see you like that."

"Why not?"

"I don't want to put ideas into her head."

The major's mind was immediately set at rest, for he considered himself a fine-looking man, which indeed he was by normal standards, particularly in uniform. However flattered he might feel, though, he didn't forget that he still hadn't had an answer to his question. "Who was this person who came to see you?" he inquired.

"A cadet," she said in an offhand way. "Someone from Captain Ratshelm's company. He brought me some books. A well brought-up boy, too, with beautiful manners."

The major seemed quite satisfied with this information. "Yes," he said, "there's nothing wrong with our human material and it's in good hands here, if one excepts Krafft."

"Which reminds me, we're still short of a girl. That is if we really must have this fellow Krafft this evening."

"You could invite Fräulein Bachner, the general's secretary."

"Can I believe my ears?" asked Felicitas Frey in dismay. "You want to invite that creature?"

"It was only a suggestion," the major assured her.

"The general's mistress, as everyone knows perfectly well."

"There's no proof of it," said the major. "I beg you for heaven's sake to be more careful, Felicitas. As you may have noticed, the general isn't the sort of person with whom one can take liberties!"

"Nor am I," said Felicitas.

"But I ask you," said the major. "Can one really blame people? There's no telling where the shafts of love may fall."

"Well," said the major's wife suddenly, smiling subtly, "I *suppose* you may be right."

"There you are, you see!" cried the major. "Besides, it might not be at all a bad move to have this girl with Lieutenant Krafft! I wouldn't give too much for the general's chances, if we did."

When she was alone at last Frau Frey shook her head sadly and heaved a deep sigh. She smoothed out her dress, and in doing so discovered a fine feminine sweep to her hips. They weren't particularly full, but they were firm. She had been a good rider once.

Then she picked up the telephone.

"My dear Fräulein Bachner," she said sweetly. "I've always wanted to invite you here. Won't you do me the pleasure?"

"What pleasure is that, ma'am?"

"The pleasure of paying me a little informal visit. I'm giving a small party here—very select of course, I need hardly add."

"Of course, ma'am."

"You'll come, then, my dear Fräulein Bachner?"

"I'd love to, but when?"

"This evening. It'll be a very great pleasure for me!"

"For me too, ma'am," said Sybille Bachner, bringing the conversation abruptly to an end.

Felicitas went straight to her husband. He had lain down in the hope of snatching a little sleep, a fact she noted with a certain resentment. While she worked herself to the bone he lay down and slept.

"Archibald," she said, quite friendly all the same, "I've succeeded!"

"What have you succeeded in doing this time?"

"I've persuaded this girl Sybille Bachner—she's coming."

"Bravo!" said the major with a yawn. "That should liven things up all right!"

The select party of officers trotted down the hill toward the little town in twos and threes.

"I feel just as if I were one of the cadets," said one of them.

"It's worse than being a cadet," said another. "For this time it's a woman who's giving us orders. What a fine lot of little fellows we are. We shall be sized up, examined, and put through our paces just as we put the cadets through theirs."

"We're in for a thoroughly lousy evening!" declared Lieutenant Rambler of Number 4 Company emphatically.

"It seems to me more subtle than that," suggested Lieutenant Webermann. "A blend of status-seeking and charity is what we're in for. Motherly instincts coupled with a brave display of class-consciousness. All in all a most remarkable phenomenon."

"Those long words of yours are too much for me, my dear Webermann," said Rambler. "What I can't stand is the time limit which my lady commanding officer imposes. What sort of social life is it that's governed by a timetable?"

The prescribed social activity began punctually at eight o'clock in the evening and ended at eleven o'clock on the dot. But it wasn't just Frau Frey's feeling for punctuality which was responsible for this; everything was in fact part of a carefully calculated plan. Each of the officers was detailed to fetch one of the young ladies from their homes not a minute too early, but at the exact moment which would enable them to enter the major's house precisely on time. The end of the evening too was ruled by the clock in the same way. The parents of the young ladies could calculate almost to the second when their daughters could be expected back at the family hearth. In this way the major's wife sought as far as possible to prevent any undesirable detours on the way home.

"One'll have to act like lightning," Lieutenant Rambler said ruefully. "There'll be no time for any refinements. It'll be a matter of seconds. What a rotten business!"

The other officers refrained from expressing an opinion. Few of the young ladies were in any way disposed to the sort of lightning action which Rambler had in mind; they wanted a slow and thorough conquest. A formal engagement was in most cases an indispensable preliminary to the achievement of one's objective.

"The whole thing's a rotten unnatural arrangement," insisted Rambler, who was something of an expert in this field. "In fact I'd almost like to say, it's an offense against the healthy instincts of the German race!"

"Welcome! Welcome!" said the major to each of them as they entered the house.

He stood in the corridor, beaming at his guests, with his Knight's Cross flashing on his chest—hero and organizer, officer and man of the world.

It was he who received the arrivals, handing them on to his wife, who then also bade them heartily welcome. The idea of a discordant note in such a house seemed out of the question.

"This person Sybille Bachner hasn't come yet, Archibald," Frau Frey whispered. "What can she be thinking of?"

"How should I know," said the major, rather nervously.

"And this man Krafft isn't here either. We really had no need to invite either of them. I follow your wishes far too easily, Archibald. Perhaps it's a mistake. Anyhow, let's start now, shall we? Or do you want me to wait any longer?"

A general conversation which passed for animated was now set in motion. The "young people," that is to say, the young ladies and their officer escorts, had gathered around the "older generation" consisting of Frau Frey, Major Frey, and certain ladies of local eminence who had been invited as a guarantee of the extremely respectable nature of the occasion. Among these were the wife of the local Party leader (a man who managed also to be simultaneously burgomaster, deputy area Party leader, and commissioner for agriculture)—a moon-faced, forty-year-old country girl with the voice of a cowhand and a laugh like a sheep's; the wife of the local pastrycook and hotelkeeper, leader of the local German Girls' League, an ungainly masculine sort of

woman with a Gretchen hair style and a surprisingly unctuous voice; and the wife of the building contractor, straight-
forwardly nicknamed The Millionairess, who was an angular
beauty with lively theatrical gestures designed to remind one
that she had once been a performer of distinction at some
unassuming municipal theater.

At the moment the dominating topic of conversation was
the requests program on the German radio. "It really amounts
to a whole new popular art form . . . it's so pure . . . and
gay, if you except one or two of the serious recitals . . .
tears came into my eyes when I heard 'Homeland, Your
Starlight' . . . my husband said there's no one can equal the
Germans for depth of feeling . . . and 'Bombs on England,'
what a tune! . . . What a frightful pack of shopkeepers those
people are, they can't bear us having Central Europe as far
as the Urals. As for the colonies where that awful Churchill
of theirs simply wants to sit and soak . . . but the most
beautiful of all was 'Mother, Dear Little Mother' . . ."

"Yes," said the major with enthusiasm. "There's something noble and spiritual about us still. Compare our culture
with the convulsive spasms that beset them over in America
with that degenerate jazz of theirs."

It was at this moment that Sybille Bachner made her appearance. She stood in the corridor, looking through the open
doorway into the "salon," a slim, rather pale figure with her
hair hanging down attractively over her shoulders. Her excellent proportions were shown to full advantage by her simple blue dress. She stood there, waiting patiently.

"She's almost eighteen minutes late," said the major's wife
indignantly to her husband.

"And she's come alone," said the latter, equally indignant.

"This man Krafft has simply failed to collect her," said
Felicitas Frey. "How disgraceful! When everything had been
so perfectly planned, too! The man's utterly impossible!"

"Scandalous behavior," agreed the major. "I won't forget
it so easily."

But Frau Frey maintained her composure.

"Welcome!" she cried to Sybille Bachner, and then handed
the general's favorite over to her husband to present to the
other guests.

The older women looked at Sybille appraisingly, the
younger women with some distaste, for they sensed competition. The officers were pleasantly surprised, and started
trying to decide if it would be all right to flirt with her or
whether she should be regarded as "bespoke." It seemed

inadvisable, to say the least, to encroach on the general's private property in any way.

"What do you think of her?" asked the girl beside Rambler.

"I like the look of you better," he whispered to her.

"I should hope so."

"I've given you proof of that."

"Rather too convincing proof, perhaps," she said.

"What do you mean by that? Just a figure of speech or . . ."

"Or nothing," she said, with such an intimate look that he was immediately highly suspicious.

"Yes, our young ladies, God bless them!" said the major with paternal enthusiasm to the older ladies he was sitting with. "I only have to cast eyes on them to realize what a bright future lies before our children."

The young ladies were still sitting there waiting patiently and rather shyly. They gave the impression that they were listening eagerly to a conversation which they were quite prepared to regard as elevated.

At the same time they stole secret glances at their escorts, being all set to admire them on hearing that they were far and away the best of the officers: specially selected to teach at the training school which was a sort of university for the defense of the Fatherland. All of these officers were decorated, most of them with the Knight's Cross, and all were strongly suspected of harboring the ambition to become a general one day.

With so much masculine glamor all about them the temperature rose appreciably. Some of the young ladies were perspiring freely, a fact, however, which seemed neither particularly to impress the officers nor to put them off.

"You weren't being serious," whispered Rambler to his lady. "What you hinted just now can't be right."

"I'm afraid so," she said.

"But it can't be!" said Rambler in alarm. He found it hellishly difficult to look about him as if nothing had happened.

"Yes," said the major in ringing tones, "one has to have a sense of poetry, even as a soldier. One must be able to appreciate true greatness. Theodore Körner for example!"

This provided the company with a new topic. The major was an exemplary host and took care to provide a variety of pleasant topics of conversation. Now it was culture's turn, with particular reference to literature.

"You know it's all so deeply Nordic, it appeals at once to

one's innermost soul . . . I read the Edda over and over again—it gives me new courage—by which I don't mean to say that without it I wouldn't have courage . . . but if we didn't have our German soul . . . how completely decadent those French are, utterly shameless, no wonder we beat them in five weeks. And then the Americans, simply gangsters, not to mention the Russians . . . and then there's the whole of our legacy, the legacy of our blood, our blood and our homeland, the soil, the earth . . . you know my husband says, 'When I breathe in the scent of German soil, I'm not ashamed to shed tears' . . . and do you know, one page of the book—which is bound in half calf, with gold leaf—was sopping wet the next day!"

Lieutenant Krafft arrived eventually. He looked quickly about him and then went across to the major's wife. He made a very sketchy bow and said, "Good evening, Frau Frey."

"Good evening," she said coolly.

Lieutenant Krafft turned to the major and said, "Please excuse me for being late—duty kept me."

"Don't mention it," said the major, maintaining face with difficulty. "Duty of course must always come first."

"Yes of course, Herr Major," said Lieutenant Krafft, slipping away from the cream of the assembled company and making his way across the room to Sybille Bachner. He sat down beside her with a sigh of relief.

"You must excuse me," he said to her under his breath. "Actually I was meant to escort you, but the train was thirty minutes late."

"Has Frau Barkow arrived?" asked Sybille. She was obviously extremely interested.

"Yes," said Krafft. "I took her to her hotel. And the general was already there waiting for her."

"What sort of women is she, Herr Krafft?" asked Sybille after a short pause.

Krafft looked at her and the ghost of a smile flickered across his face. Her curiosity was very transparent. "Frau Barkow is a lady of about forty," he said. "The general seems to know her very well—he was on Christian-name terms with her."

Lieutenant Krafft now began to take a closer look at the guests. General conversation seemed to be flagging slightly. I hope it's not anything to do with me, thought Krafft, somewhat perturbed. He listened to the words that flew about his ears. They didn't seem to him to make any sense at all. And he looked around for a drink of some sort. But it wasn't yet time for the bowl of punch.

"The man's manners!" whispered the major to his wife. "Intolerable!" He stood up and moved away. He thought he'd go and see how the drinks were coming along in the kitchen.

Meanwhile the major's wife tried to get the hopelessly desultory conversation back on the rails again. The officers made some effort to support her, as was only proper, for after all she was their commanding officer's wife. The local young ladies continued to maintain a passive attitude, being fearful of committing some terrible intellectual blunder, though in fact such a thing would have passed quite unnoticed.

"Are you quite sure?" asked Rambler anxiously. "Do you really think—?"

"It looks like it, yes."

"Perhaps you've miscalculated?"

"What do you mean by that?" asked his young lady in astonishment.

"I mean perhaps you've made a mistake? In the calendar, if you see what I mean?"

"I can count perfectly well," she said.

Damn it, thought Lieutenant Rambler. To hell with these social occasions! And the ladies in particular.

The young ladies sat there very stiffly, leaning forward slightly to show themselves to their best advantage. Yet even now there was something utterly unapproachable about them. They all smiled charmingly and laughed in silvery tones, mostly in the right places, being very conscious of the need to prove worthy representatives of their little town, at any rate as long as there were any spectators about. There were a number of "good matches" among them, each with attractive dowries appropriate to their position; the burgomaster's daughter, for instance, small, buxom, animated, with a broad behind like her mother's. It was true she was always the first to start perspiring, but on the other hand she already had a couple of lodging houses in her name, and a sizable piece of building land between the town and the barracks. Then there was the filling-station owner's daughter, sole heiress not only to the filling station itself but of the adjoining workshops and the car-hire business and car agency that went with it—a slim, doll-like creature with a neat little face but long yellow teeth. Rambler's girl was the niece of the building contractor, the man who not only had built the barracks but had provided all the necessary additional buildings as well. This girl, a full-bosomed creature, who was always breathing heavily, put one in mind rather of a thoroughbred mare. She was interested in both sport and politics, and was the local leader of the German Girls' League. Her uncle the building contractor, who was childless, was, as everyone in the town knew, very attached to her.

All of which Lieutenant Rambler was at the moment busy turning over in his mind. He was already beginning to see the whole matter in a different light. As they put it so neatly in German Girls' League circles, children are a guarantee for the future. . . .

"What are you thinking about?" she asked him. "You're smiling."

"I'm thinking about you," he said. "About us and our future."

"I always knew I could trust you," she said.

"I'm an officer," he replied. "I know my duty."

"We women know where our duty lies," said Felicitas Frey. "We wouldn't be women, German women, if we didn't."

Thus at last she had hit upon another topic of conversation: good works and feminine obligations, particularly in war-time.

". . . as my husband says, a woman must never forget that she is a German woman, particularly in times like these. We visit the hospital at least once a week, if there's nothing to prevent us . . . and how grateful they always are, our dear boys . . . I always take them flowers, my husband's roses even, I know nothing abuut them of course—Archibald, I say to him, one mustn't be grudging, not even with that special Hindenburg variety—they're a quite magnificent rose, you know, white as alabaster, a symbol of purity, spiritual purity of course . . . and how their eyes light up when I arrive, they can hardly find words to thank me . . . one has lost an arm, just think of it, the right arm too, but he laughed and said to me, 'I'm left-handed anyway.' What a sense of humor, it brings tears to my eyes."

"Do you think I could have something to drink?" asked Lieutenant Krafft loudly.

The guests reacted to this with either dismay or astonishment, according to temperament. Frau Frey's reaction might be said to have been one of outrage. After she had succeeded in recovering herself, she said, "It's much too early for that, Lieutenant."

"Not for me it isn't," declared Krafft. The way she talked had turned his stomach. He was badly in need either of a drink or of some fresh air.

The major's wife said sharply, "If you don't feel well, Lieutenant . . ."

"I was going soon anyway," said Krafft, rising to his feet. "There's still something I have to do for the general."

"In which case," said the major's wife, "don't let us detain you."

"I'll go too," said Sybille Bachner, also rising to her feet.

"Just as you wish!" said Felicitas Frey stiffly.

"It's been a delightful evening," Sybille Bachner assured her.

"And I, too, can say nothing but thank you!" said Krafft.

They went, leaving a long icy silence behind them. Felicitas Frey's heavy breathing was distinctly audible. She seemed about to burst. Then the major appeared, flashing a devastating look at his wife though a broad, benevolent smile covered his face. The smile was a little unnatural perhaps, but it stayed there all right. He was living up to his own motto: be a match for every situation! His voice rang out jovially, as he cried, "Now, then, I think we can get on with the really jolly part of the evening. Let's have a little dance, ladies and gentlemen. What about 'The Seagull Flying to Heligoland'? Or 'The Little Flower on the Heath Whose Name Is Erica'?"

The first record ground out its music, and a few couples got up obediently and went into the next room and began to dance. The older generation's conversation slowly got under way again.

But the major took his wife aside, very discreetly as he thought, and said to her, "That should never have been allowed to happen, Felicitas! We'll go into it all thoroughly later, I can promise you!"

"We'll get a little peace now," said Barbara Bendler-Trebitz, the major's wife's niece. "I know the form; once the punch is served we get a break out here in the kitchen which should last at least half an hour. What are we going to do in the meantime?"

"Whatever you like, fräulein."

"Why do you keep calling me fräulein? Is it a sort of joke?"

"But it suits you so well, fräulein."

Lance-Corporal Gemme was standing by the kitchen table. He had been detailed here from the officers' mess, or rather by Captain Kater, as a punishment for allegedly having broken one of his best bottles of red wine. And between six and eight hours' help for the major's wife was really no light punishment.

However, there was something to be said for this niece, who now stood on the opposite side of the kitchen table from Lance-Corporal Gemme. The trouble was she *was* the major's niece, so one had to proceed with considerable caution.

"Do you often go to parties like this?" Barbara asked.

"No, thank God," said Gemme, immediately pulling himself together and adding, "I mean, no unfortunately."

"This sort of thing bores you stiff, I suppose."

"Oh, I wouldn't say that," said Gemme warily.

"Anyway you're here."

Barbara edged her way around the table toward him. Gemme made a slight tactical withdrawal. But Barbara pursued him. "You don't really need to call me fräulein—I'm the kitchen maid here, you know."

"But you're the major's niece too."

"And you find that frightening?"

"Frightening? Well, you don't think that with a lady of the officer class I can simply . . ."

"What?"

"Well you know what I mean, though I never said anything, mark you I never said a word. All I said was that you were the major's niece, and that you're of the officer class."

"Oh, hell," said Barbara with conviction, "that lot leave me cold."

Gemme pricked up his ears. "Do you really mean that?"

"I'll say!" said Barbara.

Gemme looked about him. The kitchen door was shut. There wasn't a sound from the corridor. The guests were all in the drawing room, where the phonograph was playing—dancing was in progress. The punch had been taken in and the bowl had been at least half full. The major had discreetly taken his personal flask. No one would be very likely to come into the kitchen. So Gemme took the decision, and Barbara with it.

"You can hold me tighter than that," she said, to his amazement. "I'm no little officers' doll."

"But you're marvelous, girl!"

"Well then," she laughed, a little shrilly.

"Is there a lock on the door?" asked Gemme with some urgency.

"Come on, we'll go into the dining room. No one will disturb us there."

"What matters to me," said Major Frey emphatically, "is my reputation. It matters more than anything, Felicitas!"

"You don't need to bellow at me like that," she said. "Your manners have left a good deal to be desired lately. My house is a clean house, a decent house, a hospitable house, and anyone who fails to respect the fact forfeits any consideration from me!"

They glared at each other—he truculent, she indignant. It never occurred to them to lower their voices, for the guests had gone, the house was empty, and Barbara presumably was asleep. Even if she wasn't asleep, Herr and Frau Frey had long ceased to think of her.

"What's at stake here is my honor, my authority, my career itself! Doesn't that matter to you any more? I've trusted you, looked up to you, adored you! And what about you? What's got into you? Have you taken leave of your senses?"

"You don't understand me," she said in a plaintive, bitter voice. "You've never understood me."

"All we're discussing here, Felicitas, is how much understanding you have for *me*! I'm in command of Number Two Course here, and now my whole position is threatened. All right, if you don't like this fellow Krafft, then try and ignore him, don't take any notice of him, cut him. I don't like him either. That doesn't mean I throw him out of the house! Not that you seem to be satisfied even with that. You've managed to offend the general's secretary as well, of all people! I won't stand for it! No one would stand for it. The general doesn't allow himself to be provoked without retaliating. And that's why I expect you to set the whole matter straight as quickly as possible, and to leave nothing to chance! How you do so is your own lookout!"

Felicitas Frey collapsed into a chair.

"You've never understood me," she repeated. "You've never realized how I felt, deep down inside."

But he was no longer listening. He had left the room to clean his teeth.

She sat there slumped in her chair thinking, what can have come over him! Gone was all the attention he used to pay to her, gone all his chivalry and youthful charm. The devoted tenderness, the delightful submissiveness of the loving husband and dutiful lover—all were gone. All gone, gone. What now, Felicitas?

"I won't be treated like this," she said, pulling herself together. "I simply won't stand for it. I'll teach him!"

* * * *

Intermediate Report No. 5

THE CURRICULUM VITAE OF
CAPTAIN CONRAD KATER,
OR BLESSED ARE THE RATS

Ephraim Gottlieb Kater, the winegrower, is my father. My mother is his wife, Klara, born Klausnitzer. They live in Triebenbach, a village about seven kilometers north of Trier. It was here that I was born on July 17, 1900, and here, too, that I spent my childhood and schooldays.

We live in a small slate-gray house. It's all very primitive. We're often hungry but never thirsty. For we own a vineyard. Yet the wine that grows there is always slightly sour. It's difficult to sell. So my father drinks most of it himself. And when he does so he sings very loudly and fervently. Love songs. Sometimes I join in, but only after a fashion, because I don't know the words. And Mother stands there too. Her face is gray, like the stones of our house. I have six brothers and sisters. And the people of the neighborhood say, "The wine your father can't sell is responsible for that."

I'm always glad to help my mother. My six brothers and sisters don't much like to. Luckily for me they're stupid and lazy. I can usually get the better of all of them by insisting on helping Mother, particularly in the kitchen. I carry wood about, peel potatoes, and even weight the flour. Stirring the pot is what I like best. Particularly when there's no one in the kitchen. Then I quickly taste a few spoonfuls. Sometimes I burn myself doing this, but this way I almost always get enough to eat. And it makes the others furious, so that some of them even cry with rage. But all this is simply because they don't help their dear mother enough.

The boy who sits next to me at school, the fat boy with stupid eyes, always has lots of money. His father is a butcher with fingers like sausages. His sister is fat too and her lips are like two rounded rubber pads. They all smell of fresh sausage. And the sausage soup they eat at home, which comes straight out of the steaming caldron, is absolutely first class —it has lumps of meat floating about in it and barley and bits of broken sausage. I often eat with them. And the fat sister with the Negroid lips pushes her knee against mine, though this doesn't worry me in the slightest.

I put out my hand. It doesn't tremble. I see that the palm of my hand isn't very clean. And above it I watch the cane descending. I feel a burning sensation. Again the cane comes thrashing down on this hand of mine, and again and again. Red stripes appear; they make a crisscross pattern, run parallel, shoot off in opposite directions, like roads on a map. I can feel the burning sensation on the palm of my hand right up into the back of my head. But I go on holding out my hand, and it still doesn't tremble.

The woman I've brought the parcel to is sitting on the sofa. She feels my arm. "You're strong," she says. "Not so bad," I say. She draws me closer and her fingers slip inside my tunic and work their way across the muscles of my chest. "You really are very strong," says the woman. Her voice has grown softer. "And you," I say, seizing hold of her breasts, "you're not exactly weak." "No," she says.

When my schooldays were over I worked for a time on my father's property, mainly on the administrative side. In 1917 I volunteered for the front as a matter of course. I was fortunate enough to be accepted, and after a short period of admirable basic training was posted to a unit in the east. After the official end of the war I remained true to the colors, fought on in Upper Silesia, and joined our Führer's movement from the earliest days. In order to earn my living and at the same time serve higher political ends I traveled through southern Germany selling selected brands of goods until the hour of decision struck.

"We've hardly enough to eat," says my father after fortifying himself with a jug of wine. "Things go from bad to worse, it's all becoming too much for me. If it goes on like this, we might as well give up the ghost—on empty stomachs too. But thank God some of you are old enough to go into the army. Off you go and volunteer, you pigs! My one hope is that the war will last a long time."

Our heads reel; the ground sways in front of us and our eyes swim. Our clothes stick to our bodies with sweat. But it's all for the Fatherland, says our corporal. We hurl ourselves down in the mud and heave ourselves up again. Someone collapses, to be followed five minutes later by someone else. The corporal's voice grows hoarse, but he never stops shouting. We creep toward the latrine on the edge of the parade ground. "In you go!" shouts the corporal in charge of our training.

He knows how to play the piano, this comrade of ours with the girl's face. He thumps away on the keys and the empty bottles dance about on top of the piano. I go and join him and play chopsticks on the keys with two fingers. It makes a noise like glasses breaking. I go on drinking and playing chopsticks and it still sounds like glasses breaking. A Polish woman is standing in the doorway. Her name is Sonia, or something. She stares at the rotten piano, which is hers, and we lay her down on top of it, while the fellow with the face like a girl goes on playing. This Sonia looks around wildly, but she can't scream because someone has stuffed a sock into her mouth. Then she drums her legs, but we hold them down. And all this on the piano which belongs to this woman Sonia anyway.

One of the best, this fellow Hauser. They call him "Bruiser." He's an officer, but he doesn't lay it on; he just wants to be one of the boys. But he's got real personality, and in every situation commands complete authority and respect. He's been wounded in his right arm so he holds his pistol in his left. He knows Upper Silesia like the back of his hand. He's got a real feeling for people, provided they're German. I am entrusted with the organization of supplies for the entire Free Corps run by Hauser. It's small, but always in the thick of things, and thus always has a healthy appetite. I'm in my element here. I keep us well supplied for as long as the fighting lasts.

"Corporal Kater," Bruiser Hauser says to me one day, "our mission is completed. But there'll be others in the future, and the important thing is to know where to find them. Are you coming with me?" I say yes. It's an honor to be called upon by Bruiser Hauser, and turns out very much to my advantage too. The real Germany never forgets its heroes. So we move to Munich.

It isn't just modesty that prevents me from joining Adolf Hitler's, the Führer's, inner circle. There's a lot of work to be done even in Bruiser Hauser's entourage. But we march on November 9, 1923, providing the stable rear guard as it were, and we help to prevent complete catastrophe by holding firm. Bruiser Hauser and I succeed in escaping the clutches of the law. Stobmeyer, the wine merchant, a man with strong nationalist principles, gives us shelter, and we celebrate the fact to good effect. For Stobmeyer has a respectable cellar.

"A fine drop of stuff," I say appreciatively. "Delicious, with a nice bouquet and a delicate enduring aftertaste." "I can see you're something of an expert, friend!" says Stobmeyer familiarly, though he was never more than an ordinary ranker. But we aren't petty about such things. "Yes," I say modestly, "I know my stuff. I'm more or less in the trade myself. My father owns a vineyard in the Trier district." "Excellent!" says Stobmeyer enthusiastically. "I can always use sound reliable people. What about it?" "Well," I say after some hesitation, "if I can do a comrade a good turn, why not?"

Long years in the service of the firm of Stobmeyer, Munich —Stobmeyer Gin, Stobmeyer Bitters, Stobmeyer spirits of every sort. Forty-five per cent alcohol it says on the label. A modest start at first, footslogging with a brief case. Then a suitcase and travel by rail, third class. The first car follows shortly afterward, a car and delivery wagon combined. Soon after that, my own office and the founding of three branches. A secretary. Finally the Mercedes—though without a chauffeur of my own at first. And all this on a modest 15 per cent of the profits.

Girls all over the place, relatively good bargains most of them. Yet in this respect, too, steady consolidation and expansion. Ordinary barmaids at first, now and then a frigid little shopgirl, various chambermaids from third-class hotels. But none of this is anything more than a transitional phase. Later I find myself attracted more and more to ordinary, simple, modest people; they know how to make life pleasant and comfortable for one. But the so-called finer trimmings certainly have their charm too—girls picked up at bars, hostesses, night-club singers, and little creatures found at dances. The climax is undoubtedly the double-bass player of a women's dance orchestra staying in Nuremberg at the time. With her I seem like some musical instrument in the hands of a virtuoso.

Yet never for a moment do I lose sight of the really important things in life. Those restaurant proprietors whose nationalist principles are sound always get special prices— even at the expense of the firm of Stobmeyer, which thus gets a chance to further the popularity of the cause. But there are also many important conferences, in back rooms and at night. We have visits from Old Comrades' organizations, which of course always receive preferential treatment. All this goes hand in hand with an extensive campaign for German brandy. Finally the popular Stobmeyer Bear's Tooth is put on the market, invariably accompanied by a richly illustrated brochure bearing the legend, "The Teutons Camped on Both Sides of the Rhine"—one half of a couplet to which every good German knows the other half, "And German Brandy Their Only Wine!"

"Comrades," I say on January 30, 1933, "the hour for which we have waited so long has struck at last!" There are tears in my eyes. For we are drinking a Stobmeyer Feuergeist for the occasion—50 per cent alcohol.

With the opening of the new era and the upsurge of a new and vigorous fighting spirit I find myself growing more and more anxious to put my modest resources at the service of greater Germany and the Führer. My commercial activities thus have to take second place to a military career. Because I'd been a corporal in the Great War and decorated, I had completed my first period of reserve training by 1934 and this was soon succeeded by others. By 1936 I was a second lieutenant and in 1938 a first lieutenant of the Reserve. It was with this rank that I took the field in 1939 being engaged in a number of important sectors. In 1940 my promotion to captain followed, with a simultaneous award of the War Service Cross Second Class. In 1942 I was posted to No. 5 Officers' Training School, where I took over the Headquarters Company with such success that in the same year I was awarded the War Service Cross First Class.

The unforgettable German springtime of 1933—a magnificent new impetus in every field, not excluding of course my own. A welcome expansion of business, the foundation overnight of yet another branch, long conversations with Stobmeyer on the subject of partnership. A romantic and moving moment in the Hotel Königshof—crates of empty bottles—our comrades already asleep in the rooms reserved for them and their companions—soft music coming up from the bar—and I sit there musing in an armchair with the order book in front of me. And to the word "Stobmeyer" I add the words "and Kater." Stobmeyer and Kater, Distillers, Wholesale and Retail.

The upsurge of morale continues far into the German summer of 1933. I spend a lot of time traveling about in the Mercedes and am constantly delighted both by the new spirit of confidence I find abroad and by the gradual increase in purchasing power. Remarkable, too, the understanding for the new higher values, among which is a growing sense of family. I grow fed-up with being alone—which of course has nothing to do with advancing years, but with Edeltraut Marquardt. A lovable woman, very sound, very German, full of promise. She owns the hotel called The Silver Crown in Stüttgart. A house with an excellent reputation, splendidly decorated in the finest German tradition, doing plenty of business and highly profitable, Edeltraut already has three children—two from her first marriage, and one born out of wedlock. Her husband made off some years ago—an insatiable lust for adventure or something; in any case no businessman.

"Edeltraut," I say, "you need a father for your children, aren't I right?" "It could be," she says, looking at me in eager anticipation. "They're dear children," I say. "I only know them slightly, but one senses people's qualities. What do you think, wouldn't I be a good father for them?" "Certainly," says Edeltraut, leaning against my shoulder and adding, "How nice of you to think of the children and not of the hotel." "But please, my dear," I say, "the hotel means nothing to me!" "Good," she says happily.

Morale remains at its peak until the spring of 1934. I have my hands full—and with other things besides the wedding, which is due to take place on January 30, 1934. The date is well chosen. A German wedding and the celebration of the first anniversary of the assumption of power—a double festivity but only one bill to pay. The principal witness is Bruiser Hauser, now in the SS and a member of our Führer's personal bodyguard. Hitler himself gives him leave to attend my wedding, a very special honor. The second witness is Stobmeyer, the Munich businessman whose nationalist convictions are so sound. He, however, seems rather absent-minded on the day, even a little depressed; perhaps he is beginning to realize that I am his superior in business, perhaps because very little Stobmeyer spirit is drunk on this particular evening. But our schnapps after all is for customers, we have better things to drink.

I build up a vast network of agents. Stobmeyer is already well known in five of the new administrative districts, thanks to my own tirelessness and skill. My first objective is to get the branches into my hands and then the firm itself. The next step will be the hotel business, starting with The Silver Crown. But just as I am thinking along these lines I get a telegram which says, "Presence in Munich urgently required." I go there and what do I find? Stobmeyer in tears, beside himself, at his wits' end. The whole firm's ruined. And why? Because this fellow Stobmeyer, the idiot, turns out to be anything but a fellow Aryan! Who would have thought it? There's this man, nationally conscious to his finger tips, an old front-line fighter, a supporter of patriotic organizations—and he's not an Aryan! Unbelievable! "You've let me down very badly," I say bitterly. "Let's hope there's something to be saved from the wreck."

But there's nothing to be saved from the wreck. Everything's ruined. Instead of talking it all over with me in advance and putting things in order, instead of handing the firm over to me in time, either putting it directly into my hands or in the form of some fictitious agreement, all this wretched fellow thinks of is his money—the work I've put into the firm never crosses his mind. Of course I pull every string I can—after all, I have friends and comrades in high places.

"Hauser, old friend," I say, "you've got to help me. After all, you know the right people. A word from you and the head of the District Bureau for Industry and Commerce will give me a free hand."

"Kater," says Bruiser Hauser, "I'm surprised at an intelligent fellow like you thinking he can turn to me. You've landed me in a nice mess. How could you dare link my name with this Stobmeyer creature of all people as a witness at your wedding. If that comes out I'm finished. And then I'll have finished with you, Kater. Listen now, get yourself out of this mess as fast as you can, clear out of the picture and look sharp about it. The best thing would be to disappear for a time. Why don't you just go off and do some military training? As an officer of the reserve you'd have nothing to worry about, and afterward we'll see what can be done."

My first period of training with the reserve. Thoroughly successful—superior officers who understand things and, like all decent fellows, know how to enjoy a drink. My most important activity is to work on the spirit of comradeship—at the highest level, too, for as an applicant for a commission I'm allowed into the officers' mess. Bruiser Hauser, plagued by a bad conscience probably, pays me a visit. He's a real big shot in the Führer's bodyguard by now, wearing a magnificent uniform with the Pour le Mérite, and an ADC as well. There's a party in his honor that evening and I sit between him and the battalion CO. Finally I am released with the rank of senior sergeant and a note on my file, "Eminently suited to be an officer of the Reserve."

Back again then to commercial life with fresh strength and courage. The firm of Stobmeyer no longer exists, yet a man with fight in him always looks to the future. For there's my dear wife Edeltraut's hotel. "Darling," I say, as we sit cozily side by side, "we've got to have a serious talk some time about The Silver Crown." "But there's nothing to talk about, Conrad, my dearest," she says naïvely. "There is," I say. "I want to take the whole business into my own hands." "But you can't, my dearest Conrad," she says. "It isn't my hotel, you see. It belongs to my first husband and he's made it over to the children. I simply run it under the supervision of a lawyer."

A second period of training with the reserve. Much like the first, only even more intensive, more thorough, more successful. Very gradually my deep disappointment over the despicably underhanded behavior of my wife begins to disappear. I've been too good-natured, too trusting. I should have insisted on having it all down properly in writing beforehand. And anyway, there's Hilda—her surname is neither here nor there. Hilda from the flower shop, the cuddly little creature with whom I spend my leisure hours, and who so loves to ride in my Mercedes and adores new clothes. Otherwise utterly unselfish. Fresh and reinvigorated I return home with the rank of lieutenant.

War breaks out. I learn the fact ahead of time from an inside source—Hauser. We're sitting in the Künstlerhaus in a private room on the top floor. Thoroughly first-rate people all around me. The elite of the Party. Alas, from the ideological point of view, rather than the economic. Fortunately, though, there are some little girls from the chorus of the State Light Opera Comany as well; charming little things who certainly know their stuff. Refined, adaptable, and astonishingly gay, thoroughly well trained one might say. Pretty tough altogether. Not cheap exactly, but they'll accept influence as payment, so that it's the State that pays the bill. Rough male voices, smoke, bubbling champagne, girlish laughter, heady perfume. Then a telephone call for Bruiser Hauser. "This is it," he says when he comes back. "It's begun." And he disappears, handing his girl friend over to me, so that I now have two of them. And when next morning I wake up between them, our brave troops are already over the Polish frontier.

A succession of honorable and responsible positions, first of all in the field of recruiting—an important yet very routine job. Next, head of a commission of inspection in the same area—doubtless very important, too, yet not really quite suited to my own particular gifts. Animated correspondence with Bruiser Hauser, and then, thanks to his good offices, I'm put in charge of a commissariat camp at Coblenz. And finally, the peak of my career to date, I'm made commandant of the town of St. Pierre, after the victorious ending of the campaign in France. There I concentrate on supplies for the troops, the improvement of sanitary conditions, and maintaining contact with the civilian population.

"Johanna," I say to the girl, "has it occurred to you at all to wonder why you're here?" "Yes, because I'm hungry and need money," she says. "And besides, my name's Jeanette, not Johanna." This rather puts me off my stride and I say nothing at first. I look around the room—it's in the Hôtel Trois Roses, an old-fashioned, out-of-date dump that's anything but clean. What a people, what a country, what lack of morale! "You speak our language, Johanna," I say. "That's because I come from Alsace," she says. "We speak both French and German there. That has its advantages sometimes—now, for instance." "Your whole heredity is German," I say with passionate conviction. "Don't you feel the language of your blood speaking within you?" "No," she says, "I don't."

Oh yes, it's an exhilarating experience to be a German, but dangerous, too, sometimes. In St. Pierre, where I am commandant, there are certain elements known as the "Maquis" at work—footpads, sneak thieves, murderers, arsonists. One goes in fear of one's life. When three of them are hanged, three dozen more appear in their place. Deplorable country. They've no feeling for our interests there, no good will toward us. Our friendship means nothing to them. Genuine disappointment finally compels me to turn my back on them —certainly not the increasing discomfort or anything so ignominious as fear. But I receive an honorable summons from the homeland: an officers' training school requires an experienced, reliable, and trustworthy officer. I fill the bill admirably.

16 *THE GENERAL SPEAKS OUT*

"I NEVER THOUGHT I'd find myself sitting opposite the man with my son on his conscience," said Frau Barkow to Major-General Modersohn. They were sitting opposite each other in a private room of the hotel called The Golden Ram, in Wildlingen-am-Main.

After greeting each other coldly they had sat down to dinner, and on account of the servants had remained silent throughout almost the entire meal. Now, however, they were alone. Wine and a carafe of water stood on the table. No one would disturb them unless they rang the bell which hung between them.

Neither spoke. The décor of the room was typical of the solid peasant tradition of that part of Franconia; heavy but attractive furniture, a carefully carved sideboard, leaded stained-glass windows, with elaborately embroidered curtains hanging in front of them. Moreover the room was meticulously clean, as the general noted with some satisfaction.

"No," Frau Barkow repeated bitterly, "I would never have thought it. But now it's simply too much for me—I no longer have the strength to battle with anyone. Not even you."

The general listened attentively, but apparently unmoved. He accepted her reproaches as if she were speaking from some hideout in which he couldn't reach her. Then, choosing his words with remarkable care, he said, "I expected you at the funeral."

"I was ill," said Frau Barkow. "I collapsed when your letter came."

Frau Barkow avoided his glance. She had always found it difficult to confront this immobile, uncommunicative face of his, and now she had neither the wish nor the courage to do so. Always it had seemed as if he surrounded himself with walls of bulletproof glass.

Modersohn tried to recognize what was left of the girl he had known as Suzanne Simpson. The soft brown eyes? Certainly—even though they had now lost much of their warmth. The calm sweep of the forehead, the inquisitive nose? These too were almost unchanged, though marked now by finely drawn lines. The mouth, the gentle mouth, always a little weak and indulgent? No, that had changed; it was now no more than a wide slit, and the lips were cracked and colorless.

"It's over twenty years since we last saw each other," he said thoughtfully.

"Twenty-two years," she said bitterly. "Exactly twenty-two years and three months. I see it all as clearly as if it were yesterday."

Modersohn, too, tried to conjure up the past. But he found this difficult. The pictures from his past were torn and faded, covered with the dust of time. Only very hazily was he able to make out one or two things: 1921—late autumn—the woods a riot of color—bright yellow and blood red, interspersed with the last traces of brilliant green—a horse, a stallion, called Hasso, yes that was it, Hasso von Wangenheim—a black lacquer hunting carriage with a black roof and red upholstery—then a girl in a green coat, smiling at him warmly, the face indistinct but lovable, soft, immature —the brown eyes of a doe—Suzanne Simpson.

"I was on the threshold of my career then," said the general thoughtfully. He poured a little wine into his glass, added a lot of water, and drank.

"And today?" she asked, not without some curiosity. "Where are you now? At the height of your career?"

"Perhaps at the end of it," said Modersohn, drinking again.

"And you expect me to feel sorry for you after all that's happened?"

The general shook his head almost angrily.

She recognized the gesture at once. This dark, stern gesture of rejection, this cold, consciously cultivated inaccessibility, this abrupt closing of the gates against all feeling —she knew it only too well. She had never been able to forget it.

"If only one knew how the life one tried to live was going to look . . ." said the general.

"Then you'd live it in just the same way all over again, Ernst."

"No, Suzanne," he said firmly. "No. I wouldn't do that. I'm quite sure of that now."

"You always wanted to be an officer, Ernst—that and nothing else. You had no wish to be a friend, or a husband, or a father."

"It's true, Suzanne, it was like that once. All I wanted was to be an officer. But that's over now, for good and all. In this world we live in it's no longer possible to be an officer without running the risk of becoming a criminal too."

Suzanne Barkow looked Major-General Modersohn full in the face for the first time that evening, and in her eyes there was an expression of incredulity and horror. It was as if she were suddenly doubting her companion's identity altogether. How astonishingly he had changed!

But the pictures were indelibly imprinted on her memory: Lieutenant Modersohn of Number 9 Infantry Regiment, a serious, hard-working, sincere young man, full of a quiet, vigorous energy, and, in the little free time he had, of a calm, restrained sense of fun. He would sit up half the night studying maps, military regulations, and the literature of war. Respected by all his comrades in an almost astonishing way. Highly esteemed by his superior officers and clearly destined for a great and glorious career. At forty-four a major-general and commanding officer of an officers' training school, with the highest decorations, and tipped for a post in the High Command. And he of all people no longer wanted to be an officer!

"Even if I had married you then, Suzanne, things wouldn't have turned out any differently. It would simply have been all that much more distressing. But I'm alone now, and that's a good thing. I don't need to take anyone into account. I have no ties; there's no one I can harm. I can do whatever seems right to me."

"Does that really compensate for anything, Ernst?"

Frau Barkow looked at the white tablecloth. Almost mechanically, she drew the glass which he had filled for her toward her. But she didn't drink from it. "It was very difficult for me at first after you'd gone," she went on. "But I got over it."

She had never been able to get over it. Her eyes which were full of sorrow gave her away. But she went on bravely. "Soon afterward I got to know Gottfried Barkow; I had no hesitation in marrying him. He was a good man, a gentle husband, and a loving father. That's what people usually say, I know, but he really did have those qualities."

Gottfried Barkow had been a textile merchant, a decent, highly respected businessman, thoroughly good and worthy, jovial in an almost embarrassing way, and always helpful. He worshiped his wife, loved his wife's son, and let him know it. He regarded his wife as a wonderful gift that had been bestowed on him, and though he couldn't offer her any very dazzling career, or intoxicating happiness, yet he gave her security. He was killed in 1940 near Verdun, only a few miles from the spot where his father had been killed in 1916.

"I've followed your life," said Modersohn slowly. "Mutual friends have kept me informed."

"I know," she said simply. "And I have always known how you were, and how things were going with you."

"I've written to you from time to time, over the years, although I didn't want to try and force myself on you or to influence you in any way. All I wanted was for you to be certain that if you needed me I was at your disposal."

What a terrible word in the present context, thought Suzanne Barkow. At your disposal! How, though? With money, with word and deed, with the backing of his name? And was that all? Too much for any one moment, too little for a lifetime!

But even then, twenty-two years and three months ago, he'd been at her disposal, pale, profoundly shaken, but utterly honorable, and true to his own code of behavior. His eyes were cold and dark, like the deep waters of some lake beneath a crystal-clear sheet of ice. Then, too, he had made the same remark, "I am of course ready to take all the necessary consequences. Please believe that I'm wholly at your disposal!" And she had answered, "No, never, not in any circumstances!"

And their ways had parted like two branches of a river. His life had flowed onward. Hers had trickled away into the pools and ponds of everyday living.

"I should have gradually forgotten you," said Suzanne Barkow. "One forgets so much in life; time heals almost all wounds. And with the passage of the years it all seemed less and less of a tragedy. There were even times when the memory was tinged with friendliness. One day perhaps it would all have seemed just a beautiful unfortunate incident, if it hadn't been for my son, Bernd."

"You brought him up perfectly," said the general.

"I almost thought you'd say something like that," said Suzanne bitterly. "For twenty years I too thought that I was bringing him up well, being a wise influence on him. But today I know how wrong I was."

Bernd Barkow, her son, later lieutenant and section officer of an officers' training school, blown to bits and buried in Wildlingen-am-Main. Once a boy like a hundred thousand other boys, with the face and quiet friendliness of a child, devoted to his mother, industrious and attentive in school, always among the first in sports and games. But the taller and the more mature he grew, the more his face set, the more recognizable became the figure of a new and dashing young Modersohn. It was the searching look of his cold gray eyes that had first struck his mother with wonder and amazement.

"Did your husband know Bernd wasn't his son?" asked the general.

Suzanne nodded. "He also knew who Bernd's father was; or perhaps I should say he knew who begat him—for my husband was always like a father to Bernd, a kind, just, and thoughtful father."

But in one respect she had been less of a wife than her husband had deserved. In her son she had found again a man she had known long ago, a man who once had whirled her to the very pinnacle of happiness only to let her come crashing to the ground again. But in spite of the betrayal all she remembered was the glorious soaring happiness. It had been a state of utter liberation which she could never forget. And so she began to accept her betrayal. She started trying to see in Bernd Barkow a Bernd Modersohn. She encouraged everything in her boy which she thought she recognized as Modersohn-like virtues. She strengthened him in his powers of resolution, which seemed hesitant at first; she encouraged every sign of self-discipline; she directed his attention to history, and finally to military history. And she molded a youth who was eager and honest, full of the desire for knowledge, more and more determined to become an officer.

"I ought to have taught Bernd to hate such a career," said Suzanne Barkow.

Major-General Modersohn said nothing. It was as if his face had been turned to stone. He had placed his forearms on the table and folded his hands. The skin around the knuckles showed grayish white.

Bernd had been determined to become an officer like his real father, whom he had never seen and of whom he knew nothing. Modersohn had felt a secret pride when he first learned of this in letters from friends, and a feeling of gratitude toward the boy's mother. He had followed Bernd's career very carefully.

"He was a good soldier," said Modersohn.

"But why did he have to die? Why did you have to send for him and make him die here!"

"I wanted to see him," said Modersohn.

When the major-general was appointed commanding officer of Number 5 Officers' Training School, he had put in a request for Lieutenant Barkow—a procedure which presented no particular difficulties. And he had seen his son. He saw a tall, serious young man, with cool gray Modersohn eyes, and a controlled energy in his movements; a well-brought-up boy full of quiet self-confidence. The sight of him forced a treacherous blush of surprise and joy into the general's cheeks. In no other moment of his life did he have to fight so desperately for self-control.

"So you saw him," said Suzanne Barkow. "And I gave my permission in writing. That was a mistake, too, though there's nothing I can do now to put it right."

"I saw my son," said General Modersohn, deep in thought,

"and in the few hours Bernd and I spent together, I felt nothing but gratitude. For the second time in my life I experienced what for want of a better word is called happiness. Two moments of pure joy in the whole of my lifetime."

But there was more to it than that. The general didn't say that in his conversations with Bernd he had been overwhelmed by a sense of anxiety bordering on fear itself.

This son of his was an exact replica of himself—hard, determined, and relentless. It had been an unnerving and at the same time fascinating experience to recognize himself in his son like this. Everything was repeating itself all over again as if life simply went around and around in circles. This son of his was an officer and nothing but an officer, ready to fight and if necessary to die, like generations of officers before him, for a cause known as the Fatherland, or rather for the sense in which they understood that word.

But the general had realized that a true officer's life in this sense was no longer possible.

Modersohn had tried to explain this to his son, who had no idea that it was his father who was talking to him. He had tried to explain how it had all come about. Prussia had gone, and the standards of Prussia had vanished with her. Previously the cry had been for Family, Home, and Fatherland; now the slogan was One People, one Reich, one Führer! The soldier no longer simply fought other soldiers, or defended his homeland and protected his fellow countrymen. Today, as in the days of the mercenaries, the soldier had to fight whole ideologies, different faiths, power blocs. And, worst of all, he had to tolerate crimes and even sanction them and participate in them himself. Germany had lost her honor. The man who had deprived the Germans of their honor and turned officers into criminals was called Hitler. Around him were ranged third-rate hacks and sycophants, the procurers and pimps of politics, together with those narrow-minded, thick-skulled Germans who thought of themselves as some sort of elite and imagined that their country was the center of the world. A despicable attitude which had to be attacked and condemned. And no weak benevolence for those who themselves showed no mercy, whose own violent hatred knew no bounds. This was what he impressed on Lieutenant Barkow, his son. And the latter had understood him, which was why he'd had to die.

"You gave me this son," said Frau Barkow with a heavy heart. "And with you he died. You ploughed a furrow straight across my life and then destroyed it. Or do you consider your-self innocent?"

"No," said the general. "I'm guilty, and I'm determined to expiate this guilt whatever the consequences."

The light from the lamp fell on the half-empty glasses and the wine glowed blood red. They seemed to have nothing more to say to each other. The sounds from the restaurant suddenly became very distinct and audible.

The general asked permission to take his leave, but not without first making plans for the following day. Lieutenant Krafft was to fetch Frau Barkow from her hotel about nine o'clock and take her to the cemetery. He had orders to leave her alone by the graveside for as long as she wished. The florists in the market place, three doors away from the hotel, had already been told to make up a wreath to Frau Barkow's instructions and to include a double ribbon for which the in-scription would also be given them. This was to be followed by an inspection of the training school, with Lieutenant Krafft still acting as escort—and in particular, a visit to Section H for Heinrich, in which Lieutenant Barkow had been serving at the time of his death.

"In the afternoon," said the general, "I shall be at your disposal from two o'clock onward if that suits you. I still have a few small personal mementoes of Bernd, some photo-graphs, some of his work, two books of his with notes in the margin—I'll hand these over to you if you agree."

Suzanne Barkow nodded. The general accompanied her through the restaurant to the lobby of the hotel, where he asked for the key to her room, and said good-by to her at the bottom of the stairs. Then he turned to the hotel propri-etor, who was standing attentively in the background.

"Put everything down to me, please," said the general, and strode quickly out into the night.

"You've got a lot to learn, still," said Captain Kater patronizingly to Irene Jablonski. "One can see that."

They were sitting in this same hotel, where a private room had also been reserved for them. They, too, were en-sconced in an atmosphere of typical Franconian peasant solidity. The landlord knew how to look after his favored guests. On the one hand the general meant excellent publicity for him. On the other, relations with Captain Kater were materially rewarding. For Kater could always be counted on for anything from a useful tip-off to the loan of a truck, provided the arrangement was on a reciprocal basis.

"Do you know the difference between Sekt and Champagne?" Captain Kater asked, drawing pleasurably at his cigar.

Irene Jablonski anxiously admitted that she didn't. "I don't know anything about either of them, but I'd very much like to learn. Would you help me, Captain?"

"Why not? I'll help you with all sorts of things, my dear!"

"Oh, will you really? I know awfully little, you know, and I'd like to know a tremendous lot. Other girls of my age are much more advanced than I am."

"Yes, well," said Captain Kater thoughtfully, "why not?" He looked at the girl opposite him. The little thing was only a child really, and for that reason utterly charming. But at least she was over sixteen, which was reassuring.

"Have you any idea why I've brought you here?" the captain asked.

"Because you are a good man!" said Irene enthusiastically.

"Well, yes—there are a number of different ways of being good, of course, but that's true enough. I like you, my little one."

"I'm so pleased. I like you too."

This wasn't exactly a lie, but a slight exaggeration. She was genuinely grateful to him. He'd brought her to the smartest restaurant in town and had given her wine and a lot of delicious things to eat. She felt happy and content.

"We like each other," declared Kater. "That's marvelous."

"You're always so correct and honorable, so fatherly!"

Captain Kater started. He looked into the blue, trusting, childlike eyes in front of him and a terrible suspicion stirred in his mind. Could this little thing really be so naïve, or was she perhaps really being extremely cunning? Just some sort of hard-boiled little hussy? But surely she couldn't already have the experience of a practiced operator? She was far too young, disturbingly young in fact!

"Fatherly," he repeated thoughtfully. "Do I seem like that to you, Irene? Well, maybe. I'm not so young as I was."

"But you're not at all old," Irene reassured him at once with thoughtful insistence. "You're mature, and I like mature men. I can't bear young whippersnappers."

"That's understandable," said Kater, feeling better at once. "These inexperienced young fellows usually make fools of themselves. They cause more trouble than they're worth. They simply don't know how to live."

"But one can trust you, that's the point. I'd always like

to be close to you, best of all in an office. Please, haven't you got anything for me?"

"Well, I'll see."

"Oh thank you so much."

"Steady, though," said Kater, beginning to backpedal. "I didn't say I would, you know. I only said I'll see.'

"But that's enough, coming from you, Captain. One might have one's doubts if it were someone else, but not with you."

"Well, all right, my little one, but if that's so then I've earned a reward, haven't I?"

"Of course. Only how can I give you one? I've nothing to give."

"Well, we'll see about that. What about a little kiss, for instance?"

"Will it be all right?"

"Why not, my little one?"

"May I really?"

"Come here. Come closer. Closer still. Well now, what about it?"

"Thank you."

"But not on the forehead, girl. What do you think you're doing? Or were you considering me as a father?"

"No, of course not! But I'm so terribly embarrassed. I've never done anything like this before. Is that better?"

"It's a start anyway. You'll have to practice. Have another try."

"I can't now. I must be going."

Irene Jablonski quickly slipped back to her place again. She seemed extremely embarrassed, even highly agitated. Kater looked at her with some satisfaction.

"Don't be so shy, girl!" he said. "And why be in such a hurry? We've plenty of time."

"Yes, but I have to be at work in the kitchen again tomorrow morning."

"No, you don't. You can let yourself oversleep, I'll see it's all right."

"Oh, that's very kind of you. Thank you so much, Captain. But I must be off all the same."

"No, don't. What, with the evening only just beginning? We can have another drink here and then you can come home with me and er—see some of my etchings."

"Another time perhaps, Captain. I'd love to, you know. Only now I really must be going."

"But why, in heaven's name?"

"Someone's expecting me, Captain."

"Someone's expecting you? Who?"

"The girl I share a room with. Elfrida Rademacher. Do you know her?"

"Do I know her!"

"She's waiting for me next door in the restaurant. She said that if I wasn't on time she'd come and fetch me."

"Just like her! Does she know you're with me here?"

"Oh yes," said Irene Jablonski. "I talked it all over with her beforehand. She knows all about this sort of thing. So good-by, Captain. And thank you for everything. I'm so glad I'm going to be able to work in your office in the future."

A thin mist hung in the air. It hovered about the old half-timbered houses in strips as if someone had deliberately torn it up. The streets seemed deserted.

The general's footsteps echoed through them. He put up the collar of his greatcoat and sank his head inside it. He was alone, striding down the street toward the hill where the barracks lay.

The inhabitants of this little town numbered about twenty thousand, and were indistinguishable from those of many other little garrison towns. The barracks here seemed to tower up into the sky like some massive concrete diadem, lying to the west of the town so that the setting sun rested on them for a few minutes after leaving the town itself. In that moment they stood out in sharp, glowing silhouette against the horizon, and seemed both dark and menacing.

The general had never thought of his profession as a pleasure exactly, but it was a long time since he had regarded it as a menace. What he had tried to do was to master a hard, difficult, and humble calling. It was his view that it should be followed in solitude, on much the same sort of principle as that of many monastic orders. Live for others— for mother and children, for the poor and the tormented. Die for them if need be.

Service, thought the general. Service! But who was he serving?

His road to the barracks was that taken over and over again by the so-called civic dignitaries of the town. The last time they had taken it was when he had been installed as commanding officer here. They all came to see him—the burgomaster, the local Party leaders, two master carpenters, an undertaker, representatives of the local housewives, the Civil Defense, and the Red Cross—a responsible and representative deputation of citizens, which had bidden him welcome as the new commanding officer and had assured him that they were proud and happy to have him and his men among them. They spoke of the good relations which existed between the military and the people of the town, and expressed their wish and hope that they would continue like that, if possible even be intensified.

The general had looked at them without a word and simply left them standing there. Whereupon these creatures decided that he must be a man of great character, highly worthy of esteem and respect. His calculated brusqueness sent a shudder of pleasure through them. A big man had given them a kick in the pants, thus enabling them to feel a very close sense of contact with him.

The general strode toward the barrack gates, with an expression of utter disgust on his face—disgust with himself as well as with everything else. Few could share his attitude, that was clear to him. What was it that drove him to keep up this desperate search to find these few? Fate, it seemed, had marked him out. He had never felt this so clearly as on this particular evening.

As he strode through the gate, replying punctiliously to the sentry's salute, he looked up at the building in which his staff was housed. The windows of his own office shone darkly in the night. But at the next window his sharp eyes spotted a tiny chink of light—his secretary, Sybille Bachner, seemed to be working in the anteroom.

The general went into the building, up the stairs, and into the anteroom. He opened the door and saw Sybille Bachner sitting in the room face to face with Lieutenant Krafft. A bottle and two glasses stood on a table between them.

The general stopped in the doorway. Krafft quickly got to his feet. After a moment's hesitation Sybille Bachner also stood up.

"Lieutenant Krafft and I were badly in need of something to pull us around," she said.

"Why?"

The general stood there motionless.

"We've been to one of Frau Frey's little evening parties . . ."

"I understand," said the general. He nodded curtly and walked through the room to his own quarters, leaving the door open behind him. Sybille Bachner followed him and said, "We were just leaving anyway."

The general took off his greatcoat and laid it across a

chair. He returned to the anteroom, followed by Sybille Bachner. Krafft was on the point of leaving.

"Lieutenant Krafft," said the general, "I can understand why you should need a drink after an occasion of that sort. What I don't understand is why you should need to have it in my office."

"Yes, sir," said Krafft calmly.

"Is that your bottle of cognac, Lieutenant?"

"No, sir."

"Take it with you nevertheless. Take Fräulein Bachner, too, if you like."

"We were just about to say good-by to each other, Herr General," Sybille hurriedly explained. "And if there is anything else I can do for you . . ."

"It's possible," said the general. And he went over to Lieutenant Krafft, stopped in front of him, scrutinized his face carefully, and asked:

"How far are you on with that matter of ours?"

"Not much further, sir," said Krafft.

"Don't waste any more time," said the general forcibly. "Try and come to some conclusion. I want to know, to know exactly, as soon as it's humanly possible to know. Be prepared to be sent for about this pretty often in the future, Lieutenant. For the time being, however, I no longer require you."

The lieutenant glanced quickly across at Sybille Bachner. But she wasn't looking at him, having eyes only for the general. Krafft produced a regulation salute, and left.

"As for you, Fräulein Bachner," said the general, looking at her candidly, "I'm sorry if I've disturbed you, but you'll understand that it could hardly be avoided."

"It's for me to apologize, Herr General," said Sybille. "And you didn't disturb us, really you didn't."

"Well, I only wish I had," said the general, smiling bleakly. "I don't grudge you your diversions, provided they don't take place in the office. Lieutenant Krafft isn't a bad choice, for all his limitations."

"There's a lot to be said for him," said Sybille warmly. "But he's not the one for me."

"Who is, then?"

Sybille stared at the general with big round eyes. Bewilderment and dismay mingled with a momentary flicker of hope. She was almost prepared to believe that an indirect proposal had been made to her, though her reason refused to consider the possibility.

"I think it's time to clear up a possible misunderstanding," said the general, drawing himself up to his full height. "It hasn't escaped me that you feel a certain sympathy for me, Fräulein Bachner. This has always struck me as pleasant, if superfluous. I shouldn't like to lose you. Assistants like you are hard to find."

Sybille found herself in the grip of a powerful emotion. The whole world seemed suddenly bathed in a harsh and glaring light. She was hardly able to think at all as she searched desperately for some sign or indication that might give her the slightest ray of hope.

"Fräulein Bachner," said the general, "I want to see the training schedules for Number Two Course for the coming week—the detailed schedules, not just the general plan. And with them the comments of Number Six Company's commanding officer. In three minutes, if you don't mind. After that you can go."

17 *NOT EVEN BICYCLING IS NEGLECTED*

"ZERO FIVE THIRTY hours and a fine morning!" cried the duty cadet. "Up you get, you lazy sods! Off your arses! Thank God for a new day and get those blankets aired!"

For the cadets the day began like any other. There was no sign of anything unusual afoot. On the contrary everything seemed absolutely normal—the shrill blast of the morning whistle, the routine cries of the duty cadet, the thick, foul stench of the atmosphere. They tumbled off their mattresses and stood about dumbly for a few seconds before the bitter cold got them moving.

"Out of it, you lazy bastards!" cried the duty cadet. "Lift up your hearts! Off with your nightshirts!"

The nightshirt was, so to speak, the regulation clothing for the cadets for the period between lights-out and reveille. Only officers were allowed to wear pajamas, provided by the army clothing department in three different patterns and five sizes in a price range between 28.40 and 34.80 Reichmarks. At this stage in their careers, however, cadets had to wear nightshirts—white ones only, moreover. A breast pocket on the left-hand side, while frowned upon, was not expressly forbidden.

The "Clothing Regulations—Night" had been drafted by Major Frey, commanding officer of Number 2 Course, who was an acknowledged master of this sort of minutely detailed instruction. And if, as it so happened, hardly a single cadet in the whole of H Section stuck to this Special Order number 78 of his, there were special reasons for that.

For Lieutenant Krafft was still a new boy, and the cadets didn't hesitate to exploit the fact. Krafft couldn't possibly be expected to know all the various refinements devised by the course commanding officer, and the cadets therefore asked him innocently enough, "When it's very cold is it permissible to wear additional clothing at night?"

All unwittingly the newly appointed section officer had replied, "I don't care what you wear!"

The cadets of H Section therefore rose from their beds muffled in the most remarkable garments. Quite a few were wearing socks or had wound scarves about their bodies. Some wore all or part of their underclothing. Two had pulled on cardigans over the top of everything else.

Kramer, Weber, Amfortas, and Andreas, and Hochbauer of course, noted the muffled figures partly with indignation, partly with anxiety. One morning all this mollycoddling was bound to come to the notice of Captain Ratshelm, and unpleasantness would inevitably follow. When Ratshelm inspected his cadets at reveille he liked to see them wearing nightshirts as stipulated in the regulations.

"Come on now, all that whining and teeth-chattering won't help you!" cried the duty cadet.

The cadets of H Section, who slept in eight separate rooms, took off their night shirts and everything else they had on. Then with yawns they reached sullenly and sulkily for their games clothes. The first half hour was the worst period of the whole day, comparable only to the tactics period with Captain Feders. The day always opened with fifteen minutes of early-morning physical training.

Today it was Lieutenant Krafft's turn to take this period. Experience had taught the cadets that there were certain advantages to this, for each officer had his own methods and Krafft's were more tolerable than most.

"Warm yourselves up, boys!" he would say, and calmly smoke his first cigarette of the day as he watched to see that no senior officers came to disturb them.

"What about a little run, friends!" cried Lieutenant Krafft to his cadets.

This wasn't a suggestion, or even a request, but an order.

The cadets trotted off at once, at no very great pace, for the sleep was still in their bones.

"Always the same," groaned Cadet Mösler. "The same thing morning after morning. I'm fed up with it!"

It seemed to be just like any other morning, yet something did happen which no one took any notice of at first. Lieutenant Krafft said, "Rednitz, come here a moment, will you?"

"Aha!" said Cadet Kramer, continuing to lead his section in the run. "What's this fellow Rednitz been up to? Trouble of some sort, doubtless."

It was with mixed feelings that Rednitz left the group of cadets trotting sullenly around and around the sports ground. Conversations with superior officers were hardly ever pleasurable, particularly not the first thing in the morning, and he therefore approached his section officer with a cautious grin designed to test the situation.

This amiable grin of his was returned at once, creating a thoroughly congenial atmosphere. Though Rednitz really didn't know much about Krafft, he had discovered that at least he wasn't the holy terror some officers were.

"My dear Rednitz," said the lieutenant, "I'd like to put to you a question which you don't need to answer if you don't want to, although I'm convinced you can answer it."

These words put Rednitz on the alert at once. All his suspicions were aroused. The form of address alone—"My dear Rednitz"—dispelled the last sluggish traces of sleep. Rednitz sensed at once that something out of the ordinary was being demanded of him, and he looked at the lieutenant with sharp, inquisitive eyes.

"The situation is as follows," said Krafft, choosing his words with care. "Frau Barkow has arrived, the mother of Lieutenant Barkow. I've been given the job of looking after her, presumably because I'm her son's successor. And in the course of the morning, probably during the period between eleven and twelve, I shall be introducing Frau Barkow to our section."

Krafft paused calculatingly to let his words sink in, and thought he detected a flicker of understanding in the cadet's bright, humorous eyes, which certainly were not lacking in cunning.

"Yes, sir," said the cadet keenly.

"That's to say, Rednitz, Frau Barkow will be getting to know those cadets who were present on the occasion of her son's death. Now I've never been quite clear how his death occurred. I'm not clear, either, who actually may have, more or less, willingly or unwillingly, accidentally or intentionally, had a hand in his death. And this gives rise to a peculiar situation which you can help me to solve."

"Me, sir?" asked Rednitz, putting as great a distance between himself and the subject as possible.

There was no mistaking the cadet's extreme disinclination to discuss the matter. This fellow Krafft was trying to draw him onto dangerous ground. He, Rednitz, was now in a position to secure the lieutenant's good will, but only if he were prepared to betray his comrades. Alternatively, he could pretend to know nothing and keep his mouth shut, though by doing this he would annoy the lieutenant or, worse still, might make an enemy of him.

"Rednitz," said Krafft, seeming to guess the cadet's thoughts accurately enough, "don't think I want to use you as some sort of stool pigeon. All I want from you is something to go on. Just think what might happen. Frau Barkow could get into conversation with one or other of the cadets, give him her hand, and possibly even thank him. And I feel that there are some in this section who ought not to find themselves in that position—cadets, who either didn't want, or weren't able, to understand Lieutenant Barkow, who had no time for him, or even perhaps hated him."

"Well," said Rednitz cautiously, after a considerable pause, "what I'd suggest, sir, is that Frau Barkow should turn to me. I can shake hands with a clear conscience."

"Only you, Rednitz?"

"Oh, a whole lot of others as well, sir. Certainly everyone sitting on the benches at the back."

"Not those sitting in front, then?"

Rednitz stared at the lieutenant in astonishment. He felt thoroughly ill at ease. For it seemed to him that utterly against his will he had allowed himself to be lured into a trap. He groped for words, and the more he groped the clearer it became to him that every second that passed was merely making his personal catastrophe worse. For his silence signified assent.

"All right, Rednitz," said Lieutenant Krafft finally, giving the impression that he had neither guessed nor discerned anything of importance. "I had hoped you might be able to help me. But since this doesn't appear to be the case—not that this is your fault in any way, of course—treat what I have said to you as confidential. In fact forget it altogether, if you will. Thank you, Rednitz."

Cadet Rednitz turned about and ran off in pursuit of his section, to resume his place in the ranks. His youthful brow was deeply furrowed, for he was thinking hard. What seemed to him particularly ominous was the way in which the lieutenant had made everything so easy for him at the end. It was conclusive proof of the extent to which he had let himself be caught napping and had allowed this fellow Krafft to see through him.

"What did the slave driver want?" asked Kramer, the section senior.

"He just wanted to know who it was who had Lieutenant Barkow on his conscience," explained Rednitz, raising his voice to arouse attention.

"Ass!" said Kramer with some amusement, feeling certain that this was just another of Rednitz's rather questionable jokes. A number of the other cadets laughed, too, but cadet Andreas, running between Hochbauer and Amfortas, called out indignantly, "That's nothing to joke about, man!"

"Tell that to your neighbor!" replied Rednitz.

"And while you're about it," cried Mösler, "tell him to take a running jump at himself as well. Tell him he has my full permission to do so."

"He won't forgive you for that," Rednitz warned Mösler.

"I hope not," said Mösler, undismayed.

But Lieutenant Krafft had now finished his first cigarette of the day, and throwing it away into the middle of the parade ground, he blew his whistle. The morning physical training period was over.

Sections G and I now separated from Section H, and Krafft's cadets trotted up to him, came to attention, and waited for their section officer to dismiss them.

"There's a change in this morning's timetable," Lieutenant Krafft announced. "The first period, military history, will be dropped. The fourth period will be taken by me. No particular subject. In case I'm late, the section senior will read over Special Order number ninety-four and discuss it with you. The first three periods will be taken by Captain Feders —tactics instruction."

"Shit," said Mösler with some force.

"Friends," said Captain Feders with eager anticipation, "today we at last have sufficient time in which to examine our subject a little more thoroughly. I'm glad to see you appreciate the fact."

The cadets sat submissively on their benches without any illusions, sensing trouble ahead.

The first crisis occurred over the disappearance of two motor bikes which all the cadets had forgotten to mention when drawing up a large-scale inventory of supplies together on the blackboard.

"Half-wits, blockheads, nincompoops!" pronounced Captain Feders with grim satisfaction. "What a bunch of boobs! What a miserable useless lot! Do you realize what it means to forget two motor bikes? It means that two dispatch riders have nothing to do, two men hanging about idling their time away. But not only that—it could jeopardize the entire communications system, which in turn could mean a failure of supplies, and all sorts of disasters entailing fatal casualties. All this and worse, you hopeless dopes, just because out of sheer stupidity two dispatch riders are left lying about with nothing to do."

The cadets accepted Feders as some sort of infliction from on high. They bent over their notebooks and pads, scribbling away as hard as they could in an innocent enough attempt to escape from it all. At least, this way, they didn't have to look their tactics instructor in the face. It required nerve to sit there waiting for that gimlet glance of his.

"Damn it," muttered Rednitz.

Rednitz saw clearly enough that it was Feders' intention to make the training school a sort of foretaste of the hell that awaited them. What was Lieutenant Krafft up to, though?

But it was almost impossible to pursue irrelevant thoughts successfully in one of Captain Feders' periods. His remarks had something in common with a skillfully laid mine field. It was all too easy for a cadet and all his dreams of becoming an officer to be blown sky-high in them. So that even Rednitz took some trouble to concentrate on what his tactics instructor was saying.

"There's one final proof of your collective idiocy," said Captain Feders, thoroughly enjoying himself. "When I explained the initial situation to you just now, I went so far as to ask if everything was clear, and whether anyone had any comments to make or whether any further explanation was needed. And you just sat there like a bunch of dummies. Well, I was setting a trap for you, because I had quite intentionally made a mistake. Now I'd be glad if you'd tell me what it was."

A mistake? The cadets racked their brains trying to think what it could be. But they knew well enough that this was just a waste of time. At the beginning of the period Captain Feders, in outlining the initial situation, had overwhelmed them with between twenty and twenty-five different map positions, and dozens of different figures, symbols, and timings.

"Right, then," said Feders. "Between positions fifteen and seventeen I placed a burial assembly point, which is nothing but a lot of crap, as you should have realized at once. However, your brains seem to have completely atrophied."

The cadets, or rather the majority of them, still didn't know exactly where the mistake was. Had the position been wrong? Had the wrong map reference been given? Was a burial assembly point perhaps superfluous in the circumstances, or useless, or just premature? What a confusing range of possibilities! This was the sort of thing that made them regard tactics simply as a matter of luck. Trying to master tactics with Captain Feders was like trying to put up an umbrella in a hurricane.

"There's no such thing as a burial assembly point," announced Captain Feders with relish. "Not in battle at any rate. You may later wish to lay out cemeteries to our glorious dead, but there's no time for that in war itself. An assembly point for half-wits, however, seems to have something to recommend it; the entire section could be marched straight there."

The cadets noted it down in their notebooks. "No burial assembly points in battle."

"Why not?" continued Feders. "Quite simple. Transport facilities exist for the fighting troops and for supplies—equipment, rations, and ammunition. If a man is killed, he's buried. Preferably where he falls. Though of course not at the entrances to houses, in streets, indoors, near supply dumps, or in actual fighting positions. Coffins are superfluous. A ground-sheet will do, provided, that is, that a ground-sheet is used which can no longer be employed for any other purpose; that's to say a ground-sheet that's torn or riddled with bullet holes. Beechwood makes the best sort of cross. Officers with a certain amount of foresight, moreover, will always see to it that there's an adequate supply of ready-made crosses in store. To sum up: in war we have corpses but no burial assembly points."

In their passion for learning the cadets accepted even these remarks with equanimity. Feders looked at his watch and closed his book. The cadets breathed a sigh of relief.

"Talking of corpses," said Feders in conclusion, "Lieutenant Krafft will be bringing a guest to see you during the next period—Lieutenant Barkow's mother. You'll finally have the chance to show her what a hard-boiled lot you are. Try to look Frau Barkow straight in the eye—honorably and respectfully, in a manner befitting future officers."

"Ten minutes break!" cried Cadet Kramer. "And I would remind you that smoking in the classroom and the corridor is forbidden."

"You don't need to look," said Mösler pulling a crumpled cigarette out of his tunic pocket.

"I have a very keen sense of smell, Mösler."

"Well," said Mösler, looking for a match, "a little stink more or less, here, won't make much difference."

Kramer didn't reply. He acted as if he hadn't even heard, and busied himself with the class log.

Not a few cadets used the break to write up their notes. Those who sat on the benches at the back of the classroom formed a separate group from those in front, where Hochbauer now began elaborating the theory that corpses could provide excellent cover, though of course only in conditions of severe frost. At the back Mösler was giving one of his special performances—"For fighting troops only!"—in which he told jokes of a familiar kind about a certain widow—all very crude and vulgar, but popular all the same. He had soon collected about him a sympathetic audience who were roaring their heads off. Mösler found the applause encouraging, and in his enthusiasm overlooked the fact that Hochbauer and his satellites had joined the throng and were standing there listening with grim expressions on their faces. At the end of the next dirty joke Hochbauer pushed his way ruthlessly forward, planted himself in front of Mösler, and said savagely, "Dirty swine."

"Mösler. Pleased to meet you," said the cadet, pulling off an old, rather cheap joke that was always effective. This time, however, it didn't seem to strike anyone as very funny.

"You're a dirty rotten bastard," said Hochbauer to Mösler.

There was a certain amount of justice in this, at least in the present circumstances, and normally Mösler would not have taken too much exception to it. But since it was Hochbauer of all people who was here setting himself up as a guardian of morality, decency, and propriety, Mösler felt extremely indignant. So with some force he said, "I can see why *you* need to play the man of honor here. I expect you'll even manage to sing a hymn of praise to Lieutenant Barkow's mother and express your sympathy to her. I wouldn't put it past you either to convey your thanks for the opportunity to try your hand at grave digging."

It was at this moment that Hochbauer struck out, slapping Mösler's face hard with the palm of his hand. Mösler, furious with rage, tried to rush at Hochbauer, but two cadets, Amfortas and Andreas, grabbed hold of him and Hochbauer hit him again, with the same hand on the same spot.

Mösler looked around for support and tried to wrench himself free. But Rednitz had gone to the latrines. Egon Weber was smoking a cigarette outside in the corridor somewhere and the other cadets felt themselves to be strictly neutral. Only Böhmke, the poet, gasped excitedly for breath and shouted at Hochbauer, "You can't do that!"

"Hold your tongue," said Hochbauer.

At which moment Kramer shouted anxiously, "Take your seats, men! Break over!"

Hochbauer turned around without a word and made for his place in the front row. His satellites covered his retreat for him. The cadets sat down in their places and opened their notebooks, Mösler massaged his right cheek brooding on revenge, and Böhmke, genuinely indignant over what he had seen, repeated over and over again, "But you can't do that!"

"Cadet Böhmke," cried the section senior, "you will take up your usual post as lookout."

Obeying meekly, Böhmke went out and took up his usual observation post at the corridor window, whence he had a good view of the approach to the classroom block and was thus able to keep a lookout for Lieutenant Krafft.

"You gave it to him, all right!" said Amfortas appreciatively to Hochbauer.

"The swine asked for it," said Hochbauer forcefully.

Amfortas struck a warning note. "Of course," he said, "he won't just take that. He'll shoot his mouth off as soon as Rednitz is there to give him covering fire."

"It's time things were brought out into the open," said Hochbauer. "It can't go on like this. Either these fellows have got to shut up of their own accord or we'll stop their mouths by force. There's no other possibility!"

"Quiet, please, men!" cried Cadet Kramer in his capacity as section senior. "The section officer will be here any minute, and while we're waiting for him, we'll start the period as instructed."

Kramer looked about him challengingly, but no one showed any inclination to flout his authority—not even Mösler, who had much to brood on, as Kramer was pleased to note. He unfolded Special Order number 94 and prepared to read it out.

But Cadet Rednitz was still not present. Questioning elicited that the missing man had last been sighted reading some lurid trash in the latrines. Kramer immediately sent out a search party, but he was smart enough to do so without depleting Hochbauer's bodyguard.

Rednitz finally appeared seven minutes late, followed by the search party. Kramer demanded the explanation he was not only entitled, but indeed obliged, to ask for. If one were not forthcoming he would unfortunately be compelled . . .

"I've been improving myself with *Military Regulations*," declared Rednitz promptly, "and they were so thrilling that I completely forgot all about time and place."

Kramer was suspicious, and the carefree gaiety which more than immediately threatened to envelope the section annoyed him intensely. Taking a stand therefore on his authority he tired to make clear to Rednitz that he knew perfectly well what had been going on. "Since when have *Military Regulations* had lurid covers with naked women on?"

"Always, as far as I'm concerned," said Rednitz, who seemed quite unimpressed by this thrust. "I always conceal my copy of *Regulations* in this way, so that my comrades won't think that I'm just another careerist too." The word "too" carried a subtle but unmistakable emphasis.

"Hypocrite!" muttered Hochbauer.

"Quiet, please!" cried the section senior, managing not to look directly at Hochbauer as he did so, so that his order seemed directed at the room in general. "And you, Rednitz, get to your place at once. I'm now going to read out Special Order number ninety-four."

This Special Order number 94 was one of Major Frey's numerous administrative masterpieces, and bore the title, "The Care and Use of Service Bicycles Together with the Allotment and Return Thereof." It consisted of fourteen paragraphs.

Kramer read out this remarkable intellectual effort in a loud, clear voice, emphasizing the various shades of meaning, pausing slightly at every comma, slightly longer at every full stop, and slightly longer still at every new paragraph. It was as if he were proclaiming articles of war, or the Party program, or even a new Constitution.

Among other points of which Kramer notified them was the following: "Standing on the left-hand side of the bicycle the rider grasps the handlebars, one hand on each handle. The left pedal should by now have reached its lowest point."

"Not only the left pedal," commented Cadet Rednitz, lovingly putting some finishing touches to a little man he had been drawing on his writing pad. He expected a snigger of agreement from Mösler, who sat beside him. But Mösler remained silent. Finding this odd, Rednitz turned his full attention on his friend.

Meanwhile Kramer was droning on. "The rider now places his left foot on the left pedal, evenly distributing the weight of his body and simultaneously swinging the right foot, without undue vehemence—which would in fact, hamper the requisite equilibrium—off the ground and slightly forward at the same time . . ."

The cadets let the words pass harmlessly over their heads. Some made notes as always, but most just dozed off, thinking vaguely about lunch or the tactics period they had just survived or the forthcoming visit of Frau Barkow.

"The bastard hit me in the face," Mösler muttered to his friend. "While you were in the latrine."

Rednitz saw at once that this wasn't just one of Mösler's jokes. His face, which normally always wore an amiable expression, was now black with rage.

"Hochbauer?" he asked slowly.

"Who else?" said Mösler. "The swine hit me in the face—twice."

"Why?"

"The usual. I told him the truth."

"You didn't hit back?"

"They grabbed hold of me. What could I do? Run to you in the latrine?"

Rednitz nodded thoughtfully. Then he said, "He won't do it again. I'll see to that."

Mösler's spirits began to revive. "The first chance I get," he said, "I'll give it to him—that is, if I can manage to find him without his bodyguard. I'll make mincemeat of him."

"You leave that to me," said Rednitz. "For the excellent reason that Hochbauer, being your physical superior, would make mincemeat of you."

"Then just give me a little assistance," insisted Mösler. "You or Egon Weber. You're my comrades, aren't you?"

"We're your friends, Mösler, which is a good deal more. But one thing I promise you. Hochbauer will pay for hitting you like that, and he'll pay a heavy price too. Just leave it to me."

Kramer was reading on steadfastly from Special Order number 94:

"If a breakdown should occur, the following procedure is to be adopted:

"(*a*) the responsible superior officer should be informed,

"(*b*) an attempt should be made to repair the breakdown,

"(*c*) the store from which the bicycle was drawn should be informed regardless of whether the breakdown has been successfully repaired or not. A distinction should be made between the following types of breakdown: puncture (rear and forward wheels), wheel breakdown (also rear and forward), pedal, chain, frame, handlebar, and saddle breakdown."

There then followed an exhaustive description of every single type of breakdown with exact instructions on how to carry out preliminary repairs. With this went a painfully detailed list of tools, patching equipment, and other accessories. The cadets were, however, prevented for the time being from acquainting themselves further with such subtleties for just then Böhmke shot into the room in his usual state of excitement and announced, "Lieutenant Krafft approaching and the lady with him!"

Kramer hastily marked his place in Special Order number 94 and raised his voice to give his section its word of command as if it had been a considerable body of troops parading before him.

"Attention!" he roared. "Beg to report to the lieutenant— Section H all present and correct, sir!"

"And this, dear lady," said Lieutenant Krafft, indicating the cadets, "is Section H for Heinrich."

After a short pause he added, "Gentlemen—Frau Barkow."

The cadets stood stiffly to attention. Krafft showed no signs of preparing to put them at their ease. He led Frau Barkow up to the platform, which gave her the best view of the room.

The cadets carefully scrutinized Lieutenant Barkow's mother, who stood before them small and helpless and ill at ease. They saw a pale face, and eyes that were friendly and tragic at the same time.

Frau Barkow looked out a little uneasily at these fine, upstanding young men, seeing for the most part only smooth, inquisitive faces. In certain eyes she also thought she detected a gleam of sympathy. With an effort her lips parted, and it seemed for a moment as if she were going to say a few words. But Krafft gave her no time.

"These classroom barracks have two rooms," explained the lieutenant. "This one is almost exclusively reserved for Section H—tactics instruction, general instruction, political instruction, ten to fourteen hours a week under the direction of the section officer. Here is the desk your son stood at. When the cadets are doing written work we keep behind it most of the time. If you would be so good as to follow me, madam, you'll see that the only view from the windows is of the transport sheds, which makes it easier for the cadets to concentrate . . ."

While Krafft was saying all this and accompanying Frau Barkow around the room, he kept a wary eye on the section itself, particularly the front rows. But he saw nothing that gave him anything to go on. All the faces remained stiff and immobile. A little too stiff, a little too immobile, thought the lieutenant, watching Hochbauer, Andreas, and Amfortas and the others in the front rows. But to present them with a deliberate challenge now wouldn't have been fair to Frau Barkow. She was a human being, who had already won his sympathy, very much against his will and without any effort to do so on her own part.

At the cemetery he had seen her standing just as she stood now in front of the cadets, with an air of quiet, tragic acceptance about her. No wild, choking grief, no stammered words invoking pity, no demands for cheap, easy comfort. Just this simple acceptance of the inevitable. A wall of invisible glass about her, as with the general.

"I hope, madam," said Lieutenant Krafft finally, "I've shown you everything that might interest you."

"Thank you, Lieutenant," said Frau Barkow, unmoved.

"One of our cadets will escort you to the barrack gates, madam. Cadet Rednitz, to be precise." And with that the lieutenant opened the door. Frau Barkow nodded once to the section, which remained at attention in front of her. She gave Krafft her hand, and left. Cadet Rednitz stumbled, uncomprehending, after her.

Lieutenant Krafft, however, turned back to his section at once, knowing quite well that what the cadets were wondering at that moment was, why Rednitz particularly? But he gave them no time to think the matter over.

"Sit down please," he said. "Get ready to write. You have exactly twenty minutes. Subject: an obituary notice for Lieutenant Barkow. Right, off you go."

18 *THE TEMPTATION OF THE COMPANY COMMANDER*

CAPTAIN RATSHELM was privileged to be a witness to a most significant situation. Major Frey, Commanding Officer of Number 2 Course, found himself sorely troubled.

"I must confess," said the major confidentially, "that a good deal that's been going on under my command lately has given me food for thought."

The captain nodded, for it affected him deeply to hear that a superior officer had been forced to devote himself to serious thought. They were sitting opposite each other in the major's office, where Captain Ratshelm felt proud to be enjoying the major's confidence. He felt chosen, so to speak, since out of three able company commanders, the major had preferred him. What an honor! A pointer surely to his prospects for promotion.

"The major can count on me whatever happens," the captain assured him.

"My dear Ratshelm," said the major courteously and confidentially, "you find me worried, and not least on your account."

The captain stopped nodding at once. Indeed he was utterly astounded, as his face showed. For he felt certain he had done his duty at all times.

"Your work, my dear Ratshelm," the major hastened to explain to him, "leaves nothing to be desired. I'll be glad to assure you of that at any time. But even the most exemplary work may find itself undermined, and it's just this that seems to be happening in your case."

"Certainly, Major," said Captain Ratshelm rather stiffly. "But all I can do is to point out abuses and ask for them to be remedied. The appointment and dismissal of section officers, or even of tactics instructors, does not, unfortunately, fall within my province."

"Nor in mine," said the major softly with a regretful

smile and casting a quick glance upward as if to suggest that the source responsible for such things—i.e. the general —might be said to be living in the clouds.

"Let us just think this matter over together, my dear Ratshelm," continued the major with marked solicitude. "The situation is as follows. I have three company commanders below me and am perfectly satisfied with all three of them— though with you in particular, my dear fellow. But they suffer at present from the misfortune of having at least one officer immediately subordinate to them—if not two—who may be undermining their achievements. And I ask you, what's to be done about it?"

Ratshelm had no idea just then. It seemed to him that the superior officer in question, in this case the major himself, ought to seize the initiative. He had no doubt that this was what would happen eventually. But since his co-operation had been sought, it seemed that he would have to take up some standpoint, and he therefore said, rather vaguely, "Perhaps we again ought to try to ask the general . . ."

The major laughed out loud—a curt laugh with a very bitter ring to it. It left the captain in no doubt as to what he thought of his suggestion. There was a hint of criticism in it, too, if not actually accusation.

"My dear, excellent Ratshelm," said the major. "We are, I think, agreed that nothing, absolutely nothing, should prevent us doing our duty." The captain vigorously nodded agreement.

"And therefore we shouldn't allow ourselves simply to knuckle under to certain questionable manifestations of despotic behavior. This lady's semiofficial visit to the barracks, for instance—I find it disquieting."

"So do I!" agreed the captain.

"Not even my own wife," said the major, warming to his theme, "have I ever permitted to attend one of our cadets' classes. Such a thing not only interrupts the smooth flow of training but damages the whole pattern of military life as such. It offends its basic principles. All my soldierly instincts revolt against it."

Again Ratshelm could only agree, and the major now felt certain of victory. Captain Ratshelm was like a phonograph that he had wound up—all that remained to do was to put on the right record.

"Right, then, my dear Ratshelm. What we need now are facts and still more facts! As solid and indisputable facts as possible. Because theories and insight alone aren't going

to take us any further. You're the man at the source of
things. Keep your eyes and ears open, and as soon as a
favorable opportunity presents itself don't hesitate to strike.
Do you follow me?"

"Entirely, Major," Captain Ratshelm assured him.

"I knew I could rely on you, my dear fellow. And I'm
sure I couldn't have found a better man for the job."

"Isn't my wife there?" asked the major, looking about
him hopefully.

"She's gone to see the burgomaster's wife," said Barbara, looking at Frey with interest. She had seen at once that
he was in a particularly good mood. "It'll be two hours at
least before she gets back."

"Fine, fine," said the major contentedly. "I'm delighted to
think she's getting this little change."

"Yes," said Barbara, "everyone needs a little change
from time to time."

As he took off his coat the major glanced sideways at his
wife's niece. Funny girl, he thought, makes great cow's eyes
the whole time, always seems rather slow and tired. Bed-
worthy, you might say. Yes, that was it! The girl had a sort
of sluggish sensuality.

"Anything you'd like?" asked Barbara, looking at him with
her head rather on one side.

"What did you say?" asked Frey in bewilderment.

"I asked if you'd like something—coffee for instance,
or a cognac?"

"No, no," said the major with relief. "Later perhaps. I
think I'll do a little work now."

"Shall I wake you later?"

"Yes," said the major, slightly irritated by her forthright approach. "You can wake me just before my wife comes
back."

The major went to his workroom, to pass straight from
there to his bedroom. He lay down on the bed, stretched
himself out, and looked up at the ceiling.

His self-satisfaction seemed justified. His conversation
with Ratshelm had been a masterpiece of successful diplo-
macy. On the one hand he had condemned someone without
ever naming him or yet leaving any doubt as to whom he
meant. On the other hand he had put forward a number of
demands without having had to dress them up in the form
of a direct order. The task he had set Ratshelm was a

difficult one, carrying a lot of responsibility—and his own, the major's, responsibility for it was as good as nil!

"Have you taken your shoes off?" asked Barbara from the door.

"Don't disturb me," said the major indignantly. "I'm thinking."

"You can do that without your shoes on," said Barbara. "Shall I take them off for you?"

"And my trousers while you're about it, I suppose!" cried the major indignantly.

"Why not?" asked Barbara lazily. "You don't need to be embarrassed in front of me. I know how you look in your underpants."

"Get out!" said the major. "I'll take my shoes off myself."

"But be sure you do," said Barbara. "You know your wife can be very cross if you make the bedclothes dirty."

The major watched her go. Just look at her, he thought. The little thing had handsome shoulders and an unexpectedly narrow waist. A bottom like a horse, too—which was intended as a compliment, for the major had a weakness for horses. But he forced himself to relinquish this line of inquiry. Any sort of affair with his wife's niece was of course quite out of the question. He concentrated on other things, trying to think out a new special order. Its number would be 114. The subject: Use and Storage of Winter Clothing, Particularly in High Summer Temperatures, and with Particular Regard to Inadequate Supplies of Preservative Materials.

"Are you cold?" asked Barbara. She was standing in the door again, eyeing him with her great cowlike eyes.

"No," he said in a tone of rebuff. "I'm rather hot."

"Perhaps you've got a temperature?" she asked, coming closer.

"No, I'm completely normal!"

"Really?" asked Barbara, almost hopefully.

"Yes indeed—and now please don't disturb me any more. I think I'll have a little rest, or at least try to have one! Do you begrudge it me perhaps?"

"But I don't begrudge you anything," Barbara assured him with a smile. "I just wanted to bring you a blanket."

The major lay on his back and looked up at her. Everything about her seemed large and well rounded. And the major, too, began to smile. Not that Frey lusted after his wife's niece, but it flattered him to know that she was so keen on him. His power of attraction for women had of course always been enormous.

"Now tell me in confidence, Barbara," he said, sitting up a little. "What sort of relations do you have with men? What I mean is, is there one man who's closer to you than any other?"

"What do you mean by closer?"

"Well, for instance, how do you like Captain Ratshelm? He'd make a good match, wouldn't he? And you know your aunt would be delighted."

"But not Ratshelm!" said Barbara indignantly.

"Why not, Barbara? What have you got against him?"

"Well," said Barbara frankly, "I can't imagine him in bed—in bed with a woman, I mean."

The major shuddered slightly. He had expected directness but not quite such plain speaking as this. What a strange girl she was! Shocking! And here he'd been living under the same roof with her for months now and not seeing at all the sort of girl she was!

"I'd much prefer Lieutenant Krafft," Barbara assured him frankly. "But he's fully occupied at the moment. He's said to be getting a good return on his money."

"Who says so?" asked the major, partly indignant and partly extremely interested. "What's he up to?"

"He's having an affair with this girl Elfrida Rademacher, didn't you know? Even in the movies, they say!"

"Unbelievable," said the major. By that he meant two things. First, what Krafft was up to—and this piece of information was of particular interest to him; but second, what he found almost unbelievable was that Barbara of all people, whom he'd always considered fairly stupid, should be the one to know. "Tell me, how do you happen to know this exactly?"

"Oh, one hears it around."

"But what sort of people does one hear saying it? Who says such things? Who've you been talking to about it?"

"Oh well, like now, with you for instance."

"Barbara, I'll have to tell your aunt about this."

"Why? Do you want to make her suspicious?"

"You can go now!" he ordered. "That's quite enough!"

"But what is it you want?" asked Barbara honestly. "You asked me a question and I answered it. I told you that Lieutenant Krafft seems to me a real man. What's wrong with that? You seem to me a real man too."

"Out of here, Barbara! Or I may overreach myself!"

"Really?"

"Get out of here at once! I'm tired and I want to go to sleep."

"Ah, that's different," said Barbara, and left.

"At ease, gentlemen!" cried Captain Ratshelm to his three section officers. "Please don't take any notice of me. I'm here not as your company commanding officer, but only to take part in a little sport."

Captain Ratshelm, wearing tightly fitting shorts and a sleeveless shirt, mingled with his cadets.

"If it doesn't upset your plans, gentlemen, I'd very much like to suggest some ball games."

"Of course, Captain," said Lieutenant Webermann, the senior of the three section officers of Number 6 Company. He blew his whistle and shouted, "Ball games!"

The cadets immediately split up into groups and teams for the various ball games—handball, punchball, and so on.

As if by mere chance the captain joined Section H for Heinrich, which came as no surprise to the initiated. But this time Ratshelm made what he considered a particularly clever move, electing to play *against* the team of which his favorite was a member, that is against his fellow sportsman, Hochbauer. In this way Ratshelm was, as it were, able to see Hochbauer clearly and thus take particular delight in the neat and graceful movements of such an uncommonly fine specimen of humanity.

Of course Captain Ratshelm won the first game straight away. Hochbauer accepted his own and his team's defeat with equanimity. He even let it be seen that it was a pleasure to be beaten by such a remarkable opponent. The cadet's spirit of sportsmanship struck Ratshelm as being altogether exemplary.

Lieutenant Krafft watched these goings-on contentedly enough. Knowing that his section was in good hands, he went over to Lieutenant Dietrich for a short conversation. This presented no difficulty, for Dietrich's section was playing against Lieutenant Webermann's, and Webermann had quite enough imagination and endurance to keep both groups permanently on the move.

"My dear Krafft," said Lieutenant Dietrich as the two of them strolled undisturbed across the sports ground, "has it ever occurred to you to wonder why our company commanding officer should have developed such an extraordinary fondness for sport?"

"Has it occurred to you, then, Dietrich?" Krafft asked, interested.

"Certainly," said the other with some amusement. "And I assume I've come to the same conclusion as you. But like you I consider it wisest to keep my mouth shut. Or perhaps you don't agree?"

"I agree with you entirely, my dear Dietrich," said Krafft thoughtfully, following this up immediately by asking, "Why are you trying to warn me?"

"Perhaps simply out of the spirit of comradeship," Dietrich now said, no less frankly, and a mocking smile appeared on his intelligent face. "Perhaps just to remind you that you're only one officer among several dozen others here, and that there's such a thing as *esprit de corps.*"

"Now really, my dear Dietrich,' said Krafft going over to the defensive. "I hope you're not trying to tell me not to foul my own nest, because if so, you've come to the wrong address. Perhaps you ought rather to warn Captain Ratshelm?"

Lieutenant Dietrich, who was always very reserved, was one of the quietest of warriors, a man of intelligence and education. So he said cautiously, "I mean only that we all have our weaknesses. What matters is not that such weaknesses exist, but whether or not we give in to them."

The two officers now had to break off their conversation, for Captain Ratshelm brought the games period to an end ten minutes before the usual time. But Ratshelm had just won a game of punchball with resounding success—the perfect climax to an afternoon's sport.

"Off to the showers!" the captain shouted to the cadets.

It was quite usual for Captain Ratshelm to take a shower with them, and there were even sound practical reasons why the cadets should have no objections. The taking of showers, like everything else, was supposed to be carried out in accordance with a carefully elaborated routine, for hot water had to be used economically. A company commander, however, could order variations in the routine, and since this was what Ratshelm almost always did, the cadets welcomed his presence.

These shower regulations were laid down in Special Order number 53 and the prescribed procedure was as follows: The bathers were to position themselves under the showers— there would follow two minutes of hot water—bodies were then to be soaped—and this would be followed by two minutes more of water which started hot but grew gradually colder and colder though never descending below eighteen degrees centigrade.

When, however, Captain Ratshelm joined a shower group personally, the prescribed limits were freely overstepped. For he simply gave the order, water on—water off—increase the temperature—hold the temperature—and what usually took between five and seven minutes might be stretched to as much as a full quarter of an hour.

"Water on!" cried Ratshelm. "Hot tap full on!"

He was a man in love with cleanliness. For him a snow-white handkerchief was a sure sign of culture. White was his favorite color—pure snowy white, milk white.

Here among his beloved cadets he breathed in all the freshness and cleanliness of nature. New-mown hay, a glass of fresh milk, lake water lapping around the reeds, simple delights for the senses of the unsophisticated—he was a man given to the enjoyment of such things in the simple way.

"Hold the water there!" he cried. "Temperature at thirty."

Cadet Hochbauer stood close beside him. They smiled at each other through the cloud of steam and spray. And this smile told of masculine pleasure in a common activity. The youthful torsos of the cadets stood like a veritable wall of bodies around the slightly fuller figure of their captain. Spluttering, laughing, hurling happy snatches of conversation at each other, destined for masculine ears alone—it was all a magnificent romp, a fine uninhibited display of true comradeship.

"Water off!" cried Ratshelm. "Soap yourselves!"

While they rubbed and massaged their wet bodies with soap, Cadet Hochbauer said to the company commander he esteemed so highly, "That goal of yours, sir, which brought the score up to five was absolutely unstoppable. No one could have touched it."

"Yes, well, it wasn't a bad one, though I say it myself," said Ratshelm, offering the cadet his piece of soap, which was of superior quality and richly scented. "Go on, take it, Hochbauer," he added. "Pass it on to the others when you've finished."

The others found this gesture deeply touching. For the captain's soap was obviously a remnant of the booty from France, whereas their own soap had very little lather and gave off a harsh smell of disinfectant. Presumably it had been manufactured from the bodies of dead animals—at least one hoped they had been animals. In any event Captain Ratshelm's soap was the big attraction of the shower. It vanished like snow on the top of a red-hot stove.

The captain was delighted to have given pleasure to his beloved cadets. His heart warmed at the sight of these joyful creatures of nature being baptized, as it were, in the hot gushing waters.

"Perhaps we ought to select a special team of our own from within the company, sir," suggested Cadet Hochbauer, soaping his armpits. "With you as captain. I'm sure no one in the training school would be able to beat us."

"Not a bad idea, Hochbauer," agreed Captain Ratshelm. "We ought to discuss it. Best make a start right away this evening. Come and see me, bringing a first provisional list for the team if you can. I have the feeling this might be well worth doing."

"I have the same feeling, sir," agreed Hochbauer with humble gratitude.

"Water full on!" cried Ratshelm. "Maximum temperature."

"You've been looking rather tired lately," said Captain Kater to Elfrida Rademacher.

"Do you find that my work's deteriorated?"

"In no way, my dear Fräulein Rademacher. Please don't misunderstand me. I didn't mean that as a reproach, it was simply a statement of fact—made, one might say, out of pure friendly concern."

"You really needn't worry, Captain," Elfrida assured him. "Have you anything else for me to do—I mean any work?"

Elfrida was standing in front of the captain, the commanding officer of the headquarters company, who was sitting behind his desk. He had slipped right down in his chair. He glanced up intimately at his principal secretarial assistant.

"Fräulein Rademacher," he began, "just sit down for a moment. There's a small matter we have to discuss."

"By all means," said Elfrida. She again took hold of the chair on which she usually sat while the captain tried to dictate to her, though he rarely managed to give her more than a few key words. This was enough, however, for there were hardly more than a couple of dozen standard letters and Elfrida knew them all.

"As I was saying," continued Kater, rubbing his hands, "I've had the feeling lately that you've been overdoing things. You're working too hard. You really ought to do less here in the office. Take a break now and again, have a cup of coffee, call someone up or do anything else you feel like doing. Well, what do you say to it? A more restful time here in the office might suit your private life quite well, mightn't it?"

"What do you mean, Captain? That you want to cut down on the work here in your office, or to increase your staff?"

"You're a bright girl, Fräulein Rademacher, I always knew that."

"I gather then you want to increase your office staff, Captain."

"In order to take some of the load off you, Fräulein Rademacher. Perhaps also to do my good friend Krafft a favor."

"Ah," said Elfrida. "I know who you'll be taking on. Irene Jablonski, if I'm not mistaken."

"You're really marvelous," Kater assured her in ringing tones to conceal his own astonishment. "You've got it in one! But that's just it—we both know quite a lot about each other. We'll be taking this girl Irene Jablonski on here, then, if you agree."

"And what do you hope to achieve by that, Captain?"

"A great deal," he said energetically. "First of all, I'm encouraging the younger generation, giving new blood the chance to prove itself. The principle of learning from experience, you know, Fräulein Rademacher. It's one of the necessities of our time."

"But I'm afraid Irene can hardly do anything but work in the kitchen. She's not a secretary, you know."

"She's eager to learn and I'm convinced one could teach her anything in time."

"She's still very young, Captain."

"That's no disadvantage, do you think?"

"Irene Jablonski is still only a child at heart."

"That can be an advantage too. Besides, the little thing's eighteen. What's the matter with you, Fräulein Rademacher? Instead of being grateful to me because I want to take some of the load off you, you throw up a whole series of unreal objections."

"Obviously you see them as unreal, Captain."

"What do you mean by that?" Kater now asked indignantly. "Are you trying to stop this girl Irene Jablonski from coming here?"

"Quite the contrary, Captain, I welcome the idea!"

"How do you mean?"

"I mean you're doing me a favor by bringing Irene Jablonski here."

"I'm doing *you* a favor?"

"But certainly! You see, Captain, I feel responsible for Irene. She needs someone she can trust to look after her. And I can do that particularly well if she is working with me. So you're making it all much easier—which is why I'm grateful to you. You'll see, Captain. I shall look after Irene as a lioness looks after her young."

"Cadet Hochbauer reporting as ordered, sir."

"Really, my dear fellow," said Ratshelm, "there's no need to be so formal! Let's call your presence here just a friendly visit, shall we?"

"Certainly, sir. Thank you very much indeed."

"Come here, my dear fellow, sit down beside me. True comradeship knows no distinctions of rank, though it always respects them. It's a matter of tact, you see, which is something you clearly possess. Come on, closer, Hochbauer, closer!"

Captain Ratshelm received the cadet in his room, which was as bleakly furnished as all the other rooms in barracks, though a skillful touch here and there had added a certain charm. A gaily colored peasant rug from the Balkans lay on the table. A blue, white, and red cushion looked as if it came from France. Russia had contributed a samovar, beneath which a little brazier was now burning. The captain was making tea for himself and his visitor.

They drank the tea. Hochbauer permitted himself to remark that it tasted excellent. "Doubtless the way in which it was made!"

Ratshelm accepted the compliment with a smile and explained that the tea came from India. It had been requisitioned from Holland and sold in Belgium, whence it had found its way from the black market to a canteen and from there back to the black market again and to certain young girls, one of whom was the friend of a comrade of his. "A rotten business really—I don't like having anything to do with it. But since she kept on telling me she wanted to give me anything I liked, I finally had to accept her tea!"

Cadet Hochbauer laughed, though with a certain restraint, and said, "I feel that women, with their essential instability, have only partially succeeded in matching up to the great ethical challenge of these heroic times in which we live."

"Certainly," agreed Ratshelm, "we're living in an essentially masculine era."

"Which is why it's so worth-while living in," said Hochbauer solemnly.

The captain nodded, and silently laid a hand conveying profound assent on his visitor's arm. A rough, rugged feeling of tenderness welled up inside him. Just as Hagen von Tronje, he thought, had once put his strong arm around the shoulders of his companions and drawn them toward him so that they might be closer to the heart which beat only for them and the impending struggle ahead.

There was silence for a time. The captain basked in a sense of noble harmony, though he couldn't help noticing the grave, almost gloomy expression which fell across his cherished guest's face like some dark shadow. After a little superficial conversation about the selection of the team and preparatory training, Ratshelm asked sympathetically, "What's on your mind exactly, my dear Hochbauer?"

"You're very observant, sir," said the cadet, apparently hovering between embarrassment and admiration.

"Yes," said Ratshelm, "I have a sixth sense where the feelings of my men are concerned. I usually know more than I let on. And in your particular case, my dear Hochbauer, it hasn't escaped me that lately, in the last few days, you've been looking a bit unhappy."

Hochbauer lowered his handsome head slightly and said, as if after deep thought, "The death of Lieutenant Barkow has affected me more than one might think—I don't mean the fact of death itself, because that's something every soldier has to accept as a matter of course. But what worries me is that there seems to be a certain conspiracy afoot not to let the dead man rest in peace. And since I know that you, sir, set great store by openness and frankness"—here Ratshelm nodded assent—"I must unfortunately say that Lieutenant Krafft seems to be going out of his way to try and clarify the circumstances in which Lieutenant Barkow died."

"Ah," said Captain Ratshelm, making it clear at once how much this interested him, adding, "But what is there to clarify? All the inquiries have been concluded—even the court-martial inquiries which always seemed to me superfluous, though naturally unavoidable in the circumstances."

"Lieutenant Krafft seems to doubt the official findings."

"What? He doubts the findings of an official inquiry? That's impossible. Did he actually say such a thing?"

"No, sir, not in so many words. But I'm absolutely sure that Lieutenant Krafft is now himself studying all the details of Lieutenant Barkow's death."

"Incredible," said Ratshelm, shaking his head. "Simply absurd. What's the point? What can he be up to?"

"I assume Lieutenant Krafft is trying to pin guilt on someone, sir. And I can't help feeling that he's trying to pin it on me."

"Impossible!" exclaimed Ratshelm. "There are not the slightest grounds for thinking that his death was anything but a perfectly ordinary accident."

"Unfortunately, sir," said the cadet in a restrained but passionate tone of grievance, "it might in the circumstances be possible to put a different construction on it."

"But not pointing a finger at you, my dear Hochbauer!"

In a tone which seemed genuinely full of regret the cadet then said, "A most unfortunate amount of tension existed between Lieutenant Barkow and myself from the very beginning. There's no denying that, I'm afraid. And Lieutenant Krafft is bound to discover this sooner or later if he hasn't discovered it already."

"My dear Hochbauer, it's well known that tension is often productive of the highest achievement. True harmony in fact can only be effected by the conflict of opposites." It was not without an ennobling sense of the excellence of his own thinking that Captain Ratshelm heard himself speak these words.

"But there are some conflicts, sir, which can never be resolved. This war we have undertaken is an example. Don't you agree, sir? No German can tolerate opposition to Germany?"

"Of course not!" cried Ratshelm vehemently. "He who is not for Germany is no German!"'

"And our Führer is the personification of Germany, isn't he?"

Captain Ratshelm confirmed this with considerable emphasis. The idea had been drummed into his head and he believed it along with several million others. To him nothing seemed more self-evident; the Führer, the Reich Chancellor, the Supreme Commander-in-Chief of the Wehrmacht—he personified Germany! As the Kaiser had personified the First Reich, Frederick II Prussia, and Hermann the Germanic tribes. The belief was unshakable. Any other belief was high treason. And high treason was punishable by death . . .

Here Ratshelm brought himself up short. His imagination was running away with him . . . the sight of Hochbauer made the decision easy—a youth capable only of the noblest deeds! Anything else was inconceivable.

"I wouldn't have believed it," said the cadet, with a gesture that was almost touching in its helplessness, an Egmont filled with sorrow at the shortcomings of the world, "but Lieutenant Barkow didn't have the slightest respect for our Führer, let alone admiration or love. And worst still, he doubted our Führer's capabilities. He criticized him and even insulted him."

"This is terrible," said Ratshelm, trying to imagine Hochbauer in that appalling predicament; a noble youth filled with the purest ideals of Schiller—"To the Fatherland, to all that's dear, hold fast!"—inspired by the fiery spirit of Körner—"Thou sword beside me, flashing brightly!"—steeped in the sublime ideology of Fichte, Arndt, Stein, and others—"Unworthy is the nation that is not happy to pledge all for its honor!" This was the spirit which fired German youth. This was what sent them hurrying to the colors in their aspiration for higher things! They wanted to become officers of the Führer, to identify themselves with the lofty greatness of the times, with this decisive hour, this sublime moment in history in which the fate of the whole world was being decided. And then they found themselves up against someone like Lieutenant Barkow.

"That's really terrible," said Ratshelm again. It took him a little time to recover. Finally he asked, "But why, my dear Hochbauer, didn't you come to me before?"

Hochbauer, who now saw exactly where to aim, immediately landed another direct hit. Lowering his blond head he explained, "I was too ashamed."

This affected Captain Ratshelm profoundly. His German soldier's heart beat fiercely. His breast swelled with sublime feelings of comradeship and a tear stole into his honest blue eyes.

The captain got to his feet, walked solemnly over to Hochbauer, and put an arm lovingly around the young shoulders of this kindred spirit, this brother-in-arms, fighting with him for the true Germany.

"My dear young friend," said Captain Ratshelm, speaking out with manly simplicity, "I share your sense of shame. And not only that—you can rest assured not only that I understand and respect your attitude, but that I am with you. Don't be afraid; I am by your side and you can depend on me. If need be, we'll fight together, shoulder to shoulder, in this affair—fight on to final victory."

* * * *

Intermediate Report No. 6

THE CURRICULUM VITAE OF
MAJOR-GENERAL ERNST EGON MODERSOHN,
OR THE SOUL OF A SOLDIER

Name: Modersohn, Ernst Egon, born November 10, 1898, in Planken, district of Stuhm. Father: Modersohn, Maximilian, agent on the Planken estate. Mother: Cecilie Modersohn born von Knobelsdorf-Bendesslhen. Childhood and early schooldays spent in Planken, district of Stuhm.

A flat expense of whitewash—the walls of my room. The furniture is limited to the barest necessities: table, chair, stool, cupboard, chest of drawers, bed, washstand, all made of crude, rough wood, heavy and solid, not glued or nailed but simply dovetailed. Not a picture on the walls. The little courtyard adjoining the big house is visible through the narrow windows. I listen to the sounds of the new day coming up to me, the clanking of cans and buckets, the whinnying of horses, and the voice of the coachman talking to the animals.

"Everyone has his duty in life," says my father. This is delivered neither as a challenge, nor as a warning, nor as an order, but simply as a self-evident statement of fact. The first duty I can remember had to do with Hasso, the sheepdog. I am five and once a day I have to brush, comb, and clean Hasso for about ten minutes. Finally I have to take Hasso to my father, or if he's not there to my mother, of if she's not there to the groom Glubalker, who looks after my father's horses. "Ernst," Glubalker tells me, "every animal must feel that someone cares for him. That's the main thing. If he can't he deteriorates or goes wild. And it's the same with human beings."

"The bull from Sarrnitz is coming today," says my father at lunch, looking at my mother. Mother looks at him as if about to say something but thinks better of it. Then my father looks at me and says, "You'll help me hold the brown cow." "Don't you think he's too young?" asks my mother. To which my father replies, "You mean you think Ernst isn't strong enough to hold the cow while she's being covered? All right, I'll give him a helping hand." Which is what happens—just as everything happens as my father says. The men on the estate call him simply "Herr Major." And the bull from Sarrnitz is strong and wild, and leaps onto the cow so heavily that all my strength is needed to hold her. And my jacket gets covered with the foam that falls from the cow's mouth.

One of my duties is to keep my room clean. Every morning I air the bed. Every evening I carry up fresh water in two jugs. Father decides how far the window shall be open, at night. However, it's the duty of Emma, one of our maids, to clean the floor. In summer I get up at six, in winter at seven, and I go to bed at eight and nine respectively. Sometimes my father wakes me in the middle of the night, when a mare foals, or when deer break into the kitchen garden, or when, as in 1906, the coach house catches fire. The next morning I'm allowed to sleep late, for the extra amount of time taken by the night's interruption.

Father says little, and Mother still less when Father's there. She sings sometimes, when she's alone; she has a beautiful voice. But she isn't the one who tells me stories— Glubalker does that when Father and Mother aren't there and he's off duty. Glubalker tells me of war and the emperor and of his brother who killed his wife. "He split her skull with an ax," he says. "She betrayed him, you see, and when one human being betrays another it's right to split his skull with an ax. That's what's called justice." "Is that really justice?" I ask my father. And he says, "It's the servants' idea of justice!"

Fransen, the schoolteacher, has a voice like an old woman, though he's barely twenty-five, with bright blue eyes and pink skin like a pig. His hands keep moving about the whole time, and sometimes they seem to fly around each other like fluttering birds. He seems to creep rather than walk. "He's afraid of me," I tell my father. "Nonsense," says my father, "what makes you think that?" "He's afraid of me," I repeat, "because I'm your son—the son of the agent on the big estate."

The next day my father comes to the school with his riding whip in his hand. Fransen practically starts whimpering when my father speaks to him. His back is bent like a bow and his hands tremble like the leaves of a poplar. "Herr

Fransen," says Father when the three of us are alone in the empty classroom, "this boy here is your pupil. He's here to learn. And he is also here to learn to obey those who are set in authority over him. You may be a milksop, Herr Fransen, but for him you represent authority by virtue of your office. So act accordingly. And you, Ernst, are to conduct yourself accordingly."

I sit on the same benches as the village children, and the food I bring with me for lunch is no more than theirs. I wear the same clothes as they. And I don't only attend lessons with them, I do my homework with them too, and Father likes me to play with them as well. We let loose a whole lot of fish into the lake; we crawl through the drainpipes at the level crossing, we dam the brook, and flood a meadow. "Ernst," my father says to me, "you children have caused a great deal of damage—did you have any part in it?" "Yes, Father," I say. "Will you tell me the names of the boys if I ask you for them?" "I'll tell you their names if you insist, Father, but I beg you not to insist." "Good, my son," says my father. "That's the end of the matter. You can go."

Primary school at Planken, in the district of Stuhm, between the ages of six and ten (1904-08). Kaiser Wilhelm Gymnasium, in the district of Stuhm, between the ages of ten and eighteen (1908-16), where I graduated. In 1916 I volunteered for the army.

Outwardly summer follows summer in an identical pattern. I get up at five. At 5:45 I have breakfast. At 6:10 I set out on the two-mile walk to the station at Romeiken; 6:52 to 7:36 I'm on the local train, fourth class, between Romeiken to Stuhm. From 8 A.M. to 1 P.M., lessons in the Kaiser Wilhelm Gymnasium in Stuhm; 1 P.M. to 3 P.M., first session of homework in the third- and fourth-class waiting rooms of the railway station at Stuhm; 3:07 P.M. to 3:51 P.M., return on the train from Stuhm to Romeiken, and thence on foot to Planken, arriving there about 4:30 P.M. Here I do the rest of my homework, which is followed by instruction from my father, with stable duty, supper, and bed. And so on, day after day throughout the summer.

During the winter months—from the beginning of November to the end of February—I live at the Pension Victoria for schoolboys in Stuhm, Schillerstrasse 32. The pension is owned by Frau Hannelore Rohremeister, the widow of a staff officer. A severely disciplined life, from Monday morning to Saturday midday, all according to a strict time-table, including supervision of homework. From Saturday afternoon to Monday morning I stay in my parents' house at Planken.

Three others share my room with me. There are two beds on each side of the room. Smoking is forbidden. To drink alcohol is to invite expulsion. The light is put out at ten o'clock. Meals are taken together. Everyone has his own space to work in, two yards apiece, carefully measured out and marked in what were once white lines on the wooden top of the communal table. Every four weeks Frau Rohremeister writes reports on us, which have to be shown at home and then signed by our parents.

Frau Rohremeister orders me to report to her in her room. "Ernst Modersohn," she says, "you're a decent, reliable boy, which is something I appreciate." I don't reply. "I think you're someone I can trust," she continues. I still don't reply. "Which is why," she concludes, "I'm considering appointing you room senior." "What are the duties of a room senior?" I ask. "Well," she says, "he enjoys my confidence and helps me keep order. He keeps an eye on what the others are doing and saying and reports these things to me." "I'm sorry," I say, "but these are not duties for me."

"There's a price to be paid for everything," says Dr. Englehart. "And for every syllable you get wrong you'll bend over and receive one stroke. We'll see who holds the record." Fussman holds the record. There's never a Latin class in which he doesn't get beaten at least five times. "I'll never let anyone hit me," I decide. "It's all very well for you to talk," says Fussman. "You know everything anyway."

My father's face is ashen gray and his left forearm is just a bloody mass of pulp. He has slipped and fallen on the rotating chaffcutter. "Cut my sleeve off," he says. "And the shirt too. Bind up my arm. And have the horses harnessed at once, I must get to the doctor." That's all he says. He carries himself even more erect than ever. A week later he is standing in the courtyard again. He never mentions the fact that his left arm is crippled forever, and no one else mentions it either.

"Modersohn," says Dr. Englehart, entering the classroom, "stand up! I know you're a brave lad." He comes and stands in front of me and says, "I've just seen from the latest casualty list that your father, Major Modersohn, has fallen on the field of honor as a brave soldier in the battle of the

Masurian Marshes. You can be proud of him. The headmaster has given you three days' leave."

"Mother," I say, "I want to volunteer as soon as I can."
"Why?" is all she says. "I can't tell you, I just have to. Like Father."

1916: basic training in Infantry Reserve Battalion No. 779. Posting to No. 18 Infantry Regiment at Grolman. First experience of the front: autumn 1916 in the west, on the Douamont Sector. Made lieutenant: 18.1.1918. At the end of the war I returned to Planken in the district of Stuhm and started working there as an agricultural foreman.

"Modersohn?" Colonel Treskow asks thoughtfully. I stand before him in my fatigues, covered in filth, drenched in sweat. Colonel Treskow, who has a wooden leg, is inspecting the recruits. "Modersohn?" he asks again. "I had a comrade with that name. Major Modersohn from Planken" "He was my father, sir," I tell him. "He was a good soldier," says Colonel Treskow. "Try to be worthy of him." Then he stumps off again on his wooden leg.

The tavern's name is The Prussian Eagle, and its landlord is the uncle of one of my comrades. We are celebrating our departure for the front. The place is full of girls, some of whom have just come from the hospital and are in nurses' uniforms. A good deal is being drunk, and the lights are low, and voices raised. A girl pushes up against me. "Come on," she says, "let's go outside." "I'm staying here with my comrades," I tell her. "Don't you like me?" she asks. "No," I reply. It's the truth. But she can't stand the truth and she says, "What extraordinary people are becoming soldiers these days!" It's useless to explain to her that one doesn't become a soldier—one either is one or one isn't.

Pale moonlight. A landscape of shell craters. Ominous silence. Flares hissing upward and flickering as they go out. The sweet stench of corpses. I clasp the cold machine gun tightly to me. Beside me a comrade with his head on his arm—either sleeping or dead. And the feeling slowly creeps over me that behind me, mute, immobile, urging me on, stands a man—my father.

Colonel Treskow stands beside me, watch in hand. "Seven minutes to go," he says. He's been back at the front two days and taken over the regiment. He wants to lead the attack on Hill 304. He stumps up the stepladder. "One minute to go." Then he hurls himself over the top, stands erect, and stumps off in the direction of the enemy, two steps, three steps—he shudders, staggers, and falls. I throw myself down beside him. With his last gasp he says, "Never give up, Modersohn, comrade-in-arms, never give up!" and he falls back dead.

Champagne. The last few bottles unearthed from all sorts of places and opened in my honor. Shabby, worn-out, bloodstained tunic carefully cleaned and adorned with a lieutenant's shoulder straps. Officers all around me, serious, solemn. "To you, brother officer," they cry. The clinking of glasses. To Kaiser, Reich, and Fatherland! The end is just around the corner but seems a whole world away. No morning. They all know that true values are eternal.

"Now, my lad," a cavalry officer says to me a few hours later, "you can visit the officers' brothel if you want to. What about it?" "No," I reply.

Return to Planken. A new agent has taken father's place. Mother lives in the gardener's house. There's room for me there too. "The main thing is that you're still alive, my boy," says my mother. Everything seems strange, unnatural. The homeland is no longer what it was.

Everything seems changed. Only what is within us remains unaltered.

1919-21: agricultural foreman in Planken, district of Stuhm. 1921: entry into one of the units from which the Reichswehr developed. Later: transfer to No. 3 Infantry Regiment with the rank of second lieutenant. 1926: promotion to first lieutenant. 1930: captain. 1934: major. 1937: lieutenant-colonel. 1939: colonel. 1940: major-general.

A nation that lives in misery grows ill. The Great War had demanded too vast an effort. So the people sickened, grew greedy for profit, and weak and anemic. No one seems to look to the morrow. The towns decay, the countryside bleeds to death. Mother grows even more silent than before. People's faces become distorted with greed, and their eyes gleam impudently with lack of shame. "Why won't you sleep with me?" says the wife of the agent who has taken my father's place. "Because you revolt me," I say to her, thinking to myself, Because you're a part of the whole travesty of life in a country for which millions of men died.

Four events stand out in that unforgotten summer. My mother dies—quiet and smiling to the last. One morning she simply doesn't wake up. Then the new agent, my father's

successor, strikes me in the face in the center of the courtyard in front of all the men, on the grounds that I've been
trying to molest his wife. I don't say a word. I leave. Third:
I put on uniform again. Then I meet Suzanne. All in that
one summer—death, humiliation, pride, and love.

All the rest of my life is work, and loneliness, and the
attempt to give meaning to a soldier's life.

I have nothing further to report.

19 *THE EVE OF GREAT EVENTS*

THE NIGHTS at the training school were too short. The official time for lock-up was 2200 hours, after which there had
to be absolute quiet in the barrack area, at least from the
cadets, the only exceptions being made for those using the
"permitted working period" which extended up to 2400 hours.

The rules for this permitted working period had of
course been formulated in one of Major Frey's remarkable
special orders. This particular one bore the number 27 and
contained the following passage among others: "Lighting
facilities should, where practicable, be shaded by paper,
cardboard, or other material, so that those intending to sleep
should not be disturbed; but particular care should be taken
to see that the material utilized for such shades is as fire-
proof as possible and installed at a certain distance, at least
one or two inches, from the bulb in question."

At about this time of night, then, in the barracks the cadets began to hang copies of the *Völkische Beobachter,* and
Training Notes, and pants, and string vests over the light
shades. Notebooks, maps, writing pads, and copies of *Military
Regulations* lay on the tables. About one cadet in three
worked, or wrote letters to his family and girl friends, or
sat there simply brooding because he didn't want to go to
sleep. For the leaden sleep which always seemed to last
such an appallingly short time was followed by a rapid and
brutal awakening.

A few held whispered conversations, though even these
were a breach of Special Order number 27, which plainly

laid down that, "In consideration for those seeking sleep no conversations of any sort are permitted, not even muttered or whispered conversations. Only brief orders and instructions are permitted, and volume should be restricted to the minimum."

So from 2200 hours onward only an occasional murmur was to be heard in the cadets' barracks. The members of the headquarters company had slightly more freedom, since the canteen remained open for them until 2400 hours. Here, however, the slightest suggestion of rowdiness would have brought the duty officer on the scene at once.

Things were of course quite different for the officers of the training staff itself. It was part of the cadets' education that this should be so. Applicants for a commission needed to be made to realize how desirable was the goal to which they aspired.

The officers could come and go as they pleased. For the mess was theoretically open at all times. They could, if they liked, have the light on in their rooms and apartments all night, pay visits, hold conversations, play games, drink, go in and out of the gates as they pleased. They could also, of course, wander all over the barracks—for instance, keeping an eye on the cadets under their command if they thought this necessary. The only thing that restricted them at all from the point of view of space or time was the training program itself.

All this was the theory, but in practice it worked out rather differently. For in the general's view an officer was on duty at all times. He had full liberty to do what he liked, but naturally this was a liberty he did not exploit. The general saw to that.

No one could fail for long to be aware of the general's supervision. He not only hovered in spirit everywhere like some vast ominous shadow—he actually kept on appearing in person all over the place at the most awkward moments. Few managed to escape his prying eyes; he was as likely to turn up among the coffee carriers as in a washroom, the barrack blocks, the transport sheds, or the hospital.

This permanent thundercloud hanging over the training school led to the formation of other subsidiary clouds. For the two course commanders, the six company commanders, and the eighteen section officers took to swarming about as he did. In the training school at Wildlingen-am-Main, at almost any moment, at least one pair of eyes was on watch.

Yet the nights were dark, the area of the barracks large,

and there were many out-of-the-way corners, hiding places, and secret routes. Soldiers with battle experience knew how to look after themselves. And even Modersohn couldn't be everywhere at once.

Cadets Rednitz, Mösler, and Weber, Egon, were conversing uninhibitedly at the tops of their voices. They were able to do this without causing serious disturbance, because they shared a room with Cadet Böhmke, the poet, who when reading *Faust* was lost to the world about him.

"I appeal to your sense of comradeship, all of you," implored Mösler. "You've got to come."

"Why?" asked Rednitz. "Just to hold the light for you?"

"There's something in this for everyone," Mösler promised. "I guarantee that. The main thing is that none of the girls should be left out, for that only gives rise to professional jealousy. If all have the chance to participate, it's like life at the front. If one person has a thing, all the others want it too."

"What sort of girl would I get?" Cadet Weber inquired. "I'm not particularly choosy, but I don't like other people's leftovers. For instance, is she the right size for me? Is she keen on doing her stuff for the troops?"

"A splendid creature!" declared Mösler, molding a figure in the air. "Just right for a strong man like you. Besides, she works in the kitchen."

The last remark seemed to strike home. For an old soldier like Weber a kitchen maid had the same sort of charm as a ballet dancer for an old roué. His misgivings melted away. "All right," he said condescendingly. "If that's the way it is, I'm on. I'll do it for your sake, Mösler."

"What about you, Rednitz?"

"I'm tired," said Rednitz with a yawn.

"It'll wear off," urged Mösler. "I've got a really marvelous little doll for you—petite, pretty, lively as quicksilver. She'll be all over you before you can count three."

Rednitz remained unmoved. Again he explained that he was tired and wanted to go to sleep. His friends begged him not to be a spoil-sport. They asked him the question that seldom failed to be effective: was he yellow perhaps? But Rednitz wasn't to be caught that way. He merely laughed.

"The thing is," admitted Mösler finally, "my girl lives in the same room as the other two and they all know how to take care of themselves. They're all keen, but they're obviously not quite such a hand at it as my little one. So they rather cling together. To put it bluntly, my girl will come only if she can bring the others along with her."

"And where's the great event to take place?"

"In the gym. I've hired the entire equipment store for the evening, with an elecric heater and the mats thrown in."

"How did you fix that?" asked Weber.

"Quite simple," explained Mösler proudly. "I happened to catch the fellow in charge of equipment in there with his girl friend. So I simply explained to him that either he'd find himself in trouble or he must let me in too. So, now's our chance —I fixed the whole thing up in the canteen just before lockup. In twenty minutes the girls will be waiting by the window in the corridor at the back of their quarters. From there over the lawn, into the gym, and on with the gymnastics."

"What are we waiting for?" cried Weber, jumping up eagerly.

"I'm not going creeping about the place on my stomach," said Rednitz. "I'm much too tired for that. If we must go, we'll do the thing properly."

"What do you mean?" asked Mösler.

"Steel helmet, greatcoat, and rifle," said Rednitz. "We'll set off as if we were an extra guard coming off duty. It's the best possible disguise. We can march right down the main road of the camp like that, and I guarantee that no one will ask any questions."

"It's too dangerous," objected Mösler.

"It's dangerous whichever way you look at it," said Rednitz. "So either we go in full gear or you must leave me out of it."

"All right, come on!" cried Weber, Egon. "To arms, comrades."

Captain Feders stared at the basketmen behind the glass wall. They were lying in little fenced-in beds like children's cots. The whole room was bathed in a dim, reddish light. For them, too, it was night and they lay there lost in oblivion.

"They sleep almost completely normally," said Dr. Krüger, who was standing behind Feders.

The two friends were the only people in the bare observation room. Sometimes the doctor would keep watch on his patients quite alone for hours on end. And sometimes Captain Feders would keep him company.

"You dope them with morphia?" asked Feders.

"Not all of them," said the doctor with the disfigured face. "Only some, though I vary the doses even with them."

"You could put them to sleep forever if you liked?"

"If I liked, yes," said the doctor in his strangled voice. His face never altered. It was as if he wore a stiff death mask in the hideous costume ball of war.

Feders was sitting on a chair, placed back to front. He had put his arms over the back and was resting his chin on top of it. His eyes were almost closed. Softly he asked, "Why don't you do it?"

Dr. Krüger didn't answer. It wasn't the first time he'd been asked this question.

"Why don't you do it?" repeated Feders. "Why don't you increase the daily dose of morphia until these wretched remnants of human beings topple over the edge into a merciful death? They've only a few steps to go. Or are you afraid to take the responsibility?"

"I'm already absolved of that," said Krüger wearily. "I have express permission to kill in certain circumstances—"

"Why don't you, then?"

"I can't commit murder," said the doctor.

"But you'd only be putting a stop to endless torment. You'd be conferring a release, using sleep to relax the continuous strangle hold of death."

Dr. Krüger's face was no longer capable of expression, but he raised his hands in mute supplication and then let them fall helplessly to his side. Almost inaudibly he asked, "How many men have you killed so far, Eric—knowingly and willingly?"

"I don't know exactly," said Captain Feders thoughtfully. "But it must have been quite a number." And he thought of hand grenades dropped through basement windows; of a machine gun emptied into a moving bush; of an entrenching tool jabbed into an artery—he was a holder of the close-combat clasp in silver.

After a while he said, "It's better to be a corpse than one of these basketmen. There are only two ways of redeeming them—either by putting them on show in the market places of mankind as martyrs to mass madness, or by liberating them from a world in which everything is so easily forgotten, in which conscience has no place and life simply isn't worth living."

The doctor shook his disfigured head. "A man without legs and without arms is still a man," he said. "You, Eric, can do everything except sleep with a woman. And I can't show my face any more, but I can do everything else. So long as a man can see, so long as a man can hear, so long as he can still speak and think and feel, he lives in the sphere of creation and has a part in it. The world is never empty and dead so long as just one of the sensory perceptions continues."

"No," said Feders vehemently, "I want to live completely or not at all."

"Then could you kill them?" asked the doctor gently. He waited for his friend's answer, but none came.

"If you really could, Eric, I wouldn't stop you doing what the regulations permit. More than that—what they expressly recommend. Well, Eric, shall I show you how it's done?"

Captain Feders looked searchingly at his friend's scarred and mutilated face, which seemed to be glowing strangely. His hands shook slightly as Feders, as if seeking help, reached out for them.

"We really completed a remarkable piece of work today," said Captain Kater, rubbing his hands contentedly. "But that's how it should be—never a moment's hesitation when duty calls."

Kater was in the staff company office speaking to his closest collaborators, Sergeant-Major Rabenkamm—a sergeant-major to his finger tips—and Elfrida Rademacher, and Irene Jablonski, his new secretarial assistant.

The quarterly stock-taking always took up a great deal of time, though not of course Kater's. He had first-class assistants on whom he was able to rely implicitly. His own participation consisted solely in appending his signature to the completed document.

"Really," said Captain Kater appreciatively, "a most excellent piece of work. I'm extremely happy about it."

"It just requires the date, sir," said the sergeant-major, "and then it's ready for you to sign."

"Not before I've checked it right through once again," said Kater. "I'm a stickler for accuracy in this sort of thing. You might say stock-taking inventories are a unit's visiting card. Naturally I require mine to be flawless."

The sergeant-major glanced quickly across at Elfrida Rademacher, who smiled mischievously. Both realized that the CO of the headquarters company was putting on one of his little solo acts again, "correctness" being his theme of the moment. And not very convincingly performed either. Irene Jablonski was the only one who hadn't seen the performance before, and she now turned her childlike eyes up at Captain Kater in admiration.

"Right," said Kater, "I'd be glad if you'd complete the inventory."

"It'll take only a couple of minutes, sir."

"Please don't rush things. Slowly does it—more haste less speed is my motto in these matters. Look through every detail of the thing once again, don't let the smallest inaccuracy escape you."

"It's really all in order, sir."

"Check it all the same! When you've done that, I'd be glad if you'd bring the document to me in my quarters—in, say, half an hour's time. And so as not to take up too much of your time, it'll be quite in order to send Fräulein Jablonski with it."

Captain Kater nodded paternally to Irene and left the room.

Whereupon the sergeant-major collected the papers, entered up the date—a matter of a few seconds—and said, "There we are."

"That's all for today, then," said Elfrida. "High time too—I've got a date. And you will be off to your billet, Irene—is that clear?"

"But I've got to go and see Captain Kater!"

"No, you haven't," said Elfrida firmly. "You should be in bed by this time. Off you go to your room. In ten minutes I shall come and see if you're in bed."

"But the captain said . . ."

"Captain Kater obviously forgot about time. That's all for you for today. Don't argue, Irene."

Irene Jablonski obeyed and trotted off sulkily.

"I don't want to interfere," said the sergeant-major quietly, "but you do realize what you're doing, Fräulein Rademacher?"

"Just as much as you do. But you don't need to worry about that. I accept full responsibility, as the saying goes. And you are to take the requisite documents to Captain Kater. Just think of how astonished he's going to be when he sees you instead of Irene."

Major-General Modersohn interrupted his night's work to listen to the ice-cold rain beating against the window panes. He rubbed his cold, damp hands. His head throbbed. He had a fever, as almost always when the weather changed.

He forced himself not to think about his physical condition. Later on, back in his quarters, he would swallow some quinine with a lot of water.

He summoned his ADC. Either the ADC or a clerk had

always been there lately when he went on working after normal hours, though never Sybille Bachner alone.

"If you please, Lieutenant Bieringer," said the general, "I'd like you to prepare the training schedules right up to the end of this course."

"Up to the end of the whole course?" asked the ADC in astonishment.

The general stared at him in silence, and Bieringer hurriedly repeated, "Training schedules up to the end of the course—very good, sir."

"How many days will you need for that, Lieutenant?"

"Three days, sir."

"Three days from now, then, Lieutenant."

"Very good, sir," said the ADC.

"Please tell Fräulein Bachner I'm waiting for her work. That's all for the moment, Lieutenant Bieringer."

The ADC disappeared into the anteroom, where he stopped for a moment thoughtfully at the door after closing it carefully behind him. Then he wandered slowly over to his desk, uneasily turned over some of his papers, and looked across at Sybille Bachner, who was sitting at her typewriter.

Finally Lieutenant Bieringer asked cautiously, "Have you any idea what's up, Fräulein Bachner?"

Sybille Bachner interrupted her work and looked up in surprise. It was extremely rare for the ADC to make a confidential remark of this sort to her, and she wasn't one to let its significance escape her. However, all she said now, in a way that sounded far too innocent to be true, was, "No."

"I can't help it," said the ADC, "but it all looks to me damnably like some sort of closing-down procedure. What are you actually working on at the moment, Fräulein Bachner?"

"On the final assessments that are drawn up at the end of every course."

"Already?" asked Bieringer with genuine concern. "The course has got almost six weeks to run yet. Or do you mean you're just making out one or two individual reports?"

"No, Lieutenant. Nearly all of them are now ready. The few exceptions are of officers on Number Two Course, including part of Number Six Company."

"I don't understand it at all," said Bieringer thoughtfully. He had never wholly succeeded in penetrating the general's mind, but then Modersohn's instructions had never been as obscure as this before. Staring thoughtfully ahead of him

Bieringer said, "That must mean that the general is packing up here."

"Why should he do that?" asked Sybille anxiously. "Maybe he's going on leave?"

Bieringer shook his head. "The general had leave only last summer just before we took over this pigsty. No, no— there must be something else behind all this."

Sybille Bachner felt confused. She had noticed the same signs as the ADC but hadn't dared to mention them, because she had no wish to think of the possible consequences. It was relatively simple for Lieutenant Bieringer—the general would take him with him. But he wouldn't take her.

"Anyway, the general's waiting to see your work, Fräulein Bachner."

Sybille nodded. Then she opened the top drawer of her desk, where her mirror was. She propped it up on the desk, and without showing the slightest embarrassment at the presence of the ADC, stared into it.

Lieutenant Bieringer watched her furtively. He saw her shake up her hair and tidy it with her slightly plump but elegant hands. Then she undid the clasp which kept her hair in place at the neck and let it fall in soft waves about her shoulders. Then she combed it through carefully and began to smile. Bieringer smiled, too, but not without a certain cynicism.

Sybille Bachner got to her feet, threw a last searching glance at the mirror, picked up the folder containing her completed work, and took it in to the general.

Modersohn looked toward her, or rather toward the folder that contained the work. He put out a hand for the folder, took it, opened it, and looked inside. After a few seconds' pause he asked, "Anything else, Fräulein Bachner?"

She summoned all her strength and asked, "Do you mind my new hair style, General?"

"No," said Modersohn without looking up from his work.

For a moment Sybille felt almost happy. Bleak as the general's reply was, it proved one thing that was of the greatest importance to her; namely that he had noticed her new hair style. So he did notice her appearance after all, even when seeming to look straight through her. This "No" of his could be said to amount to a curt approval. Her eyes lit up.

"Fräulein Bachner," said the general, "I would like you to give some thought to what I am about to say. If your work here in staff headquarters had to come to an end, where would you prefer to work? I give you three days in which to tell me. That's all for today. Thank you, Fräulein Bachner."

Marion Feders, the captain's wife, walked uneasily into her bedroom, where she switched on the little lamp and looked across at her husband's bed. It was empty and hadn't been slept in.

The sight seemed to increase Marion Feders' sense of unease. She turned around wearily and looked back into the living room, where Lieutenant Seuter, the Minnesinger, was standing. He filled a glass with brandy and held it up to the light before drinking it down with unmistakable pleasure.

Marion Feders shut her eyes for a moment. After a few seconds she went across to her bed and lay down on it on her back. The light shone in her eyes, and with a quick nervous gesture she turned the lampshade around toward her.

She looked back into the living room again. The Minnesinger was fiddling unsuccessfully with the knobs of the radio trying to find a station with the right sort of music. He crossed to the window and looked at the barometer hanging there; it stood at Variable. Then he looked at his watch, and poured himself out another glass of brandy.

"Are you nearly ready?" he asked.

Marion Feders didn't reply, though she heard him clearly enough. Her face was a stiff mask in which only her eyes betrayed her unease.

The officer began to unbutton his tunic, moving toward the bedroom as he did so. His steps were those of a man marching calmly and confidently toward an objective. But he stopped in the doorway, and stared in astonishment at Marion Feders on the bed. "What's the matter with you?" he asked.

Marion Feders looked at him. She saw his polished, handsome, athletic figure, his possessive hands, and his superior smile—the smile of a man who has every reason to feel satisfied with himself.

"What's the matter with you, Marion?" he repeated with slight irritation. "Are you ill?"

"No," said Marion Feders.

"Are you afraid your husband might come back?" He looked at his watch again—a splendid object, waterproof, unbreakable, with luminous figures and a built-in stopwatch. "He never comes back before midnight when he's been out in the country. By the way, where is it he goes off to? Still, that's beside the point. We can be quite sure we won't be disturbed before midnight. So what's the matter? Aren't you going to undress?"

"I don't want to," said Marion Feders.

Now he was really astonished. Although as a man of the world he knew all about feminine temperament, this was somehow the last place he had expected to find it.

"You don't want to?" he said, sitting down beside her on the bed. He bent over her and laid a hand on her knee.

"I don't want to any more," said Marion Feders. "I can't go on. Five minutes' thrill in twenty-five hours' emptiness, followed by twenty-four hours' revulsion! A sickness of the body which disappears with the years, a sickness like acne or whooping cough. It's a transitional phase like everything else—like being weaned or growing out of diapers, or cutting teeth."

"What on earth's all this nonsense," he said, smiling indulgently. "Those aren't your own thoughts—someone's been putting them into your head."

"I've been thinking things over," she said. "This is no solution."

"Come, come," he said loftily. "You're not exactly opposed to the idea."

She felt his hand beginning to move. It left her knee and slid slowly upward. Her muscles tensed as his hand reached her hips and then slid down again.

"I don't want to," she said to herself.

The truth was, she could no longer bear to see her husband suffer in silence, to see the grim, tortured face which he imagined he hid from her. He had insisted that she should take every freedom—but true freedom, as she now thought she saw, lay only in deciding how one wanted to live. And she wanted to live with him, with her husband. It was as simple as that.

Again Marion Feders said, "I don't want to."

Lieutenant Seuter only laughed, taking her refusal for a subtle form of provocation, a longing to be taken roughly. Well, why not? Setting-to with a will, he hurled himself at her, but found to his astonishment that she lay cold, stiff, and motionless as a stone.

"You revolt me," she said.

This was too much for him. He got to his feet, adjusted his uniform, and strode out without so much as another glance at her.

Captain Ratshelm spoke almost solemnly. "It's always the great ideas that get men on the move," he said.

"As for instance those of our Führer," agreed Cadet Hochbauer.

Ratshelm nodded. "But it's the great deeds," he continued, "that *keep* men moving."

"If every officer thought as you do, sir, we might have won this war long ago," said the cadet, burning with enthusiasm. "But unfortunately all officers don't."

Captain Ratshelm lowered his head as if in genuine sorrow. With anyone else who was not an officer he would by now have demonstrated his strong feelings of solidarity with the officers' corps, immediately putting forward the argument that all officers think correctly—some might express themselves differently from others, but an officer's morale in itself is always faultless. If the war were not yet won, he would have continued, it's the fault neither of the officers, nor of the noncommissioned officers, nor of the rank and file, provided their officers remain of this caliber. If there *were* something delaying final victory, it should be looked for elsewhere. For example in the tragic material superiority of the enemy, who tried to make up for his lack of true soldierly qualities by fantastic production figures, or in the shameless, unappreciative attitude of the civilians, who tolerated all sorts of grumbles and defeatists in their midst, or in the unwilling, treacherous foreign workers, who let themselves be incited by communist agitators and potential traitors of every sort. And so on and so forth. But the officers were the last people to be blamed. All this is what Captain Ratshelm would have said to any other cadet. But to him Hochbauer was the great exception. He already thought and acted as an officer.

"We officers," explained Ratshelm, "aspire to perfection. But the enlightened among us—and in all modesty I number myself among these—have realized that there's no such thing as perfect perfection. The most you can hope for is to get somewhere near it, though of course you must try and get as near as possible."

Captain Ratshelm was thoroughly enjoying himself. He felt loved and honored like some teacher and friend well loved by grateful pupils. Plato came to mind, listening attentively at the feet of Socrates, whom he was destined to make immortal one day.

The comparison seemed to Ratshelm a happy one. Ever since he had come to the training school he had dreamed that fate would provide him with an occasion such as this. It seemed to him that he was a man who was full of knowledge and within a striking distance of wisdom, but he had to spend most of his time preoccupied with routine duties, drumming elementary principles into the heads of willing but not exactly brilliant young cadets. And all the time he had been longing to found a sort of school for the propagation of advanced ideas, in which a whole philosophy of soldiering could be devloped. So far he had had no chance to do this, but now Hochbauer had come into his life and the noble youth hung on his every word.

"Perfection, as I was saying, is the ultimate goal. But it can't be reached without rejection of the imperfect, always assuming of course that the imperfect allows itself to be recognized. You see what I'm driving at, my dear fellow? I can't help thinking of Hermann of the Cheruski, who had weaklings even in his ranks. Again, among the twelve apostles of this fellow Christ there was a traitor called Judas—though we don't exactly want to stray into ecclesiastical territory. After all, we're the first nation to have shaken off the medieval influence of the Church and to have started a whole new glorious chapter of our own in world history. Don't you agree, my dear Hochbauer?"

His dear Hochbauer agreed readily enough.

"Sir," said the cadet gratefully, "you've made it all very clear for me. How well you put it, sir, when you said perfection can only be achieved by the rejection of the imperfect. It reminds me of a story I read once, which has always moved me, about one of Frederick the Great's officers sitting in a tavern and hearing another officer slander the king. He rose to his feet, drew his pistol, and shot the traitor down, crying out as he did so, "A dirty dog who doesn't love his king!"

"Yes," said Captain Ratshelm thoughtfully. "Those were great historic times."

"But we mustn't let this spirit die out, sir!" said the cadet, all afire.

Captain Ratshelm gravely nodded his assent. What it was exactly that he had just sanctioned he didn't know. He was thinking only of the great heroic traditions—of the Spartan mothers who were so proud of their dead sons, provided all their wounds were in front; of the great king who cried to his soldiers, "Lads, do you want to be immortal"; of the guard dying but not surrendering; of the emperor demanding of his troops that they should kill fathers and brothers if need be—this was the world of Captain Ratshelm. The best of all possible worlds.

Elfrida Rademacher stretched contentedly, laying an arm across Karl Krafft's chest. "It's marvelous," she said.

He found it marvelous too. For five minutes he had been able to forget everything except the woman beside him. All had vanished—the war, the training school, the little town, and the simple room they'd found, which belonged to a friend of Elfrida's who had gone to the movies with another friend. Her husband, who worked on the railways, was busy sending men and materials backward and forward across the length and breadth of Germany.

They lay on the sofa exhausted, listening to their heartbeats. And it seemed that they could hear their two hearts beating as one.

But what they heard was not the sound of their heartbeats, but of a fist beating against the door. Then a high voice breaking with excitement cried out, "I've caught you at last, you filthy slut! I'll make you pay for this! Open the door at once! I'll kill the fellow!"

Elfrida and Karl sat up, listening in astonishment, with worried expressions on their faces. They looked at each other in dismay.

"It must be my friend's husband who works on the railway," said Elfrida.

It soon appeared that her surmise was correct. The railwayman thundered on the door as if trying to get an entire freight train moving with his naked fists.

"Caught you in the act, you slut!" he roared. "But I'm going to break the fellow's neck now, destroy him like some mangy dog—and you as well, you whore."

Kraft went to the door and said, "Don't shout, man, you'll wake the whole house up. Your wife isn't here."

"What!" roared the railwayman furiously. "Do you think I'm an idiot? When I've seen you through the keyhole with my own eyes!"

Elfrida now ran over to the door and shouted, "But I'm not your wife! Do be reasonable!"

The furious railwayman had no intention of being reasonable. He felt certain his honor had been besmirched. "I'll deal with you, you whore! You can't take me in like that."

Krafft saw that it was pointless to try and calm this maniac who was so determined to avenge his honor. The only thing left now was to get dressed as quickly as possible and leave the place in haste with the minimum amount of damage done.

In the meantime the fellow's roaring had waked the whole house. A crowd collected to enjoy the curious scene and express their indignation or simply indulge their lust for violence. A sinister murmur arose and swelled to a torrent of abuse. The people were seething with righteous indignation.

"Give me a pistol," the irate railwayman bellowed. "I'll kill the dog! And that sow with him!"

Judging from what could be heard through the door, some people seemed to be trying to calm him down. Elfrida and Karl dressed as fast as they could. The railwayman kept on leaping at the door like a man possessed.

"Let me deal with this," said Elfrida.

Karl Krafft shook his head. "This is a man's job!" he said. Carefully turning the key in the door, he flung it open quick as a flash just as the furious railwayman was about to hurl himself against it. The fellow came whirling through the air to avenge his honor, stumbled, and fell headlong on the carpet.

Krafft hurriedly shut the door behind him, warding off a number of curious spectators in order to do so. He simply seized hold of the nearest man to him and using him as a bowling ball pushed him into the others. The most difficult of the operation was thus taken care of. All that remained now was to exploit the German vassal mentality to the full. With this in view the lieutenant went across to the railwayman, planted himself in front of him, and fixed him with a threatening stare.

The man who only a few moments before had been so anxious to avenge his honor was now visibly confused, and not only by his heavy fall on the carpet. The unexpected sight he now found himself confronted with in his own home left him dumb with amazement. He had felt certain he was catching his wife in adultery, instead of which he now found himself face to face with people he'd never seen before. On top of it all he saw an officer in full uniform standing over him, who turned out to be the man he had been threatening so violently.

"Name?" demanded Krafft.

"Behnke," returned the man promptly.

"Occupation?"

"Railwayman."

"Done your military service?"

"Yes, Lieutenant," said the railwayman in confusion. He had even been considered for an NCO's course.

"Then kindly leave us in peace here. Your wife is at the movies. Dismiss."

"Very good, sir," said the railwayman, now utterly bewildered. He shambled off.

The three cadets—Rednitz, Mösler, and Weber, Egon—were cosily settled with their girl friends. They lay strewn across mats in the gymnasium equipment store in positively bohemian abandon. The scene was bathed in a soft, rosy light from the electric heater and the radio. Three bottles stood beside them.

"Friends!" said Mösler. "Atmosphere is all-important on these occasions!"

It was Cadet Mösler's view that he had been born into the wrong century altogether. He saw himself possessing all the qualities of a dandy or true epicure. Instead, fate had landed him in the middle of this filthy war.

Not that this prevented Mösler from pursuing his pleasures with a certain style. It was just that certain adjustments had to be made, the prescribed supper by candlelight, for instance, having to be replaced by a simple schnapps at the bedside.

"The sacrifices I've made during this war!" he declared. "They defy description."

His feeling for décor had survived anyway—subdued lighting, soft warmth, and above all, music. Without music—a radio set in the present instance—Mösler found it impossible to work up the right mood. And though it had taken him almost twice as much trouble to organize this music box as it had to organize the three girls—music there had to be.

"I like piano music best," he said enthusiastically. "Chopin or Schumann, though Mozart'll do. When you close your eyes and switch out the light, you feel bathed in moonlight. In France we used to drink champagne as well, but we didn't bother about caviar. Champagne and caviar together seem vulgar to me, unless the champagne's from the Crimea, of course."

"You'll be relieved to hear I haven't brought any caviar," said Cadet Weber, Egon. "A strong schnapps isn't too bad, though, eh, my girl?"

The girl by Weber's side smiled primly. She was a fat, buxom little kitchen maid with aspirations toward higher things. Her head was full of notions of the great world, and the life of an officer's wife would have suited her admirably. She hoped this fellow Weber would be able to put her wise on one or two points of etiquette. "Isn't schnapps considered rather vulgar in some circles?" she asked him.

"My dear child," declared Weber gaily, "the circles you speak of consider nothing too vulgar. Sophisticated people have a pretty complicated love life, too, you know."

"Wouldn't it be an idea to dance?" suggested Mösler.

Rednitz shook his head anxiously, and Weber said, "What's the point? Besides, we ought to be careful about noise."

"I've thought of all that," said Mösler grandly. "The gym is particularly well placed, some distance from the main road and far from the regular beats of the sentries. Besides, I've done the blackout very conscientiously with boxing mats, which have the additional advantage of insulating sound. We could easily have the radio on louder if we wanted—no one's going to disturb us unless some officer suddenly takes it into his head to come and practice on the horizontal and parallel bars in the middle of the night, though I don't think even our officers are quite as far gone as that."

The girls laughed. They found the cadets very amusing. Most of their little adventures consisted of hurried scuffles on service blankets or doorsteps, without any finesse about them at all. This time things were delightfully different. This was a real little party.

The girl at Mösler's side was practically purring with pleasure. Rednitz's girl was certainly slightly bored, but she had hopes, even though her cadet hadn't made much effort to stimulate her so far. Weber's buxom little kitchen maid on the other hand was burning to find out more details about the customs of the officers' corps.

"Does it actually matter very much what sort of background an officer's wife comes from?" she inquired.

"In the first place," said Weber, "there's no such thing as an officer's wife—when you get to that stage you become an officer's lady. And then it doesn't matter where you come from."

"Really?" asked the girl eagerly.

"Certainly," said Weber. "There was once even a field-marshal who married a prostitute—that's to say, she used to walk the streets a good deal before he married her. But as I said, as the wife of a field-marshal, she was of course a lady. Even our beloved Führer was a witness at the wedding."

"Ah, yes," said the girl dreamily. "My heart beats quite differently every time I think of the Führer."

"Shall we move off together somewhere?" asked Weber, imagining this to be a favorable opportunity. "Come on— let's go into the gym itself."

But the girl didn't want to, or at least not yet. The information she had gleaned about the origins of officers' ladies interested her considerably. There was no doubt that officers, or at least aspiring officers, took to her. The boys just wouldn't leave her alone. This boy Weber was a fine, upstanding fellow, who would obviously have a splendid array of medals one day. And what a handsome couple she and he —or she and some other equally upstanding young fellow— would make! She saw herself shaming many an officer's lady —that dried-up old she-goat, the major's wife, for instance.

"Are you coming?" asked Weber impatiently. But his question came too late. Cadet Mösler had already waltzed out with his partner, so that the gymnasium was occupied for the next half hour.

"Could you imagine me as the wife of an officer?" said the girl, pursuing the subject stubbornly.

"But of course," said Weber, cocking an ear into the night, for he thought he heard a suspicious noise. But it seemed he was mistaken—it must have been the wind or a distant truck. He pulled the kitchen maid and all her social ambitions toward him. Damn it, though, it was the sort of night that made one uneasy.

Major Frey went into the kitchen for a glass of water, to find Barbara sitting at the kitchen table cutting her toenails. He looked first at the toenails, then at her feet, and then at her legs.

"Tell me, Barbara," he asked brusquely, "don't you feel rather ashamed of yourself?"

"Why should I?" she replied, looking at him with big round eyes.

"One simply doesn't cut one's toenails in the kitchen," said the major severely. "Kindly take note of the fact."

Whereupon he slopped out again in his large, warm felt slippers back to his workroom. Here sat his wife, Felicitas, reading a book—a particularly fine German book, of course. She raised her eyes and looked at him without expression.

The major sat down at his desk and began to write.

"What are you working at, Archibald?" asked Felicitas.

"At a special order, my dearest," said the major.

"What sort of special order?"

"It's a sort of omnibus special order this time, Felicitas.

I'm combining a whole number of different small points. Haircuts, for instance, late passes, nomenclature——"

Felicitas nodded and went on with her book, which was one of those the excellent Captain Ratshelm had sent her by that nice boy Cadet Hochbauer. Involuntarily she sighed.

"Anything the matter, Felicitas?" asked the major, attentive at once.

She replied in the negative without glancing up at him, and appeared simply to go on with her reading. He bent over his special order, but without any real concentration.

"What do you make of the Christian name Egon?" he asked suddenly.

"Appalling," she said.

"My view too," agreed the major.

"A distant cousin of my mother's was called that," explained the major's wife. A thoroughly worthless fellow—no officer, of course."

"All the same," said the major, "a man can't really help his name. It's given him at birth or at his christening."

"I'm well aware of that, Archibald."

"What I meant," explained the major, "was this: we live in times when unnecessary ballast in a person's name can be dispensed with. Take the name Grabowski for instance— that's Slav. But because he's a German he decides to call himself Grabow, which I think you'll agree sounds very Prussian. The necessary legal procedure is a pure formality. In my opinion a German officer ought to have a German-sounding name. And Christian names must be suitable too. Fortunately a man usually has two of these. I simply won't tolerate names like Egon. It sounds like some name out of a comic strip."

Felicitas Frey yawned. It wasn't only her husband's lecture that made her do this. She held the book up in front of her face and yawned again. But the book again reminded her of the pleasant, glossy-haired young cadet who had given it to her. Again she smiled dreamily, and her husband interpreted her smile as a thoughtful, friendly expression of agreement.

"Actually I feel sorry for the cadets," she said unexpectedly.

The major looked up puzzled, finding it difficult to make sense of this remark. "What makes you feel sorry for them?" he asked.

"Yes," said Frau Felicitas, "I do. How, I ask myself, do these young men spend their evenings?"

"Well, they work. What else should they do?"

"I remember so well the cadets of my youth," she said, smiling absent-mindedly. "In those days there were dances, parties, concerts, excursions, grand balls."

"But really," said the major, shaking his head soberly. "We're not in Dresden or Berlin, my dear. And besides, this isn't peacetime. There's a war on, you know."

"All the same," said Frau Felicitas stubbornly, "everything should be done to prevent the young people from forgetting the social graces. They're so important in establishing human relations, in encouraging a proper sense of respect for rank and standing. Aren't I right, Archibald?"

"Of course," said the major. "Only you must remember we're suffering from certain restrictions at the moment."

"I don't forget that," she said, mildly enough. "But I'm beginning to find this problem absorbing. I'll devote a little time to it, if you'll let me—it'll be in your own interest in the end. Could you tomorrow ask the excellent Captain Ratshelm to send me some more books? By the same means as before."

Elfrida Rademacher hurried through the icy rain to her quarters, where she found a sentry barring the way. "You're to come to Captain Kater," he said.

"Won't tomorrow morning do?" asked Elfrida.

"It's a service matter," said the sentry. "The captain is waiting for you in his office." This was a summons that Elfrida couldn't ignore. She went across to the staff company building and reported at once at the CO's office.

Kater looked ostentatiously at his watch as she came in. Then, grinning knowingly, he said, "Pretty late, eh?"

"If I'd known you were waiting for me," said Elfrida tartly, "I shouldn't have hurried so much."

Captain Kater winced. He didn't like the way she'd been talking to him lately. But he kept the grin on his face and, with a twinkle in his eye, asked, "Did you have a good time at any rate?"

"I don't know what you mean by that," said Elfrida. She wanted to make it quite plain that she had no use for conversations of this sort. "I can't think what you want at this extraordinary time of night. If it's Irene Jablonski you want to talk about, that can certainly wait until tomorrow."

"What can have put such an idea into your head?" asked Kater disingenuously. "What are you trying to suggest? That girl doesn't interest me in the slightest."

It was clear to Elfrida Rademacher that by stopping Irene

from going to his room she had struck him a blow which he wasn't easily going to forget. He was already taking his revenge.

"Sit down, Elfrida," said the captain.

"My name is Rademacher," she said.

"All right then, Fräulein Rademacher," said Kater irritably. He was absolutely determined to get even with this creature. There were certain things that people could do to him only once.

"Fräulein Rademacher," said Kater, pulling a well-filled wine glass out of the large cupboard in his desk and taking a drink from it, "several times recently you've been very late getting back either to barracks or to your own quarters."

"That's my affair, Captain," said Elfrida firmly.

"Not entirely," said Captain Kater, fortifying himself with another powerful draught of wine. "Where, under what circumstances, and with whom, you spend your time is not altogether unimportant. And since it is I who am responsible for you, you must permit me to give the matter a moment or two's thought. Nor can I feel indifferent about the gentleman with whom you spend your time."

"What are you getting at?" asked Elfrida.

Kater grinned to himself in a superior fashion. He knew exactly what he was getting at. The day now only had a few more minutes to live, but three things had happened in it that warned him he must hurry. First, his subordinate, this girl Rademacher, had dared to inferfere in his most personal affairs. Secondly, the general had demanded from him a final report summarizing his activities. Thirdly, Judge-Advocate Wirrmann had written him a personal letter of some urgency.

"I've got a soft spot for you, Fräulein Rademacher. But what worries me slightly is the fact that I also have a certain sympathy for this Lieutenant Krafft of yours. I like the fellow, and find it regrettable that my feelings should be so little reciprocated."

"That's nothing to do with me," said Elfrida discouragingly.

"You can take it from me," said Kater, continuing as if he hadn't been interrupted, "he's badly in need of friends at the moment. I know at least two people who would be glad to be rid of him."

"And I think I now know a third."

Captain Kater grinned. He felt positively flattered. "No, no," he said cagily. "Of course if I wanted to, I could—but why should I, when it's a friend who's involved? On the other hand I have certain quite specific obligations as an

officer. For instance if I knew of any immoral conduct or behavior prejudicial to good discipline I would have to report it.
But do I know of any? Sometimes my memory plays me
tricks. And there are some things which in certain circumstances I'm prepared to ignore, just because I always make a
point of standing by a friend. But I need to be quite clear
about who is my friend and who isn't."

"Why are you saying all this to me?" asked Elfrida with
some feeling. "You should say it to Lieutenant Krafft."

"Look here, my pretty child," said Captain Kater. "I'll be
quite frank with you—there's no one listening to us. Right,
then. This Lieutenant Krafft of yours is a pretty smart fellow,
I've absolutely no doubt about that at all. If I try and talk
him over to my way of thinking he will try and make me
commit myself more than I want to. Which is why I make
use of you. You will in fact tell him all the things that I
would find it difficult to put to him with the requisite clarity.
If, however, something should go wrong—then naturally I
haven't said anything at all. Do you follow me? I've simply
been discussing some service matters with you and that's all.
If you, as Lieutenant Krafft's mistress, were to try to maintain the contrary, then you would both find yourselves involved in a scandal. And this man Krafft of yours would
come a real cropper, you can be sure of that."

"I see," said Elfrida. She felt disgusted, but resigned. She
thought of what had happened that night. The fat would
really be in the fire when Kater heard about the brawling
railwayman.

"Right, then!" said the captain with satisfaction. As if
there were now no more need for dissimulation he placed the
bottle and the glass on his desk. "Why do we have to spend
hours beating about the bush when we really understand each
other perfectly well?"

"All right," said Elfrida Rademacher, "I'll talk to you."

"Listen, dear child, this fellow Krafft has got to put his
cards on the table. What I want to know is this; what sort of
relationship existed between the general and Lieutenant
Barkow, and the general and Frau Barkow? He must have
discovered that by now. He hasn't been escorting the lady
around for hours for nothing. I'll tell him what else I want to
know later. Right—and if the good fellow says nothing,
unfortunately I shall then have to do my duty in the interests
of morality and good discipline. There is another possibility,
of course, Elfrida. You could, so to speak, sacrifice yourself

for him, though sacrifice is hardly the right word. That would be most welcome to me. For I really have a very soft spot for you."

Lieutenant Krafft sauntered slowly across to his quarters. The cold rain began to change into thick, lumpy snowflakes. His greatcoat weighed a ton, his face glistened with moisture. But none of this bothered him. He badly needed to cool off.

The business with the railwayman had been tricky. If the story were to find its way up to the training school there might be trouble. The general wasn't going to stand for any nonsense like that. Modersohn himself had told him not to lay himself open to attack . . . but it was all very well for the general, who had no Elfrida Rademacher.

The lieutenant slowed his pace still further and listened to the night. A heavy stillness lay all about him—no sound of music, no distant train, no church clock striking, nothing.

Suddenly, however, Krafft heard soldiers' boots approaching in step across the concrete. Certainly there wasn't much life in their marching, in fact it sounded altogether pretty slack, but after all it was past midnight—the men were tired and not expecting to be observed. This became clearer and clearer as they approached.

The party which marched past Krafft consisted of three men, two sentries apparently, led by a third—shadowy figures in the snow and darkness. The leading soldier suddenly saluted, surprisingly smartly.

Lieutenant Krafft brought his hand up to the peak of his cap and looked after the party in some astonishment. There was something unusual about such a clear-cut salute in almost pitch darkness. Captain Ratshelm would have noted the fact with satisfaction, but it made Lieutenant Krafft suspicious.

His eyes followed them more closely. And something about the men's gait, particularly that of the leading man, seemed familiar to Krafft. His excellent memory went into action at once, and he cried out in surprise, "Isn't that Rednitz!"

The soldiers pounded on with a slight increase in pace. It was the only thing they could do in the circumstances, in the hope that the person who'd called after them would wonder if he hadn't made a mistake. Krafft, however, hurried after the three musketeers and gave the order, "Squad—halt! Squad —about turn!"

And there in front of him stood Rednitz, Mösler, and Weber, Egon. In the faint light from a street lamp their faces were pale with dismay. They gazed at Krafft like prisoners on whom sentence has already been passed, but in whom hope of mercy is not yet entirely extinguished. They didn't say a word, not in fact having been asked to say anything.

Lieutenant Krafft sensed at once that something was wrong, and quickly set his mind to work. It wasn't their turn for sentry duty. No special duties had been allotted, no exceptional orders given. Moreover the fellows smelt of alcohol. "You'll report to me in five minutes," ordered Lieutenant Krafft. "Attention! Squad—about turn! Squad—quick march!"

They trudged off with drooping shoulders and sagging chins.

"What are we going to do now?" asked Weber anxiously when they got back to their billet.

"Perhaps," suggested Mösler hesitantly, "we could just tell the lieutenant we were practicing sentry duty."

"Half-wit!" cried Rednitz.

The cry awoke the fourth man in the room, Cadet Böhmke, who pushed his tousled head out of the blankets. The copy of *Faust* lay on his pillow. "Are you back already?" he asked amiably.

"Act dead," said Rednitz. "You've heard nothing, seen nothing, and know nothing. You were reading *Faust* and fell asleep over it. You haven't a clue what we've been doing in the meantime. Is that clear? Krafft will make mincemeat of you if you say anything else. And we'd like to spare you that. Three casualties are enough for one night."

"Very decent of you," said Böhmke gratefully. And in proof of his gratitude, he quoted the lines:

> *"For the noble soul has power*
> *To compass all if wise and swift."*

Then he crawled under his blankets again.

"We're done for," said Weber glumly. "He can do what he wants with us."

"The only question is," said Rednitz thoughtfully, "what does he want to do with us?"

Their fate lay in Krafft's hands. He could see to it that they were expelled from the training school the next morning, which would mean farewell to all thoughts of a commission and back to the ranks for them.

"There's not much sense in trying to cover things up, is there?" asked Mösler gloomily.

Rednitz was realistic. "Not with Lieutenant Krafft," he said.

"But we must leave the girls out of it," insisted Weber,

Egon. "We've got to be chivalrous. Or should we fall back on the story that we were seduced?"

They soon saw that it was hopeless. They slunk across to the door of Lieutenant Krafft's room, knocked gingerly, and went inside. They stood there crestfallen. It was as if they hadn't the courage to look their section officer in the face.

Lieutenant Krafft, however, said, "Now listen, friends. I'm glad you hadn't gone to bed, because I want a little talk with you. I'd like to ask you one or two questions about the death of Lieutenant Barkow. Now get this straight; these questions interest no one but me. If you answer them fully and honestly, I won't have any other question to ask. Is that clear?"

The cadets nodded. They were faced by two alternatives: either to be expelled from the training school, or to tell the truth.

"We'll tell the truth," declared Cadet Rednitz.

20 *PLACING OF THE CHARGE*

"YOU'RE going to write an essay," Lieutenant Krafft told his cadets. "Time: half an hour. Subject: *Dulce et decorum est* . . . it is sweet to die for the Fatherland! Right, off you go!"

Thus did Lieutenant Krafft place his charge. With some satisfaction he sensed that no one seemed to have taken in the fact. The cadets looked up at him anxiously for a moment before staring into space and wracking their brains. They had had to put up with a whole host of idotic subjects like this in their time, and one more or less made little difference.

"Come now, friends," said Krafft encouragingly, "what are you waiting for? Didn't someone once say, 'Death follows hard upon the heels of men?' Well, then, before he finally catches up with you it might be as well to spare a few moments' thought for him."

Lieutenant Krafft lounged over his desk, regarding his section with the eye of a placidly watchful Saint Bernard. He looked very tired. But some of his cadets had passed an equally restless night——Rednitz, Mösler, and Weber, Egon for instance. Krafft had certainly put them through it. It had been three o'clock in the morning before they had been able to crawl exhausted into their beds.

But Krafft had spent a further hour writing up his notes. Dawn broke before he finished, and it was in the harsh light of the new day that he realized what his next step would have to be. The lieutenant had written up these notes on little sheets of paper in a meticulous hand which bore some resemblance to print. In an abbreviated and concentrated form they contained everything that seemed to Krafft important. Their contents were as follows:

Sheet 1—CADET WEBER, EGON: Lieutenant Barkow was an officer through and through; nothing else counted for him, neither the Party nor the Führer. Certain cadets, like Amfortas, Andreas, and of course Hochbauer, place the Führer above everything. They like to talk of themselves as officers of the Führer. This led to disputes in which Lieutenant Barkow's attitude remained adamant. The cadets in question inevitably began to be afraid they mightn't survive the course. (Weber, verbatim, "They were on their knees. Hochbauer was the only one who wouldn't knuckle under.") Nothing special seemed to happen at the locator post during the engineering exercise. (Weber, verbatim, "But of course I wouldn't put anything past some people.")

Sheet 2—CADET REDNITZ: Lieutenant Barkow never lost a chance to make it clear that this was a course for people who wanted to become officers, not one for people who wanted to get on in the Party. Lieutenant Barkow's favorite slogan was, "You can only serve one cause properly. Either the army or the Party." To which Hochbauer objected that the army was the Führer and the Party was the Führer, too, so it was all one. Barkow's reply was that this was nonsense. He who wished to be a soldier must either be a soldier or nothing at all. At the locator post during the engineering exercise a number of different fuses were prepared for the main charge as part of the exercise, and one of them was eventually used with a burning time of five seconds. It was prepared by Amfortas with the assistance of Hochbauer and Andreas. (Rednitz, verbatim, "Eight men took part in the final stage, three of whom at least were asleep on their feet. But there are always people who take any chance to push their way to the front.")

Sheet 3—CADET MÖSLER: Lieutenant Barkow always had a will of iron. (Mösler, verbatim, "Like a pocket edition of the general, one might say.") The lieutenant certainly embodied all the soldierly ideals, but Hochbauer had his ideals, too, and never ceased proclaiming them. (Mösler, verbatim, "Perhaps this was all humbug on Hochbauer's part. In any case, he stood very low in Barkow's estimation. Perhaps that was why he sheltered so much behind his Führer.") Just before the explosion, when the fuse had been lit, Hochbauer shouted, "Take cover as fast as you can!" (Mösler, verbatim, "And so we did; because Hochbauer's no fool. It was then that we felt pretty sure he knew exactly what was happening.") There were plenty of fuses and charges lying about, and it was always possible for small quantities to disappear without anyone noticing.

These were the three sheets of notes which Lieutenant Krafft had prepared. He read them through thoughtfully. A lot could be deleted, a certain amount could be condensed, and perhaps one or two things could be written off as exaggeration. However, that still left more than enough with which to lure his prey into the trap.

The cadets were now writing away furiously. Lieutenant Krafft left his desk and wandered down through them to the wall at the back of the classroom. Here he stopped and watched them thoughtfully as they sat hunched over their work. The virgin sheets of paper began to be covered with letters from which words, sentences, and eventually whole paragraphs grew. Explosive material indeed, and of considerable force, too, with luck. *Dulce et decorum est*—

"I don't want to disturb you, my friend," said Captain Feders looking into the classroom, "But could I have a word with you a minute."

"Of course, Captain," said Krafft, leaving his observation post at the back of the room.

Feders had come as far as the front row, where he peered curiously over the shoulder of one of the cadets. When he saw the subject of the essay he looked up at Krafft with a twinkle in his eye.

The captain turned to the cadets and said, "Don't utterly kill yourselves over this essay, friends. I want a little breath left in your bodies for when I take you myself later."

The cadets looked up at Captain Feders and laughed appropriately. They felt this was expected of them. But their laughter sounded very forced, since they realized that Feders must have understood at once what a tricky subject they had been set. This business of the sweetness of death for the Fatherland had at first seemed just a routine bit of nonsense to be smothered in platitudes, but slowly it began to dawn on them that they were really in deep water. It was going to be a job to get anything down at all.

"They seem quite happy," said Captain Feders. "Let's go out into the corridor for a moment."

"Keep an eye on them for me, will you, Kramer?" said Lieutenant Krafft to the section senior. "I don't want any talking, understand? And I don't want to find similarities of thought between people sitting next to each other or behind or in front of each other. That would amount to intellectual pilfering, and I've no wish to train a lot of criminals."

"You'll have plenty of time for that sort of thing when you become officers," added Captain Feders.

Feders and Krafft then left the section to themselves, walking out into the corridor and across to the window, where they could talk without fear of being overheard.

"What are you up to with this sweet death of yours, my dear Krafft?" inquired Feders with a wink.

"Captain," said Krafft bluntly, "do you find it at all conceivable that one or perhaps more than one of our cadets could have intentionally blown Lieutenant Barkow to kingdom come?"

"Of course," said Feders unmoved. "These things happen. The percentage of such cases is of course very small, but presumably only because the fear of superior officers is always disproportionately greater than the hatred felt for them."

"Captain, I'm talking about fact."

"I'm talking about facts too," said Feders. "I've known a soldier in peacetime to bash his corporal's skull in with a rifle during rifle drill. The man had been bawled out by the corporal, got excited, and lashed out at him. Again, right at the beginning of the war I knew a lance-corporal who drove a sergeant-major over a steep embankment. The truck and the sergeant-major were a total write-off, but the lance-corporal managed to jump clear just in time. Then again, the CO of the company next to us was brought down while leading his men in an attack. He'd been shot in the back—twice, as a matter of fact."

Obviously Feders was no longer capable of being surprised by anything. He found death child's play.

"So," continued Feders, "you think Lieutenant Barkow was done in by some of our cadets and that he was stupid enough to allow it to happen? Well, the cadets seem to have pulled it off very neatly. Lucky for them. You're not seriously thinking, my dear Krafft, that you might succeed in finding the culprit at this stage?"

"But if I should in fact succeed in doing so, Captain?"

"I'll be the first to help you bring him to account, Krafft. But don't fool yourself, my dear fellow—the birds have flown long ago."

"I'll try and tempt them back again!"

"Well all I can say is, the best of luck to you, Krafft, my dear old sportsman! But do be careful how you handle your guns—they can be fixed so that they go off in your face, you know."

"We'll see," said Krafft, who didn't find the conversation particularly encouraging.

"Typical of you," said Feders grimly. "I've seen this coming, Krafft. For days now I've had a suspicion of what you were up to. God knows who put you up to it! You're trying to shift a dunghill with your bare hands. You're the born suicide candidate. Basically you're rather like me. I'm sorry for you, Krafft, because I like you."

"I like you, too, Captain Feders."

Feders stared at Krafft, and nodded. He felt suddenly very bitter. He clapped the lieutenant roughly on the back and nodded again, being unable apparently to find the words he wanted. He turned brusquely on his heel and walked away.

"Was there anything else, Captain?" Krafft called after him.

Feders stopped and looked back. "Quite right," he said. "I wanted to ask you if you'd take my place during the next class. All right?"

"Of course," said Krafft. As a matter of routine he added, "You've told the company commander and the course commander, I suppose?"

"Neither," said Feders, now quite himself again. "I have some private business to attend to; in fact I want to appeal to my wife's conscience over the Minnesinger. She seems to have slung him out last night. What do you make of that, Krafft?"

"I'd be delighted, if I were you."

"But you're not me, Krafft, and a few days ago I would have told you, you were lucky not to be! Now I don't really know whom one ought to feel more sorry for—you with your damaged brain, or me with my damage elsewhere."

"Everyone has their own problems," said Krafft, "not least your wife."

"But I mean this, Krafft. I don't want to deprive my wife of anything. Why does she fight me on this?"

"Because you've at last succeeded in getting her where you wanted her, Feders."

"How do you make that out? I warn you, you're on dangerous ground here."

"Ah, what the hell?" said Krafft carelessly. "You meddle in my affairs—I'm going to meddle in yours. You and I are beginning to get the measure of each other."

"Well, all right, what do you imagine you've discovered?"

"Something very simple and obvious, namely that a substitute will never be anything but a substitute. You're deliberately rubbing your wife's nose in the fact. You refuse her nothing—on the contrary, you offer her everything. Simply so that sooner or later she shall find out that it's all not nearly so desirable as people think. But she's already learned that; she can hold back now. She's cured. She's back where she belongs. And all this in an astonishingly short time, wouldn't you say, Feders?"

"Krafft," said Feders, visibly moved, "now I see the sort of person you really are. Hitherto I've taken you for something of a starry-eyed idealist. But that's wrong. You're not going blindfolded into this adventure of yours, as I supposed—you know exactly what you're doing."

"You go and send the Minnesinger packing and talk things over with your wife."

"Not yet," said Feders. "Because there's one thing I've learned from you, Krafft, and that is to have patience. You know how to wait. I'll do just the same."

Once again the captain turned as if to go, but again he stopped and looked back at Lieutenant Krafft, seeming to hesitate. Then he came right up to Krafft again, planted himself squarely in front of him, and said slowly, "Just to go back to this Sherlock Holmes role of yours, my dear Krafft, it won't be enough for you simply to hunt down the culprit and identify him. You mustn't overlook the fact that there were obviously several people involved in the affair, even though one was presumably the ringleader. But just consider this: what you have to cope with is a ringleader, several accessories and accomplices, and a whole host of onlookers with more or less of an idea of what happened. The questions you have to ask yourself are these: Why is there so little conclusive proof? Why does everyone keep quiet? Why does there seem so little to go on? Why are these nothing but assumptions, suspicions, hypotheses?"

"This has occurred to me, too, Captain."

"I should hope so, my dear fellow. And what conclusions have you come to? Presumably you'll need a confession if you're going to take the matter to a court-martial. Or did you intend to play the judge yourself? I wouldn't put it beyond you. If you want to get the guilty party, Krafft, what you'll have to do is to isolate him, cut him off from his clique, break his influence—get him quite alone. Then you can strike. Aren't I right, Krafft?"

"That is exactly what I'm doing," said the lieutenant simply.

"Good," said Captain Feders. "But make your will first."

"Time up," said Lieutenant Krafft to his cadets. "Collect the work, Kramer. Ten minutes break."

The cadets left the classroom and pushed their way out into the corridor, where they split up into small groups.

"It's easier to die than to write about it," declared Egon Weber grimly.

"Quicker, too," said Mösler.

"What I'd like to know," said Rednitz, "is what made Lieutenant Krafft set this subject—there must be something behind it."

"Difficult to tell," said Mösler. "The lieutenant may simply have been too tired or too lazy to do any teaching."

"The sweetness of death," said Weber pensively. "To hell with that!"

"However," said Rednitz, "I assume your indignation didn't prevent you from declaring that you were ready to make a sweet sacrifice of yourself for the Fatherland."

"What else is one to do?" asked Weber with resignation.

"It is so sweet to sleep for the Fatherland," said Mösler grinning. "That'll do me as a theme for an entire course."

"I've collected the work, sir," announced Cadet Kramer, the section senior.

"Put it on my desk," said Krafft.

"Very good, sir," said Kramer, taking the work and piling it up carefully in front of Krafft. He spent a lot of time doing this.

The lieutenant scrutinized the cadet carefully. Kramer was an uncommonly keen type, there was no doubt of that. The man felt drawn toward Hochbauer and his clique, it seemed. Here then was a chance to remove one stone from the wall that had to be dismantled. There certainly wasn't much time to lose.

"Tell me, Kramer," asked Krafft, "how long have you been section senior here?"

"Since the beginning of the course, sir."

"And do you intend to remain section senior to the end of the course?"

The cunningness and directness of this question left Cadet Kramer completely at a loss. He wracked his brains for an answer, but could find none. Lieutenant Krafft maliciously gave him any amount of time.

Kramer had spotted the significance of the question at once —his post as section senior was in danger. It was a post which involved a certain amount of extra work, but which also entailed considerable privileges as well. For a section senior stood as it were halfway between the cadets and the officers who trained them. He was the connecting link, the intermediary, the man with both parties' confidence, the man through whom things got done. He had been specially selected, and unless he went completely to pieces would inevitably pass out near the top of the course, provided, that is, he didn't make off with the spoons or rape the commanding officer's wife or forfeit his job some other way. The point was that it lay within Krafft's power to depose him.

"I wouldn't like to lose you, Kramer," said Krafft with devastating friendliness, "but I'm afraid that's just what's going to happen if you continue to neglect one of the most important aspects of your job here, by which I mean the need for strict impartiality. You are responsible to me for the whole section, not just for a group within the section, and you're not to show favoritism to any one clique or group. It isn't your job to apportion blame or deliver judgment— you will kindly leave that to the officers in charge of you. What you've got to try to achieve is complete objectivity. If you are not quite sure what that means, you can always ask me. Do you follow me, Cadet Kramer?"

"Yes, sir," said the latter in some consternation.

"And you see that my remarks are fully justified?"

"Yes, sir."

Kramer saw it all. There was no other choice for him; from now on he was determined to be ostentatiously detached, thus leaving himself unhampered to pursue his final goal of becoming an officer. This goal could only be achieved with the assistance of Lieutenant Krafft; without it he hadn't a chance, unless of course some third section officer were to take over before the end of the course, which, though not beyond the bounds of possibility, was unlikely.

"Well," said Krafft, "I look forward to our future co-operation, then."

"Yes, sir."

Meanwhile Krafft had begun to look cursorily through his cadets' essays. They seemed on the whole to be exactly what he had expected. Only one appeared wholly to absorb him. Indeed he seemed delighted by what he read—it obviously exceeded his wildest expectations. He put this effort, which meant so much to him, carefully to one side.

Meanwhile Kramer busied himself with the class logbook. He had sat down in his place and had started writing up his entries, but kept glancing up at his section officer.

"Might I ask you a question, sir?" he finally ventured to ask.

"Well, Kramer?"

"Might I be permitted to ask, sir, whether you have any particular wishes with regard to our future co-operation?"

"Kramer," said Lieutenant Krafft affably, "in your capacity as section senior you, so to speak, represent me in my absence. Isn't that enough? All you have to do is to think what I would do. It's really quite simple."

"Very good, sir," said Kramer submissively.

"Besides," continued Krafft, "I'll naturally let you know when I have any special requests. There's nothing at the moment. Your next job will be to bring the break to an end. In five minutes' time, let's say. Between now and then I'll look through the rest of the work."

"Break over!" the section senior shouted down the corridor. "Come on now, double up! No hanging about! Or do I have to come and get you?"

The cadets streamed back into the classroom. They in no way resented Kramer's slave-driving tactics, which were all part of the general style to which they had grown accustomed. They merely cast a furtive glance or two in the direction of their section officer, and, as experienced judges of the moods of superior officers, recognized that their lieutenant was obviously in rather a good one, a fact which they noted with relief. It was almost with a sense of eager anticipation that they resumed their places.

"Right, then, let's begin," said Lieutenant Krafft.

The section senior immediately emitted the prescribed roar of command as if on the barrack square. The noise was deafening. Presumably he wanted to show how splendidly he discharged his duties. "Attention!" he bellowed and made his report.

Krafft acknowledged it. "Take your places!" roared Kramer.

The cadets flopped into their places like so many sacks of flour dropped from a great height.

Krafft eyed his eager retinue with a certain ambivalence, taking his time over this in a way which gave rise to considerable unease. Finally the lieutenant pointed to the pile of essays in front of him and said, "Friends, after a cursory glance through these I can't help asking myself how it is you're all still alive, since according to your own assurances it is so incomparably sweet to die for the Fatherland."

The cadets winced, but continued to look at their lieutenant with interest, for they had learned, particularly from Captain Feders, to be wary of being caught off their guard by their officers.

"That each of us has to die," said Lieutenant Krafft, "is just about the one thing in our lives that can be forecast with absolute certainty. The only thing we don't know is when and in what circumstances. The possibilities are extraordinarily numerous, from the infant who chokes on his bottle to the old man whose heart simply wears out. Between these two extremes there's an astonishing range of so-called natural and violent deaths, violent-natural and natural-violent, and among these is death on the so-called field of honor. And this field of honor can be a flower-decked meadow or a dung heap, a romantic babbling brook or a filthy puddle. Death's repertoire is inexhaustible."

The cadets began to eye each other furtively, realizing that the work which had cost them so much effort had turned out a failure, and a pretty serious one at that, at least in Lieutenant Krafft's view, which was, after all, the only one that counted. This theme of *Dulce et decorum est* had obviously been some sort of subtle trap.

Lieutenant Krafft picked up some of the essays, apparently quite at random, and quoted from them. "Here for example Cadet Mösler writes, 'Even the ancient Greeks were glad to die for their Fatherland.' That may well be, or rather it's exceedingly difficult to prove they weren't. Besides which, there have always been a few people who were glad to die— suicides for example, and of course heroes. But when Cadet Amfortas writes here among other things 'There is no finer death,' I really can't help wondering. I can think of more than a few forms of death that are at least as fine as that on the battlefield. And Cadet Andreas seems to have discussed the subject of his essay with the Lord God in person, for he writes, 'Providence has chosen the soldier to die the most splendid death one could conceive of.' All I can say to that is, let the chosen ones then push forward so that those less favored by the Almighty may be left to survive!"

The cadets were beginning to realize that the occasion was not without its humorous aspects. Laughter made itself heard here and there warily at first, though gradually growing less and less inhibited.

Krafft now reached out for the essay he had put carefully to one side. "Here," he said, "I've discovered a particularly splendid piece of confectionery—quite the most sugary thing we've got on the whole subject. Permit me to offer you a piece of it. I quote, 'For the noble ones of history death is a sheer delight, to be regarded as the crowning moment of a hero's existence. It is sweet in the sense that it opens up vistas of immortality.' And I ask myself, How is it possible for a normal human being to churn out muck like this?"

Cadet Hochbauer now rose to his full height and stood there very pale. Heroically he acknowledged that this over-weening flight of fancy was his. Presumably he felt that there was no other choice left to him.

"Lieutenant," he said, "what I meant by what I wrote was that death for the Fatherland was the most honorable death there was."

"Even that's disputable," said Krafft, "though not, I freely admit with everyone. Personally I can think of quite a number of other honorable forms of death—but not a single one that is in any way sweet. Still less 'sheer delight!' Man dies on the battlefield. Sometimes it takes a fraction of a second and sometimes it drags out for days."

"That it is sweet to die for the Fatherland," returned Hochbauer stubbornly, "surely has to be accepted as an incontest-able legacy from classical times, Lieutenant, and expounded accordingly. Today this saying adorns many of our war memorials and triumphal arches, it's to be found in textbooks, and is quoted on all solemn occasions."

Krafft, who actually seemed to welcome Hochbauer's stubbornness, said, "A few thousand years have passed since certain sharp-practicing bards of rosy antiquity first mouthed this drivel about the sweetness of death for the Fatherland. In the meantime, although men have become essentially no cleverer, they have been able to amass a certain amount of experience—though their memory, particularly with regard to war, is lamentably short. Yet by now it has managed to get around that war itself is anything but sweet. It was only a few decades ago that some poet sang:

> *"Today a steed to match the best,*
> *tomorrow a bullet through the breast."*

But war makes nonsense of the poet's fancies. It seldom kills anyone cleanly through the breast. It tears them to shreds, bursts them open, squashes them flat, pulverizes them. No trace of sweetness anywhere."

"But that, Lieutenant," said Cadet Hochbauer, with haughty disdain, "is the view of people like Remarque and Renn and Barbusse!"

The cadets looked horrified, realizing at once how dangerously effective was this last argument of Hochbauer's. It was intended as a knockout and had been ruthlessly delivered. It was just like old times again. It might have been Lieutenant Barkow standing there instead of Lieutenant Krafft—Barkow whose reaction had been one of cold contempt. But Lieutenant Krafft actually beamed as if he'd just been handed a very welcome present. The cadets were flabbergasted by so many astonishing twists and turns.

Krafft did in fact have some difficulty in concealing his sense of triumph. The lieutenant had now got Hochbauer exactly where he wanted him. His victim was ready for the knife; all he had to do was to drive it home.

And Krafft said simply, "I note, Hochbauer, that you have the impertinence to attribute the views of our Führer to Herr Erich Maria Remarque."

The effect of this sentence was immediately to erect some sort of mighty pillar right there in the middle of the room, a pillar against which Cadet Hochbauer found he had unwittingly cracked his skull. He looked about him in stunned amazement, unable to grasp what the lieutenant had said. His face wore an expression of utter bewilderment. Hungry for sensation, the cadets pricked up their ears, and they began to realize that a rare drama was being enacted in front of them.

With an air of utter helplessness Hochbauer asked, "Our Führer?"

Krafft nodded with grim pleasure, "Yes indeed! I'm speaking of our Führer, Hochbauer. And I'm not going to have you comparing him with Remarque. I find it scandalous that you should cast aspersions on him and indeed insult him in this way. How can you hope to become an officer if you're not even prepared to respect the views of our supreme commander-in-chief?"

Hochbauer felt completely at sea. Had he really made a mistake—he of all people, who considered himself one of his Führer's truest and most loyal soldiers? He could find nothing to say. The cadets stared open-mouthed.

"You ought to take a look at Adolf Hitler's book *Mein Kampf* sometime, Hochbauer," said Krafft. "Clearly you haven't found time to read it, but I strongly recommend it to you. Or do you perhaps not intend to become one of our Führer's officers? It almost looks like that to me. And I'm afraid I'll have to draw my own conclusions."

Hochbauer stared uncomprehendingly at his section officer. What had happened was too appalling! If he had heard right, doubt was being cast here on his attitude to what was for him the most important thing in life. His Führer mattered to him more than anything in the whole world!

Krafft now proceeded to inform the man who had once been widely accepted as one of the Führer's most loyal disciples, that Adolf Hitler, the front-line soldier of the First World War, considered a battlefield no place for saccharine sentiments. Nowhere was there any mention of the "sweetness" of death—quite the contrary, the Führer had emphasized that dying was anything but a delightful business. And with ruthless persistence Lieutenant Krafft rammed home his point until Cadet Hochbauer came to realize that he ought to be thoroughly ashamed of himself.

The incident profoundly affected the entire section. The cadets had witnessed the destruction of a legend of invincibility. Cadet Hochbauer had for the first time been heavily defeated—and with his own weapons, too. And Mösler almost moaned with joy, saying, "He's knocked him cold!"

Lieutenant Krafft concluded as follows, "Hochbauer, I shall have to reserve the right to designate your remarks as seditious. Where the Führer's concerned, I know no mercy. Take note of that."

21 *ORGANIZATION OF LEISURE*

"Gentlemen," cried Cadet Mösler on waking, "today is Saturday—the big day for all would-be officers! Let us rejoice, then, and from midday on make merry. This evening we'll have something of a party."

Whereupon Cadet Egon Weber rolled out of bed with a huge yawn and declared, "Friends, when I get up on a Saturday the only thought in my mind is which bed I'm going to get back into again."

"I see it's a problem," said Rednitz, pulling on his sports clothes.

"I'll say it's a problem, man!" replied Weber. "You know, there's something that worries me. It looks very much to me as if the planning staffs are falling down on their job. How are we to win the war, I ask myself? Isn't it clear that these people's shortsightedness endangers final victory itself, if it doesn't actually sabotage it altogether?"

"Is anything wrong?" asked Rednitz, pretending to be very anxious. "Shall I report you sick?"

"Let me finish!" cried Weber indignantly. "What sort of idiotic planning is this, I ask myself. How can a staff officer who is even half a normal human being plant an entire training school in a godforsaken area like this? The man must be an impotent or a homosexual. For I'm afraid the middle-aged female civilian population doesn't really begin to match up to our standards."

"Bravo!" cried Mösler appreciatively. "You should put in a petition about it."

"I mean to say, friends—no vacation home in the neighborhood, no high-class girls' boarding school, not even a women's labor service camp! Nothing but emergency solutions available!"

The registry of births of the little town of Wildlingen-am-Main contained abundant evidence to this effect. Every officers' training course left its mark on the files—contributing on average between thirty and fifty official illegitimate

321

births apiece. The rest never found their way into the statistics at all. The usual explanation, "It was one of the cadets!" never got anyone very far. There were hundreds of cadets in every course, and it was incredibly difficult to tell one from the other.

Practical men like Mösler were quick to appreciate the advantage this gave them. "You should never give your real name," he confided to his friend Rednitz. "Recently I've taken to saying my name was Hochbauer. Adolf Hochbauer, too, which is rather good."

Rednitz was no longer in a mood to think any joke about Hochbauer very funny. He had been feeling this even before the man had hit the defenseless Mösler in the face.

"Ah," said Böhmke, the poet, thoughtfully, "the Eternal Female!"—thus in a way beginning the day with a quotation from Goethe. He looked around with satisfaction.

"Our friend Böhmke has once again cast a most revealing light on the problem," said Weber. "What worries me, comrades, is the fact that the girls are beginning to get a bit above themselves here. In normal times the kitchen maids were delighted if any Tom, Dick, or Harry paid attention to them. But now it has to be at least a cadet, and if possible one who looks like becoming a general. What's happened to the world?"

"Won't your girl come out with you this evening?" asked Mösler wryly.

"You'd never believe it," declared Weber, "but the little slut has started making conditions. She wants to be accorded full social status. But I'll soon knock that sort of nonsense out of her if I have to smash up half of Wildlingen in the process."

"Have you got something against me?" Cadet Hochbauer asked Rednitz, who was busy washing opposite him in the washroom. Rednitz looked up quickly but refused to let himself be interrupted.

"I'm not against you, and I'm not for you," he said, calmly soaping his chest.

"It would be a pity, don't you think, if we were to misunderstand each other?" said Hochbauer with almost a touch of courtesy.

"No," said Rednitz, "I really couldn't care less."

"I could, though," said Hochbauer with slightly more emphasis. "Perhaps we ought to make an effort to try and understand each other sometime. It might work out to our mutual advantage."

"A waste of time," said Rednitz, splashing water over his chest. "I'm not looking for advantages, especially not from you."

Hochbauer went back to his room, opened his cupboard, and began to dress. On the inside wall of his cupboard door there was a picture of the Führer—greatcoat fluttering against a stormy background—searching glance directed into the distance—genial lock of hair—vigorous toothbrush mustache poised between receding forehead and boxer's chin—Hitler as war leader, in four colors.

Hochbauer felt it was high time he reviewed his present position at the training school. Lieutenant Krafft's performance yesterday had made it more necessary than ever. Though the cadet still couldn't make out where he had gone wrong on the subject of the sweetness of death for the Fatherland, one thing seemed certain to him—his position was in danger. Not only were some of the cadets like Rednitz and his friends against him, but even his own section officer.

Hochbauer looked about him. The other cadets in his room still seemed weighted down with early morning lassitude, their movements were slow and sluggish. They seemed to take no notice of Hochbauer. He had to face the question of whether there was any significance to this. Were they doing it intentionally? Were they trying to isolate him?

The first person Hochbauer put to the test was Andreas. He seized him by the arm and said, "I've left my handkerchief in the washroom. Will you go and get it for me?"

"I've got to clean my boots first," said Andreas sullenly.

"You mean you won't?" asked Hochbauer slowly.

"Yes, all right, I'm going," said Andreas, but he sounded rather bad-tempered about it. "I'm not one to refuse when a friend asks me to do something for him."

"Fine," said Hochbauer. This set his mind slightly at rest. He let go of his friend's arm and began to smile in his cool, superior way. "You can save yourself the walk to the washroom. I remember now I brought my handkerchief with me."

"Oh, good!" said Andreas with relief. He seized his boots and went out into the corridor.

Hochbauer watched the man go. He hadn't been particularly helpful, but then he hadn't been blatantly unco-operative either, and it was quite possible that he wasn't properly awake yet. However, one had to be on one's guard. Every position had not only to be conquered, but, once conquered, held.

So Hochbauer went over to Amfortas, planted himself squarely in front of him, looked at him in a searching, friendly way and asked, "Will you take my things to the classroom afterwards?"

"Can't you take them yourself?" asked Amfortas.

But no sooner were the words out of his mouth than he realized what was up. He didn't wait for Hochbauer to press him.

"If it'll help you out," he hastened to reassure him, "of course I'll take your things. I suppose you want to go to the latrine just before."

"Correct," said Hochbauer, not without a certain sharpness. But as if trying to enlist the other's sympathies, he immediately followed this up by asking, "You don't imagine I'd try and take advantage of you, do you?"

"Of course not," said Amfortas almost bursting with loyalty.

Hochbauer nodded solemnly. What he did was never done for himself, but for Germany. It was for Germany that he collected a small group about him, for Germany that he was prepared to face every sacrifice—a fact which alone justified him in demanding sacrifices from others. He was firmly convinced that he himself was completely unselfish, and since, in Germany at least, good always triumphed, his companions were fully aware of their obligations both to him and to the cause. Not that this awareness didn't have to be tested from time to time. It was also one of the eternal laws of nature that good could triumph only at the expense of much that was bad.

The impeccable nature of his own views was once again immediately brought home to Hochbauer during the first class of the day, in which that universally respected figure, Captain Ratshelm, took the entire company. His subject was the oath of allegiance to the Führer and supreme commander-in-chief of the Wehrmacht.

"The oath of allegiance is a soldier's most sacred undertaking," concluded Captain Ratshelm finally. "Do you understand? Right, windows open—there's a terrible stink in here again. Long break."

The company commander signed the entries in each individual section's logbooks with a bold, almost artistic flourish of his pen. When he had done this he called Cadet Hochbauer over to him.

Hochbauer appeared at once, almost as if he had been waiting for the summons. He came to attention in front of Ratshelm in exemplary fashion and beamed at him in a decent, modest sort of way.

The captain smiled equally modestly. He leaned forward slightly and asked, "Would you do me a personal favor, Hochbauer?"

"Certainly, sir!" cried the cadet.

"Frau Frey has expressed a wish for further reading matter," said Captain Ratshelm confidentially, "and if I understood the good lady correctly, she would like you, my dear Hochbauer, to be the means of conveying her the books in question. This afternoon at teatime, moreover. That's a sure sign of confidence. Not only is the good lady a person of culture, but she also has considerable influence."

"Thank you, sir," said Cadet Hochbauer warmly.

He returned to his companions. The gloom of the early part of the morning was now forgotten. The section's respected and influential commanding officer held him in high esteem, he had been selected to act as liaison with senior officers' circles.

"What did the CO want with you?" asked Andreas.

"A personal commission," said Hochbauer loftily.

"Yes," said Amfortas, "he seems to trust you."

"Well," said Hochbauer, "we understand each other."

Others pushed forward interestedly. It hadn't escaped them that Ratshelm had picked out Hochbauer for something, and they wanted to know what it was.

"Gentlemen," said Hochbauer with a patronizing air, "don't press me. But quite between ourselves, I've been invited to Major Frey's house this afternoon."

The cadets muttered among themselves. Their reaction gave Hochbauer a pleasantly exalted sort of feeling which lasted the whole morning—for the next three hours, in fact, during which the first important written tactical examination of the course was held. Hochbauer completed it in exactly two and a half hours—and, he felt sure, without a single mistake.

He didn't encounter Lieutenant Krafft again that day. And this too contributed to his increasing feeling of self-confidence.

"I'll tell you one thing," he declared. "So long as we have people like Captain Ratshelm or Major Frey in charge of us, nothing can go wrong. Skill and talent will always triumph in the end. You mark my words!"

"Rifle inspection!" cried the duty cadet. "Come on, get your arses off the ground. Line up for the last event of the day!"

It was 1400 hours. Official duty for the day usually ended with rifle inspection. Once this was over, the cadets could count on having the rest of it free.

"After rifle inspection," announced Cadet Kramer, "I've got a special order to read out."

"Another one!" cried the cadets in unison.

The proclamation of the latest special order nearly always took place on a Satruday. This was part of Major Frey's deliberate intention. For in this way the energetic course commander hoped to instill something of his own spirit into the cadets before they dispersed for their various weekend pleasures.

First, however, the cadets waited for their section officer. But he failed to show up. Lieutenant Dietrich of Number 1 Section appeared in his place.

"All rifles ready for inspection?" asked Lieutenant Dietrich brusquely.

"Yes, Lieutenant," said the cadets. Any other answer was unthinkable.

"Then that's rifle inspection," announced Lieutenant Dietrich, walking off and leaving the astonished cadets gaping.

And that, for all practical purposes, was the end of duty for the day, the end of duty for the whole week. What now followed was merely boring and superfluous routine—the reading out by the section senior of the latest special order, which bore the official number 131.

The cadets fell silent, though hardly any of them listened properly. Their minds wandered off. Most of them were already preoccupied with thoughts of the coming evening. Some lounged on their rifles, treating them like shooting sticks. Others dozed off. Cadet Mösler, in the rear rank as usual, was able to clean his fingernails with his bayonet, undisturbed.

The first section of the special order dealt with walking-out passes, preparations for walking out, correct dress (with particular regard to accessories such as handkerchief, paybook, and prophylactic—the latter with special stress on the need for hygiene), and behavior in public, et cetera. All this was kindergarten stuff for recruits, but decked out at uncommon length.

"Can't you read any faster?" one of the cadets asked the section senior affably.

"Surely it's just enough to read the headings," suggested someone else.

Mösler's helpful contribution was that the special order should be hung in the latrines where everyone could read it at his leisure.

"Silence!" roared Kramer indignantly. He had been extremely sensitive in the last few days, whenever his authority as section senior seemed called in question. "Or does anyone here want to try and stop me doing my duty? If so, let's hear from him immediately." And then, as if afraid that someone might actually respond to his suggestion, Kramer added, "Anyway I've nearly finished."

With a certain haste he announced, "Next section: Nomenclature. With particular regard to national and racial requirements."

The cadets stood there patiently letting even this pass over their heads. In so far as they listened at all they learned that names were not just mere matters of sound, they were indications of origin, ideology, and general attitude. No true German—and certainly not an officer—wanted to be called Karfunkelstein or Greczinski, or Isaac or Ivan. These were Jewish or Slav names and therefore un-German—they must be regarded as undesirable, burdensome and unworthy—"Egon, for example, is simply a joke name."

"What did you say Egon was?" asked Cadet Weber in alarm.

"Simply a joke name," explained Mösler with delight. "Haven't you got ears? According to your major and course commander you're the owner of a joke name."

The cadets roared with laughter. Even Hochbauer joined in the general merriment.

Kramer alone tried to preserve gravity and dignity. But he very soon saw that it was hopeless. He gave up reading the rest of the order and yelled, "Duty over! Dismiss."

The cadets surrounded the indignant Weber, Egon, and pushed him along into the barracks. Everyone was in splendid form.

"It must be a mistake," said Weber. "It simply must be an error of some kind."

"An officer," declared Mösler with delight, "never makes a mistake; and certainly not when he's a major and in command of a course at an officers' training school. One thing is certain. As Egon you're extremely unlikely to survive the course. It is of course conceivable that a joke figure might become an officer, but when he even has a joke name as well, naturally that's the end of the joke."

"I can't believe it's anything but a mistake!" repeated Weber, shaking his head.

"Yes, but a mistake on your part," said Mösler with a grin. "You should have protested against this name of yours back in the cradle. The fact that you didn't is proof 'you weren't embryonic officer material."

"Friends," said Egon Weber, putting an end to the discussion, "I hereby solemnly declare that anyone who in the future makes fun of my Christian name will have the living daylights pasted out of him regardless of whether he's a major, a course commanding officer, or anything else. Is that clear, friends?"

It was crystal clear.

"Let us then gather up our strength," cried Mösler collapsing on his bed, "and embark upon our leisure hours as fully refreshed as possible."

Every Saturday in this region was dominated by a very simple arithmetical proposition. About eight hundred of the thousand cadets streamed down into the valley. These then divided themselves between the two movie houses, twenty-eight restaurants and bars, and the seventy to eighty available girls and temporarily solitary women, including those of the outlying areas around Wildlingen-am-Main. Anything to which this absurd imbalance might give rise had to take place in the short period of time between 1800 and 2400 hours.

The officers of the training school were very little better off than the cadets. Some escaped to Würzburg, though this was a laborious business, involving a great deal of time and requiring the general's permission. Those who were married or engaged were the lucky ones. Anyone trying to secure a foothold in one of the bourgeois families of Wildlingen also had something to do on a Saturday. But for the rest there was little choice but to follow the general's example and work. Yet, unlike him, they permitted themselves long breaks, which were spent in the officers' mess. Here they were at the mercy of Captain Kater.

"Gentlemen," Kater was in the habit of saying, "I'm not inhuman, whatever people may say about me. I will gladly give my permission for one small bottle of wine among three persons. Further provision may be made after consultation with me."

"Permit me, ma'am?" asked Cadet Hochbauer. "May I be allowed to offer you a few books on behalf of Captain Ratshelm."

Felicitas Frey smiled with studied good will. "How charming! And how are you, Herr Hochbauer?"

"Very well, thank you, ma'am," he replied, adding, "it's most good of you to ask."

The atmosphere in which Hochbauer found himself struck him as civilized. He was asked to sit down and take a cup of tea, and although he had always loathed tea, here it seemed enjoyable—a fragrant and exquisite luxury served by a lady with a gift for ennobling even an idiotic British custom such as this. Besides, he seemed to have heard that the Führer preferred tea too—and Indian as well; which undoubtedly had something to do with the fact that the Indians also could claim Aryan origin.

"Of course I don't want to keep you, Herr Hochbauer," said Felicitas Frey.

"There's no question of that, ma'am," the cadet reassured her warmly.

"I'm sure," said Felicitas with an understanding but rather agonized smile, "that there's a young lady waiting for you somewhere."

"Not at all, ma'am," insisted the cadet truthfully enough. "I've no time for anything like that."

"That could be a great pity," suggested Felicitas Frey, and her smile became a shade more understanding.

Hochbauer felt sufficiently encouraged to reply, "It seems my experience, ma'am, that young ladies, even of the best families, are often lacking in the deeper qualities."

"You may well be right there," admitted Felicitas eagerly enough.

"Young ladies of today," said Hochbauer, feeling his way, "seem lacking in sensibility, in, what for want of a better word, one might call culture. I don't mean that as a reproach. It's probably an inevitable condition of wartime. And it is of course something we've just got to put up with. But I find it regrettable all the same."

"Your feelings do you credit. And I can well imagine how painful you must find such shortcomings."

"I manage to overlook them, ma'am, for nearly all my time is taken up by work. And when I feel the urge to enjoy myself in a cultivated atmosphere of this sort, I remind myself of all the many things more demanding of my effort and attention." Thus their conversation prattled gaily on as they drank their tea and began to feel that they were achieving a real mutual understanding.

Felicitas Frey even went so far as to say, "I've found our meeting most enjoyable."

But at this point their meeting was rather rudely interrupted by Major Frey himself. With a quick wave of his hand he motioned the cadet, who had jumped ceremoniously to his feet, to sit down again, and turning to his wife said, "I've got to speak to you urgently."

"Can't it wait till later, Archibald?"

"It's most urgent," the major insisted, leaving the drawing room.

"A pity," said Frau Felicitas in a tone of genuine regret. "I've found our conversation thoroughly stimulating, Herr Hochbauer."

So had Cadet Hochbauer. Yet he had no choice but to take his leave, kissing her hand in appropriate fashion.

"I do so hope," she said, "that we shall have another stimulating conversation of this sort before long."

"It would be an honor for me, ma'am."

"I hope a little more than that," she said flirtatiously.

"It would be a great pleasure for me, ma'am," he replied, and strode off like some young Germanic god, or so it seemed to Felicitas.

"Felicitas—please!" called the major from the next room. "It's urgent. Very urgent!"

"Just look at that!" said the major to his wife.

"Archibald," she said icily, "I must record with regret that your manners have recently left very much to be desired. How could you interrupt us so rudely in the middle of a conversation?"

"Oh, what the hell!" rejoined the major brusquely. "You can't ask me to start taking notice of cadets. Who takes any notice of me, I'd like to know? I've matters of great importance to discuss with you. Now will you just take a look at that!"

The major laid a heavy hand on a sheet of paper in front of him. Felicitas resentfully took a step closer and looked at Special Order number 131.

"This," said the major sullenly, "simply shouldn't have been allowed to happen. But it has happened, even though I took the trouble to consult you beforehand, Felicitas. But either you failed to take into account the consequences of your advice, or, what is worse, you have regarded as insignificant certain things which in fact are of the utmost concern to me—all-important, in fact. To put it plainly, Felicitas, you've let me down badly."

"I simply don't know what you're talking about," she said indignantly. She felt misunderstood, harassed, bullied. "I spend my whole time trying to help you and give you support. I even go to the trouble of trying to sound out your cadets for you. And what thanks do I get? You hurl abuse at me! What is all this about?"

The major handed his Special Order number 131 to her without a word. It bore a stamp from the general's office of that day's date, and one sentence in it had been underlined with green pencil which the general alone used. The sentence ran, "Egon, for example, is simply a joke name." In the margin beside this sentence there was a single note of the general's, a dangerously laconic comment, also in green pencil, which ran, "Noted. Ernst Egon Modersohn, Major-General."

"This is a ghastly catastrophe," said the major. He felt shattered. "It should never have come to this. Egon apparently is the general's own Christian name. You've let me down, Felicitas—quite simply let me down."

"You can't just blame me for your own mistakes," she said.

"If you'd been on the alert," he insisted, "this would never have happened. But apparently the things that are of importance to me mean nothing to you."

"You're an ungrateful beast," she replied fiercely. "What would you be without me?"

"A quiet and contented human being, I expect," said the major.

"I see," said Felicitas Frey stiffly. "This is very serious. It's clear to me that I mean nothing to you, Archibald. I see you no longer love me. You would never have abused me like that if you did."

She rushed out of the room, slamming the door behind her.

"If she doesn't come to her senses soon," spluttered the major, "there'll be real trouble!"

Cadet Hochbauer stood in the market place of Wildlingen-am-Main. He still felt rather carried away by his experience of mutual harmony with a high-ranking officer's lady. He wasn't quite sure what to do next.

Several possibilities lay open to him. He could either take

the road to the barracks, to his books, *Military Regulations*, and notes, or he could take a thoughtful walk through the frozen, capitulated wastes of nature, or, finally, he could indulge in spiritual relaxation in the form of a worth-while film like *Ohm Krüger*.

Hochbauer came to a sudden decision and took himself off to the movie house. This went by the high-sounding name of the Film Palace, and here, wedged in among the goggling audience, he gave himself over to the elevating, ideologically stimulating film on the screen.

Hochbauer watched with rising indignation the cruelties of the British as they mowed down the defenseless population of South Africa or tortured them in concentration camps so that they died in their thousands of hunger, thirst, and exhaustion, cursing perfidious Albion. And these brave, stouthearted, honest South Africans were not racially inferior creatures, not dirty colored people, dangerous undesirable foreigners of an inferior species, or even Jews—but Boers, of pure Aryan stock. They were men and women of the highest racial qualities who were being terrorized by these dehumanized sadists intoxicated with power, the British. Hochbauer almost trembled wth indignation. Some people sitting near him opened their mouths wide, perhaps in astonishment, perhaps just to stuff themselves with sweets.

Confirmed in his convictions, which were strong enough in all conscience, Hochbauer left the movie. He looked up at the sky as if to ask the Lord God whether what he had just seen in the film could be reconciled with the rest of creation. But then he remembered in time that he had severed all connection with religion, out of conviction and on the advice of his father. He had been quite right to do so, too. The British prayed to God.

Hochbauer felt in need of a drink. And this gave him the idea of wandering over to the bar that went by the name of The Gay Dog. There, as he knew, the greater part of the section were in the habit of meeting every Saturday evening. There they would have something of a party under the leadership of the section senior, Cadet Kramer.

This bar called The Gay Dog lay on the banks of the Main and could be reached in ten minutes by walking through a number of winding side streets that led off from the market place. Hochbauer took his time. He wandered slowly past the old half-timbered houses, eyeing them almost tolerantly. Symbols of a narrow-minded, unenlightened epoch, he thought; very pretty and cozy, but crumbling and antiquated. Doomed to destruction! The storm of the new era would sweep them all away. They were no more than historic ruins, from which new life would blossom thanks to the energy and efficiency of the German people.

Hochbauer walked into the taproom, and was immediately engulfed in a cheerful wave of sound. The atmosphere was suffocating. The place was packed with cadets. There were only one or two girls sitting about the room—rare spots of color in a sea of field gray. The swinging doors which led into the other rooms were wide open, and Section H for Heinrich sat ensconced just behind them. Hochbauer raised a hand in greeting.

"Good to see you!" Kramer called out to him. "Make room, fellows."

Hochbauer's appearance aroused a certain amount of interest, for until now he had always kept away on occasions of this sort. However, as he made his way past the chairs he said, "One has to be a bit sociable now and again."

Mösler looked him in the eye and said, "Let's hope we both mean the same thing by sociable. But I suppose we'll soon see."

"I'll tell you one thing, friends," said Captain Feders, shuffling the skat cards for the next deal. "If anyone here thinks he's going to take the pants off me, he's got his work cut out."

The laughter that followed had an almost cheerful ring about it. The voices sounded rough and brittle, with a thin falsetto quality, but a certain cheerfulness was unmistakable. The only thing was that no one laughed very loudly.

Feders' phrase about taking the pants off him was also a technical term of the game of skat which they were playing— himself, Krafft, and Krüger the medical officer. All three were sitting in the Villa Rosenhügel wearing white doctor's overalls over their uniforms. But they weren't alone, for each had a partner.

"Don't be too deadly with your shuffling," said Krafft to Feders.

Krüger, the medical officer, flashed a quick warning glance at Krafft with his single eye. Krafft had just made a blunder. It was true that his remark sounded harmless enough, the sort of remark any cardplayer might make, but certain subjects were taboo here, and among them were alcohol, women, and death.

For these three officers' partners were basketmen who

hung in the air behind them. They dangled low from the ceiling in their harnesses so that they could see almost comfortably over the shoulders of the people in the chairs.

The man hanging behind Lieutenant Krafft bore the number 73. His face was gaunt, crude, and deeply lined, the face of a workingman who had spent much time in the open air on building sites, in woods, and on trucks. All that Krafft knew about him was that his name was Willie.

"Now we'll really give them a pasting," said Willie. "This time we'll show them—eh, Lieutenant?"

"It should be easy enough," said Krafft, nodding to his partner. "We've got a good start."

"We ought always to play together," said Willie, otherwise number 73. "We back each other up very well, eh?"

"I'll say!" said Krafft. "The others haven't a hope. We ought to organize a championship here—we'd win it easily."

Krafft picked up the cards Feders had dealt him, sorted them slowly, and looked back at his partner. They had a very promising series of hearts. And two jacks as well. Krafft slid the forefinger of his right hand across the good cards. Willie's head nodded as he muttered his consent.

Krafft looked around the table, and noted with satisfaction that the doctor was no longer keeping an eye on him. He must be behaving all right, then. Captain Feders gave him a quick, grateful look of appreciation.

These skat parties were Feders' idea, to which the MO had agreed only with reluctance. The experiment had been preceded by a series of chess games. And a further necessary provision had been the setting aside of a special "games room." For the number of basketmen who could play was strictly limited to the number of partners who could be found for them.

The preparations were extremely complicated. Before there could be any question of a patient taking part in such a game Dr. Krüger gave him a thorough mental, physical, and psychological examination. The delight of those selected, usually without the others knowing, was always tremendous, and Krüger had to see to it that they didn't become too excited. He couldn't afford to let the game turn into some sort of special treat. So he always had to choose the partners very carefully. These partners were normally the hospital staff, and always included the doctor himself, and very often Captain Feders. This was the first time Krafft had taken part.

"Got a cigarette?" asked Willie behind him.

Lieutenant Krafft looked quickly across at Dr. Krüger, who nodded almost imperceptibly. Krafft lit a cigarette, took a puff, and gave it to Willie, otherwise number 73, putting it into his mouth for him.

Willie inhaled deeply and contentedly. He never took his eyes off the cards which Krafft held up in front of him in his right hand. "Now we'll show 'em, eh, Lieutenant!"

Lieutenant Krafft began to call his hand. This should really have been Willie's job, but he was busy smoking. With his consent, however, Krafft raised the bidding. The other two basketmen replied. They did this slowly on the whole, often after a whispered consultation with their partners. But it was for them alone to decide—it was their game. The three officers merely lent them their limbs and now and again gave them advice.

Krafft hesitated. He didn't want to raise the bidding further without a consultation with his partner. He turned around to Willie and took the cigarette out of his mouth. "What do you think?" he asked. "Should we go higher?"

"The sky's the limit!" cried number 73. A harsh light shone down on them, falling on the cards in the officers' hands and lighting up the faces of the three basketmen staring at the cards. Their faces were very different. One was crude and sharp, another soft and flat, another quite deformed—split from the middle of the skull to the left side of the chin. All three thought of nothing but their game. Krüger's single eye glinted amiably, showing that he was enjoying himself.

"You're a good partner, Lieutenant Krafft," said the doctor.

"He certainly is," confirmed Willie without hesitation. "Which is why we're now going to take a chance. Grand slam!"

"Right," said Krafft. He put what was left of the cigarette back into number 73's mouth. Then, on instructions from his partner, he played the jacks and followed them with the entire set of hearts. He slammed one card after another down onto the table.

"With the fist!" cried Willie, holding the cigarette between his teeth. "Always bring your fist down on the table! Really bang it down!"

And Krafft put his fist at Willie's complete disposal. At this moment the two of them were as one, though they were both quite unaware of the fact. Together, in an utterly trivial piece of activity, they had succeeded in banishing the shadow of death.

"We must try and keep this up, my friend," said Krafft to number 73 after they'd won the game.

"Comradeship's a fine thing," said Cadet Hochbauer in the back room of The Gay Dog. "I'm all for it, but it's got to be reciprocal. You won't find me wanting."

Hochbauer pushed his way onto a bench between Kramer and Amfortas. He wore a cheerful, conciliatory, good-humored expression, and began scrutinizing more closely the thirty cadets there in all. The size of the party was presumably due to the fact that the section senior had managed to establish excellent relations with the landlord. For in front of each cadet stood a jug of wine, and in addition there was a well-filled fifteen-liter jug under Kramer's seat. He was in the fortunate position of having a whole barrel at his disposal, acquired in exchange for a couple of cameras. All in all, Kramer was remarkably popular. His section couldn't have wished for a better section senior.

"Drink up, Hochbauer!" said Kramer patronizingly. "That's what it's there for!"

He looked about him triumphantly, and over to the next table, where cadets of another section were sitting. These had practically nothing to drink at all. The landlord had merely granted them one small jug of wine each. Kramer made it clear that this was the sort of thing that happened if one didn't have the right man as section senior.

"Your health, fellows!" he shouted, and his men gladly responded to the toast. Kramer felt sure that he had put his two cameras to the best possible advantage. In the future, he thought in his innocence, his cadets would always be glad to give him their respect.

Hochbauer's eye fell on one or two of the ladies—little kitchen sluts, by the look of things. These girls, who were questionable enough by any standards, were sitting down at the far end of the table, where Mösler, Rednitz, and of course also Weber, Egon, were to be found. Weber, Egon, however, astonishingly enough, didn't seem to have a lady of his own. To make up for this he was staring hard at a fleshy rustic beauty sitting with the cadets at the next table.

Hochbauer seized his glass and emptied it at a draught. The sight of this unabashedly primitive female made him shudder. Just a lump of flesh, he thought with revulsion— no charm, no grace, no ladylike airs such as prevailed in higher officers' circles.

"Tell me, Hochbauer," Mösler inquired with a wink, raising his voice embarrassingly, "why don't you ever bring a nice girl along with you? Can't you manage it, or is it that you just don't want to?"

"Of course a handsome boy like that could have any girl he liked," said one of the girls at the back with the air of an expert.

"Looks aren't everything, you know," said Mösler provocatively. "It's the machine itself that counts. And you know, there are some who don't want to because they can't."

Hochbauer was about to jump to his feet in indignation, but Kramer laid a restraining hand on his arm. He was responsible for the evening and didn't want people to start fighting. He looked after the drinks, and it was up to him to see that perfect harmony prevailed.

So Kramer ostentatiously placed the fifteen-liter jug on the table and cried, "Friends, speech is silver and drink is golden. With us everyone can get drunk in his own way."

"How right you are," said Mösler, immediately conciliated by the sight of the fifteen-liter jug. "Pass the thing over here and give my way a chance. I can't talk when I'm drinking, and when I look into my glass I don't need to look at Hochbauer. Like this it might turn out to be a quite pleasant evening."

So the jug wandered across the table, and from there back to the cellar to be refilled. The cadets at the next table were looking very glum. Kramer reckoned this a real personal triumph; he was delighted by the mounting spirit of cheerfulness among his own section. A really harmonious little evening, he thought.

In the true spirit of comradeship, Kramer made a real effort to pacify Hochbauer, speaking convincingly of other people's crude geniality, of gay mischievous spirits who shouldn't be taken too seriously. "You just have to laugh at them," he said, "and they're delighted. They're like children, you know; they don't mean any harm."

"But the infantile behavior of this fellow Mösler and his friends gets on my nerves sometimes," said Hochbauer, refusing to be appeased.

Kramer continued to try and talk him around. He was determined to make the evening a success, but while devoting time to Hochbauer in this way he completely failed to notice what was happening at the other end of the table where Weber, Egon, was sitting.

Cadet Weber had been a good deal less talkative than usual on this particular day. He had even gone without his afternoon sleep, so darkly overwhelming was the brooding sense of unease that had settled on him after the reading of Special Order number 131. In the course of his life as a soldier, Weber, Egon, had had to let many a provocation and insult pass over his head. There had been the NCO in charge of him as a recruit, for instance, on whose orders he had had to crawl seven times through the latrines on his belly. There had been a sergeant who had humiliated him by making him take off his socks on the public highway. There hadn't been many people about, but his feet had turned out to be anything but clean. And then again there had been that girl in France, in Dreux, who had tried to empty the contents of a chamber pot on top of him. All of those things which he was able to have a good laugh about once they were over. But the present case was different. His name had been made fun of in front of the entire training school. It was a name he had in fact always been rather proud of, without of course ever letting this be known. What was more, he had succeeded in giving it a certain prestige; he was known as that smart fellow Egon, or that sharp fellow Egon, or even Egon the Muscle Man, or Egon the Heartthrob, all of which testified to particular qualities of his. And was Egon now suddenly to be a name damned in high places as nothing but a joke?

"I've got to get drunk today," he said suddenly. However, this painful affair of his name was not the only thing eating Weber, Egon, just then. Something else was worrying him too—a something else with long dark hair sitting at the next table with some cadets from another section. These cadets were, in Weber's view, a flabby, spineless lot, supervised by an officer known by the revealing name of the Minnesinger.

"I have a great desire to tear that outfit apart," he confessed to his companion.

The girl next door thrust out her magnificent bosom and occasionally cast a glance across at Weber, which he chose to interpret as a challenge. For since the night in the gym equipment store he had been on pretty intimate terms with her. Apparently he hadn't paid sufficient attention to her soul, though, for she wanted to feel not only desired but respected and honored as well. She wanted to walk out with him and be treated as a lady.

Egon Weber leaned forward and stammered, "Come over here and sit with us, Erna."

"Can't you see I'm in company?" Erna replied majestically.

"There's better company here," Egon Weber assured her.

The cadets around Erna began to show signs of impatience. One of them, who almost looked Weber's physical equal, said, "Mind your own business, little man. Can't you see the girl's with us?"

"But she's my girl," said Weber, trying to sound as agreeable as possible. "I established my rights to her some days before you, isn't that so, Erna?"

"You're not a gentleman!" said Erna, disavowing him. "I must ask you to leave me alone."

"Did you hear that?" asked the beefy cadet from the other section. "This lady wants you to leave her alone."

"Come over here, Erna," said Egon Weber. "You don't want to spend the whole evening, and possibly part of the night, with that bunch of half-wits!"

"Shame on you, Egon!" said the girl.

"*What's* his name?" asked the beefy cadet in delighted astonishment. He had picked up the fateful word at once. "Can I have heard aright? Egon? Did you hear that, fellows? His name's Egon! And that, as we know from Special Orders, is a joke name!" They roared with laughter.

Cadet Weber rose to his feet, pale and trembling. He went up to the beefy cadet, and without a word hit him on the chin with his fist. The beefy fellow crumpled up at once and with glazed eyes slipped in slow motion to the floor. His face set in an expression of astonishment.

Mösler jumped up ready for battle and shouted, "Out of the way, ladies. Clear the ring! Into them, fellows!"

Whereupon, Mösler, not without a certain skill, caught a chair that had been slung at him, tottering slightly but just managing to hold steady. Then he swung the chair over his head and hurled it back as hard as he could into the middle of the opposing section.

With that the battle began in earnest. Weber's arms had transformed themselves into flails, which came whirling down on every head within reach. Mösler ran in under their opponent's guard and carried the battle far into their rear. Rednitz, who was of a practical turn of mind, dismantled a number of chair legs and distributed them among his allies.

Kramer rushed forward indignantly in an attempt to separate the antagonists. Without any hesitation Hochbauer followed him into the fray. Someone near him had used the electrifying word "coward." Apart from which, he couldn't overlook Kramer's call for assistance. Moreover he was on principle a man of order. And so Kramer and Hochbauer scurried forward with Amfortas and Andreas in their wake in true Niebelungen fashion.

"Take it easy, men, take it easy!" roared Kramer.

Immediately afterward he fell silent. One of the chair legs which Rednitz had distributed and which had fallen into the enemy's hands came whirling down on top of him. He sank beneath the table, pulling his fifteen-liter jug down with him. Fortunately there was very little wine left in it. What there was splashed over his face and soaked through his uniform.

Cadet Hochbauer, who was doing his best to separate the combatants, suddenly received a tremendous blow on the back. He staggered forward straight into the middle of the enemy section, where he was left with no alternative but to defend himself for all he was worth—it seemed to him that he was fighting for his very life.

The noise was deafening—the smashing of glasses, the cracking of chair legs, the splintering of tables, the screaming of girls, the groaning of men—here and there a great gurgling cry. The landlord roared and bellowed appeals, at first for reason, then for some sense of decency, and finally for the police.

Within five minutes the whole thing was over, the bar had been completely broken up and the enemy section routed. Panting heavily, bleeding, and with the light of victory in their eyes, H Section remained in possession of the field.

"Gentlemen," groaned Mösler happily, "that's what I call really taking time off!"

Intermediate Report No. 7

THE CURRICULUM VITAE OF
ELFRIDA RADEMACHER,
OR DESIRE AND OPPORTUNITY

My name is Elfrida Rademacher. I was born at Neustadt on the Inn, on September 21, 1919. My father's Christian name was Ernst—he was a foreman in the repair shops of the State Railways. My mother's Christian name was Margot— she was born a Gutsmut. I have four brothers and sisters, all a good deal older than me. My childhood was spent in the town of my birth, which was where I went to school.

The sloping ceiling of the little room is just above my head. It is rough and cold to the touch. I lie on a mattress be-

neath it and can touch it with my hands. It has been rotted
with the rain, and I press hard against it, but it holds firm.
The whitewash comes off on my hands and I push so hard
that my arms tremble, but the ceiling still doesn't give
way. I lie there alone staring up at it for hours. All I
hear is the rain. Then I don't even hear the rain any more.
This sloping ceiling and I are the whole world—there's no
one else in it, not even my mother. Slowly the ceiling begins
to come down on top of me—or is it I who am floating
up to the ceiling? I feel helpless, unable to move or speak,
as if caught in some giant press. I scream and am immediately so terrified that I lose my voice altogether. For
I'm expressly forbidden to make a noise.

The dog I play with has long hair that reaches to the
floor. You can tie it around his ears, or under his belly, or
you can weave it into plaits on his back. Ordinary days
of the week I tie a blue bow on his coat, on Sundays a green
one, on high days and holidays I like it to be red; but on
my parents' birthdays it must be yellow. The intervals between each change of bow seem terribly long.

There are a lot of colleagues of my father's downstairs
in our little house, celebrating his birthday. They make a
tremendous amount of noise—I hear their booming voices
come floating up the stairs. When one of them laughs all the
others laugh with him. But it remains a mystery to me what
they're laughing at. I don't understand what they're laughing
at. I don't understand what they're saying. I climb out of
bed and tiptoe over to the door in my bare feet, very, very
quietly. I open the door and look down into the hall, which is
like a narrow passageway, and there by the cellar door
stands my father holding an armful of beer bottles. He is
as white as chalk and gasps for breath. His features are distorted. He collapses and dies.

I have a high temperature and the moon looks down on
me. She comes into the room and sits down on my bed. I
stretch out my hands toward her but she slips away. Then I
try to push her away, but she won't go. What am I to do with
her?

Sometimes I'm allowed to go and visit my friend Marina.
One day she looks in the mirror hanging in her mother's
bedroom while I stand beside her. Her face wears a thoughtful, rather worried expression. Looking at herself in the
mirror, Marina slowly begins to undo her dress. She strips
it from her shoulders, and lets it fall to the ground. She pulls

her vest over her head and throws it to one side. Then she says, "You do the same." And I do the same. We stare at each other a long time.

The governess who teaches us German, scripture, and history has incredibly beautiful hands with fine elegant fingers and pink nails that gleam like ivory, filed into a semicircle. These hands dance across the blackboard with the chalk. They lie on the page of the lesson book, glide before me explaining words that I don't hear, reach for my own hand —and this unsettles me. I lay my cheek against this wonderfully beautiful hand, feel the velvety softness of the skin and breathe the scent of lavender. "But Elfrida!" she says. "I want to be like you one day," I tell her. And she takes my head in her hands, looks at me sadly and says, "Better not."

There's a man in our house now, taking Father's place. Mother does whatever he wants. My brothers and sisters have left home. There are only the three of us, and he's always staring at me. His eyes rest on my hands at meals, follow mine as I read my school books, and watch me form the stiff, straight letters. His eyes are fixed on me as I draw the comb through my hair, or lace up my shoes, or wash the dishes. And Mother says, "Go to your room at once!"

Certain days are torture to me. When at last I find myself alone on these days I shut my door, bolt it, and draw the chain across. Then I take up my position in front of the mirror and stare into it, leaning forward to stare as hard as I can into my eyes. It's as if I'm under some sort of spell. All I find there is exhaustion and emptiness. My skin is flaccid and gray, and the pores are enlarged—the sight disgusts me. I lie down and think of what is happening inside me and feel a dragging pain seeping endlessly through me. My blood is rotten, I think. I am filthy and bad. I dread these days.

The man living with my mother usually slaps me on the bottom as he passes me, and he passes me whenever I scrub the floor of the house. That's all he does. He just slaps me, without hurting, briefly, flirtatiously, as if it were just a little joke. I wait for him as I cross the floor on my hands and knees, or stand there bending, knowing he'll come. And every time I shudder. It's almost as if I had a great desire to feel it, as if I longed for it. I don't move. I keep quite still, closing my eyes and wondering when he'll go further than that? But always he moves on.

The boy kneeling with me by the flower bed has strong hands which plunge into the earth and tear it up as he packs around the plants with his firm, strong fingers. And I think to myself, if they wanted, these hands could break the plants, tear them up and throw them away, with just as much firmness and strength. Later on, when I feel these hands on my body, first on my shoulders, then on my back moving up my shoulder blades, I push him away from me. I don't want to have to feel these hands that touch earth and flowers and food and people. I think what a filthy thing my body is, and how it nauseates me, and I burst into tears.

Between 1933 and 1936 I worked as an apprentice to the firm of Halliger, in the main office. At the end of this time I did a year's service as a farm worker and then until 1938 worked in a number of different offices, mostly as a shorthand typist. I was called up in 1940. And this was how I came to Wildlingen-am-Main.

"How old are you, girl?" the elder Halliger asks me. "Nearly fifteen," I tell him. "Almost unbelievable," says the elder Halliger. "You look older, and I know why, too. You don't laugh enough! Isn't that right? You don't answer. Come on, then, laugh!" "I can't laugh to order," I say. "You can't laugh at all," says the elder Halliger. "Not even at a little garden gnome like me." And then I do have to laugh, for he does look exactly like a garden gnome, and even says so himself! "If only you knew, my girl," says the elder Halliger, "what a hellishly funny world this is, you'd never be able to stop laughing."

It's a large office and I'm alone most of the time. The strong smell of seed corn is all about me. I revel in it because it is stronger than the smell given off by the human beings there. Sometimes the elder Halliger sits opposite me at his desk—without saying much. But from time to time he winks his right eye at me, and I always have to laugh because he looks so funny. And then he says, "Life's a funny business, isn't it?" And I find I have to agree. It does seem like that whenever he's there.

The storekeeper is a man called Kroppke. He looks at me in the same way as the man who's taken my father's place at home. One day when Kroppke is standing in front of me, with his order book in his hand, gaping at me, the elder Halliger quietly unbuckles his belt and slashes him across the buttocks. "Little man," he says to Kroppke, "don't stand there gaping like an idiot—you're quite idiotic enough as it is!" Kroppke blushes scarlet and leaves the room. Halliger turns to me and says, "It's only a respite for you. Sooner or later everyone loses control of himself. And then usually there's no one there to put the young fellow in his place."

Two men wearing raincoats stand in the office—dark gray raincoats, though it isn't raining. "Halliger," says one of them, "your time is up. We've been very patient with you, but you wouldn't keep that great mouth of yours shut. So now you've had it. You're coming with us." The elder Halliger gets to his feet, takes his hat and the brief case which he's kept ready in his desk for months now. Before he leaves the room he turns to me once more and says, "Funny world—isn't it?" He goes out and I never see him again.

The girl leader in charge of me during my year as a farm worker is called Charlotte—Charlotte Kerr. She's a big girl with broad shoulders who walks like a man. But she's good; at least, she's always good to me. "Have you got a boy friend, Elfrida?" she asks me. "No," I tell her. "Then I'll find one for you. It's good for the health. You need a boy friend to keep you happy—it's about the only thing a man's any good for. You'll soon see that." "My health's all right," I say, "and I feel fine. I don't need a boy friend. Besides, I'm always so tired after work that all I want is to go to sleep." "Well anyway," says Charlotte Kerr, "that just shows what a wonderful thing a year on the land is."

I don't want to return to the little house and the man who has taken the place of my father. And I don't want to go and live with any of my grown-up brothers and sisters either. They're strangers to me now, almost as much of a stranger as my mother. For my mother has said to her new man, with a glance at me, "If you find her so attractive I don't mind. I'll take anything from you. I love you, you know that." And so I left. All I want is to be alone. But haven't I always been alone?

The man who is now my boss suddenly starts behaving quite differently. I always used to watch him sitting at the desk in front of me. He had a thick, squat neck and was always very carefully shaven. His thick mass of brown hair stopped quite abruptly and gave way to smooth gray skin. It was as if he were naked somehow, though very upright and clean and correct. Below his neck came broad, powerful shoulders, a slightly hunched back, and then the chair engulfing the rest of him. That was how I used to see him. Now he is suddenly standing in front of me with his arms around me. I am too tired to try and push him away. And I think, it'll have to happen one day; and if it isn't him it'll be someone else. Later I think, why did it have to be him?

The pile of rubble in front of me was once the little house where I lived. This was where I spoke my first word, where I learned to walk. People used to laugh here. This was where my father died. This was where I dreamed and wept, this was where Marina and I felt each other's bodies and sensed the rottenness of the world. Here—where the brick walls now lie shattered and the broken beams point at the sky, where the grasses fade and the trees die. And here, they say, somewhere beneath all this, lies my mother. I turn away unable to shed a tear.

"The sexual instinct has its proper function just like anything else," says the man in spectacles, leaning right back in his armchair. "For instance, we use our hands to take hold of things with, our eyes to see with, and our ears to hear with. This is all part of the law of nature, so there can't be anything unnatural about it. Do you see?" "No," I reply, "but I suppose I'm shortsighted." "I can offer you a good job," says the man in spectacles, smiling at me thoughtfully. I nod my head. "Your arguments are very convincing," I tell him.

The man in front of my boss looks up submissively. His whole presence conveys his willing subservience. His eyes are trained on my boss and remind me of a dog's eyes, of the eyes of the dog which I had as a child and whose coat I used to twist into plaits and decorate with bows. "Very good, sir," he says, "certainly, sir," and goes out again, bowing his way out backward. The boss smiles with satisfaction. And I smile, too, making no effort to conceal my contempt. Men, I think to myself. What servile creatures they are! I'll never feel weak with them again.

The first one seized hold of me impatiently, consumed with lust, and he was in a hurry. From then on I avoided him like the plague. The second was a man I had known since my schooldays, without ever having taken much notice of him. Our life together was compressed into three nights, after which he had to leave for the front, where he was killed. The third wooed me tenderly and patiently. He'd had a lot of experience, and when he finally told me he was married, he seemed to me to fade away into a sad, gray nothingness. The fourth fell upon me during an air raid when I was almost helpless with fear and had drunk too much. After I had run off there was a second raid, and the shelter we'd been in caved in on top of him and buried him alive. The fifth was the fiancé of my childhood friend Marina. She lent him to me, as she put it, and I couldn't resist him because he was handsome as a god, though utterly depraved. I became engaged to the sixth until Marina took him away from me, and he accepted this as if it were the most normal thing in the world. And that's how it was. I was surrounded by men, but there was an emptiness inside me which no one seemed able to fill. Could no one really fill it?

Then one day everything changes! He doesn't look at me. I don't know what it is he's looking at, or where he's looking, or why he doesn't look at me. His eyes are somewhere else, but I feel his hands. And his voice says, "I'm tired and weak. If I had my own way I'd like to sleep forever and forget. Don't expect anything. Don't hope for anything. But stay with me—for as long as things last." As long as things last, I think. That is all I think. This man's name is Karl Krafft.

22   SUNDAY IS A DAY LIKE ANY OTHER

FATE, which, as is well known, never ceases to pursue its course, betook itself early on a Sunday morning down the hill toward Wildlingen-am-Main, panting slightly and bearing the features of Captain Kater of the headquarters company. Though he had breakfasted magnificently he left the barracks wearing a solemn expression. There were good grounds, too, for the serious air he was at such pains to convey, for he was on his way to church.

Not that Captain Kater was a particularly pious man. He was simply on his way there for the sake of appearances —also to make contacts. Naturally he was never anything but a soldier, even in church.

Captain Kater blinked in the blinding morning sunlight. He had a friendly response for everyone who greeted him, and there were quite a few such people. Kater was a well-known figure in Wildlingen-am-Main.

For as the man in charge of the headquarters company, Captain Kater was in constant contact with the civilian population. He bought in bulk. He traded, bartered, and retraded. He was full of advice, of tips, and general information. He could even, if he liked, supply transport, gas, and men. Above all, he carried weight in the town. By contrast with Captain Kater's influence, the local administrative officer was little more than a jumped-up messenger boy, for the administrative officer had his regulations to stick to and in any case hardly counted as a proper officer at all.

Captain Kater enjoyed the confidence of a wide circle of people, and enjoyed it in the best sense of the word. If a new vintage of the excellent Franconian wine was ready for tasting, Captain Kater would be invited to taste it. If there was a new building to be opened or a respected citizen to be buried, or if some local society was holding a celebration, Captain Kater's absence was unthinkable. And the local newspaper, the *Wildlinger Beobachter,* would report next day: ". . . Among those present we observed Captain Kater, representing the officer in command of our officers' training school, Major-General Modersohn . . ." Or: " . . . Captain Kater conveyed the sincere good wishes of all in a few well-chosen words . . ." Or: ". . . Among the numerous mourners was Captain Kater, who read a moving address and laid an appropriate wreath . . ."

It was an essential part of his duties to do what was fitting and appropriate. However unpleasant these duties might seem at times, they brought certain considerable advantages with them in the long run. Even visits to church usually paid off. For this picturesque little town, far from the great highways of the world, was still touchingly old-fashioned in matters of religion. Even influential Party members went quite regularly to church.

So in the square in front of the church, Kater was able to meet the deputy burgomaster, who ran the town bank, and a number of other respected merchants, local officials, and presidents of societies. He was continually flattering the ladies and chumming up with the men, thus enjoying considerable popularity and being generally reckoned a dashing and excellent fellow.

After Kater had succeeded in initiating several promising little bits of business, he proceeded to enter the church, where he pushed his way forward to one of the front pews and pretended to sink himself deep in prayer in full view of the rest of the congregation.

Humbly he lowered his eyes, taking advantage of the opportunity to examine his shoes. He was able to confirm that they had indeed been cleaned, though not perhaps with that extra thoroughness which would have given them a true spit-and-polish. This set him thinking of his orderly, a slovenly fellow, who unfortunately knew too much for it to be possible to fire him. While Kater was turning these things over in his mind to the gentle sound of organ music, a powerfully built figure pushed his way in beside him, and he heard a subdued, conspiratorial sort of voice mutter, "God be with you, Captain."

Kater glanced carefully up from his shoes and recognized the man beside him as Rotunda, a respected citizen and vineyard proprietor who also owned the inn called The Gay Dog. Kater's solemn expression gave way to a discreet, friendly smile as he whispered back, "God be with you, Herr Rotunda."

They exchanged a furtive but hearty handshake below the level of the pew. The organ swelled to introduce the choir. There was a rustling of prayer books.

Kater had a particularly soft spot for this man Rotunda. Many was the time the captain and some of his boon companions had eaten together in the snug back room of The Gay Dog, where delicious trout and enchanting wine were to be had. For Rotunda had one of the finest cellars in the whole of the Franconian winegrowing area. His Wildlinger Mainleite surprised even the most fastidious connoisseurs, while his Wildlinger Harfe had been praised by no less a person than Reichsmarshal Goering himself. Kater could put a few bottles of this noble wine to good use at any time, the '33 vintage preferably—Sylvaner, or even Trokkenbeerenauslese.

So the captain now leaned forward confidentially and asked, "How are you, my dear Rotunda? And how's business?"

"Bad," whispered Rotunda with some feeling. "Very bad."

"That's most regrettable," Kater whispered back. He listened for a while to the singing of the choir. An all but celestial piano was doing its best to compete, thus making further conversation very difficult. Kater dealt with this handicap by staring solemnly into space for a while until he heard Rotunda whisper in his ear. "Yes, those fellows broke up the whole place yesterday evening—"

"Some trouble over women, presumably."

"Too true," said Rotunda, thinking to himself that it was always the same with the cadets—if they didn't get enough to drink they raised hell, if they got too much to drink they raised hell. If things continued like this, the takings, which were easy enough to come by in all conscience, wouldn't even cover the damages. "Can't you do anything about it for me?" asked Rotunda cautiously.

The captain pretended to be thinking hard. He too found that the cadets were always the same; a fracas of one sort or another occurred almost regularly down in the town. They were usually hushed up or dealt with on the quiet. Once the cadets had sobered up after a row they were usually willing to pay the damages, and few landlords wanted elaborate investigations which presented far too great a potential threat to their licenses. With Captain Kater on their side many an awkward situation could be got around. "Have you still got a bottle or two left hidden away somewhere?" he asked.

"For you, of course, always, my dear Captain," Rotunda assured him.

They were now able to converse together without embarrassment, for the whole congregation had joined in a rousing hymn and the organist was pulling out every stop.

"Normally I'd turn a blind eye to this sort of thing," the landlord and vineyard proprietor assured him, "but this time the cadets really went too far. It was the work of an entire section."

Captain Kater made a show of joining lustily in the singing. He asked, apparently without any special interest, "I don't suppose you know which section it was?"

"Oh yes," replied Rotunda, "this time I know perfectly well who it was. It was Section H of Number Six Company."

Captain Kater's mouth stayed open for a short time without actually saying anything, then he shut it firmly. A twinkle came into his eye. His knobbly face positively radiated satisfaction.

He said softly to Herr Rotunda, "What you tell me interests me very much, my friend. I'll certainly take up the matter out of friendship for you. How many bottles did you say you could spare at the moment?"

"Twenty?" suggested Rotunda warily.

Captain Kater nodded agreement. It should be enough for a start—he didn't want to be petty, after all. Besides, he would in fact have been very glad to take on such a promising case without any fee at all. "We'll arrange the details later," he whispered, and joined in the singing with gusto.

After the service the captain made a few more detailed inquiries of Herr Rotunda. "You see," said Kater, "one can never be too thorough if one really wants to help in the right way."

"You can't imagine how grateful I am to you, my dear Captain," Rotunda assured him. "I'm certain this painful matter simply couldn't be in better hands."

"You can rest assured of that, my dear fellow. Ticklish matters of this sort are a specialty of mine."

"My dear Captain Ratshelm," said Kater at the top of his voice, "I'm most terribly sorry to have to disturb your Sunday afternoon nap, but I see no alternative."

"Please don't apologize, my dear Kater," said Ratshelm with formal politeness. "One way or another we're on duty all the time. Well, what can I do for you?"

Captain Ratshelm looked rather anxiously at the book in which he had been browsing. It was a dictionary, and in the course of his reading Ratshelm had just reached the word "Reich." This was a word which with all its various permutations and combinations covered twelve pages all together —Reichsakademie, Reichsarbeitsdienst, Reichsautobahn, etc., etc. It was only with some reluctance that Ratshelm put this impressive Reichsdictionary to one side.

"I don't quite know how to begin," said Kater, affecting a show of embarrassment. "The confidential matter I want to discuss with you doesn't strictly come within my sphere at all. But there's such a thing as responsibility toward a comrade, and that is something I have no wish to shirk."

"I appreciate that," Ratshelm assured him.

"I'd hoped you would," said Kater gratefully. "Let me be quite honest with you."

But Captain Kater began by talking of his visit to church, which he described as a semiofficial one. He took pains to explain to Ratshelm that by virtue of his office he couldn't help acting as a sort of liaison between the training school and the civilians down in the town. He begged Ratshelm not to become impatient with him.

Thus did Kater achieve his objective and succeed in making Ratshelm impatient. Ratshelm began to show distinct signs of restlessness. Kater then came to the point. A bar had been broken up down in the town, there had been physical violence—the peace-loving landlord had been subjected to extortionate threats—filthy songs had been sung. "And all this was the work of Section H for Heinrich."

"Impossible!" cried Ratshelm indignantly. "You must have made a mistake, Kater."

"I never make a mistake," replied the other firmly, "especially in matters like this."

"Utterly impossible," repeated Captain Ratshelm. "I can't believe that anything like the whole of Section H is involved, or even the greater part of it. There are of course unreliable elements in H for Heinrich, which I certainly wouldn't go out of my way to protect. I'm even inclined to think that this particular section contains a greater number of shifty customers than any of the others—due to a certain regrettable appointment on the personnel side . . ."

"You mean Lieutenant Krafft?" inquired Kater eagerly.

"I don't feel justified in being more precise than that," answered Ratshelm severely, adding immediately, "You have in fact hit the nail on the head. But however that may be, it can't be possible that the entire section is involved in this scandal. For it contains a few young men of quite exceptional caliber—the finest type of officer material we have."

"I'm sorry," maintained Kater, sticking to his guns, "but almost the entire section was involved. Thirty of them at least."

Ratshelm shook his head in consternation. Even the worst of influences could hardly be held solely responsible for something of this magnitude. If it were true, Captain Ratshelm's ambition to become a course commander was seriously endangered. For the extent to which he himself had failed as company commander would inevitably be taken into consideration as a factor.

"Right then," said Captain Kater with satisfaction. "I'll leave you to your problems. You will of course let me know how things develop. But I do strongly advise you to deal with the matter as quickly as possible. Otherwise the injured party may himself well feel compelled to inform the police, and then the fat will really be in the fire. Quite apart from anything else, the general will have to be brought into the picture, and you know what that means."

"Impossible," said Captain Ratshelm, with a shake of his head, "utterly impossible!"

There were times when he talked to himself like this to make up for what he regarded as his impenetrable silence in the presence of others. When he was alone he released himself from such strict self-discipline. He would discuss things with himself, deliver lectures, make speeches, and administer reprimands. He also experimented with suitably effective gestures.

"Something must be done about this!" he told himself. "First, though, I must make sure that my instinct hasn't let me down."

In order to clear this up for a start, Captain Ratshelm ordered Cadet Hochbauer to report to him at once. One glance at Hochbauer was enough to dismiss all wishful thinking from his mind. The cadet's youthful Grecian profile was slightly battered—disfigured by a piece of sticking plaster and a number of purple bruises—while the submissive expression on the cadet's face cried unmistakably, *mea culpa!*

"You, too, Hochbauer!" Ratshelm reproached him.

"Sir," declared the cadet, "I am ready to draw whatever conclusions about my behavior you think fit."

"But how could such a thing happen?" asked Ratshelm. He looked straight at Hochbauer, and the latter stood up to his searching glance unwaveringly. It became clearer and clearer to the captain that there must have been some serious justification for what had happened. When even his finest and most promising cadet saw occasion to intervene, then the provocation must have been great indeed.

"I assume there must have been something behind all this, Hochbauer?"

"Certainly, sir," replied the cadet at once, adroitly seizing the lifeline that had been thrown him. "I was trying to put a stop to a quarrel and found myself involved in a fight in the process."

"Aha," said Captain Ratshelm, "so that's it." He thought hard for a moment, and then continued with conviction and relief, "I knew it must have been something like that."

"My friends and I, including the section senior, did everything we could to end a quarrel that the other side had provoked. But they set upon us and left us with no choice but to defend ourselves."

"Fine, Hochbauer, I believe you. As I see it, you and your comrades were trying to re-establish law and order, but though you did your utmost you were unfortunately unsuccessful—that's it, isn't it?"

"We did everything in our power, sir."

"And how did this quarrel start, my dear Hochbauer?"

"That I can't say, exactly, sir. All I know is that a member of one of the other sections declared that one of our comrades, Cadet Weber, had a joke name. Whether or not he was right about that I can't say. But I do know that this statement was made in public, in the presence of civilians, even including some of the opposite sex."

"Females of doubtful reputation? I hope you had nothing to do with them, Hochbauer?"

"I abhor that type of creature, sir."

"Right, my dear fellow," said Ratshelm, now thoroughly satisfied with the information the cadet had given him. "We'll soon clear this up."

Hochbauer proceeded to answer certain questions; such, for instance, as how many cadets had taken part in the brawl and what their names were. He also gave exact times and as far as possible precise details of the way in which the defensive action—or rather the abortive defensive action—had begun and ended.

"May I assure you, sir, how deeply I regret this turn of events."

"Perfectly all right, my dear fellow. It certainly wasn't your fault, I'm quite convinced of that."

"I'm deeply grateful for your confidence, sir."

"You've nothing to thank me for, Hochbauer," said Ratshelm, giving the cadet his hand. "Let's hope we soon have time for another of our little private chats."

"That's a great relief anyway," Captain Ratshelm reassured himself. "Not that I feel entirely happy about it yet."

Pacing up and down his room, Ratshelm gesticulated to himself as if having to convince an excited and attentive audience of the significance of what he was saying. A really first-rate piece of creative thinking seemed to be germinating.

"Firstly," he said, "the possibility that the bar may in fact have been broken up cannot be altogether ruled out. Secondly, however—an extenuating circumstance—honorable motives may well have lain behind its destruction. Thirdly, however, there's no getting away from the fact that physical violence did take place."

These were weighty problems indeed and the more he turned them over in his mind the clearer he became that all this was too much responsibility for one man. He had to find someone who would relieve him of part of it—as substantial a part as possible.

With this in mind Captain Ratshelm went off to see Lieutenant Krafft.

Immediately on arrival the captain found himself confronted by a most questionable and to him most objectionable sight. A female was sitting on the bed. And she stared at the captain and company commander quite unashamedly, and indeed with positive curiosity.

Ratshelm stood stiffly in the doorway, speechless at first, waiting for some explanation from his section officer. But no explanation was forthcoming—Krafft clearly regarded any such thing as superfluous. He merely said, "Yes, Captain?"

"I beg your pardon," said Ratshelm with some restraint, "but I didn't expect to find a lady here—it's not usual, you know."

"May I introduce Captain Ratshelm," said Krafft, turning easily to Elfrida. "And Captain, may I introduce my fiancée —Fräulein Rademacher."

"That, of course," Ratshelm hastened to reassure him, "is something quite different."

He immediately switched on the chivalry, strode up to Elfrida, and without a moment's hesitation declared, "It is a real pleasure for me to make your acquaintance."

Ratshelm said this even though he knew perfectly well who Elfrida Rademacher was, where she came from, where she worked, and almost everything else about her there was to know. But the word of an officer was good enough for him. This was an officer's fiancée he had in front of him. There was no more to be said. "My heartiest congratulations, Lieutenant."

"Thank you, Captain."

Krafft didn't feel too happy about the sudden brain wave which had led him to proclaim Elfrida his fiancée. But it was, he thought, certainly the most convenient solution, at least for as long as he remained at the training school.

"I beg your pardon, Fräulein Rademacher," said Captain Ratshelm formally, "but I'm afraid I shall have to take your betrothed away. We have a service matter to discuss together."

Elfrida Rademacher seemed rather amused by her new role as an officer's fiancée. She nodded graciously to Captain Ratshelm, in the approved style of Wildlingen officers' ladies. This leisurely yet courteous drawing-room manner was one she affected surprisingly well. But to Krafft she turned with a contented smile and said sweetly, "Run along, then, darling, but don't keep your poor little fiancée waiting too long."

Krafft had some difficulty in controlling himself. He realized that his little fiancée would have a number of surprises in store for him from now on, but there was no time just then to envisage them in detail.

For Captain Ratshelm was urging him out of the room. They passed first into the corridor and then out onto the parade ground. Ratshelm looked about him to make sure that they would not be interrupted. Then without further introduction he came straight to the point.

"Lieutenant Krafft, do you know what your section was up to yesterday evening?"

"No," said Krafft, truthfully enough.

"Your cadets were involved in a brawl yesterday evening, Herr Krafft."

"I thought something like that must have happened," replied Krafft without showing much interest. "I noticed my men were looking rather the worse for wear today."

"Is that all you have to say?" demanded the captain indignantly.

"What else should I say?" returned Krafft innocently. "What the cadets do with their spare time is their own business. As far as I'm concerned they can split each other's skulls open as much as they like provided it doesn't interfere with the way they do their work. Why should we get ourselves involved in all sorts of high-powered proceedings when all they were doing was probably just fooling around a bit? Let's just assume that the cadets had a snowball match, or that they all fell down some cellar steps, or bumped into a bedpost in their eagerness to read standing orders."

"They've broken up a bar," cried Captain Ratshelm angrily, "and what's more, in the presence of civilians, including women."

Krafft looked closely at the captain and then asked him slowly, "How do you know all this? Has someone reported it?"

"I've merely received a private piece of information to this effect from a brother officer."

"Forget it, Ratshelm," Krafft advised him.

"It came from Captain Kater!"

"Then certainly forget it!" said Krafft. "You'd be playing with fire. If the cadets really have made fools of themselves in some way, give them time to iron it all out themselves. Take my advice, Captain, wait until you get an official report, either from the police or from some other quarter. I'll bet you you'll never hear another word about it."

"That won't do, Krafft," cried Ratshelm indignantly.

"Things can't be dealt with like that—not under my command anyway."

He had hoped that this fellow Krafft would immediately spring to his assistance, unhesitatingly accept responsibility, push ahead with an inquiry and seek out the guilty and absolve the innocent. But in fact the fellow had the effrontery to offer him advice about how to keep out of trouble. He of all people, Captain Ratshelm, a front-line soldier with numerous decorations, in charge of the training of future officers!

"Krafft," said Ratshelm severely, "I give you an official order to notify Captain Feders, in his capacity as tactics instructor, of these deplorable events. You will further request him to be ready for a conference with Major Frey. And this of course applies to you too. The exact time of this conference depends on special circumstances, but in any event it will be some time during the afternoon. Is that understood, Krafft?"

"Certainly Captain," said the lieutenant slowly. "If that's how you want it, by all means go ahead. But I wouldn't if I were you."

"But you're not me!" cried Ratshelm angrily.

"Fortunately," said Krafft.

"Your views," said Captain Ratshelm with unmistakable repugnance, "sometimes seem to me thoroughly reprehensible. I say this to you quite frankly because it's part of my principle to be frank. I find your approach positively dangerous."

"Who for, Captain?"

"I've no wish to enter into an argument with you, Krafft —not now, at any rate. I'm going to see the major now. And you will kindly do what I ask you."

"Most certainly," the lieutenant assured him.

"And how are you feeling, dear lady," Lieutenant Krafft said to Elfrida Rademacher.

"Pretty silly," said Elfrida. "And I'm beginning to be worried about you. You don't think enough about the way you do things."

"You're wrong," said Krafft. "In fact the opposite is almost always the case. I usually do things only when I've worked them out very carefully beforehand."

Krafft stood opposite Elfrida, who was still sitting on his bed. After his conversation with Captain Ratshelm he had returned to his room at once. He had a large number of things to do, but most important of all was what he had to discuss with Elfrida.

"Anyway," she said, "I thought that a pretty risky joke of yours."

"It wasn't a joke," said Krafft.

"All right then, it was a brain wave, a brilliant move. You wanted to get out of an awkward situation, and you introduced me as your fiancée. Aren't I right?"

He smiled, sat down beside her, put his arm around her, and said lightheartedly, "But you played along very nicely, Elfrida."

"Well, yes—for your sake," she said with some hesitation. "And at first the role rather amused me."

"Then let's keep it that way," suggested Krafft. "The times are serious enough—why should we give up something that amuses us?"

"Do you mean that?" she asked shyly.

He looked at her with pleasure and said, "It's like this, you see—everywhere I've been I've got fiancées; two in Silesia, three in Poland, four in the Rhineland, seven in France, and one in Russia. That's the way I do things."

"No, it isn't!"

"Well," he said, suddenly very embarrassed, "perhaps you're right. Anyway, one has to make a start sometime."

"Karl," she said softly, "I've never put any pressure like that on you."

"That's why I'm doing it, girl!"

It had indeed been a sudden brain wave to introduce her as his fiancée, but there had been a certain amount of subconscious preparation for it.

"Good, then," she said simply, kissing him lightly, carelessly almost, on the cheek, for she was embarrassed herself now.

"The only thing I'm afraid of," he said gaily, "is that we won't find time or opportunity today to celebrate our engagement properly. For if I'm not much mistaken, we've got a couple of geese here trying to pretend they're swans. I just want to help them into the water if you don't mind."

"I don't mind what you do."

"Just stay that way, then," he said, putting his arms around her.

"I'll always stay just how you want me, Karl."

He stiffened a moment, freed himself, stared at her for a few seconds, and said, "Elfrida, you must promise me one thing. You must never try to adapt yourself to what I do.

You shouldn't try and think as I do. You must even avoid behaving as I do. You must stay as you are, not be some sort of echo of me, some sort of extension or shadow. Do you understand?"

"Don't worry about that, please. And don't hang about here any longer. I'm busy now. I've got to think out how to set about being engaged."

"Do that," he said, laughing with relief.

Krafft walked out of the room and picked on the first cadet he found in the corridor. He ordered him to fetch Cadets Kramer, Weber, and Rednitz for him, within three minutes at the latest.

The three cadets appeared immediately. They came to attention in front of Krafft and looked at him with wary humility. They were anything but easy in their consciences —in fact they were scared stiff. And seeing little grounds for hope, they had come prepared for the worst. Yet what happened next was the last thing anyone had expected. Lieutenant Krafft simply burst out laughing. The sight of the colorfully patched and bruised faces in front of him seemed to fill him for some seconds with helpless mirth. The cadets smiled sheepishly, glancing at each other furtively.

The victorious fracas had been stimulating at the time, but the awakening the next morning had been cruel indeed. And someone had spread the ominous news that in the previous course a whole section had been "sent packing"—to the front, that is—because of some communal breach of the training school's regulations. Yet a cautious hope had arisen. If anyone could help, it would be Krafft. They had in fact been on the point of sending a delegation to him. But would he be willing to help? Now it seemed almost as if he would.

"What gay dogs you look!" cried Krafft, thoroughly enjoying himself.

The cadets immediately realized that the lieutenant knew all about it. He even knew the name of the inn in which their Pyrrhic victory had been won.

And Kramer began helpfully, "If we might be allowed to give the lieutenant a report . . ."

"I'm not interested in any report about the way in which you spend your spare time," said Krafft. "I've only got you here to tell you a little story I've just thought of."

The cadets stood in stunned silence, realizing at once that their section officer had no desire to be made any sort of accomplice. But on the other hand he refused to sit in judgment. So what was he up to?

"During the campaign in France," the lieutenant went on easily, "I once appropriated a cellar full of wine. A magnificent affair. I was really proud of it; particularly at the moment when I appropriated it. But soon afterward, the very next morning, I think, it became clear to me that I had no right to do anything of the sort. And not only that. What I had done was a punishable offense. Several of my superior officers had, however, by now got wind of it, having been put on the scent by a third party. Well now, how shall I put it? When my superior officers came to inspect the cellar I was alleged to have appropriated, there simply wasn't a cellar there."

The cadets took Krafft's point. Their faces brightened, and they looked gratefully at their lieutenant.

Cadet Kramer said, "May I request permission for myself and my comrades to go into town, sir? We have a little business to attend to there."

"Permission granted," said Lieutenant Krafft.

The cadets executed an eager about-face and hurried off. After a moment's reflection Krafft called Rednitz back. The cadet came smartly to attention and looked at the lieutenant with an almost conspiratorial smile.

"One question," said Krafft. "Quite between ourselves, Rednitz, did Hochbauer take part in this?"

"And how, Lieutenant! He didn't want to at first, but he was given no choice. I went so far as to lend him a helping hand. He shot into our opponents' rank like a cannon ball."

"And who, or what, do you think, Rednitz, was responsible for the fight?"

"Strictly speaking, Special Order number one hundred and thirty-one, Lieutenant," explained the cadet with a grin. He noticed a look of slight bewilderment pass over his section officer's face, and realized that Krafft obviously knew nothing of the particular significance of this special order. "It reached the section at mid-day on Saturday and was then, as usual, read out on the spot. In this special order it is stated among many other things that the name Egon, for example, is a joke name. And it was just that which the opposing section threw in Cadet Weber's teeth. He reacted promptly."

"Which section was it, Rednitz?"

"Section B for Bruno from Number One course, Lieutenant."

For the first time Krafft showed a positive reaction to the cadet's report; he smiled. Krafft knew now that at the forthcoming conference he could reckon on the support of Captain Feders. For Section B for Bruno was the Minnesinger's. It was a factor which might well prove decisive.

"Very useful information, my dear Rednitz," said Lieutenant Krafft. "I can make use of it. But now I won't detain you any longer. After all, you and your comrades have urgent business to attend to down in the town."

"I imagine it'll be settled in an hour, Lieutenant."

"Let me know the result immediately, Rednitz—wherever I may happen to be at the time. Even if you should have to fetch me out of a conference!"

This secret and extraordinary conference began at 1600 hours in the office of the commanding officer of Number 2 Course. It was relatively short, and, for some, ended in a most painful manner. The participants were Major Frey, Captain Ratshelm, Captain Feders, and Lieutenant Krafft— the last three in their capacities as officers directly responsible for the training of the accused Section H for Heinrich.

"Gentlemen, I'm appalled!" were the course commanding officer's opening words. He sat in his chair erect and dignified and full of self-importance. "I regret to have to disturb your Sunday rest, gentlemen," continued Major Frey. "I too would have preferred to spend it in the peace and harmony of my own fireside. At this very moment my wife is, as you know, receiving the ladies of the married officers under my command. The situation which has, however, so carelessly been allowed to arise compels me to forego the pleasure of being with them. What have you to say about it, Lieutenant Krafft?"

"Nothing, Major," declared Krafft simply.

The course commander seemed to gasp for air for a moment. Then, with sudden sharpness, he said, "The section for which you yourself are primarily responsible comes to blows in a public bar like a lot of lumberjacks, and you have nothing to say?"

"First of all," returned Krafft calmly, "I consider it unproven that any brawl and consequent destruction of the bar did in fact take place. If it did, it would then be necessary to establish whether Section H for Heinrich were guilty, partly guilty, or perhaps completely innocent. For it seems that some of those who took part in this row were cadets who hitherto have enjoyed an unusually high reputation. Is that not so, Captain?"

Ratshelm jumped at this. "That is indeed a point to which particular attention should be paid," he said. "One might almost say that the finest and most promising cadets of all were involved in this unfortunate affair. It really does make one stop and think!"

"All of which gets us precisely nowhere!" said the major, obviously determined to cut an impressive figure. "And don't forget, Lieutenant Krafft, that ultimately the entire responsibility rests on you."

"I'm very glad to accept it, Major," Krafft assured him nonchalantly, "though I'm still not quite clear what sort of responsibility you mean. In order to get a clear picture one shouldn't omit the other section involved in the affair—B for Bruno, as it happens."

"Which?" asked Feders incredulously.

The lieutenant eagerly gave full particulars, and Feders, taking no notice of anyone, simply burst out laughing.

"I don't see what there is to laugh at, Captain!" said the major in astonishment.

"Really, Major?" said Captain Feders. "I must say I find the whole affair extremely comic!"

"I'm sorry, Captain Feders," replied the major with some asperity, "but I don't. Might I ask you to take it as seriously as possible?"

"I'll try," said Feders, winking at Krafft, "but it's going to be difficult."

"The very origin of this row seems a little peculiar," maintained Krafft. "What they were quarreling about was whether or not the name Egon was a joke name."

"It can't be true!" said Feders, now feeling on the top of his form again. "It's too absurd."

"I also find this statement of Lieutenant Krafft's grotesque," agreed Captain Ratshelm all unknowing. "You can't seriously tell us that an idiotic remark of that sort was responsible for an outbreak of vandalism."

"Unfortunately that is precisely the case," declared Krafft. "One of the cadets considered the offensive use of the term 'joke name' an insult to his honor, and accordingly sprang to his own defense. As for the alleged remark being an idiotic one, I'm sure the major wouldn't agree with that."

The three men looked at the major, who had now become thoroughly uncomfortable. A mild flush had spread over his features that were usually so dynamic and warlike. He seemed upset, and his fingers drummed nervously on the table top.

But in the approved tradition Major Frey now attempted to reply to an attack with a counter attack. "I gather from your astonishment, gentlemen, that you seem regrettably unaware of my Special Order number one hundred and thirty-one. This seems to me to throw a curious light on the way in which my written orders are received. The order in question left my office around ten hundred hours and should have been read on the same day between twelve hundred and fourteen hundred hours. The company commanders and tactics instructors should have thus had ample time in which to acquaint themselves with it. But obviously absolutely no one seems to have seen the necessity for such a thing."

This was in fact true enough. Orders came in, were signed for, promptly passed on again, and only very occasionally read. This obviously came as a painful surprise to the major. His carefully thought-out, beautifully polished special orders, the tangible fruits of his soldierly intellect, were going unread. Even by the otherwise reliable Captain Ratshelm. Most depressing.

"But none of this," said Krafft, preparing to go in for the kill, "alters the fact that it was the description of Egon as a 'joke name' which was the actual cause of the brawl."

"An error," the major assured him hastily, anxious to get away from this delicate subject as soon as possible. "Simply an error."

"The row between the cadets?" asked Krafft ingenuously.

"The description of Egon as a 'joke name,'" said the major quickly. "But don't let's bother about that—we're remedying that."

"However," said Krafft with a persistence that was beginning to be most painful—particularly for the major—"it was this error which was responsible for—how was it that one of the gentlemen put it?—the cadets behaving like a lot of lumberjacks. 'Egon a joke name' was the slogan under which the battle was fought—always assuming that the alleged destruction of the bar did in fact take place. But don't you think it might be better, cleverer, and easier if we were to assume that nothing happened at all?"

The major didn't immediately say "No" to this. And this struck those present as very remarkable. Frey sat at his desk like some royal coachman on his box—upright, fully arrayed, a dependent, but not in any unworthy sense. He had reached a point where all he wanted was that someone should give him some clear line on how to proceed. He looked about him inquiringly.

It was at this moment that one of his orderly clerks appeared and announced that a cadet from Section H for Heinrich wished to speak to his section officer on a matter of urgency. Frey gave permission for this, simply because it provided the secret conference with a breathing space. For the next few minutes he didn't have to explain anything or make any decision.

All the major did, after Krafft had left the room, was to ask, "Well, gentlemen, what do you say?"

The gentelmen had nothing to say, or rather nothing definite. Feders showed himself to be completely uninterested. Ratshelm made it clear that he preferred to agree with whatever the major's opinion might turn out to be when he finally discovered what that was, but Frey didn't seem to be particularly interested in helping him over this.

The major was quite clear about one thing—namely that if he were to pursue his original intention of making the matter into an issue, he might be the one who suffered in the end. If the general were to learn of the catastrophe that had resulted from the phrase about Egon being a joke name, the consequences would not bear thinking of. Ernst Egon Modersohn would tear Major Frey limb from limb.

But at this moment Lieutenant Krafft reappeared and declared cheerfully, "Gentlemen, I have just learned from one of the cadets of my section that the whole unsavory matter has been cleared up. Herr Rotunda, the landlord of The Gay Dog, not only declares that he has no wish to file a complaint, he is even prepared to testify to the fact that what took place was no more than a misunderstanding. Fundamentally, yesterday evening was a normal evening like any other."

"What on earth's all the fuss about, then?" asked Feders.

The major heaved a great sigh of relief, as what had seemed like a commanding officer's nightmare slowly dissolved. He was saved. Luck had favored him as it always favored really able people. He felt like a new man. And in the approved manner of a superior he immediately remounted the high horse from which he had momentarily tumbled.

"Gentlemen," he said in a tone of authority, "now that it has been established that some of you have made a mistake I can state quite openly that this was really what I expected from the start. And I find myself all the more surprised by some of your individual reactions. You, Captain Ratshelm, ought never to have bothered me with a matter that was so hopelessly unclarified. You, Captain Feders, should conduct yourself with a little more gravity in such matters in the future and refrain from describing a complex investigation as a 'fuss.' Finally you, Lieutenant Krafft, could well concern yourself a little more closely with your section; for the concluding report which you have just made should have been made at the very outset of our conference. However, you know, gentlemen, that I am not a petty man. I hold nothing against you. Thank you, gentlemen."

After the three officers had left their commanding officer the latter felt confident that he had once again mastered a difficult situation in exemplary fashion. He therefore took a snow-white sheet of paper and wrote upon it the memorable words which would soon either astonish or delight the entire training school, from the general himself down to the humblest cadet:

ADDITION TO SPECIAL ORDER NO. 131

SUBJECT: Correction.

A regrettable misprint has accidentally found its way into the above order, Section III, paragraph 2c. The word "Egon" is to be deleted. The word actually intended was "Ede."

Signed: FREY
MAJOR

Officer Commanding No. 2 Course

23 *AN INVITATION AND ITS CONSEQUENCES*

"SHE ISN'T THERE," said the corporal to Captain Kater.

"What do you mean?" asked Kater angrily. "Has she disappeared?"

"No, Captain," said the corporal, "but she must have gone out."

"Gone out?" asked Kater slowly. "How could she do that?"

The two of them, the CO of the headquarters company and his orderly corporal, were talking of Irene Jablonski, the new assistant.

"Didn't I expressly order Irene Jablonski to be on duty?" asked Kater irritably.

"Yes, Captain."

"Then why isn't she on duty?"

"Fräulein Rademacher decided otherwise."

"Who?" asked Kater in alarm. "That Rademacher creature? How does she come into it?"

"I don't know, Captain," said the orderly corporal patiently. "She merely said that if the captain wanted her for anything she'd be at your disposal."

"Ah!" said Kater, pricking up his ears. "She said that, did she?"

"Yes—if the captain wanted her for anything."

"All right," said Kater, thoughtfully, "you can go now."

The corporal left the captain's quarters. But Kater stood there in thought for some time. Then he shook his head with a smile and said, "These women!" After which he crossed to the window.

Captain Kater's binoculars were of excellent quality—German workmanship of course. They were intended for use by officers of the training school. But what Captain Kater was using them to observe was neither the behavior of the enemy nor that of his own soldiers. His eyes were trained across the road onto the barrack block opposite, where the female civilian staff lived.

Captain Kater concentrated his attention on the windows of a room on the first floor, where Elfrida Rademacher had her quarters together with Irene Jablonski and one or two other girls. At this precise moment the room seemed to be empty.

Kater put down his binoculars, wondering what game these girls could be playing with him. Things were of course by no means as simple as they appeared at first sight. If this girl Rademacher made out that she wanted to protect little Irene, that was of course only a pretext! It would slowly emerge that the Rademacher girl wanted a go herself. She just couldn't manage to come out into the open with it.

"And why not?" Kater asked himself. For this girl Irene was after all only a novice, and, though by no means without charm, was hardly to be compared with Elfrida Rademacher, who was a magnificent example of a mature woman.

He realized that she had been absorbing more and more of his attention lately. Her difficult attitude might well be simply due to frustration. And the episode with Krafft was a passing affair. After all, she was no fool. She must sense the precariousness of the lieutenant's position. Clever girls like her always changed horses in plenty of time.

Kater leaned forward slightly as if this would enable him to see better, and through his binoculars spied Elfrida Rademacher, who had just entered her room. She had switched on the light and was looking about her. Apart from her, the room was empty. Thoughtfully she began to unbutton her blouse. And as she did so she crossed to the window and drew the curtains.

Captain Kater lowered his binoculars. With a certain haste he finished dressing.. He was wearing his full regulation uniform, for he intended to set out on a round of inspection. And since what he intended to inspect was the female civilian quarters, he naturally couldn't do so wearing nothing but a dressing gown. It's true it was customary to carry out such inspections accompanied by the senior female civilian employee, but he was entitled to act alone in emergencies and he felt justified in regarding the present situation as a sort of emergency.

With one last glance in the mirror Kater left the room. He could feel sure of making a really distinguished impression. He strode down the corridors, walked out of the headquarters building, crossed the road, and entered the barrack block, over the entrance to which was written in large letters:

WOMEN'S QUARTERS
ENTRY BY UNAUTHORIZED PERSONS STRICTLY FORBIDDEN

But of course he himself was an authorized person, for the notice itself bore the signature: KATER, *Captain and Commanding Officer of the Headquarters Company*.

In front of the door number 210 Kater stopped and once again nervously adjusted his uniform. After looking carefully about him, he entered without knocking.

The sight which met his eyes was well calculated to raise his blood pressure. Elfrida Rademacher was standing there, leaning forward slightly in front of her wardrobe, dressed only in panties and a brassière. Her figure fully came up to his expectations.

Elfrida Rademacher straightened up and looked at him inquiringly. She betrayed no particular surprise or embarrassment. She was used to men undressing her with their eyes, and thought to herself that Kater was therefore at that moment seeing only what he had already seen in imagination a hundred times before.

"What do you want here?" she asked with apparent indifference. "And why don't you knock?"

"I wanted to bring you an invitation, Elfrida," he said rather huskily.

"Rademacher to you," she declared snubbingly. "Besides, I'm not accepting any invitation from you. Kindly leave the room, or at least turn around until I put on a dressing gown."

"Why not stay as you are?" said Kater. "It doesn't worry me."

"But it does me," said Elfrida. With that she turned her back, reached for a dressing gown, and threw it around her.

Kater snorted. He had a strong desire to sit down—to lie down, if possible. But Elfrida's amused glance contained a cool snub which afforded him little hope.

"Listen," said Kater huskily, still standing by the door, "you don't need to pretend with me. I know what you're after—and it suits me perfectly. I know you're a sensible girl, and thoroughly expert in these things. And I find you most attractive."

"But I don't find you at all attractive," Elfrida assured him. It sounded very convincing, though not of course to Captain Kater.

For Kater felt he had seen through her. It was all simply a question of price, he thought, and he was fully determined not to be petty about this aspect of things. "We'll soon come to an agreement," he said. "You come and see me about ten o'clock."

"I'm sure that would suit you very well," cried Elfrida, with a laugh.

"It suits me admirably," he replied. "After ten we'll be quite undisturbed."

"You forget," said Elfrida, "that I'm engaged to Krafft."

"That makes no difference," Kater assured her with a grin. "It doesn't worry me in the slightest. I might almost say quite the contrary—it makes things even better. For it will make you all the more ready to do me the honor. A word from me and this so-called fiancé of yours will be out of the training school. Never underestimate my influence, Elfrida, and always remember that I know more than is good for you. I only need to go to the general tomorrow morning and whisper one or two particulars in his ear. If you really want this so-called fiancé of yours to come to a sticky end . . . well then! Any time after ten—and don't keep me waiting too long, Elfrida, I'm already rather impatient."

"Well, you'll have a long time to wait," said Elfrida. "I'm busy this evening—and for months and years to come."

"You'll come around," Kater assured her. "I guarantee you that. But I'm prepared to be co-operative—you can send a substitute. Irene Jablonski, for instance. Best come yourself, though, Elfrida. Why should we put off what's bound to happen sooner or later anyway?"

Elfrida Rademacher looked in the mirror. She was utterly calm and cool and unruffled. And she thought with surprise that her skin was quite different—fresh and clear and smooth —and her brain was working quite differently too, these days. All that tiredness and dullness seemed to have left her. She had someone to treasure now. She'd changed—it was like being given some wonderful present. But did life really give presents like that?

She had neither the time nor the wish to bother herself with any more such questions. Someone was waiting for her. That was all that mattered.

She dressed hurriedly and wrote a note to say where she was going, which she left on Irene Jablonski's bed.

Then she ran out of the building across the main street of the barracks to the block which lay rather to one side, in which Section H was billeted.

The room she entered had wooden walls that were cracked and blackened with smoke. In it stood a battered army bed, with a shabby strip of carpet running up to it. Here also stood Karl Krafft, waiting tenderly for her. He smiled, radiating a wonderful feeling that this was all the most natural thing in the world. Whatever he did, she felt safe with him.

She threw herself upon him as if seeking sanctuary with him. "At last," she said, "at last!"

"Don't be so impetuous!" he said, putting his arms around her. "Either you've got a bad conscience or you've just had an unpleasant experience."

"Kater's been making a nuisance of himself," she told him.

"Never mind," he said soothingly. "His whole existence is a nuisance."

"Can he do you any harm?" asked Elfrida.

"Even a louse can do harm," he replied calmly.

Elfrida told him what had happened. "What am I to do?" she asked, when she had finished. "Shall I just slap his face next time?"

"Simply don't listen to him. Try to look straight through him as if he just didn't exist. Remember you're what they call a lady now, Elfrida—an officer's fiancée!"

"I'm not going to find that easy, Karl, I can tell you."

"You'll soon get used to it," he said. "After all you're a woman, and very adaptable."

"Yes, I'm that all right," said Elfrida. His spontaneous gaiety had a wonderful effect on her. She nestled up to him and put her arm around his neck. "I love adapting myself to you, Karl," she said.

Gently he freed himself. "You'll have a chance to practice your role of officer's lady at once. We're invited out."

"We're not staying here this evening?" she asked in some disappointment.

"Not to begin with," he said. "We've got to go and see Captain Feders and his wife. They want to meet you. Don't you find that rather flattering? An official invitation, so to speak."

"The first of my life," she said in embarrassment.

"Life's full of surprises."

"But Captain Feders of all people?"

"Do you know him?"

"No, not personally. I only know what people say about him—about him and his wife."

"Forget it, Elfrida. People say a lot of things about us too."

"You like this man Captain Feders, don't you? I can tell that from the way you talk about him. Or is it his wife you like?"

"I'm interested in both of them. They're unusual people. In Captain Feders and his wife you'll be meeting two people with very different problems from ours. Come on, let's go."

They strolled arm in arm through the barracks. Fresh snow had fallen. The gleaming whiteness was like some sort of Christmas idyll. Their hands reached for each other. They were radiant with happiness. The engaged couple were beginning to get used to their engagement.

"Welcome to the lovers of Wildlingen!" cried Captain Feders.

Krafft smiled. "Have you just invited us here to gape at us?" he asked.

"You've got it in one," said Feders, leading them across to his wife. "We could hardly wait to clap eyes on a couple who were actually happily in love, isn't that so, Marion?"

Marion Feders greeted her guests with some reserve, almost shyly. She was obviously afraid of being confronted with people who might look down on her.

"It's very kind of you to ask us," said Elfrida to Marion, adding frankly, "It's the first official invitation I've had."

"Poor child!" cried Feders cheerfully. "And it had to be us of all people!"

"A difficult start isn't necessarily a bad start," said Marion affably.

"Thank you," said Elfrida. "You really do make things easy for us."

Marion Feders smiled at Elfrida Rademacher and offered her a chair. She was finding that her fears were unjustified. The girl seemed genuinely sympathetic—simple and uncomplicated and possessed of a full-blooded rustic beauty.

They grouped themselves around a low table which already had glasses and a bottle of vermouth on it.

"Actually, of course," said Feders, "we ought to be drinking champagne. But we are neither Croesus nor Kater. And any drink among friends is a good drink."

They drank the first glass in silence.

"The news of our engagement seems to have got around astonishingly quickly," said Krafft.

"The telephone has taken the place of jungle drums in our society," said Captain Feders. "And while savages are barbarically open about it, technology turns us into a lot of furtive whisperers. The good Captain Ratshelm, that awful old woman, had barely learned of your engagement before he was on the phone. And naturally the first person to whom he breathed the sensational news was the respected wife of his commanding officer."

"Well, that saves us sending out engagement notices anyway," said Krafft.

"But it won't save you from the curiosity of your commanding officer's wife," said Feders, filling the glasses again. "The major's lady will certainly want to examine the lieutenant's fiancée very closely. Prepare yourself for the most impossible questions, Fräulein Rademacher. For example: do you come from a respectable or at least a well-to-do family?"

"My father was a foreman in the railway repair shops," declared Elfrida Rademacher without embarrassment. "In addition to which, he used to sing in the choir."

"Very admirable, the major's lady will say." Feders began to warm to this game—and to Elfrida—and mimicking the commanding officer's wife's voice he continued, "And what about your education, boarding school and all the rest of it?"

"Primary school, that's all."

"Ah, well, the major's lady will say, let us hope you have a certain native wit, that can make up for a lot. But what about your health now—from the point of view of childbearing?"

"One'll have to put it to the test."

Captain Feders burst out laughing. "Splendid," he said. "If you keep your end up like that the old bitch won't bother you any more. Fräulein Rademacher—once again, welcome." He raised his glass. "Your health."

"And what about the major's lady from the point of view of childbearing?" Elfrida asked. "That's a question I could put to her, if she grills me like that."

"My dear Fräulein Rademacher," declared Captain Feders in amusement. "Allow me to draw your attention to one of the most important rules for raising armies, creating states, and fighting wars successfully. It's epitomized in the phrase, the oxen do the threshing of the king's corn. By which I mean that since wars require victims, it's the soldiers who have to provide them. Similarly wealth requires money—the small men have to provide it. Again, states need citizens— the people must provide them. Generals are seldom killed, statesmen are never poor, and ladies of high society do far less to promote the birthrate than ordinary women of the people. Which is why it is not really surprising that certain females make a great fuss about motherhood without actually being mothers."

"You may be doing Frau Frey an injustice," Marion Feders suggested. "I sometimes get the impression that she has genuinely maternal feelings."

"Do you really think so?" asked Feders. "When she married she was thinking not of children but of careers. It wasn't until her husband had been highly decorated and was suspected of being on his way to a staff job that she married him at all. The idea that she of all people might have maternal feelings seems to me rather far-fetched. How do you make it out, Marion?"

"You know I'm not particularly fond of Frau Frey—"

"I've always known you had excellent taste!"

"—but just recently at one of her ghastly coffee parties for officers' wives she talked about the young cadets with great warmth, and with a remarkable openness that was quite unusual for her."

"What does she know about our cadets?" said Feders.

"She never meets anyone outside officers' circles. She hasn't started inspecting the sections yet, thank goodness."

But Marion Feders was unwilling to yield—and besides, she had noticed that Lieutenant Krafft was listening to her with lively interest. "I think you're wrong," she said. "Frau Frey certainly knows at least one of the cadets."

"Could it be the one who brings her books from time to time?" asked Krafft cautiously.

"Yes," said Marion Feders promptly, "that's right. How did you know?"

"Quite simple," Krafft explained. "Every cadet who leaves the barracks whether on duty or private business has to report to his section officer. Special Order number thirty-nine."

"And who's the lucky man?" asked Feders curiously.

"The right one," said Krafft. "The very man you're thinking of."

"Well, well," cried Feders. "This could prove grist to your mill, eh, Krafft? Always provided, that is, you can keep it turning. But if it would help you in any way, I'll gladly send the excellent major's lady a few books at an opportune moment—in the same way, and by the same man."

"Most gratefully accepted," returned Krafft.

"May I ask what we're talking about, actually?" inquired Elfrida.

"My dear good Fräulein Rademacher," said Feders gaily, "we're talking about the excellent system of controls by which it is possible to detect the rejects in our factory—always assuming that one knows how to make proper use of the equipment."

They drank each other's health, and it was suddenly as if they had all known each other for ages. Frau Marion relaxed and smiled, and Elfrida looked radiant with happiness. It was a great pleasure for her to find the notorious Captain Feders such an amusing conversationalist.

"I admire your courage very much, my dear Krafft," Captain Feders assured him. "What you do you do quite openly. In the case of your engagement, now, that's understandable enough. But I hope you don't intend to proclaim a similar sort of engagement to justice herself. I warn you; in Germany this lady goes a-whoring from time to time."

"My husband loves making remarks like that," said Marion Feders with a smile at Elfrida.

Feders laughed and raised his glass.

"Come on, Fräulein Rademacher," said Marion Feders, getting to her feet. "Let's go into the next room. I want to show you how an officer's wife lives. Presumably you know the sort of existence she can expect already."

They withdrew into the next room.

When they were alone and had once more drained their glasses Krafft said to Feders, "I think I see your particular problem at the moment—it concerns the basketmen. Previously you were quite sure that death was the only possible salvation for them. Better die, you told yourself, than go on living like this. But now you can't say that any more, for in the meantime you've discovered that the merest spark of life is enough. Even fragmented existence knows what it is to have hope; hope for a book, a picture, scraps of music, a game of skat—or even the love of a woman."

"You're a sly, low-down sort of fellow, Krafft," said Feders brusquely. "You remind me of my younger brother. No one could ever make him out. He was killed one day trying to stop some runaway horse which trampled him to death. However, he had saved the lives of two other people—a prostitute and a swindler."

"I feel quite up to runaway horses," said Krafft seriously. "I've had some experience with them."

"They may turn out not to be horses at all but tanks. Armor-plated with prejudice. Powered by lies. You look out, Krafft! You may well be taking on more than you can tackle."

"All I have in mind at the moment," said Krafft, "is a relatively small and routine bit of business. It's now ten o'clock, and I couldn't bring myself to keep Captain Kater waiting. He's waiting for my fiancée at the moment."

"At this hour of night?" asked Feders in surprise. "Some service matter?"

"Quite the contrary—strictly private."

"Ah," cried Feders with pleasure. "I see. You want to announce your engagement to him."

"That's no longer necessary—he knows about it already."

"And all the same he . . ."

"For that very reason, presumably. He's got so far as to say that it does not worry him in the slightest. So you'll excuse me. And if I might leave Fräulein Rademacher here in the meantime, I'd be most grateful. I won't be more than a quarter of an hour."

"Take me with you," Feders pleaded, "I beg you. Do me the favor!"

Krafft thought for a moment. "Perhaps," he said, "it would be better if there were no third person present as witness."

"Quite the contrary," insisted Feders. "The safest thing is a witness who will testify in all circumstances that you handled him with velvet gloves. So what are we waiting for?"

"All right, then."

Feders rubbed his hands in anticipation. "My dear Krafft," he said, "you're giving me great pleasure."

"I don't see anything particularly pleasurable about it," said the lieutenant.

"You soon will," returned Feders. He went over to the door of the adjacent room, opened it, and said, "I just wanted to inform the ladies that we intend to take a little stroll—we'll be about half an hour."

"What are you up to?" asked Marion Feders.

"We plan to cool down any over-heated spirits we may come across."

"Well, that can't do any harm," said Elfrida.

They left the guest house. A narrow gleam of light shone from behind the curtains of the general's room. Feders waved a hand in that direction. "Presumably the old man is working away at some standard work on the ethics of being an officer, with particular regard to the historic traditions of Prussia."

The eagerness with which Feders was obviously looking forward to the coming meeting made Krafft apprehensive. As they approached the headquarters building he asked hesitantly, "Don't you think it might be better if I were to talk to Captain Kater alone?"

"Certainly not, my dear fellow! I want to do the right thing by you."

"But really this concerns only me."

"You're wrong, my dear fellow—it concerns your friend just as much as your fiancée. Besides, you should think of this in practical terms, Krafft. If you punch Kater on the nose, it could in certain circumstances be interpreted as a physical assault on a superior officer. But if I do it, then at the most it's a rather crude attempt at comradely persuasion. Now that I've got a sod like that in my sights at last I'm not going to let him get away."

Feders hurried on. He went up to Captain Kater's room, pushed open the door, and cried, "Visitor to see you, Kater!" Then he stood back to let Lieutenant Krafft enter.

Kater, who was already in his dressing gown, got to his feet. At first he was merely indignant at this brusque intrusion on his evening vigil. Then astonishment overcame him;

finally he became uneasy, and his hands began to shake as he straightened his dressing gown.

Lieutenant Krafft walked up to him and said, "My fiancée Fräulein Rademacher, is unfortunately unable to come and slap your face herself. It's my intention to spare her the trouble."

"What do you want with me?" cried Kater, scurrying for shelter behind a chair. "I don't know what you're talking about. And how dare you speak to a superior officer like that!"

"We're not talking to a superior officer at the moment, but to a dirty swine," said Feders with a friendly grin. "And we are taking the liberty, as you have already heard, of representing Fräulein Rademacher. Right, then, come on—put your fists up!"

Kater stood there rigid. He looked helplessly about him, obviously searching for some way of escape. But he had two powerful obstacles in front of him. It was useless to call out, because hardly anyone else lived in the headquarters building. This freedom from disturbance, which had previously seemed such an amenity of the place, suddenly revealed itself as a dangerous trap. So there was no choice left to him but to try and talk his way out. "But gentlemen, I assure you, there must be some mistake here."

"On your part, yes, Kater," said Feder, looking about him preparatory to action, "but not as far as we're concerned. You're just a lousy sod. Is that clear?"

"If you ever try to bother my fiancée again," announced Krafft firmly, "I'll knock hell out of you."

"You're threatening me," snapped Kater. "I can have you court-martialed for that."

"You'll be in the hospital first," cried Krafft.

"Now steady, friends, steady," said Feders. "First of all, there's no question of threats—I'll testify to that on oath. We're just having a little chat here. We mean no more harm than you do, Kater. Clear? And never forget, it's the word of two against one—two witnesses who have fought at the front against the word of a desk soldier—and we know that always carries a lot of weight with court-martials."

Captain Kater saw that if these furious visitors of his were in earnest his position was utterly hopeless. He backed to the wall, feeling weak at the knees.

"Let's get down to business then," said Captain Feders. "What about a refreshing drink, Kater? At least we've got everything set out here."

Kater motioned toward the table with a trembling hand. A number of bottles and glasses stood on it, presumably intended as a prelude to a night of debauchery.

Feders walked carelessly over, picked up one of the bottles, and looked at the label. He shook his head disapprovingly and let the bottle fall to the ground, where it smashed. The schnapps splashed all over the carpet and the furniture. A strong, heavy smell of alcohol pervaded the room.

"Not good enough for us!" declared Captain Feders laconically. "What can you be thinking of? A lousy fruit brandy? You won't get away as cheaply as that!"

Feders picked up one bottle after another and dropped each in turn on the floor, where they all smashed. Then he searched through the cupboard and chest of drawers and brought further bottles out into the open. All suffered the same fate.

The various different sorts of schnapps—all high-proof alcohol—made a fearful stench. The atmosphere was literally "thick with alcohol." The floor was a mass of broken glass and covered by a giant puddle. Kater stood in the middle of it in his slippers, looking helplessly about him and trembling in every limb. The vandals were upon him! He was at their mercy—for the moment at any rate.

Feders looked around the room. But his satisfaction still wasn't complete. So finally he said, "It's much too cramped in here—don't you agree, Krafft?"

The latter nodded and said, "The bed seems superfluous to me."

"Quite right!" said Feders. "It's been worrying me all the time. Besides, we've got to protect our brother officer from himself."

They joined forces and took the bed to pieces, heaving the different parts of it out into the corridor. Then they smashed up anything else that was left to sit on. When they finished they turned the key in the door from the outside.

Kater was now thoroughly humiliated. But before finally cutting him off from the outside world altogether, Captain Feders said, through the door, "Very many thanks for an extraordinarily pleasant evening! It's certainly something we'll talk about afterward—if anyone should ask us about it."

24 *A QUESTION OF INFLUENCE*

CAPTAIN KATER was almost blind with rage. And his rage continued throughout the extremely uncomfortable night of his humiliation and into the following afternoon. It was with rage still in his heart that he sailed down the hill toward Wildlingen straight into the burgomaster's office.

This burgomaster, whose name was Hundlinger, was both district Party leader and district commissioner and thus a man of some importance and influence, with his finger in every pie. Nevertheless, Hundlinger had Captain Kater shown in at once, for Kater himself was a universally respected figure. It set Kater's mind at rest to have this amount of notice taken of him: he felt it a flattering tribute to his personality. Here at least people knew how to value and respect him, here at least he was someone.

"And what can I do for you, my dear Captain Kater!" cried Hundlinger. For him the captain was a valued liaison officer between the training school and the population, an embodiment of one of the three pillars of the greater German Reich—the Wehrmacht. The other two pillars—Party and State—he, Hundlinger, embodied himself.

"I thought I'd just look in, as I was passing," said Kater disingenuously.

"Always delighted to welcome you," replied Hundlinger, no less disingenuously. He had seen through Kater in the first ten seconds. Hundlinger knew from long experienne that Kater was an extremely cunning businessman who never did anything without an eye to the main chance. Hundlinger was thus prepared for Kater to make all sorts of demands, which suited him very well, for he had all sorts of demands of his own to make on Kater.

"Yes, well there is one thing bothering me," said Kater finally, with evident frankness. "Something to do with Herr Rotunda."

"Aha!" said Hundlinger, thinking to himself, Rotunda, a small vineyard proprietor and landlord of The Gay Dog; a

Party member of relatively recent date without much influence. Small fry, in fact. But of course there was no need for Kater to know that.

Kater now really pitched into Rotunda, hoping to start off an avalanche which would sweep Krafft, and perhaps Feders too, together with their entire section, to disaster. This fellow Rotunda, declared Kater, had left him shamefully in the lurch. The man was an innkeeper of doubtful repute—weak, easily influenced, and utterly unreliable. Not the right man for such times as these.

"He appealed to me to help him. I had no thought of getting anything out of it for myself but I'm not inhuman, so I intervened on his behalf up at the training school. But what does this fellow Rotunda do? He suddenly backs out altogether. He lets himself be talked out of it by the cadets and simply carries on as if nothing had happened. Of course the cadets had themselves been got at. And now there I am looking a real fool, just because once again I've tried to play the honest broker in the interests of the civilian population, while all I get for my pains is ingratitude and misunderstanding."

Hundlinger put on a thoughtful sort of expression. The material side of the business was quite clear in his mind—not much to be made out of it—a truck for a week, at the most. Unless, of course, Captain Kater had some special personal stake in the affair, which was always possible. A crafty fellow like him wouldn't make a full-blown intrigue out of a trifle without good reason. A telephone call would have sufficed. So what lay behind all this? Hundlinger continued to fish for information.

"Just leave it to me," he said generously. "I'll have a talk with Rotunda and make him see he must do as you say."

"That's not quite what I meant," said Kater immediately.

Hundlinger pulled his massive frame together in his chair. At the same time he made a mental note to increase his price. He would now ask for two trucks, for two weeks, with drivers, drivers' mates, and gas.

"I'll do anything for you, my dear Captain," he declared. "After all, our collaboration has always been extremely profitable and must of course continue. I'll—er—keep Rotunda in line myself, without bringing your name into it."

"We understand each other perfectly," said Kater. "But there's one more point I'd like to make—namely, that I regard it as imperative for Rotunda to address himself to the general in person. The general in person. That's most important."

Whereupon they clinched the deal. The officers' training school would put a working party with two trucks at the disposal of the town of Wildlingen-am-Main for two weeks, nominally for "relief works." Gas to be paid for by the training school. Work to be determined by the burgomaster. Hundlinger for his part contracted to "clear up the matter under discussion."

They separated as they had met; brothers under the skin— guardians and custodians of public property and patriotic feeling. "There are still some Germans one can rely on, thank God!" Thank God indeed. Their two hearts beat as one.

Hundlinger, the civilian ruler of Wildlingen, now got to work with astonishing speed and with complete success. One telephone call sufficed. A private hint of a possible checkup on the way Rotunda's business was being run was enough to get him to agree to everything.

"I don't want to influence you, of course, in any way, my dear Rotunda," said Hundlinger, entirely in his capacity as district Party leader. "I'm merely giving you a piece of advice."

"I quite understand, District Leader," said the latter humbly.

"What you do, you do entirely voluntarily. I am not giving you any orders. If things ever come to the point where I have to give orders, my dear Rotunda, then I warn you I can be utterly ruthless. At such times friendship means nothing to me and only the Party's interests count. We don't want it to come to that, now, do we?"

"Of course not, District Leader."

"Right, then, my dear Rotunda, we understand each other. It's just as I expected. So go straight up and put the matter before the general—the general in person! That's all you have to do."

"I'm very grateful to you for seeing me, Herr General," said Rotunda, the landlord.

"Don't beat about the bush, please," said Major-General Modersohn. "What is it you want to see me about?"

Rotunda presented his case succinctly. There had been a brawl, his entire bar had been destroyed, insults had been hurled at civilian guests—all this had been the work of Section H for Heinrich. In the course of this recital, however,

Rotunda began to feel thoroughly uncomfortable. Not because his conscience was plaguing him at all, but because of the feeling that he was talking to a statue.

Modersohn sat as usual quite motionless in his chair. His face seemed turned to stone, and his eyes never flickered, remaining trained on Rotunda throughout. When Rotunda had finally come to the end of his statement the major-general merely asked, "Have you put all this in writing, Herr Rotunda?"

"Yes, indeed, Herr General!" cried the latter enthusiastically, almost relieved to find that the silent giant could speak. Rotunda had automatically leapt to attention. The instinctive reactions of a German civilian did not desert him; he was glad to pay his tribute of respect to the military. Slightly awkwardly, yet happy to be able to respond to a high-ranking officer's command, he handed the general his written complaint. "I took the liberty of preparing it in the form of a sort of informative report."

Modersohn took the sheet of paper without moving a muscle in the upper part of his body—he merely stretched out his hand. He laid the manuscript down on top of his desk and said; "You'll be hearing from me, Herr Rotunda."

Rotunda, the landlord and vineyard proprietor, saw at once that his audience was at an end. He shot up a hand in the Hitler salute, but the general took not the slightest notice of it. Modersohn was busy reading the document through slowly and apparently with great thoroughness.

"Heil Hitler, Herr General!" cried Rotunda.

"Good day to you," said the general without looking up.

"Fräulein Bachner to see me, please," ordered the general.

Sybille came tripping into the room wearing her hair long and wavy with a well-fitting beige dress. She took up her position in front of the general, with her left foot placed attractively at a slight angle, and said, "Yes, General?"

Major-General Modersohn cast a quick, surprised glance at his secretary. Her appearance had been becoming more and more feminine recently. But Sybille detected no particular expression of disapproval in his eyes, which made her very happy. Less than three seconds later she realized that she had not the slightest grounds for her happiness.

"Take a memo," said the general dryly, getting down to business. "Accompanying document to Number Two Course Headquarters. Urgent. Comment required."

The general put the document which Rotunda the landlord

had handed him down on the right-hand side of his desk. Which meant, dealt with—exit! Modersohn never handed a document directly to his secretary.

"That's all," he said in conclusion.

This embarrassing document landed half an hour later on the desk of the officer in command of Number 2 Course, Major Frey. The first thing he read was the general's own laconic note, "Comment required," which was simply one of the usual formulae and had no particular significance.

But then the major read the accompanying document written by Rotunda and this upset him considerably. He even turned slightly pale.

The major's modest pallor was understandable enough, first because of the resuscitation of something which Frey imagined had already been dealt with, and secondly because this meant—and the color of the major's face slowly turned from white to red as he realized the fact—that his embarrassing Special Order number 131 might now once again come up for discussion. The matter was extremely serious! If the general were to discover that this unfortunate special order of his had been the immediate cause of the brawl, the consequences didn't bear thinking of. Frey saw himself involved in a series of desperate complications.

But the major, too, was a man who knew his military practice. He was well aware of the advantages of sticking to the prescribed methods of procedure. Not only did they, if properly handled, provide one with a breathing space, they also made it possible for a really skilled person—and he considered himself such—to shuffle off responsibility, preferably onto the people below him.

Major Frey therefore enlarged the document before him wih the following note: "Most urgent! Passed for immediate appropriate comment to the CO of No. 6 Company."

Thus the file automatically drifted on a stage further. Its next resting point was Captain Ratshelm, who first read his commanding officer's note, then the general's, and finally Rotunda's document itself.

Ratshelm was, as ever, ready to respect the views and decisions of his superiors. More than that, he was as ever anxious to emulate them and follow their example. He didn't much like the way things were developing, but had to accept the inevitable, and thus promptly handed the whole business on one stage further.

Captain Ratshelm's addition to the file ran as follows:

"Extremely urgent. Detailed comment required without delay. Passed to the responsible quarter—Section Officer of Section H for Heinrich."

This file, which had now been handed on three times, finally reached Lieutenant Krafft.

The lieutenant was in the middle of a class on paper work and correspondence when it arrived. He, too, first of all read the bald annotations of his superiors. He noted immediately that "urgent" had transformed itself into "most urgent" and that this in its turn had finally become "extremely urgent." But Krafft derived no pleasure from this. He saw at once that Rotunda's document was a dangerous business, and he read it through twice, concentrating on it carefully.

His cadets seemed to sense that there was something unpleasant about what he was reading, and they began to feel uneasy. With the sure instinct of sorely tried, carefully watched, perpetually supervised candidates for a commission, they smelled trouble. Their section officer's expression told them more than enough.

"Gentlemen," announced the lieutenant finally, looking up, "while we're on the subject of paper work I won't keep from you a good example of a properly formulated complaint from the civilian population that comes to hand. Listen well."

Once again Lieutenant Krafft had had a really bright idea. He read through the whole of the document in front of him without omitting a single word, beginning with the letter heading and the date—March 5, 1944—and ending with the annotations of the officer in command of the company.

When Lieutenant Krafft had finished, a heavy silence settled over the class. Kramer, the section senior, snorted indignantly. Rednitz's eyes opened wide. Hochbauer bit his lips. Mösler simply said out loud, "What a lousy dirty trick!" Whereupon not a few cadets nodded vigorously, muttering agreement.

"Friends," said Krafft restrainingly, "I forbid you to make any personal comment. What we're concerned with here, in the first instance, is simply an illustration for our lesson. I don't want any polemics, nothing but concise, matter-of-fact comments. Do you see?"

The cadets were beginning to understand. They had learned a lot during the four weeks in which Lieutenant Krafft had been their section officer. He had taught them to look for the essentials and avoid the pitfalls. He had freed them from the jungle of written regulations in a downright but effective manner, and the process was now slowly beginning to bear fruit. Just because of this, the lieutenant was now in a position to acquaint them, under the threadbare guise of "paper work," with a matter that was red hot.

Mösler was one of the first to realize what was up, and naturally reacted after his own fashion. He got to his feet beaming, and declared, "I recommend that the following addition should be made to the document under consideration: 'Urgent! Most urgent! Extremely urgent! Duly passed, by section officer, via section senior, with the request for a detailed, immediate, and extremely rapid comment, to Cadet Hochbauer, who according to his own view of himself knows everything and can explain anything.'"

The secion burst out laughing with relief. The laugh was at the expense of Hochbauer, who looked daggers at Mösler. Lieutenant Krafft, however, generously overlooked this diversion. "Responsibility for documents of this sort usually rests with the last officer to receive it," he explained. "So just try and pretend for a moment that you're already officers. I'm curious to know how things will develop."

Rednitz now put up his hand and received permission to air his views. He rose to his feet and declared, "A report, whatever its origin, should first be tested for its veracity. It's by no means rare for the contents then to turn out not to fit the facts at all or at least only very inaccurately."

"Quite possible, Rednitz," admitted Lieutenant Krafft. "But you overlook the fact that this particular file is dated today."

"There must be some misunderstanding," gulped Kramer. "We cleared the whole matter up to everyone's satisfaction."

For Rednitz there was something a little too blatant about Kramer's comment. "When one looks into these things more closely," he said, "a word in the right place, in conjunction with adequate compensation, is often enough to settle matters to everyone's satisfaction without the need for any written complaint at all."

"How would such an arrangement work out in practice?" asked Krafft curiously.

The information the lieutenant received was exhaustive and complete. For instance, you go to the man concerned, give him your hand, are very friendly with him, explain to him how it all happened, try and win him around, offer him generous compensation, even eventually give him additional money for his pains, and finally shake hands on it again.

In this way Krafft learned every detail of the conciliatory action which his cadets had taken on the Sunday without ever having had to ask directly. Everyone was only too eager and anxious to give him the details. Admittedly there was a small group around Hochbauer which took no part in this spontaneous demonstration of confidence but maintained a noncommittal attitude of reserve throughout. Even this attitude, however, was welcome to Krafft.

"Extremely interesting points of view," said the lieutenant, closing the file again. "I'm now going to leave you alone for a period. The section senior will take command in the meantime, and so that you don't get too bored, you'll write me a letter of condolence on the occasion of the death of my second cousin. She died the day before yesterday. Is that clear?"

The cadets looked utterly astonished for a moment, and then broke into broad grins. This was a real piece of vintage Krafft again. They were no longer capable of being surprised by anything he thought up—the only thing that worried them slightly was his failure to specify a definite length of time for their letter writing. How many minutes had they got? Presumably it depended on where Lieutenant Krafft was going—to the toilet, to his billet, to see his company commander, or even down to Wildlingen for a glass of wine.

Meanwhile Krafft had buckled on his belt and put on his cap. Yet before he finally left he had one more shaft in store for them. He was already at the door and the section senior had shouted "Attention!" and the cadets were standing there like pillars of salt, when Lieutenant Krafft turned around again and said quietly but very precisely, "Hochbauer, you could have taken somewhat greater part in our communal attempts to settle this affair—at least as much as you did in the brawl itself, in which you were not unprominent."

Thus was Cadet Hochbauer once again unmistakably branded. He sat very erect and upright on his bench, not daring to make any comment. Caution seemed required, for the majority of the cadets were in sympathy with Krafft at the moment.

"Gentlemen," said Cadet Egon Weber amid general approval after Krafft had gone, "we're really in the shit now. But if anyone can get us out of it then it's our lieutenant."

"How's he going to do so is a mystery to me," said Mösler. "After all, he's not a magician."

But Böhmke, the poet, loosed off one of his quotations from *Faust*:

> *"For the noble soul has power*
> *To compass all if wise and swift."*

"I'd like to speak to the general," said Krafft.

Lieutenant Bieringer, the ADC, looked up from his work. He thoroughly disapproved of the visitor's manner and tone. This wasn't the way in which soldiers, and above all, officers, were expected to behave in these sacred precincts. Bieringer, however, astonishingly wasted no further time on such thoughts, but merely looked toward Sybille Bachner, who said affably, "The general is expecting you."

"Me?" asked Krafft incredulously.

Sybille nodded. "He's been expecting you for the last hour. Go straight in."

Krafft cleared his throat. Things were moving so rapidly that he felt he could hardly keep up with them. He pulled himself together, adjusted his uniform, and walked into the general's room, as usual without knocking.

"Well?" asked Modersohn, looking the lieutenant over with steely eyes. "Carry on."

"Sir, I've come about the brawl in which my section was involved, in the bar known as The Gay Dog."

"Leave out the preliminaries," said Modersohn. "Come to the point, Lieutenant."

"Sir," said the Lieutenant, "this fellow Rotunda's complaint is founded on fact. The brawl did take place and had the usual origins: alcohol, women, the general atmosphere of the place. But the next day my section went to clear the matter up, and Rotunda was won around. Whereupon to all intents and purposes the matter was closed. But a day later someone got this fellow Rotunda to change his mind, clearly with the express purpose of striking at me."

"Who got him to change his mind, Lieutenant?"

"Captain Kater," said Krafft firmly.

"Why?" asked the general at once.

"For several reasons, sir."

"Which reason in particular, Krafft?"

"A woman, sir," said Krafft. He was convinced that his greatest chance of extricating himself from this affair without harm lay in complete frankness. "The person in question is Fräulein Rademacher."

"I've heard of the lady," said the general, rising to his feet. Then, after a significant pause, he said, "Lieutenant Krafft, first of all I congratulate you on your engagement. Then, however, I must express to you my disapproval—not on account of the brawl, these things happen—but on account of the inadequate manner in which the affair was handled. I dislike it when the task of clearing up after my officers falls to me. Kindly arrange for Herr Rotunda to come and see me without delay. Further, inform my ADC that Captain Kater is to report to me as soon as possible. You, Lieutenant, will hold yourself at my disposal. That's all for the present."

Shortly afterward Major-General Modersohn had what was commonly referred to among his entourage as a "field day."

The first person who sprang to attention in front of him was Captain Kater.

"Captain Kater," said the general, probing ruthlessly, "did you take any part in the affair of the brawl in The Gay Dog?"

"If I may explain, sir . . ."

"Yes or no, Kater?"

"Yes, sir, because I thought . . ."

"I'm not interested in what you thought, Captain—only in what happened. This affair has severely damaged the reputation of the officers' training school. Prepare to hand over your job as CO of the headquarters company. I will make arrangements for your replacement. Until this occurs an officer will be attached to you without whose consent you are to make no further decisions in the future. The officer I have in mind is Captain Feders. You are dismissed now, Captain Kater."

The second person the general got in his sights was Herr Rotunda.

"Herr Rotunda," said the general, "I've read your complaint and made the relevant inquiries. And I'm wondering whether you really wish to press this complaint, or whether perhaps you might not be making a mistake."

"General," said Rotunda with remarkable modesty, "I'm doing no more than insisting on my rights here."

"No one denies them to you, Herr Rotunda. I'd merely like to put another point of view to you."

"And what would that be, General?"

"Herr Rotunda," said Modersohn solemnly, "if everything in your report should in fact turn out to be true, and if I were thus compelled to carry out a full-scale investigation, an example would presumably have to be made of the guilty cadets."

"After all, the law is the law, General."

"Of course, Herr Rotunda, and I am just pointing out to

you some of its inevitable consequences. Right, then, Herr Rotunda, should it transpire that your complaint is justified, then I should have to put your bar out of bounds to all troops. The ban would be widely advertised. Moreover I would reserve the right to apply to the burgomaster and district commissioner for your bar to be closed altogether."

"But," stammered Rotunda, utterly flabbergasted, "you can't do that . . ."

"Oh yes I can, and will," said Modersohn. "Unless of course there's some mistake about your report and you wish to withdraw it."

The wildest pictures flashed through Rotunda's mind—the door of The Gay Dog heavily barricaded; sullen, menacing-looking sentries standing in front of it; a notice in the *Wildlinger Beobachter* which read: "Germans—boycott Rotunda!" He shuddered. The thoughts continued to race through his mind—Rotunda—enemy of the people—hunt him down, smash his property—he has no right to it—give his wine to the pigs—he has shown himself unworthy of the times in which we live, a subversive influence and a traitor—liquidate him!"

But most of all Rotunda's mind focused on one point. An idea had suddenly occurred to him. It seemed like a sheet anchor. For what was it that he had promised the burgomaster, district Party leader and district commissioner? Merely to go and see the general and put in his complaint! That was all. Nothing else had been agreed. What was to come of the complaint had never been discussed. It was therefore with considerable relief that Rotunda hastened to declare, "It was a mistake, General. I withdraw my complaint."

The third person the general had up before him that day was Lieutenant Krafft.

"Lieutenant," said the general, this time in a tone of pained regret, "you've been a disappointment to me."

"I'm sorry about that, sir," said Krafft.

"So am I," said Modersohn. "I've already asked you once not to embark on any questionable adventures, so that I should not again have to intervene on your behalf. I requested you to concentrate instead on a certain matter which I considered important. Why are you not doing so?"

"It all hangs together, in a sort of way, sir," ventured Krafft.

"This brawl and your engagement? The enmity of Captain Kater and your running controversy with your course commander and company CO? All this is in some way connected with Lieutenant Barkow, or alternatively with the man who blew him to pieces?"

"Sir," said Krafft, risking all in one last bold leap, "I have never let the matter out of my sight for a single instant."

"And what progress have you made, Krafft?"

"I could give you now the name of the only cadet it could possibly have been, sir, but I still lack the final proof. However I am on the point of obtaining it."

Major-General Modersohn stood back from Krafft as if this enabled him to see him better, to make more certain of him. His eyes—now steely gray, and hard as ice, never left the lieutenant's face for a second. But the severe aloofness of his manner gradually relaxed.

"Good," said the general. "You've still got a few days Krafft. But then I want to see results one way or the other! See you don't get involved in any more incidents! I warn you, you can't count on any more help from me. Now leave me alone."

* * * *

Intermediate Report No. 8

THE CURRICULUM VITAE OF CADET OTTO MÖSLER, OR THE JOYS OF THE CAREFREE

My name is Mösler, Otto. I was born in 1922 on May 1. The name of my birthplace was Klein-Zachnow, district of Lückenwalde. My father, whose Christian name was also Otto, was then working on the state railways. My mother, Emma, was born a Kressenfuss. We lived, at first, in Klein-Zachnow, where I went to primary school.

The horse in the stable at home is called Wilhelm—Wilhelm III, in fact, for it's the third horse called Wilhelm. Besides, it belongs to my grandfather, who is very loyal to the Kaiser, and a policeman by profession. Grandfather Kressenfuss, my mother's father, is like a little king in our village—when the great landowner von Keibel isn't about. And von Keibel is seldom about. He's almost always in Berlin, playing at politics. So my grandfather, the policeman, has a free hand and orders the entire village around, including his own daughter, my mother. He also orders my father around, who curses him in secret.

"That oaf gets on my nerves," says my father of his father-in-law. "He's a good man," says my mother. "Besides, we live in his house. You must earn more money before you can afford to sneer at him."

Grandfather Kressenfuss, the policeman, can do everything. He rides, ploughs, mows, arrests people. When he sings in church, you can hear him from the inn. But when he sings in the inn, the entire village hears him. He has a whole milk can filled with beer, which he places in front of him and drinks to the dregs. He stands there with feet astride, his shiny face red as a beet, with the beer running out of the corners of his mouth, onto his collar, and the teacher, who can't drink anything, says, "A decent stomach rejects alcohol." And all Grandfather, the policeman Kressenfuss, has to say is, "Miserable worm!"

"I'm fed up with this life of ours," says Father. "I've got to get out of here, or I'll suffocate." "You're certainly never going to amount to much on the railway," says my mother. "You aren't even an official." "That's because I don't want to be an official!" replies my father. "But after all I'm still young. I'm going to make my own way in life. I'm off to Berlin!" "And what's to become of Otto and me?" my mother asks. "You'll follow on afterward," says my father, adding, "As soon as I've made good."

The brass band plays, a flag flutters in the breeze, and the ex-servicemen's association marches past. Von Keibel, the big landowner, takes the salute. He has put on his reserve officer's uniform for the occasion. One of my uncles is marching in the front rank, another in the third, and another in the eighth. I am singing with the school choir—leading it in fact. Mother waves a handkerchief at my uncles. Grandfather Kressenfuss is in his element, being responsible for law and order in his role as village policeman. Yet when von Keibel speaks of Germany, of the shameful Treaty of Versailles, and of the stab in the back, my grandfather also furtively wipes a tear from his eye—the left eye. I pass him a handkerchief.

The uncle in the fourth rank is a particularly nice man. Since Father went to Berlin, where he too is playing at politics, this uncle has become particularly attentive to Mother. He's always very nice to me and knows exactly what sort of chocolate I like best. He seizes me by the hair and shakes my head and laughs—he laughs at me and at my mother. And he also sometimes laughs when he is with my mother in the next room. But mostly when he's there I just hear him groaning.

"Order is what we need," says Kressenfuss the police-man, my grandfather. He drinks up his beer and stares thoughtfully ahead of him. "You're my daughter," he says to my mother, "which is why you know the meaning of the word 'order.' " Again he takes a drink of beer. "You," he says to me, "are my grandson. One day you too will know the meaning of the word." "I already know the difference between right and wrong," I tell him. He nods and smiles, and pushes his beer toward me and lets me take a drink.

Suddenly my father is there again. He's doing very well—you can tell from his suit and the way he talks. "I've made good," he says, "I'm onto a good thing at last. We're on the threshold of a new era, and I've seen it coming in time. I'm with the Secret Police now. Doesn't that surprise you?" We are indeed surprised. My grandfather's mouth drops wide open. And my mother asks, "Is it well paid?" "Best of the lot!" says my father.

In the summer of 1933 we moved to Berlin, where my father's job was. We lived in the Uhlandstrasse, Charlotten-burg. In 1936 my schooldays came to an end, and I was apprenticed to a firm of plumbers called Rahmke.

Here in Berlin things aren't so very different from Klein-Zachnow. There are just more people about, but they are no different. Instead of two inns, there are two hundred, perhaps even two thousand. But people are the same everywhere when they're drunk. In the village there were four or five swindlers, seven adulterers, and one thief; one man seduced children, six adulterated food stuffs, two were drunks—and it's just the same here in town, except that here there are hundreds and hundreds more of them. The streets are straight here, like furrows in the fields, and cars stand about like horses, and in the bars beer actually comes out of the taps. And, wherever one looks, swastikas and the color of shit. Here, too, there are uncles who pay particular attention to my mother when Father's away. All just as in Klein-Zachnow—except that there are more of them here, many more.

Her name is Magda and she lives in the house with us. I'm very fond of her and she is fond of me. She must be around thirty. She is always either standing up or lying down. She does her standing up on the corner of the Uhlandstrasse and the Kurfürstendamm. She does her lying down in her bed alone when I'm with her, but with someone else when the door's shut. "Poor boy," she says to me sometimes and hugs me tight. I find myself panting for breath. But she is full of warmth and everyone is very fond of her. Including my father, whenever he's at home.

"Otto Mösler," the teacher asks, "what do you want to be when you grow up?" "I don't know!" "But you know everything else!" says the teacher. "Not that, though," I reply. "Well," he says, "you must have some particular inclination, haven't you?" "Well yes," I say, "best of all I'd like to be Magda's steady." "Shame on you!" he cries. "How could you say such a thing!" Which makes it clear that even he knows perfectly well who Magda is.

"The boy knows too much," my mother tells my father one day when he comes back home. "That's better than knowing too little anyway," replies my father. But my mother says, "He's learning all sorts of filthy things!" "Not from me," says my father. "You ought to set him an example," my mother replies, "he needs one badly." "You may be right," returns my father . . . "I'll try to take a bit of trouble with him sometimes, and teach him what life has to offer."

"Otto," my father says to me, "your schooldays will soon be over and then you'll have to learn a decent trade." "Can't I be what you are?" I ask him. "Better leave that alone, Otto," says my father. "That's not for you. Look now, your grandfather was an official, and that was good enough for Klein-Zachnow. But being with the Secret Police I get to see quite a bit of life. I know where the best pickings are to be had. They say that trade is the basis of all prosperity, but a trade and a business together is the way to grow really fat."

The plumber to whom I and another boy are apprenticed is called Rahmke. "You've got to learn to look at our clients from two points of view—their arses and their purses. After all we're plumbers, and customers are going to be content only if they can settle down to their business comfortably. We must make it our aim to see that they can. So remember purses and arses. And note that the two usually go together. That's what's called psychology. For only someone who's in a position to eat a lot is in a position to . . . well exactly!" We see what he means at once, for he's a great joker besides being a good businessman. I tell Father about this and he says, "That old swine Rahmke's got a marvelous sense of humor!"

She doesn't seem very experienced, but I'm told this heightens the charm. We go on the Ferris wheel for the third time; and the ground flies away from us, and the lights flicker and every now and again she lets out a scream—

for example when, as if I just wanted to hold on, I make a grab at her breast, which is round and firm. And I ask myself, "Is she only playing up, or doesn't she really want to?" But then she starts clinging to me and her fingers fasten on my thigh. I take her off to get a breath of air in the dark at the back of the fairground. I find her very attractive, I'm absolutely mad about her, and it's the first time it's going to happen. But suddenly she pushes me away as if she's taken leave of her senses. She hits me and screams, "You swine!" and runs away. I stare after her, thinking she can't be normal.

"Listen to me a moment, Otto," my father says to me. "You're no fool, which is a good thing. But you haven't had much experience of life so far, which is why I'd like to put you wise about a thing or two. The most important thing of all to learn is that there's no one you can't break in the end. Anyone you like can be reduced to pulp, given time. The only difference between the so-called strong man and the others is that it takes a little more time to bring him to his knees, that's all. Today I had a fellow up in front of me for interrogation—a complete softy. He was sweating by the end of an hour, slobbering after two hours, and after three hours' interrogation he was looking about him like a stuck pig. The man bored me. Another three hours and he'd told me everything I wanted to know. Tomorrow he'll swear anything I tell him to, and for the time being even believe it himself. For the time being. But not the day after tomorrow, though it's too late by then. You see, Otto, that's how men are. Everything about them is imperfect, even their weakness."

I've been saving for this moment for several weeks. I go into Magda's room, put the money down in front of her, and say, "Is that enough?" "You little idiot," says Magda. "Put your money away at once." "Don't you want to?" I ask. I feel terribly disappointed. "Oh, you little idiot," says Magda. "Who said I didn't want to? But why do you want to pay for something you can have for nothing? Don't look so stupid. Close the door."

My apprenticeship ended in 1939. I was called up the same year for military service. I served in various units and was finally recommended for a commission and posted to the officers' training school.

Being in the army is really very like being at school. There's not much anyone can teach me—I know most of it already. But anyone in a position of authority likes to make his authority felt. Well let him, if it makes him feel happy! As far as I'm concerned, it makes no difference to me whether a man behaves like a peacock or a stuck pig.

"Otto," my father says to me when I come home in uniform for the first time, "you're a man now and I want to talk to you like a man. Put a few bottles of beer on the ice, Emma, and leave us alone. What we have to discuss isn't for women's ears. Right, Otto, now there are just the two of us I want to tell you my views on life. Namely, I don't think anything of it at all! Got me? Absolutely nothing at all. It's all a lot of shit.

"Otto, I've seen a lot of corpses in my lifetime, and quite a number of corpses who were still alive. Produced on the conveyer belt—not only by us, but by the force commonly known as life. For what becomes of a man? He turns into a corpse. That's all there is to it. That's life, Otto. Never forget it!"

One gets to know people in a war like this. There's some monster of a human being cowering behind every corner; some megalomaniac superior officer, some whimpering coward, some fanatical idealist, some drooling general—to hell with the lot of them!

I can't see properly any more. My skull throbs, and my eyes keep closing. Someone yells my name and I force myself to open my eyes. My head swims and the bottles standing in front of me on the table seem to dance about and the dim light dances with them. And through the smoke, through the empty sea of bottles, through the light, I see the girl lying on a sofa. And I see an open mouth, with a little spit dribbling out of the corners, I see her swaying breasts which seem to be coming up toward me. And my comrades hurl the naked girl at me. But I feel ill, I vomit! Man, am I drunk! Man, did we laugh!

Gottlieb Degersweiler feels drawn toward me for some reason. He doesn't seem to have much luck with women and I help him with them sometimes. This has its advantages, for Gottlieb is a military policeman and has friends in the baking and butchering companies. From time to time he puts on a private show for me. The badge around his neck which identifies him as a military policeman shakes lightly as he wrenches the brief case away from the officer. The latter makes a grab for it, but Gottlieb closes his hand over the man's fingers and bends them back. The officer tries to pull his rank. But Gottlieb simply says, "Shut your trap, man." The brief case is locked. Gottlieb demands the key from the officer, but he won't give it up. Drivels on about official papers or something. Gottlieb rips the brief case open with his bayonet. Contents: cigarettes and tinned foods. It's always the same. "Confiscated!" says Gottlieb. "Under arrest!" says Gottlieb.

Her name is Marita Schiffers and I've got her away from a major. This hasn't been difficult, because the major is a tired man and Marita has tasted blood. She is abandoned as war itself and as obedient as the rawest recruit. She'll do anything I ask of her. She rolls over at a touch. I go to her during the day, at night, in the early morning, and say "Come on!" and she does whatever I say. I feel I need her because she makes a sort of sense of my life. She does this for me because she can't help it. Because she wants anything I want, because my wants are her only wishes. The world is in the palm of your hand if you only realize it.

But then comes the day when I have nothing but digust for Marita Schiffers. I return her to the major, who is deeply touched. He almost weeps for joy and is anxious to show his gratitude. Which is how I get recommended for a commission.

25 *CADET HOCHBAUER SLIPS UP*

"A REPULSIVE FELLOW," said Cadet Hochbauer with feeling, looking at Lieutenant Krafft as he stood at the instructor's desk. Naturally Hochbauer said this only in a whisper, and even his close companions seemed not to have heard. Nevertheless he said it, which showed how honest and outspoken he was.

For Cadet Hochbauer had recognized that Lieutenant Krafft was no friend of his. Though it didn't require any great effort to recognize it, Hochbauer had done everything he could to shy away from it. Now, however, he had no doubts left, and for the first time intended to draw his own conclusions.

Hochbauer was always prepared to tackle people who saw things differently from him. He saw the world as a place full of obstacles in which the man who desired victory had to fight for it first. He knew all about the vermin that had to be crushed if anything was to be achieved. St. George, who had killed the dragon, had always been one of his heroes, in spite of his ecclesiastical origin. Hochbauer's own dragons of course bore foreign, Jewish features, or looked about them with hypocritical Christian meekness, or, like this fellow Krafft, barred the way to true progress with boorish, barbaric cunning. "Scum!" hissed Hochbauer to himself.

"Gentlemen," said Lieutenant Krafft, holding a bunch of papers up in the air, "I recently went so far as to inspire you to write me a formal letter of condolence on the occasion of the supposed death of my second cousin. Well, I have the result here, and I can tell you that not only do they come up to my wildest expectations, they even exceed them."

The cadets sitting behind Hochbauer laughed inanely, or so it seemed to him. Most of them were simply guided by the herd instinct, which was inevitable enough, for after all, exceptional people were rare—it was just their rarity that made them exceptional. Hochbauer considered himself exceptional enough, but recognized that membership of an elite brought specific obligations with it, such as the conquest of evil, the rejection of vulgarity, and the removal of all obstacles to progress.

Lieutenant Krafft, however, thought Hochbauer, was more than a mere obstacle to progress, he was a positive menace. The longer Hochbauer observed him, the clearer did this seem to become. Take this officer's appearance alone—how aggressively scruffy it was, how boorish his whole manner! None of that lean gracefulness which betrayed an inner tension. No awareness of membership of the Führer's masterful elite. Nowhere a trace of the classical good looks which denoted racial purity. A wily road-sweeper of war—that was all he was.

"I freely admit," said Lieutenant Krafft with a wink, "that I was deeply impressed by my section's sympathy on this tragic occasion, and I wouldn't like to miss this opportunity of reading out a few particularly moving lines. For instance my bald announcement wasn't enough for Cadet Berger, who took the trouble to buy a newspaper and wrote: 'I have read the tragic news in the papers, and now, my dear Herr Krafft, the painful loss which you have just sustained crystallizes into unbearable certainty.'"

The cadets laughed. Hochbauer turned and looked at them contemptuously. This fellow Krafft, he felt forced to admit, was a thoroughly subversive element. The very yeast of decomposition, as Treitshke had put it. Constructive thinking was entirely foreign to his nature. He was lacking in all moral purpose, and had no sense of the German people's dedication to eternal values. The fellow Krafft was an embodiment of all that was depraved and poisonous and alien to the German race. He must have Jewish blood somewhere.

"Cadet Mösler," continued Krafft, reading from the messages of condolence, "even discloses a secret affair of the heart in the following remarkable passage: 'Still crushed by the news of the decease of your cousin, whom we treasured so dearly, I search in vain for the right words . . .' Well, that last remark is to the point, all right; and as for the dearly treasured cousin of whom several others also wrote, I can only hope that no one was trying to establish closer relations with me with a view to getting through the course more easily."

Hopeless, thought Cadet Hochbauer. No sense of greatness, of profundity, of worth or dignity. No word about the Fatherland, the German people, the German Reich and its Führer. Nothing but these subversive cynical phrases. And this at a time when the final struggle was at hand. At such a moment as this, the fellow was confusing the simple yet sensitive minds of a few wretched, trusting, easily seduced cadets. On examination it amounted to treason.

Naturally Lieutenant Krafft had no idea of the devastating criticism he was being subjected to. To the unrestrained delight of the majority of the cadets he calmly continued to quote from the various messages of condolence. "Our friend Böhmke unleashes a veritable volcano of emotion and writes: 'Now she is gone from you, most honored Herr Krafft. She was so young and yet has faded from our sight. I feel for you in your agony. It is barely supportable, and yet it had to be.' "

This passage was greeted with a roar of laughter, but Cadet Hochbauer still didn't entirely give up hope. It was still possible even at this stage that the lesson might develop a serious turn. A number of possibilities existed. For instance there was the thought that the German word for cousin ("Cousine") was of foreign derivation and appeared to require Germanization. Furthermore the subject of death announcements and letters of condolence as a whole lent itself to discussion, with particular reference to exemplary, heroic bearing in such great times as these. Hochbauer felt himself thoroughly capable of giving a constructive note to the period himself. He sat up very straight and looked toward the lieutenant, thus indicating in the approved manner that he was ready and willing to be asked to speak.

But Lieutenant Krafft looked straight past Hochbauer, neither quoting from the cadet's message of condolence nor putting a question to him. It was as if, for Krafft, Hochbauer had simply ceased to exist.

There followed a further seven or eight extracts, which led to further outbursts of hilarity. Just another ruse to win over these gullible cadets, thought Hochbauer contemptuously. They had to be protected in their own interests.

But Lieutenant Krafft now concluded, "I must say I'm deeply moved," and without changing his expression in the slightest added dryly, "When sympathy is expressed in this form it really must be a positive pleasure to die."

Hochbauer wrote this sentence, or rather the essential part of it, down in his notebook, and again looked up inquiringly at Lieutenant Krafft.

The next subject for discussion was disciplinary punishment, with particular attention to the way in which it was formulated, recorded, and carried out. For this purpose the section officer let one of the cadets read from official regulations, while he himself leaned against the wall at the back of the room, apparently staring disinterestedly into space. He even yawned once and all he said was, "Louder! Otherwise everyone here will fall asleep."

Hochbauer continued to take stock of the situation. He became more and more convinced that if he was to survive the course successfully—and if possible come out on top— some decisive step was required. There were a number of elements in his favor: Captain Ratshelm the company commander had unmistakable feelings of warmth and sympathy toward him. Captain Feders, the tactics instructor, always gave his work the highest marks. He even had a certain intimate contact with Major Frey, his course commander. Lieutenant Krafft was the only obstacle, and one that was becoming increasingly insuperable.

"It can't go on like this indefinitely," remarked Cadet Hochbauer rather more loudly than before—for Krafft was now at the back of the room.

The cadets in Hochbauer's vicinity instinctively bent low, pretending to be completely absorbed in their notes. Hochbauer laughed contemptuously.

"If you've anything to say, Hochbauer," cried Krafft promptly from the back of the room, "kindly say it out loud so that everyone can hear it. Well, what is it?"

"Nothing, sir," replied the latter stiffly.

"So you've nothing to say, and you admit it! Well, that's something. Sounds most convincing in fact. But in that case one can't help asking how strong your convictions really are?"

"Tell me, Hochbauer," asked Amfortas, his roommate, confidentially when they were back in their billet. "Has this Lieutenant Krafft got something against you?"

"I've got something against him," replied Hochbauer nonchalantly. "And he knows it and doesn't like it."

They were alone in the room. The midday break had just started and it was a good opportunity for a private conversation. Hochbauer motioned to Amfortas to help him off with his boots. The latter clamped each boot in turn between his legs and willingly allowed himself to be kicked in the backside. Merely to promote a congenial atmosphere during this procedure, Amfortas remarked, "What can he have against you—with the connections you have?"

Hochbauer allowed Amfortas to sit down on the bed beside him. The cadet felt honored and smiled gratefully, knowing very well the advantage still to be found in being on good terms with Hochbauer. There were for instance the numerous food parcels from which Hochbauer's closest circle of friends always derived benefit. There was his roommate's copious knowledge of military subjects, which from time to time made difficult homework much easier. And there were his excellent connections.

"What you call my connections," Cadet Hochbauer explained to Amfortas, "aren't just a matter of chance, you know. There have to be certain prerequisites for them— ability, aptitude, special talents."

"All of which you have!" Amfortas assured him. He was hoping in particular to benefit from Hochbauer's ability in tactics next time—he always had difficulty in formulating his orders clearly and precisely.

"Well yes," admitted Hochbauer after a certain show of hesitation, "I am one of the best at tactics."

"*The* best!" Amfortas insisted hastily. "There's no doubt about that at all."

"Well I won't deny it," admitted Hochbauer. "And as far as Captain Ratshelm, our company commander, is concerned, I am on what you might call intimate terms with him."

Amfortas nodded. This was well known. "He's got plenty of time to spare for you!"

Hochbauer gave his comrade a quick searching glance but found nothing but innocent friendly enthusiasm on his face.

"Captain Ratshelm and I," said Hochbauer, "pursue the same studies together, strictly in the line of duty, of course."

"Of course!" said Amfortas like some sort of echo.

"It's only Lieutenant Krafft I don't like." And quite suddenly, to test him, Hochbauer asked, "Or do you rather like him?"

Amfortas hotly denied any such suggestion. He always agreed with Hochbauer as long as he was with him. Though Hochbauer's star, which had once shone so brightly, now seemed rather on the wane, it was not going to be possible to disregard or oppose him in the foreseeable future. However powerful this fellow Krafft might be, Hochbauer was closer.

"This Lieutenant Krafft disseminates some rather remarkable views, don't you find, Amfortas?"

Amfortas found that he did. "You can say that again," he replied. "His views are more than remarkable."

"You mean the frivolous way he talks about the death of a human being, for instance?"

"Yes, that for instance."

"You too get the impression that nothing's sacred to him, not even the Reich and the Führer himself?"

"Exactly!" said Amfortas innocently.

"Well if that's so," said Hochbauer with devastating logic, "you ought to put it in writing in the form of a report or complaint—perhaps even as a basis for an indictment."

"But . . ." stammered the cadet opening his eyes wide. He had been caught utterly unawares. "But I can't . . ."

"Oh yes you can, Amfortas, I mean that very seriously. And I accept your suggestion. You'll write down everything you've just said—today, too, what's more."

"But what happens if I do that, Hochbauer?"

"You can safely leave the next step to me, Amfortas. After all, you're my friend and comrade, aren't you?" He looked severely at the cadet, who had now turned pale.

"No," gulped Amfortas desperately. "I won't do that. You can't make me do that. One dirty job's quite enough!"

Hochbauer looked about him; they were still the only people in the room. There was no one to disturb them. The midday break and still some time to run, and the other two inhabitants of the room had orderly duties to perform.

Cadet Hochbauer seized Amfortas and pulled him off his

feet. Then he hurled him across two stools to the floor. Leaping after him he grabbed hold of Amfortas's tunic again until the seams threatened to burst. Amfortas was once again lifted off his feet and for several seconds found himself staring into a cold, pale face that might have been made of stone.

With a compelling softness, and yet with a voice as sharp as a razor, Hochbauer said, "Never say that again! Never again let me hear you say I made you do anything dirty. Forget that Barkow business, or I'll kill you."

Cadet Hochbauer slowly dropped one hand from Amfortas's chest, and with it struck him two vicious, violent blows in the face in quick succession. He left his victim standing there, and without even looking back walked away to his own locker, from which he calmly pulled out his copy of *Military Regulations—For Service Use Only*. He opened it without a tremor and began to read.

Hochbauer was certain he'd acted correctly. You had to use force to appeal to a man's courage and sense of honor from time to time. Man was a weak creature, and being perpetually exposed to subversive influences, had to be trained to stay on the straight and narrow.

Cadet Hochbauer sat down and began to write a letter, not even deeming the figure of Amfortas worthy of a glance as he sat smarting under his punishment with burning face in the corner.

Hochbauer's letter was addressed to his father, the commandant of the National Socialist Political Training School. It began harmlessly enough in vague and general terms, with Hochbauer assuring his father that he was in the best of health. Then the cadet inserted a few elevated and high-sounding patriotic phrases about National Socialism and Greater Germany. With these he was gradually feeling his way toward his real goal. Next he inquired after his father's brother, who had an important job in the Ministry of Justice. This brother had a nephew in the Führer's headquarters, and was in turn a close friend of a judge-advocate general at the Army High Command.

Hochbauer's letter continued as follows:

While I have learned to set the highest store by many of my superior officers, among them my most admirable company commander, Captain Ratshelm, I have come across one officer whose activity genuinely disturbs me, and not only myself, but a number of other cadets as well. I hesitate to describe this officer as subversive in his attitude, but that really seems the only effective word for it. This man is not only of a sadistic temperament but allows himself to indulge in derogatory remarks about the German people, the Reich and the Führer—in a particularly sly way, moreover, which is very difficult to pin down. It seems to me that such men have no right to be officers, and that it really would be acting in the best interests of the community if responsible people in authority were to concern themselves with questionable creatures of this sort. The man I am referring to here is a certain Lieutenant Karl Krafft, at present a section officer in No. 6 Company at No. 5 Officers' Training School.

There followed a few concluding generalities culminating in best wishes for his father's health and well-being and a vigorous "Heil Hitler." As a postscript he added:

Please give my best wishes to my excellent uncle, your brother, in the Ministry of Justice. I'm sure he'd be glad to see this letter. As always your loving and obedient son.

Hochbauer sealed up his momentous letter, considering how further to consolidate his followers' loyalty. He had to ask himself whether Andreas needed the same treatment as Amfortas and what was the best way of getting Kramer to react most favorably. While he was preoccupied with these thoughts, the duty cadet appeared and put down a packet of books.

"Hochbauer," said the duty cadet, "an order from Captain Feders! You're to deliver these books this afternoon to Frau Frey immediately after duty. Captain Feders says she'll be expecting you."

"All right," said Hochbauer with a show of indifference, though in fact overwhelmed by a sense of pride and satisfaction. "You can put the books down there on the table."

The duty cadet seemed rather taken aback, and said, "You just act as if it were the most normal thing in the world."

"It's nothing special for me," explained Hochbauer. "I've been down to the course commander's house several times already. I've even been to tea there."

The duty cadet let out a low whistle of respect. That this particular confidential task should have been given to Hochbauer by the "sea-green incorruptible," Captain Feders, spoke volumes in itself! A great honor and privilege for Hochbauer.

Hochbauer also regarded this commission as an indirect mark of respect. He began to tot up the various proofs he had of people's confidence in him. There was Ratshelm's affection, Feders' mark of respect, and perhaps too he could count the good will of the major's wife, who was an influential woman. All these could be reckoned decisive trumps in his hand.

"Well, Amfortas," asked Hochbauer, with his eye on the packet of books that had been entrusted to him, "do I get the document I want by tomorrow, or not?"

"Of course," said Amfortas wearily. He too had been deeply impressed by the fact that even Feders was now beginning to single out Hochbauer. "I hope you'll make proper use of it, though."

"You can count on me to do that," said Hochbauer, toying thoughtfully with the parcel of books.

Afternoon duty passed quickly, though not quickly enough for Hochbauer. It was spent in instruction around the sand table. The exercise: the sending of a section into action. Half-experienced cadets could do this sort of thing in their sleep. For them it was no more than dreary routine with the one advantage that it contained few dangers for their final assessments. Hochbauer allowed his thoughts to drift in the direction of Felicitas Frey and the various possibilities she offered. Krafft allowed him to pursue these thoughts undisturbed.

The instruction around the sand table ended as abruptly as it had begun. Lieutenant Krafft simply said, "That's all for today," and made off.

Hochbauer turned to his neighbors.

"He simply doesn't know how an officer should behave," he said. "Anyone dispute that?"

No one wished to dispute this with Hochbauer. In any case he didn't give anyone time, adding, "This fellow Krafft has only been to Major Frey's house twice so far, but I've now just been invited for the third time. That tells you everything, doesn't it?"

The closer circle of Hochbauer's friends was astonished, regarding their acknowledged leader with wary envy as he got ready to go out.

Hochbauer even changed his socks, and rubbed his almost beardless chin tenderly with an astringent after-shaving lotion. But he refused to change his handkerchief when the obliging Amfortas offered to help him out.

"Handkerchiefs, my dear fellow," said Cadet Hochbauer,

now at the top of his form, "are for wiping away tears or snot. I have no use for them at all."

Hochbauer picked up his parcel of books. First he had to go and report to Lieutenant Krafft, his section officer, in the prescribed manner. "Right, comrades," he said, "now we'll see who really counts around here—a tactics instructor or a section officer."

The cadet found the lieutenant seated at his table, leaning slightly forward. Yet Krafft wasn't working as at first appeared. He was simply staring at a piece of bread and cheese he was on the point of devouring. Hochbauer came to attention and said, "I request your permission to be allowed into the town, sir. Captain Feders has ordered me to take a parcel of books to Frau Frey."

"Permission granted," said the lieutenant idly, without looking up or disturbing himself in any way.

Hochbauer was paralyzed with astonishment for a few seconds. What? he asked himself. No uniform inspection? No awkward questions? No objections of any sort? What could this mean? Did Lieutenant Krafft have no interest in him at all?

These were the thoughts in his mind as he made his way down the hill into the little town. With Krafft any explanation was possible—a subtle feint, temporary exhaustion, slowly developing indifference, new-won confidence, an evasive maneuver in response to pressure, intelligent recognition that the game was lost . . . but of all possible explanations Krafft could certainly be credited with the least pleasant. And the thought threw the cadet into considerable gloom.

The gloom, however, lightened immediately at the sight of Felicitas Frey. A mature and dignified lady, full of charm and beauty and acknowledged to have the best possible connections, smiled at him. "Welcome, my dear boy," she said. "I bid you heartily welcome."

With youthful ardor he bent over her well-manicured hand, and kissed it with a certain noble rapture. When he looked up again he was delighted to see that Frau Felicitas was blushing modestly. "It's a great honor for me to be here," he assured her glowingly.

"It's a great pleasure for me to see you!"

They started talking about books. A heavy Madeira was served—the major's favorite drink, which had so often been effective in raising his spirits. But it rarely appeared nowadays, for Madeira was in short supply and was reserved for very special occasions. And though Hochbauer didn't quite realize what an unusual privilege was being bestowed on him, he sensed it from the tender glances Frau Frey was giving him.

"If you'd rather have tea," she said, "I'll gladly make some. Only it will take a little time. I'm quite alone in the house—my niece is out and won't be back until late this evening, and my husband is working on something. The general has ordered another tactical exercise which could last until midnight."

"Yes," said the cadet rather wearily, "that could well be."

"Would you like to, then?" she asked amiably.

Hochbauer looked at Frau Felicitas. He hadn't quite understood her. He leaned forward slightly.

"I mean—would you like to have some tea?" Felicitas corrected herself in some embarrassment.

"I'd like whatever you'd prefer, ma'am."

They at once started talking about books again, this time discussing the sort of literature which dealt with fierce battles and stirring victories, with the German character, with manly strength, and feminine charms.

"Regal qualities," said Frau Frey, sipping her Madeira, "regal qualities have never been exclusively confined to the person of a sovereign. There are those among the sovereign's retainers too who have something regal about them."

"How right you are, ma'am!" Hochbauer assured her. "In our own time too, of course, one finds these exceptional human beings, though today they bear different names."

Thus did the words of the books they discussed catch fire and warm them with their blaze. And the soft blue shadows of twilight stole into the room and wove themselves invisibly about them.

In order not to disturb the emotional harmony, Frau Felicitas lit a candle, which shed a soft honey-colored light. The Madeira gleamed with secret reflections. It could also be seen that the bottle was getting low. But, without changing their theme, they had just arrived at an extraordinarily moving point in the conversation—the notion of the queen and her pages or alternatively the special qualities of the sovereign and her right to command obeisance, her duty to let herself be worshiped.

"This aspect of service," Hochbauer assured her in a low voice, searching for her enraptured eyes, "is a tribute to the simple queenly quality to be found in every woman of standing, recognized and lauded as such by the nation's finest writers."

"A quality of timelessness, do you mean?"

"A quality specifically for these times of ours in which true greatness has once again become the only standard and in which it is love's task to inspire the struggle for our existence so that, strengthened in ourselves, we can march forward to final victory."

Felicitas Frey felt carried away with wonder. The candle shed a golden light which tinged the whole world with its gentle gleam, a world which in this moment revolved around two human beings only: a queen, and the humble page at her feet, glowing with loyalty and inspired by a noble passion.

She stretched out her hand toward him and he seized it and pressed his hot face against it. But it was not only her hand of which he took possession. As if drawn by magic in search of support and protection and yet at the same time bestowing both these things himself, he felt his way up her arm to her shoulder—and all this was done without a word, in the strong but gentle spirit of service.

From this moment onward Felicitas Frey forgot everything except herself and her page, whom she let have his way. But the room they were in dissolved, her life and its orderly everyday routine disappeared in a whirlpool of queenly feelings. And even the major ceased to exist. Gone were all the hopes he had failed to fulfill; forgotten the disappointments that he had meant to her—all gone!

Later, very much later, she said, "Here—take my handkerchief!"

Hochbauer hadn't wanted to pull out his own handkerchief. Its condition was quite unsuited to such a moving occasion. He should have brought another cleaner one. For the uses of a handkerchief were not, as he had said, confined to snot and tears. That at least was something he had learned in the course of that hour.

So he took her handkerchief, of transparently thin bluish fabric, looked for a moment at the elegant, clearly legible monogram F.F., then made use of it and put it away in his pocket as a trophy.

26 *AN EVENING AMONG COMRADES*

"LISTEN," said Cadet Kramer. "What do you say to a section party one evening?"

"A communal blind, you mean?" said Cadet Mösler. "Well it's all right by me. Always provided there's enough to drink. The rest'll take care of itself."

But Hochbauer would have nothing to do with the idea. "I haven't the slightest intention of indulging in that sort of rowdyism," he said.

"Friends!" cried Cadet Kramer, calling for silence. "There's no question of a blind or rowdyism. What I'm suggesting is simply an evening on which we can all get together as comrades."

"Well," remarked someone, "if there's nothing else for it . . ."

"Is it really necessary?" asked Amfortas, inspired by Hochbauer.

"Comrades," said Cadet Kramer loudly and looking around challengingly at his section as they sat before him in the classroom, "I've thought it all out, as you might guess."

The cadets looked at each other and grinned. They knew their Kramer. He always liked to seize the initiative to prevent anyone else from doing so. Particularly where parties and similar, organized sparetime activities were concerned. On such occasions his enthusiasm knew no bounds, for he was able to play top dog unchallenged.

"It's like this, you see," said Kramer. "The first object, as I said, is simply to promote the spirit of comradeship. But then we've got to invite Captain Feders and Lieutenant Krafft in order to create a congenial sort of atmosphere. Because it's time for the mid-course assessments."

This clinched the argument.

"Right, then," said Kramer, "my proposal is carried unanimously, as I expected it to be. Anyone who doesn't join in simply proves that he doesn't know the meaning of the word comradeship. And no one wants to come under that sort of suspicion, I imagine. Attendance, then, will be regarded as a duty!"

"Permit us, sir, to invite you to a little party we're giving!" Cadet Kramer said to Captain Feders in front of the assembled section. The tactics instructor saw through the invitation at once. "Aha," he said affably, "so you want to put me in a good mood for the mid-course assessments."

"The party's been planned a long time," Kramer assured him gravely.

"But the moment's particularly opportune, eh?" laughed Captain Feders carelessly. "Well there's one thing I can assure you of, friends, as far as I'm concerned you can give me a gala dinner, stand on your heads, and sing the Horst Wessel, but it won't affect my view of your performances in the slightest. However, this evening I'll have a little talk with each of you, and tomorrow you can try again."

There was no way of avoiding these mid-course assessments. They were intended to provide as brief and concise an indication as possible of the work of the cadets to date. The assessment was made as a result of a personal conversation between pupil and instructor.

"Each of you come to me in turn," said Captain Feders sitting down in a corner of the classroom. "Three minutes for each."

With Captain Feders this procedure developed as one might have expected. Feders castigated each in turn as "oaf," "half-wit," "idiot," and—his highest form of praise!—"goose-stepper." He took no pains to conceal his view that not a single cadet was fit to become an officer. Not even Hochbauer. However, the latter did at least get classified as a "goose-stepper," which was commendation of a sort.

Then it was Lieutenant Krafft's turn with them. "I want to see you one by one," he said.

The section officer conducted his mid-course assessments in his own quarters. Unlike Feders, he took his time about them, conducting amiable conversations with each of the cadets.

"My dear friend," Lieutenant Krafft would say by way of introduction, "let us now try and see what we make of each other."

Then the section officer put to his cadets one or two questions which sounded harmless enough but were very confusing at first sight. For instance, "How do you rate comradeship?"

Most of them rated it very high indeed. They declared that comradeship was the first necessity, a genuinely manly emotion, an indispensable quality in any soldier—in short, something to be striven for, to be respected, and practiced at all times.

"And what about comradeship with those who show no comradely feelings?" asked Lieutenant Krafft as an afterthought.

Quite a few stumbled over this. But Krafft remained friendly, and his final words seemed to carry hope so that they all went away invigorated and content.

"Not too bad," admitted most of them.

"The whole tone of the thing was as undesirable as ever," said Hochbauer to his friends.

But Cadet Kramer declared firmly. "You see what a difference it makes to show feelings of comradeship at the right moment. Our invitation worked wonders—it's the only way of explaining such splendid results."

Only later did it transpire that the assessments from Lieutenant Krafft had all been fatally identical. Not only that; on closer examination they all proved to be of an impenetrable ambiguity. For Krafft's standard summing-up had run as follows: "My dear . . ."—here the relevant name was inserted—"if you carry on as you have been doing there can be no doubt about how the course will end for you."

However, the cadets put as good a face on this as possible. After all, it was a fact that at least 80 percent of all candidates for a commission did survive such courses. These were the official figures. Officers were badly needed for the war. The factory couldn't afford to allow too many rejects; steady production figures were the order of the day.

"Anyway," said Lieutenant Krafft to his section in conclusion, "I hope you yourselves have learned something from this. Dismiss!"

"You play extraordinarily cautiously," said Felix, whose number was 33.

"That's just my way," said Lieutenant Krafft, still hesitating about his move.

Felix examined his partner calmly and closely with his large, dark eyes, which had soft beauty about them. There was a smile on his face, but it was a smile of almost mask-like stiffness.

Lieutenant Krafft avoided Felix's glance by concentrating on the chessboard in front of him. Beyond it dangled the helpless body in leather harness. Number 33 was one of the more fortunate of the basketmen. He had learned to love books, knew something of music, and played chess.

The latter accomplishment was particularly fortunate; all Felix needed was a partner with hands. He only had to notify him of each of his moves to be able to enjoy the game to the full. With the purely mechanical help of an orderly or a nurse, two basketmen could play chess together, though only very few of them knew the game.

"Does my rather slow technique bore you?" asked Krafft.

"No," said Felix. "For in the first place I've plenty of time, and secondly I find your method of playing chess very interesting."

"I know I'm unconventional. I don't stick to the basic principles at all."

"That's an advantage," said Felix politely. "You know how to surprise your opponent and confuse him by an unusual move. What I don't know is whether this is intention or accidental."

"It's just my way of doing things, I suppose."

They fell silent for a time. Felix made his laborious depositions alone, nominating first the piece's old position on the board, then the new position, which he gave by a grid reference of two letters and two figures.

They were alone in the room, between white walls and illuminated by a harsh light from the ceiling. For number 33 couldn't see very well, his eyes watered continuously. From time to time he bent his head forward and laid it on a sort of ruff around his neck to wipe away the fluid from the corners of his eyes.

"What are you here for?" asked Felix suddenly.

"To play chess with you," said Krafft, moving his bishops four squares ahead. At the same time he buttoned up his doctor's coat that he always wore over his uniform on these visits. "Your move."

"What sort of a wound have you got?" inquired Felix. It hadn't occurred to number 33 that the lieutenant in front of him might be physically undamaged. Anyone who spent his time in these rooms was marked in some way, and even if there were no visible external signs there must be something missing—a large section of the lungs, a part of the stomach, or a kidney. Perhaps shell splinters were making their way slowly through his body toward the heart? Perhaps his blood was turning to water? Perhaps he had lost his sense of balance?

"Let's not talk about that," said Lieutenant Krafft. "Let's concentrate on the game."

"Do you sometimes have this depressing feeling that it's all so utterly pointless?" persisted Felix. "You know, hanging here wouldn't be quite so bad if one felt that there were some reason for it. Let's suppose I'd blown up a bridge to save the lives of others, and that that was how it had happened—all right, why not? Or suppose I'd struck a general in the face before the assembled company and had been shot for it—well, one would at least know why. But I was asleep at the time. And when I woke up I was as I am now."

"You're not the only one to stumble on death in his sleep," said Lieutenant Krafft with exaggerated nonchalance.

"And you?" asked Felix undeterred. "What happened to you? Have you ever thought about why you were crippled?"

"All that happened to me was that they tried to remove my brain," said Lieutenant Krafft. "But that's not so bad. For most people the brain is a more or less superfluous part of the body. Look out, though, your queen is in danger. Check."

"I can't see properly any more," said Felix, number 33. "My eyes are watering too badly. Let's stop playing for today, if you don't mind."

"I don't mind," said Lieutenant Krafft.

"So—the brain," said Felix with his eyes closed. "And was that pointless too? Or did you manage to save the lives of your comrades, or protect women and children or do something that had some point in it? Or even anything which you thought at the time had some point in it? No?"

"Let's stop now," said Lieutenant Krafft dully.

"Do you know," said Felix, the basketman who bore the number 33, "if I were still capable of doing something I'd try to make some sense out of this wretched life of ours. Utter some infallible truth, unmask a murderer, die for someone, preserve a shred of beauty, nail a lie, tend a garden, or something like that. Do you understand what I mean?"

"Yes," said Krafft. "I feel exactly the same."

"Right, fellows, the party's on!"

The section had all assembled in The Gay Dog, the choice of which Kramer regarded as particularly clever. For the triumphant navigation of a treacherous reef—in other words the complaint put in by Rotunda the landlord—called for celebration too. The fact that they were all sitting here was the surest sign that their triumph was complete.

"I beg to report to the officers: Section H all present and correct!" cried Kramer.

The section rose to a man. The section senior strode up to Feders and Krafft, came to attention, and stared straight between them. Kramer considered this good tactics. Wishing to avoid giving one officer precedence over the other, he slammed his report in at both of them.

"We seem to be in this together," said Feders to Krafft.

The cadets of H Section now all sat down at a well-laid table arranged in the shape of a horseshoe, with the tactics instructor and the section officer in the places of honor in the center. An almost solemn atmosphere prevailed at first; an atmosphere of clean-shaven faces, newly clipped hair, carefully pressed dress uniforms the trousers of which had spent at least one night under the mattress, and of restrained jocularity, subdued voices, and carefully controlled movements. In short a thoroughly superior atmosphere such as they had learned to enjoy at the communal midday meal with their section officer.

"Comrades," said Cadet Kramer, "I suggest we sing a song."

"Hear! Hear!" cried the cadets eagerly.

"May we ask you, sir," said Kramer, turning with humble attentiveness to Feders, "to tell us which song you would prefer?"

"Well if you really mean it," said Feders, "then I'd like 'The Lüneburg Heath.' "

" 'On the Lüneburg Heath!' " announced Kramer at the top of his voice. "A special request from the captain. One, two—three!"

The cadets burst into song, singing crudely and heartily with more volume than quality. Captain Feders listened to the well-disciplined din with a wintry smile.

But in the open doorway stood Rotunda the landlord, watching his guests with evident satisfaction. He could hardly have wished for anything better. These were decent, solid, well-brought-up young fellows. It seemed almost inconceivable that these were the same lads who only a few days ago had reduced the bar to a heap of ruins in such a fantastically short time.

But now they roared out "The Lüneburg Heath" and yelled of the joys of the chase and of the vine and of love, with forty mouths opening and shutting as one. Forty pairs of eyes glanced with furtive relief at their officers; the tactics instructor and the section officer both seemed satisfied. At least neither showed any signs of going over to the offensive. With a last joyful burst the song came to an end.

"Captain Feders has the floor!" announced Kramer the section senior.

Feders started, and rose to his feet. He cleared his throat and said in his usual clipped tones, though mildly for him, "I don't recall asking anyone here for the floor, precisely because there's no one here in a position to give it to me. But since I am on my feet, I'd like just to draw your attention to one small detail. Namely to the fact that this is fortunately not a tactics class. As a private individual, however, I'd like to say this to you; never go bragging about your achievements, or using big words or regarding yourselves as supermen! Treat everything and everyone with the deepest mistrust, but, above all, yourselves. And now, if you can, forget everything I've said, at least until tomorrow."

The cadets appeared to listen to this attentively, and some even nodded, although none was clear whether they had been treated to a sheer piece of mischief or a pearl of worldly wisdom. When in doubt it was usual to look thoughtful, in a not unoptimistic manner suggestive of having the situation under control. They drank Captain Feders' health, after of course first asking his permission to do so.

Kramer, whose only interest was that the evening should proceed entirely according to plan, now rose to his feet again. He turned to Krafft, and formulating his request with the requisite care said, "Might we ask you, sir, to tell us your favorite song and grant us the permission to be allowed to sing it."

" 'In the Field with Stone for Pillow,' " said Kraft.

Kramer smiled happily. He had expected Krafft to name this song and had taken the precaution of practicing it with the section beforehand. Kramer had noticed before that "In the Field" was Krafft's favorite song; perhaps it was the only one the lieutenant knew, perhaps he really did like it, but what mattered was that he had requested it, and that his section now complied with his request.

Their voices were heavy with sentiment, pregnant with destiny. The words were gloomy and foreboding, as if issuing through a nostalgic vale of tears.

"It's enough to make you howl," whispered Mösler to his cronies between verses. "Can someone lend me a handkerchief? Mine's too dirty. Besides, I've only got one and it's at the wash."

A few of them, among them of course Böhmke, the poet, seemed genuinely moved by this song:

> *In the field with stone for pillow*
> *Stretch I now my weary limbs!*

Even Krafft seemed to listen with a certain sympathy—and indeed this was quite genuine. Krafft was lost in himself, carried away by the melancholy tune that was half hymn, half popular melody. It was a song of the firelight and the hearthside—no sort of song for a march.

As the last bar faded away—and not a few of them found the song far too sloppy, soft, and tame—Kramer, the section senior, took things into his own hands again. Cloudy melancholy was as unsuitable a start to a congenial evening of this sort as unrestrained hilarity. Proper organization was what counted at such moments, and Kramer now turned to Krafft and invited him to say a word.

"Cheers!" was Krafft's only word, and thus without more ado he brought things to the point for which everyone had been waiting. Before the cadets had time to be astonished he raised his glass and drank to them. This inspired a certain cautious gaiety.

"Right, fire away!" said Kramer. "You may smoke and talk now!"

So they began chattering among themselves, most of them putting up a show of being cheerfully at ease, without at the same time making much noise. Their topics of conversation could hardly have been more innocent. Not a word was spoken that wasn't fit for the ears of an officer.

From time to time they sang a song, long recognized as the surest way of keeping out of trouble. And the songs, which had been carefully selected, were almost entirely free from any crude suggestiveness either sexually or politically. The mood thus remained serene throughout.

They were all relieved when Captain Feders and Lieutenant Krafft started making preparations to go.

"The next time you feel like breaking a place up," said Captain Feders with a grin, "try at least to find out the conditions for doing so and the prices beforehand. It's also a good thing to have a few culprits ready. The whole situation must be cleared up at least by the time the police arrive. The best excuse of all, of course, is the war. That makes everything in order. It's much simpler to set fire to a village or wipe out a town in the name of justice, peace, or freedom than to smash a wine bottle out of excessive exuberance. However, I'm in no way suggesting that infantile spirits should be allowed to have their fling."

Lieutenant Krafft, however, had the last word. He said, "I want you back in barracks by midnight, friends, but without any singing or noise or monkey business. Apart from that, have a good time."

"Now we can really enjoy ourselves!" cried Cadet Kramer.

His statement was entirely superfluous, for barely had the two officers left the room than the officers'-mess atmosphere dissolved altogether. There was a veritable avalanche of noise. Glasses were emptied with disconcerting speed, and a bare minute later the first of the cadets was standing on his chair trying to make a speech.

"Comrades!" he cried. "Now we're really among ourselves at last: back with your glasses and on with the booze."

"Steady now, fellows!" said Cadet Kramer anxiously. "Take it easy!"

But in a flash the cadets had shown how easy they intended to take it. Some roared for the landlord, demanding drinks, reinforcing their demands with all sorts of unmistakable hints. And Rotunda much preferred to see wine flow rather than blood. Above all he wanted no more trouble with the burgomaster or the general. Moreover a glance at the clock reassured him somewhat; there was hardly more than an hour to go. Let them get drunk, then—they wouldn't have time to get fighting drunk.

"I'll see that everyone gets his due," Rotunda promised cooperatively. "After all I'm no spoilsport!"

"Cut the cackle!" cried the cadets.

The landlord hurriedly disappeared. Three minutes later the first stone jug was brought up. A roar of delight greeted its appearance.

Once again Kramer, as section senior, sought to keep the evening within bounds. So, yelling at the top of his voice as if he were on the barrack square, he ordered, "Comrades —a song!"

" 'In Hamburg there I Met a Maid'!" cried Mösler at once, and before Kramer could protest, the group around Mösler had taken up his suggestion. Kramer sat down resigned. He had had the right idea, but he had also made a mistake. What he should have done was not just order a song but lay down which song was to be sung. Now they were bawling out this song, which without any exaggeration might be described as thoroughly disgusting. This hymn to the eager woman of pleasure would have been excusable coming from ordinary soldiers, Kramer decided, but was utterly deplorable and absolutely impossible coming from officer cadets for whom he was responsible.

Nevertheless Kramer joined in too, because he was unwilling to destroy the community spirit. But when they came to the part about the "Thaler," which, in the pimps' jargon, the girl willingly paid out for "her work on the street," Kramer's voice faltered. And when the landlord even bolted the swing doors to spare the few citizens in the taproom any undue embarrassment, the section senior began to see his little mistake as a disgraceful failure on his part. This made him furious.

"You should never have allowed a song like that!" Hochbauer admonished him.

"It's none of your damn business!" returned Kramer, losing his temper. His own awareness of his failure stuck in his throat.

"There's no reason why I shouldn't drop a hint!" said Hochbauer with some annoyance.

"Do better yourself if you can," said Kramer, like some angry bull. "I've long suspected you of trying to become section senior in my place." This went home to Hochbauer, who didn't reply. Of course this had always been his wish, though he had never mentioned it to anyone. Certainly this man Kramer had proved himself something of a broken reed lately, and a new section senior really did seem necessary; but there obviously wasn't the slightest chance of being appointed against the will of the section officer—that was the snag.

In the meantime this very popular song was being brought to a conclusion. Both Hochbauer and Kramer made a show of joining in, keeping each other under furtive surveillance throughout. Each expected the other to apologize to him, and both waited in vain.

In the end it was Hochbauer, the cleverer of the two, who was prepared to give in first. It seemed to him inadvisable to make an enemy of Kramer as well, for he had enemies enough as it was. In Hochbauer's eyes Kramer was just a harmless idiot, a willing tool if properly handled.

But Hochbauer made no immediate attempt to try and win the section senior over, for the noisy bunch at the lower end of the table was already in full cry. The loud-mouthed Mösler now got to his feet and shouted, "I hereby insist that our dear comrade Böhmke read us one of his own poems—preferably on the subject of love!"

Böhmke put up a show of resistance, for he wanted to be implored to do so. And entreaties duly followed, to the accompaniment of many high-spirited and even coarse remarks, which the poet took for compliments, which in a way they were. Finally, after further pressure, Böhmke declared that he would indeed be willing to read one of his more recent works, but unfortunately was not in a position to recite one on the subject of love. For those examples of his output which he had with him—purely by chance of course!—were on the subject of war and nature.

"In no circumstances!" cried Mösler, as spokesman of the undisciplined rabble. "You won't get anyone to listen to a poem about war, let alone a cadet. Love is what we want!"

"But at the moment," replied Böhmke defensively, "I really haven't got a love poem on the books!"

"What sort of a poet do you call yourself!" cried Mösler to everyone's delight. "You must write one immediately! Go off into a quiet corner and lie down at once. No one will disturb you, I guarantee that. We'll simply post a guard over you: someone on whom one can rely, like Hochbauer."

"Couldn't we sing a song instead," suggested Hochbauer. "For example, 'On the Far Side of the Valley'? What do you say to that, Kramer?" But Kramer managed to neither agree nor disagree. Mösler leapt forward like a tiger leaping onto the back of an elephant. It was almost as if he'd been waiting for this excuse, for any excuse, to get at Hochbauer, and he shouted at him, "Are you against love, then, in some way?"

This question certainly wasn't meant harmlessly and was put in as provocative a manner as possible. The cadets began to show an interest in the turn of events. They nudged each other and even broke off their conversations, some leaning forward in curiosity, others gradually stopping talking. Finally all were leaning forward in their seats with a certain eager anticipation. They realized that they had front-row seats for the show. It was necessary only to look closely at Mösler and Hochbauer, who were wearing the determined expressions of gladiators.

"Well, what about it?" asked Mösler aggressively. "Have you got something against love as such?" In this sort of way enemies in the wars of religion must have asked each other why they didn't confess the true faith. Mösler at any rate was carrying on as if he were the champion of mankind.

Hochbauer turned to Kramer and asked, "Do I have to put up with this?"

The latter replied discouragingly, "I don't see why he shouldn't ask you a question"—this complying with Krafft's injunction to remain strictly neutral. Besides, someone who wanted to oust him from his post as section senior could hardly expect to count on his support.

"Well, what about it?" asked Mösler bitterly. "So you're against love, are you? You'd rather hear a poem on the subject of that Captain Ratshelm of yours, I suppose. Perhaps you even believe that love and the captain are one and the same thing?"

The cadets watched the two adversaries tensely—this time it looked like war to the knife. What was plainly the larger group, led by Rednitz and Weber, supported Mösler. A smaller but certainly no less effective group sympathized with Hochbauer. A third group, under Kramer, maintained, to begin with, a strict neutrality. And Böhmke, the poet, felt unhappy and bemoaned his fate, for he had been ready to call upon the muses, whereas this bunch of philistines was interested only in Mars.

Cadet Hochbauer was almost the only person to sum up the situation correctly. For some time now he had recognized that the good old days in which he could bash Mösler in the face as he pleased were over. He had known that part of the section, inspired by Krafft, was against him. What he hadn't known was that this part was so dangerously large. A physical quarrel therefore was out of the question; he would probably have no chance.

For these reasons Hochbauer settled for a tactically clever, well-ordered retreat. He managed to force a quite plausible smile, and said, "Why are you trying to pick a quarrel with me, Mösler? I can't see what you're after. These insinuations of yours are so ludicrous—I couldn't care less about them."

Mösler took a few seconds to recover from this. For a moment or two he looked almost like someone who's taken a run at an obstacle that turns out not to be there. He shook his head angrily, like a horse that finds its manger hasn't been properly filled.

"Did I hear right?" asked Mösler returning to the fray. "Are you denying the tender bond of noble sympathy that exists between you and that beloved captain of yours?"

"What utter nonsense!" cried Hochbauer, even managing a laugh—a remarkable demonstration of self-control. Not only did he parry splendidly, he even went over to the offensive, exploiting to the full every one of his opponent's weaknesses. With a certain audacity, he declared, "I am completely normal, if that's what you mean. I'm at least as normal as anyone else here, and certainly as normal as you, Mösler."

"Just listen to that!" cried Mösler in some perplexity, vainly looking about him for support. The neutral group was growing larger, and Mösler cried rather excitedly, "Just say that again!"

"You can even have it in writing," declared Hochbauer. "At least I don't spend my whole time with those eager little girls that anyone can pick up by the dozen any time. They're too crude for me. I prefer real ladies from the very highest social circles."

"Just listen to that!" Mösler repeated with a gasp, being unable to think of anything else to say at the moment.

Hochbauer was enjoying his unmistakable sense of superiority more and more with every second. Those cadets who adhered to his cause looked at him with admiration, and some of the neutrals, headed by Kramer, hastened to nod sympathetically. This gave Hochbauer a terrific boost. He found himself utterly despising these pathetic little pedlars of banal emotions, these squalid practitioners of the crudest pleasures. He could barely conceal his ironic smile.

Finally he said, "I could tell you things that would open your eyes for you. None of your common dirty little tramps for me. Something quite different! Those people who are constantly shooting their mouths off about their squalid little adventures would never dream of anything like it."

And with this, Hochbauer pulled a bluish gossamer-thin piece of fabric out of his breast pocket, to the general admiration and astonishment of all. Indolently he waved this touching object—a handkerchief obviously—backward and forward in front of him and smelled it for a moment, savoring it deeply.

The cadets stood there wide-eyed and open-mouthed. Rednitz in particular seemed riveted by this remarkable performance. Hochbauer, however, with an elegant gesture, simply put the handkerchief back in his breast pocket.

"I'd like to get a closer look at that sometime," whispered Rednitz to his friend Mösler.

Mösler, however, wasn't listening. He was preoccupied in trying to discover a new angle from which to attack Hochbauer. Moreover he thought he'd found one. "So that's it!" he cried excitedly. "According to you, you're one of those romantic heroes who enjoy their pleasures and keep silent about it. You can tell that to the Marines, or even to Captain Ratshelm. Anyone can trot out fairy tales like that!"

"No, that won't do!" cried Böhmke with poetic fervor. "A lady's name must always be taboo!"

"Balls!" declared Egon Weber. "And what do you mean by 'lady'? The mechanism's always the same."

"You just want the address for yourself," cried Amfortas aggressively.

And Egon Weber roared back, "What do you mean the address! Anyone in skirts will do for me. As for what you choose to call eager little girls of ours, I won't have them insulted! Certainly not by someone who gives himself airs as a ladies' man and just thinks of us as figures of fun! Who dares call my name a joke name? I'll bash him to pieces and take him up in front of the general whose name, it now appears, is also Egon. Do you realize that?"

"Comrades!" roared Kramer, trying to pacify everyone. "Comrades, this won't do!"

It wouldn't do. The cadets could see that, all right. Egon Weber's sweeping tirade had rather confused them all, and a certain clarification of the issues seemed required. The extremely interesting subject on which they were embarked mustn't be allowed simply to founder altogether.

"May I say something?" asked Rednitz quietly.

"No!" cried Hochbauer immediately. "Not you!"

"Let him speak," said Kramer in the interests of neutrality. "He may have an idea."

"It seems to me," said Rednitz, while everyone listened attentively, "that this is a relatively simple matter. Our friend Mösler accuses our comrade Hochbauer of being capable of unnatural feelings. And it seems to me that this is a serious insult which we mustn't let our friend Mösler get away with. We must be fair, after all."

"There now!" cried Amfortas. "The first sensible word spoken in this whole business." And he wanted to say more, but Hochbauer signaled to him to keep silent.

"Well, go on!" cried Kramer encouragingly.

"As I was saying," continued Rednitz, "we oughtn't of course to put up with insults of this sort. So it's now merely a question of proving the contrary!"

"How do you suppose that can be done?" asked Kramer.

"Nothing easier," explained Rednitz. "Hochbauer must bring us clear conclusive proof to the contrary. It shouldn't be so difficult for him, being the sort of person he is, and having the sort of success he has with the ladies!"

"Typical!" cried Hochbauer, rejecting the idea indignantly. "I won't have anything to do with these sordid little girls of yours. I've too much pride for that!"

"If that's all you're worrying about," said Egon Weber, a man of considerable experience, "it's easy to help you. There is, in this pretty little town, a child—are the doors shut, fellows?—well I tell you—milk and honey she is. Your mouth'll water at the mere sight of her. Glamorous as a film star and pure as a girl from the choir. Guaranteed virgin—I promise you. Compared with her a so-called lady is nothing but an old cow. Maria Kelter is the child's name."

This suggestion went much too far for Kramer, and Rednitz seemed to agree with him. But Mösler roared, "Hochbauer will never make her! I know the little girl—I can't even make her myself!"

"That doesn't mean a thing!" said Hochbauer angrily.

"You haven't a hope!" countered Mösler immediately. "You haven't got the guts. You'll never make her. If you pull it off, you can call me what you like in the future. You can kick me up the arse in the presence of the entire section. You have my word for that as an officer cadet!"

"I accept your offer!" declared Hochbauer with grim determination, looking very pale. He drew strength from the encouraging and respectful glances flashed at him from all sides.

"Bravo!" roared the cadets in chorus.

"Done! The bet's on!" cried Mösler. "Will ten days be enough for you?"

"Five days will be enough," declared Hochbauer. He was absolutely determined to maintain and increase his respect at any price. Even this price.

27 DISASTER DAWNS

THE FIRST PEOPLE to get up in the barracks every day were the kitchen staff—the guard woke the relevant personnel at four A.M. They rolled out of bed, dressed while half asleep, and then shuffled off to the kitchen block, where they lit the fire under the coppers and sulkily brewed up the thin liquid officially known as coffee.

Five A.M. was the hour for certain mess orderlies, the transport squad, and those with special distribution jobs. Shortly after five the officers on special duty got up—and with them usually the general. The duty cadets in the various companies were wakened around the same time.

Reveille for the headquarters company, or for the ordinary rank and file at any rate, was at five-thirty. The NCOs usually had about an hour longer in bed provided they weren't on early duty. Certainly Captain Kater, the CO, was never seen in his domain at anything like this time, unless of course he was returning from a night-long session in the mess or from some extensive celebration down in the town.

The barracks as a whole began to wake up properly at six: eight hundred cadets—encouraged and incited by sixteen duty cadets—left their beds cursing and grumbling with the shrill din of whistles and the brisk cries of their dutiful young persecutors in their ears. The principle upon which everything was conducted was that the more noise that was made the easier it was to wake up.

Exactly a quarter of an hour later the cadets, still slightly dizzy with sleep, streamed out into the open, fell in in sections, arranged themselves into companies, and were then taken in charge by the section officers whose turn it was to do early duty. The tedious and often perfunctory early-morning physical training now started at six different corners of the parade ground simultaneously. This lasted exactly fifteen minutes, unless one or other of the section officers was too cold or tired or simply had no stomach for it, which in turn depended on whether or not a high-ranking superior officer—even perhaps the general himself—was in the vicinity.

With this over, the barracks automatically turned itself into a well-organized ant heap. Those whose job it was to get the coffee streamed off to the kitchens; the cleaners armed themselves with buckets, mops, and brooms; one group of cadets occupied the washrooms, and others the latrines, while still others gave a final polish to their boots, or merely dozed off again. Not a few actually began eating.

Toward seven the rest of the officers got up, together with the NCOs of the headquarters company, and even those members of the female auxiliary staff who were billeted in barracks. The officers trotted off to the mess, where they devoured their modest breakfasts with a great deal of chatter.

They faced the day's duties with the same sort of feelings as the cadets.

Official duty began, according to the timetable, on the stroke of eight.

For Lieutenant Krafft this particular day started cheerfully enough. Together with Captain Feders he made his way toward the headquarters company block, where both were looking forward to a little diversion at the expense of Captain Kater.

"You really mustn't miss this," Feders assured Krafft. "Since the general put the good Kater in my charge, his life has suffered something more than a mere shake-up—his whole attitude has changed. Kater is beginning to feel pretty small, and naturally I'm doing what I can to help him do so."

Feders and Krafft, the tactics instructor and the section officer, were free to pay this little visit together, because the first period of instruction that day was being taken by Captain Ratshelm, the company commander. He was lecturing the assembled cadets on ideology and trying to bring home to them the particular importance of dying for an ideal. After all, though every war has been fought for something different, this has always been a constant factor. The task of purveyors of so-called ideology consists merely in stuffing the heads of half-wits in every country under the sun with high-sounding phrases—which, experience shows, presents no particular problem.

Captain Kater, however, found himself with little time these days to think of higher things. Captain Feders, who had been set over him as a sort of commissar, overwhelmed him with a mass of trivial activity.

There was no set time for the daily visitation, which usually lasted an hour. Captain Feders appeared just when he felt like it. On this particular day that meant eight o'clock in the morning. Captain Kater was ready to receive him.

"Sit down, Kater," said Feders by way of greeting. "Lieutenant Krafft is keeping me company today, so that I don't get too bored with the childish work I have to do here. I hope you don't mind, Kater?"

"Don't push it too far, Feders," said Kater angrily, entrenched behind his desk. "You've got me in your power at the moment, but it can't last forever."

"Now really, my dear Kater," said Feders amiably, "please don't talk like that! I always find threats rather stimulating—which can't work to your advantage in the long run." He sat down comfortably and motioned Krafft to a chair.

Captain Kater mumbled something imcomprehensible, though unmistakably hostile. On the general's orders he now had this fellow Feders hanging around his neck all the time, and Feders was playing with him as if he were some cadet at the training school—him, a fully grown captain! The fellow even insisted on his keeping regular working hours, from eight to twelve and from two to six. This in itself was something that had never happened to Kater before in all the time he'd been an officer.

"May I see the folder containing your work?" asked Feders amiably.

Captain Kater nodded sullenly and pushed the folder at his elbow across to his overseer. Captain Feders picked it up, opened it calmly, and began to read through it. At the sight of the very first sheet of manuscript he pulled a well-sharpened red pencil out of his pocket, shook his head with a smile, and drew a thick line right across the page from the bottom left-hand corner to the top right.

"My dear Captain Kater," said Feders, "I wish you wouldn't keep using these inaccurate terms! I haven't confiscated . . . . this is of course intelligent enough, for after all, who likes to commit himself? There is however a basic mistake here which would be reprehensible even to an NCO. Do you know what I'm referring to?"

"Come on, tell me!" growled Kater. A murderous look which didn't escape Feders for a moment smouldered in his eyes.

"The mistake lies in the heading, my dear Kater," said Feders readily. "You've used the word 'Report' but a report should contain nothing but facts and be as brief, concise, and comprehensive as possible. As soon as you start 'believing'—which in any case a soldier never does, that's the Church's business—as soon as you start 'assuming,' or putting forward an 'opinion,' then what you're writing is not a report, but a commentary. Isn't that right, Krafft? You as an instructor in written procedure should know best."

"You're quite right, Captain," said Krafft.

"I'm glad to hear it," Feders assured him. He turned to Kater and said courteously, "May I ask you, my dear fellow, to take note of this and act accordingly in the future?"

Kater growled impotently, "Just you go on like this!"

"Only too delighted!" said Feders courteously, promptly obliging.

Of the twelve papers in the folder Captain Feders objected to nine; the rest were simply filled-in forms. After each reprimand, Kater grew smaller and smaller.

"What about brandy, now?" asked Feders finally, as Kater's instruction in paper work came to an end. "Have you got any?"

"What more do you want!" cried Kater, helplessly writhing. "You've already confiscated all the drink I had!"

"My dear Captain Kater," said Feders, "I wish you wouldn't keep using these inaccurate terms! I haven't confiscated anything. I have merely listed certain goods and placed them in safe custody: a measure which you seem to have overlooked. Besides, it isn't a question of your drink—you were merely responsible for it, weren't you? So, what about it—have you any brandy or haven't you?"

"All right," said Kater, imagining that in this way he would be able to buy himself a respite from persecution for at least a day. "I'm not niggardly about these things!" He opened his desk and fished out a full bottle of Rémy Martin and three glasses.

Feders smile appeared to approve these preparations, until he said, "You can put your glasses back where they came from, Kater. I never said anything about wanting to drink the brandy; I merely asked you if you had any. Because I had a suspicion that you might still have some under the counter. And I must confess this annoys me, because a few days ago I asked you for a complete list of your supplies and there was never any question of making allowances for private stocks."

Kater had been caught out again, and looked at Feders with undisguised malevolence. "There'll be a day of reckoning for all this!" he said, and it was clear that he had in mind not only Feders but the general as well.

"If our friend Kater could have his way he'd murder me, and the general too, I dare say," commented Feders crisply. "But he can't, so he's hoping for a miracle. But as everyone knows, these are few and far between. And until the miracle comes, my dear Kater, I'm afraid you're delivered over to the leveling instrument of justice. So just put this bottle of brandy down on our list, will you? And think quickly whether you've got anything more hidden away. Would you like me to assist you?"

"Do you want to carry out a search?"

"Not a bad idea, Kater. But for the moment there's something else that interests me more. There are five private cars in the transport pool, aren't there? Two of these are in reserve; one is kept permanently at the general's disposal; another is held for the course commanders whenever they require one; and finally one car is alloted to the CO of the headquarters company. Isn't that right?"

"Yes," said Kater, "that's right. The CO of the head-quarters company needs a car all the time—for day-to-day requirements, keeping up contacts and so on."

"All quite in order and above board," said Feders. "Except for one small detail. For all practical purposes you are no longer the CO here—I am; so the car is not at your disposal, but at mine, from now on. Kindly take the necessary steps. And that's all for today, my dear Kater."

On this particular day Number 6 Company was down for ground training from nine to twelve. The theme, according to the timetable: platoon action. Site: the locator post. Supervision: company commander and section officers.

The three sections of Number 6 Company—G, H, and I—left the barracks at close intervals. The march to their destination was short, which meant that an even sharper and closer eye than usual had to be kept on the cadets.

Lieutenant Dietrich, in charge of Section I, avoided all complications such as talking in the ranks, inattentiveness, and superfluous questions by making his men march with their gas masks on. Lieutenant Krafft kept mostly to the rear of Section H in order to be able to observe them better. He hardly ever reprimanded anyone, but nothing escaped him.

Lieutenant Webermann, on the other hand, the officer in charge of G Section, seized the opportunity to impart all the fun of the barrack square to the march. He shouted at them constantly and was continually finding fault. One cadet was marching "with his nose in the mud"; another was "mistaking his rifle for an umbrella"; a third was "marching so stiffly he might be on stilts"; yet another was swinging his arms too hard; several were dragging their feet, and almost all failed to "range the horizon with their eyes." "What a rabble!" cried the section officer several times.

Captain Ratshelm, now pressing forward, now falling to the rear, liked to keep stepping aside onto rising ground to enjoy the picture his cadets presented. It seemed to him a splendid one—not without good reason, for he stood for the most part at points where he was clearly visible and every time the cadets saw him they thrust out their chests, picked up their feet, and sang more loudly. Not because he was Ratshelm, but because he was their company commander. What he enjoyed was the manly litheness of their youthful stride, the spring in their joints, the light in their eyes, the tension in their hips.

Once arrived at the so-called locator post—a mile and a half, or twenty minutes' march, from the barracks—the sections dispersed over the training field. Those who were keen on simple physical training, like Dietrich's section, kept to the vicinity of the quarry. But those who, like Krafft's section, set store by the minimum amount of interference in their activity withdrew to the woods.

Once here, Lieutenant Krafft deployed his men in open order with cover on the flanks and cover against snipers in the trees. Camouflaged by their ground sheets, which they wore buttoned up as capes, and carrying full battle equipment, including entrenching tools, they trotted over the terrain, keeping a sharp lookout for the imagined presence of the enemy. Battle readiness then! "Wait till you see the white of their eyes."

Only Böhmke, the poet, seemed to take no particular part in this game. He made no attempt to scan the horizon for the enemy, but kept his eyes thoughtfully on the ground. Krafft noticed this with some astonishment and called out, "Böhmke, are you playing the part of an advancing rifleman or merely looking for mushrooms?"

Böhmke's reply made it clear that the poet wasn't always as wrapped up in his own thoughts as was commonly supposed. He had a sizable share of native wit. For, to Krafft's delight, he explained, "I'm keeping a lookout for mines, sir."

"Then keep your eyes skinned," said the section officer. "It would be a pity if you were to tread on one."

The men enjoyed the joke. It added to that air of good relations between the lieutenant and his section which seemed to have developed quite noticeably during the last few days. The cadets had recognized that Krafft possessed two important qualities which make it tolerable to treat any superior officer with respect; he had an understanding of his men, but at the same time wouldn't allow any of them to take advantage of him. Some had come to feel really fond of him, and the number of those who had no time at all for him was growing smaller and smaller.

"Dig yourselves in!" ordered Lieutenant Krafft.

This gave the cadets plenty to do for the next ten minutes, and Krafft once again had time to consider how to adjust the balance of power in his section to his own advantage. He knew exactly where to apply the pressure. It was merely a question of finding the most effective method of doing so.

Krafft's mind was preoccupied as he watched the cadets at their work. It could be assumed that the largest mound of earth denoted Hochbauer's position. The lieutenant went over toward it.

"Hochbauer," said Krafft, "get the section to fall in and practice target indication."

"Very good, Lieutenant," returned Hochbauer promptly. "Section, fall in! Target indication practice!"

Hochbauer would have passed on the order with equal promptness even if it had been completely meaningless—if it had run for instance: "Prepare for drawing and quartering! Quick march—direction of hell!" That there was indeed a slightly devilish twist to this phrase "target indication," Hochbauer knew perfectly well, though he didn't show it. The section had wrestled bravely with this subject for the first time a few days before, for it was one that couldn't be grasped completely from written regulations. Battle orders, fire orders, battle dispositions, all these things could in general be laid down fairly precisely in advance—but not target indication, because in this the terrain itself was the decisive factor.

Hochbauer collected the section around him, and, just as Krafft had anticipated, immediately transferred responsibility to Rednitz. The excellent Rednitz was no fool, thought Hochbauer; he would save the situation, or else expose himself to ridicule, which would of course be preferable.

The cadets pricked up their ears at once.

Rednitz knew quite well that "target indication" was one of those few subjects which even Hochbauer himself hadn't mastered, so he came out carelessly with "Distance one thousand—single bushy-topped tree."

"Wrong," interjected Lieutenant Krafft calmly.

"Wrong!" echoed Cadet Hochbauer.

With astonishing speed Rednitz switched to another tack. Thanks to Krafft's tip, he had recognized Cadet Hochbauer's Achilles heel at once. With extraordinary humility he asked, "Where did I go wrong actually, Hochbauer?"

"Tell him," Krafft ordered Hochbauer.

But Hochbauer didn't know what the mistake was. He stood there uneasily looking about him for help. He bit his lips and turned pale. But no one came forward to save him. The bosom friends Rednitz and Mösler restrained Egon Weber, while the rest of the cadets peered keenly in the direction of the "single bushy-topped tree" a thousand yards away.

"Hochbauer," said Krafft very softly, "we'll pass over the fact that you are insufficiently acquainted with military history. The fact that you show insufficient recognition of our Führer's efforts is certainly regrettable. But that you should be behindhand in even the most elementary basic principles fills me with astonishment. To give you a chance to think over the matter in peace, Cadet Weber will take over the section in your place."

Weber came swaggering forward and Hochbauer, blushing profusely, withdrew. He was trembling with indignation at his failure, and at the fact that Krafft should have discovered what was perhaps the one point on which he felt himself regrettably inadequate. This, he decided, was a defeat, and all the more shaming since it had been brought about with so very little effort.

Weber, Egon, therefore took over the section. He looked around it appraisingly. Although he was one of the few who knew his stuff on this particular subject, he was reluctant to complicate things unnecessarily. He noted with some surprise that Rednitz was signifying that he wished to speak.

"I see where my mistake was now," declared Rednitz with a completely innocent expression. "I forgot to give the direction. The correct target indication should therefore run: straight ahead, one thousand, bushy-topped tree. Two fingers left, toothbrush-shaped bush. Enemy machine gun."

"Correct," said Cadet Weber, looking across at Hochbauer with a slight shake of the head. Hochbauer now became aware for the first time of the full extent of Rednitz's slyness; he had simply acted as a decoy, and Hochbauer had fallen into the trap.

"Quite right," said Lieutenant Krafft, satisfied. "Why couldn't we get there right away?"

Between eleven and twelve o'clock the general had two conferences, one after the other, with the two course commanders of the training school. But whereas the commander of Number 1 Course had used up only twenty minutes of his prescribed time—the results of his course met all the general requirements—the commander of Number 2 Course, Major Frey, had already been sitting there five minutes over the prescribed time.

The general didn't bother to comment on this. He had merely looked up at the clock once and in doing so had raised his eyebrows. This could be taken as a devastating reproach, and made the major feel extremely uncomfortable.

The general never spoke very much, but now he had been silent for a full seven minutes. A single figure seemed to preoccupy his mind—namely, 63 per cent. He compared it with all the other figures in front of him. They were all between 81 per cent and 87 per cent. This meant that every section had achieved the required percentage with the single exception of Section H for Heinrich.

"How do you explain this remarkable difference, Major?"

Major Frey felt tempted to say that there was no explanation at all for it, or at least no clear one. He had simply received the figures in front of him and had dutifully passed them on. He himself had rather wondered at them but had raised no objection. "Of course these are only the mid-course assessments, not the final results, and therefore I suppose they will be improved upon."

"Is that all that you suppose, Major?"

The major gradually began to feel that the temperature in the room must be rising. "I think it seems a very arbitrary assessment; the methods of examination are, after all, well established."

"What else do you think, Major?"

"These figures will, I believe, certainly be altered in the final analysis."

The general's eyes narrowed. He said, "You suppose, you think, you believe! Don't you know anything?"

"General," the major now said, with the boldness of those who have hardly anything left to lose, "Captain Feders' figures have always been very arbitrary, with every course. But now that this Lieutenant Krafft of all people is collaborating with him, the situation is obviously very bad. I'd almost like to say that between the two of them they're sabotaging our work here; they are thoroughly disrupting influences—these figures alone are proof enough of that."

"Captain Feders," said the general coolly, "is acknowledged to be the finest tactics instructor we have—he is in fact responsible for the standard pattern of tactics instruction in all training schools. And Lieutenant Krafft too seems to be a man of unusual qualities."

"Certainly," the major admitted at once, "both know their jobs—I won't deny that."

"When two officers of this stamp," said the general, "combine to declare that only sixty-three per cent of all cadets are fit for commissions, and not, as is usually maintained, an average of eighty-four per cent, what conclusions do you come to, Major?"

Major Frey refrained from coming to any hasty conclusions. He wasn't quite clear where the general was heading. And so he said vaguely, "It's always possible to make mistakes, of course."

The general closed his eyes for a moment; it was an effort for him to conceal his contempt. "Just consider this, will you, Major. What if these two officers happen to be right in their assessments, and the others wrong? Perhaps our entire system is wrong, or incomplete, or in need of improvement. Perhaps we are in fact sending out from each course twenty per cent of officer cadets whose qualifications are sadly deficient? Do you know what that could mean, Major Frey? Have you ever given any thought to that?"

"Yes indeed, General," maintained the major firmly, with a powerful jerk so that his Knight's Cross shook vigorously. Of course he had never spent a moment on such misplaced thoughts. What was the general thinking of? Almost 40 per cent wastage—and that in the middle of a war, on the threshold of final victory? That would have been a catastrophe indeed! No honest German had thoughts like that. It would be tantamount to a failure to recognize the whole point and purpose of a training school.

"Are we then a factory, Frey?" demanded the general.

The major was on the point of saying yes, for in a certain sense this was true. They made officers here, in the same way as elsewhere they made kitchen utensils, steel helmets, and shells. The only difference was that their activity here was far more complicated, more responsible, and significant. There you had machines, workers, and engineers—here spirit, ideology, and a staff of dynamic officers. The final product—the lieutenant.

But it was pointless to say this to the general, and slightly dangerous too, for the man's egocentricity was notorious. However, Major Frey was, in his own estimation, not the man for cowardly evasions; he merely fought after his own fashion. He therefore declared, "These intermediate figures of Captain Feders and Lieutenant Krafft don't seem to be in any way the result of scientific examination, but rather proof simply of a very arbitrary method of procedure."

"Is this just another of your suppositions?" asked Modersohn keenly. "Or have you concrete proof this time?"

"May I draw attention to a comment of Captain Ratshelm's," asked the major. For of course he had no intention of committing himself personally in this matter. "According to this there seem to be fundamental differences in the style and method of assessment. Particularly significant in this respect—I'm quoting Captain Ratshelm's opinion here —is the case of a cadet called Hochbauer. This cadet starts with some not inconsiderable advantages. He comes from an old, highly respected military family. His father is even commandant of a National Socialist training college . . ."

"Major, I'm not particularly interested in his origins. The only thing that concerns me is a person's achievements."

"That's my opinion too, General. I merely allowed myself to quote Captain Ratshelm's view. At any rate this fellow Hochbauer does seem remarkable in so far as there are some extraordinarily contradictory opinions about him. Lieutenant Krafft, for example, regards Hochbauer as quite unfit to become an officer. Captain Feders maintains that, from the point of view of tactics, Hochbauer is unusually gifted, but otherwise he agrees with Lieutenant Krafft's opinion. Finally Captain Ratshelm considers that Hochbauer is in every respect fitted to be an officer; that he is in fact quite outstanding."

"That's interesting," said the general. "Kindly see that I have the relevant documents on the subject by this afternoon at the latest."

From twelve to two o'clock was down on the timetable as midday break. Yet this interval bore not the slightest resemblance to a "break," even lunch being eaten "on duty" in the strictest manner.

But before this took place, the rough traces of the morning's work had to be removed. If there had been classroom instruction the relevant notes had to be quickly completed and put away. If the cadets came from outdoor duty their equipment had to be cleaned. They had to change their clothes in any case; lunch was eaten in "best" uniform, whenever it was "official," which was the case on five days of the week, from Monday to Friday.

The cadets were kept constantly under pressure, and their timetable was extremely tight. Twelve five: return from work. Twelve five to twelve fifteen: finishing touches to the morning's work, such as putting away of rifles, equipment, writing materials, or overalls. Twelve fifteen to twelve twenty: change for lunch, including hair combing and nail cleaning. Twelve twenty to twelve thirty: fall in for lunch; short inspection of uniform and cutlery by the section senior; march off to kitchen number two; enter same; take up positions around the tables to which the section was allotted. The tables had been pushed together and covered with paper tablecloths. Finally: wait for the arrival of the section officer.

The section officers usually appeared at twelve thirty-five; at any rate hardly ever later than twelve forty. Each took up his position behind the place at the head of the table that had been reserved for him, and listened to the section senior as he reported the section all present and correct. He would then call out, "Text for the meal!"

The "mealtime texts" were an old tradition. In the time of the Kaiser they had consisted mainly of His Majesty's own sayings. In the time of the Weimar Republic the situation had been helped out by profound sayings of "great German soldiers," and there was certainly no lack of these. And now there were constant quotations from the Führer. So long as Krafft was in charge of the section a certain spirit of "free-for-all" reigned: each man in turn fired off anything he liked. The exact order of rotation was determined either alphabetically or by the section senior or by someone occasionally having something he very much wanted to get off his chest.

On this particular day it was once again Cadet Böhmke's turn—his comrades were usually perfectly willing to delegate this function to him. And as usual Böhmke quoted from his beloved *Faust,* and spoke his favorite lines:

> *"For the noble soul has power*
> *To compass all if wise and swift."*

"Right, then, gentlemen, *guten Appetit!"* cried Lieutenant Krafft, sitting down.

The cadets followed their section officer's example. They too sat down, and began to taste their soup. There was no conversation at first, but this didn't mean that the cadets were brooding on the text for the meal; it meant that they were hungry. Even the watery, insipid potato soup was welcome.

Kramer sat on Krafft's right and Rednitz on his left, which was neither accident nor calculation but the result of the daily rotation of seating. The section officer alone was the only man who never sat anywhere else than at the top of the table. And while Cadet Mösler at the bottom end was indulging in an elaborate piece of tomfoolery about Goethe's "civilian German," Lieutenant Krafft turned to his section senior and asked, "Know anything about homosexuality, Kramer?"

"Yes, indeed, sir," said Kramer. "It's said to exist, but is an offense."

"And doesn't someone who knows of such an offense but fails to report it commit an offense himself?" asked Rednitz.

Both Krafft and the section senior were fortunately spared the responsibility of having to answer the tricky question, for at that moment an orderly appeared and announced that the lieutenant was wanted on the telephone—urgently, on a matter of importance.

Krafft responded to the summons without delay. Before going, however, he ordered that lunch should continue in his absence. Which in practical terms meant, If I'm not back after the soup, you can carry on with the so-called roast and gravy, in fact if you like you can also consume the watery gruel and syrup that passes for pudding.

It was Captain Feders on the telephone. His voice sounded far less calm than usual, rougher, more urgent, and insistent. "You must take over my classes this afternoon, Krafft. I haven't time for any of that nonsense—I must get out to the Villa Rosenhügel."

"Has something happened there?" asked the lieutenant.

"Not yet," said Feders hurriedly, "but there's been an official murderer of some sort around there for the last hour—a major-general of the medical corps, a man steeped in the Greater German medical ethos and with full powers to suit the times. I don't know yet what'll happen."

"All right, Feders," said Krafft at once. "Of course I'll take over the afternoon classes. And if I can help you in any other way, let me know."

That was the end of the conversation. The lieutenant returned to his place. As he had expected, the cadets were already on the second course, the so-called roast. According to the kitchen chart, each helping was meant to weigh a hundred grams; in addition, the ration prescribed two hundred and fifty grams of potatoes, together with a gravy partly reinforced with water but nevertheless carrying a strong, all-permeating smell which signified it to be a product of wartime chemical ingenuity.

As Lieutenant Krafft sawed his way through his tough slice of meat, he turned to Kramer and said, "This afternoon's tactics class is canceled. There'll be ground training in its place."

And Cadet Rednitz pricked up his ears and inquired, "What shall we be concentrating on, Lieutenant?"

"There's one subject on which we've some leeway to make up," said Krafft warily. "A subject on which a start was made but which had to be interrupted. Well, today we'll see the matter through to the end."

Kramer looked at his section officer uncomprehendingly. But Rednitz had got the point. He said, "Engineer training. Demolition of a bunker. Like the time Lieutenant Barkow died."

"Exactly," said Lieutenant Krafft, squashing a potato. "Make all the necessary preparations."

Afternoon duty began at two o'clock and usually lasted until five.

Once again the sections fell in and streamed off to their various working destinations laid down in the timetable: the classrooms, parade ground, gymnasium, training ground, and so on.

Section H first armed themselves with engineering equipment from number three equipment shed: spades, axes, crowbars, sledge hammers, explosives, and fuses. Those cadets allotted to the job signed for every item, down to each individual strip of insulating tape. A good half hour thus went by before the section finally marched onto the training ground.

No sooner had they arrived at the locator post than a time-wasting piece of work awaited them. For a bunker which was to be demolished had first of all to be built. But a solid bunker took time. Forty men were fully engaged for ninety minutes in building something that was to be blown sky-high in a fraction of a second. So the cadets hacked and shoveled busily away, and in order that their work shouldn't be altogether unsystematic, Krafft got them to dig a trench as well.

Meanwhile in the barracks the assessment of the cadets proceeded apace. The officers collected plus and minus points and noted them down in their memory or their notebooks. The documents mounted up in the orderly room: intermediate assessment number one, intermediate assessment number two, one long tactics paper, two shorter ones; three tests apiece on the section officer's instruction, an essay on ideology, various performance tables for sport and physical training, a medical report and lists of equipment and other instruction material issued, such as compass, special maps, and geometrical instruments. Each cadet had a fat folder to himself. For every four cadets there was one man whose work was devoted wholly to them. To every forty cadets two officers; to every fifty cadets one woman.

Direct contact between the female staff and the cadets had recently been strictly prohibited. This had been carelessly overlooked in the earlier courses, with the result that various members of the female staff put not only their persons at the disposal of the cadets but also any files they wished to see, as well. Under Major-General Modersohn, however, the female staff never came into direct contact with the cadets.

Thus Elfrida Rademacher worked for the CO of the headquarters company, Marion Feders for the staff administrative officer. Since they had become acquainted they often telephoned each other, and from time to time sought each other out on duty, with a file under their arms, which usually provided an adequate excuse for an hour's gossip.

Recently they'd been meeting mostly in the headquarters company—and not only because Kater still had some real coffee left in store. They had realized that Captain Kater now always gave them a wide berth, pretending not to see them at all. What neither of them noticed, however, was that Kater made a note on each occasion of the time and duration of their all-unsuspecting conversation.

"I'm worried," said Marion Feders. "I've been getting more and more worried about my husband lately. He seems to have changed in such a strange way."

"What you mean," said Elfrida Rademacher no less frankly, "is that it's your husband's friendship for Lieutenant Krafft that worries you."

Marion Feders nodded. "Don't you feel they make an unusual pair?" she asked. "They've been hatching all sorts of dangerous plots together since they got to know each other."

"I don't understand much about all that," said Elfrida evasively.

"But you do feel it, don't you?"

"I haven't any influence with Lieutenant Krafft."

"But you're engaged to him!"

Elfrida smiled. "We love each other; at least we think we do. That doesn't give me any rights over him!"

Marion Feders looked at Elfrida Rademacher thoughtfully. With some affection she said, "You love him very much, don't you, Elfrida? You do everything you can to stop him acting stupidly. Because they're marked men, these two, as anyone who knows them at all well can see, however much they may try to keep themselves to themselves. I'll tell you quite frankly; at first I was glad when these two outsiders became friends, but I'm gradually becoming afraid."

"You'd like them to separate, Marion?"

"Yes," said Frau Feders with surprising vehemence. "Together they represent a danger—or rather they invite danger; doubtless for the best of motives. If we manage to separate them, this danger is automatically halved. It's up to you, Elfrida."

"Why me?" asked Elfrida Rademacher. "Why should I be the one to succeed, anyway? I've only known Lieutenant Krafft a few weeks; but Marion, you've been married to Captain Feders for a long time."

"You know what sort of marriage it's been, and what it's turned into since my husband was wounded. I haven't much influence with him. But with you, Elfrida, it's all different, very different, it seems to me. And that's why you must do everything you can to split them up before it's too late."

At the locator post Lieutenant Krafft had placed his men carefully in preparation for the final round.

He himself got the charge ready. Eight cadets designated beforehand remained in his immediate vicinity. The rest waited under cover fifty yards away. Everything seemed set.

It was a crystal-clear day. The trees stood out sharply silhouetted against the pale blue sky. The ground was frozen hard; it was like concrete underfoot. Every breath turned to frosty vapor. But none of the cadets were cold.

They watched in silence everything the lieutenant did. They watched his calm, punctilious movements; they heard his curt, clear instructions, all obviously very carefully thought out. He seemed to be even more in control than usual, and his face wore a constantly serious expression.

Gradually the cadets realized that what was planned here was nothing less than an exact reconstruction down to the smallest detail of the situation that had led to Lieutenant Barkow's death. The equipment lay in identical quantities in the identical places, and the cadets themselves formed the same groups as they had then.

Lieutenant Krafft began to place the ten-kilo charge. He knelt down on the freshly dug earth and looked up; eight cadets were standing around him. Two of them, Andreas and Hochbauer, were in his immediate vicinity; three—Kramer, Weber, and Berger—were standing a few yards away; the

other three—Mösler, Rednitz, and Böhmke—were away to one
side.

"Who was assisting Lieutenant Barkow at the time?"
asked the lieutenant.

"I was," said Cadet Hochbauer. He tried to sound calm
as he said it.

"Then try, Hochbauer, to act in exactly the same way
with me as you did then with Lieutenant Barkow."

"Very good, sir," said Hochbauer with apparent keenness,
"I'll try to do that."

Hochbauer went over to Krafft's side and knelt down beside him. Both of them now put the charge in position, and
packed it around firmly with a few stones and handfuls of
sand. The fuse snaked away across the ground past some
clods of earth.

When this had been done the lieutenant got to his feet. He
left the site earmarked for the explosion and looked for a
moment at his watch. Then, hurrying slightly, he went over
to the main group of his section about fifty yards away
across the terrain. Once there he turned to Cadet Amfortas.

"Amfortas," he asked, "where exactly did you sprain your
ankle?"

Amfortas was visibly nervous. He hastened to point out
the spot—a rabbit hole; he was standing only a few yards
away from it. When Krafft asked him what had happened
next, Amfortas said, "Lieutenant Barkow was called over and
came across just as you did just now, sir. He took a look
at my foot and then ordered me to get under cover. That
was all."

"Right then—down you go—under cover!"

Lieutenant Krafft crossed the fifty yards or so of open
ground and returned to the smaller group. Several times he
looked at his watch; more than four minutes had gone by.
When he came back to the spot at which the explosion was to
take place, he asked, "What's been happening here in the
meantime?"

"Nothing," said Cadet Hochbauer.

"And what happened on the previous occasion, with Lieutenant Barkow?"

"Nothing either, sir," maintained Hochbauer, looking toward the other cadets.

"Andreas," Krafft asked the cadet who stood in his
immediate vicinity, "did you notice anything on the previous
occasion?"

"Nothing, sir," Andreas assured him immediately. "Nothing at all."

Krafft persisted with the same question to each of them in turn, though he thought he knew what their answers would be. Kramer, Weber, and Berger didn't remember having seen anything—they had been talking together. Mösler, Rednitz, and Böhmke declared that they hadn't been in a position to see anything from where they were. Krafft immediately put this to a test. It was correct; neither the charge nor the fuse lay in these cadets' field of vision.

"Take cover," said the lieutenant. "Hochbauer will stay here."

The cadets turned on their heels. They were plainly glad to have got away from this fiendish game. The precision with which death was being reconstructed was getting on their nerves. Hurriedly they trotted off to cover.

Krafft and Hochbauer alone remained behind. The lieutenant closely scrutinized the cadet, who didn't flinch for one moment. No word was spoken for a long time. Neither betrayed the slightest sign of nervousness.

"Now I know how the whole thing was done," said Lieutenant Krafft. "Lieutenant Barkow was called over to Amfortas. It took him four minutes to get there, examine Amfortas's foot, and get back again. A lot can happen in four minutes. Just take a look at your watch, Hochbauer."

With quick, unobtrusive movements Krafft removed the stones and the sand that had been packed around the charge. He took out the fuse and detonator and replaced it with another, which he had ready in his greatcoat pocket. Then he pushed the stones back around the charge and filled up the gaps with a few handfuls of sand. "Now how long did that take me?"

"Not quite three minutes," said Hochbauer hoarsely.

"So that was it," declared Krafft.

The cadet forced a smile and said, "A remarkable theory, Lieutenant."

Krafft continued, "The rest of the practical arrangements were as follows."

The lieutenant now placed the end of the fuse and a match against the rough side of a matchbox. After a quick look at Hochbauer, Krafft wrenched the box away, the match flared up, and in the same moment the fuse began to hiss. When that was done, Krafft scrutinized the cadet more carefully than ever.

But Cadet Hochbauer simply stared wide-eyed at the glowing spot, which with a gentle hiss rapidly made its way with ever-increasing speed toward the charge. His face was white as snow. His fists were clenched tight with excitement. Then he hurled himself forward. He threw himself down on top of the charge and wrenched out the fuse.

He sat on the ground as if all strength had been sapped from him, his limbs trembling. In his eyes there was wild, undisguised rage. Panting he cried, "And if I did do it, you'll never be able to prove it."

"You did it," said Lieutenant Krafft softly.

"Yes I did it!" said Hochbauer, triumphant but at the same time quite out of control. "And I had a right to do it. At least as much right as you had to try and blow one of us up just now, or even both of us. Because obviously that was your intention. I at least confess to what I did. Only to you, though. To no one else. For no one can prove anything. No one. And you know that perfectly well, Lieutenant Krafft!"

"Your confession is good enough for me," said Krafft quietly. "And I've seen now that your nerves are weak, Hochbauer—you won't be able to see this thing through. You'll weaken—sooner or later I'll get you. For I've discovered several weak points of yours now; two of them are called Amfortas and Andreas. The only advice I can give you is to make your will."

"You'll never get me," said Hochbauer. The light of battle shone almost feverishly in his eyes. "I've got nerves of iron!"

"Your nerves are pitiful, Hochbauer. And you've no more sense than a fly. You took me for an idiot who would risk getting blown up on your account. But I'm neither a fool nor anxious to commit suicide. Just take a look at the detonator I substituted—it's empty. There was nothing for the burning fuse to contact. It was a trap, and you fell into it."

The day's work ended at about five, but no one was officially released from the treadmills until seven. It was merely that the bulk of the officers forsook their training, teaching, and supervisory duties during this period.

For those two hours the cadets could breathe rather more freely and feel slightly less closely observed. The timetables laid down, in rotation, periods for cleaning and mending, rifle cleaning, homework, choral singing, voice practice, or even Bible study—the latter, however, was extraordinarily rare, and, being voluntary, usually took place after duty hours, by which time even the keenest believer could be guaranteed to feel tired.

Officers rarely showed up during these two hours, though of course they had to be reckoned with at all times. It was usually the job of the section seniors to take the sections through the relevant routine.

On this particular day the danger of an officer's inspection was extraordinarily slight. For Major-General Modersohn had summoned the officers to another tactical training scheme—this time before dinner, which at least meant that there was some possibility of a time limit. At any rate it was scheduled to begin at half past five, and though dinner in the mess was usually served at seven fifteen, it might be nine o'clock or later before the general declared himself satisfied.

"I hope it doesn't last too long," said Captain Feders nervously. "I simply haven't got the time—I must get back to the Villa Rosenhügel before anything terrible happens."

Krafft saw that Captain Feders, who was usually so sure of himself, was for once showing signs of strain. "Is it serious, Feders?"

"Could be, Krafft! I must get away from here. If the general extends his tomfoolery for more than an hour I'll simply get up and leave. I couldn't care less."

"Well," said Krafft, "I'll see what can be done about it."

With that the lieutenant left the group of officers waiting in the large anteroom, and against all the rules of ceremony stationed himself in the hall. Here he waited for the general, who appeared a few minutes later accompanied by his aides.

Lieutenant Krafft saluted, looked into Modersohn's cool, penetrating eyes and said, "I request permission to leave the exercise early in company with Captain Feders. For reasons connected with the matter in hand."

Bieringer, the ADC, who was standing behind the general, shook his head in dismay and rolled his eyes. He was within an ace of wringing his hands in horror. This was a miiltary *faux pas* of the first order—a lieutenant accosting the general! In the presence of all the assembled officers, too!

Modersohn regarded Krafft with his cold, gray eyes for several seconds. Then he said, "You have an unusual hair cut, Lieutenant." With that he left Krafft standing there, and with Bieringer scurrying at his heels, walked into the anteroom. Lieutenant Krafft trotted slowly along behind.

The commander of Number 1 Course, that is to say the highest-ranking officer present, made his report to the general, who acknowledged it without a word. He merely nodded, signifying that the officers were to take their seats; then he went over to the center table, sat down at it, and waited until there was complete silence. Then he said, "Lieutenant Bieringer, please."

Forty pairs of eyes stared at the ADC. Lieutenant Bieringer announced, "Tactical exercise, subject: major fire in the barracks. For the second time. Situation as on the map."

"Unbelievable," Captain Feders whispered to Krafft. "The old man won't leave it alone. What can he have hatched up for today?"

The ADC unrolled a huge wall map over one of the boards in the background. It was a map of the barracks, scale one in a hundred, and had obviously been specially prepared. Black outlines and a confusing mass of red circles, streaks, wavy lines, and elliptical shapes, all denoted the seat of the fire, which had already reached a pretty advanced stage.

Captain Feders took in the situation at a glance. He seemed to be the only person who succeeded in doing so. "Gentlemen," said Feders, and for a moment his practiced confidence overcame his nervousness and anxiety, "this is utter chaos. I've seldom seen such a mess. Nine-tenths of us are going to come a cropper this time." But then suddenly his delight in the tactical masterpiece collapsed, and he muttered gloomily to Krafft, "If the general works this thing out properly we'll be sitting here till midnight. Damnation!"

Damnation!—that was what the other officers thought too. The general watched them, motionless from behind narrowed eyelids. His expression was utterly impassive.

Meanwhile the ADC, as usual, read out the list of duties to which people had been allotted. As always, no one had been forgotten; everyone had his part to play. Even the two course commanders were roped in, one as provisional burgomaster, the other as railway commandant—a sure sign of the scale the operation could be expected to assume.

Thus no one was really surprised when one of the officers was even appointed "commanding officer of number 5 training school" for the duration of the scheme. This role, which at first appeared to be quite an honor, fell to Captain Ratshelm. He rose proudly to his feet.

"I've always thought Ratshelm a bastard," said Feders. "But not even I would wish him what he's in for now."

A bare four minutes later the accuracy of Feders' forecast became unmistakably clear. The general intervened at Ratshelm's very first order, which ran, "Cordon off the barracks!" Within two minutes Ratshelm was reduced to a nervous wreck, for Modersohn proved to him that to cordon off the barracks in a situation such as this was simply to commit suicide. "Even a cadet could see from a glance at the map that the fire couldn't possibly be fought properly without help from outside." Hence the inclusion of a provisional burgomaster, hence the nomination of a railway commandant, hence the inclusion of all the fire brigades in the region. And so on and so forth.

In nine minutes Ratshelm was finished. His appointment as commanding officer of the training school was rescinded and he was allotted an auxiliary chain of firefighters equipped with buckets. Ratshelm staggered back to his seat and collapsed. He didn't know what had hit him.

Major Frey sat there hunched and pale. He alone began to suspect what all this was really about. His morning conversation with the general was now bearing fruit in a way that endangered his very existence. He too began to fear for his dignity and position.

But before continuing with the slaughter the general announced with complete impartiality, and in exactly the same cool, objective manner in which he usually gave his instructions, "Captain Feders and Lieutenant Krafft are released from all further participation in the present exercise."

"You don't need to come with me, Krafft," said Captain Feders. "What I have to do can be done alone." As Krafft merely shook his head, he added darkly, "And don't you try and stop me doing it!"

They tore along the icy roads in the car, skidding recklessly around corners with the headlights dimmed to narrow slits. But the snow shone through the evening darkness and the roads were empty. The lonely, forsaken atmosphere of the home front was all about them. It was a far cry from those great arteries down which the forces of destruction were kept constantly supplied.

The captain sat at the wheel, the lieutenant beside him. They had left the driver of the car behind in the barracks as Feders was entitled to do now that he enjoyed full authority as CO of the headquarters company. The engine of the clattering jeep whined shrilly as it raced along.

"The major-general of the medical corps whom you'll find there," explained Feders, "is an unctuous swine grunting about ethics and armed with full powers. He wants to do away altogether with those wretched fellows hanging there in the villa."

"Step on it, Feders!"

"This old thing won't do any more. But we won't be too late, thanks to your intervention with the general. I arranged for the medical general to have dinner in a hotel I know, where he can guzzle his way through liver and blood sausage and stuff himself to the eyebrows. Then I want to serve him a little pudding that'll stick in his throat."

"And if he turns out to be a man of decency and sensitivity who doesn't want to do away with anyone, what then?"

"Then I'll be happy to weep on his shoulders, Krafft."

They turned off the highway and the car hurtled down side roads toward the Villa Rosenhügel. The area wasn't closed— the gate was open, the barrier up. They ignored the sign which read "10 kilometres an hour" and drove up to the main entrance, where a car was already standing. This was the medical general's Mercedes; the heater was on and his chauffeur was asleep in the front—he too had had his fill of country fare and the excellent Franconian wine.

Feders and Krafft jumped out and hurried to the door. Krüger, the MO, was already waiting for them under the lamp. The pale light fell on his face and made it seem even more ravaged and mutilated than usual. "Welcome, Lieutenant Krafft," he said, putting out his hand.

"Well?" asked Feders.

"Nineteen," said Krüger.

"The swine," said Feders. He went ahead into the hall, where he stopped and said to Krüger, "You keep out of this, Heinz—you go to your basketmen, they need you now."

They left Krüger behind, with his head sunk low on his chest, and passed through a number of empty surgeries to the MO's office. There sat the man they were looking for— the major-general of the medical corps, a small pinkish gentleman, with a smooth, round, benevolent-looking face and watery blue eyes. His hands were folded politely in the manner of a well-behaved child. He looked up from a document before him with evident satisfaction. Then he took in his visitors.

"Ah, here you are again, my dear fellow!" he cried to Captain Feders. "I was thinking I'd have to move on without being able to say good-by to you, and we had such an excellent conversation this afternoon. What's more, the dinner, which I owe entirely to your consideration for my welfare, was really excellent. And the wine, my dear fellow—Veithöchshemier Wölflein, Auslese, 1933—a poem. But what's the matter? Don't you feel well?"

"You've finished your work here?" asked Feders, coming closer. He made no attempt to introduce Krafft. The latter closed the door behind him and leaned against it as if intending to block the exit.

"Yes indeed," said the major-general of the medical corps, slightly taken aback, but in no way uneasy. "Work carrying a heavy responsibility which I have to bear myself—yes, indeed I've finished it. With the result that might have been predicted. It certainly wasn't easy for me; but I have my duty to do here, a painful duty, certainly, but unavoidable. You know how it is—the diagnoses, the requirements of the moment, one's moral convictions."

"You're simply going to wipe out nineteen human beings just because you take it to be your duty?"

"No, just a minute please!" said the medical general, gradually becoming uneasy. "Things aren't quite as simple as that. There are various factors here, Captain, which I can't explain to you in a few words—as a layman you wouldn't understand them."

"Try to explain them to me, all the same."

"I don't see what the point would be," said the general. His rosy complexion had now turned a blotchy red. "I am a doctor, after all, and as such it is my duty to preserve human life, certainly. But it's also my duty to alleviate pain. And death can be a release. Moreover, I am a soldier too . . ."

"And a member of the Party, I presume."

"There's such a thing as putting people out of their agony," said the general. "It's something you don't refuse even to horses. And then think of the demands of the times! First, there's the release from insanity, from eternal sickness, from the torture of endless vegetation. But think too of this: the hospitals are over-crowded; doctors are short; so are trained nursing staff. There are three seriously wounded men waiting for every bed . . ."

"Hold your tongue!" said Feders.

"I beg your pardon," said the general in astonishment, quite certain that he must have misheard.

"I said you were to hold your tongue," said Feders calmly. He snatched up the document which lay in front of the general, trying to grasp what was happening.

"It's quite simple," said Feders, tearing up the document he had just read. "You will have to write your report all over again. And you'll come to the conclusion that none of these wretched people—not a single one of them—is to be assisted into eternity. Do you understand?"

"But this is . . . this is . . ."

"Extortion!" said Lieutenant Krafft from the door. "Which is always preferable to murder!"

Krafft advanced slowly toward the major-general of the medical corps, who was now utterly disconcerted. As he did so he unfastened the holster of his revolver. When he reached the table he drew his revolver and put it down noisily. "Right, come on then," he said threateningly. "Prepare another report, on the required lines."

"All right," said the general, pale and choking, "I yield to force."

"You've got fifteen minutes," said Feders, placing the typewriter on the table and putting in a sheet of paper.

The general of the medical corps began to type with trembling fingers.

Meanwhile Feders drew Krafft over toward the door, where he said in a whisper, "You must do something else for me now, Krafft—for me and our friends hanging there in their baskets. Get this general's car and driver out of the way. Tell the driver quite simply that you're both going on ahead, to the barracks if you like, and that I'll be bringing his boss along later. Will you do that for me?"

"All right, Feders. But see you do your work properly—otherwise we'll both be for it. And I want to live a little longer. There's something I've still got left to do."

The daily timetable ended officially at seven o'clock. From this time onward no duty was allotted—though it was certainly expected. The fact that there was nothing on the timetable didn't mean that there was nothing to do for long.

But at least there was now a certain amount of freedom. Thus supper, which was taken in the billets themselves, could be dallied over and prolonged. It was possible too to take a stroll to the canteen, though the beer admittedly was pretty weak and watery. And anyone with cultural aspirations could make his way to the so-called reading room, where fine German magazines such as *Reich*, *Signal*, and *Our Wehrmacht* were available, with a radio emitting stirring popular tunes.

All this was possible, but it took time. Because, timetable or not, a whole series of things had to be done. For instance, uniforms had to be brushed, weapons and equipment cleaned, notes completed, and written work finished. In addition to which, there were the preparations for the following day's work.

Any thought of leaving camp in the middle of the week was usually beyond the bounds of possibility. It was in one sense a question of time, but it also depended on the attitude of the section officer. The rare permits to go into town at the end of the day's duty could usually be obtained only by someone who (*a*) could give assurances that he had put all his affairs in order; (*b*) could prove that he'd made all the necessary preparations for the following day's work; and (*c*) was in a position to put forward a satisfactory reason for his request.

Every conceivable sort of reason could be advanced, but it had to sound serious. The most popular were so-called semiofficial reasons, such as the need to buy writing materials, or get photographs for identity papers, or darning material for uniforms. Far more suspicious were the reasons of a cultural sort such as the wish to visit a film of national significance, or to borrow books, or visit certain buildings. These always raised deep misgivings, for even though the section officers knew perfectly well that the cadets only wanted to go into town for wine, women, and song, they felt entitled to demand a really convincing sort of excuse.

On this particular day the section officers were not available—as late as eight o'clock they were still being put through their paces by the general in the mess. In such cases it was the section seniors who had to decide on the requests for walking-out passes—in theory, at any rate; in practice, things usually worked according to Cadet Mösler's formula.

Mösler appeared in front of Kramer and declared, "I'm just going down into town, to the café."

"What you mean," declared Kramer, determined to exercise his authority, "is that you're asking for a walking-out pass."

"Now don't start giving yourself airs," said Mösler, unimpressed. "I'm clearing out, and you can enter me in your list. I'm just telling you as one comrade to another."

"And what reason are you giving for the pass?"

"I leave it to someone of your acumen to find a plausible reason."

"No, it's not as easy as all that!" exclaimed Kramer angrily. "You'll have to give me some sound reason."

"All right, then," said Mösler agreeably, "women!"

"But I can't put that down on my list!"

"Then simply put down, fostering relations between the Wehrmacht and the civilian population."

With that, Mösler just left Kramer standing there. But he didn't leave the barracks at once. He went over to see Weber again first, and with him had a short but significant conversation in which they reached complete agreement.

After this Weber went to Rednitz and told him of his conversation with Mösler. Rednitz listened and said, "You do what you like!" Weber took this as agreement and wandered off.

Now it was Hochbauer's turn. Weber took him on one side and began, "I hope you remember your bet."

"Of course," said Hochbauer indignantly. "And I'm going to win it too."

"You haven't much time left, Hochbauer."

"You leave that to me, Weber."

"But you're not going to give a comrade the brushoff when he offers you a helping hand?" said Weber humbly. As always when introducing a beautiful thought such as comradeship into his conversation, he fixed the person he was talking to with an unwavering eye. "And besides, today provides a particularly favorable opportunity."

"You don't need to tell me that, Weber—I'd thought of that already myself."

"Well fine," said Weber. "Everything's perfect. We'll all come down in the role of discreet witnesses. Between ourselves, Hochbauer, and entirely in confidence, your position within the section isn't altogether happy just at the moment. You've an urgent need to do something about it, and here you've got a really first-class opportunity. Show them you're a man, Hochbauer! You've a real need to."

So it came about that Kramer had to put up with a complete invasion of people asking for walking-out passes. Mösler was followed by Weber, who had taken over the role of a sort of umpire in the events anticipated for that evening. Böhmke appeared with him, though he had as yet no idea what was going on; he had been chosen as an expert. Then came Hochbauer, accompanied by Amfortas, ready to lend his friend every assistance. After these came the camp followers, eight in number.

Kramer was desperate. But since he'd already given Mösler a pass he could only cast a benevolent eye on the frivolousness of the others. He himself, however, like Rednitz too, apparently, would have nothing to do with the affair.

At first everything proceeded in a far less complicated way than had at first been supposed. Hochbauer put this down to the impact of his personality, in which he wasn't altogether wrong. He won the admiring respect of his comrades hovering about him.

The first stage went as follows. The cadets waited about in various groups in front of the local Cultural Hall, where a German Girls' League evening was in progress. As experienced observers had anticipated, around eight thirty the girls of the League came pouring out into the open. Among them was the victim, Maria Kelter. As prearranged, Weber now went into action and began annoying the little girl in most convincing fashion. Hochbauer came up, told him to stop annoying her, and undertook to take Maria Kelter under his protection.

"Thank you very much," said Maria Kelter gratefully. "That was very nice of you."

"It was no more than my duty," Hochbauer assured her with a seriousness that was very engaging. "And I must apologize for this fellow, who is, after all, a comrade of mine." This made an excellent impression. "May I escort you?" he added.

"I'd be delighted," said Maria Kelter. Her voice seemed to suggest that she was blushing, but the streets were unlit.

The second stage went like this. In the Café Popp, usually known as the Café Puff, Hochbauer was sitting with the little girl called Maria Kelter in a corner reserved by Weber. They were talking away pleasantly, and the girl found herself more and more carried away with admiration for the handsome and elegant young cadet. At the moment it seemed that she was the only thing in the world that mattered to him. A few other cadets, who made a harmless enough impression, were also sitting about in the café. When Hochbauer repeated his order for two cups of tea, he himself received pure rum, in a tea cup of course—a stirrup cup provided by Cadet Weber, who had put his connections here to good use. He was a regular customer in the Café Puff.

"Actually I hardly go to bars at all," confided Maria Kelter.

"That does you credit," Hochbauer assured her promptly, and was delighted to note the respectful glances he was getting from his comrades sitting behind Maria Kelter.

"I'm more of an open-air girl," she said.

"I'm all for the open air," said Hochbauer, spotting the opening. "A walk in God's good air is the most beautiful thing in the world. Even now in winter. Don't you think so?"

Maria Kelter thought so too. So she didn't hesitate to follow Hochbauer and enjoy some of the nocturnal beauties of nature in his company. She also enjoyed looking up at the imposing, slender figure of her escort, who seemed to her the very picture of chivalry. Humbly and shyly she nestled up against him as they walked along.

Then came the third stage. A number of cadets, with Weber at their head, made their way carefully forward toward the war memorial in the municipal park, where Hochbauer and Maria Kelter had already arrived. This was a site which had often proved its worth and was much used of a Saturday. Its many steps and pedestals offered all sorts of excellent opportunities.

"Please don't," said Maria Kelter suddenly in an agitated voice. In astonishment and bewilderment she added, "You can't do that!"

"He's actually making it!" said Weber in a tone of appreciation to Böhmke, who was peering beside him into the semi-darkness. He had been able to pick up one or two scraps of conversation, although the couple themselves remained partly out of sight. Now Hochbauer forced the girl down onto the stone steps and they disappeared from the view of the spectators altogether.

"What's going on there?" asked Böhmke in some agitation.

"I'll give you three guesses," said Weber.

"But he mustn't do that!" Böhmke was beside himself. "The girl's resisting, can't you hear?"

"Oh come off it, man!" said Weber roughly. "They all carry on as if they meant to resist, the first time! That's all part of it. And this little one's no better than any of the others. To think that she actually turned me down! It never occurs to her that Hochbauer's merely a third-rate substitute for myself."

"You're all a lot of swine!" stammered Böhmke angrily. He was trembling with indignation.

"Ah, what the hell," said Weber. "We're men, aren't we? It goes on all the time."

Elfrida Rademacher and Karl Kraft were side by side on the camp bed in the lieutenant's room in barracks. There couldn't be much objection to engaged couples visiting each other. And it was possible to lock the door.

"Karl," said Elfrida Rademacher softly, with some wariness, "I've had the silliest wishes sometimes—particularly lately."

"Well forget them again quickly," Lieutenant Krafft advised her. "There's another three months to Christmas."

"I've been wishing we could be together more, Karl," she said. "I love you, after all, and I want to live with you as long as I possibly can."

"Now, Elfrida," said Karl Krafft seriously, "have I ever made you any promise of that sort?"

"No."

"Have I ever given you any grounds for misunderstanding about this?"

"No, Karl."

"Good, Elfrida. That's clear, then. We love each other, but we made up our minds never to think about how long this love can last. It may last a long time—it may end any day. Some order that may already have been signed can tear us apart at any moment. You could wake up one day and find me no longer there. It could be tomorrow. So let's get used to the idea and say no more about it."

"But Karl," she said, "it could all be much less dramatic than that. This is your first course; there'll be at least two or three to come—we've probably got months ahead of us. And in a war of this sort that's a tremendously long time— it should be a happy time for us, Karl. I'd like to feel sure that it could be."

"Don't do that, Elfrida."

"Why don't you just stick to your work here!" cried Elfrida with some vehemence. "That way we could be sure of at least six months together. Instead of which you get yourself involved in things beyond your control, with people who could get you in trouble."

"I think it's getting late," said Karl Krafft calmly. "Too late. You ought to go."

She got up and stared at him, distraught and uncomprehending. She saw that he was smiling. It was a smile that concealed pain.

"Elfrida," said Lieutenant Krafft, putting his arms around her, "you try telling a donkey that it doesn't do him any good having long ears. Try telling a bull that red's a nice color. You'll have more success than you'll have in trying to protect me from myself."

He helped her into her coat, put on his own, shut the door, and let her out into the corridor. There stood Cadet Rednitz with the dim light falling on his face. He saluted without a sound.

"May I have a word with you a moment, sir?"

"Have you been waiting for me, Rednitz?"

"For the last quarter of an hour, Lieutenant, but I didn't want to disturb you."

The lieutenant nodded. So the cadet knew all about his private life and probably even caught a word or two. Well, so long as it was only Rednitz it didn't matter. Krafft turned to Elfrida, "Go on ahead a bit, my dear—I'll follow you. Or do you intend to delay me some time, Rednitz?"

"Three minutes, Lieutenant, no more."

Lieutenant Krafft went back into his room followed by Rednitz. The crumpled bed was very obvious, but Rednitz seemed to take no notice of it. He looked straight at the lieutenant.

"Sir," said the cadet frankly, "may I ask you what you said to Hochbauer this afternoon at the end of the engineering exercise?"

Krafft didn't seem in the least astonished at this question; even if he was, he didn't show it. He looked at the cadet with equal frankness. "You don't really need to ask, Rednitz," he said. "You know quite well already."

"And the result, sir—may I know that?"

Krafft looked at the cadet more closely. It was an honest face, full of trust, and above all, sympathetic. So after hesitating for a moment, the lieutenant said, "I won't ask you why you want to know, Rednitz—all I can tell you is that Hochbauer admitted what he'd done."

"Well, everything's clear then," said Cadet Rednitz.

"Unfortunately it's not at all clear, my dear fellow," said the lieutenant, lowering his head. "What we have here isn't a confession, but simply a statement that was not made in front of witnesses and which Hochbauer will therefore deny, as he's already told me he intends to. What I need to complete the picture, Rednitz, is proof, and I haven't any—not one single piece of convincing proof. That's to say I've found a murderer but can't bring anything against him. But that's the way it is, Rednitz. Is that what you wanted to know?"

"If that's really how it is, sir, then perhaps there's another possibility. A way around it that nevertheless would lead to the desired goal. Or were you thinking of letting the whole thing drop?"

"Go on, man! Speak up! What have you got in mind?"

Cadet Rednitz produced three things. First: a fairly comprehensive and very accurate list enumerating in detail each occasion on which Cadet Hochbauer had paid a private visit to his company commander, Captain Ratshelm, with a precise record of the times. Witnesses were listed, and their evidence noted.

Second: a delicately woven blue handkerchief, slightly soiled, and adorned with the monogram F.F., which stood for Felicitas Frey.

Thirdly: the address of a certain Maria Kelter, who lived in Wildlingen-am-Main, Kranichgasse, 4, with the following accompanying particulars: Municipal Park, War Memorial, about 2350 hours.

"Rednitz," said Krafft with conviction, "this should do the trick."

The barrack day came to an end officially at 2200 hours with the sounding of lock-up.

The canteen manager turned out the last of his guests and switched off the light in the bar. The sentry barred the main gate and closed the small one beside it, leaving it unlocked. Another member of the guard set out on his rounds.

The pickets responsible for order and discipline went into action: the duty lieutenant for the headquarters company; the duty cadet for the various training companies, and the girl on duty for the civilian female employees in barracks. They made their rounds through their own territories, each noting who was present and who was not—the absentees requiring to be checked against leave or pass lists. Generally speaking all was in order.

This evening there was great activity in the mess. The officers had only just finished swallowing their dinner, for the tactical training exercise had, as prophesied, turned out to be interminable and had continued long past the usual time. Numerous victims lay strewn about the field, chief of whom was Captain Ratshelm. Now, however, each officer was allowed half a bottle of wine, and badly needed it. At least all now knew what to do in the event of a major outbreak of fire.

Many of the cadets were still not asleep—most were working and thus maintaining the regulation silence. In Section H, however, the atmosphere was still very lively. They were celebrating Operation War Memorial, initiated by Weber and successfully carried out by Hochbauer. The participants, who had returned rather late, had got in over the fence.

Only Böhmke took no part in the celebrations. He had been

the only person to return from the operation in time, and he had poured out his heart indignantly to Rednitz. Now he was seeking further comfort in *Faust,* and lingered a long time over the passage which ran:

> *Resolute, now claim your hour*
> *Though the throng may quail and drift;*
> *For the noble soul has power*
> *To compass all if wise and swift.*

The communications section, however, was extremely active at this time—a very rare occurrence. The two girls on duty here had hardly any time for the cadets paying court to them. The air-raid warning system demanded their attention —a number of enemy aircraft had been reported.

"Oh, what the hell!" said one of their visitors. "They won't come here. I bet they haven't even got this place on their maps."

"Make yourself comfortable, girl," said Captain Kater. "Make yourself at home, in fact. Or don't you like my room?"

"Oh yes," Irene Jablonski assured him, looking curiously about her, "I like it very much here."

"Sit down, then," said Kater. "Wherever you like. On the bed, for instance."

"Thank you," said Irene politely, doing as she was told.

She liked what she saw very much. The room seemed to her extravagantly large. Five or six girls usually had to put up with a room this size. And there was a carpet here, too. Colored curtains of some heavy material made an unusually decorative effect. The bed was covered with a sort of fur rug.

"You can take your shoes off if you like," said Kater generously. "Your feet must be cold with this fearful weather we're having. And it's easy to catch cold."

"Oh, I don't mind about the weather," said Irene.

"Take you shoes off all the same," Kater advised. "You can put your feet under the rug. It's nice and warm there."

Irene Jablonski followed his suggestion. She was a willing, humble sort of girl. And she felt honored; the other girls were sitting around in their wretched little rooms or stuck away in some corner or other—she, however, was paying a visit to the CO, Captain Kater himself.

"I'm going to open a bottle of champagne today," began Kater, "in celebration."

"Oh fine!" said Irene Jablonski, hugging herself with delight.

Kater opened the window and got the bottles that he'd been keeping outside in the cold. Then he produced a couple of elegant champagne glasses—officers'-mess property. He sat down beside Irene on the bed and said, "Well, here we go!"

He filled the glass, the champagne bubbled over onto her dress. Kater went to considerable lengths to wipe it off, while she giggled affectedly, for she was very ticklish.

"Let's have a drink," suggested Kater.

"Oh, that's lovely!" cried Irene taking a sip. In fact she didn't particularly like the champagne, which tasted to her rather like soda water.

Suddenly she pouted and said, "You haven't had much time for me these last few days. I thought you'd forgotten me."

"It's true, child," said Kater, "but one can't unfortunately always arrange one's life as one would like to. I have my duty to do, you know, with all its little problems. My hands are full all day long sometimes."

Kater saw with satisfaction that Irene nodded understandingly. Or at least she did her best to understand. Fortunately, he thought, she was endowed with a certain innocence, and this, as he had learned, had its advantages.

In any case this seemed as good an opportunity as any. Feders was driving around the countryside somewhere with his bosom friend Krafft. Elfrida was with Frau Feders. The barracks had closed down for the night. He wasn't likely to be interrupted.

"That stain on your dress is worse than I thought," said Kater. "Take it off—I've got some marvelous stuff for removing stains."

"I don't really know—"

"It's warm enough in here, isn't it?"

"Should I really?"

"Why not?" said Kater, as if it were the most natural thing in the world. "We're quite alone here. And we mustn't let that spot stay there. It would be a pity on such a nice dress. Besides, I'll get you another one if you like."

"You're so good to me," said Irene.

"Come on, then, girl—don't be embarrassed. Come closer —I'll help you. There, that's better. A bit closer. There you are!"

Irene Jablonski pulled her dress over her head.

"That's better, isn't it?" Hurriedly he filled the glasses

again, taking a good look at her as he did so; graceful, feminine thighs, positively provocative breasts, and a sensuous mouth, with moist lips slightly parted. Kater's hands began to tremble. Once again the champagne overflowed, this time unintentionally, and poured onto his trousers.

"Well look at that!" he said. "They'll have to be cleaned too, won't they?"

"It looks like it," said Irene Jablonski gravely.

At this moment the telephone began to ring—relentlessly, continuously, without a pause. Kater looked first at Irene Jablonski, who had leaned back on the bed, then at the telephone which wouldn't leave him alone. Finally he picked up the receiver and cried, "Damn it, what is it? At this time of night! Can't you leave a man in peace! . . . Ah, I see," he added a few seconds later. "That's different. I'll come at once."

"Do you have to go?" asked Irene softly.

"Yes," he said. There was a note of genuine regret in his voice.

"A pity."

"There's an air-raid warning," said Captain Kater. "Get dressed again."

Captain Feders steered his jeep through the night in the direction of Wildlingen. The medical corps general sat beside him clinging tense to the door handle. They were driving fast and the road was bad.

"You might at least have spared me this," said the medical corps general with a groan. "I've done everything you've asked of me. It really was unnecessary to divert my car."

"Nothing's unnecessary and you're not going to be spared a thing!" cried Feders, stepping on the accelerator.

The general's hat fell forward onto his forehead. He tried to make himself more comfortable but lost his balance altogether. His pink face was distorted with fury.

Suddenly Captain Feders jammed on the brakes. The jeep shot across the surface of the road like a sleigh, turned toward the edge of the road, struck a sandy patch, and came to a halt the wrong way around with a screech of brakes. The medical corps general cracked his head against the windshield and started to moan.

"Shut up!" said Feders roughly, and his passenger fell silent immediately.

Feders cocked an ear into the darkness. The sound of sirens could be heard from Wildlingen—air-raid sirens howling with monotonous regularity.

"That suits me fine," said Feders.

"What are you going to do?" asked the medical corps general anxiously.

"I'll tell you exactly," declared Captain Feders, turning to his companion and looking him straight in the eye. The general's face was glistening with sweat. "I'm going to dispatch you into eternity so that some poor creatures can continue to live a little longer."

"You're joking," gasped the medical corps general. "I've already done everything you wanted. I've confirmed for you in writing that all the patients stand a chance of recovery. You've got that officially. Which makes everything all right. You meant that as a joke now, didn't you?"

"My dear man," said Captain Feders, "what do you take me for? I know the rules of the game! Besides, there's nothing I wouldn't put past you murderous bastards. Someone who can finish off the sick to get empty beds or fulfill some Greater German fantasy or other is capable of any dirty underhanded trick. I know what'll happen. As soon as you're out of my clutches you'll rescind everything and nineteen basketmen will be promptly finished off. What's more you'll report both me and Dr. Krüger. That's why there's only one course open to me. It's logical, isn't it?"

"I assure you nothing like that will happen," said the medical corps general. "I give you my word, my word of honor."

"I don't give a damn for the word of honor of a man who can kill the sick. My only choice lies between a murderer like yourself and nineteen helpless human beings. Who knows how many hundred others you may have on your conscience? No, it's no use. You'll have to go. It's the only thing to do with your sort."

The engine roared, the jeep shot forward, the general was hurled back into his seat, and the monotonous howl of the air-raid sirens mingled with the whine of the engine into a hellish crescendo.

The captain shouted, "Let them come! And let's hope they drop their bombs. Then I'll just throw you onto a pile of corpses. If not, I'll drown you in the Main. That way I'll at least have done one good deed in my life!"

They didn't hear the drone of aircraft above them. They didn't hear the whistling of the bombs. They merely saw what looked like mushrooms exploding all around them with a glaring, blinding brightness. Their eardrums seemed about to burst. The jeep rocked wildly and the general cowered in his seat.

Feders trod wildly on the brakes, stalled the engine, and hurled himself on the medical corps general. With features distorted with frenzy he dragged him out of the jeep.

But as Captain Feders raised his pistol a powerful blow knocked it out of his hand. A sheet of flame stabbed agonizingly at his eyes. Then the blast knocked him over and flung him into the dirty snow.

A few seconds later the captain picked himself up. The overturned jeep was a complete wreck, while beneath it, hunched and pale, lay the body of the medical corps general.

"I couldn't even do that myself," said Captain Feders dully.

The flames from the burning houses were all about him. The acrid smell of devastation hung on the air. Human cries mingled with the howl of the air-raid sirens. But the captain simply stared helplessly in front of him.

A small group of enemy bombers—probably not more than six or eight in all—appeared over Wildlingen at 2243 hours. It took them exactly three minutes to drop their bombs, and at 2246 hours the danger was over.

They left behind them a heap of ruins on the eastern edge of the town; four complete streets and fifty-eight houses destroyed, and two hundred and seven fatal casualties including one general of the medical corps and a cadet who had overstayed his walking-out pass. The rest were civilians.

"We've been lucky again!" commented Major Frey, after assuring himself that the market place, and with it his house, remained undamaged.

Every fire brigade in the area poured in; the barracks too contributed their share of disciplined activity. The tactical exercise on the "major outbreak of fire" had indeed borne fruit. Everyone was full of admiration for the prophetic instinct of the general—it almost looked as if he had ordered the attack himself, though not even Captain Ratshelm dared to put it quite like this.

The burgomaster, district Party leader and district commissioner, also visited the scene of the catastrophe, though he soon left again for he had a lot of organizing to do. Before he left, he declared to the bystanders with a certain pride, 'It was our railway station they were after—after all, it's an important junction."

The statement rather upset some of the officers, who felt that their importance had been overlooked. One of them said out loud, "Of course it was the training school they were after. But they're such bunglers they missed by two miles. That would never have happened with our fellows!" The barracks stood quite undamaged on the top of the hill, illuminated by the light of the fires from the burning houses in the valley. Not a tile was missing from its roof, not a single window pane had been broken.

By three o'clock in the morning the worst was over; the troops were able to return to barracks. Some of the cadets' overalls were bulging prominently—among other things, they had managed to rescue several hundred bottles of Steinwein from the flames. So, though they were tired, they were not unhappy.

The general, however, before going to bed said, "Tomorrow morning, training program as usual."

* * * *

Intermediate Report No. 9

The Curriculum Vitae of Cadet Heinz-Horst Hochbauer, or The Honor of a Murderer

I, Heinz-Horst Hochbauer, was born on March 21, 1923, the son of Captain Heribert Hochbauer, a serving officer, and his wife Victoria, née Sanders-Zoffhausen, in Rosenheim, Torplatz No. 17. At the express wish of my father I joined a number of patriotic associations at an early age, which benefited my general education considerably and enabled me successfully to complete my four years in primary school —also in Rosenheim—without any particular effort.

My father throws me up in the air, but only if I cry "Hurrah." It's our favorite game. Father's powerful arms snatch me up and I hover, shouting, over everyone and everything. Below me the furniture and the people, including my mother, who laughs heartily, and my brothers and sisters, who stare up at me. Tiny distorted faces below me and eyes flickering with envy. For it's obvious that it's me my father loves best. I am the only one he throws up in the air. "Hurrah!" I cry with delight.

All my brothers and sisters—whose names are Hugo and Harold, Helga and Hermione—are born, as I was, around March 20. This is because our mother's birthday is on June 20, which is also the day on which my parents got married. Father is a very busy and much traveled man, says our mother. "He travels for Germany, for the future Reich, for the coming Führer!" But he never forgets his family, thinks of us day and night, and once a year—on June 20—returns home, passes us all in review, dispenses justice, lays down the broad principles for our education, and begets a further increase in the family. Then he returns to the struggle again. And Mother says, "He's a superman!"

Flies can go on walking even when one of their legs has been pulled off—even with two of their legs off too, so that one can choose which leg to pull off—front or back, left or right. But if one pulls their legs off diagonally—that is to say the front left-hand one and the rear right, then they lose all sense of direction and collapse. "Flies," says my mother, "spread dirt and disease—they are disgusting and must be killed."

Men keep on appearing—Father's men. They bring messages and money; they leave packages and take others away. Some of the men stay with us a few days, some on the floor of the sitting room, but some also in the bedroom, in my father's place. They're all called "uncle" by us children, most of them hold military ranks, and those who stay in the bedroom are almost all officers, war heroes, like Father, with plenty of decorations. "Real daredevils!" my mother always says. "I owe it to Father to treat them kindly, for the future of the Reich rests on their shoulders."

"My dear boy," my Aunt Chamberlain-Schipper says to me, "learn to recognize distinctions between people, and you'll learn all about life. Because human beings are not equal even before God. There are always some people of inferior quality. Even everyday life grades people by rank into those in authority and their subordinates. Be like your father—be a leader, get a following around you." Aunt Chamberlain-Schipper must know what she's talking about, because one of her relations was a great philosopher, whose thoughts shook the whole world, so people say. My father has said of my aunt, "We hold these things in our hearts, but she has them in her brain too."

My friend Conrad and my other friend Karl Friedrich

stand with me in the corner of the school yard where the dustbins are. The others are running around and the girls are playing hopscotch by the benches at the entrance. They jump about laughing stupidly and sweating; one of them is a fat girl with pigtails dangling down her back. This is Elfrida, whom everyone always calls Elfie. We size her up carefully because she has told tales on us and must be punished for it. We decide to cut off her pigtails in the hall, where we'll lie in wait for her with a sack and the scissors which we've borrowed from Elfrida's father's business. In fact this is too mild a punishment for what she has done. Personally I think we should tear her hair out by the roots; it would be no more than she deserved.

The members of the youth club stand before me. I am their troop leader. Aunt Chamberlain-Schipper has designed our pennant—a black Celtic cross within a white St. Andrew's cross on a red background. Mother has sewn our pennant and one of my brothers carries it. (Father provided the material, says Mother, from his special fund for the promotion of patriotic effort.) We have lit a midsummer bonfire and our faces are aglow. "Pile it on!" I shout, and twigs and branches and planks are thrown onto the fire. The splendid flickering glow from the fire shines on our faces, our eyes are ablaze, and my voice vibrates with happiness. "Pile on more!" I shout, and bales of straw are now added to it, with a bottle or two of paraffin, a tin of gas. Everything's been perfectly organized. And I shout "Now jump! Everyone after me! Anyone who doesn't follow is a coward!" And they all jump. There's no place for cowards in our lot.

"Hochbauer," says my teacher, whose name is Marquardt, "I've heard you've founded a national society among the pupils. Is that correct?" "That's correct," I say. "Is it forbidden?" "Not by me," says Marquardt, the teacher, "not if it's a national society. One can't stop people doing what's right!" I tell my father this, and Father tells his friends, one of whom is an education inspector. So it comes about that one fine day Marquardt the teacher is made headmaster of our school. "Justice always triumphs in the end," says my father.

Since my performance in primary school was above average it was taken for granted that I sould continue my education at a higher level. To this end I was sent to the Prince Eugen High School in Neustadt in 1932, Neustadt being chosen partly because this high school enjoyed the services of particularly good teachers and also because this was where my Aunt Chamberlain-Schipper lived, whom my father had singled out to complete my education. And here I stay, playing a full part in the magnificent development of the ideology of the Reich, until 1940, when I graduated with distinction. Immediately afterward of course I volunteered for the Wehrmacht and had the good fortune to be accepted at once and enrolled as an officer cadet.

It is a solemn moment which completes and at the same time provides the climax to my basic schooling in my home town. The youth club I founded is incorporated in the Hitler Youth. The drummer boys beat furiously on their drums. For the last time our pennant flutters in the breeze, to be lowered with honor. Kopelski, a regimental leader in the Hitler Youth, comes up to me; his face is deadly serious, his eye moist with emotion. The drums seem about to burst, they're beating so furiously. "In the name of the Führer!" cries Kopelski. He takes our own pennant and hands over the pennant of the Hitler Youth. And, as arranged beforehand, I am appointed group leader.

Father drives up in a car this time—an eight-cylinder Mercedes—an official car. Father in a light brown tropical-style uniform with cosmopolitan air. He's wearing his Pour le Mérite. And his laugh drowns the noise of the engine. There's a chauffeur sitting beside him, an ADC and an orderly behind him—and all in splendid, light brownish khaki. "Fall in!" cries my father good humoredly. And then he reviews his family and his eyes light up at the sight of me, for I am wearing a brown shirt too. "My dear sons," he says, "you've seen the signs of the times!" "I am your son," I say with simple pride, and he enfolds me in his arms.

I get up crying, "Garlic!" Wassermann, the assistant master, looks at me wide-eyed. "What do you mean, Hochbauer?" he askes naïvely. I repeat, "Garlic! There's a smell of garlic in here. No one can work in a stink like that." "Hochbauer," says Wassermann, the master, "control yourself please." "The stink of garlic is driving us out of the room," I say. "We can't be expected to breathe the same air as certain people." "Get out!" cries Wassermann, the master. "Have you considered who it is you're throwing out?" I ask. "Get out!" he repeats. I go. But fourteen of my comrades leave with me, as arranged. Three days later the classes are organized and all racially alien elements are withdrawn from us. We have won, though not all along the line. Wassermann continues to teach there, but only foreign languages in the sixth and fifth grades.

We put a notice on Wassermann's desk: "Jews not wanted." He picks it up and puts it in his pocket without a word. We make a complaint about this confiscation of personal property. Wassermann is requested to give the notice back to the owner. He no longer has it. He is told to find a similar notice. When he tries to go into a shop to buy one, the shop people, who are very nationally conscious and have been tipped off by us beforehand, turn him out. Finally there's nothing else for him to do but to have a notice made just like it. But the printer, who has also been tipped off by us, knows his duty—he insists that he can only print a notice like this if he gets an order for at least fifty at once. Wassermann places the order —there's no other choice left to him. Then we get hold of the fifty notices and hang them wherever Wassermann goes —outside the lecture room, his apartment, his cellar, the entrance to the school, every lavatory in sight. Wassermann disappears from the town. Now victory is really ours.

It's June again, 1934, and again Father drives up in his official car. But it isn't Mother he wants to see, but Aunt Chamberlain-Schipper. Besides, it's nighttime and the chauffeur, the aide, and the orderly wait outside in the street in the darkness. "Matilda," my father says to my aunt, "the situation is serious. But you've got good connections, you must help me. After all, you're related to one of the philosophers the Führer swears by." Father tells his story and I listen with burning cheeks, for I am allowed to be present. A quarrel is about to break out inside the party; the chief of staff of the SA, Röhm by name, a former wartime comrade and a good friend, intends to bring about a reshuffle of power within the leadership of the Reich. "Has he got a chance?" asks my aunt shrewdly. "Not against the Führer," says my father. "What are you hesitating for, then?" says my aunt. "Your place is at Hitler's side." "You may be right," says my father. "But what's my surest way of getting there?" "The quickest way, pursued with the greatest possible frankness."

A few weeks later my father has taken off his brown uniform. He's wearing a black one now. The color suits him splendidly. "He looks devastating in his black uniform," says Mother. "And his Pour le Mérite shows up much better now." My Aunt Chamberlain-Schipper takes me to one side and says, "You have witnessed a historic occasion—never forget it! Your father was confronted by the most difficult decision a man can ever have to make. It was a question of loyalty.

To whom did he owe it? To his comrade, or to the Führer? The answer is 'To the Reich'—which is embodied in the Führer. You must never forget this—Germany comes before everything! Even if thousands and thousands have to die for it!"

Her name is Ulrica—her nickname is Bubsie, but that's neither here nor there. She is a darkish blonde, very shapely, and her step is firm and springy. She laughs a lot at everything under the sun—a fresh, jolly, unabashed German girl. A year older than me, though this makes no difference, apart from the fact that she's much more experienced. Together we are in charge of the sport and physical training camp at Frundsberg on the Ammersee—a thousand young people, including three hundred and seventy girls—different tented camps, but a communal kitchen, a communal parade ground, and communal staff quarters. At our very first private conference Ulrica lowers the tent flap over the entrance. "We must get to know each other properly first," she says. "That's always the most important thing—the rest then falls into place."

But three days later Liebentraut appears. He's the district leader and a member of the Reich Youth-Führer's staff. He inspects the camp and is lavish with his praises. "I like it here, comrades," he says. "I'm staying. There's nothing to beat communal physical training." And he stays, taking up his quarters in the staff tent. Ulrica can barely conceal her annoyance. "He's undermining the congenial atmosphere we've built up," she says. For Liebentraut, the district leader, while dedicated like us to the common cause, thinks that the sexes should pursue it separately. So Ulrica is banned from the staff tent. But between the two of us, Liebentraut and me, a wonderfully genuine friendship develops. When the communal camp comes to an end, I am promoted senior group leader.

Then there's Söhnig the coward. A tall, gawky fellow with spectacles and a stoop. Brother of a girl whose outward appearance is extremely exotic and who therefore makes a far from Germanic impression. The Söhnigs come from the Rhineland; presumably some of the colored occupation troops have left their mark on the family. Thier mother is still said to speak French at home sometimes. Söhnig anyhow—Kurt is his Christian name—shows none of the team spirit, won't join in the communal games, refuses to jump from the ten-foot board. We haul him up the tower by ropes. He resists furiously, coward that he is, flailing with his arms, kicking out, and even spitting. He moans and howls, entreats and whimpers like a baby. But we tie him up, yank him to the top, and then push him into the water. Heart attack. Done for. Just shows the sort of milksop he was.

Investigation. Interrogation, inquiries. "Who was there?" asks the headmaster. The whole class gets to its feet, including me. "Whose fault was it?" asks the headmaster. The whole class sits down again after me. "But how could it happen?" asks the headmaster. "It was a heart attack," I say. "That's been proved. And he got this heart attack out of sheer fright. It was his own fault." "Most regrettable," says the headmaster, squirming uncomfortably, "but nothing can be done about it." "And besides, there's a war on," I say. And everyone knows what that means; cowards like him have no right to exist. "Hochbauer," my classmates say to me afterward, "you saved us. If you hadn't answered up to the headmaster like that, we wouldn't have stood a chance of graduating, and that would have been a frightful thing." "Ah well, you know, friends," I say, "all you need is guts and a sense of purpose—nothing can go wrong then."

After I had volunteered for military duty along with the whole class and had completed my basic training, I was immediately posted into the field; but unfortunately not until after the end of the campaign in France. However, by February 1941 our unit was in the General-Government of Poland, and from there we were able to take part in the campaign in the east right from the start, first of all in the double battle at Byalistock and Minsk, where I was awarded the Iron Cross Second Class. After further action against the Bolshevik enemy of the world and after being specially selected for a regimental course and an officer-cadets' course at Dresden, I was posted to the Officers' Training School at Wildlingen-am-Main.

Dompke, the corporal in charge of recruits, never lets up. He's the sort of man who never gives in about anything—a real whole-hogger. Down into the mud, up out of the mud—mud everywhere—in the corners of one's mouth, in one's ears, around one's neck, and the rest of one's body streaming with sweat. But Dompke never lets up. We measure the length and breadth of the barrack square a hundred times over, until the first man collapses. "Hochbauer," says Dompke, "Do you feel you're being maltreated?" "No, Corporal." Dompke likes this. People always like the truth. I'm breathing fairly regularly, my pulse is beating almost normally, my heart flutters only once or twice when under pressure. I know that the body has to be steeled if it is to remain fit. As I steeled my boys in the Hitler Youth. It's part of the system, part of the whole educatonal pattern. Idlers, weaklings, and cowards are the people who complain of maltreatment at such times; that's one of the ways one recognizes them.

The partisans stand against the wall at the back of the school staring at the mud. There are three fellows and one woman—the only way you can tell that this filthy, ragged creature is a woman is by her long hair. Our company has fallen in and is staring at the partisans, then at the lieutenant, who steps out in front. "I want volunteers," says the lieutenant. "This rabble here"—he points at the partisans—"set fire to a house last night and killed two of our comrades. Right, then—volunteers forward." I step forward, and my comrades in my section follow me to a man. "It's what I expected of you," the lieutenant says to me.

Father is commandant of the SS political training school at Pronthausen. A vast complex of buildings with elements of early Germano-Celtic style, set in a heroic landscape. All directly under the Führer through the Reich-Führer SS. Father and Mother and the younger children live in an idyllic villa with a fantastic rose garden—the official residence of the commandant. Marvelous days on leave between two battles. The climax—I am allowed to accompany Father as he inspects the ranks of the future SS leaders. A fine speech from Father on the theme of loyalty! One evening Father asks, "What's the name of your regimental commander—Warnow, isn't it?" "Yes, Father," I say, "Colonel Warnow." "His son is at my training college," says Father. "Give the Colonel my regards when you get back to the front."

"I'm delighted, my dear Hochbauer," says Colonel Warnow. "Absolutely delighted to hear my son's making such good progress and that he's in such excellent hands as your father's. Is there anything particular I can do for you?" I ask to be sent into action again. But we're not very favorably placed in our regiment. We're seldom lucky enough to be allowed up to the front. "Corporal Hochbauer," Colonel Warnow says to me, "I'll take you under my wing for a bit. You'll be transferred to me in the regimental staff. No objections! You'll soon see. Wherever I am, war follows."

Midsummer night in Russia. The glow of the half dark. Hot

enough to make you sweat. The colonel takes off his tunic. We're having a private celebration of his award of the Knight's Cross. As his personal aide I'm allowed to be present, too. The colonel unbuttons his shirt and finally pulls it over his head altogether. We're sitting in the hall of a country house—the whole thing a bit primitive, but improved by a certain Germanic feeling for décor: fleecy blankets over the chairs, flowers in cut-glass vases, flags, and a portrait of the Führer on the walls. A crate of Crimean champagne is brought up—twenty-eight bottles for seven men. The temperature rises. The colonel takes off his trousers too and, to cool himself, pours a glass of champagne over his manly chest. Other officers follow his example. Wonderful moments of true masculinity. "My dear Hochbauer," Colonel Warnow says to me, "I swear to you, my boy, you're a born officer."

The colonel says this because I played a considerable part in the heroic action which led to his award of the Knight's Cross. I can claim to have been the first to have spotted the weak point in the enemy sector. For the battle signals were passing through my hands; four tanks destroyed on one hill showed where the weakness lay. The colonel personally led the break-through with all his reserves—we fought so hard that over four hundred of our comrades lie where they fell. "Hochbauer," says the colonel afterward, wiping his driver's blood from the windshield—the fellow hadn't managed to get under cover in time—"there's one thing we must never forget. No sacrifice is too high for victory in a just cause!"

28 *TRUTH IS DANGEROUS*

THE NEXT DAY Lieutenant Krafft was determined to make a clean sweep of things. In a few days he felt it would be too late. But he still had the courage to see it through.

Krafft first asked Captain Feders to take his place in the day's program. Feders immediately agreed without any questions, merely saying, "So, the hunt is up! I remember once getting a wild boar in my sights, but the good Lord himself took a hand in the matter and the wild boar was struck by lightning. What do you say to that?"

"Perhaps," said Krafft, "you were trying to encroach on the good Lord's territory. He never seems to like that very much. With me the matter is somewhat different. You might say I intend simply to present Justice with the reverse side of the picture. There's no particular risk in that—everyone knows the lady is blind."

"Off you go, then, trouble maker. I'll keep our section at it in the meantime." •

Krafft left the barracks and went down into the little town. The eastern part of it, which had been destroyed in the air raid, was still smoking, and now stank considerably more than the night before.

The Kranichgasse, however, to which Krafft made his way, seemed to have been spared. It was here that he found Maria Kelter. He had a short, revealing conversation with her which passed off satisfactorily enough. He acted as if he had a duty to perform; a painful one certainly, but unavoidable. This was a method which hardly ever failed to impress the brave subjects of the Reich, not least its innocent young girls.

After this, Krafft returned to the barracks, directing his steps toward the building where the commanding officer lived. There he made his way straight to Major-General Modersohn's anteroom. He greeted Sybille Bachner briefly, but not without warmth, and said to Lieutenant Bieringer, the ADC, "Could I speak to the general, please?"

"Quite out of the question," replied Bieringer. "The general's in an important conference at the moment with a delegation from the Party and municipal council of Wildlingen about the clearing up of last night's bomb damage."

"How long will it last?"

"At least another hour."

"I'm afraid I can't wait that long. Please tell the general I'm here. I need three minutes, that's all."

"My dear Krafft," said Bieringer, somewhat dismayed, "what are you thinking of! You should know our general by now—he never lets anyone interrupt him. Particularly not when there's a third party present. No one can do it—neither you nor I."

"Presumably you've never tried."

Krafft turned from Bieringer to Sybille Bachner. She gave him a confidential smile and he looked at her inquiringly. Then she got up and said, "To save you the trouble of trying to persuade me, Herr Krafft, I'll go of my own accord—

the responsibility is mine, but it's you who are taking the risk."

"I might as well get your posting ready in the meantime, Krafft, if you're really so determined to have it," said Bieringer. "Disturbing the general in the middle of a conference is sheer madness!"

But Sybille Bachner went over to the door which led into the general's study. She straightened her dress, hastily adjusted her hair, and went in.

Krafft and Bieringer stared at the closed door. Bieringer feared the worst, while all Krafft could do was to hope for the best.

After a relatively short pause the door opened again and the general appeared, with Sybille Bachner smiling behind him. Modersohn strode over to Lieutenant Krafft and gave him his hand. Bieringer collapsed in his chair with astonishment.

"Well, Lieutenant Krafft," asked the general, curt as ever, though warmly enough, "what can I do for you?"

"General," said Lieutenant Krafft, "I request you to institute expulsion proceedings."

"Against whom?"

"Against Cadet Hochbauer, General."

Modersohn didn't move a muscle. Only his eyelids narrowed slightly. There was a rough edge to his voice as he said, "Expulsion proceedings are an unusual step. Do you think you have sufficient evidence to justify the procedure? Moreover is your evidence such as to ensure a positive conclusion?"

"I have no doubt of it." Quietly Lieutenant Krafft added, "It's the only thing to do."

The general hesitated for several seconds, then asked, "When?"

"Today, General," said Lieutenant Krafft unhesitatingly. "Early afternoon would be the best time—I'll have everything ready by then."

"Permission granted," said the general. He turned to his aide. "Take all the necessary steps, Bieringer. Expulsion proceedings against Cadet Hochbauer, Number Six Company, Section H for Heinrich. On the basis of evidence provided by Lieutenant Krafft. Chairman of the commission of inquiry Commanding Officer of Number Two Course, Major Frey. Composition as usual. Beginning fifteen hundred hours. Preliminary report, to be fully confirmed first thing tomorrow morning. If there's anything else that's not clear, Bieringer, please refer to Lieutenant Krafft."

The ADC looked down at his notes in consternation. He was utterly amazed. Sybille Bachner smiled encouragingly at Krafft. The latter had eyes only for the general.

With the same measured stride as before, Major-General Modersohn made for the door, but here he stopped for a moment and turned. Then something utterly unprecedented occurred; the general nodded to Lieutenant Krafft before closing the door behind him.

It was some time before Bieringer recovered himself. With heavy irony he asked, "Has the lieutenant any further orders for the staff?"

"Not for the moment," said Krafft, looking gratefully across at Sybille Bachner. "Or perhaps just one, Bieringer —try and make clear to the course commander that these expulsion proceedings are of a highly official nature, and not just some convenient provisional solution."

"I understand," said Bieringer. "You want me to make clear to Major Frey that any mistakes he makes in this business may be turned against him. Moreover you attach particular importance presumably to there being no exploratory conversations beforehand. Everything that is to be revealed should be kept for the proceedings themselves. Yes, I'll certainly let the course commander know that. What exactly is this little game you're playing, Krafft?"

"You'd better ask the general that," replied Krafft.

"Aha," said Major Frey significantly. "I see."

"The general wishes expulsion proceedings to be instituted," explained Bieringer on the telephone. "The results are to be positive and clear cut."

"Of course," Frey assured him. "I understand that."

But in fact he didn't understand at all. He stared for a long time at the telephone he had just put down. He had received an order from the general, with additional comment from Bieringer—very definite comment too. And yet what was it exactly Major-General Modersohn wanted?

This was a problem requiring profound thought. To this end Major Frey had himself driven home, taking a brief case full of documents with him. After a lavish midday meal in the studied peace of his own house, he intended to get to the bottom of it.

"Dear Felicitas," he said to his wife as he tasted his soup, "I've been detailed to conduct official expulsion proceedings."

"Do so, then," said his wife without much interest. "You

shouldn't find that difficult. You know your procedure and all the various rules and regulations—they can leave it to you quite safely."

Felicitas had become rather absent-minded lately. He didn't really need her advice—he merely wanted to make a little conversation in the course of the meal.

"Expulsion proceedings of this sort," he said, as his niece Barbara brought in the roast, "have been extraordinarily rare hitherto. There've only been five of them in the whole history of our training school. And not one of those under Modersohn. But of course this has no particular significance."

"Not for you, certainly," said Frau Frey.

She was plainly uninterested. She didn't want to know any of the details, not even the name of the victim. She seemed to have succumbed to a sort of apathy of late. It was noticeable even at meals.

The major withdrew to his study. Frau Felicitas went to lie down. But Barbara prepared a strong, sweet cup of coffee.

The major wanted to think the matter over further by himself, but Barbara wouldn't leave him alone. She bent over him, put down the coffee, and looked at him with soft velvety eyes. "Do you want a brandy afterward?" she asked.

"No," he said, "I've got to work."

"But you ought to rest a little in the meantime," suggested Barbara.

The major, however, bent over his papers, trying to concentrate. A whole series of questions had to be cleared up. What did the general really want to happen? How did he want things to go? Which documents would he want to see? Which needed to be edited, and which could be thrown away as unimportant? And finally the most important question of all. Since these were the first expulsion proceedings held under the general's command, it was quite possible that he was really opposed to the whole business altogether! Problem after problem!

Frey felt something warm pressing against his back. It took him some seconds to realize that this was his niece Barbara leaning against him.

"Have you taken leave of your senses?" he hissed.

"Don't carry on like that," said Barbara solemnly. "I'm only looking at you for a moment. I don't mean any harm."

"Well, stop it at once," he said with an effort. "Your aunt might come in at any moment!"

"She's asleep," said Barbara softly. She leaned over him.

Her lips were moist and slightly parted. They touched his ear.

"You forget," he said, "that your aunt is my wife!"

"And why not?" asked Barbara with a giggle.

Archibald Frey went over to the defensive, though not exaggeratedly so; by his gestures he might conceivably have been simply maneuvering himself into a better position.

"Aren't you ashamed of yourself?" he muttered. "It's broad daylight!"

"Anyone can do this sort of thing at night," said Barbara sliding onto his lap.

Archibald Frey, as if trying to push her away, let his hand rest on her bosom. As he did so he caught sight of his wrist watch and saw that it was very late. Alarmingly late.

He jumped up hurriedly and Barbara slid to the floor. From there she looked up at him with hungry eyes.

"Get up at once," said the major. "This is quite impossible. Do be reasonable! You must never forget that I'm married to your aunt, happily married too. Don't laugh like that, I mean it. And besides, I haven't any time at the moment. There are more important things to be done first. We'll have a talk later!"

By 1500 hours all preparations had been made. Major Frey intended to begin punctually, to the minute. He had set aside classroom number seven in which to hold the proceedings— slightly off the beaten track, and thus free from interruption, but at the same time well heated.

The following were required to attend: Captain Ratshelm, Captain Feders, Lieutenant Krafft, Cadet Hochbauer. In addition to these there was a reliable corporal to keep the minutes, and one other corporal to be at the major's disposal and act as runner if necessary.

The room had been suitably arranged. There was a table in the center for the major, with a number of files on it and a row of chairs in front. Two other tables, temporarily unoccupied, stood to left and right.

The officers and men participating had already arrived and were sitting in silence. At first no one knew exactly what was up. Major Frey seemed completely engrossed in his files. Krafft stood there stiffly, not even noticing the friendly, ironical glances of Captain Feders. Hochbauer, preserving face as much as possible, looked longingly across at Captain Ratshelm, who returned an encouraging smile. The two corporals sat staring vacantly into space. What excitement could any aspect of life at a training school conceivably hold in store for them?

The major cleared his throat and announced solemnly, "I hereby open the expulsion proceedings instituted against Cadet Hochbauer, Heinz, born at Rosenheim on twenty-first March nineteen hundred and twenty-three, at present stationed at Number Five Officers' Training School, in Number Six Company, Section H for Heinrich."

Whereupon Captain Ratshelm at once spoke up, "I propose that the expulsion proceedings be quashed on the grounds that there is no case to answer."

Lieutenant Krafft now intervened, "I propose," he said, "that Captain Ratshelm be released from further participation in these proceedings on the grounds of prejudice."

Captain Ratshelm flushed hotly and cried, "I forbid anyone to voice such a suspicion."

"It's not a question of suspicion," returned Krafft promptly, "but of fact, and I'm in a position to prove it!"

"A disgusting slander!" cried Ratshelm indignantly.

"Gentlemen, gentlemen!" cried the major angrily. "I beg of you! You're not in the mess here!"

Frey struck the table with his fist to show he meant business. He felt quite dismayed. The proceedings had hardly begun, and already they threatened to degenerate into anarchy—and what was worse, in the presence of lower ranks. Where would all this end?

"I propose," said Captain Feders, "that we first discuss this matter *in camera,* so to speak."

"Just what I was going to propose myself," said the major with relief. "Right, then. All below the rank of officer will leave the room!"

Cadet Hochbauer and the two corporals obeyed at once, delivering ceremonial salutes, as the major noted with satisfaction. When the door had closed behind the other ranks Captain Feders said jovially, "We shouldn't wash our dirty linen in public. I'm for keeping this matter between ourselves and thus shortening the whole proceedings. What's clear is that Krafft and I are for expulsion. I recommend Captain Ratshelm to abstain from voting, and you, Major, are of course impartial."

"I'll do nothing of the sort," cried Captain Ratshelm leaping up at once. "I am strongly against!"

"Two for," said Feders unmoved, "one against. So you're outvoted for a start. And if you're clever you'll come around to our way of thinking and accept it."

"All I'm concerned with is justice!" declared Ratshelm pompously.

"Gentlemen, gentlemen!" implored the major. "It really can't go on like this! These are official expulsion proceedings. They can only be conducted by"—here the major looked down at his notes—"by the discussion and consideration of clear-cut arguments for and against until the best possible solution is arrived at, preferably involving the unanimous verdict of all participants. A decision has got to be reached in any case—a postponement is as unusual as a transfer to higher authorities."

The major looked around him inquiringly. In order to prevent his officers from getting at one another's throats again he stuck to the approved method of dealing with this sort of problem, that's to say he tolerated what he could not prevent, and at the same time tried to lay down certain well-ordered rules of procedure. "Gentlemen," said the major, "the task of conducting these proceedings falls upon me. I expect to get every support from my officers, without wishing to influence their views in the slightest. Lieutenant Krafft has assumed the role of prosecuting counsel against Cadet Hochbauer. It would seem fitting if one of the other officers were, so to speak, to assume the role of defense counsel—Captain Ratshelm might seem best fitted for this, while I would like to regard Captain Feders as an unprejudiced expert. Do you agree to that?"

"All right, then," said Feders.

"Accepted, sir," said Ratshelm, obedient as ever.

"Not accepted," declared Krafft stubbornly. "I continue to oppose Captain Ratshelm's participation in any form."

"Kindly justify that point of view!" ordered the major sharply before Captain Ratshelm could make his protest heard.

Frey had realized that Lieutenant Krafft was determined not to give an inch in this matter. It seemed a pure waste of time to try to get him to change his mind, so that practically speaking the only thing to do was to try to get over the hurdle as quickly as possible. This was best achieved by getting Ratshelm to keep silent. The major therefore said, "I will ask you, Captain Ratshelm, to reply to such objective arguments as may be brought forward with equal objectivity."

Captain Ratshelm responded, as was to be expected, with "Very good, sir."

At a sign from Frey, Krafft now stepped forward. He took

a sheet of paper out of his brief case and put it on the table in front of the major. "Here," he said, "is a list of occasions during the past two weeks on which Cadet Hochbauer has paid visits to Captain Ratshelm."

"What's all this underhanded snooping!" cried Ratshelm indignantly. "It's as bad as the Gestapo!"

"That last remark," said Feders with a grin, "might in certain circles be interpreted as treasonable."

"I didn't hear it," maintained the major promptly.

Ratshelm recognized his mistake at once, and willingly confessed, "Of course I didn't mean the remark like that. Subversive activity is entirely contrary to my whole nature—I abhor it. It follows that I can never have made any remark of that sort."

Krafft was ready to leap again, and the major continued, "I can't see why the fact that a cadet visits his company commander should be in any way significant."

"An occasional visit would be quite normal, but constantly repeated visits must in the circumstances be considered abnormal—particularly as one of these visits lasted for three hours and more."

"Three hours and more?" asked the major in astonishment.

"Unless, of course," suggested Feders with a grin, "the cadet is in some way related to our respected captain, or is his brother-in-law, or married or engaged to him."

"This was simply a case of my doing my duty," said Ratshelm defensively. It was clear that this attack had gone home. "It is the primary task of every training officer to show both leadership and encouragement to gifted young cadets, it is every educator's duty to concern himself with his pupils."

"Three hours and more?" repeated the major in astonishment. "With all due respect, Captain Ratshelm, isn't that a little too much for one cadet? After all, you have a hundred and twenty of them to educate."

"But this one, Major, has quite special qualities, uncommon talents—he's a shining exception."

"We, however," said Krafft, "who are his immediate superiors, are of a very different opinion. Not only with regard to this cadet's qualities—we also see his relation with Captain Ratshelm rather differently. And the cadets in my section have discussed the matter very openly among themselves."

"I don't altogether understand you, Krafft," said the major, still rather at sea. "What are you getting at? Are you trying to suggest that Captain Ratshelm has been favoring a relation? Or have you the impertinence to hint at corruption of some sort, blackmail, or something like that?"

"I consider it utterly beneath my dignity," said Ratshelm, purple in the face, "to take the slightest notice of such accusations."

"Will you please be explicit now, Krafft!" demanded the major.

"Careful, Major!" advised Feders amiably. "You're on thin ice here, though it does you credit if you haven't yet realized the fact. Anyhow, Major, there's only one other explanation possible—affection—human, or rather masculine affection. Of the sort that Plato had for his pupils, or Caesar is said to have had for some of his young legionaries, or Frederick the Great for certain of his aides de camp . . ."

"Enough!" cried Major Frey in alarm.

At last he had realized what he was involved in. He, a normal, decent, healthy soldier and superior officer, was on the point of stumbling over a bucketful of filth. If he were to go a step further the consequences could be unforeseeable. "No further words are necessary!" he said.

Major Frey immediately took steps to safeguard himself. "Captain Ratshelm," he said, slightly reproachfully yet not without understanding, authoritatively enough and yet with a measure of comradely good will, "I value the fact that my officers should devote themselves to the welfare of the cadets entrusted to them. But really one can go too far in that direction, as seems to have been the case here. I can't approve of your action, but at the same time I can't condemn it. I accept, however, that you were inspired by the purest of motives."

"I assure you, sir," declared Ratshelm in ringing tones, "that all I was concerned with was the maintenance of a high standard of service achievement. I rate Cadet Hochbauer as far and away the best and most gifted officer cadet on this course. I'd put my hand in the fire for him. And as I said at the beginning, I considered expulsion proceedings against a cadet of this type absurd, if not downright slanderous."

"Captain," said the major, disturbed by this final phrase of Ratshelm's, "I beg you to remember that I am in charge of these expulsion proceedings. Therefore there can be nothing either absurd or slanderous about them."

"I'm sorry, sir. I beg you, sir, to allow me to withdraw this remark."

Major Frey graciously granted this request. He had found the weakest link in the chain, and its name was Ratshelm.

This fellow Krafft was as firm as a rock. Only dynamite would remove him. Frey went on, "A certain partiality, which I couldn't go so far as to call prejudice must, based on the situation as it looks now, be charged to Captain Ratshelm. I do not consider, however, that this need interfere with the proceedings. So let us get on with the matter. Lieutenant Krafft, please."

Krafft stepped forward and said, "I accuse Cadet Hochbauer of committing rape."

"Ridiculous!" expostulated Captain Ratshelm. "Utterly absurd! Cadet Hochbauer would never do anything of the sort."

"How can you be so sure of that?" asked Feders with interest.

"It is a question of morality!" cried Ratshelm, almost trembling with indignation. "Cadet Hochbauer has particularly strong principles in this respect."

"Major," said Krafft, "I offer proof of my allegation. The girl's name is Maria Kelter. She is to be found at the moment in canteen number two where she is at our disposal should we require her. Shall I ask one of the corporals to go and fetch her?"

"Ridiculous!" cried Captain Ratshelm furiously. "Have the girl brought here if we really want to make fools of ourselves."

The major, who was already beginning to break into a slight sweat, nodded reluctantly. "We'll have the girl in," he said. "But first of all let us examine Cadet Hochbauer more closely. I hope to have your general approval if for the time being we dispense with all protocol and the presence of the lower ranks. Agreed? Good! Then we can proceed. Please, Lieutenant Krafft."

Krafft went into the corridor. He made Hochbauer enter the room first, and only then he ordered one of the corporals to fetch Fräulein Maria Kelter from canteen number two without delay. Meanwhile Hochbauer stood facing the commission of inquiry—a tall, athletic figure with glossy blond hair, looking utterly self-composed. He stared straight past Krafft, avoiding Feders' eye as well. Then, however, he espied the benevolent, encouraging glance of his revered Captain Ratshelm, and, thus strengthened, turned to Major Frey, whom he regarded with humble attentiveness.

"Cadet Hochbauer," said the major fussily, "you stand here before a commission of inquiry. Those present are all known to you personally. It is our task to determine whether or not you should continue to remain at the training school. There is no appeal against any decision we come to—in other words it's final. Should our decision be for expulsion, it would be announced officially, and a copy of the announcement would be attached to your personal file. Such expulsion would of course mean the end of your military career; you would lose your status as a cadet and could never become an officer. It goes without saying that before this commission you will speak the truth the whole truth and nothing but the truth. Is that clear, Cadet?"

"Yes, sir!" cried Hochbauer very correctly and in a manner that made an excellent impression on the major.

"Let us get down to business, then."

"Excuse me, sir," said Cadet Hochbauer, who mistakenly felt himself obliged to offer some sort of self-justification, "may I point out that my case, in so far as there can be said to be a case against me at all, has already been closed. Officially too, by the judge-advocate attached to the officer in charge of training schools. Any resumption of the proceedings is invalid, unless carried out by the same court-martial. If any new suspicious evidence has come to light, Judge-Advocate Wirrmann should be informed. Any other course of action is out of the question."

Hochbauer looked at the faces of the four officers, who stared back at him in amazement. He put their reactions down to sheer astonishment, and prepared to enjoy himself. He imagined that his plans for these proceedings had been flawless. He had carefully assessed everything that was likely to be thrown into the scale on both sides, rehearsed likely witnesses, manufactured evidence and affidavits—nothing could take him by surprise! However, as Hochbauer looked across at Krafft he began to feel uneasy, for the lieutenant's eyes were sparkling with satisfaction.

"What the hell are you talking about, man?" boomed Major Frey.

Hochbauer noticed that now even Captain Ratshelm was shaking his head warily, which considerably increased the cadet's sense of unease. Feverishly he tried to think, but it was hopeless—all his elaborate preparations collapsed like a pack of cards. What had gone wrong? He had been prepared to meet a frontal attack, and here was this fellow Krafft slyly trying to trip him up. While still shaken he became aware of the voice of one of the corporals behind him announcing, "Fräulein Maria Kelter, sir!"

So that was it, thought Hochbauer. Desperately he tried to concentrate. What was Krafft up to? And what was this all?

What was there to come, what were they driving at? Hochbauer looked across to Ratshelm for help, but Ratshelm was busy regarding, with visible repugnance, the girl who had just come into the room.

Maria Kelter—small, pretty, extremely embarrassed—stepped slowly forward. Five pairs of eyes followed her, some of them just curious, others uneasy. A deep blush spread over her thin face.

The major first of all sent the corporal out into the corridor again. Then, in a voice in which the undertones were positively paternal, he addressed himself benevolently to Maria Kelter. First of all he thanked her for coming, and assured her that he appreciated it very much. Next he asked her, by appealing to her frankness, to help him in his search for the truth. "I assure you you can count on my utter discretion—and that of the others present here, too, of course. Not a word that's spoken here will go beyond these four walls. Can I count on your co-operation, Fräulein Kelter?"

"Yes," she said.

"Excuse me, please," said the major, slightly raising his bottom off the chair. "I've forgotten to introduce myself. I am Major Frey—one of the commanding officers of this training school. You can address me quite simply as Major."

"Yes, Major," said Maria Kelter.

"Right, then, Fräulein Kelter," said the major. "Were you assaulted?"

Maria Kelter looked up terrified and glanced helplessly about her.

Captain Feders put in a word of explanation. "An assault and rape aren't the same thing. What the major wants to know is, were you, Fräulein Kelter, compelled by the use of violence to grant your favors to someone to whom you were not prepared to give them voluntarily?"

"Yes," said Maria Kelter.

"You've answered the first question that I put to you," said the major with a flourish. "Now to the next one. Was it Cadet Hochbauer?"

"Yes," said Maria Kelter, almost inaudibly.

"It can't be true!" cried Captain Ratshelm, turning pale. "Hochbauer, say immediately that it isn't true!"

But Hochbauer hung his head. It was clear from his face that he was thinking desperately hard. He had to find a way out of this. Finally he said, "This will be cleared up in time. It was more in the nature of a mistake, a misunderstanding."

"Ah!" said Feders. "You wanted to rape someone else, then."

"No, certainly not!" exclaimed Hochbauer promptly.

"This girl then!"

"But it wasn't rape!" cried Hochbauer.

Captain Ratshelm barely heard this exchange; the words went over his head. Only one thing had any meaning for him, and this was seared into his brain. Hochbauer had done it! This ethereal youth under the filthy spell of sex! This lofty idealistic paragon besmirched by life at its crudest level! Captain Ratshelm's whole world collapsed, and the name of the man who had brought it down upon him was Hochbauer!

"Now I must ask you to be very precise," said the major. "When you, Hochbauer, maintain that there was no rape you thereby maintain that Fräulein Kelter is not speaking the truth. What about it, Fräulein Kelter—do you uphold your previous allegation?"

"Yes, Major," she said softly, but unmistakably clearly. "It took place against my will."

"Hochbauer," challenged the major, "have you anything to say to that?"

"I was under the impression," said Hochbauer, "that a certain understanding had been arrived at."

"Fräulein Kelter," said the major again, "what is your reply?"

"I was taken by force," she said.

"Did you resist?" inquired the major, with a certain interest.

"Yes."

"Did you cry for help?"

"I don't know. No."

"Why not?"

"It was pointless. We were in the park. There was no one anywhere near us. And perhaps I did cry out, though not very loudly."

"I think, sir," said Lieutenant Krafft, "we can spare ourselves the details. That's quite enough. I regard the matter as clear."

"So do I," declared Feders.

"And you, Captain Ratshelm?" inquired the major.

"I," said Ratshelm, choking with revulsion, "find this whole affair utterly nauseating. The sooner we bring it to a conclusion the better."

He cast a quick, devastating glance at Hochbauer. Hochbauer, however, had no time at the moment, and little inclination, to think of the deep disappointment he had caused his captain, being wholly preoccupied with the search for a way out of his predicament. Suddenly he thought he saw one.

He looked at Maria Kelter and said quickly, "Maria, I'm terribly sorry about all this. I didn't want it to happen. Do please forgive me. Certainly I've behaved unpardonably, but I'm prepared to take all the consequences, Maria. All. I'll go and see your parents today and ask for your hand. But you mustn't say I took you by force."

"Suborning the witness," said Feders expertly. He winked at Krafft.

"Sir," said Krafft vigorously, "I ask you to put a stop to this." But Maria Kelter said quite quickly, "Now I come to think of it, Major, perhaps it was love after all."

"Yes, certainly," said Hochbauer, who saw Krafft's trap disintegrating, "and I'm ready to take all the consequences— this very evening, Maria."

"Steady now, steady!" cried the major, who saw that the time had come once more to take charge of the proceedings.

In itself, the way in which the affair was developing was not unwelcome to the major. A rape in his domain was a real blot on his escutcheon; a rash and precipitate action, however, though regrettable, was not an offense. An engagement solved all problems at a stroke. It was hardly possible to think of a better argument for the quashing of these expulsion proceedings. And why should he do stubborn fellows like Krafft a favor? The question now was how to make sure of bringing the whole matter to a successful conclusion.

"Right, then, Fräulein Kelter," said the major self-importantly. "First of all you maintain that violence was done you. Then you maintain that it was not. What makes you change your mind?"

"Well, Major," said pretty Maria Kelter, casting a quick possessive glance at the handsome Hochbauer, "I've been thinking things over. I see now that it didn't actually come to the . . . the final . . . so that it actually it wasn't really a proper rape."

"It didn't come to the final . . .?" asked the major, furrowing his brow.

"No," said the girl, "not actually. At first he was like some wild thing, and I had to defend myself. But when it came to it—well, he simply couldn't . . . if you know what I mean . . ." She fell silent.

Captain Feders roared with laughter. He was quite out

of control, holding his sides and looking for a moment as if he were going to fall off his chair. Those present looked at him as if he were a creature from some other planet. "My God," he cried, "what a marvelously funny place the world is!"

"I hope, Captain Feders," said the major angrily, "that you will pull yourself together so that it will be possible for you to follow the further course of these proceedings. First of all, Fräulein Kelter, we thank you for your valuable co-operation. You can go now."

Maria Kelter smiled agreeably. She smiled particularly agreeably at Hochbauer. "I'll wait for you," she said tenderly and yet with a certain emphasis, and tripped out of the room.

"And with that," said the major, "everything seems to be cleared up. We can wind the affair up. Or do you think I'm making a mistake, Lieutenant Krafft?"

"Yes, Major," said Krafft, "I think you're making a grave mistake. And I'm sorry about this for your sake. Or am I to assume that you too have reached an adverse verdict?"

"How could I—on the insufficient evidence you've produced so far, Krafft?"

"Perhaps this will make you change your mind, sir!" And while everyone watched attentively, Lieutenant Krafft took from his brief case a fine and delicate piece of blue fabric; a slightly soiled handkerchief, with the monogram F.F. well in evidence. He put it down on the table in front of the major.

The major stared at it as if an extremely poisonous snake were coiled in front of him. His face slowly distorted into a mad, grimace-like smile. In a flat voice he inquired, "What's all this?"

"You must ask Cadet Hochbauer that, sir," said Krafft relentlessly. "This handkerchief was found in his possession. It shouldn't be difficult for you to determine its origin."

"What does this mean?" screamed the major like a wounded animal.

Everyone looked at Hochbauer. He was white as a sheet. He could find no word of explanation. Nothing that would sound plausible.

"You swine!" cried the major, utterly losing control of himself. "You filthy cur! You dare to lay hands on my . . . my . . . out with you! Get out of here before I kill you!"

Hochbauer turned and left the room with head bowed. He even forgot to salute.

The major, however, continued to stare at the handkerchief in front of him. His face was the color of a beet. Those present looked tactfully away, even Feders.

"Sir," said Lieutenant Krafft at length, "I vote for expulsion."

"So do I," said Feders.

"We can't tolerate depraved characters like that," declared Ratshelm in a trembling voice. "There's no place for him here. He was unworthy of my sympathy. Expulsion!"

"And your vote, Major?"

"Out with the swine!" he cried, and it was as if he were waking suddenly from a long sleep. "Out with him! And with the rest of you as well. Go on, get out! Don't stare at me. I want to be alone. I just want to be alone!"

In the night that followed these expulsion proceedings Captain Feders and Lieutenant Krafft practically drowned themselves in alcoholic gloom. They cursed a world that forced them to commit murder in this way. But Marion Feders and Elfrida Rademacher had presentiments of fear.

It was in the course of this night that Captain Ratshelm wrote his request for a posting; he humbly and urgently begged to be sent to the front. Major Frey also spent his time writing—a new special order. He wanted to make it unmistakably clear to the cadets what morality demanded in certain difficult situations.

In the same night Cadet Hochbauer came to the conclusion that his honor was ruined, his self-respect destroyed, and his career finished. Thus the conviction took root in his mind that his life was forfeit—only a dog would want to continue to exist in these circumstances.

He wrote a farewell note, took his rifle, and shot himself.

29 *DEATH HAS ITS GLORIES*

CADET HOCHBAUER'S death took place, as was established later, in the early hours of the morning on March 21, 1944. "Beginning of spring," said the calendar. The exact time was 0505 hours. The scene—a particularly unfortunate and painful circumstance, this—was the latrine at the far end of the barrack block.

It was here that at about this time Cadet Mösler had

found himself trying to deal with a persistent stomach ache. As he sat there half asleep, musing gently with his eyes shut, a sharp report suddenly made him jump.

Mösler's own account was as follows: "I started up, thinking I couldn't have heard properly. That sounded like a shot, I said to myself. But then I thought it couldn't have been a shot at that hour. I stumbled over to the door, pushed it open, and there I saw it!"

Fortunately for Mösler, as things turned out, though he was the first person on the scene of the incident, he wasn't the only one there. The duty cadet, Berger, had also heard the shot. Berger had just got up, but unlike Mösler was wide awake. He heard the shot and hurried out into the corridor toward the latrine, where the sound of the shot had come from.

And here in the dim lighting Berger saw someone lying on the floor. It was a cadet in full uniform with a rifle beside him. The back of his head was a mass of blood.

"That looks like Hochbauer!"

Now for the first time the horrified Berger saw Cadet Mösler, who must have appeared on the scene almost at the same moment.

"My God!" cried Berger, appalled. "What's the meaning of this?"

Mösler said nothing. He knelt down and looked at the man lying there, without touching him. Then he raised his head and said, "He's done for!"

"He's dead!" cried Berger, looking wildly about him with a hunted look. "Oh no! What do I do next! What am I meant to do now!"

"Start by shutting your trap," said Mösler. "You'll rouse the whole section with the din you're making! The best thing would be to go and tell Lieutenant Krafft first."

"Yes, I'll do that!" cried Berger. "That'll be the best thing."

But it was too late. Other cadets had been waken by the shot and the subsequent yelling of the duty cadet. They ran toward the latrine and into the room, where they gathered around the body in sleepy stupefaction.

Cadet Mösler turned to Berger and said, "You must cordon the room off—at least until you receive further orders from the section officer."

"What am I to do!" cried Berger helplessly. "I can't stand guard here and at the same time go and tell Lieutenant Krafft."

"Come on, now, fellows, don't stand around here!" said Cadet Kramer, the section senior, who had at last arrived on the scene. He pushed his way forward to see what was going on, and what he saw made him turn pale.

However, even in this situation Kramer remained the ever-reliable NCO. He took charge of things at once and gave the order, "Everyone out of the room. Berger, you stand guard on the door. Mösler, you go and tell Lieutenant Krafft. I'll keep watch here."

"How much longer are we going to be kept out of there?" asked some of the cadets with a certain anxiety as they withdrew into the corridor. When Lieutenant Krafft appeared, wrapped in an old blue- and white-striped dressing gown, visibly pale and wearing a tired, vacant expression, they made room for him in silence. Cadet Kramer was standing inside. He saluted and made his report. "An unexpected development, sir. Cadet Hochbauer shot, just after five o'clock."

Krafft strode stiffly over to the body. He bent over it and looked down at it a few seconds. Then he straightened up, and his face seemed even paler than before.

"Suicide presumably," said Cadet Kramer.

Krafft nodded almost imperceptibly, without saying a word.

"The usual thing, it seems," continued Kramer, apparently little moved. He was determined to make a good impression and show the extent to which he was master of every situation. "The rifle is loaded, then water poured down the barrel, the barrel put in the mouth and the trigger pulled with the toe. A dead certainty. Never fails to work—instantaneous too."

"A ground sheet," said Lieutenant Krafft.

Kramer passed the order on. "Berger," he said, "a ground sheet at once!"

"But I need my ground sheet," stammered Berger, who saw his immaculate piece of equipment in danger. "We've got ground training today."

"Then take Hochbauer's ground sheet, idiot!" cried Kramer, irritated by this obvious lack of initiative.

Berger disappeared, but other cadets pushed their way forward. Among them was Amfortas, who muttered under his breath, "Who knows whether it really was suicide, with this fellow Mösler around?"

Mösler rushed at Amfortas, but Rednitz held him back. "Calm down," said Rednitz. "One corpse is enough for the time being. Everything'll sort itself out in a minute."

Meanwhile Berger had come back with a ground sheet. He had taken his own in the end, because it had occurred to him that Hochbauer's ground sheet was of considerably better quality and he would be able to appropriate it later. Hurriedly he covered the dead man over with the ground sheet and declared, "Order carried out, sir."

"Kramer," ordered Lieutenant Krafft, "will you see that all the responsible officers are informed of the following particulars: Section H for Heinrich, shortly after five o'clock, suicide of Cadet Hochbauer. Send one man each to the tactics instructor, to the company commander, to the course commander. I will inform the commanding officer of the training school myself. In the meantime this room will be cordoned off and a guard put on it—no one is to enter unless I'm there. In the absence of further orders the timetable will be followed as usual. Dismiss!"

Lieutenant Krafft went into the washroom, took a cold shower, shaved, and went back to his room, where he quickly dressed. When he had done this, he tried to get the general by telephone.

But only Lieutenant Bieringer was at the other end. The ADC informed him that the general was not available that morning—he'd gone to Würzburg for a conference.

"But it's important!" said Krafft on the telephone. "The general must be informed at once!"

"But really, my dear Krafft," said the ADC jovially, "what's so special about a suicide? They happen every few months or so. No need to get excited! I'll send along Captain Schultz, the legal officer—he'll deal with everything."

Captain Feders was the next officer to appear on the scene. He called out hurriedly to Krafft even before he got there, "Is this true, or just another trick of yours, Krafft?"

"Unfortunately not," said the lieutenant, getting the duty cadet to open the door.

Feders took in the scene at a glance. He turned to Krafft and said, "A rotten business!"

"You could put it another way," said Krafft gently.

"You mean the triumph of justice. Don't worry, Krafft, no one's going to deprive you of that! Right, to your places! Here come the body snatchers."

Major Frey and Captain Ratshelm now arrived, the company commander, against all the rules, striding along two paces ahead of his CO, while Frey seemed to have some difficulty in keeping up with him—a stiff, dignified figure striding along behind a determined avenger.

"This should never have happened!" said Major Frey. "It's

deplorable, quite deplorable!" He shook his head in consternation.

But Captain Ratshelm pushed his way past the major and strode up to Hochbauer. He stopped close beside him and stared down at him for some seconds. His face was ravaged with grief, and his arms hung loosely at his side. But his fists were clenched.

Slowly he raised his eyes and fixed them on Lieutenant Krafft. In muffled tones, as if speaking through a filter of cotton wool, yet clearly audible, he said, "You alone are responsible for his death. You have this man on your conscience!"

"Don't be such a fool," said Captain Feders, roughly pushing his way forward and at the same time thrusting Lieutenant Krafft into the background. "What's all this about, friend!"

"I can substantiate what I say!" declared Ratshelm, darkly menacing. "A man has been killed here, and I demand that someone be made to answer for it."

"My good man," shouted Captain Feders at the top of his voice, "what's happened here is that someone's dispatched himself into eternity, and that's altogether his affair. Drop the heroics! People like this boast and brag and make themselves out great heroes, but when it comes to the test they take the cowardly way out!"

"You're insulting a dead man!" said Ratshelm.

"Oh come off it!" shouted Feders. "I'm trying to make a living man see sense!"

"Gentlemen, please!" cried Major Frey.

The commanding officer felt it his duty to intervene. The quarrel was a painful one, since cadets were present in the shape of the sentry on the door and the ubiquitous section senior.

"Gentlemen," said Major Frey when peace had been restored, "I understand your feelings! I too am affected by this tragic affair—after all, I'm the officer with the ultimate responsibility. But we've got to proceed with complete objectivity. So I must request you to restrain yourself, Captain Ratshelm, and to forego conjectures which cannot be substantiated, and which it seems to me are extremely unlikely to be substantiated. You, however, Captain Feders, are requested to be rather more careful about the way you express yourself—particularly as you are not alone here!"

"But someone must be made to answer for this," said Ratshelm wildly.

Captain Feders immediately pushed forward again. "You've got a one-track mind, Ratshelm. If someone's going to commit suicide no one can stop him. The actual cause of it can be something quite trivial—a sudden depression, a pair of socks missing, or even expulsion proceedings."

"In which he was systematically destroyed by Krafft!"

"You had your share in it too, Ratshelm," said Feders calmly.

"Gentlemen," intervened the major, "speculation will get us nowhere. We must confine ourselves to facts, and this suicide is an indisputable fact. The reasons for it are of secondary importance—and I completely agree with Captain Feders that there are a thousand possible reasons. I don't want any wild speculation, particularly when it's based on prejudice. Do you understand, Captain Ratshelm?"

Ratshelm had the audacity not to reply. He stood there stiff and unapproachable.

"And you, Lieutenant Krafft," pursued the major, "have you also got absolutely nothing to say? What's your opinion?"

"I haven't got one," said Krafft.

"Right, then," said Frey in a choked voice. "Let's hope the legal officer gets here soon."

The legal officer, Captain Schultz, a member of the general's own staff, did in fact arrive soon afterward. His official role was that of administrative officer, but in fact he was a sort of maid-of-all-work and thus "legal officer" along with everything else.

Captain Schultz was a farmer by profession, a squat man of medium build with a face like a potato and a quiet, imperturbable approach to life. He had the habit of sniffing the air like a hound. There was no particular significance in this, but it always made a good deal of noise because Schultz almost always had a cold except when in the presence of the general.

Schultz strode onto the scene and sniffed about him. His first positive action was to turn to Ratshelm and say amiably, "Get out of the line of fire, will you? Or have you taken root there?"

Ratshelm stepped obediently to one side. Schultz pushed a little closer, took a look at the corpse and the area around it, and then asked, "How long has he been lying here?"

"Almost three hours," answered Krafft.

"But why on earth?" asked Schultz in astonishment. "Do you want him to spend the winter here?"

"We thought," said Krafft in some astonishment, "that there'd have to be a full investigation."

"But why?" asked Schultz, shaking his knobbly head in irritation. "Why make it all so complicated? The man's dead, that's clear. Why leave him lying here for hours? He's blocking the way to the latrine."

Major Frey tried to express a disgusted disapproval. Captain Feders grinned. Krafft was unable to restrain his amazement at such unexpected calm. And the cadets in the open doorway realized that they were being given some unscheduled instruction of a quite special sort.

Only Captain Ratshelm was indignant, and he made no attempt to conceal the fact. "You'll want to make out a report, of course."

"Yes, of course," said Schultz promptly, "there's no way of avoiding that. But we can always do that later—in the course of the day, let's say, when we're less pushed."

"And the question of guilt?" inquired Ratshelm bitterly.

"Guilt?" The legal officer was absolutely astounded. "Where do you get that idea? This is a straightforward case of suicide. That's all there is to it. Or has some sort of farewell note been found giving further particulars?"

"No farewell note or anything like that," said a clear voice from the door where Cadet Rednitz was standing. He looked across at Lieutenant Krafft as he spoke.

"All the better," said Captain Schultz the legal officer. He found it easy to take the reactions of the various bystanders in his stride. "These farewell notes can cause a lot of trouble, though no one really takes them very seriously. A lot of rubbish mostly, written under circumstances which can hardly be described as normal. Utterly misleading—full of false hints, exaggerations. Worthless, in fact. I'm always glad when there isn't one."

But Ratshelm wouldn't let the matter alone. "But that can't stop you from investigating the cause of suicide."

"Captain Ratshelm," said the major sternly, "it's my view that we should respect Captain Schultz's methods. I think he knows his job."

Captain Schultz made a splendidly self-deprecating gesture and said, "It's all a matter of routine. You learn by experience. This is my fifth suicide. I could do the whole thing in my sleep now. What you soon get to realize is that however much trouble you take and however hard you try, you'll never really discover the true reasons for a suicide. So why bother? Take the corpse away and have a coffin made. The best thing would be to spread sand down here, then scrub the floor and put down some Lysol. My office'll look after the paper work in the course of the day. Anything else, Major?"

"No thank you, Captain," declared Frey with relief. He accompanied the legal officer out into the fresh air. They disappeared in the direction of the mess.

Captain Feders turned to Captain Ratshelm. "Do be reasonable, my dear fellow," he said. "Go home and calm down, and don't do anything stupid."

"I shall do my duty!" said Ratshelm stiffly.

And when they carried the corpse out he followed solemnly behind it.

"Well, Krafft," asked Feders anxiously, "got cold feet?"

"What a frightful lot they are!" said Krafft wearily.

"They're the lot we're fighting the war for."

"What does death amount to, really?" said Krafft. "It's much more difficult to live honorably than to die honorably. And to die dishonorably—well, it's an offense to the living."

"These fellows have spent their time yelling 'Germany Awake!'" said Feders. "But it's beginning to dawn on me that what that really means is, Germany disintegrate! You try and explain that to these brave officers of ours, though. The moment they hear high-sounding words their whole reason automatically clouds over. Do you think you're immune, Krafft?"

"They'll have to beat me to death, Feders—that's the only way they'll get me to die for them!"

"How modest we've become all of a sudden," said Feders with a tired smile, putting his hand on his friend's arm. Then he walked sadly away.

The morning passed uneventfully enough. Lieutenant Krafft and his section went out to the training field and there practiced what was down on the timetable: operational patrols from an entrenched position for major reconnaissance.

The section did what was required of them. Yet there was a colorlessness about the morning's activity—no funny remarks, no arguments, no amusing incidents. It was suddenly like being in any of the other sections. At all events there was no talk of Hochbauer—officially; he was dead. And no one wanted to talk about his death.

Krafft allowed his section a great deal of freedom on this particular morning. He gave no sort of lead, and didn't bother to keep them under proper control. He merely observed that in the break period a much larger group than usual gathered around Rednitz; the abandoned sheep were looking for a new leader. Rednitz accepted the role with considerable skill.

Before ordering them to return to barracks, Krafft called Rednitz over to him and said, "Rednitz, how was it you were able to say that Cadet Hochbauer left no farewell note?"

"Because I had a look, Lieutenant," said the cadet candidly, "immediately after the tragedy occurred. I thought of it at once—Hochbauer was always a terrific writer."

"And you say you found nothing, Rednitz?"

"Yes, Lieutenant, that's what I say."

Krafft looked his cadet straight in the eye. Rednitz smiled— a smile full of warmth and affection. At that moment Krafft had the feeling that everything was easy and manageable, that whatever might be in store for him it would not have been in vain.

"Make your report," said the general, almost before Krafft had had time to enter the room. "I've just come back from Würzburg. I want to know what's been happening."

They stood facing each other. Krafft made his report, and the general listened without a word. Only when the lieutenant had finished did Major-General Modersohn say, "Sit down, Krafft." His voice sounded unusually gentle, almost hesitant.

"Krafft," said the general after they had both sat down, "this isn't the solution I wanted."

"It's a solution all the same," said Krafft.

"No," said the general firmly. "I wanted him to be handed over properly to justice. But you've driven him to suicide. This is no atonement. This is escape, cowardice, fraud."

"General," said Lieutenant Krafft, still respectful, but without a trace of subservience or any particular regard for discipline, "Cadet Hochbauer confessed to me, to me alone, that it was he who killed Lieutenant Barkow. But it can't be proved."

"If there were no other possibility of convicting him, this confession would have had to suffice, Krafft."

"A confession, General, is never any use on its own— particularly not when it's a private confession, as it was, without witnesses, not even an affidavit. When it's a question of one person's evidence against another's, then it's the people giving the evidence who count. And here you have a lieutenant of no particular standing faced by a cadet who claims to be a zealous National Socialist, and whose father is a commandant of an SS training school."

"None of that must count," said the general stiffly. "We're soldiers, after all—and nothing but soldiers."

"That's just where you're mistaken, General. A soldier's life is no longer what it was in the glorious days of Prussia, or rather what it was said to be. The soldier as a guarantee of order and decency, justice and freedom, is all just a fairy tale today, and people like Hochbauer make that crystal clear. The soldier in the service of an ideology has to be a Nazi or an anti-Nazi. There's no third possibility."

The general didn't speak for a long time. But his eyes looked sad. It was a sadness in which there was no pain—a sadness born of knowledge and understanding. Krafft was quite prepared to be put in his place in that cold, concise manner which the general had made all his own. But all Krafft heard was the single phrase, "Go on."

"If I'm faced by a powerful enemy, General, who thinks and acts quite differently from me, who comes from a different world and with whom I have nothing in common but the language, then I have to try and defeat him by his own methods. I have no other choice."

"And you feel that the end justifies the means, Krafft?"

"I've overestimated these people. They're less stable than I thought. They live between the two extremes of crime and cowardice, only they call these things by different names. They call the one proving themselves and the other self-sacrifice. They've destroyed Lieutenant Barkow, and they're ready to do anyone else in—as they always have been and always will be. Yet the moment they have to answer for any of this they plump for suicide. They perform the most prodigious feats so long as their madness keeps them going—they're a gift to the narrow-minded technician, a joy to emotional fantasists like Ratshelm—and they see to it that anything worth-while left in Germany goes down with them."

The general avoided Krafft's eye. It almost seemed as if he wanted to have nothing to do with him. "What are you going to do now, Krafft?"

"I consider that I've completed the task you set me, General. A murderer has murdered himself. I didn't intend it to happen, but now that it's happened I accept it—it's a solution of a sort. For who can say what would have happened once the wheels of justice began to turn!"

"And what about me, Krafft? Do you think it's possible for me simply to wash my hands in innocence?"

"General," said the lieutenant emphatically, "you haven't soiled your hands. You gave me the job of examining magistrate, and against my will I've been turned into an executioner. What's happened is my own affair—and I've no intention of trying to shirk the blame. Why should I? For if what we do here, General, if what goes on all around us, is the decent, honorable, unsullied life of the soldier, then this world is beyond me. It's valueless and fraudulent. A haven for crooks, for sneak thieves, and sadists without a glimmering of conscience. It's a world that nauseates me, and there's no point in living for it."

Major-General Modersohn stood up suddenly. He crossed to the window and stared out—a slim, angular silhouette against the harsh light of the snow and the wintry sun. He was silent for a long time.

Then he turned to Krafft, just as suddenly and abruptly as he had got up. "You seem bent on savoring all the consequences," he said. "Well, you're going to have your way!"

Swiftly the general crossed to his desk, where he picked up a long sheet of paper and held it out to Krafft. "There," said the general, "read that. This teletype message came in half an hour ago."

Krafft took the sheet and began to read. It ran as follows:

FROM: The Officer Commanding All Training Schools
TO: The Officer Commanding Training School No. 5

Take over investigation into death of Hochbauer. Investigations on the spot to be suspended pending arrival of our representative with full powers, Judge-Advocate Wirrmann. Latter to be given every assistance. Judge-Advocate Wirrmann is already on his way.

Signed: OFFICER COMMANDING ALL TRAINING SCHOOLS.

"Just let him come!" said Krafft.

30 *THE HUNT IS ON*

JUDGE-ADVOCATE WIRRMANN arrived that very day, reaching the training school late in the afternoon, and entering it at once like a bloodhound taking up the scent.

Of course Wirrmann behaved very correctly, and reported without delay to Major-General Modersohn. He was not kept waiting unduly. The general received him standing up.

Wirrmann discharged his disciplinary obligations in exemplary fashion. He saluted and made a formal report, being particularly concerned to do everything as correctly as possible. He wanted to give the impression that he had come to deal with only a routine affair.

Modersohn asked, "Why have you come in person? And why all this hurry?"

"Well," said Wirrmann evasively, "this is rather an unusual case."

"I don't see how you can say that yet," said the general. "Unless of course either preliminary investigations have already taken place or certain preconceived notions exist in your mind. The first is not the case and the second is not to be the case. Besides, you haven't answered my question, Judge-Advocate."

"General," said Wirrmann, whose pale gray complexion was slowly turning a vivid red, "may I point out that I am not seconded to the training school—I am merely instructed to co-operate."

"Exactly what constitutes co-operation, Judge-Advocate, is something that I alone decide here. And I hereby order you to make me a daily report, starting tomorrow, at a time of which I will inform you later. That's all for the present, Judge-Advocate."

Wirrmann left the general and the staff building as quickly as he could, filled with a cold rage against Modersohn. The humiliations to which this inveterate reactionary was constantly subjecting him were developing an obsessional hold on his mind.

As usual, Wirrmann once again took up quarters in the guest house. Yet hardly had he entered the room allotted to him and thrown his brief case and suitcase onto the bed than he picked up the telephone. The first person he spoke to was Captain Kater; the second, Captain Ratshelm. He invited both gentlemen to come and see him.

Kater, who had the shorter distance to come, appeared first. He greeted Wirrmann with open arms. "There you are at last!" he said joyfully.

The judge-advocate shook his outstretched hand. "I think we've got everything just where we want it, my dear fellow," he said. "Anyhow, I'm grateful to you for your prompt notification."

"But really, please! It was only my duty!"

"Without this express hint from you, my dear Kater," said the judge-advocate courteously, "I would have overlooked this vital matter, for the moment at least. For this suicide was merely listed in the daily routine reports which go from here to the commander of training schools every midday—listed without further particulars. But your call put me on the alert —and here I am!"

"Do you think we'll be able to get anywhere?"

"Confidentially, my dear fellow, we're already there! I've just come from talking to the general, and quite between ourselves, Kater, I came away with a very definite impression. All I'll say is that I met with the typical reactions of a man with something to hide. But he can't hide it from me! Without wishing to boast, I might say that no one's ever succeeded in hiding anything from me yet."

"Yes, fine—but don't underestimate Modersohn."

"My dear fellow, I might just as well say to you, don't underestimate me! But enough of that. Let's come to the point. What's it look like to you?"

"Well," said Kater thoughtfully, "I gave you the essential facts on the telephone. This poor cadet has obviously been brutally harried to his death by Lieutenant Krafft. And the decisive factor seems to be that this fellow Krafft is a quite particular favorite of the general's."

"That doesn't sound too bad at all," said Wirrmann thoughtfully. "In fact it sounds quite promising. But if we have nothing but assumptions to go on we're not going to get very far."

"This is no assumption of mine," declared Kater with satisfaction. "This is a statement by Captain Ratshelm."

"That sounds more like it," said Wirrmann. "But before

coming here I also telephoned Captain Ratshelm. He was unusually excited, and was recommending an investigation by court-martial, but he didn't say anything about this fellow Krafft being responsible for the cadet's death. What if he denies he ever said such a thing?"

"He can't do that," said Kater. "Captain Ratshelm made the statement not only in front of me but in public, at the scene of the tragedy in the presence of three officers and a number of cadets. He quite openly and categorically accused Krafft. There can be no going back on that."

"Well," said the judge-advocate with extreme satisfaction, "if that's so, then Captain Ratshelm will have to stand by it, come what may."

Captain Ratshelm himself appeared shortly afterward. He saluted with a certain hearty formality and showed himself co-operative and full of interest from the beginning.

"You can't think what pleasure it gives me to be able to count on your valuable co-operation," Wirrmann assured him.

While a number of general noncommittal remarks were exchanged, principally on the initiative of the judge-advocate, Captain Kater saw to it, after his fashion, that a congenial atmosphere was established, conjuring up a bottle of Steinhäger and a box of cigarettes out of his brief case. He presented both of them to their honored and most welcome guest, but then opened them immediately himself.

After a brief, friendly toast, Wirrmann came to the point at once. He nodded vigorously toward Captain Ratshelm and said, "So you, my good sir, are what might be called my star witness."

"Me?" asked Ratshelm, visibly shaken. "What do you mean by that, exactly?"

"Quite simple," the judge-advocate assured him with invincible friendliness. "It's you who have provided the basis for my investigation. No one can deny that you've rendered that service."

"May I ask what you're talking about?" inquired the captain.

"My dear fellow, don't hide your light under a bushel. You were the one who leveled the accusation against Lieutenant Krafft in public, as you might say. You now merely need to prove your statement. That's all."

"Excuse me, please," said the captain, shifting uneasily on his chair, "but there must be some misunderstanding. I'm naturally glad to render you any assistance you may require, but you'll have to pass me over as a witness, I'm afraid."

"Quite out of the question, my dear fellow," Wirrmann assured him, still relatively amiably. "I can't do without this evidence of yours under any circumstances. Justice is at stake here, my good sir, and you simply can't get out of it."

"I've my own reasons," said Ratshelm.

"And those are?"

"I'm sorry, but I can't reveal them."

Wirrmann frowned angrily. His beady little eyes narrowed. He looked across at Captain Kater both challengingly and reproachfully at the same time.

Kater appreciated this glance for what it was worth. He jumped into the breach at once. Something about which he cared passionately was at stake. Cautiously he said, "I think I can understand our friend Captain Ratshelm. He thinks he's now faced with a choice between his duty and his honor."

"Ah!" said Wirrmann, though he saw clearly enough that something was escaping him. "Carry on, please."

"Yes," said Kater ponderously, "I think I know the fly in the ointment here. You're a friend of mine, my dear Ratshelm, and I beg you to let me speak frankly. Right then. Our friend is afraid, and with some justification, that if he's forced to give official evidence he might get rather painfully entangled in this whole affair. Lieutenant Krafft is his acknowledged enemy and he won't hesitate to slander Captain Ratshelm in the vilest way if Ratshelm opposes him."

"That's just how it is," said the company commander gloomily.

"Right then, be quite frank now," urged the judge-advocate, who had got the point. "What is it you've done?"

"Nothing! Nothing, of course!"

"Good—then what are you afraid Lieutenant Krafft will reproach you with?"

Ratshelm fell silent, overcome with shame, yet without any loss of dignity. Once again Captain Kater felt obliged to leap in. This time he no longer beat about the bush. He didn't want to delay the hour of his triumph any longer than necessary. "Let's have some plain speaking," he said. "This fellow Krafft maintains quite simply that our friend Ratshelm has had unnatural relations with Cadet Hochbauer—homosexual relations, not to put too fine a point upon it."

"Damnation!" cried Wirrmann. He seemed completely to lose control for a second or two, a small, nervous little man wearing an expression of utter dismay. "God in heaven! This puts the lid on it." The judge-advocate jumped up and began pacing up and down the room with quick little strides.

Captain Ratshelm looked at him for a moment, and then asked indignantly, "But you don't believe I'm guilty?"

Wirrmann snapped this up at once. He made for the captain, crying, "What's that? You mean you're innocent?"

"Of course!" urged Ratshelm.

"But this is marvelous!" cried Wirrmann, immediately weaving a whole new chain of ideas—or length of rope perhaps. "That suits us splendidly! Plain defamation, then—in fact it's more than that; it's a deliberate slur on a man's character, a baseless accusation punishable by imprisonment. That'll help bring this fellow Krafft a step nearer his grave!"

"At the cost of my reputation and my honor!"

"Steady now," said Wirrmann, pressing his palms together, "steady! We've got to think this through very thoroughly. We can't afford the slightest mistake."

The judge-advocate sat down again and pushed his chair closer to Captain Ratshelm. He declined refreshment from the Steinhäger bottle, wishing to keep a clear head. "You must answer some questions, my dear Ratshelm. First of all, are there any witnesses?"

"What for?"

"But my dear fellow!" cried Wirrmann, slightly irritated. "The only thing that's going to be any help here is complete frankness! Right, then. Are there any people who witnessed your unnatural activities with Cadet Hochbauer?"

"Of course not!" cried Ratshelm, blazing with indignation.

"Good, very good!" said Wirrmann, satisfied. "That's the worst out of the way. Still, we must leave no stone unturned. It's the only way to find the truth. Right, then. Are there any witnesses who have caught you partly clothed or alternatively unclothed with a cadet?"

"Certainly not, sir!"

"All the better! That takes us one step further. But still it's not everything. Next question. Are there any witnesses who have observed exchanges of affection between you?"

"Sir!" roared Ratshelm. "What do you take me for?"

"For a man of honor, Captain!" Wirrmann hastened to assure him. "But unfortunately that's not the point. What matters is what Krafft takes you for, that's what we've got to get to grips with. So kindly answer my question."

"No!" cried Ratshelm, blushing with shame. "No exchanges of affection!"

"I'm fully aware of the delicacy of your feelings in this matter, Captain, please believe that. And I only wish I could respect them. But I can't—in your own interests. So I'm compelled to draw your attention to one or two details. Legally an exchange of affection may be regarded as taking place in any of the following instances: excessively long handshake, an arm around the shoulders, a hand feeling its way down the back, a slap on the buttocks."

"There's been no question of any of that," cried Ratshelm.

"In other words you can guarantee that there are no witnesses to anything like that?"

"Yes indeed, that's exactly what I mean."

"And there's no letter, no diary, no sheet of paper in Hochbauer's writing which might also suggest or provide evidence of such a thing?"

"No, I don't think so."

"You don't think so? Does that mean it's improbable but not altogether beyond the bounds of possibility?"

"It's beyond the bounds of possibility!" said Ratshelm, choking with indignation.

"Excellent, quite excellent!" said the judge-advocate rubbing his hands. He now permitted himself a Steinhäger. He looked across at Kater expressively.

"Captain Ratshelm," he continued, "the decks are clear, then. You have no choice but to give evidence against this fellow Lieutenant Krafft. On two grounds: first, because you'll thereby be doing your duty; but also because you will thereby be forestalling Krafft. This matter is a pure question of self-preservation. Fortunately you can be sure that you will receive every understanding from me—and a fair hearing into the bargain."

"But I'll be risking my reputation," said Ratshelm anxiously.

"Man cannot live without risk," said Wirrmann, confident of victory. "You know the famous phrase, not even the good can live in peace . . . well, that applies to you. But I'm giving you a great chance to clinch the matter; with my help you can forestall this stab in the back. All you need to do is to bring out your evidence; we'll edit it together. But it's essential we should be absolutely frank with each other, so that together we can take the wind out of this fellow Krafft's sails."

"And you think," asked Ratshelm hopefully, "that there's no danger of things going wrong?"

The judge-advocate shook his head. He acknowledged the appreciative glance from Captain Kater. Then he picked up his brief case and said, "I will now confide to you, my dear friends, something which I must ask you to treat with the utmost confidence."

Captain Kater and Captain Ratshelm nodded agreement. Wirrmann took a file out of his brief case, opened it, and began to turn over the pages. Finally he found what he was looking for—the copy of a letter. He tapped this with the forefinger of his right hand and looked significantly at his companions.

"Here," he said with some solemnity, "I have a letter from Cadet Hochbauer to his father, the commandant of an SS training school. This letter, which was written a mere two weeks ago, came into my hands by a circuitous route—in confidence and with the request that I respect that confidence. And I must confess, gentlemen, that this letter is a document of the most enormous importance in view of what has taken place here in the meantime. The culprit is named openly here. And though that doesn't exactly have the force of proof itself, nevertheless another part of the letter means a great deal to me. This is concerned with you, Captain Ratshelm."

"With me?" asked the latter, not without some apprehension.

"Yes indeed," said the judge-advocate, folding his hands, thus giving a very pious air to the whole proceedings. "And I confess openly this part of the letter moved me profoundly. This was the reason I immediately got in touch with you by telephone so frankly, Captain Ratshelm, on hearing the news of the cadet's death. For this part of the letter tells of the trust and admiration which this cadet felt for his esteemed company commander. For you, Captain Ratshelm! A testimony of faithful devotion."

Captain Ratshelm cast his eyes down with emotion. Wirrmann and Kater watched him, sizing him up, and in no way were they dissatisfied with what they saw.

Ratshelm, much stirred, declared, " 'His trust shall not be in vain,' " adding firmly, "Judge-Advocate, please count me in on this in every respect. I am wholly at your disposal."

"Right then!" said Wirrmann, unable to conceal his triumph any longer. "The die is cast. Captain Ratshelm—I congratulate you on your decision. My dear Kater—pour us out another glass. We've got a long, hard night in front of us. First we must draw up our friend Ratshelm's evidence. Then we must go through the cadets of Section H for Heinrich with a fine-tooth comb. And you, my dear Ratshelm, will give me the names of all those who were friendly with Hochbauer—

and the names of his enemies. And when you've done that, we'll have our friend Lieutenant Krafft in to see us."

"All in the course of tonight?" asked Kater in amazement.

"Time presses," said the judge-advocate authoritatively. "And besides, I've something even bigger in mind. I'm aiming at Krafft, but I intend to hit the biggest prize that's ever fallen to me in my life!"

Judge-Advocate Wirrmann moved rooms from the guest house to Number 6 Company. Captain Ratshelm's office was made his headquarters for the night. The captain himself was assigned the task of protecting the flanks, or in other words keeping Lieutenant Krafft at bay. The latter, however, seemed completely uninterested. Besides, he was busy with Elfrida Rademacher.

Judge-Advocate Wirrmann had the cadets marched in to him one after the other. Each was allotted between five and ten minutes, simply as part of the sounding-out process. This procedure took almost five hours, from 1900 hours to midnight.

But Wirrmann's energy seemed inexhaustible. If his cold, ferocious determination should succeed in bringing down the greatest prize of his career, then the post of a judge-advocate general, to which he aspired, would be within his grasp.

Wirrmann's methods were of classical simplicity. The creation of a reliable witness took place in three phases:

First phase: Wirrmann made it clear who he was, how far his influence extended, and who was behind him. He suggested to his prospective witnesses that he was in a position to decide between success and failure for them, between freedom and imprisonment, glorious promotion and ignominious expulsion.

Second phase: Wirrmann made himself out to be as human as he possibly could. He even endeavored to show fatherly feelings. At any rate he made a great point of being completely understanding. There were certain human weaknesses —here a wink!—to which he was not altogether a stranger. He opened his heart to people in the hope that they would open theirs in return.

Third phase: Wirrmann appealed to common ideals and to the grim need to draw together in the face of the enemy. He talked of Germany and service to the Fatherland in a voice not altogether free from emotion, an effect which he managed to reproduce forty times over almost without effort. A challenging fanfare on behalf of justice formed the peroration— justice which only an absolute swine would try to evade.

"With due respect," suggested the astonished Ratshelm, "wouldn't it really be much simpler to address this threefold appeal to the assembled section and not to each cadet individually?"

"Simpler? Of course," said the judge-advocate, taking the captain's admiration elegantly in his stride, "but not more effective! The appeal to the individual, a personal and confidential appeal, always goes much deeper. This has been proved over and over again. It nearly always pays to take trouble."

"Quite astonishing," admitted Captain Kater. "And yet permit me a question, my good sir. Why go through so much formality? Simply turn the heat on these young fellows. Then you can get anything out of them you like."

"No, no, no!" declared the judge-advocate with conviction. "Such methods may be employed where a certain suspicion exists already and you have certain things to go on. But not here! Here I have to create willing witnesses. I have to talk to them like a friend, have to open up each as if he were some sort of treasure chest. In short I need their co-operation— they are to sing for me and must be under the impression that they're doing so voluntarily."

Judge-Advocate Wirrmann's methods were completely justified by results. With meticulous detail he separated the sheep from the goats. Shortly before midnight he saw his way relatively clear. Of forty names, only five were now left on his list: Amfortas and Andreas, Hochbauer's henchmen to the last, now isolated and cut off from the others and thus automatically driven into Wirrmann's arms; Böhmke and Berger, the one sensitive, the other good-natured, highly approachable if one talked to them nicely, naïvely unsuspecting, and still maintaining a belief in justice; finally Kramer, the section senior, much too obviously concerned for neutrality and ostentatiously impartial, who wouldn't be much use but couldn't do much harm either.

Wirrmann worked on the five he had selected, both individually and in small groups. He took his time about it. Slowly he succeeded in building up an uncommonly sinister portrait of Lieutenant Krafft. Admittedly the whole thing wasn't entirely easy going. For instance, just before midnight, Cadets Rednitz, Mösler, and Weber reported again. Without having been sent for.

"We beg to be allowed to give certain evidence," said Rednitz, the group's spokesman.

"I haven't asked for it!" protested Wirrmann.

"But we've come here voluntarily."

"That is quite unnecessary!"

"We beg to differ," said Rednitz respectfully. "We believe that we have certain important evidence to offer."

"Whether your evidence is important or not," said Wirrmann in slight agitation, "is for me to decide, if you please."

"But you can't very well decide before you've heard it." The three cadets stood there like rocks. Their eyes twinkled impudently as they looked at the judge-advocate.

Wirrmann looked around to Captain Ratshelm for assistance. The latter recollected that he was, after all, the company commander here, and in his capacity as such ordered the cadets to dismiss. They hesitated for only a moment. Then they saluted and trotted out, slamming the door behind them.

"Extraordinary manners," remarked the judge-advocate.

Kater said, "This is all Krafft's influence. You can see how badly we need to get rid of him."

It was just at this moment that the door which had been slammed reopened, and in walked Lieutenant Krafft, comparatively politely. He came to a halt, looked around the room, and said, "Good evening."

Captain Ratshelm winced at this ostentatiously civilian form of greeting, and said in a tone of rebuke, "I don't remember asking you here, Lieutenant Krafft."

"That wasn't really necessary," returned Krafft crisply. "I came of my own accord and in your interests."

"In any case," said Kater acidly, "you're not wanted here."

"Just what I wished to say to you, Captain," said the lieutenant politely. "You've been wanted elsewhere for some time by your immediate superior, Captain Feders. He wants to talk to you urgently."

"Now, at this time of night?"

"Captain Feders has no qualms about sending for you at any time, but I dare say the later it is, the less pleased he'll be to see you."

With that, Captain Kater was temporarily eliminated. He took his leave and disappeared. Kater felt fairly certain that Feders didn't want to speak to him at all. But what was even more certain was that Feders wouldn't hesitate for a second to back up his ally.

Meanwhile Captain Ratshelm was intent on delivering this stubborn section officer a knock-out blow. But Wirrmann intervened and said, rather surprisingly, "I'm delighted to see

Lieutenant Krafft. I was just on the point of asking him to come here."

"In case you'd thought of interrogating me, Judge-Advocate," said Krafft politely, "I must ask you to stick to the regulations. I demand the presence of someone to take down my statement and the exclusion of third parties, particularly those who are more or less involved in the case and are clearly prejudiced."

"Do I have to put up with remarks of that sort, Judge-Advocate?" demanded Ratshelm.

"Ignore it, Captain," the lawyer advised. "Besides, I think I'll shut up shop here for tonight. I'd just like to have a little private conversation with Lieutenant Krafft, though. You'll permit it, Captain?"

Ratshelm took his leave of Wirrmann and walked out, passing Krafft without so much as a glance. His firm steps, strongly accentuated by the flagstones in the corridor, echoed through the night.

"Now that there are just the two of us," said Wirrmann, beginning to smile, "let's talk quite frankly."

"Judge-Advocate," said Krafft, "as section officer I am responsible for the cadets of my section. That is to say I will not tolerate anything which is not strictly in accordance with existing regulations. By that I mean informal interrogations, particularly when they're held in the presence of a third party of doubtful repute. An offense of this sort is more than a mere formal mistake. Therefore I not only lodge a protest against it; I intend to file a report about it. And I demand that in the future all inquiries and interrogations should take place in the presence of our legal officer, Captain Schultz."

"What are you getting so excited about, Lieutenant?" said Wirrmann with a deprecating gesture. "This is all quite unnecessary, because you're rather too late, I'm afraid. But please sit down, so that I can explain things to you more fully."

Krafft sank into one of the chairs, stretched out his legs, and looked at the judge-advocate. Wirrmann smiled—it was anything but a friendly smile, and made it unmistakably clear that he felt on top.

"Yes, you're too late," repeated the judge-advocate. "Admittedly you can make things a little difficult for me because of my methods of investigation. But you can do nothing to erase the results already acheived."

"I can produce directly contradictory results, if you really want."

"I am convinced you'd manage to do just that—after everything I've heard about you. You're the type who doesn't stop even at murder, Krafft."

"Of people of your sort, no, Wirrmann."

The judge-advocate's eyes opened wide. No one had ever called him simply "Wirrmann" in this unceremonious way before—or at least not in a situation of this sort, where he was faced by someone of lower rank. He took a deep breath and forced a tortuous smile.

"I see you're quick to exploit every situation," he said somewhat laboriously. "Well, I've no objection to that. There are only the two of us here and no witnesses, so we can talk to each other completely honestly. I welcome that, Lieutenant."

"I too, Judge-Advocate."

Formal order was restored, and the game was able to continue. It was like the start of a boxing match; the opponents shook hands before setting about each other.

"Right, then," said Wirrmann. "My inquiries have shown me quite clearly how to tackle this. I've found at least two cadets who categorically indict your methods. Two other cadets either directly or indirectly confirm their statements. Others can doubtless be found. You know from your own experience, Lieutenant, how easy it is to mold opinions into explicit points of view. In short, if you so wish it, I can have you up before a court-martial without any trouble at all."

"What do you mean, if I so wish it?" asked Krafft, pricking up his ears.

"Aha!" cried Wirrmann with evident satisfaction. "I see you have a real feeling for subtleties. You're on the alert all right. Well, I am fully determined to instigate court-martial proceedings, and since, sir, I'm a master of my subject, the outcome can hardly be in doubt. But there's a special aspect to this case. Because two alternatives present themselves—and I must confess I find one of them infinitely preferable to the other."

"What alternatives?" asked Krafft, leaning forward.

"Well, in the first place, I could proceed exclusively against you, against a section officer, against—excuse my frankness, won't you?—against a relatively insignificant lieutenant. And I'd like to emphasize expressly that this value judgment has nothing to do with your personality as such, but only with your rank. There is, however, an alternative, which I should much prefer—but that would be possible only with your assistance, Lieutenant."

"Who do you want to use me against?" asked Krafft.

"Let us say, against the current system of training here, against the outdated and reactionary methods by which officers are formed, against a thoroughly questionable prevailing atmosphere. Surely such things must be the concern of every good German."

"You've got courage," admitted Krafft in astonishment. "But perhaps it's no more than blindness."

"I know what I'm doing," said Wirrmann, "and I'm counting on your intelligence. If you're absolutely determined to sacrifice yourself, all well and good. But I can hardly believe you'll be so foolish, if I guarantee to get you out of trouble. All you need to say is 'Yes' and we'll start collaborating at once. We'll work out a plan together. Then no interrogation will take place without your cognizance, and you'll be able to take part in everything right up to the drawing up of the indictment. I'm sure you'll realize I'm making you the most favorable possible offer in the circumstances. Will you accept it?"

"Now I see what you're after," said Krafft. "It's the general's head you want."

"All I'm interested in is justice," insisted Wirrmann, "and I'm determined to get it. And you'll have to realize this; it's either the general or you, though for you, Lieutenant Krafft, there does exist a choice."

* * * *

Intermediate Report No. 10

THE CURRICULUM VITAE OF CADET WILLI REDNITZ, OR THE PLEASURES OF POVERTY

My name is Willi Rednitz. My mother, Clementine Rednitz, is a domestic servant. I was born in Dortmund on April 1. I don't know the name of my father. I spent my youth in Dortmund, where my mother was employed.

I squat in the kitchen where my mother is at work. I squat

in the corner under a table. People usually can't see me here though I can see everything. I'm not really meant to be with Mother when she works. And she works very hard. But she likes me to be there. She always smiles when she sees me— even when the sweat is running down her face and her hair hangs in strands, even when she's carrying a load or on her knees scrubbing the floor. She doesn't say much, but she smiles.

"What's that boy doing squatting there, Clementine?" says the good lady of the house. "He ought to go out and play in the park. Fresh air will do him good." My mother says nothing, but I leave at once. "I don't mind going, Mother," I say. In the garden at the back, near the servants' entrance, stands the Generaldirektor. "Well, Willi," he asks, "are you going off to play again?" "Yes," I say. He nods and gives me a slab of chocolate, a piece of cake, or sometimes even a mark. Anything that's edible I eat up at once. But I save all the money, for my mother's birthday.

Mother and I have a room in a little house at the back of the Generaldirektor's villa, in the place where all the servants live. Herr Knesebeck lives here too; he's the gardener and everyone just calls him Karl. He's a friend of mine. "Life is like a garden," he says. "A few flowers, a few bushes, a few trees and lots and lots of grass. Acres of grass. Masses of grass. And tenacious weed. A garden is just like life." "The dog has walked all over the lilies," I say. "Can't anything be done about it?" "One plants new lilies—and if a dog walks all over them there's nothing one can do about it."

"You're hanging about in the kitchen again, Willi," the good lady of the house tells me. "I'm sitting with my mother," I reply. "Haven't you anything better to do?" "No," I say. "Then show me your hands, Willi." I show them to her. "Let me see if you've washed your neck." I let her see. "Lift up your right foot." I lift it up. "And now your left foot." I lift that up too. "Well, yes," says the good lady, "he's not dirty. He can stay if he likes." And she goes away. Again my mother smiles at me without a word. But I say, "Do you know, Mother, I'm not really as clean as all that. My feet are terribly dirty, because I've just been running about outside without any shoes on. But when I come into the kitchen I always put on socks and shoes."

We play on the canal as well as in the park. It's Sunday, which means that my mother has a great deal of work and the good lady keeps on coming into the kitchen. So I am out on the canal again. I've got a new white sailor suit to make me look like some well-brought-up child. But I don't look like one. They always play in exactly the same way whatever they've got on. But I just stand about, quite stiffly, without bending, without leaning over, without sitting down. Because my suit is brand new and very white, and has cost a great deal of money—almost as much as my mother earns in a whole month. Irene calls me a "spoil-sport," and Thomas pushes me and I fall into the deep, dark, dirty canal. This isn't really dangerous, because I can swim, but it's a very terrible thing, because I've got on my new white expensive suit. I daren't go home to Mother. I hide away in a corner in my wet suit and freeze. I stand there until late in the evening, when my mother comes to fetch me. I'm freezing and trembling, and suddenly hot all over. But Mother says, "It doesn't matter, Willi—your suit'll wash." That's all she says.

From 1927 onward I go to the primary school in Dort-mund. In 1935 when I leave school, I spend a year at the commercial school at my mother's request and another year at the higher commercial school. Then I work for almost a year as an employee of the soap firm, Braun and Thomas, also in Dortmund. In the spring of 1940 I'm called up for military service.

Philip Wengler, the fat boy, won't sit beside me on the school bench. He says his father owns a big restaurant and I haven't even got a father. He says this to our teacher, whose name is Buchenholz. This fellow Buchenholz gives Philip Wengler the fat boy a box in the ear, which echoes around the room. The next day the father of Philip the fat boy comes running into the classroom and yells at Buchen-holz, "How dare you raise your hand against my son!" Buch-enholz tells him why he did it. Then Wengler, Philip's father, goes up to Philip and gives him a box on the ear him-self, which echoes around the room. "He deserves it," says Wengler, "considering he was there before I even met his mother." From this day on Philip Wengler is my friend and I love my teacher Buchenholz. In all the subjects he teaches me I get top marks.

"Mother," I say, "when you marry, I'll have a father." "You have a father already," says my mother, "but he doesn't want you to know he is your father."

"If that's so," I say, "then I haven't got a father. But still you can marry if you like." "Willi," says my mother, smiling at me, "it's not so difficult to become a mother. To find a man one loves and who loves one is much more difficult. Most difficult of all is to find a man who goes on loving one and whom one goes on loving." I don't quite understand that, because Mother is very very beautiful. It seems to me that every one must love her as I do. Perhaps only the lady of the house doesn't. But she can neither marry Mother nor be my father. And that I find a comfort.

I have two friends apart from Philip Wengler: Hilda and Siegfried Benjamin. The Benjamins have a toy shop but that isn't the reason why they're friends of mine. I like them. They're clever and have nice parents. And Herr Benjamin is a particularly good father. Sometimes he even sings his children songs that sound both German and foreign at the same time. I think, "I'd be very happy to have a father who spoke in a foreign language if he would only sing me a song sometimes."

Then I find such a man. He has dark skin and a name that sounds French—Charles, the people call him. And Charles can sing in a deep voice, and rolls his eyes as he does so, which is very funny. He likes buying schnapps in the bar, and he wrestles for money, because he has to live, after all, and everything's expensive. Sometimes he sings to an audience too, if someone plays the piano. I squat at the back of the storeroom, between crates, until he notices me. "You shouldn't be here, Willi!" says Charles. And I say, "But you sing so nicely." "It's very late, Willi—you must go back to your mother. I'll take you home." "Oh please do," I say. "Mother will like that."

Charles takes me home to Mother. He sits in our room and drinks a cup of coffee. Charles is very embarrassed and keeps on apologizing. But Mother says, "It was very nice of you to bring Willi home. I'm afraid I'm not always able to look after him." "I need a father," I say, "but it's so hard to find one." Charles often gets the chance to take me home to Mother.

"Clementine," says the lady of the house to my mother, "I'm a generous, broad-minded person and very easy-going. But there are limits even with me. Your boy Willi is really going too far, it seems to me. It's not enough for him that he spends his time with Jews—he's now bringing colored people into the house as well. I'm not going to stand for that. See that it stops at once, if you value your job here." "I'm not going to see that it stops, madam," says my mother.

"People who are nice to my son are much more important to me than any job."

"Clementine," says the Generaldirektor, "be reasonable, I beg you. Don't be so petty. Apologize to my wife and there'll be no more said." "There's no more to be said," says my mother. We leave the house and take a room that's much smaller than our last one. Mother works in a bank, from five till eight in the mornings. In addition to that she also works in a shoe factory, between seven and nine in the evenings, making everywhere very clean and nice. But on Saturdays and Sundays she's allowed to help in the restaurant which Philip's father owns. This goes on until Siegfried Benjamin has his accident.

Siegfried Benjamin is run over by a truck while playing in the street. His left leg is practically snapped off, there's a deep gash in it, and it's bleeding badly. Siegfried howls with pain and the others just stand around gaping. The truck has driven on—its driver obviously didn't see what had happened. But I cut down a piece of cord hanging from some scaffolding and put a tourniquet on Siegfried's leg. I've read about this in a book. Then we take planks from the scaffolding, make a stretcher, and lay Siegfried down on it. We carry him to Dr. Grunewald, who lives two streets further on.

"My respects, Willi," says Dr. Grunewald, after he's examined Siegfried, cleaned the wound, bound it up, and set the leg. "You didn't do at all badly there. How did you know all about that?" "Read about it," I say looking about me. "But it isn't very clean here," I say. "Now listen a moment, my little man," says Dr. Grunewald, "my instruments are impeccable and so is my surgery." "Well yes," I say, "but the waiting room isn't as clean as it could be, neither is the hall." "But what's one to do?" says Dr. Grunewald, shrugging his shoulders. "I have to look after my patients—I haven't any time for anything else." "You need a woman, someone to keep it all clean here," I say. "A woman like my mother." Three days later my mother at last has a good steady job and a nice room too—we move into Dr. Grunewald's house.

Her name is Charlotte Könnecke. She goes to our school, but she's in the top grade. Her father is a post-office official, and she is marvelously beautiful. She always wears bright clothes, and her hair, which is long and brown and silky, blows about in the wind. When there is no wind she shakes her head from time to time and her hair hangs down like a wonderful thick curtain. I stand and stare at her as she comes to school, as she goes home, as she walks to the baths in the afternoon, or in the park, or as she crosses the streets. She's much older than me—two years older than me—two years older, and she doesn't see me or doesn't want to see me, because it wouldn't be suitable. "Charlotte," I often say to myself as if in a dream. And I say to Mother, "If I have a sister she's to be called Charlotte." And I say to Dr. Grunewald, "Charlotte is the most beautiful name in the world." "There are other beautiful names too," says Dr. Grunewald. "You'll soon see." "There can't be a more beautiful one," I say with conviction. And once I'm allowed to carry her satchel. This happens on September 13, 1933, between 1205 and 1211.

I'm allowed to carry my beloved Charlotte's satchel because she isn't well. She's having a child. She's only just fourteen, and the child is said to be by her stepfather. I am miserable and I cry and hate the world.

"Willi," Dr. Grunewald says to me, "I've heard you've been crying. That's good, it makes one feel better. I cry too, sometimes—not often but sometimes." I look at Dr. Grunewald—he's an old man, his hair's quite white, his face is deeply furrowed, as if a plow has been at work on it, but his eyes are quite young. Does he really cry too? "Be glad you can cry," he says to me. "Great emotion is what makes life beautiful, deepening and broadening it. Only those who know torture can feel joy." "You're like a father to me," I say. "I can't think of a better son," says Dr. Grunewald.

Philip Wengler, the fat boy, is the first to go. The restaurant which his father owns is broken up till it's nothing but a a heap of rubble. Then the remains are set on fire and burned to the ground. Herr Wengler, the father, lies in the hospital. His spine is damaged. He says to Philip and me when we come to visit him, "Don't hold opinions of your own, boys, or they'll beat you up and make cripples of you. There are always some who disagree with you and they can't bear anyone else to think differently. But if you do have the misfortune to develop opinions of your own, keep them to yourselves—for God's sake, keep them to yourselves. Otherwise they'll beat you to death!" Two days later Herr Wengler dies. And his wife, Philip's mother, disappears. An aunt takes Philip to live with her—he goes a long way away, somewhere far up in East Prussia. I've never seen him again.

Herr Benjamin has put on a little cap. A big silver candelabra stands on the table and we sit around it—Frau Benjamin, Hilda, and Siegfried and me. The candles burn solemnly, and Herr Benjamin says, "Willi, you were always a good friend of our children, and we've all got to like you very much. But tomorrow we're going away to a foreign country and perhaps today is the last time we'll ever see each other in this life. We want to thank you for everything, Willi. And we ask you to forget us."

I tell all this to Dr. Grunewald, and ask him why, but Dr. Grunewald looks away and weeps.

Then comes the day when even Dr. Grunewald is no longer there. Someone else takes over his practice. From that day onward Mother hardly ever smiles again when strangers are about. But she still smiles at me. And once she says to me, "Try always to look on the bright side. Otherwise all this poverty and misery will suffocate you."

With the beginning of the war I was sent to the front. I was in action in Poland, then in France, later in Russia, almost always with the same unit. In 1941 I was promoted corporal, in 1943 sergeant, and simultaneously selected to be an officer cadet.

Poland: in a little wood near Mlawa a mutilated German airman—his eyes gouged out, his sexual organs cut off. In Mlawa, a Polish family, the man with his skull split in two, the woman split up the lower part of her body, and between the two corpses a child trying to hide in terror. In Praha, in the villa of the president of the Polish railways—an officer cuts pictures from their frames, a corporal excretes into an antique marble bowl. Further on—a group of German soldiers, surprised in their sleep, lying there with their throats cut. Warsaw, a man dangling from the bars of a window above the street. A man looking rather like Dr. Grunewald.

France: two men entangled with each other in a vast pool of blood and red wine, with stiff hands grasping at each other's throats—a Moroccan and a German grenadier. A bunker near Verdun, filled with the mutilated remains of human beings, stinking pulp—among them faded bones, and bits of skull of unidentifiable nationality left over from the previous world war. A bed with a Frenchwoman on it, and on top of her a German soldier, and under the bed the woman's husband—all of them dead and all about them the ruins of the house demolished by a bundle of hand grenades.

Dreux in France: the tomb of the Valois, former kings

of the country. A pair of lovers, lying among these tombs. Phonograph music coming from a tower room in the castle. The bawling voices of drunken soldiers all going off to the brothel together. An old Frenchman, who stands there in a trance, a child being scolded by a railwayman. An officer sitting in his billet reading Voltaire. A long, wild, appalling scream, going on and on, a scream that rings out over the rooftops of Dreux and yet no one seems to hear it except myself; the scream of a man gone mad.

Intervals at home again in Dortmund. Home? Mother smiles and I immediately forget a lot. The doctor who has taken over Dr. Grunewald's practice can never look any of us straight in the face. But Erna, his assistant in consulting hours, has great big eyes which like to stare and be stared at. The second night she comes to my room and lies down beside me. "What is one to do?" she asks. "After all there's a war on." "Well, all right," I say. "After all there's a war on." She reminds me of Charlotte.

The campaign in Russia: mountains of corpses—Polish officers. The work of the Russians. Further mountains of corpses—Polish Jews. The work of the Germans. Strange fruit hanging from the trees—partisans, men who fight the partisans, commissars, men who liquidate the commissars. Corpses used as parapets; corpses used as paving stone; corpses used as fuel. And on the far horizon a fire as if the whole world were ablaze.

Here in Russia near Charkow a girl called Natalie. Snatched at the last moment from three drunken fellows who are trying to rape her—Russians in fact—quite by chance—assistants at a German supply unit, where it's relatively easy for them to get hold of schnapps. Two of them now have to go to the hospital, for I shot at them with my carbine. Natalie is panting desperately. I try to calm her down. Dark brown eyes, beseeching help and looking at me gratefully, full of trust, full of hope. I share my rations with her. She fixes her dress somehow. She is breathing excitedly, seizes my hand, and it seems she wants to kiss it though it's filthy. I drink some of the schnapps the fellows have left behind. I put my arm around Natalie and feel her trembling. I drew her to me and then do just what the others wanted to do with her. Natalie doesn't resist, but she weeps, and I stumble out into the night, overcome with shame.

Next morning I go back again. I know that I love Natalie, it's like loving some hard and yet sweet and unavoidable destiny. This feeling for another human being overwhelms me. I've never known it before, never thought that such a thing was possible. I want to shout it out to the clear frosty morning, so that it's heard all over the world, across all the fronts. When I push open the door of the house in which Natalie lives, I see her lying in front of me in the middle of the room on her back, with her dress torn. Hunched up. Covered in blood. Dead.

As to the details of what's called a military career, there's nothing special to report. I've done what's commonly called one's duty. I was promoted regularly and selected to be an officer cadet as a matter of course. Why, I can't say. What for, I don't know. All I do know is this: I'm a poor man. And because I know that, I try and look on the bright side.

31 *FAREWELL AND NO REGRETS*

THE NEXT DAY passed like sand through an hourglass; the hours ran through with monotonous regularity. Everything seemed as normal: the timetable, the breaks, the meals; the dull, automatic thought processes. The officer factory was working full blast. None of the machines seemed out of order in any way.

Even Lieutenant Krafft did all that was expected of him. He too seemed to function strictly according to the timetable. He got up punctually, breakfasted in the mess, took his section out on ground training—concentrating on patrol work —and ate together with the cadets at midday. He seemed completely his normal self. His remarks were no less frequent or effective than usual. Perhaps his tone of voice wasn't quite so carefree as usual. But no one noticed that.

The afternoon timetable laid down the inevitable classroom instruction for the first period. This time the rather curious subject was "Care of Relatives." The cadets gathered in the classroom and arranged paper and pencil in front of them. They were all set to write one of the usual essays, and the prospect made them yawn.

Yet when Krafft appeared on the scene, his first question was, "Care of relatives—what's that supposed to mean?"

To which the cadets were unable to find the right answer, not least because they took no particular trouble to do so. Why should they? This was a completely new subject for them, and in any case they were there to be enlightened and instructed or at least prompted into understanding. So they merely embarked on one of their usual guessing games. Cadet Mösler's contribution for example was, "If for instance the sister of a soldier comes on a visit, then I take care of her—provided of course she seems worth it."

But the laughter which greeted this was of no great volume.

Kraff noted down each argument in turn, but made no comment on them. He seemed preoccupied with his own thoughts and even stared out of the window for minutes on end. Only when the cadets' on the whole rather vague collection of ideas began to seem exhausted did the lieutenant turn back to them.

"So you really don't seem to find this subject particularly relevant," said Krafft. "And you're not altogether wrong. The military machine is interested only in the soldier who serves it—in no one else. This naturally doesn't mean that superior officers show themselves unfriendly if their soldiers' relatives turn up from time to time. In peacetime there used even to be social occasions—a company dance, for instance, an excursion for the NCOs and their relatives, a ladies' night in the officers' mess. But all that's a long way off now, and not likely to concern us for some time in the foreseeable future. In short, a soldier's relatives play no part in our program, with one single exception. Now what could that be?"

The cadets had no idea. They stared dully at their section officer. Had any of them ever bothered about their relatives at any time? Not so far.

"There is one case," said Lieutenant Krafft, "in which an officer finds himself forced to make contact with a soldier's nearest relative, which is if the soldier is severely wounded or killed. What happens in that case?"

"The company commander, or alternatively his deputy, writes a letter of condolence."

"And what form should this letter of condolence take? What in fact does it look like? Has anyone here ever seen such a thing?"

Kramer, the experienced corporal, put up his hand. "A letter of this sort should be as comprehensive as possible, and written in longhand. Only when casualties are exceptionally heavy and fighting is continuing can they be typed."

"And the content of such letters?"

"A few specimens are laid down in the relevant handbook. But basically it can be said that the more personal they are the better."

Krafft seemed barely to be listening. The almost indifferent way in which he imparted his technical information emphasized all the more clearly the macabre character of the theme. "What points are there to bear in mind in such letters, and what points to avoid?"

The cadets threw the sentences back at Krafft as if they were playing handball.

First, the positive points. Essential was: "fallen for Führer and Reich." Less usual: "fallen for the Fatherland." Always important: "in faithful and exemplary execution of his duty." Always welcome: "unforgotten . . . will continue to live in the hearts of his comrades."

Next, the negative points—that's to say points to be avoided at all costs. Essential: no description of suffering. Whenever possible: no detailed description of the cause of death. Obviously: no criticism of his soldierly or human qualities. And in no circumstances any remarks which might suggest a disastrous military operation of senseless casualties.

The general theme should be that to die on the battlefield was to die honorably—and this of course included dying in hospitals, on training grounds, and within all military establishments. Anyone who dies is basically a hero. The indispensable phrase then: "in pride and sorrow."

"So there it is!" said Lieutenant Krafft flatly. "And that's how it's been for several hundred years. The form and content of this sort of letter of condolence is always the same, only a few of the details changed. Once it used to be 'For King and Country.' Then 'For Kaiser and Fatherland.' Now it's 'For Führer and Reich.' And always on the field of honor. And never senseless. Just think about that a bit if you have the courage. That's all for today, my heroes."

The section was dismissed. Only Cadet Rednitz remained behind. He put the class log down in front of Krafft and waited until he had made his entry.

When that had been done the lieutenant suddenly said, "Rednitz, I was working with Captain Feders on the section's final assessment last night. Because the course is nearly over. Do you want to know how you've done?"

"No, sir," he said truthfully.

"Why not, Rednitz?"

"Because I'm sometimes not sure whether I really want to get through this course at all, sir. There are moments in which I begin to wish that I need never become an officer."

"Rednitz," asked the lieutenant, "are you tired of this life, or something?"

"Not yet, sir. But the more I think about it, the less sense there seems to be in it all—as things are at the moment, anyhow."

"Then try and change things. You're still young. I'm only a few years older, but I'm already an old man—tired, used up, resigned. You're still different, Rednitz. You mustn't give up."

"In a few days this course'll come to an end, sir, and we shall separate forever. Most of them will soon forget what you've tried to teach us here—you and Captain Feders each in his own way. You've taught us to think for ourselves and see for ourselves and sometimes you've stirred our consciences. But I'm afraid that you haven't always been forthright enough—it wasn't possible for you in the circumstances. And it's just this that makes me wish not to become an officer at times. For if someone like you can't break down the barriers, what hope is there for a little fellow like me?"

"Rednitz," said the lieutenant gravely, giving the cadet his hand, "if you should ever remember me later, try not to feel sorry for me. Everyone must work things out in his own way, because in the last resort everyone is alone."

The cadet left the room. Lieutenant Krafft didn't watch him go. He collected his things very deliberately, cast one last brief glance around the empty classroom, and smiled as if saying farewell. Then he, too, left.

Outside the classroom block the lieutenant met Captain Ratshelm, who seemed to have been waiting for him. Ratshelm's manner was very official and completely impersonal.

"As you know, Lieutenant Krafft," he said, "Cadet Hochbauer's funeral will take place tomorrow in the customary manner of this training school, like Lieutenant Barkow's. The actual burial will be preceded by a short ceremony at which it's usual for the relevant section officer to make the funeral oration."

"I know that, Captain," said Lieutenant Krafft, "and I'm all prepared for it."

"Don't you think," asked Ratshelm coolly, "that in the circumstances it might be better for you to stand down?"

"No I don't, Captain," said the lieutenant evenly. "I'll make a speech according to custom. I consider this to be my duty, and I maintain my right to fulfill it."

"And the investigation pending against you?"

"Has no interest for me, Captain. An investigation is in no sense a judgment. I shall make the speech unless the general decides otherwise."

Lieutenant Krafft brought his hand up to the peak of his cap with a slight smile, and leaving Captain Ratshelm standing there, simply walked away. He had some hours' work to put in with Captain Feders yet. The final assessments for the section had still to be written.

Feders and Krafft were working together in the captain's quarters. Marion Feders and Elfrida Rademacher were trying to help them by typing out what the officers dictated. Not a minute was wasted. Krafft kept pressing stubbornly on.

"My dear Krafft," said Captain Feders finally, "why the devil are you treating all this like piecework? We've still got eight days but you're behaving almost as if the course came to an end tomorrow."

The two women looked first at each other, and then at Krafft. He seemed to be concentrating exclusively on his assessments. He didn't look up as he answered. "The date matters to no one but me. These assessments must be completed before Judge-Advocate Wirrmann can start gathering me in with his rotten harvest. Do you understand? Nothing that's extracted from the cadets in the course of this inquiry must have any influence on our final assessments. In case of emergency you must be able to swear with a clear conscience that we concluded them beforehand."

"If necessary," said Feders, "I'll swear a whole host of other things with a clear conscience too. Because all that matters is to get the better of those two bird-brains, the course commander and the company commander. They're always saying they want people to give everything they've got. Right —we'll show them!"

Elfrida Rademacher and Karl Krafft said good-by to Captain Feders and Marion, and left. They walked side by side across the main road, past the building which housed the general's staff, and Elfrida said, "They're very nice people, these Federses, aren't they? And they're very brave."

"Yes, brave as a cat clinging to the person who's trying to drown it, brave as a circus tiger jumping through burning hoops. Our life's like that these days!"

Elfrida took advantage of the darkness and the absence of passing traffic to nestle close to him.

Elfrida said softly, "You've changed, Karl. You've changed a great deal lately."

"Well," said Krafft defensively, "perhaps I'm showing my true face now. But I hope you remember I warned you."

"Karl!" she said. "That wasn't meant as a reproach."

"I'm a hopeless case, he answered brusquely. "And the best thing for you would be to realize that and forget about me—I'm not a very pleasant memory."

"Don't worry, Karl," she said tenderly.

"We're there," he said, pointing to the building he lived in. "Good night, Elfrida."

"I want to stay with you," she said.

"I've still got a lot to do tonight."

"Will I disturb you, Karl?"

"The course commander wants to see me. That could take a long time."

"I'll wait out here on the road."

It was a night without frost. There was a blue-black sky with barely perceptible strips of cloud, and a fitful wind which brought the thaw. In the fields the snow melted and drained away. The winter itself seemed to be trying to creep away.

Karl Krafft drew back. "You simply won't understand me!" he said with some force. "Whatever I say you just smile! I've tried to warn you of the dangers and you find that funny. Are you so sure I love you?"

"Oh," she said, "it isn't like that! The fact that I love you is enough for me."

"It would be a good thing if it were," he said, and he tried to say it harshly. "You mustn't believe I love you! Perhaps I even love this strange profession I'm caught up in. Perhaps I even love these oafish cadets because I feel they're going to suffer. And perhaps I love this statue of a general— in the same way as one loves some daydream."

"So many things loved by one man," she said casually, "and not a single woman to be jealous of. I wish I could see your face now."

"I am, as you know, a man who likes to be fair and just about things," Major Frey declared.

He looked at Krafft as he said it, bestowing trust, pleading for understanding. His handsome hero's face smiled mechanically. He hadn't known happiness since the day on which his wife's infidelity had been made public.

"I'm a friend of justice too," Lieutenant Krafft assured him.

Major Frey fingered his Knight's Cross a little nervously. It was always the same gesture, as if he wanted to reassure himself that this outward mark of his exceptional bravery was still there.

The course commander pressed his section officer to take a seat. He did this with almost exaggerated courtesy. He wasn't far short of offering him a cushion to sit on, and he turned the lamp away so that the light didn't strain his visitor's eyes unnecessarily. "Cigars? Cigarettes? Anything to drink? Cognac, liqueur, a glass of wine?"

"Thank you. Nothing but a bottle will do—that is if you have one."

The major forced a laugh. A joke had been made, and this sort of thing improved the atmosphere. Something like that was needed, for he had a delicate task ahead of him. Whether or not he was successful depended on this fellow Krafft.

"Yes, my dear fellow," said the major, "tomorrow they will be burying Cadet Hochbauer. With almost full military honors—an order from the officer commanding all training schools, passed on without comment by the general. So I don't need to make any comment on it either."

Once again Frey fingered his Knight's Cross, looking down as he did so at his desk, where there was a comment from the general on another matter. Then he gave Krafft a keen, searching look and continued, with some effort. "My dear Lieutenant Krafft, what I wanted to see you about was the funeral oration which you were down for."

"Which I'm going to make," Krafft corrected him courteously.

"Which you are going to make, certainly. But, and here we're on tricky ground, don't you think that perhaps we ought to think this matter over very carefully?"

"I've heard Captain Ratshelm's arguments, Major, and I don't accept them. I had, however, reserved the right to submit to any decision of the general. May I ask if any comment of his on this subject is available?"

"Yes," admitted the major reluctantly, "there is one."

"And what does it say, Major?"

"Well, the general agrees."

Krafft leaned back in his chair. "Then everything's clear."

"Certainly, formally, yes." The major searched for his handkerchief, for his palms were sweating.

"My dear Krafft," he went on, "we must now talk to each other as man to man. I don't want to compromise Captain Ratshelm in any way, nor am I in any way afraid of anything, but this fellow Ratshelm—quite between ourselves, Krafft—is absolutely beside himself with rage. He'll stop at nothing. He's even prepared to bring the unfortunate story of Hochbauer and my wife into the open. A subject on which you, my dear Krafft, have shown considerable tact, I must admit. But one can't count on such a thing with Ratshelm. He's going to play every card in his hand. And he can afford to, because—and this is in confidence—he's already put in his request to be transferred to the front. Besides, he's very thick with this judge-advocate fellow. So, my dear Krafft, we must try and keep cool. Let us show caution and intelligence, and skip this funeral oration. Agreed?"

"And the general's decision?"

"Well," declared the course commander hopefully, "there's something rather special about this decision. For what the general in fact says is, 'if Krafft wants to, then he's to do so!' Now that means quite categorically, Krafft, that if you don't want to, then you don't need to do so!"

"I'm sorry," said Lieutenant Krafft, "but I do want to!"

"There's a light in your room," said Elfrida Rademacher as they approached the barrack block where Section H were billeted.

"I probably forgot to switch it off."

"But you've been out all day, Karl!"

"Well then it must have been my orderly. But we'll approach as quietly as we can—I don't want any of my cadets to lose any sleep."

They went into the anteroom—Lieutenant Krafft's room lay immediately to the left. A series of fitful, muffled, and distorted sounds were audible—gusts of wind tearing at the barrack walls . . . the snoring of the cadets.

Krafft opened the door into his room. And there in the light of the lamp, sitting in front of the papers on his desk, was Major-General Modersohn. Just as he normally sat in his own office; stiff, erect, and unapproachable. Though this time the general smiled.

"Come in," said the general, "you live here, after all."

Krafft approached and saluted mechanically, while Elfrida Rademacher stayed in the doorway, at a loss what to do.

"Good evening, Fräulein Rademacher," said the general, rising. He strode over to Elfrida, offered her his hand, took hers, and bowed slightly over it.

"General," Krafft ventured to explain, "Fräulein Rademacher is my fiancée."

"I know that," said the general. "I've already expressed my congratulations to you, Lieutenant. But I don't remember there being any regulation which permits officers to receive their fiancées in their quarters."

"If you will permit me," Lieutenant Krafft hastened to say, "I will conduct my fiancée to her own quarters."

"Lieutenant," said the general, "I shall have to call you to account for this offense in any case, so your fiancée might just as well stay now. It's all on the same bill, so to speak. So don't bother to move, Fräulein Rademacher."

Elfrida smiled gratefully at Modersohn. She moved gracefully across the room, past the general and his lieutenant, to the bed. Krafft felt himself blushing.

"I intend to disturb you only a short while," said the general. He sat down at the lieutenant's desk again and signed to him to be seated. Krafft pulled up a stool and sat down expectantly.

"Lieutenant," said the general, "have you discovered what Judge-Advocate Wirrmann is up to here?"

"Yes, General!"

"Perhaps you would be so good as to tell me."

"This fellow Wirrmann," said Krafft, "wishes to bring me to book, and in such a way as to bring you down too, General."

"Excellent," said the general slowly. "Your observation is excellent, Lieutenant. And what do you think this fellow will achieve?"

"Nothing," said Krafft decisively. "Nothing that I don't want him to."

The general's blue-gray eyes, normally so cold, lit up. "Listen carefully, please, Lieutenant, and note that for the moment I don't wish to hear any reaction from you. Right, then. I expressly give you permission to inform Judge-Advocate Wirrmann that it was I who told you to conduct inquiries into the death of Lieutenant Barkow."

"I think that would be inappropriate, General."

"No comment, please, Lieutenant Krafft. I want you to think about this. I repeat, it was I who told you. I asked you to proceed by any method you thought suitable, and made no attempt to restrict you in any way. I alone bear full responsibility. Is that clear?"

"Quite clear, General."

"That's all I wanted to say to you now, Lieutenant Krafft. We'll be seeing each other again tomorrow, when you make the funeral oration. Not only Number Two Course but the entire training school will be present. Good night, Krafft. Good night, Fräulein Rademacher."

The general strode off into the darkness.

"What did he want?" asked Elfrida, staring after him.

"He wanted to help me save my skin," said Krafft. "And he quite deliberately made you a witness so that I could retire to my warm bed in peace and with a clear conscience. But that's not what I'm going to do!"

Lieutenant Krafft stared at the harsh light and tried to concentrate as he leaned over his desk filling sheet after sheet with his small, neat hand. He was putting his funeral oration down on paper.

Elfrida Rademacher lay on his camp bed watching him. Her eyes looked tired and her smile was wan and pale. She looked at the tense, serious face above the white paper and at the nervous hands forming the letters.

Krafft propped his head in his hands. His gaze was directed intently into space. Visions of death formed around him in the darkness, took shape and color—the dark colors of a man's last hour—a feverish flood of blue dissolving into an earthy brown, reeling into the inconceivable black of total extinction. And again and again the flaring red of fire, of blood, of the sunset.

Elfrida stretched herself uneasily on the bed, sank into a dreamless exhaustion, and finally slept, silently, with her lips apart. A smile of anticipation flickered across her face.

"Nothing must be left out," said Krafft softly. "For every truth that remains unspoken is the beginning of a lie."

Exhausted, he dropped his hands. Twelve closely written pages lay in front of him. He felt free and happy and tired as never in his life before.

He stood up, undressed, and lay down beside Elfrida. Without opening her eyes she made room for him, yet almost in the same movement drawing close to him. Her legs entwined themselves around him, she took him in her arms, and he sank into a well of oblivion, deeper and deeper in search of the depths of infinity.

A wave of bliss surged over him obliterating him altogether. His life was over.

32 *THE CALL OF DESTINY*

THE THREE SECTIONS of Number 6 Company were allotted special duties on this particular day because the gymnasium had to be transformed into a funeral parlor. Normally this was a fairly easy task. But Lieutenant Webermann of Section C, the sheepdog, was in charge of operations today, and kept his men at it nonstop.

The cadets in Webermann's section were usually known as "the hares," because they were always on the run. Apart from which, Webermann was a born organizer. When for instance, as here, he had a hundred and twenty men under him, at least a hundred were working, regardless of whether the job was the installation of field latrines, or dugouts, or the preparation of a hall for a movie. On this particular day it just happened to be a funeral.

First of all, then, the gym had to be turned out completely, then the equipment had to be put in the adjoining rooms or behind the building, the floor scrubbed, scraped, and polished, the windows cleaned, and the walls dusted. There were to be no foreign bodies about the place, no duckboards lying about in the corners, no cobwebs on the wall, not a particle of dust on any of the polished surfaces.

Meanwhile, in accordance with a precise plan of action, every available bench was brought from the canteen, the dining rooms, and the classrooms. These formed the rear rows, and were followed by chairs of simple design, brought from the same buildings, which constituted the middle rows. Finally, from the billets and offices came chairs of superior design, which provided seats for the officers in the front rows. And a special high-backed masterpiece, from the officers' mess, was placed right in the center for the general.

"What a business!" groaned one of the cadets, who thought himself unobserved since he could see no sign of Lieutenant Webermann. The reason he couldn't see him was that he was standing just behind him. And Webermann was famed for the sharpness of his hearing. "Why all this fuss?" continued the cadet. "All we've got here is a suicide, as far as I can see."

"What you've got here are a lot of chairs!" interrupted Webermann. "And for the time being you're not required to see any further than that. I've expressly forbidden talking while at work. I don't want to hear anything but words of command here. Is that clear?"

"Yes, sir," answered the cadet, seizing four chairs immediately and trying to escape from the sheepdog as fast as possible.

"Halt!" cried Webermann severely. "You will report to me at twelve-thirty midday and nineteen-thirty in the evening —for three consecutive days. In full equipment. We'll have a little talk about how orders are to be interpreted!"

But even that wasn't enough. Webermann wasn't a man to do things by halves. He put his whistle, which was always at the ready, to his lips and blew a devastating blast. Everyone froze. The lieutenant shouted, "Semicircle around me at the double!"

The cadets left whatever they were doing and rushed together to form a semicircle around Webermann.

"Listen a moment, men!" he cried, which wasn't strictly necessary since they were already listening. "A half-wit here has just thought fit to question an officer's intelligence. It suddenly occurred to him to try and think for himself. You have to do that now and again, but not when an officer has already done your thinking for you. For anything an officer does or orders to be done is always right. Understand?"

"Yes, sir!" roared the cadets in chorus.

"Above all," continued Lieutenant Webermann, "I don't want to hear any nonsense about suicide. In the first place there was no one there when it happened. He might just have been cleaning his rifle, or who knows what else might not have happened. And besides, men, we're not a church. The fellow's dead, a funeral ceremony has been ordered, and that's all there is to it. I don't give a damn about anything else. Back to your work now—at the double."

The cadets scurried off.

And so the décor was completed. A row of barrels was

brought in and planks were set on top of them to form a bier. Trees in pots, taken from the officers' mess stores, were set alongside, together with candelabras borrowed from church. Flags were hung at the back, not least to conceal the crumbling dirty white walls. Flags on the side walls—for there was no shortage of flags—also served to cover up the glass of the windows very effectively. Subdued reddish lighting streamed through and created, to Webermann's way of thinking, an appropriately solemn atmosphere.

Then the coffin was dragged in without much ceremony, put on the bier, and covered with the Reich war flag. Webermann personally supervised this with a ruler, for he attached great importance to accuracy. He had the coffin shifted three times before he was satisfied.

But then Webermann discovered that the steel helmet was missing. A coffin with the war flag but no steel helmet was for him like a field gun without a shell. "Slovenly bastards!" he cried. "Go and find a tin hat from somewhere —the first decent one you can lay your hands on—so that the funeral can really get going!"

Splendid candles of special quality were burning on the bier. The church down in the town had made them available, thanks to Captain Kater's connections. On either side of the bier and between it and the candles stood a cadet from H Section, motionless in full-dress uniform with rifles reversed. Sensibly Kramer had allotted this role to Cadets Amfortas and Andreas.

Slowly the gymnasium began to fill up; one company after the other marched in, wearing full service dress. They were received by Lieutenant Webermann, who in turn was supervised by Captain Ratshelm.

Webermann operated according to a precisely calculated seating plan. He was the only man to move about quite uninhibitedly and even raise his voice occasionally.

"The officers are requested to sit in the two front rows— rank captain and above in front, lieutenants to the rear. The cadets should move in from the right."

Number 6 Company arrived first, fifteen minutes before the official time. Section H sat in front, immediately behind the officers. Among these was Lieutenant Krafft, who passed almost unnoticed with a brief case under his arm. Next to him sat Feders, remarkably still, and taking no part in the muffled conversation going on all around him.

Judge-Advocate Wirrmann had found a place next to Kater on the right-hand end of the front row.

Lieutenant Webermann's cadets had taken up their position to the left of the coffin. For Section G was to act as choir in the ceremony. This was determined neither by accident nor by a whimsical decision of Webermann's, but by the fact that his cadets really were better suited to the role than anyone else in the training school. Webermann always made a great point of chorus singing. Not that he was particularly musical. He was inspired solely by practical considerations. Experience showed that singing strengthened discipline and bolstered morale. So he had them singing at every available opportunity, especially since he was lucky enough to possess a young choirmaster among his cadets. They sang on the march, on their social evenings together, and, to the delight of the officers' ladies, on national holidays. Why then shouldn't they also sing at a funeral?

At five to ten the course commander, Major Frey, appeared. His medals shone and sparkled as if he had given them a special cleaning for the occasion, which indeed might well have been the case. His boots too shone radiantly. Altogether he cut a splendid figure. The commander of Number 1 Course had had to go to Berlin for a staff conference, with leave attached, so Frey was able to feel himself the second most important man in the training school. Which he did, as was plain to everyone.

At a signal from Captain Ratshelm everyone rose—ceremonial regulations demanding that on occasions of this sort loud words of command should be restricted in confined spaces. However, everything took place with extraordinary precision. Frey nodded in acknowledgment and returned the salute. When he had done this he signaled to the cadets to sit down. They collapsed like a lot of puppets.

Major Frey now carried out a little solo performance of his own. He went forward to the coffin, where he stopped for a few seconds with a great show of reverence and emotion, keeping his back to his audience, who regarded his large pair of baggy trousers with some amazement.

Finally, thinking he was unobserved, but in fact in full view of eight hundred spectators, Major Frey looked at his watch. It was two minutes to ten. The course commander thereupon brought his performance to an abrupt conclusion, for the general could be expected at any moment.

Exactly on the stroke of ten o'clock Major-General Modersohn himself appeared, accompanied only by his ADC.

All present sprang to attention and tried to look him fearlessly and openly in the eye, as they had been trained to do.

The general strode slowly past his cadets, as if eying each of them individually, one after the other. His cool, searching glance then transferred itself to the officers—no one was overlooked. What's more, everyone knew that he had not been overlooked.

"Begin!" said the general.

Now follows the unabridged version of Lieutenant Karl Krafft's oration as taken from the documents of the court-martial in which it reappeared as exhibit number 7.

"General! Gentlemen! Dear comrades-in-arms!

"Today we are burying a dead man. This is, after all, the most normal thing in the world—particularly in these great and heroic times into which we have been born. For the paths of glory do indeed lead but to the grave.

"Millions go to their graves without anyone noticing them. When they came into the world, at least there was a mother to moan for them. But as they left the world, their final cries were drowned by shell bursts, bombs tore them to shreds, and dust and rubble buried them. If they still had a mother, perhaps it wasn't until some weeks later that she first wept—or not even then, so as to keep her last vague hopes alive.

"In these short years of ours, millions of dead have fertilized the earth. Men have marched over them, vehicles have ground them into the mud; they have been buried with pickaxes and spades—as one buries treasure, or rubbish. And corpses have become transformed into cold casualty figures whose precise accuracy no one can determine. For death seems no more than some gigantic process of decay in a world that is profoundly sick.

"At certain moments, in these terrible times of destruction, candles are lit for Death, men gather around and make speeches, often full of the greatest, most miserable lies in the world. He did not die in vain, people say. His memory will live forever. Thus they sing the dead man's praises. A hero's death, they say, is the most beautiful death in the world.

"Yet there's little connection between beauty and death. All too often it is neither heroic nor contains any mystical quality, being merely bloody, and squalid. It offers not the slightest occasion for glorification, singing, or praise.

"Death expunges nothing from the life that preceded it.

Death is neither exculpation nor atonement—it marks no more than a conclusion. At the same time it's also, we hope, a transition—though here on earth it is the end of everything.

"There's only one question that can be asked in the face of death. And this question is not why did he die, but how did he live?

"All of us who stand close to death—whether we accept the fact or refuse to admit it—all of us should ponder these questions. We should do so as thoroughly and frankly as if we were about to die tomorrow. Not only because we follow a profession which makes death an everyday affair, but because we are actually in a position to order others to their death, indeed because we can't help demanding it of them.

"This presents us with the most difficult and inscrutable problem we have to live with—one that is as old as mankind. What we do and are compelled to do, directly contravenes those commandments which we believe to be of divine origin. This is a matter between each one of us and his God alone—if not on this earth, then, we must hope, in a better world. But no one can absolve us of our responsibility toward our fellow human beings, not even God himself. This is something which can't wait for the afterlife; it must be worked out here and now. By each single one of us.

"We are soldiers—or believe ourselves, or claim, to be soldiers. It doesn't matter whether we are officers or cadets. The degree of responsibiity of each individual may vary with his rank, but in principle it doesn't alter—this is something which is indivisible. We are soldiers.

"There was a time, comrades, when soldiering was a clean, straight-forward profession. In those days the operative words were: serve—protect—defend. And if, human nature being what it is, the soldier never wholly succeeded in living up to this ideal, the point was that this was the ideal to which he aspired. Such an ideal wasn't just wishful thinking but an integral part of his existence.

"To serve! This presupposes humility. The deed for its own sake—not the glory which may possibly become attached to it. To protect! This presupposes some knowledge of what is worth protecting. It implies a feeling for beauty and at the same time tolerance. To defend! Only he who has known love can know the urge to defend. But anyone who has ever loved—how can he bring himself to kill?

"The soldier must want to serve—to serve mankind and

life itself. But the man who truly loves his home, his fellow countrymen, and his country must also know that there are others who do the same and are ready to do as much for them as he is. This makes the life of a soldier so enormously difficult that only stillness and humility can give it meaning.

"A slogan which once used to try to sum up this stillness and humility ran: 'Let appearances speak true.' It didn't say everything, but it was a good slogan. It suggested a way of life. And it has no truck with the sort of ideology to which military men pay lip service in order to secure their own advancement.

"A soldier's life shouldn't consist exclusively of marching and being victorious and dying. He too may be permitted to consider that a thousand years in God's sight are but a day. And he must know that his mother is not the only mother in the world. The knowledge will be a heavy burden to him, but then being a soldier at all is a terrible burden unless one is a criminal or an idiot.

"A lot of nonsense is usually talked about tradition. Tradition is a handing on of values, not an end in itself. Flags and ceremonies and battle honors and heroes—these are not important. What is important is the knowledge of actions performed without self-interest. And if the dead have something to teach us, it is seek not death, but life!

"It is easy enough to give orders. But it's hard to set an example. And most difficult of all is to serve selflessly. This becomes impossible when there is no one and nothing left to make sense of such service.

"For the point of life is not just to have a roof over one's head, something in the pot, and a car in the garage. And no one's life can make sense if he's trying to win living space by creating corpses.

"A true soldier doesn't just howl with the pack. As soon as he stops trying to make sense of his existence, his existence ceases to be justified. One thing he certainly is not is an errand boy for power politicians.

"The soldier must say Yes when he thinks Yes. But when many say Yes and think No, when they feel forced to say Yes, though they think No, or when they say Yes for the sake of their careers, their own comfort or self-interest while their consciences tell them No, the point has been reached where true soldiering dies out altogether. And not only soldiering. This is death's great triumph. For when conscience dies, mankind dies with it.

"The true face of a soldier is not seen in victory—defeat

alone reveals it clearly. Any wild beast can be victorious. But to recognize defeat and look it in the eye requires something more than the courage of a mameluke. Only he who has preserved a glimmer of sanity can do that. And who is strong enough for that?

"For the great fear is that the spring of life itself may dry up. After the successful gamble comes the threat of loss. The so-called soldiers disclose themselves as gamblers. At the very best they are military practitioners more or less adept at the technique of destruction—and as such profoundly contemptible.

"When soldiering in the true sense disappears, murderers come to the fore. Hate becomes the order of the day. Opponents turn into enemies, and enemies into devils. Then it is always one's own side whose principles are right, the other side whose principles are wrong. The only justice is that which serves one's own side, injustice is that which prevents it from winning by every means and at any price.

"And so it comes about that the soldier lies—whether officer or cadet. He lies to himself. He refuses to believe that what he is doing is senseless—has become senseless or perhaps always has been senseless. When he is finally forced to realize this, he no longer has the courage to accept the truth. Then comes the worst stage of all; he hides his thoughts from his fellow soldiers. He lies to them too.

"Then the whole edifice collapses like a house hit by a land mine. He who believed himself to be a soldier finds himself a criminal; the man who thought to serve an ideal finds himself the thug of an ideology.

"It's all really quite simple. The soldier must respect what he serves. He who consciously serves a criminal becomes his accomplice. But he who is of good faith and yet cannot distinguish between a criminal and a true soldier will be the victim of his own blindness and his own stupidity. There are times in which it's possible to be led astray. But when it becomes clear that these times are times of lies and crime, there is no room for comfortable double talk or cowardly evasion; murderers are capable of nothing but murder.

"It's really even simpler than that, comrades-in-arms. The true soldier despises popular glory. The cheapness with which it is earned makes him blush. If soldiers are turned into conscienceless mercenaries with no other wish than to boast about themselves for hours on end, if they sanction crime simply because it brings them honor and respect, the responsibility for this failure lies with those who have betrayed the profession of soldiering—even though they did so only out of weakness, because they were helpless and powerless and stupid as a flock of sheep.

"The true soldier, comrades-in-arms, lives a life of responsibility. In silence. He wishes to serve.

"Death absolves us from none of this. It lets no one out. It in no way releases us from responsibility. The way one lives is the only thing that counts. Let us, comrades-in-arms, try to live like soldiers. If that is still possible!"

Lieutenant Krafft's speech struck his audience like a thunderclap. However, it was a little time before the mourners realized that something quite out of the ordinary was happening, for most of them had pretty thick skins, and who would have expected the occasion of a straightforward funeral oration to be abused in this way?

The officers were the first to react, one or two of them soon beginning to prick up their ears. But it wasn't long before they dozed gently off again in the manner of such occasions. People thought they must have misheard. It seemed the only explanation. For who in Greater Germany would speak out of turn like this unless he was tired of life?

The second reaction which followed some minutes later was one of incredulous amazement. At first this was felt only by the officers and cadets. Someone shook his head vigorously as if he thought he must be dreaming, though those capable of thinking for themselves gradually began to show an interest. They were still inclined to believe that what they had heard were just a few ill-considered or carelessly formulated phrases which the speaker would soon return to and correct in the opposite sense.

One of the first to show visible signs of uneasiness was Captain Ratshelm, who nudged Captain Kater excitedly. The latter started out of a half-sleep and was merely irritated at first—not with Krafft, but with Ratshelm. Then he too began to prick up his ears.

Captain Ratshelm shifted uneasily in his chair, clearing his throat with a good deal of noise. He looked about him trying to catch the eyes of people who thought as he did and shared his indignation. Finally he leaned forward in the hope of getting Major Frey to say something.

The major in his turn looked at Major-General Modersohn. The latter sat immobile in his high-backed chair as if carved from wood, not unlike some medieval figure on a choir stall. Only the color of his face, instead of being a deep rich brown, was ashen gray. His eyes seemed to be staring intently into the far distance.

It was not only Major Frey who was looking to the general. Other officers, full of growing uneasiness, were doing the same. Finally they were sitting on the edges of their chairs ready to spring into action at any moment. A sign from the general, the merest gesture, a word muttered under his breath, and they would have leaped like one man.

But the sign was not forthcoming.

Captain Feders leaned back in his chair enjoying the remarkable occasion with something almost like a happy smile on his face. From time to time he looked indulgently at Judge-Advocate Wirrmann, who was sitting beside him writing busily.

Wirrmann's fingers flew across the paper and he panted triumphantly with the effort. When the speaker paused for a moment, the judge-advocate growled "He's done for himself now."

"Scandalous!" hissed Captain Ratshelm indignantly. "Utterly scandalous!"

At that moment it so happened that the general began to move. Slowly he turned his head in Ratshelm's direction. The officers followed his every move excitedly. The general's cold, dominating eyes gave Ratshelm a devastating look that lasted several seconds.

The captain shrank into himself, and the other officers avoided the general's gaze, pretending simply to be listening to the speaker. They felt it inappropriate to show any reaction at all. The general showed none either.

So by the end the audience was listening to these remarks in spellbound silence. Of one thing they felt certain—the epilogue to this speech would be a fearful one.

When Lieutenant Krafft had finished he collected his notes and without looking at anyone returned to his place. A paralyzing silence reigned in the hall. Each of the lieutenant's steps was painfully audible.

Then the general rose—slowly, almost as if it were an effort, as if it caused him pain. His glance swept over the faces of the officers, who rose simultaneously—distraught faces in which he discerned dismay, helplessness, and anxious uncertainty.

Feders, however, made a quick grab for the judge-advocate's notes, which took Wirrmann completely by surprise.

"Extremely interesting!" said Feders, letting the individual sheets slip from his fingers to the ground as if by accident.

They scattered under the chairs, ending up under the officers' boots.

"Dismiss!" ordered the general with something like a smile on his lips.

The officers moved off at once, marching across the judge-advocate's notes, driven by an urgent need to get out into the open air. Wirrmann, however, with a throttled cry, threw himself on his knees and tried to collect his notes. Captain Feders made a great show of trying to help him, but by the time they had finished there were at least three pages missing.

"I'll be only too glad to help you reconstruct this edifying oration, Judge-Advocate," declared Feders amiably. "Unfortunately your documents are very incomplete. I hope that won't put you out at all."

"It won't worry me," rejoined Wirrmann furiously. "Even if I had only one page of notes—it'd be enough to send him to the gallows!"

It was on the evening of this day that Lieutenant Krafft was arrested.

33 *THE NIGHT THAT BROUGHT THE END*

THEY HAD BEEN stopping in Wildlingen-am-Main for two days now, at the hotel known as the Rising Sun—an officer called Bogenreuther and two corporals of the Secret Police whose names were Stranz and Runke. They were on a special mission, directly responsible to Judge-Advocate Wirrmann. Their car—a much-battered six-seater—stood outside the front door, while they themselves sat in two rooms at the back of the hotel waiting. They passed the time playing skat, as they had done for the whole of the past two days.

"I won't say it's boring exactly," confessed one of them, "but I would rather have a more solid sort of assignment."

The others didn't answer. They looked at their skat cards with passionate interest, peace-loving citizens enjoying a harmless little game of cards, in a good-natured atmosphere of fun and trust, even though they did occasionally try to steal a glimpse of each other's cards.

"Wirrmann must put in a bit of an effort if he wants to hold his job," said one of them, sorting his cards carefully. "He's hardly done anything worth-while lately. It could come to be regarded as incompetence."

"I don't know, he's booked two sergeants in the last month."

"Chicken feed," said the third contemptuously. "As the state prosecutor said recently, the real traitors are higher up."

They exchanged smiles. Their civilian clothes gave them a solid bourgeois appearance. One looked like a fairly successful businessman taking his evening apéritif. Another might have been a reputable official of some sort, or a cashier in a local bank with a position of responsibility—accounts made up weekly. The third, on the other hand, might have been manager of a prosperous little factory, a rather crude fellow perhaps, but with a definite sense of humor. There was something infectious about his throaty laugh.

"Wirrmann wouldn't get anywhere without us," he said. "He works on the so-called intellectual plane. He's not a practical man at all. But it's we who soften his people up for him. Let's have a drink on it—at Wirrmann's expense, of course."

"We'll finish the game first," said the cashier. The others nodded obediently. So he presumably was the officer.

The door opened. The landlord looked in and said, "One of the gentlemen is wanted on the telephone."

The cashier rose, taking his cards with him, and leaving the door open so that he could keep his opponents under observation from the next room. He wanted to make it as difficult as possible for them to cheat.

When he came back he winked amiably. "Wirrmann's got one," he said. "An officer too—even if he is only a lieutenant."

"Things are moving, anyway. But of course we'll finish the game first."

"No," said the officer of the Secret Police, throwing down his cards, which hadn't been particularly good. "Duty first—especially as Wirrmann hinted that we may be in for a long night."

"If that's so," said one of the corporals jovially, "then why not a spot of pleasure first? What's all this about a long night, though? I can deal with a man an hour, if really pushed."

The others joined in his hearty, good-natured laughter.

Lieutenant Krafft stood in the center of his room and looked about him. Elfrida Rademacher sat on his bed watching him with her dark eyes. A half-filled suitcase stood on the table directly under a center lamp. "I don't expect I'll need much," said Krafft thoughtfully. "And I don't want to clutter myself up with things."

"You ought at least to take two pairs of socks," said Elfrida, trying to say it in a thoroughly practical sort of way.

Karl Krafft looked at her for a moment. Then he reached into the cupboard and obediently took out two pairs of socks. But he felt embarrassed and irritated. He threw the socks into the suitcase. Turning to Elfrida he said brusquely, "Well, come on! Start attacking me! I'd rather you swore at me than just helped me pack my suitcase."

"Underclothes are always important," said Elfrida, "particularly at this time of year. I'd take an extra set if I were you."

"I haven't got an extra set," said Krafft.

"Then I'll get you another and send it on after you."

Krafft looked at her. He felt touched and thoroughly uneasy. He had expected her to react differently. He had said to her, "I've got to go away." And her answer had been, "Then I'll help you pack."

The lieutenant surveyed his meager possessions: two uniforms, a few shirts, two pairs of boots, and a pair of shoes, together with a handful of books and a sheaf of papers. That was all he had after five years of war.

"Take the books for yourself," he said. "And my papers too."

"Yes," she said.

"You can burn them if—if you want to."

"You can rely on me."

"Elfrida," he said intently, going up to her, "why don't you ask me why I'm going? Why don't you want to know how long I'll be away?"

"Why should I ask these things?" said Elfrida. "When I know the answers already."

He wanted to take her hands. But just as he was about to do so he stopped and went rigid, listening. He had heard footsteps, firm footsteps, approaching his door. Elfrida tried to smile at him.

"I think this is it," he said. Having said it he straightened up and looked toward the door, which opened and revealed Judge-Advocate Wirrmann. His eyes flashed across the room as he closed the door behind him, but in such a way as to leave it open a fraction.

"You're pretty late," cried Krafft. "I've been expecting you for some time."

"All the better," said Wirrmann in some surprise. "All the better. But I hope you appreciate the seriousness of your position, and don't imagine that you can play fast and loose with me. May I ask what the young lady is doing here?"

"My fiancée," said Krafft. "I hope I'll be allowed to say good-by to her."

"Of course," said Wirrmann at once. "We're not inhuman, after all. But make it short and painless. We've got a lot of work ahead of us tonight."

"What sort of work, if I may ask?"

"We've got to work out your confession together, Lieutenant Krafft. And we'll manage it, however difficult you try and make it. I haven't been idle all day, as you might imagine. I've collected a whole heap of individual testimony—very effective and convincing, too, some of it. I know my business, believe me. And I tell you at once, you'll confess! Everything I want you to! Even if I have to work on you for weeks."

"But, really," said Krafft with a smile, "if that's all there is to it, you can have anything you like from me."

"Really?" asked the judge-advocate, rather taken aback. "And you're not going to try and deny your subversive, treasonable speech or play it down in any way?"

"I know you've lost some of the notes you made of it," said Krafft sympathetically. "Which is unfortunate, of course."

"We shall reconstruct the speech," returned Wirrmann promptly. "Responsible officers are prepared to help with it. And after all, I was a witness to it myself."

"What are you getting so worked up about?" asked Lieutenant Krafft with maddening cheerfulness. "You can have the whole speech from me. I've kept my draft, Judge-Advocate."

With that, Lieutenant Krafft put his hand into his left sleeve and drew out the manuscript, which he held out to Wirrmann, who seized it avidly. Excitedly, Wirrmann cast his eyes over the closely written document. They were ablaze with triumph.

Krafft turned toward Elfrida, gave her his hand, and said, "Good-by, Elfrida. And thank you for everything. It's been wonderful for me to have you in my life."

Elfrida held his hand tight, but only for a few seconds.

Then she tried to smile, as if to show that she wasn't crying. She knew he wouldn't have liked to see that. "Good-by," she said bravely. She couldn't say any more, but she continued to smile for as long as he could see her.

Judge-Advocate Wirrmann, however, held up the draft of Krafft's speech and said, "What are you playing at? What's behind all this? Why are you giving me this speech? Is this another of your tricks?"

"Come on," said Lieutenant Krafft, closing his suitcase. "We won't keep your stooges waiting in the corridor any longer."

"Now I see it," cried Wirrmann indignantly. "You're trying to slip one over on me. You're trying to shield the general. You're determined to put a spoke in my wheel somehow."

Lieutenant Krafft picked up his suitcase and walked out without looking back. The judge-advocate rushed after him. The door closed.

For the first time Elfrida Rademacher began to cry.

At about 2200 hours Captain Feders made a round of the billets, deputizing for the section officer, who was otherwise engaged. He stared at pale, frightened, uneasy faces. Section H had split into two groups. On the one side, the sheepdogs, eager for action—on the other, the sheep cowering anxiously in a corner. Around all of them prowled the wolves.

"Excuse me, sir," inquired Kramer, the section senior, confidentially, "will the course now simply be broken off or will we get a third section officer for the rest of it—or what?"

"Don't you worry, Kramer," said Captain Feders cheerfully. "You need only one officer to tell that the greater part of this section are a lot of sheep. You can safely leave that to me—quite safely."

And with that, Kramer was mentally struck off Feders' list. Others followed. Anyone who in a tricky situation thought only of the possible consequences to himself was unfit to command anybody; of this, Feders was firmly convinced.

He almost preferred types like Amfortas and Andreas, who showed their satisfaction openly. The tide had turned in their favor again.

There were different reactions among the others: cautious curiosity, feigned indifference, gnawing anxiety—all concealed with some effort behind the façade of discipline. Some were already in bed behaving like ostriches. Others stood stiff and awkward in Feders' presence.

"Any more questions?" inquired Feders before moving off on his rounds again.

No one dared to put forward any of the questions that Feders had hoped to hear. This worried him, and his smile became a shade grimmer. He began to tell himself that it was his own fault if no one found it easy to confide in him, for he had always treated them like a lot of sheep. But to hell with it, weren't they just that? Didn't their reactions prove it to the hilt?

To complete his round, Feders moved on to room number seven, where the first thing he became aware of was a great cloud of smoke. In the middle of it sat seven cadets staring at him. Rednitz rose from among them and reported the room all present and correct.

"Keep the noise down," said Feders with a warning gesture. "The smoke generated in here attracts enough attention as it is. All you need is some alcohol to put courage into you."

One of the cadets hurried to open the window. The others stood around their respected tactics instructor, who looked as if he was just about to embark on a period of instruction. Feders drew up a stool and sat down. The cadets also sat down, after hesitating for a moment. The captain looked at his men and the men looked at their captain.

"We were discussing whether to come and see you, sir."

"And what decision did you arrive at?"

"We were all in favor," said Cadet Weber.

"Good." Captain Feders nodded. "You wanted to come and see me—I've come to see you. Not a bad basis for a talk, eh? Well, what is it?"

"Sir," said Rednitz, "it's about Lieutenant Krafft—we've been thinking about him. Have you heard, sir, that Lieutenant Krafft has been arrested—just an hour ago?"

"I've heard it, and expected it."

"It's a filthy rotten business, we think."

"That's what I think too, friends—what else?"

"We're not prepared to allow it, sir," said Rednitz. The cadets sitting around him nodded their agreement.

The captain regarded the cadets with some emotion, which, however, he took pains to conceal. All that happened was that his ironical smile disappeared. He looked at each of them in turn: at the handsome Rednitz with the sharp eyes, the burly Weber, the cunning Mösler, the honorable Berger, and Gundler and Cremel, who never opened their mouths (which led one to infer that they only spoke when spoken to and only did what they were told). But all those whom Feders saw in front of him were determined to act on their own—what they didn't know was how to do so most effectively.

"Well, well," said Feders. "It is with utter astonishment that I learn that there are certain things that you're not prepared to allow. Things instigated by the court-martial authorities; things approved of, or at least tacitly condoned, by a whole row of superior officers; things which in the sort of state we enjoy must be considered utterly normal, even if you are not prepared to allow them."

"Exactly," said Cadet Mösler, "that's just how it is."

"Look here," said Feders, placing the palms of his hands together, always a sign of deep satisfaction with him, "if that really is so, then there's an ugly and very important word for it which you may all bring down upon yourselves. That word is mutiny!"

The cadets didn't flinch. Feders didn't even succeed in surprising them particularly. The captain found his spirits rising; these fellows were beginning to think for themselves. Quite a triumph!

"Sir," said Cadet Rednitz, "we think there's every reason to suppose that an error of justice has taken place. If certain of our superior officers do nothing about it, that's because they don't know the circumstances. We do know them, though. And that's why we think we've got to act."

"Bravo!" cried Feders gaily. "So you want to act? And how are you going to do so? And at what price?"

"Any price," cried Cadet Weber, thumping the palm of his left hand with his right fist.

"That's to say," interjected Rednitz, "we're determined to do everything we can. One thing is that we all want to give evidence in favor of Lieutenant Krafft. And we want to ask you, sir, to make it possible for us to do so. We also wanted to ask you to tell us how best to set about it."

With amazing courage Böhmke, the poet, cried out, "If our Lieutenant has been arrested just for uttering a great truth, then Goethe ought to be burned too. For in his *Faust* he said almost exactly the same thing when he wrote:

> *How the hosts in ordered manner*
> *All the pleasant landscape mar,*
> *Following his lying banner*
> *Like the silly sheep they are.*

Those present were slightly taken aback by this fiery quotation. Weber shook his head and said soberly, "We've made extensive inquiries. We're certain of this much—the judge-advocate has brought some of his henchmen with him, one over- and two under-henchmen. They've requisitioned a whole row of cells down in the town. That's where the lieutenant is at the moment. And it's where these fellows have installed themselves. In short, a few people like me, handy with their fists, and we'd soon clean the place up."

"A risky business," said Captain Feders, in deadly earnest. "What then?"

"Yes," said Mösler, giving his imagination full rein, "well, then we'll get hold of some transport and take Lieutenant Krafft off in the direction of the Swiss border. It's said to be possible to get across still on Lake Constance."

"For who to get across?" asked Feders. "Half Section H including their tactics instructor? Don't be funny!" Angrily he added, "You've let me down. This isn't a game of cowboys and Indians. You're just a pack of idiots letting your imaginations run riot. And that's the end of the lesson."

"Have we forgotten something important, sir?"

"Certainly," said Feders. "You've left out the most important factor of all. You've omitted to find out what Lieutenant Krafft thinks. You're trying to fix all this up over the head of the man it's in aid of. What do you take Krafft for? A dreamer who's blindly stumbled into an adventure? A fanatic running his head against a brick wall? A weakling whose knees buckle at the crucial moment? Friends, this man is neither a babe in arms nor a fool. If he had wanted to evade so-called justice he could have done so. Which is as much as to say that nothing should be done without asking his opinion, without his knowledge, or even without his express approval."

"Sir," asked Cadet Rednitz calmly and attentively, "have you spoken to Lieutenant Krafft about all this yourself?"

"No," said Feders. He was surprised to realize that he had neglected to do so, and what was more, that he confessed his neglect so readily in front of his cadets.

"Wouldn't it be a good thing to try and straighten this out, sir? You're the only person still in a position to do so, Captain."

"Yes," said Feders. "I will."

A harsh cone of light shone down on the open files. They lay on a crude, broad-topped, battered wooden table. Behind it sat Wirrmann, hunched, grim, restless. In front of it sat Krafft, tired, calm, patient.

The walls were grayish white and covered with marks —walls badly in need of redecoration, much-washed, with traces of sweat and spit and blood on them. By the heavy wooden door stood one of the corporals of the Secret Police, Stranz, yawning widely and at the same time managing to preserve his friendly grin.

"This is sheer suicide," said Wirrmann without looking up. "You never stop incriminating yourself, although I offer you one way out after another."

"You forget that your way out doesn't necessarily appeal to me," said Krafft indifferently. "What else do you want to hear?"

"You've only one head, you know," Wirrmann reminded him.

"And that's one too many," said Krafft. "In these splendid times in which we live in Germany today, a head that even begins to think for itself is either a luxury or a sign of carelessness. Anyway it's more than I can cope with. Do what you like with it."

"Unbelievable!" muttered Wirrmann. "I've seen a lot in my time, but never anything like this before."

"It was high time you did, then."

The judge-advocate was given no chance to renew his astonishment, for at that moment a loud noise broke out in the corridor, gaining in volume with every second. The door was banged open. Wirrmann prepared to take cover behind the table. A crowd of people burst into the room, and from this crowd Captain Feders detached himself.

"Wirrmann," cried Feders, slightly out of breath, "if you don't want me to pick off your watchdogs like a lot of rabbits, kindly call them off double quick."

"What do you want?" cried Wirrmann excitedly.

"Good evening, Krafft," said Feders, offering the lieutenant his hand. "How are you?"

"Well," said Krafft, taking his friend's hand, and shaking his head almost imperceptibly with disapproval. But Feders appeared not to notice this, drawing himself up in front of the judge-advocate and saying, "I'm here with full powers from the general."

"The general has no powers with regard to the work I'm engaged on," roared Wirrmann promptly.

"The general," declared Feders angrily, "has appointed me legal officer. You have arrested a member of the training school. We dispute your right to carry out this arrest. In accordance with existing regulations we are entitled to demand access to the documents. Moreover we have already been in touch with the officer commanding all training schools, whose subordinate you are."

"This is a special case," said the judge-advocate, pugnacious again, now that he seemed free from any immediate threat, "and I am subordinate only to the German High Command itself."

"That doesn't alter the fact that the responsible legal officer is entitled to be shown all relevant documents on demand. So do you want to make me resort to force to obtain my rights?"

The judge-advocate retreated slightly in the direction of the dirty, grayish wall behind him, whence he took in the scene —Krafft sitting patiently beside the burly captain with the determined, vengeful expression—behind them Stranz and Runke, ever-reliable, pistols in their pockets, safety catches off, ready for action. Nothing much could go wrong—Wirrmann began to breathe more easily. Pulling himself together he caught sight of the glance which Lieutenant Krafft gave the intruder.

"Aha!" said Wirrmann, pressing a little closer. "I begin to understand—the two gentlemen are friends. I should have thought of that at once."

"To hell with that," said Feders defiantly. "Friends or not, I'm here in my capacity as legal officer, and that's that."

"Just as you like," said Wirrmann, thoroughly co-operative. "I haven't the slightest objection to making use of a good rewarding friendship. Quite the contrary, I might say—particularly in the present circumstances."

"What are you getting at, man?" asked Feders warily.

"You must know," said Wirrmann, edging forward again, "that I've a weakness for your friend here. But he's not making things easy for me. He's terribly stubborn. It could all be so simple. He needs only to be reasonable and reveal the men—or rather the man—behind him."

"The judge-advocate's quite a wag," interposed Krafft. "He's practicing for later on. If he should happen to fall on hard times he can always play the part of the jolly uncle at children's parties."

"Appeal to his conscience," said Wirrmann. "Maybe he'll listen to you. If he does, then you can take him straight off for a little private celebration. All he needs to do is to sign an affidavit I've already drawn up."

Wirrmann collected his papers and he signed to his henchmen to disappear. When they had gone the judge-advocate said, "I'm going to leave the two of you alone now for about ten minutes. All I can say is, the best of luck!" And he too left the room.

When the two of them were alone Feders asked, "What's all this about, Krafft?"

"He wants me to incriminate the general. If I'll do that he says he'll let me off."

"I see," said Feders simply. "He'd rather have the general's head. He's after the big fish. And you're not taking that way out?"

Krafft answered almost frivolously, "Really, Feders, you ought to be ashamed of yourself for asking such a question."

"All right," said Feders, "I asked it and you've answered it. Now I've got another question. Seeing you like this I'm almost afraid this is the way you want things to be. You can't help yourself. Is that right?"

Krafft rose slowly, straightened up, and faced Feders. "That's just how it is," he said. "I don't want things to be different and there's nothing I can do about it. All I know is that there must be an end once and for all to the great lie these crooks have made of soldiering. I've had enough of it."

"You're not the only one, Krafft."

"Certainly not, but someone has to make a start and say what he thinks. The thought of this cowardly swindle by which eager, decent young men are turned into cattle makes me almost choke with rage. All I wanted to do was what you are always trying to do: get people to think for themselves. They must start thinking about things at last, even if only three or four eventually come to their senses."

"There are seven in your section alone, Krafft—at least seven."

"Good," said Krafft, "then it's been worth it."

"Krafft," said Feders, and his voice sounded sad, "you've shamed us all—not least me."

"That was the last thing I wanted to do, Feders. Please believe me about that. But of all those who think as I do, I'm the most dispensable. My youth was difficult and lonely, I'm alone in the world, I have no parents, no relations—I had nothing to lose—except perhaps the thing we call honor."

"And Elfrida?"

Lieutenant Krafft looked away. He stared at the bare table top with the harsh cone of light still shining down on it.

"Elfrida," he said sadly. "That's the one thing that worries me. It all seemed very straightforward at first and very cozy. But she gave me more than I had ever expected, not just from her but from any human being. Fortunately she's strong and healthy—she'll get over it in time. What she deserves is a good, decent, uncomplicated sort of man—and she'll get one, too. I feel sure of it. I think it'll be a good thing for her in the end to lose me."

"All right, then," said Feders harshly, "you want to sacrifice yourself. I understand. I've been prepared in principle to do the same thing myself for a long time now."

"No," said Krafft, "you mustn't. No sacrifice should be senseless. No one should make nonsense of such a sacrifice, as you call it, or weaken its effect. I have made my funeral oration—that's enough. It's enough if it makes a few people think. But you've still got at least three things to do. You must go on looking after our basketmen. You must help our cadets on their way—they must return to their men with a whole set of new ideas clearly in their heads. And you must show your wife that it can never be wrong to love utterly unselfishly."

"Good," said Feders with some emotion. "I see there's no help for us. And perhaps all you're doing now is to give me a respite. How difficult it has become to *live* in Germany."

Major-General Modersohn sat at his desk exactly as he had done for months past: erect, calm, and unapproachable. His uniform was perfectly pressed, there was not a speck of dust anywhere. His left hand lay idly on the top of the desk, his right hand guided his pen.

"Is that all there is to sign?" he asked.

In front of him stood Lieutenant Bieringer and Sybille Bachner. Both nodded. They stared at him keenly. But the general seemed not to notice this; he read through the last of the documents before him.

"And with that, Herr General," said Bieringer, "Course Number Six for all practical purposes comes to an end, from the staff point of view."

"That was my intention," said the general, closing the file before him.

"Seven days too early," commented Bieringer.

"Just at the right time," said the general, getting to his feet. "Has Judge-Advocate Wirrmann arrived?"

"Yes, in accordance with your orders, General," said the ADC. "He's waiting in the anteroom."

"Then that's that," said Modersohn, looking at his trusted subordinates. In his eyes there was a depth of gratitude they would never have believed possible. "All I want to say to you both now is that it's been a pleasure to work with you. Thank you."

"But, General," said the ADC, disconcerted, "what does this mean?"

"It means," said the general, "that from now on we go our separate ways."

"No!" cried Sybille Bachner in horror.

Modersohn smiled bleakly and said, "Fräulein Bachner, we've never let personal feelings intrude into our work, let us not depart from our excellent and sensible habits at the last moment, if you please."

Sybille Bachner, breathing heavily, was trying to gain control of herself. Finally she managed to say, "I'm sorry, General," and turned and left the room.

The general watched her go. Then he said to his ADC, "You'll find my personal belongings in good order in my quarters. Dispose of them as you think fit. If Fräulein Bachner should express a wish to do anything for me, tell her that I'd very much like her to look after Lieutenant Barkow's grave—my son's grave. Now ask Judge-Advocate Wirrmann to come in."

The ADC hesitated for several seconds. He looked at the general, searching for the right words. But he quickly realized that no words could express his feelings. He lowered his head, and it was as if he were bowing. Then he left the room.

Wirrmann appeared, tense and excited. His face was lined with strain. He advanced upon the general as if approaching with the greatest courage some dangerous wild beast.

"General," said Wirrmann hoarsely, "I must inform you that in the circumstances I feel compelled to extend my inquiries to you personally. I should also take this opportunity to point out that I am acting with full powers from the High Command of the Wehrmacht."

"I am aware of that," said the general.

"I regret to have to inform you," Wirrmann managed to gulp, "that it will be necessary to subject you to interrogation. And, General, I must draw your attention to the fact that I am empowered to make an arrest."

"You can spare yourself any explanation," said the general. "Merely note this: under my command nothing takes place without my approval. Lieutenant Krafft acted exclusively on my orders. His speech was delivered with my approval. I endorse every word he said."

"That," said Wirrmann in a toneless voice overcome with astonishment, "gives me the right to arrest you."

"Let us go, then," said the general.

"Yes," said Major Frey significantly, "there you are. It just shows what happens when reliable officers aren't spotted and promoted in time."

"Yes, indeed—exactly," agreed Captain Ratshelm. "Proper appreciation should be shown of the people with the proper outlook on things."

The two sat opposite each other in deep armchairs with the soft light from a salmon pink standard lamp shining down on them. Captain Ratshelm had been only too glad to comply with his commanding officer's request that he should keep him company for a while in the major's house down in the town, where the last bottles of Madeira were also to be found. One of these stood in front of them.

So they talked on about matters of moment and significance —about the officer as the standard-bearer of his time, as the promoter of progress, protector of decency and true idealism. Neither of them—tactful, responsible fellows that they were —mentioned Felicitas Frey. But the fact that the major had already opened the second bottle of the once much-treasured Madeira seemed a sure sign that for him she ceased to exist.

"To the responsibility we bear," said the major, raising his glass, "and of which no one can deprive us."

"And which we shall continue to bear, come what may!" said Ratshelm solemnly.

"Are you still determined to leave us, my dear fellow?"

"It is my firm, unalterable decision."

They drank to each other. They listened to the sounds of the night, turning over in their minds the thought which struck them as so stirring and profound. Toward midnight they heard the sound of footsteps and voices. Judge-Advocate Wirrmann burst in, followed by Captain Kater.

Wirrmann was waving a long teletype message like some sort of pennant. His gray, haggard face was radiant with triumph. "Victory all along the line!" he cried.

Major Frey grabbed hurriedly at the teletype message while Captain Kater took possession of the bottle of Madeira. Wirrmann stood in the center basking in his triumph. Ratshelm leaned over the major's left shoulder.

When Frey had read the message and grasped its contents, he drew himself up to his full height and looked at the ceiling like some newly crowned king looking toward heaven. Solemnly he said, "I am commanding officer of the training school."

And so he was—though only a substitute for the absent commanding officer of Number 1 Course and thus only for a few days. He was in command of the training school! His secret ambition had been fulfilled. This was the most wonderful night of his life since he had been awarded the oak leaves to his Knight's Cross.

"And the general's arrest is confirmed!" cried Wirrmann. "I have him safe under lock and key. A real setback for reaction. And I've not only caught the ringleader but his accomplice as well—both of them have been dealt with once and for all. Gentlemen, I thank you for your co-operation and understanding."

"We've only done our duty," Major Frey avowed, "and we hope to continue to do so."

"I hope I shall be reinstated as commanding officer of the headquarters company," said Kater, offering full glasses all around. "With full powers, of course."

"Of course, my dear fellow," said Major Frey. "You have rendered valuable service."

"Hear! Hear!" cried Wirrmann in confirmation.

"You, however, Captain Ratshelm," said Major Frey, "are requested in the best interest of our great and good cause to withdraw your request for a transfer. For I want you to take over my job as commanding officer of Number Two Course."

"If that's so," said Captain Ratshelm, "I consider it my duty to accede to your request." His firm and unalterable decision was reversed—every other consideration must give way before the call of duty.

After Captain Kater had opened another bottle of Madeira he held a quick conversation on the telephone. "This girl Irene Jablonski," he said, "is to report to me in one hour's time—in my room. It's urgent."

But when the major found himself alone again, exhausted by the stirring events of the last few hours, he fortified himself with a final glass of Madeira and went into his wife's bedroom. She looked at him uneasily.

"Felicitas," he said with dignity, "I am now in command of the training school. What do you say to that?"

"You have deserved it as no one else has!" she assured him

quickly. "You were born for a great career, I've always known it."

"And you'll promise me always to think of it from now on!"

"I promise you, Archibald!"

"I expect you to go to a lot of trouble in the future," he said pompously. "Not only as commanding officer of the training school do I expect it, but as a man!"

"I like you," said the man, nodding agreeably. "You don't complain and you don't shout. You don't creep off into a corner and you don't try and spring at my throat. You're not afraid and you're not cheeky. You're just quiet. I like you."

The general stood in the middle of a cell twelve feet long by nine feet wide. There was a barred window six feet up the wall. A mattress, a stool, a small table. Nothing else.

The general stood there motionless just as he had stood on parades on barrack squares, in the mess, and in his office in staff headquarters—a clearly defined, unapproachable figure.

The man looking after him, Corporal Runke of the Secret Police, regarded his prisoner with friendly interest. "You're no fool," he said. "You realize what's up. And you're not going to make any trouble, eh? So I don't have to trouble you in return. You obviously couldn't tolerate that. And I must say it's not much fun for me—it's so monotonous! Right, then, turn out your pockets."

Without a word the general began to empty his pockets. There wasn't much in them—a handkerchief, a small comb, a purse. The only papers he had were his military paybook.

"You mustn't think I'm inquisitive," said the man. "Or brutal. Only when absolutely necessary. I only do my duty. And of course everyone's equal before the law—including generals, of course. A lot of people don't realize that. We had another general the other day. Man, did he yell! Tried to give me a lot of barrack square bull shit—me, of all people! But it didn't last long. I gave him a thorough going-over and he soon came to his senses. Seemed about time he realized what doing one's duty meant. Right, then—now give me your suspenders."

With an impassive face the general unbuttoned his tunic and opened it. He had no suspenders. He let his hands fall and stood there motionless and upright.

"I must have your belt, I'm afraid," said the man amiably. "That's regulations. For we have concern for the lives of our prisoners, you know. No one's allowed to hang himself, in my charge—I won't have it. I'm not a general, after all. Every corpse means trouble for me, filling out forms and all that rot."

Major-General Modersohn undid his belt and handed it to him.

"You're pretty thin," said the warder. He folded the belt in half and slapped his thigh with it. "It has its advantages, being thin. One's trousers don't fall down so easily. That looks bad, you know. This other general I was telling you about —did he have a paunch on him! Almost as big as the Reichs-marshal's. But it subsided, of course. After a few weeks he was thin as a lathe. And of course his trousers kept on falling down. Damn funny, I can tell you. Man, did we laugh our-selves sick—there he stood while sentence was being passed on him in his underpants! And that couldn't happen to you with your build. Now I'll have the laces from your riding breeches. We can't take any chances."

The general sat down on the stool. He pulled off his boots. Then he wrenched the laces out of his riding breeches, put them on the little table in front of him, and stood up again.

"Now I'll go and get you a bucket," said the man. "And a brand new one, too—because you're a general. Besides, I like you. So I'll give you a piece of advice. Let the bucket stay empty over night. Wait till the morning to do your business. Otherwise it'll simply stink for hours and your clothes will begin to stink too. And I don't like that. If you're smart you'll do what I tell you. I wouldn't like to have to give you a going-over—really I wouldn't."

The man gave a friendly grin and left.

The general, however, remained standing in the middle of the cell. Not a muscle moved. His mouth was tight shut. His eyes were closed.

In the cell next door Lieutenant Krafft lay on his mattress. The darkness was like a blanket of black snow all about him.

Krafft lay calm and relaxed, trying to switch his thoughts about. The night was one long silence. No breath of wind, no sound of a human being.

The world seemed to fall right away from him. He was alone, surrounded by four bare walls which seemed like a huge, cold coffin.

"Is this what I wanted?" he heard himself ask.

He listened to the sound of his own voice. The darkness seemed to swallow it up, smothering it as if with some huge pillow. Once again the heavy silence seemed to fall and cover him.

But then, almost like an echo, he heard other voices—picking up his own, reinforcing it, returning it to him. Finally these voices rang out loud and clear through the night.

Lieutenant Krafft sat up, incredulous. There was a look of utter amazement on his face. He heard singing. Young, lusty voices rang out through the night, not too many voices, perhaps seven or eight in all. But they were voices which destroyed his loneliness and filled the darkness with a distant glimmering light.

The cadets were singing his favorite song, "In the field with stone for pillow, stretch I now my weary limbs."

The lieutenant smiled. Sinking slowly back on his mattress, he listened with closed eyes to this melody so steeped in weariness and impending death. If was as if his blood sang too in harmony with the cadets.

In their case, he had broken the pattern of manufacture, he had succeeded in upsetting the soulless routine of the assembly line. Some of them would become officers in whose hands soldiers could remain human beings. And that was a lot, these days.

"This was what I wanted," said Lieutenant Krafft.

The court-martial proceedings against Major-General Ernst Egon Modersohn and Lieutenant Karl Krafft took place shortly afterward.

The charge specified—among other things—high treason and the undermining of the Wehrmacht's morale.

Both accused refused to defend themselves.

They were condemned to death.

The general's last words were "Long live Germany!"

"Long live a new Germany!" said Lieutenant Krafft before he died.

FINAL REPORT

MORE THAN fifteen years have passed. Some of these characters are no longer alive. Others are older, but no wiser. Only very few have tried to find a moral in what happened.

Captain Feders survived his friend and the general by only a few months. He was arrested in connection with the events of July 20, 1944, and executed shortly afterward. They hanged him on piano wire, so that it was several hours before death came to his rescue. Yet as his features stiffened there was a smile on his face.

Marion, his wife, disappeared about the same time. No one knew where she went. Just before the end of the war she was said to have been seen in Berlin as a member of a resistance group. According to another version she is said to have turned up in Swabia as the girl friend of an American officer. The only thing that can be said of her for certain is that all trace of her has disappeared.

Captain Ratshelm, however, came through both the war and his time in a prisoner-of-war camp with flying colors. He never ceased to supplement his knowledge of military matters and consolidate his character. Moreover he was absolutely certain that he had never made a mistake in his life. He worked first of all on a district council in the Rhineland, and then as an employee of a chemical firm in the same area. He is still not married, though he is once again a soldier, and a lieutenant-colonel too. He shows every concern for the men entrusted to his care and is a great succses.

Major Frey's career has been scarcely less fortunate. At first he found some difficulty in keeping his head high after the total collapse of Germany. He went through two relatively lean years, which he spent on the estate of a wartime comrade of his. Later, however, he interpreted the signs of the times correctly and went into politics. His highly respectable past and his skill in negotiation soon brought him to the fore in a national liberal democratic party. Here he fought—among other things—for respect for Germany and the right to wear decorations won by gallantry in action. On state occasions he cuts a most impressive figure in his tail coat, particularly when he wears his Knight's Cross as well.

Felicitas Frey lost her estates in Silesia, of course, but had plenty of influential relatives left in West Germany. Naturally her marriage wasn't exactly a bed of roses—her niece Barbara Bendler-Trebitz saw to that. Barbara remained very attached to the Frey family. Even when she married, later, the lucky man was a colleague of Frey's, which proved extremely convenient.

The former Captain Kater remained in the closest touch

with the Frey family. Skilled and adept as he was, he successfully overcame every obstacle. He remained a captain and CO of the headquarters company right up to the moment of final victory. Then, without ever shifting his ground, he ran a supply camp for the U. S. Air Force and was in charge of the administration of the officers' mess. A little later, since he was politically uncontaminated, he took over the administration of the town of Wildlingen-am-Main, where he performed remarkable services at the time of the transfer of a well-known optical factory from the Russian Zone. His efforts were soon rewarded by his appointment as sales manager of the very same factory. His contacts with such an exceptionally successful politician as Herr Frey were regarded as extraordinarily valuable.

Irene Jablonski on the other hand had a brief but stormy career. After Kater had thoroughly opened her eyes to her own possibilities, she began to enjoy herself and revealed remarkable powers of endurance. After Kater came a district administrator, then a district Party leader, then an economic commissioner. Her naïveté and willingness attracted men to her like moths to a candle. But then half a company of Turkmenian infantry fell upon her; she collapsed and went insane.

Judge-Advocate Wirrmann remained a pillar of justice. After all, he was an expert, and experts are always in demand. He stuck rigidly to the law—to whatever law happened to be valid at the time. So long as it was necessary he applied paragraph five of the Special Wartime Code and sentenced large numbers of people to death for their subversive attitudes. Then he became adviser to an Allied legal commission. Finally he ended up as president of the agricultural commission of a court of appeal in North Germany. Dr. Wirrmann's slogan: One Race, One Reich, One Law.

Sybille Bachner stayed on at the training school for a time after the general's execution. She first had an affair with his successor, and then married him, thus fulfilling her dearest wish, which was to become the wife of a general. But then he was severely wounded in one of the final battles for Greater Germany—by a flying bomb, as it happened—and was thereafter confined to a wheel chair. Sybille Bachner accepted her fate. She lives, a lonely, taciturn, hard-faced woman, with her husband, in a small tumbledown house on a lake in Upper Bavaria.

The forty cadets of Section H for Heinrich were scattered to the four winds. They dispersed and went back to their respective units, to their respective sectors of the front. They had survived the training school, they became officers, and soon for them Wildlingen was no more than one fleeting memory among many others.

Cadet Amfortas was killed as a lieutenant on the eastern front. Andreas became a prisoner of war of the Russians and immediately joined the National Committee for a Free Germany. Berger, Gundler, and Cremel vanished into obscurity —and with them most of the others. They took off their uniforms and joined up in the armies of workers, of traveling salesmen, of civil servants. And here, just as in that other army, they represented the solid reliable average. The sort of people who always prove useful.

Kramer, the eternal NCO, remained what he had always been, a professional soldier, who neither wished to learn anything else nor was capable of doing so. Egon Weber, the muscle man, went back home, rolled up his sleeves, and started shoving loaves into an oven. He is president of a choral society, a bowling association, and a skat club. He refused to found an old comrades association, but did found a family, which expanded rapidly. He's considered a decent sort of fellow. But whenever he suspects anyone of laying rather too much stress on his Christian name, Egon, he can be thoroughly unpleasant.

Cadet Mösler's short but cheerful career was a curious one. He had struck up simultaneous liaisons with the wife of his company commander and the wife of his regimental commanding officer. Because of this he was posted to the front, but was sent to France, where he founded a military brothel with a number of different branches. This cost him his officer's uniform. Mösler then, according to his own account, joined the German resistance. In the end he was shot as a member of the French Maquis, though this was a mistake— the lists had just got mixed up. A number of ladies of easy virtue wept for him.

Böhmke, the poet, also became a prisoner of war and was missing until 1946. Then he turned up again and started publishing articles advocating "no more war" in a number of respectable newspapers. He also did some broadcasting, and enjoyed a certain popularity on the South-West German radio for a time. After some years he couldn't find anyone to print his articles, or indeed to read them. In protest Böhmke crossed to East Germany, but very quickly came back again and then emigrated to Canada. There he worked as a lumberjack. A respectable German publishing firm even published a volume of his poems—of which sixty-eight copies were actually sold.

Cadet Rednitz retained his connections with the training school at Wildlingen-am-Main for quite a time. He kept up a correspondence with Captain Feders, and after Feders' execution, with Elfrida Rademacher. These letters were few and far between and mostly obscure, but Rednitz learned from them something of what was going on. The death of Feders came as no surprise to him. He heard that the Villa Rosenhügel was closed shortly before the end of the war. What became of the basketmen no one seemed to know. Among the few graves in the park of the Villa Rosenhügel was one which bore the name of the army doctor Heinz Krüger. The date of his death was given as April 20, 1945. The cause of his death could not be ascertained.

Elfrida Rademacher's life from then on followed a very simple pattern. She remained at Wildlingen at first, though no longer working in an office but in the stores. She was the last person to tend the grave of Lieutenant Barkow. No one tended the graves of Lieutenant Krafft and Major-General Modersohn, for no one knew where they were buried. When the war ended Elfrida Rademacher went to stay with her sister in a little town in Franconia. Here in 1948 she married a timber merchant. She is said to be a good wife to him and a good mother to her two children.

Cadet Rednitz became a lieutenant as expected, but after July 20, 1944, was involved in a court-martial for refusing to obey an order and was reduced to the ranks. After a short period as a prisoner of war he settled in the Ruhr and became a chemist in a factory making synthetic fibers. He founded a family, built himself a little house, and from then on lived exclusively for his wife and child. He it was who provided much important documentation for this book.

He handed the information over to the author in Wildlingen-am-Main on a winter's night that was still much like any winter's night of eighteen years ago. The barracks still dominated the sky line. After it had ceased to be a training school it first became a prison camp for German soldiers. Then American troops moved in. Later it was used as a refuge camp. Soon after that a battalion of the new frontier force moved into the desolate building for a time. But not long afterward the entire barracks was completely renovated for a communications school of the new army.

Now it is resplendent in all its old glory—everything is just as it was before.

As it was before? Everything?

May the Lord preserve us from that.

THE END

TAYLOR CALDWELL

One of the world's most highly-read, thoroughly-enjoyed, best-selling authors is now readily available for your reading pleasure. Look for the handsome Pyramid editions of these great Taylor Caldwell novels wherever paperbacks are sold, or use the handy order form below.

T-810   THE TURNBULLS_____75c

T-811   THE EAGLES GATHER_____75c

T-834   THE STRONG CITY_____75c

T-878   THE BALANCE WHEEL_____75c

T-879   MELISSA_____75c

N-891   DYNASTY OF DEATH_____95c

T-905   THE WIDE HOUSE_____75c

(Add 10c postage and handling charges for every book ordered. On any order of four or more books, postage will be paid by Pyramid Books.)

_____

PYRAMID BOOKS, Dept. T-954, 444 Madison Avenue, New York, N. Y. 10022
Please rush me the books circled below. I enclose $_____

T-810   T-811   T-834   T-878   T-879   N-891   T-905

Name_____

Address_____

City_____State_____

HOW TO OPEN THE GREEN DOORS

For more thrills, chills, excitement, suspense and pure reading pleasure!

It's easy. Just look for these Green Door Mysteries wherever Pyramid Books are sold—or use the handy order form below. Either way, it'll pay in enjoyment.

SPECIAL: 4 books for only $2.00, Postage Paid
(single copies 50¢ plus 10¢ postage and handling)

- -

PYRAMID
BOOKS